TEARS

OF THE

FLAMES

TEARS
OF THE
FLAMES

SISI ZHAO

Tears of the Flames by Sisi Zhao

The story, names, characters, places, organizations, facilities, and incidents in this book all came from a certain universe that resides in the author's head and are therefore completely fictional. Hence, all historical events, supernatural phenomena, and scientific research and references that are mentioned in this book should be considered as fictitious—unless proven otherwise by archaeologists and scientists in the future.

Edited by Shawna Hampton
Cover art by Jessica Cvilo
Typesetting services by BOOKOW.COM

ISBN: 979-8-9998116-8-4 (Paperback)
ISBN: 979-8-9998116-0-8 (Hardcover)
ISBN: 979-8-9998116-2-2 (Ebook)

Library of Congress Control Number: 2025918312

Publisher's Cataloging-in-Publication Data
provided by Five Rainbows Cataloging Services

Names: Zhao, Sisi, author.
Title: Tears of the flames / Sisi Zhao.
Description: Roswell, GA : Sisi Zhao, 2025.
Identifiers: LCCN 2025918312 (print) | ISBN 979-8-9998116-8-4 (paperback) | ISBN 979-8-9998116-0-8 (hardcover) | ISBN 979-8-9998116-2-2 (ebook)
Subjects: LCSH: Mothers–Fiction. | Women–Fiction. | End of the world–Fiction. | Animals, Mythical–Fiction. | Friendship–Fiction. | Fantasy fiction. | BISAC: FICTION / Fantasy / Dark Fantasy. | FICTION / Fantasy / Contemporary. | FICTION / Fairy Tales, Folk Tales, Legends & Mythology. | GSAFD: Genre heading.
Classification: LCC PS3626.H36 T43 (print) | LCC PS3626.H36 (ebook) | DDC 813/.6–dc23.

Published in Dec 2025 by Sisi Zhao
in Roswell, Georgia, United States of America

First Edition

www.sisizhao.com

To those who are seeking a purpose in life

It's not that the dots will connect one day; it's that when we look back, years and years later, we'll finally see the choices we made and the prices we paid had shaped us into who we are today and decided what we are going to do tomorrow.

For Dora and James

I've hidden a part of me inside your hearts. When you miss me, give it a knock, and you'll find me right there, knocking back with all my love.

CONTENTS

In my chest, there lies a big hole
For the choices that were made, and the prices that were paid
For the pains that were endured, and the tears that were shed
When I'm forever trapped in this prison
A world between the dead and the living
A cage I cannot break free from
For you
Again and again
To see you—
Try and fail
Trust and be betrayed
Err and rue
Change and suffer
Pursue and be lost
Grow sick and fragile
Yet I will do it again
Again and again
For you
No beginning, nor end
To see you live
To see you laugh
To see you cry
To see you love
To see you in pain, in misery, in anger, in regret, in sorrow, and in despair
To end all your sufferings
The pains, the miseries, the angers, the regrets, the sorrows, and the despairs
To see you at peace and let go
To hold and embrace your soul

It's a journey of choices
A path built with costs
I don't expect you to understand
But you already know the answer
Don't you?

Until we meet again

She put down the pen and gazed at her handwriting on the notepad; her expression hardened. Then, as if she was reminded by the noisy birds that time was running out, she looked toward the little yellow house, which was still sleeping serenely amid the sweet-smelling freshness of the early morning dew. It was a quaint little house, nestled in the middle of a grassy glade on a gentle hill. There was a good distance between the house and the woods, and she was sitting at the edge of the glade behind the house, under a maple tree.

She lowered her eyes and returned her attention to the notepad on her knees. Holding the handwritten page by a corner, she paused. But then, in a determined manner, she peeled the page off and folded it up. She reached under the notepad, took out a blank but full envelope, and slipped the page in. With the envelope carefully held in one hand, she grabbed the pen and the notepad with the other and got up.

"I'm ready," she whispered to the others.

The birds fell silent. The gentle morning breeze ceased. The trees and the animals held still. It was quiet—so quiet that everything seemed to be frozen in time.

Noiselessly, like a phantom, she approached the sleepy little yellow house, which, with its back toward her, had no idea that what was going to happen next would eventually alter the fate of this world.

As dawn arrived, mesmerizing hues of red and gold exploded from the woods and blossomed across the sky while the dawn chorus of the birds came to a deafening climax. If anyone had been watching, they might have thought it was a show of strength performed at the whim of a higher power. On second thought, however, they would have told themselves that it was just the sun, rising again.

Chapter 1 THE DEMONS

1

"**W**HAT are you looking for?"
Startled by the voice of another human being when she had thought she was the only person still prowling around Sunrise Park at this time of the day, Mira spun around. She saw a teenage boy perched on a bike, and he was staring at her with an inscrutable look on his face. Before Mira could decide whether she should answer his question, he had hopped off the bike and begun to walk it toward her, slowly shortening the distance between them.

The autumn wind danced past, swirling and twirling over the fallen leaves, tossing them this way and that. It brought a chill to Mira, who responded with an involuntary shiver and realized she was not wearing her jacket; she had left it at home when she hurried out the door, and all she had on was a sleeveless black dress.

Mira noticed then that the sun was beginning to set. It was melting into the horizon behind the naked trees and their lonely branches at the top of the hill like a giant ball of red-hot lava, generously spilling its bloodred glow onto everything in sight while quickly withdrawing its heat. The temperature was really starting to drop, and judging by the position of the sun, it was high time for her to head home. Yet she still hadn't found what she came here to look for.

The boy came to a stop when he was only a few feet away from her. He had a tan skin tone and a quite unremarkable combination of facial features that would otherwise fail to produce much of an impression on anyone if it weren't for the sparse facial hairs lounging above his upper lip and on his chin, appearing as if they were exhausted from their debut and had decided to chill out around his mouth like earthworms after a rainy day—proof that he was going through the awkward transitional phase where the magic of testosterone turned a boy into a man. Mira concluded he must be older than her, probably around fifteen.

He seemed to have been pedaling hard. His brown hair was wet with sweat, which pasted the bangs to his forehead like excessive hair gel. He was wearing a baggy gray hoodie and a pair of loose jersey shorts in solid black, which accentuated his skinny legs as a telltale sign of his lanky build. A large and bulky navy blue backpack hung heavily from his shoulders, though the proportion of his size to the size of the backpack made him look more like a kid than a man-to-be. Nevertheless, he was still at least a foot taller than Mira, and having no success in spotting any emotions on his face, Mira was starting to feel uncomfortable at the way his dark green eyes gleamed under the fading light of the dying sun.

"So, what are you looking for?" the boy asked again. His voice sounded tired and lazy, but for a split second, Mira thought something energetic had flashed across his face.

He doesn't like the way you studied him . . . said a voice in her head.

He's hiding something . . . said another.

. . . something that he doesn't want you to see, offered the third. *Something that he doesn't want you to know . . .*

"I'm looking for ginkgo trees," Mira replied to the boy absentmindedly. "I need some ginkgo leaves." She made another quick scan of the trees nearby. *Nope, no ginkgo trees.* She must have been searching in the park for over an hour by now. She was beginning to wonder whether she should just give up on the idea of using ginkgo leaves to complete her art project; yes, she would most likely have to redesign and redo the whole thing, but the deadline was tomorrow, which meant she would have to finish her project that evening, with or without the ginkgo leaves. She had told Mom she would be back by dinnertime, and now dinnertime was right around the corner. If she still wanted to try to find some ginkgo trees, she would have to hurry. With that in mind, Mira forced a quick smile to the boy as a polite way to put an end to their conversation and returned her attention to where she had left off.

Much to her surprise, the boy called from behind her, "I know where to find them."

Mira twisted around. "You do?"

There was a blank look on the boy's face, as though he didn't hear her, but he said, "Follow me. I'll show you."

Without waiting for her to reply, he hopped back on his bike and started pedaling, heading deeper into the belly of Sunrise Park.

As much as Mira wanted to follow him, she hesitated. The sun was sinking lower behind the trees. The birds and the bugs were getting noisier, urging each other to go home. Dusk was falling. She should be heading back instead.

"Are you sure you know the way?" she called to the boy.

"I'm sure." He glanced back at her over his shoulder, pedaling on as lazily as he had used his voice.

Mira took a few steps after him then stopped. Her heart was beating faster, and the three voices were getting louder in her head.

Do not follow him!

You should go home!

Cara is expecting you to be home by dinnertime!

Mira suddenly had a strange sensation that her spirit had shot out from her body and flown straight up into the sky, where it hovered and looked down at her physical self as it conversed with the voices in her head: *I just need a few leaves. Then I can finish it like I've planned.*

What if he can't find them either?

What if he's lying?

What if he wants something in return?

He's a big kid, her spirit argued. *He's probably in high school. He knows what he's doing.*

It's getting dark.

Nobody's here now except you and him.
Do not trust him. You should not trust him.

Mira blinked, and in that millisecond, her spirit seemed to have dived down and reentered her body; the next thing she knew, she was watching the boy pedaling away from her again. She shook the dreamlike feeling from her head and focused on the boy.

"Wait!" she called and ran after him. She couldn't let this last opportunity slip through her fingers after all; she didn't want to give up on the hope of finding ginkgo trees yet.

As Mira chased the bike, she heard her heart beating loudly in her chest. But in her head, it was unusually quiet, as though the three voices were angry that she had not followed their advice and were refusing to speak. Even the enthusiastic members of the dusk chorus had stopped singing, producing only an occasional chirp here and there to hush the younglings from talking to each other at bedtime. Without their active participation in seeing the sun off, Mira couldn't help noticing how quiet it had become in the park —uncomfortably, eerily quiet.

The boy was pedaling faster now. Mira picked up the pace and ran harder. Amid the uncanny silence that had befallen the park like a spell, her senses were greatly heightened. Despite the cooling temperature, she felt sweat beads forming on her skin, sealing off her pores from breathing and sending her body hairs tugging and pulling at their roots to gasp for air. Moreover, every little sound she made seemed to be amplified ten times over. She heard her heart pounding in her rib cage, producing loud echoes in her chest with a rhythm that harmonized with the bass-like thumps from the throbbing veins in her ears. She heard her own ragged breathing, wheezing like the bellows of an accordion that was being pulled and pushed in a mad rush. As she followed the bike off the main trail, she heard a new sound: the crisp, crunching noise of a mixture of dead leaves, dry twigs, and fallen branches being crushed under the soles of her shoes. Naked trees sprawled around and hunched over them, their limbs drooping wearily, as if they were still mourning the deaths of the leaves, twigs, and branches that used to be an integral part of their weathered bodies and were weeping silently as they watched their remains being crumbled under the bike's wheels and her feet.

Mira was not sure how long she had been following the boy, nor did she remember how far they had left the main trail behind them, but she noticed she hadn't caught sight of any trail marks in a while and the forest floor in this area was littered with a lot more fallen branches and dead tree trunks.

All of a sudden, the boy braked to a stop. He hopped off the bike and leaned it against a nearby tree. With her energy level boosted by the thought that they had finally arrived at the right location, Mira ran faster and caught up with the boy. Panting heavily, she looked around and asked, "Where're the ginkgo trees?"

"Over there," answered the boy, pointing straight ahead with one hand as he knelt to tug at a shoelace with the other. "You go ahead. I need to tie my shoe."

Mira wiped the sweat from her forehead and trudged forward toward a less woody area, which seemed more like an unwelcoming graveyard of more dead trees and shrubs. She told herself she would pick out a few ginkgo leaves, turn around, and run home. There was a hidden shortcut from the main trail that would lead her right back to the house. If she could run at full speed the whole time, she might still beat Dad home, then maybe Mom wouldn't be as mad, considering dinner would not be served until Dad was back from work anyway . . .

However, this decomposing graveyard was as unforgiving as it was unwelcoming. Mira's calves were soon pricked and scratched by the skeletons left behind by the ghosts of her unfriendly hosts, until they managed to make her lose her footing and trip over a fat and knotted tree root buried under the thick layer of dead leaves blanketing the forest floor. Luckily, Mira was able to regain her balance in time to stay on her feet, but a thought popped into her mind then, like a subconscious observation that had been shaken loose from somewhere deep in her brain when she tripped and had finally made its way to her awareness: *How can he remember where to find ginkgo trees in a part of the woods like this one?*

The thought made Mira freeze in her tracks. She instantly realized something was terribly wrong here, and she had only two choices: fight, or flight. She decided to fight, so she spun around to confront the boy.

But it was too late.

Before Mira could orient herself, something hard rammed her into the ground. A force, as heavy as solid metal, was pinning her down, and the repulsive heat and smell of a stranger's body were seeping into hers. Then her brain finally caught on to the signals sent from her eyes: it was the boy; he was the suffocating weight immobilizing her. His body was pressing so hard against hers that she thought he might crush her bones and flatten her into the dirt. She opened her mouth and screamed, but a hand immediately slapped down to cover it, muffling her cry of help into a high-pitched whine.

"Get off! Get off! ... Get off me ...!" Mira shrieked, but his hand was pressing her lips mercilessly against her teeth, so her voice was squeezed right back into her throat. She jerked and kicked and thrashed like a stranded fish, but it was no use; she could not break free from him. She couldn't believe such an overpowering force was produced by another human being, against which she was like a twitching bug struggling helplessly under the fingertip of a cruel and ruthless child. Painful heat was quickly building up inside her from the useless fight she was putting on, and she felt her whole body expanding from it: her bones, her flesh, her skin, and even her hair, all of it. Like a pot of water about to boil over, she felt the heat steaming out of her pores with pain, ready to erupt and explode. She couldn't breathe; she couldn't move; she couldn't even think anymore. She was burning up.

His face was right above hers—so close, so sweaty, so human, yet so demonic. His pupils dilated with an intense desire and excitement as his free hand slithered down her body and pulled himself out of his shorts in haste. With the help of his knees, he jerked apart her thighs forcibly and attacked her underpants. Drooling and grinning like a hungry wolf closing in on a defenseless lamb, he buried his face in her chest greedily and moaned. Grunting with pleasure, he fumbled impatiently to make his way through the tatters that had once protected her crotch from him. His intent was clear; he was squeezing himself into her body.

His entry set off a powerful shockwave inside her, igniting her blood vessels like a lit fuse zapping into a cave full of explosives. Searing fury erupted and exploded from within her, bursting out into a long and terrifying screech.

Startled by the inhuman noise coming from her, the boy peeled his sweaty face away from her chest and raised his head but was immediately met with an enormous pair of chilling black eyes. They stared coldly into his, piercing his eye sockets, drilling deeply into his brain and his soul while dilating his pupils to the rims of his green irises until all that was left were two bottomless black holes in the whites of his eyes.

Still burning with fury, she stared on. She saw roaring flames raging in the black holes in his face, rampaging through the dark void in his head and into the depths of its black abyss until they engulfed him in his mind. There, they chewed on his flesh, gnawed on his bones, and tore him apart piece by piece as they fed on the shreds of his remains and the screams of his soul.

The boy's face, still sweaty, was now as white as a sheet. His mouth, half-open, with drool still dangling from both corners, was producing a series of gurgling and choking sounds, as though he was gagging on his own tongue. He slipped out from her then, which only reminded her how disgusted and revolted she was by his entire being. With a screech, she kicked and flung him away. However, instead of her arms, a pair of fiery wings flapped out, passing through the boy as they projected him into the leaf litter a few yards away from her with a dull thud. The boy did not catch fire, but there was a strange yet familiar prickling and tingling sensation buzzing from her hands to her arms.

Feeling more shocked than relieved, Mira sat up and looked down: her hands and arms were not there; instead, burning flames spread from her shoulders like wings, each large enough to cover the entire length and width of her body with room to spare. They were burning so wildly that their sparks appeared to be dripping into the leaf litter around her, yet nothing got burned and nothing was set on fire. Gingerly, she moved her arms and flexed her fingers. The fiery wings moved as she moved, and the tips of the flames flickered when she flexed.

Just then, she heard the boy—the vilest creature she had ever encountered, the demon in human skin. He was scrambling to his feet, his genitalia retracting back down into his shorts like a wounded snake retreating backward into its hole.

Mira pushed herself up at once, ready to stand her ground. Her eyes soon found his, which were now as big and round as gumballs, emitting no lust but total horror and despair. The muscles on his face were twitching ghastly. His jaw had dropped open so wide that something unimaginable seemed to be crawling out from his throat. As he fought to keep his balance, his body started to convulse. It only took a few more seconds before he lost control and bolted away like a mad man, screaming at the top of his lungs:

"Devil . . . ! Devil . . . ! She's the Devil! She's the Devil . . . !"

11

Mira did not remember how she found her way home, nor did she remember walking back at all. But presently, she found herself standing at the edge of the glade in a trance as though she had been sleepwalking. The little yellow house was waiting for her quietly in the dusk in the middle of the glade; soft yellow lights were winking at her through the dining room windows. There were two cars parked in the driveway, meaning A: Dad was already home, and B: she was officially late for dinner.

But instead of making her way toward the house in a hurry, Mira did not move. She did not know how to explain to Mom and Dad why she was late, and she had no idea how to tell them about what had happened to her in the park. So Mira just stood there and stared vacantly at the house, until she noticed there was something strange about the way it looked that night: it appeared to be reflecting an ominous green tint, which reminded her of an old sci-fi movie about a league of green aliens invading Earth in their high-tech UFOs. That was when she heard a strange sound coming from the sky—a cacophonous whooshing noise charged with static, which somehow made her think of a giant shape-shifting bird formed by a great murmuration of starlings, and each of the starlings was whispering to her in a different human voice, all at the same time.

She turned around and looked up. Something gigantic and green was rotating steadily in the sky right above Sunrise Park: an enormous vortex, all lit up with an eerie yet mysterious green glow that seemed to be beamed down from another world, spinning slowly downward from the center and forming a short glow-in-the-dark funnel with an opening at the bottom. If this green vortex could cast a shadow, Mira was certain the entire Sunrise Park would be shrouded in darkness. Despite its already mind-boggling size, the green vortex was still growing and expanding, gradually but visibly. Innumerable streaks of what looked like glowing green tentacles spun out from the vortex's rim as it rotated, but they seemed to be evaporating and disappearing into the atmosphere just as quickly as they formed. The opening at the bottom was as round as a singing mouth, and it was glowing with a soft pink color, like lipstick for the green vortex. However, since the whole thing looked more like an alien portal than a natural astronomical phenomenon, it was hard to determine whether the green vortex was going to kiss Earth with its pink mouth or to suck the life out of it.

Even so, to Mira, the green vortex possessed a peculiar form of beauty that was both unsettling and intriguing, just like the strange and cacophonous noise it was producing from its pink mouth, which now sounded as if it was whispering something incomprehensible to her in an old and inexplicable tongue, beckoning her to come closer. Mira suddenly had the sensation that she was being pulled toward the green vortex and into its mouth, and she was rising higher and higher inside it as the green vortex rotated around her, until all she could see was an abyss of absolute blackness. Everything was blocked out here—the sight, the smell, the sound—save the strange and cacophonous noise, which was getting louder, and which, somehow, was making more sense to her as she spun deeper into the heart of that black abyss.

Then all at once, the noise and the rotation stopped, leaving her floating weightlessly in total silence. To her amazement, even though she was surrounded by nothing but blackness, she could see her surroundings shifting and flowing like an infinite pool of fluid. She watched as the black abyss became a dark void, then the dark void became a black hole, and the black hole split into two and became a pair, looking as hollow and empty as the ones she had seen in his eyes.

Disgust and revulsion kicked in right away, and she shrank from the two black holes automatically, like a reflex. With that, she was again standing at the edge of the glade and gazing at the green vortex from afar.

Mira felt like someone who had been yanked out of bed to her feet in the middle of a deep dream. In fact, everything that had happened in Sunrise Park that evening felt like a blurry nightmare to her now. She couldn't help but wonder if it had all been a very bad dream. Her head felt groggy and heavy. She buried her face in her hands and massaged her forehead. Then, as though she had just remembered something, she paused and lowered her hands from her eyes.

They seemed perfectly normal; there were no flames. She checked her arms. They appeared perfectly normal too; there were no wings. She flexed her fingers one by one and was relieved to see they all responded effortlessly and accurately to her commands, so she proceeded to run her hands up and down her arms to make sure they were indeed made of flesh and bones, only to find them tender and sore from many scratches and scrapes, which she had failed to notice earlier.

Mira felt her heart sink. Slowly, she let go of her arms and looked down at her dress: it was dotted with bits of dry leaves and twigs, and the skirt was badly wrinkled.

She thought about reaching under to check her underpants, but the thought was soon replaced by a sudden spell of dizziness that caused her to wobble. By the time Mira had regained her balance, she already knew there was no point in checking—it wouldn't make much of a difference to the situation, not to mention it would not change anything anyway.

So she spent the next few minutes cleaning her dress and straightening out the skirt. When she was done, she walked quietly to the house and tried the doorknob on the back door. To her relief, it was unlocked. She cracked it open slowly and, as swiftly and noiselessly as she could manage, slipped inside.

Mira was half expecting to find Mom right there in the kitchen and thought she would most likely be caught under Mom's reproachful gaze before she could sneak up the stairs to her room to change, so she was surprised to see it was all dim and quiet inside. The kitchen was empty, and there was no one in the dining room either. The only form of illumination in the house came from the three candles standing diligently on the dining table, greeting her with the same soft yellow lights that they had been waving at her through the dining room windows when she was outside.

"Mira?" an eager voice called from the living room, then Mom's head popped up from the couch as she turned to peer over the backrest. Mira couldn't see the expression on Mom's face, but she could hear it clearly in her voice: "What took you so long? You said you'd be back by dinner. Do you know what time it is now?"

Mira shifted uncomfortably in her dress. "Sorry, Mom. I got . . . distracted . . ."

"Distracted by what?" Mom got up from the couch and walked over to Mira. "You didn't get lost, did you? . . . Wait, did you forget to wear a jacket? Weren't you cold?" She was about to continue on with her questions when her innate intuition as a mother picked up an unpleasant vibe in the air that made her stomach tight. When she spoke again, her voice softened with concern. "Is everything okay?"

"Yeah," Mira answered quickly and lowered her head. She had made up her mind; she would not tell her parents what had happened in Sunrise Park. She did not want them to suffer from the knowledge of it, nor did she want to relive that nightmarish memory in any way. She wanted to forget it, every bit of it, even if she had to lie to herself to pretend it had never happened.

She felt a surge of pressure in her head, which caused her brain to buzz with pain. A burning sensation spread from her lower abdomen to her torso and limbs, sending a wave of nausea to her stomach. She felt dirty. She wanted to run away from Mom and scrub herself under a steaming hot shower from head to toe to make herself clean again.

Mom tilted her head to one side. "Are you sure?"

Mira glanced up at Mom and realized she would have to sound way more convincing than she was to avoid causing further suspicion. She put on a casual smile and said, "Yeah. I'm just a little tired from all that walking in the park. But really, Mom, everything's fine."

Mom did not seem very convinced, however. She kept her head tilted and looked at Mira with her lips pursed, as though she could tell Mira was not being completely honest with her.

Mira knew then that she had no choice but to make up a lie to cover up the truth. The only problem was she couldn't think of a lie fast enough to offer to Mom as a plausible explanation, partly because she did not have much practice in lying, but mostly because she was just not a good liar. So Mira decided to improvise a story from a part of the truth—the harmless part.

"Actually . . . I had a little accident in the park," she began slowly, reminding herself to speak as calmly as she could. "I thought I spotted some ginkgo trees off the main trail, at the foot of a big slope. I thought I could manage going down there and coming back up the same way, but I didn't expect the leaf litter would make the slope so slippery . . ."

Mom's eyes grew round as her head swung back to an upright position. She covered her mouth with a hand, but a soft whimper had already escaped: "Oh no."

"I fell and slipped the whole way down," Mira continued softly as her hands moved secretly and subconsciously to pull down on the skirt of her dress. "I tried to climb up the slope, but it was too slippery. So I had to walk along it to find a better spot to get back up. But when I did, I found myself in an unmarked area away from the trail . . . It took me a long time to find my way back to the house . . ." She lowered her eyes and, with genuine regret, added quietly, "I should have listened to you and stayed home, Mom. I didn't find any ginkgo trees after all."

Mom removed her hand from her mouth and made a half-sighing, half-grunting noise. She pulled Mira into the dining room and squinted under the soft candlelight to examine her face and arms.

"Just as I thought." Mom wrinkled her nose and made a face, as if she could feel the scratches and scrapes on Mira's skin appearing on hers as well. "Look at your arms! All these just to get some leaves?" She shook her head disapprovingly, then she dug her fingers into Mira's long, thick, curly red hair and felt her scalp.

"Um, Mom?" Mira asked cautiously under Mom's inquiring hands. "What're you doing?"

"What am I doing? Making sure you didn't hurt your head, of course!" Mom replied in a reproachful tone as she pulled one hand out of Mira's hair, holding a piece of dried-up leaf between her fingers. She frowned at it briefly and tossed it onto the dining table with a flick of her wrist. "Your hair might have saved you from a potential concussion. Just look at this mess!" She held Mira by the shoulders and made her turn to her back. "You've got a lot of souvenirs from Mother Nature all tangled up in your hair . . . Seriously, it's like you've been dragged through the woods on your head. Is your head sore?"

Mira shivered inwardly as she fought back the memory of her struggling uselessly on the forest floor under a suffocating weight. A new wave of nausea rose in her stomach. This time, it was reaching for her throat.

She swallowed hard and shook her head weakly. "No . . . I'll go take a shower and wash my hair—"

"You can't cure this mess by washing," said Mom, busily separating the curls in Mira's frizzy hair to extract Mother Nature's gifts, one piece at a time, until her fingers brushed past something hard in her hair.

Mom paused and knitted her brows. "Hold still," she said, turning her head to the side to squint at the spot where she thought she felt the unexpected resistance. But the candlelight was not bright enough for her to see clearly, and her eyes were getting sore and tired from having to focus closely in dim light, which soon made her sigh through her nose in defeat and close her eyes to ease the discomfort. While she was resting her eyes, she stuck her hands back into Mira's voluminous hair and felt around. Before long, she located what she was looking for. She got a good hold on it and, with one sharp motion, plucked it out of Mira's head.

Mira, on the other hand, was not at all prepared for the physical shock this would set off. Every nerve ending in her body, from her scalp to her toes, immediately buzzed with the numbing, burning, paralyzing sensation of a powerful electric shock. A vivid image automatically flashed through her mind, in which, a fistful of her long, red curls was dangling from Mom's hand, with a piece of her scalp still attached at one end, blood dripping and all. If Mira could still control the muscles in her vocal cords, she would have cried out in pain.

"A stone?" Mom exclaimed as though she couldn't believe her eyes. She let out a long sigh and turned Mira around to face her, holding the stone up for her to see. "This is about the strangest thing I've found in someone's hair, Little Bird." She put the stone down on the dining table, on top of the pieces of leaves and twigs she had picked out from Mira's hair earlier, then she added wryly, "Well, this and gum." She gave Mira a resigned but pained smile and gently brushed the stray curls back from her forehead. "Just look at what you've put yourself through. Scratches and scrapes on your arms, a mess in your hair, even a stone! . . . It must have been a very steep slope."

Mom pressed her lips together tightly but eventually pulled the corners of her mouth up into a soft smile and switched to a more cheerful tone. "Anyhow, for what it's worth, I think your project looks great the way it is. You don't need any ginkgo leaves, honestly."

She gave Mira a reassuring squeeze on her shoulder and went into the kitchen. With an audible sigh, she opened the fridge and started digging through the shelves. Mira had not completely recovered from the shock yet, but she instantly sensed that something was not quite right in the kitchen.

"I hope you're not too hungry," said Mom as she pulled open one of the fridge drawers. "The power went out when I was baking the lasagna. I thought it'd come back soon—apparently not. It's been what, an hour, perhaps?"

As soon as Mom had pointed it out, Mira realized where the problem was: although the fridge door was wide open, there was no light from the inside. Then it dawned on her that there were candles on the dining table because the power had gone out. She just had been too preoccupied to notice it.

"Dad said it was out everywhere in town. He thinks it'll be a few days before they can restore it for everybody. Anyway, he's down in the basement working on that old power generator, trying to get it to come back to life." Mom stepped away from the fridge holding a pack of meat and some vegetables. She closed the fridge door with her elbow and put the food down on the kitchen counter. "Well, let's hope he can work miracles. In the meantime, I think we need an alternative for dinner so we can at least have some food in our tummies and go to bed on time. Not to mention"—she gestured toward the basement—"he might use up all of our remaining candles if we don't stop him in time. So instead of the half-cooked lasagna, we'll grill some chicken kabobs. Sound good?"

Mira managed to bend her neck and give Mom a stiff nod. Mom responded with a thumbs-up and, as she washed and diced the ingredients, went on to talk about what might have caused the power outage.

But Mira was no longer listening; her attention was absorbed by something else: the "stone" that Mom had plucked out from her head. The physical reaction of it being separated from her scalp was finally wearing off. She picked it up with her still-numb fingers and brought it under a candle flame for a closer look.

This "stone" was about the size of a large almond, but it weighed practically nothing in her palm. Unlike the stones she had seen and touched before, this one had an unusual glossiness that somehow made her think of dragon scales, only smaller and slenderer. To

Mira's surprise, even though it looked dull and dark and inconspic-uous on the table, once she brought it under the candle flame, it glimmered like a rare gem, its color so vibrant it seemed to contain fresh blood that might start dripping from its tip at any moment. A golden tint floated on its surface like a thin film of olive oil, though it was hard to judge whether it was indeed glowing with a golden hue or merely reflecting and amplifying the light from the candle flame. If Mira had found this "stone" on the side of a road or in the woods, she would have thought it was a precious gem that had once adorned some mysterious ancient artifact. But she didn't find it on the side of a road or in the woods. Instead, it was plucked right out of her head. Mira had no idea what to make of it, except that . . .

Maybe it has something to do with the wings.

Mira closed her hand around the "stone" and shut her eyes. The nightmarish memory had crept back to terrorize her with vivid, painful flashbacks. Her head was throbbing, her stomach was churning, and her body was shivering. She was once again very aware of how dirty she felt. She needed a shower, a steaming hot shower, to melt and wash everything away . . .

Mom was still carrying on about her opinions on the blackout. ". . . definitely has something to do with that green . . . *thing* in the sky. I'm not a scientist, but I know it's not an aurora. I mean, just look at the way it's rotating, not to mention it's growing bigger and bigger . . ." She was marinating the chicken cubes with such dedication that she didn't notice Mira was not feeling well.

"Mom," Mira called in a tired voice, "I think I should go take a shower first."

"Oh." Mom looked up from the big bowl she was using. "Sure. Go ahead. I left one of my scented candles in your room. It should be bright enough for a shower. Good thing our water heater runs on gas, so at least you won't be washing your hair in cold water." She gave a wry chuckle and went back to coating the chicken cubes. "I hope you like the scent. It's cedar and magnolia, my personal favorite, very relaxing . . . Speaking of which, I should probably light one up for myself too so I can actually *see* what I'm doing here."

Had it been a peaceful and uneventful evening like it usually was, Mira might have snickered to herself. But it had not been one, and her mind was trapped in a gloomy haze. A hot shower was all she could think of to keep herself from slipping back into that endless black abyss.

And it worked. As the steaming water embraced her, Mira felt her mind and body grow lighter. She closed her eyes and imagined the warm steam was rising and falling like a sea of clouds. In her mind's eye, the fine mist was bouncing off her head, forming whimsical shapes in the air and tickling the candle flame, making it dance and wave. The pleasant scent from the candle was saturated with warm water vapor. She inhaled it, deeply and greedily, until her lungs were filled up by a soothing, warming sensation that made her finally feel like herself again.

Mira didn't know how long she had been standing under the shower. She didn't want to move, nor did she want to turn it off. Before she knew it, her temporary escape was interrupted by a series of loud knocks on the door, then she heard Mom's voice: "Mira! You're still in there?"

"Yeah . . ." Mira answered lazily over the sound of running water, struggling to lift her eyelids.

"Well, time to get out. Dinner will be ready in ten minutes, okay? . . . Oh, remember to blow out the candle when you leave the room. Dad can't fix the generator after all, so we'll need to start rationing."

"Okay," Mira answered, much more quickly this time, like a well-rehearsed reaction. Mom had a thing about mealtime punctuality. When the food was ready to be served, Mira and her dad must be either sitting down at the dining table or helping Mom bring the food and drinks into the dining room. It was an unwritten rule in the family that she and Dad had adhered to carefully ever since the time Mom got mad at them for not showing up in the dining room after the third call and replaced the food on their plates with low-sodium crackers. Mom said she did it because she didn't feel like her cooking efforts were appreciated. She then made her case by pointing out that even puppy dogs knew to rush to their food bowls when their owners called them to eat, and they were only getting packaged dog food, not fresh food made from scratch and cooked with love, like what she had spent the last three hours preparing for the two of them. Needless to say, it was not a lesson one could easily forget. Since that day, neither Mira nor Dad dared to show up late to appreciate Mom's cooking efforts again.

Mira turned off the shower reluctantly and reached for the towel, but she immediately noticed how sore her muscles were and how stiff her joints felt. Worse yet, every movement she made hurt and burned like fire, and her head felt so heavy on her neck that she thought her cervical spine might snap.

With great effort, she wrapped the towel around herself, wincing from the pain. With even greater effort, she dried her hair and body, as best as she could manage, until the towel brushed against her lower abdomen and triggered a swollen, raw pain there as though it was missing a layer of skin.

Finding it too painful and disorienting to bend her neck forward to check what was wrong, Mira steadied herself with the towel bar and, slowly and gingerly, stepped out of the bathtub. She used the wall to support herself and wobbled over to the sink, where the scented candle was burning as unsteadily on the vanity top as her labored breathing. Grunting in pain, she lifted an arm and swiped her hand across the mirror to wipe off the steam. She was not entirely successful in her endeavor; even so, it was enough for her to see what was causing the pain: below her belly button, spreading across over half of her lower abdomen, there was something that seemed like a big burn mark on her skin. From its reflection in the mirror, it looked almost like a bloodred tattoo in the shape of three exotic feathers lining up side by side, with the one in the middle being the biggest and the tallest, barely half an inch shy of reaching her belly button. But instead of blisters, this burn mark was filled with something that resembled lava, pushing and pulling along slowly inside it as the whole area glowed with a mesmerizing mixture of red and gold, illuminating her lower abdomen from within like a piece of freshly produced artwork by a red-hot branding iron.

Hesitantly, Mira touched it with a trembling hand. A raw, stinging pain rippled across her lower abdomen as a result and made her grimace, but she was surprised to find that in spite of the tenderness and pain, her skin was still flat and smooth to the touch, without any indication of an actual burn mark on its surface.

She dropped her hand and stared blankly at the mirror. Even though a fresh coat of steam had already reclaimed it, the reflection of her burn mark remained prominent. In a dreamlike trance, Mira was suddenly under the impression that the burn mark was coming alive. It seemed to be shifting inconspicuously yet continuously on her lower abdomen, crawling up toward her waist like three dancing flames in a slow-motion animation . . .

But Mira didn't know whether it was indeed coming alive or she was just seeing things. She felt dizzy. Her head was spinning from a splitting headache, which was intensifying between her temples. Though it was still steamy and warm in the bathroom, she was cold. Leaning heavily against the vanity top, she struggled into her underwear and nightgown. Her hair was still dripping, and her body was not completely dried yet, but she was too lightheaded and groggy to care.

A few quick knocks came from the door then. "Mira!" Dad called in a hushed and nervous voice. "Hurry up! Mom's fixing our plates. You'd better come out!"

"Coming . . ." Mira called back feebly. With one hand supporting herself on the vanity top, she opened the bathroom door. The warm steam immediately gushed out from behind her, fogging up Dad's glasses and leaving her shivering with chills under her nightgown.

"Whoa . . . heat alert!" Dad exclaimed, holding up both hands in front of his face as though he was trying to shield himself. "How hot was your shower? It's like an oven in there!" He made a face, took off his glasses, and squinted at Mira through the evaporating steam. "Mom could have finished baking the lasagna if she had left it in there with you, Little Bird." He gave her a humorous wink and wiped the steam off his lenses with a corner of his shirt. "Anyway, methinks Mom did not enjoy having to cook a second dinner on the grill out in the cold, so we'd better be sitting down when those kabobs are served."

With that, he pushed the glasses back onto his nose hastily and strode away, calling over his shoulder as he left the room, "Come on! We're cutting it close!"

Mira tried to follow him, but her legs were heavy and stiff like drying cement. Worse still, her bedroom seemed to be spinning— above her, beneath her, and around her. She held on to the door-frame, hoping the vertiginous sensation would ease off, though she was panting heavily just to stay on her feet.

The scented candle flickered behind her and suddenly flared up, casting an ominous shadow on the opposite wall of her bedroom. The shadow swayed and shook and grew into a monstrous size, then a pair of wings fanned out from it and reached across the ceiling like the unquenchable spirits of two roaring bonfires, swallowing up every inch of her bedroom in black shadowy flames.

The veins in Mira's temples were throbbing painfully. Her ears were ringing, smothering the three voices bubbling up in her head and muffling the sounds drifting from downstairs. She felt the weight of her body slipping away from her awareness as though she was entering a dream, in which, the walls of her room shifted from left to right, the ceiling shook from side to side, and the floor crumbled under her feet and collapsed, with her on it, into a bottomless void.

She felt cold, she felt weak, and she could no longer stand. Before she could call out for help, her eyes went dark, her hands slipped off the doorframe, and she finally fell to the floor . . .

She heard a voice calling her name from somewhere beyond the darkness. It sounded distant and muted, like echoes in a dream. Something cold and soothing touched her forehead, easing the pressure and pain between her temples as the liquid blackness gradually faded from her eyes.

"Hey, Little Bird." Mom smiled down at her with relief, but it was hard to miss the concern in her eyes. She moved her hand back from Mira's forehead and stroked her head.

"How are you feeling?" Dad asked in a whisper. He was holding her in his arms. She could hear his trembling heartbeats through his chest.

"I'm cold," she answered weakly.

Dad tightened his arms around her. Mom's lips merged into a line as though she was suppressing a whimper.

"You have a bad fever," said Mom in a broken voice. "We found you on the floor . . ." She bit her lip, her eyes glimmering with the reflections of the soft candlelight. "When did you start to feel bad? . . . In the shower? Or when you were at the park?"

Mira tried to nod, but her head barely moved. Her eyelids, on the other hand, were fighting to stay open.

"It's okay." Mom pressed her lips together tightly and forced a smile. "You need rest. Let's get you to bed. I'll ask Ms. Susan to come check on you, but I need you to take some medicine first, okay? . . . Anything else that's bothering you, besides the fever?"

Mira felt an uncomfortable contraction in her heart. She had a sudden urge to come clean to her parents and tell them everything that had happened to her that evening.

"Like headache, sore throat, chest pain, bellyache. . ." Mom prompted helpfully.

But they don't need to know, she heard herself say in her head. *After all, what's done cannot be undone, and the knowledge of it will only bring them pain and suffering. You should not let that happen. You will not.*

Relieved and content with her decision, Mira smiled. She was warm and cozy in Dad's arms, and Mom's voice was as relaxing as the sound of a babbling brook. She was safe. There was really no need to recall anything from a very bad dream . . .

She didn't know when or how she closed her eyes; if they had closed on their own accord, she didn't fight it.

She heard Dad whisper something to Mom, then she felt herself being pulled away from the grasp of gravity and was lifted from the floor, her body becoming so soft and light in the process that it no longer felt like she was connected to it. Before her head touched the pillow, she had drifted off into a deep slumber of nothingness.

III

Cara closed Mira's bedroom door gently behind her and led Susan down the stairs into the kitchen. She took two cans of sparkling water out from the still powerless fridge and handed one to Susan. "Is it the flu?"

Susan took the can and set her medical bag down on the floor, next to the back door. "I don't think it is."

Cara gave Susan a surprised look and gestured for her to go into the dining room, where they sat next to each other. Susan's silky light blond hair was smoothed back from her delicate face and tied into a low ponytail, accentuating her perfectly proportioned facial structure and her high cheekbones. Her eyes were a pastel blue, which always reminded Cara of the color of the sky on a beautiful day in spring. There seemed to be a perpetual smile on Susan's small, full lips, the kind that appeared both sublime and elusive, like Mona Lisa's, yet somehow made you feel as though you were in the presence of an all-seeing, all-knowing Buddha. There was no denying it, Susan Heart was a beautiful woman, and she had always been. The only blemishes on her face were the dark circles that constantly hung under her eyes, which looked extra heavy today. But knowing Susan, Cara assumed it was because she had spent another night dealing with big and important brainwork rather than going to bed on time. Truth be told, in Cara's opinion, with her fine complexion and slender build, Susan could have easily become a famous model or a popular actress. But Susan preferred to be the brainy kind, so she became a doctor instead. "The mind and the body both grow with time," she always said. "The mind can grow beautiful, but the body will only grow old." And that was precisely how Susan spent her free time: working, researching, learning, and working again. In other words, growing her mind. Sometimes Cara could not help but wonder whether Susan's body had stopped growing old because she had spent too much energy growing her mind, for even though they were both in their forties now, Susan still looked pretty much the same as when they graduated from college.

"If it's not the flu," said Cara, "it must be something that's just as nasty, otherwise she wouldn't have such a bad fever. Right?"

"The fever has definitely taken a lot out of her." Susan opened her sparkling water and let the contents sizzle and fizz as she continued. "Her heart rate is elevated, which is quite normal when you have a fever. But she doesn't cough, doesn't have a sore throat, doesn't have any congestion, and her glands are not swollen." She paused to think for a moment, then she asked, "Was there a change in her diet lately?"

"Diet change?" Cara let out a dry laugh, thinking she had heard a joke rather than a question. "No, Suze. I'm not even in the mood to cook my regular dishes these days, let alone try out new recipes. So if you were thinking about food poisoning, you can cross it off your list."

Cara put down her sparkling water and rubbed her forehead. The fatigue and stress that had been building up between her temples since the night before weighed her head down like lead. She remembered how terrified she was when she saw Mira passed out on the floor. She thought her heart had stopped then, as if it did not dare to beat or it would imply the passing of time and, consequently, add an additional second to the duration of Mira's unconscious state. Cara refused to think what would have happened to her heart if Mira had failed to open her eyes in the end, but she knew she was only fooling herself because the possibility of losing Mira had been haunting her this whole time.

To begin with, Mira had never had a fever before, let alone passed out from one. Then, when Mira's temperature reading made Cara gasp in panic, she tried to call Susan for help, only to find that neither her phone nor Thomas's had any signal, and, thanks to the power outage, both phones had lost internet connection as well. Worried and unsettled, she asked Thomas to go find Susan at her office. Thomas went but didn't return till much later. He said there was a note on the door saying the office was closed early because Susan was called away for an off-site medical emergency, and she would not be returning to the office that evening. So he went to Susan's house and waited there, hoping she would be home soon. However, in addition to the electricity and the cell signal, the internet and the radio had gone out as well, and combined with the unnerving growth of the eerie green vortex in the sky, the blackouts were starting to cause mass hysteria in town. As a result, with the traffic lights in the downtown area rendered inoperative by the power outage, the streets nearby were getting dangerously chaotic and congested. Fearing the situation would only grow worse, Thomas eventually decided he should go home while he still could.

When Cara learned about the situation on the streets, she only grew even more anxious than before. Although she didn't have the heart to put Mira in the car in her current state to drive through all that traffic to get on the highway, she found herself dwelling on the urge to take Mira to the emergency room in the city, for the haunting fear of losing another child was gnawing at the old scars in her heart again, making it hard to breathe.

In the end, Thomas persuaded her to keep Mira home. They had no way of knowing exactly how large an area was impacted by the blackouts, and there was no guarantee by the time they could get out of traffic and reach the highway, it wouldn't also be bogged down by panicked drivers eager to flee the area at all costs. Not to mention there could be many unforeseeable situations, even greater risks, driving through downtown, which was already highly on edge by the time Thomas was heading home.

So she and Thomas spent the rest of the evening in a high-strung state. They took turns staying up with Mira, taking her temperature and scooping out the melted water from the ice box in hopes of preserving the cubes a little longer so they could make a few more ice packs to cool off Mira's forehead. Even though it had been a sleepless night for them both, Cara could not deny it was mesmerizingly beautiful. The power outage had surrendered the entire town to the shadow of the night, so the green vortex was really brought to life. With the sky as the stage and the velvety black night as the backdrop, it looked like an enormous top made of glow-in-the-dark cotton candy, spinning out long strips of cotton-candy wisps as it rotated and grew, becoming more and more translucent in the process. The effect was spellbinding, like watching real magic being performed in the sky.

Cara remembered how the vortex's green glow had seeped through Mira's windows and caressed her little face as she slept. Her fiery red curly hair seemed to be fleeing in all directions from the burning heat radiating from her head, but her face looked peaceful and relaxed, as if she were not suffering and only asleep under a sleeping spell, so deeply and soundly that she was barely breathing. This made Cara very nervous. She found herself constantly holding her breath to make sure she could hear Mira breathe, and there were even a few times she had to put her ear next to Mira's nose to assure herself. The rational part of her knew she was probably being paranoid, but at the same time, the emotional part of her feared that her mind would cave if she had to face another loss in her life.

Cara felt a sudden pang of pain jabbing into her heart, pulling on her nerves and rippling to her limbs, causing her to wince. She closed her eyes and let out a sigh. She was tired, physically and mentally. The power had not returned yet; neither had the cell signal. She hadn't tried the radio in the car, but since the green vortex still lingered in the sky, she suspected it would not be any different. She wondered how much longer she could keep the rest of the ice cubes from melting completely. She wondered how much longer Mira's fever would last—how much longer all *this* would last.

"I'm sorry," she said in a remorseful tone. "It was a bad joke. It was not funny. I didn't mean to sound so sarcastic."

Susan gave her a loving and sympathetic smile, like how a mother would smile at her child when she needed to be comforted. "It's okay. I know you're tired. I can tell you didn't get much sleep last night. Thomas too. He looked like he had not slept at all."

At the thought of Thomas, Cara was overtaken by self-reproach. She knew he must have been as nervous as she was about Mira's fever, but she was so preoccupied with her own fears that she had not been the easiest to be around. She didn't even realize how tense she had been acting until early in the morning when Thomas came into Mira's room with a cup of hot coffee he had managed to make for her on the stove. Mira's temperature had finally come down a little by then, so he was smiling, but his face looked tired and haggard. There was a light stubble forming on his lower face, and there were dark circles decorating the bags under his bloodshot eyes, which were almost too heavy to hide behind the black frames of his glasses. Nevertheless, his gray eyes were still gentle and calm like mountain lakes, and there was a reassuring and warming quality to his smile. It was this smile that melted away the prickly shell of anxiety that had been clasping Cara like a straitjacket. And it was with this smile that he had told her he would go find Susan again before checking out the situation at work, and, with any luck, he would bring back candles and dinner. Although Cara knew it was not his intention to make her feel guilty, she couldn't help wishing she had been a little more supportive when he decided to try his hand at fixing the old power generator, which he had, as expected, failed to repair in the end. After all, she was the one unhappy about how the power outage had left her homemade lasagna only half cooked by dinnertime, and she was the one who had complained to him that she would be forced to cook a second dinner if the power didn't come back soon. He was only trying to make her happy.

Cara felt her throat tightening. She missed Thomas. She missed having his comforting scent by her side. She wished he were home.

"Definitely not a night I want to repeat." She stole a glance at the kitchen, half hoping to see Thomas opening the back door at the exact moment. "It's funny how slow time can be when you can't sleep. It felt like an eternity."

"Made you want to endure the fever for her, didn't it?" Susan said nostalgically as an old memory came to her mind. She leaned in and looked at her friend, her soft blue eyes empathetic and warm. "I'm sorry I wasn't here when you needed me. It must have been very stressful for you and Thomas, not knowing why she suddenly had such a high fever. For what it's worth, I think you made the right choice staying home. The situation did put a lot of people on edge last night. It'd have taken you forever just to get out of town safely. Her body needs good rest. Having a safe and comfortable place to sleep through the night definitely helped bring down her fever."

Cara lowered her head. Somewhere deep in her heart, she could feel the old scars aching again.

Susan continued. "Her temperature is at least under control now, which means whatever her body is fighting against is being diminished, so all you need to do now is let her rest. Make sure she stays hydrated, and her immune system will do the rest. You should try and get some sleep too. Your body needs it to stay strong to take care of her."

"I know." Cara sighed and leaned back in her chair. But she soon knitted her brows and asked, "What caused the fever though? I mean, she's never had a fever before. Never. She was perfectly fine when she got home from school yesterday, but within just a few hours, she had fainted and was burning like a furnace. It just doesn't make sense."

"I remember." Susan nodded. "I've always been amazed by how she seems to be immune to whatever germs are going around in town, even after she started school. To be honest, I don't have an answer for you. Like I said, except for the fever and the elevated heart rate, she doesn't have any other symptoms. If I had to guess,

I'd say it's either something that's just starting to spread, or something that has been around for a while but now has somehow triggered a much more aggressive response from her immune system. But no matter which one it is, the silver lining is considering this is her first time being sick, her immune system is functioning well to protect her health. So my suggestion is to let it run its course."

"I don't mean to be sarcastic," Cara said bitterly, "but did anyone ever tell you 'let it run its course' is not something a mom would wanna hear from the doctor when her child is sick? It basically sounds like the child is on her own to face the trial of 'survival of the fittest.' And while the mom can neither intervene nor help, nature and destiny can, and will, decide it all. Seriously, Suze, for a worried mom to hear that? That's just awful! At least tell her a little white lie or something to make her feel like she's still useful to her child's survival!"

Susan chuckled and shook her head slowly. "Well, that's motherhood for us. 'Constantly seeking the fine balance between controlling and letting go as they grow, yet it's always complicated by your love for the child—' "

"All right, all right!" Cara suddenly threw up her hands, her voice quavering. "I'm being paranoid because I can't let go! Is that what you want to say?"

Heavy silence fell upon them, as if the air had stopped flowing. Cara bit her lip and jerked her head to the side, but Susan kept her eyes on her friend. Cara had changed considerably in both her appearance and her temperament during the past thirteen years. Her shiny chestnut hair had lost its glossiness and become dry and coarse. Her sweet, cherubic face had withered and thinned into one with sunken cheeks and a pointed chin. The sparkles in her hazel eyes had been smothered by fear and doubt. And her enthusiastic cheerfulness had long been replaced by sarcasm and cynicism. Compared to the Cara she had known since high school, the woman in front of her almost looked like a different person, and it was all because of what had happened over thirteen years ago.

Susan felt her heart contract in pain at the thought of how much Cara had suffered back then. First, it was the two back-to-back miscarriages. Then, a little over a year later, Cara first lost her mother to a stroke and then, less than a week after, her father to cancer, which eventually led to the stillbirth just seven days after her father's passing. With everything Cara was going through at that time, it became the straw that broke the camel's back—as it would have with anyone who was unfortunate enough to go through the same. And then, amid Cara's mental breakdown from the consecutive blows, there was the abrupt farewell from Nina, their best friend since high school. The way Nina had left was painful, almost unforgivable. The whole thing had shaken Cara to the core and pushed her down into an emotional abyss. If it weren't for the arrival of Mira, she would not have been able to climb back up from there. Even so, all the emotional traumas from then had, undeniably, made Cara much more vulnerable than before. Sometimes, not even Cara herself knew whether she had only been hanging on the edge with her fingertips all these years to keep herself from slipping back down. Luckily for Cara, she had a friend who was determined to pull her out of it.

"No," said Susan, reaching for Cara's hands, which were now clenched into two fists on her lap. "You're not being paranoid. But I think something else is bothering you ... What is it, Cara? Is it ... about Nina? Did she contact you?"

Cara tensed up involuntarily. Her eyes widened as she tried to keep the tears from escaping. After a long moment of silence, she finally said, "I wish."

And that was all it took to surrender herself to the full force of the emotion she had been trying to suppress. Sadness swept over Cara like lamenting waves in a storm, flushing away whatever pitiful amount of emotional strength was left in her. She closed her eyes, hoping to swallow back the tears, only to feel them streaming out like spring water, silently and continuously; there was no stopping them, and there was no going back. She tried to wipe the tears away, but it was as useless as turning on the windshield wipers while driving in a downpour.

"What can I say? I expect to hear from her every day, but I also expect to hear nothing from her every day. I know it sounds crazy, but part of me feels like the reason we haven't heard from her at all is because she's never left. But the thought of that ..." Cara shook her head weakly, her voice trembling along with her lips. "The thought of that alone is driving me mad because—Why would she do that? Why would she pretend she'd left for a faraway land but hang around in secret? On the other hand, if she did leave, why is she not contacting us? Doesn't she care? Doesn't she want to know Mira? How could she stand it, not knowing her at all? How could she do that? ... I don't understand. I really don't understand ..." She buried her face in her hands, her shoulders shaking visibly with every inaudible sob she made into her palms. She didn't want Mira to hear her. She had made a promise to herself that she would never let Mira see her cry; she didn't want her to find out how pathetic and weak she actually was. She wished she could stop crying—if only that wish were enough to keep herself from acting the exact opposite.

"It's been over thirteen years, Suze," she murmured between sobs. "I don't know where she is. I don't know if she's okay ... I don't—I don't even know if she's still alive!"

Tears welled up in Susan's eyes. She pressed her lips together into a line and hugged her friend. Like an exhausted child who was ready to go home, Cara leaned into her arms willingly, resting her forehead on Susan's shoulder as tears dropped from her eyes and pattered down between them. Susan sniffled and, as if she were holding a tired baby who was whimpering as it drifted off to sleep, patted Cara on the back, softly and rhythmically, like how she used to comfort Chloe and Peter when they were upset, a long time ago, when the twins were still little, when they were still close.

Susan smiled wistfully at the thought of her kids. Her heart ached with longing for the time that she could neither turn back nor relive. "It's already been that long, huh?" She sniffled again and leaned away to look at Cara, drying her face with a hand. "You know what? I also feel like Nina has never really left. Sometimes, I get this funny feeling that she's watching us, from somewhere afar, observing our choices and actions as she disapproves of them through her own opinions, which neither of us would want to hear or acknowledge because, you know, they tend to turn out to be big ugly truths that we'd rather know nothing about beforehand." She paused, wearing a resigned smile, then she suddenly rolled her eyes in a comical fashion and groaned, "Argh, I couldn't stand how she was always right."

Cara's sobs broke into a snort. "Me too! And that I-told-you-so smirk on her face when she found out what we did had just proved her right again? That annoyed the hell out of me every, single, time!"

Susan let out a stifled guffaw. "Oh . . . I remember those! I also remember you got so irritated one day and told her to stop doing it, saying it was giving you wrinkles and gray hairs. But she just looked at you, dead serious, and told you it was only natural to have wrinkles and gray hairs because you were aging!"

Cara shook with a suppressed belly laugh "Ah . . . yes, I remember. I honestly didn't know if I should laugh or cry when I heard that. Gosh, she could be such a pain sometimes." She gave a soft sigh and, with a smile still lingering on her tearstained face, grabbed a napkin from the napkin holder and dabbed at her eyes. "We had so much fun together though, the three of us . . . Do you remember how she always made these jaw-dropping comments at the worst moments possible?" She tittered. "Remember the time when we were trying to decide if we should brave the haunted house at the carnival? Remember what she said to us? She said, 'Don't waste your time on meaningless decisions. Life is short. You may not even be alive in the next minute. Do you want this to be the last thing you do before you die?'"

Susan laughed and gave a clap. "Of course I remember! We were so spooked that we turned on our heels and ran! We must have looked like a pair of scared jackrabbits, thinking the haunted house was coming to life to get us or something ... Oh, oh! What about the time when we made her go shopping with us? I was picking out a dress, and she pretty much said the same thing to me! I swear, it gave me goose bumps from head to toe, and I was only trying to decide which dress to buy!"

Cara chortled loudly. "The dress for your first date, right? I remember. The contrast between your expressions was hilarious! You were staring at her, eyes wide like a deer in headlights, but she just looked at you with a baffled frown like she didn't know what was going on with you!"

"Oh yes, her I-don't-understand-you-people face. It was *so* Nina." Susan nodded enthusiastically and giggled. "Whenever we talked about boys, she'd put on that face, and she'd say something like"—she knitted her brow and raised her chin, then she continued in a resigned yet slightly annoyed tone—" 'Don't waste your time on unnecessary interactions. Time never comes back, no matter how much you want it to.' "

Susan's impersonation of Nina made Cara laugh so hard that she had to hold her belly. "Right! Boys were categorized as 'unnecessary interactions' in her dictionary. Remember when poor Michael came to ask her for a dance at the New Year's Eve party, but she just frowned and said, 'I don't have time for you. Please go away.' in front of everybody? Talk about being mortified! I asked her why she had to turn him down so bluntly, you know, without any sugarcoating at all; she replied with a deadpan face, saying that because it was the truth and that"—Cara cleared her throat and continued in a pretentious voice that sounded like a commercial—" 'Life is all about choices. Make good choices. Don't waste your time.' "

"And if you failed to make good choices, fear not, because instead of comforting you, she'd look at you with an annoying smirk, and she'd say, 'It hurts because your brain wants you to remember not to make the same mistake twice.' " Susan nodded along like a little girl reciting a quote from her parents. With that, they both dissolved into laughter, holding their sides breathlessly like two silly kids who couldn't stop laughing even though neither of them could tell you why it was so funny or, for that matter, what they were laughing about in the first place. It was as if they had traveled back to the good old days, when they were still young and carefree enough to laugh like this.

"I miss her," said Cara as she tried to blink back the tears that had somehow filled her eyes again.

Wearing a sad smile, Susan replied, "Me too, Cara. Me too."

Cara tilted her head back and gazed at the ceiling. With a melancholy tone in her voice, she said, "Why do you think she chose to leave like that?"

"I don't know," Susan answered softly. "But knowing Nina, there must have been a very good reason for her to make that choice. We just need to believe she made the best possible choice, whatever the reason was . . ." She looked down and inhaled deeply, then she raised her head and said, "Besides, it's not like she's completely gone from our lives." She put a hand over her heart. "She managed to leave something in here to interfere with our thoughts from time to time, like how she used to drop her mind-boggling comments on us when we least expected them. Maybe that's why it feels like she has never left."

Absent-mindedly, Cara pressed a hand to her left chest and was momentarily disappointed to feel nothing more than the slow, dull beating of her own heart. Still, she hoped Susan was right. She hoped Nina had only chosen to leave because she didn't have a better choice. She wondered whether Nina had ever regretted it, and if she had, whether it was enough for her to, one day, change her mind and come back.

Cara felt the stress on her neck disappearing. The tension in her muscles was also reducing, until, at last, she felt her body sag in the chair with fatigue like an overstretched rubber band. She drew a deliberate, deep breath and exhaled slowly. It had been a long thirteen years. Every single cell in her felt tired and exhausted.

"Suze?" she said quietly, gazing down at her knees. "I'm sorry I snapped at you for giving me parenting advice."

Susan smiled and gave her a reassuring squeeze of her hand. "It's okay. You were tired, and you were under a lot of stress from last night. It was not a good idea for me to say things like that to you in the first place."

"It's just that . . . it sounded a lot like something Nina would say if she knew what a nervous wreck I'd been about Mira," Cara added in a small voice.

"That's probably because those were her words," Susan said pensively. "That's what she said to me when I told her I didn't know how I could ever win Chloe and Peter back. Remember how mad they were at me when they found out Ben and I were getting divorced? They thought it was my fault that their father wanted to split up our family and marry another woman, so they refused to talk to me or interact with me, like they could deny me my role as their mother by pretending I did not exist . . ." She gave a soft sigh before continuing. "I didn't want to think about what she said then. It was too painful for me to digest and understand. So I pretended to not hear the ring of truth to it. But guess what? As Chloe and Peter grew into teenagers and learned to give me more attitude and headaches than ever, I finally realized what she'd revealed to me back then was the reason for all the heartaches and struggles I'd had as a mother all along. Maybe that was why I felt the need to repeat her words to you earlier . . ." She gazed into space, looking lost in thought, then an amused smile came to her lips. "Just imagine the smirk on Nina's face if she'd heard what I just said. It'd probably give both of us wrinkles and gray hairs and make us age ten more years!"

Cara let out a long wheezing laugh, breathless. Susan joined her with a suppressed giggle but soon stopped when she noticed Cara's laugh had turned into a cry.

"I'm sorry," Cara sobbed as she alternated her hands to dry her face. "I don't know why I'm crying . . . It was a joke! It was a funny joke!"

Susan didn't say anything. She patted Cara on the back and passed her a napkin.

Cara took the napkin and pressed it against her eyes. "Look at me, crying like a fountain today. I don't know what's gotten into me . . ."

Susan remained silent for a while, then she said gently, "Cara, I think you might be experiencing the Anniversary Effect."

Cara peeled the wet napkin off her puffy eyes and sniffled. "What's that?"

"It's a term to describe the fluctuations in emotion and mood one might experience around the anniversary of a . . . painful event in life," said Susan, carefully picking her words. "In your case, some of the painful events you've experienced took place in quick succession within a month. So it's possible that the Anniversary Effect of each of those events had been stacking up all this time and are only now releasing in one go, when you least expect it."

"Like . . . just now?"

"Yes," Susan replied softly. "But it's good to let it all out. Think of yourself as one of those temples in ancient Greece. The significant events in your life are like the pillars in that temple. It only takes the fall of a few pillars to weaken the entire building. So by releasing the suppressed emotions that have been stacking up within some of the pillars like expanding pressure, which would otherwise lead to cracks in the structure, you're helping those pillars stay strong for your temple."

"My temple . . ." A melancholy smile appeared on Cara's face. "I can't remember what my temple looks like anymore. I don't even feel like myself anymore. Actually, I haven't felt like myself for quite a while, ever since . . . since . . ." She drew a shaky breath and buried her face in her palms.

"I know," Susan whispered, feeling a lump in her throat. She held out a hand and rubbed Cara's back. "That's why you need to get those pent-up emotions off your chest. You want to hold on to them as memories, but they have become your burdens. You need to let them go, Cara. And you should talk to Thomas about this. It'll help."

Cara reached for another napkin to dry her face, but she didn't look up.

Susan leaned forward to catch her eyes. "There's nothing wrong with showing your wounds to the people you love, okay? Thomas is a good man. He cares about you, a lot. He knows there are wounds in your heart, but he won't be able to help you in mending those wounds if he doesn't even know what they're like, right? Isn't that what love is for anyway? To cure each other's wounds?"

Cara thought of the cup of hot coffee Thomas had made for her on the stove that morning, of his bloodshot eyes and his light stubble, of the warmth and tenderness in the way he had smiled at her. She felt a pang of guilt clutching at her chest, forcing her to look back and reflect. Deep down, she knew she had never fully recovered from all the heartbreaks that had bombarded her over thirteen years ago. There were times when she wondered whether she would ever be able to find her way back to her old self, and times when she questioned the purpose of this new self that she was turning into. But no matter how bad those times had been, Thomas was always there, loving and accepting, quietly attending to her emotions and moods while always trying his best to bring a smile to her face in his own special ways.

"Honestly, I didn't know what to expect when I pulled into the parking lot at the office this morning," said Susan, "but I definitely did not expect to see Thomas waiting there by the entrance. As soon as he spotted my car, he ran toward it, waving his arms like a man who had been stranded at sea for days and finally caught sight of a passing boat. I wish you could see the expression on his face; he looked like a kid who'd finally caught Santa Claus on Christmas Eve! I don't know how long he'd been standing there, but he seemed cold. Yet the first thing he said to me was how glad he was to have caught me at the office, because you'd been too worried about Mira to eat or sleep." She paused and made Cara look at her for emphasis. "I'm telling you, Cara, you're very important to him. He might not always know what he could do to help, but he would move mountains for you in trying."

Cara felt her throat tightening as a wave of lamentation washed over her. In her mind's eye, she saw her eight-year-old self sitting on the beach, drenched in sea water. She was hugging her legs tightly, with her face buried between her knees, sobbing uncontrollably. And there he was, the nine-year-old Thomas, wrapping her in a bath towel that he had run all the way home to fetch for her to dry her off and keep her warm.

"So don't be afraid to show your wounds to him. He cares about you, and he cares about what you're going through. You married the right man, Cara," Susan said with a wink. "Me, on the other hand . . ." She sighed and shook her head. "You know, sometimes I wonder whether things would have turned out differently for me and Ben if I had been as attentive to him as Thomas has been to you . . . We might still be together in Chicago. The kids might still think of me as a workaholic and a lousy mom. I might still be struggling between career and motherhood and still be torn between pursuing my passion and fulfilling my duties as a mother and a wife . . ." She gazed into space, a sad smile on her lips, and continued, "But then, I wouldn't have moved here, to this obscure town out of all places, trying to find my peace and my purpose again. I wouldn't have come to check on Mira today, and we wouldn't be sitting here, chatting and crying and laughing about life like when we were still roommates, when it was just the three of us . . ." She turned her gaze to Cara and gave a wry chuckle. "She was right, you know. 'Choices. Life is all about choices.'"

Cara wished she could say something to comfort her friend. Unlike Susan, she was never good at consoling people. She knew it was still painful for Susan to remember the divorce and the separation from her kids. She hated for Susan to have to go through all that. Back in college, Susan and Ben were the perfect couple, the object of envy of the entire school. No one had thought that the golden couple would choose to walk their separate ways one day —no one except Nina, who was always cynical about the necessity of relationships.

"Do you regret it?" Cara eventually asked. "The divorce."

Susan gazed up with a sharp inhale, trying to imagine what it would be like if she hadn't signed the papers, but she soon decided it was unnecessary. "No. There was really nothing left to salvage between us. Might as well open the cage to set us both free." She sighed softly, a pensive look in her eyes. "That said, if I had the ability to turn back time, I'd probably choose to do a lot of things quite differently for my marriage . . ."

She shook her head, trying to shake the thought off her mind. "Anyway, speaking about turning back time, I should get going. I still have a patient—"

A chill ran down Susan's spine and interrupted her sentence, jogging her memory about the two bottomless black holes she had seen in that patient's eyes. Her heart immediately began to race. She clutched the armrests and, focusing hard to direct her mind back to her surroundings, pushed herself up from the chair.

She caught sight of the sparkling water on the table and reached for it in a hurry. The carbonated liquid, though already a little flat, was able to ease the tightness that had clasped her throat. Feeling a bit more in control of herself, she leaned down and gave Cara a hug. "I'll come by after work to see how Mira's doing, probably around dinnertime."

Cara cocked an eyebrow. "Does that mean I have to make dinner for you as well?"

Susan gave an innocent shrug. "Well, it *is* called dinnertime . . ."

Cara rolled her eyes. "Fine. But whose dinnertime are you talking about? Yours or ours? Yours is literally our bedtime, you know. If we had to wait on you to eat, we might starve to death before you got here."

Susan laughed. "Fair enough. You don't need to wait for me. Just save me a plate."

"I can do better than that," said Cara, scratching her chin in a thoughtful manner. "I can keep you company while you eat . . . *if* there's wine."

"I'll bring the wine," said Susan, chortling as she walked toward the back door. She picked up her medical bag, opened the door, then she paused and twisted around to look at Cara. "You talk to Thomas, okay?"

Cara made a face at her, but she nodded.

Susan chuckled under her breath. "Good girl. Now go get some rest. I don't want you to fall asleep when I'm enjoying my dinner tonight; you'll drool all over my food."

And with that, Dr. Susan Heart left the little yellow house and drove off for her next engagement. She made a right turn at the end of the driveway and got onto a one-lane dirt road, which was the only way in and out of the area that belonged to Sunrise Park. She followed it to a big, open field in front of a wooded hill. The field didn't have a name on the map, but it was generally referred to as Sunset Field by the locals.

The one-lane dirt road widened into a two-lane gravel road at Sunset Field. As Susan pressed down on the gas pedal to pick up speed, memories from the night before crept back into her mind like the claws of a tenacious ghost. And even though she had turned on the heat in the car, it was not enough to stop the chills from running down her spine.

IV

Susan was just wondering why the siren was wailing right in front of her office when the blaring noise came to an abrupt stop. She asked the patient to give her a moment and stepped out into the hallway just in time to see Chief William Johnson and Officer Neil O'Brien approaching the front desk, a level of urgency in their steps.

Both officers were very tall and had a muscular build, which made Susan feel as if she were standing in front of a human wall and would have to strain her neck to maintain eye contact. Chief Johnson was in his late thirties. His big brown eyes and charming dimples gave him a boyish look, but he had successfully offset it with a full beard, which added at least ten years to his appearance. Officer O'Brien was in his mid-thirties. He was a well-groomed man with a pale complexion and sharp blue eyes, and he always seemed to be brooding over something serious. Today, however, he looked rather distressed.

"Good evening, Officers." Susan greeted them with a smile. "I take it you didn't come here for a health check?"

"Good evening, Dr. Heart," said Chief Johnson, sounding a bit distracted. "I'm afraid not. There's a case . . . quite an unusual one, and you're the only doctor whose office is still open at this time . . . and the only licensed psychiatrist in town."

Susan already knew where this was going. She nodded and said, "I see. What do you need me to do?"

"We're hoping you could come and give us some on-site assistance . . . and guidance," said the chief, "to help us proceed with the investigation."

"Of course," Susan replied. "I'll gladly offer my assistance in the matter, Chief. We can schedule a time—"

"We need your help *now*." Officer O'Brien stabbed the air with an index finger, punching an invisible button to emphasize his words. Susan was surprised to be cut off by the officer, who was known for his manners, but she was even more surprised to see the uneasiness in his eyes.

Chief Johnson gave Officer O'Brien a stern look. "Neil, Dr. Heart does not work for the bureau. Even though she's never turned down our request for assistance since she moved here, she's still doing us a favor. We're here to ask for her help, so we should respect her schedule and her availability in rendering it to us." He turned to Susan and said apologetically, "Please excuse our manners, Dr. Heart. We're still a bit, um . . . preoccupied with the investigation. We're very grateful that you've agreed to assist us again. However, due to the . . . perplexity of this case, we'd like to ask for your immediate assistance, if possible."

It was not his words but rather the look on his face that made Susan wonder what kind of "unusual" case could unsettle a man that was big and strong like a tree trunk. Whatever it was though, as someone who was always eager to study and solve a puzzling medical case, Susan was very much intrigued to find out what she could do for their investigation. Luckily, there were no more patients to be seen. Most of the people that had come in earlier had decided to cancel their appointments and left in a hurry after Linda, the receptionist hired by the previous owner of Susan's clinic, whom Susan had graciously agreed to keep in spite of the objection from her intuition, excitedly announced to everyone in the waiting area that there was a giant green UFO hovering in the sky. Since then, there had been no walk-ins. Even the office phone had been unusually quiet, with no more calls coming in for questions or appointments at all.

"Actually, I'm about to wrap up with my last patient, so I should be able to leave the office soon," said Susan.

"That's great!" Chief Johnson made a dull clap with his big, thick hands. "Thank you, Dr. Heart. We're beyond grateful."

"Glad to help, Chief. How about you gentlemen go ahead first, and I'll head over when I'm done here? Should I go to the police station? ... No? Well, give me the address ..." said Susan as she searched the pockets on her lab coat for her phone.

"I think it's best that we wait for you here," said the chief. "Traffic's building up fast. It seems like everyone's anxious to leave town to avoid finding out what's going to happen next. You'll need a police car to clear the way."

Susan pulled her phone out from one of the inner pockets. "That's very considerate of you, Chief." She smiled at him and turned on her phone screen. "I prefer not to make you wait though. I can always search for an alternate route to avoid the streets with heavy traffic ... Wait, what's wrong with my phone?"

"It's not your phone," Officer O'Brien said grimly. "It's everybody's. The cell signal went out over an hour ago. The internet too."

"What?"

"So did the power. You probably didn't notice it since you've got a backup generator here," Chief Johnson added, gesturing toward the fluorescent lights over his head. "The radio went out as well. My officers are having a hard time staying in contact with each other. According to some, the blackouts all happened at the same time, when that green thing appeared in the sky."

What he said prompted Susan to glance at the window. But instead of the green thing that Linda had referred to as "a giant green UFO," she saw a reflection of Linda's face, which was being painted on the cheeks by a big brush. Susan turned to the busy receptionist. "Linda, did you know?"

Linda snapped her compact shut and slipped the brush into her purse. She cleared her throat deliberately and looked up at Susan. "Know what?"

"The cell signal and the internet are out? And the power? The radio?"

Linda blinked innocently in Susan's direction, fluttering the unyielding eyelashes she had just strengthened with a fresh coat of the new waterproof and volumizing mascara she had purchased in the city over the weekend. "No, Dr. Heart. I've been *very* busy with reorganizing the filing cabinets. You asked me to finish that today, remember?"

Maybe it was the ostentatious makeup on her face, or maybe it was the sarcastic undertone in her voice, but for a split second, Susan thought she was back in Chicago, failing at yet another attempt to get her teenage daughter to answer a question without receiving a comeback. She forced a deep breath into her chest and turned to the police officers. "Well, I guess that explains why the office phone has stayed quiet for so long. I thought it was just one of those days where people would rather go observe an astronomical phenomenon than call in for an appointment to have their blood pressure taken at the doctor's." She slipped her phone into an outer pocket and gave it a gentle pat to make herself remember where to look for it later. "So, what caused the blackouts?"

Chief Johnson shook his head. "We don't know yet. We've never had a quadruple blackout before, and so far, we haven't received any word from the mayor. It's hard to say how bad the impact will be on the town as a whole if the situation continues throughout the rest of the evening. Whatever the cause is, I hope it can be resolved quickly"—he exchanged a look with Officer O'Brien—"and I can only hope it will not lead to an exhausting night for my officers."

" 'Tis the aliens, no doubt!" Linda butted in. "That's their UFO!" She tapped at the window with a perfectly manicured red fingernail, pointing at the green vortex that was rotating slowly in the sky. When she saw the confused looks on the officers' faces, she clicked her tongue and scoffed. "Do you not watch the movies? Electricity is the first thing that goes out when the UFOs come down! It's jamming our cell signals and the internet and the radio to prevent us from contacting Uncle Sam for help! But this is only the first stage of their plan, I tell ya. The second stage is—" She paused and quickly scanned the street in front of the office through the window before lowering her voice. "The second stage is to bring mayhem to the town so nobody knows they're taking control over us, brainwashing us, and abducting us, one person at a time!"

Susan felt a guffaw escaping her lungs, but she caught it just in time. The officers, however, were not only not in the least amused, but their expression had also changed from one of graveness to that of concern. As ludicrous as the UFO theory might sound, it did offer a thrilling explanation to the quadruple blackout, not to mention the size and the shape of the green vortex did seem too anomalous to be a natural phenomenon. Still, Susan couldn't help but wonder which part of Linda's words had led to such an unexpected reaction in the police officers. She wondered if it had something to do with the case she had been invited to assist them with. Either way, she had a feeling it was going to be a case like no other.

So Susan decided to let Linda go home. Without incoming patients, there was no point in keeping her at the office anyway. Plus, Linda was now rambling on to the officers about how to make tinfoil hats properly to shield themselves from the alien mind-controlling devices in the impending doom, which was starting to give her a real headache. Linda accepted the early dismissal by telling Susan it was her loss not to listen to the lifesaving tips on how to survive an alien attack that she had gathered from the internet over the years. Then she sashayed to the front door on her six-inch-high heels and cheerfully, in a flirtatious sort of way, waved goodbye to the officers.

Once the clicks of Linda's high heels had faded beyond the front door, along with her headache, Susan excused herself from the officers and went back to her last patient to wrap things up. After she had sent the patient on his way, she wrote a note to explain why her office was closed early and taped it to the front door, just in case any of her patients decided they would like to have their blood pressure taken after all. When that was done, she followed the police officers into the parking lot and hopped into her car with her medical bag. Chief Johnson was right; the traffic was much heavier on the streets. Even the one in front of her office was much more crowded than it usually was at that time of the day, especially in the direction of downtown. Officer O'Brien signaled her to follow them out and turned on the siren to clear the way. Susan gave him a thumbs-up from the window and trailed behind them into the street. She made a left turn after the police car and, led by its flashing beacon, headed in the opposite direction of downtown.

She followed the police car all the way to the edge of the town till they reached Sunset Field. It was a big, open field at the foot of Sunrise Park, which shared one of its hills with Cara's house. Technically speaking, this field was part of Sunrise Park, but the locals had been calling it Sunset Field for as long as she could remember, since she had moved from Chicago to this obscure town.

Presently, the police car slowed down and cut straight into the field. Due to the power outage, not a single light was lit in the area. But thanks to the vortex above them, the field seemed to be glowing with an eerie green tint, and Susan was even able to make out the silhouettes of the trees standing on the hill at the end of the field.

Feeling awestruck by the view, Susan pulled slowly into the field. Besides Chief Johnson and Officer O'Brien's car, two more police cars were parked in the middle. Their beacons were flashing, and their headlights were pointing at the same spot, where a few police officers stood around a shape that was slouched to the ground. Susan parked behind the police cars and turned off the engine.

As soon as she opened the door, she heard a soft, low humming noise that was coming from every direction in the field. At first, she thought it was some kind of white noise, but instead of inducing drowsiness, this one made her feel nervous and alert. What's more, the longer she focused on it, the more uneasy she became. And that was enough for her to confirm her initial suspicion that the source of this unsettling noise was the monstrous green vortex.

The moment her mind had completed the connection, Susan felt a chill down her spine that made her hair stand on end. A mixture of uncertainty and fear crept over her. But fortunately, as a woman of science, she was able to rely on her rational brain to remind herself that although it might seem improbable, the sensible explanation would be the green vortex was not only rotating but also vibrating, thereby producing a noise that she could only hear now that she was standing near its mouthlike center. However, she could not explain to herself how or, for that matter, why it was vibrating.

Maybe it was because of the noise, or maybe it was because Susan was now physically in the field, but the eerie green tint that was reflecting off its surface looked even more unnatural than before. It was as if something unknowable was being transmitted up into the green vortex, even though all that was visible to the human eye was the ominous color of its light. Susan took a deep breath and pushed those thoughts out of her mind. Then she grabbed her medical bag and walked over to Chief Johnson and Officer O'Brien, who had just been briefed by one of the other officers.

"Dr. Heart, I'm afraid the suspect's condition hasn't changed much since we left to ask for your assistance," said Chief Johnson, turning to Susan. Like Officer O'Brien, both his face and his uniform seemed unnaturally green, adding an extraterrestrial quality to his appearance. Susan wondered if she too looked like a green alien to the officers. "Before you examine him," continued the chief, lowering his voice, "I think it's necessary that we fill you in on how we came to find him here in the first place."

Susan waited patiently for Chief Johnson to begin, though goose bumps were already forming on her forearms.

Chief Johnson seemed to be having a hard time finding the right words to begin. He pressed his lips together, reached into a pocket, and took out a small notepad. With a deep inhale, he turned on a flashlight and flipped it open, then he finally said, "Earlier this evening, a senior couple rushed into the station to report the sighting of—and I quote—'an extremely dangerous Satanist.' According to the couple, he was spotted at dusk, not long after this green ... thing appeared out of nowhere in the sky. By the couple's account, he was staggering from utility pole to utility pole, jabbering senselessly while bashing his head against the poles—and I quote from my record here—'to trace out a satanic symbol by marking the corresponding utility poles with his blood as a sacrifice so he could channel Hell into this world and summon the Devil.' The couple was convinced that he was making good progress in his attempt, as his actions coincided with the expansion of—and I quote again—'the portal to Hell in the sky,' which they believed was the evidence of his impending success, and which, they also believed, was responsible for the total blackout of our electricity and communication systems to cripple the normal day-to-day of human society before Satan's arrival. The couple told me that was why, instead of fleeing town, they drove in to the station to report him. They were counting on us to terminate his ritual in time to prevent him from opening 'the portal to Hell,' which, they emphasized, would otherwise unleash death and destruction upon us all."

Susan shivered involuntarily as a chill crept down her spine, but she was not sure whether it was triggered by the content of the couple's account or the logic behind it.

"At the end of our conversation, the couple insisted on me sending police officers to the location where the 'Satanist' was last sighted." Chief Johnson slipped the notepad back into his pocket and turned off the flashlight. "Needless to say, we were under a lot of pressure to find the person in question right away. The good news was, once we had arrived, it only took us about five minutes to find the guy; we simply followed the utility poles in opposite directions, and he was soon spotted here in Sunset Field. The officers who saw him first observed visible bloodstains on his face and clothing. Considering it might be an indication that he could be a threat to himself and others, they determined police intervention was necessary after all. And since we could no longer radio or call each other, they turned on the siren to signal us that they'd found our guy.

"They were half expecting he would run from the police car at the sound of the siren, but he didn't seem to hear it at all. So the officers decided to approach him on foot.

"Office O'Brien and I were just arriving then . . . I should have known something was wrong. He didn't even seem to notice the police officers or the police cars. He just kept on tottering aimlessly in the field like he was under the influence." Chief Johnson paused and looked down at his feet. Then, as though something heavy was weighing on his mind, he raised his head slowly. "What happened next was a shocker to us all. Instead of following the officers' order to remain where he was and hold up his hands, he suddenly dropped to his knees and started crying for our help to save him from the Devil. This caught everyone off guard and stunned us all. The fact that the so-called 'Satanist' was begging for our help to save him from the Devil? . . . We were at a loss.

"However, just when the other officers turned to me to decide how to handle the situation, he laughed . . . It was the most sinister laugh I've ever heard and I could ever imagine hearing in my life. Next thing we knew, he was smashing his head in with a big rock from the ground, dead set on cracking his skull open." Chief Johnson shook his head, as though he still couldn't believe what he had witnessed. Officer O'Brien stood quietly by his side and stared at the ground with an expression of someone who was feeling carsick.

"Our first reaction was to stop him from causing more harm to himself, of course," Chief Johnson continued quietly after some time, looking lost in thought. "Officer O'Brien and I rushed over to grab his arms, but he . . . he flung us aside like we were feathers, like he possessed some kind of supernatural power . . . The other officers ran to us to help. It took us a while, but eventually we were able to subdue him to the ground and pry the rock from his fingers. That was when he began to scream, something about the Devil, at the top of his lungs, right before he started convulsing violently on the ground, thrashing and twisting and jerking as he screamed, like something was about to rip him open from the inside.

"Fearing that he might be having a seizure or something worse, we turned him over to examine his condition. To our surprise, under the bright headlights, one of the officers recognized him as Eric

Ekker, a fifteen-year-old boy who plays on the same soccer team with his son. What's more, he had played in their team's soccer match earlier this afternoon, acting perfectly normal.

"We're not sure why, but at the mention of his name, Eric's convulsion stopped, and he stopped screaming too. But that was it. We can't get him to answer any question to explain why he was acting this way. According to the officer who identified him, he'd been volunteering as an assistant coach for their soccer team for months, but he had never seen Eric in such a disturbed mental state before."

Chief Johnson looked at Susan then, as though he had finally returned from his thoughts. "At first, I thought we could take him back to the station to have a thorough examination there. But every time we tried to get him into the car, he would have a seizure-like episode and scream like a victim from a horror movie, each time sounding even more hysterical than before. So eventually I decided it was best to invite you here.

"I've sent two officers to look for Eric's address to contact his parents. I'm sure they'll want answers and explanations when they get here and see the condition of their son. But right now, I have none. Something must have happened to Eric after the soccer match and before he caught the attention of the senior couple. The question is, what could have happened to a fifteen-year-old boy in such a short time frame to put him into such a shocking state? Are we dealing with a misfortune or a tragedy? Who else is involved? Why did he come here after the soccer match? Where else had he been before coming here? Could this area turn out to be a part of an unspeakable crime scene? . . . There are so many questions that need to be answered before we can determine the nature of this case. But so far, Eric hasn't responded or reacted to any of them. We're not even sure whether it's because he can't hear us, or he can but just doesn't understand what we're saying anymore.

"That's why we need your help, Dr. Heart. We're hoping you can find a way to get him to talk, to give us some information, some clues. I mean, if there's something more to this that we've not yet discovered . . . if there's something real sinister going on in this part of the town that has caused him to behave like this, we need to find out what it is, and we need to put an end to it, fast."

Not too far behind Chief Johnson and Officer O'Brien, the other officers were murmuring something indistinctive to each other. Susan tilted her head and peered past Officer O'Brien in their direction, and she suddenly realized the shape surrounded by the other officers was actually a person, hunching so low on the ground that she could barely see the head.

By then, Susan already knew it was going to be a very difficult case, but she said, "I'll try my best. By the way, did you notice any physical evidence likely to suggest he was exposed to some sort of traumatizing experience?"

"That's the thing," Officer O'Brien said uncomfortably. "Based on our preliminary visual examination, there's no sign of physical assault or the like. The only injuries we can see are the wounds on his forehead, which were determined to be self-inflicted."

"In that case . . ." Susan turned to Chief Johnson. "May I know what gave you the impression that his condition was induced? You seemed . . . certain of it."

Both Chief Johnson and Officer O'Brien fell silent. Their eyes glazed over, and they became very still, looking like two wax figures from the Community Helpers section at a wax museum, only greener.

"A hunch, then?" Susan offered helpfully.

"He was screaming about a female devil," Officer O'Brien whispered under his breath. " 'She's the Devil! She's the Devil!' was all he said. But the way he screamed . . . it was like his limbs were being torn off by invisible claws, or a wake of ghost vultures was picking his insides out . . ."

"I think he saw something . . . something he was not supposed to see," said the chief. "I know the probability of someone running into a real-life she-devil from Hell should be close to zero, but after what we've witnessed this evening, I can't help but wonder whether our perceptions of what is possible and what is not possible were misconceived." He gave Susan an apologetic smile. "I have to say, on some level, it's a relief to have a woman of science to assist us with this case . . . you know, to remind us what is possible and what is not, to keep our minds from slipping into dark places."

Susan smiled back and nodded. Her heart, however, was not so sure if she could continue to provide the level of psychological relief that the chief was hoping to share with his officers. She walked past Chief Johnson and Officer O'Brien toward the shape on the ground, which was being guarded by the other officers. They saw her approaching and stepped back to make room for her, considerately turning on a couple of flashlights from the opposite direction of the headlights for her to see the boy clearly.

Eric Ekker was kneeling on the ground with his head bent low. He was hunched over a hole, digging at it with his bare hands with such determination and focus that he seemed to be looking for something he had buried there before. His fingers were covered in a muddy mixture of dirt and blood. His wrists were connected by a pair of handcuffs that appeared to be too large for his skinny hands, producing muffled clanking sounds with each digging motion he made.

When Susan was only a few steps away from him, she paused to observe his reaction. Eric didn't seem to notice her, however. He just kept on digging feverishly, all the while jabbering something incomprehensible under his breath.

Susan inhaled deeply and sat down in front of him. Then, in a voice that was as gentle and soft as a lullaby, she called the boy's name.

Eric's head jerked up; the flashlights immediately followed, illuminating a face stained with drip trails from his bloody forehead, along with his messy brown hair that was matted with dried blood. He was staring at Susan straight in the eye with a pair of fully dilated pupils that looked like two bottomless black holes in the whites of his eyes, emitting nothing but total horror and despair.

Chills shot down Susan's spine like icy darts, paralyzing her limbs. She didn't know what it was, but something from the two bottomless black holes clutched her by the throat so tightly that she could neither speak nor breathe. Worse still, as the grip on her neck tightened, the black holes seemed to be growing and merging into a dark void, a blackness so empty and large that it was swallowing her in . . .

There was a flash of light from somewhere behind her. The dark void started to shrink, and its grip on her throat began to loosen. But just as it returned to Eric's face and resumed the form of a pair of bottomless black holes in his eyes, Susan saw a flight of stairs unfolding, quickly descending into the endless depths of a black abyss in a spiraling free fall, with her on it, until eventually, it showed her what was at the end: a sea of roaring flames, the portal to Hell, the gate of Death . . . and demons, so many demons —thrashing, flailing, and convulsing in the burning sea as they screamed, "She's the Devil! She's the Devil! She's the Devil . . . !"

"Dr. Heart! Dr. Heart!" an urgent voice shouted from above her, sounding distant and muffled, as though her head were under water, reminding her of the consequences if she failed to swim up soon. Susan tried to kick the water to push herself up, but no matter how hard she kicked or what kind of stroke she used, she remained at the bottom. In a panic, Susan opened her mouth to cry for help, only to realize no sound was coming from her throat. Just as fear and despair took over her, something cold was splashed onto her face. Like a drowning man whose head was finally pulled from the water, Susan felt the much-needed air rippling across her face and gasped for breath, choking and coughing and wheezing as she did.

"Are you okay?" asked a nervous voice next to her.

Still panting, Susan turned her head slowly to look at the source of that voice: it was Chief Johnson. He was supporting her upper body with his arm. Officer O'Brien was right next to him, holding an opened bottle of water with trembling hands and dread in his eyes. The other officers stood silently behind them, looking dazed, as though they no longer knew what was not possible in this world.

Feeling the chills returning to her spine, Susan asked in a small voice, "What . . . happened?"

"I'm not sure." Chief Johnson's expression was not only grave but also distressed. "One moment, you and the boy were staring at each other in silence, the next your face was turning blue, like you couldn't breathe, and you weren't responding to us ... My instinct told me to break your eye contact with him. That was when you fell backward like a statue. Yet you still wouldn't respond to us, even though your eyes were wide open ... so we splashed your face with water ..."

"I couldn't breathe," Susan said weakly. "I thought I was drowning ... in a dark void ... a black abyss ... a sea of flames ..."

Chief Johnson either didn't hear her or chose not to. "You need to rest, Dr. Heart," he said softly. "Can you walk? You can lie down in the car for a bit while we seal off the area. We'll escort you back afterward. It's getting late anyway. We should all get some rest." He helped Susan up and gave Officer O'Brien a nudge with his elbow. "Neil? ... Neil! Go grab a blanket for Dr. Heart. Tell the team we're wrapping up and sealing off the area for the night. We'll resume the investigation in the morning."

Chief Johnson half carried Susan to her car and helped her lie down in the back. Officer O'Brien brought over a blanket and a bottle of water. Susan took the blanket, but with the drowning sensation still lingering in her chest, she didn't touch the water. She wrapped the blanket around herself tightly and stared numbly out of the opened car door. Even though the blanket was warm, she couldn't stop shivering. She forced herself to take deep breaths and focus on the green vortex to keep all other thoughts out of her head, but the image of the two bottomless black holes in Eric Ekker's eyes always managed to sneak back into her mind.

Her failure in defending the last bit of composure of her rattled self was temporarily relieved by the urgent cries of a police siren rushing their way. Susan followed the incoming police car with her eyes and noticed there was another car trailing closely behind. Both cars made a sharp turn from the road and screeched to a halt next to where the other police cars were parked. Four car doors were then swung open in a great hurry, almost simultaneously, followed by rustling footsteps running toward the middle of the field. Before long, a woman's cry pierced the sky, prolonging into a desperate howl.

Susan pushed herself up and looked toward the direction of that heart-wrenching wail. There, under the headlights of the police cars, a woman was clutching Eric's head to her chest and sobbing loudly, like a little girl whose beloved rag doll was torn apart. A man stood motionlessly next to them, his head drooping heavily from his neck.

And Eric Ekker just kept on digging.

V

Cara woke up feeling peaceful and rested. She didn't know when sleep had taken her over; she only remembered lying on the couch and thinking about her conversation with Susan. Nevertheless, it was a deep and dreamless nap, and Cara couldn't remember the last time she had slept so soundly.

She sat up and took a long and deliberate stretch, inhaling deeply. There was a sweet and cheesy aroma in the air, like the smell of fresh pizza. She turned her head and looked toward the kitchen. Thomas was in there, working busily on something over the kitchen counter with his back toward her.

"Thomas?" she called in surprise. "I didn't hear you come home. Did you get off work early?"

Thomas twisted around and gave her a big smile. "Hey, sleepy-head." He turned on the tap and washed the flour off his hands. "Well, the school was practically empty, so I didn't need to go in after all."

"When did you get back?"

"Pretty early, actually. Before ten," said Thomas, drying his hands on a towel. "Did you have a good nap? You've been asleep for a long time."

Cara glanced at the clock: it was almost six in the evening.

"Oh no!" She scrambled to her feet. "Mira! I haven't checked on Mira—"

"I came home before ten, remember?" said Thomas, smiling. "I've been checking on her every hour." He opened the microwave, took out a thermos mug, and came into the living room. "I just went up not long ago. She's still sleeping."

"And her temperature?"

"It came down quite a bit. 99.6 now."

"She did it." Cara let out a relieved sigh. "She fought it off."

"Well, technically speaking, she's not there yet. But almost. Here—" He handed her the thermos mug and removed the top. The sweet smell of hot chocolate instantly filled Cara's nose and lungs. "One hot chocolate à la Thomas," he said proudly. "I didn't want to wake you up for lunch, so hopefully this will last you till dinner, which should be ready in half an hour."

"Thanks." Cara wrapped her fingers around the mug and took a sip, savoring the rich flavor of chocolate and milk on her tongue before swallowing it slowly. The energizing warmth of the silky-smooth liquid traveled down her throat and into her stomach, spreading pleasantly to her chest and belly.

"Good?" Thomas asked eagerly. Cara nodded and made an approving noise through her nose, licking her lips.

"I don't want to brag, but I think dinner will be even better." He grinned. "I'm making garlic knots. And guess what? The lasagna you made yesterday is being baked in the oven."

Cara lowered the mug from her lips. She looked at Thomas, her eyes widening in anticipation. "You mean . . ."

Thomas laughed. "That's right, my dear wifey. No more blackouts! Everything's back on, baby!"

Cara almost couldn't believe her ears. "For real? Since when?"

"Since just about fifteen minutes ago!" Thomas stretched out his arms and flopped down onto the couch. He rested his head on the top of the backrest with his eyes closed. "Ah . . . finally. Back to the convenience of civilization." He lifted his head a little and beamed at Cara, patting the spot next to him. "Come here. I want to know what Susan said about Mira's fever."

"Well . . ." Cara sat down and snuggled up against him. "Susan couldn't tell me what caused the fever, actually, but at least she didn't find anything worrisome." She slipped a hand into his. "She said not to worry. Apparently, there's not much we can do for her except to let her rest and keep her hydrated. She said her immune system would do the rest."

"So we made the right choice staying home, then?"

"Looks like we did." Cara gave Thomas a smile. "According to Dr. Heart, being able to rest comfortably at home had really helped to bring down her fever."

"Thank goodness it all worked out in the end . . ." Thomas smiled back, but it soon grew pensive and then disappeared from his lips.

Cara noticed the change in his expression. "What's wrong?"

Thomas seemed hesitant, but eventually he gave a sigh and said, "Did Susan say anything about what it was like out there?"

"No." Baffled, Cara straightened up. "Why?"

"Well, where should I begin?" Thomas drew a long, deep breath and then breathed it out heavily. "Okay. Let's begin from this morning, after I left Susan's office for work.

"The school looked deserted when I got there, but I could tell someone had been in the parking lot earlier. Trees were covered in toilet paper, and there was a lot of trash: beer cans, wine bottles, cigarette butts . . . scattered around all over the place. But that was not all. There were obscene drawings and words written across the parking lot floor—in paint!"

Cara stared at Thomas in shock, too speechless to respond.

"There was only a handful of other cars in the parking lot, so I already knew I wouldn't be doing much teaching today. Anyway, I managed to find a relatively cleaner spot to park and walked over to the main building—that was when I realized a bunch of the windows on the lower floors had been smashed, and the walls had graffiti all over them, with more obscene drawings and words. What's worse, the front entrance was giving off a strong odor of urine."

"Ew!" Cara screwed up her face. "Who would do something like that to a school?"

"Teenagers, I think, the ones who hate school. Or maybe they just wanted to have a big wild party under the green vortex to feel alive one last time because it was 'the end of the world.'"

"The *what*?" Cara narrowed her eyes, raising her voice.

" 'The end of the world.' That was what they called it after the green vortex appeared in the sky." Thomas shook his head resignedly. "As far as I know, there are two versions going around. In the first version, the green vortex is an omen that marks the beginning of the Great Cleansing. In the second version, when the green vortex stops rotating, it'll come crashing down into our world, causing unprecedented earthquakes and floods and killing off everything on Earth."

Cara's jaw dropped. "How . . . How did they even . . ."

"Come up with all this nonsense?" Thomas shrugged. "I don't know. But they did spread quickly through the town like a contagious virus."

Cara looked at Thomas apprehensively. "What else do I not know about?"

"I didn't want to tell you last night," Thomas finally said, "but by the time I was heading home from the school, the town was already in a state of mass hysteria."

Cara sucked in an involuntary breath, clasping her mouth with a hand.

"It was crazy how fast 'the end of the world' rumor crippled the entire town," Thomas said dejectedly. "As I was driving home, I saw a lot of people out on the streets. Some were wandering around aimlessly, looking like green zombies, some were screaming at every car that drove past, some were setting up special rituals to worship the green vortex, some were praying on their hands and knees, some were wailing like they'd been sentenced to death, and some were laughing like they'd gone completely mad.

"Then there were those with signs. They chanted in groups like shamans, saying the end of the world was upon us, Judgment Day was here, and it was time to repent and face our sins.

"I felt like I was driving through an alien world. Not only because everything looked green under the green vortex, but also because I'd never expected to see people act like that in real life. I still can't believe the mere existence of the green vortex was able to bring out such a level of hysteria and paranoia in us. But when

I realized some of the people were tearing down houses to build boats and rafts, I knew the situation was getting out of hand."

Cara opened her mouth but didn't know what to say. She lowered her eyes, and they landed on the hot chocolate Thomas had made for her.

"And still, you went back out there when I asked you to . . ." She looked up and gazed at Thomas with a mixture of reproach and regret. "Why didn't you tell me?"

"I didn't want you to worry about our safety." Thomas held her gaze with an apologetic smile. "Plus, our house is far away from downtown and hidden by trees at the edge of the town, so I didn't think the craziness would spread to us that easily." He reached for her hand and gave it a squeeze. "I'm sorry, honey. I thought if I didn't tell you, then at least one of us would have a good night's sleep."

"But why didn't you say something when I asked you to go get Susan? It could have been dangerous over there, with people losing their senses like that."

"Because we needed her to come check on Mira," Thomas replied softly, his eyes warm and gentle like a summer breeze. "And I didn't want you to worry about me."

Cara felt her throat tightening. She bit her lip and elbowed Thomas in the ribs, just hard enough to show her disapproval. "You could have at least warned me about it! What if 'the end of the world' is indeed coming because there are no sane people left in town?"

Even though Cara only intended to make a joke out of it, the thought somehow brought her a pang of inexplicable anxiety.

"Was it . . . Was it as bad when you went to Susan's office?" she asked hesitantly. "Was that why you persuaded me to keep Mira home?"

Thomas didn't answer. He didn't need to; the answers were already in his eyes.

"What about this morning? Still the same?"

Slowly, Thomas shook his head. "I'm afraid it was worse."

Cara tensed up right away, but she said firmly, "Tell me."

Thomas let out a heavy sigh. "Remember what I saw at the school? Well, it didn't take me long to decide it was time to leave, so I headed downtown, hoping I could still find some candles and food at the store.

"It was . . . almost like I was driving into a postapocalyptic scene in the movies. If it weren't for the sirens constantly blaring in the background, it'd have felt like I was entering an abandoned ghost town. There were a lot of car wrecks along the way, at least twenty; I lost count after a while. They were just left there, either in the middle of the road or on the side of the street against a road sign or a mailbox or a utility pole that they'd crashed into. There were many houses and shops with broken-down doors and smashed windows. Their contents had either been ransacked or trashed, and the mess . . . It looked like garbage trucks with broken tailgates had flown past.

"So when I finally got to the store, I was relieved to see it was not only open but still intact. After everything I'd seen along the way, it was a very welcome sight—a reminiscence of normalcy, reminding me what the town was like before last night. But as soon as I stepped inside, I knew something was wrong. Instead of the usual cheesy music repeating on a loop in the background, it was filled with loud, angry voices. Some people were arguing over bottled water and toilet paper, while some were fighting over canned food, bread, and flour. There were people sweeping whatever that was left on the shelves into their garbage sacks, and there was also a group of teenage kids with carts full of cigarettes and alcohol, making a run for the exit as they cheered and laughed like they'd outsmarted the world. No one was on duty at the checkout area. As a matter of fact, all the cash registers were opened and emptied, with a few coins littered on the floor like they were dropped in a hurry. That was when I finally realized there were no shoppers at the store, only looters.

"I didn't know what I could do to stop everything from happening. I almost felt like whatever it was that had gotten into those people would get to me too if I stayed any longer. So, I left. But just when I thought things couldn't get any more absurd than they already were, I found out the bank across the street was sealed off by the police because it had been robbed."

"What's wrong with these people?" Cara murmured in disbelief.

Thomas sighed and leaned back against the couch. "I've been asking myself the same question. I can't help but think it wasn't because something had gone wrong with them, but rather, the idea that the world was coming to an end gave them a good excuse to let out their suppressed inner demons."

"You're probably right," said Cara with an air of melancholy. "Nothing's scarier than human nature at its worst." Gently, she ran her fingers through Thomas's hair and caressed his cheek. "I'm sorry you had to see all that. It sounds like a nightmare."

Thomas gave her a tired but affectionate smile. "One of the worst kinds."

"I guess there *are* some benefits of living in the woods at the edge of the town like hermits after all," Cara said wryly. "At least we're far away from all that absurdity and haven't had to deal with anything like what you've seen so far . . . knock on wood."

Thomas nodded and gave a few quick knocks on his forehead. "Knock on wood."

Cara couldn't help chuckling. "It'd better work, Pinocchio. As much as I dislike the inconvenience of living up here, I'd rather be surrounded by trees than by other people's inner demons."

"You don't need trees to protect you," said Thomas, giving her a wink. "You have me."

Cara rolled her eyes, but the corners of her mouth had already curved up. She gave Thomas a kiss and leaned into his arms, taking comfort in the warmth of his embrace as she tried not to picture the chaos and disarray that had taken place downtown.

However, her mind refused to be reined in. In a matter of seconds, it had produced some disconcerting images to project in her head, which prompted her to push away from Thomas and cry out in panic, "Susan's house! Her office! They're much closer to downtown!"

"They're fine, honey. I stopped by her house this morning before I went to her office. They were both untouched," said Thomas, rubbing her arm to calm her down. "Don't worry. Now that the blackouts are done, law and order will be restored soon. This nightmare is coming to an end."

"Hold on," said Cara, raising her eyebrows in surprise. "You went to her house first?"

"Well ... I thought I'd have a better chance of finding her at home at six thirty in the morning, but she wasn't there. So I thought she must have already left for her office—"

"But she was not at her office either, right? She said you were waiting for her when she got there." The anxiousness on Cara's face was replaced by puzzlement. "Where was she, then?"

"The police station," Thomas answered. "She said she was helping them with a case. It sounded like they ran into some troubles with it last night and she had a hard time falling asleep, so she got up early and went over to work on that case instead."

"The police station?" Cara repeated in a squeaky voice, but she suddenly remembered how the dark circles under Susan's eyes had seemed extra heavy that morning, and she finally saw the connection between the two. Feeling the weight of self-reproach on her chest, she let out a frustrated groan. "No wonder she looked like she'd been working all night! I was so preoccupied with Mira's fever, I didn't even—Argh, I should have at least asked how her night had been. I was being so selfish!" She lowered her eyes and bit her lip, but she soon jerked her head up and asked, "What kind of case? Do you know?"

Thomas shook his head. "She didn't say. I didn't want to ask either. She looked like she could use a mental break from it."

"Hopefully it's nothing serious," said Cara, though her intuition was telling her that only a few situations in a police investigation would require the help of a doctor. And out of those few situations, only the worst kinds would cause Susan to lose sleep. She clutched the thermos mug with both hands and rubbed her thumbs together nervously.

"Do you think ... it has something to do with how people behaved last night?" she finally asked.

"Honestly, I wouldn't be surprised if it did. I could hear sirens wailing in the background pretty much the whole time when I was out. As disheartening as my morning was, I doubt I'd seen every inconceivable thing that had taken place since last night." Thomas's expression grew grave, with deep furrows forming between his brows. "Actually ... when I was on my way to Susan's office last night, I saw some police cars parked in the middle of Sunset Field with their lights flashing. Several policemen had come out of the cars, and they were standing in a circle with flashlights. I don't know what they were doing there, but by the time I was heading back, the area had been sealed off."

Cara gasped. "Sunset Field?"

Thomas nodded. "It was still sealed off this morning, but it didn't look like the police had returned for anything. I imagine their manpower is stretched thin after last night ... Maybe that was why they needed Susan's help."

Cara made a feeble noise through her nose and stared at her drink. Despite her resistance, her mind had already conjured up a list of possible scenarios that could have happened on Sunset Field and resulted in the area being sealed off by the police for investigation; she shuddered at every one of them.

Thomas noticed Cara's uneasiness and put his hand on her back. "You okay?"

"As long as whoever the police is looking for doesn't climb up the hill from Sunset Field and barge into our house," Cara murmured. "I thought we were safe from other people's inner demons, being so far away from downtown."

"You *are* safe. I won't let anything happen to you and Mira," said Thomas, gazing into Cara's eyes. Then he added, grinning, "I'll protect you from the inner demons of those crazy green zombies in town. After all, I have the biggest head and the biggest brain in the family. I'll lure them away from you and Mira."

"What?"

"I'll lure the crazy green zombies away"—Thomas gestured animatedly at his head—"with my big, juicy brain."

Cara snorted and burst into a wheezing laugh. Before she could catch her breath, the oven beeped.

"Ah! Dinner's ready." Thomas sprang to his feet. "I hope all that talk of my big, juicy brain didn't ruin your appetite, milady." He winked at Cara and offered her a hand.

Still chortling, Cara let Thomas pull her up from the couch and followed him into the kitchen. As they approached the oven, Thomas suddenly slapped a hand to his forehead. "Uh-oh. I forgot about the garlic knots!"

Cara offered, snickering, "Your big, juicy brain spaced it?"

Thomas laughed. "Looks like it did!" He put on the oven mitts and took the lasagna out, then he grabbed a few cloves of garlic and began crushing them with a knife. "Just give me a few minutes to make the sauce. It'll be worth the wait. I promise."

Cara gave him a tacit smile and nodded. Leaning against the wall, she watched Thomas waltz around the kitchen like a busy bee, humming an improvised tune that sounded like the theme song from a funny cartoon. Before long, he was dipping balls of dough into a garlic butter mixture and arranging them to sit snugly against each other in a loaf pan. Within a few minutes, the pan was filled, looking and smelling deliciously promising. He opened the oven door and slid the pan in, then he started the timer and washed his hands, still humming his improvised tune.

"Thomas?"

"Yeah?"

Cara opened her mouth and felt the words blurt from her lips. "Do you hate it here?"

Thomas was drying his hands on a kitchen towel. He paused and turned around, appearing surprised and alarmed at the same time. "Huh?"

"Do you hate it here?" Cara repeated, enunciating each word deliberately as though she had rehearsed it thousands of times in her mind but was only able to say it out loud at that specific moment. To her surprise, now that she had let it out, she couldn't help but wonder what exactly held her back from asking that question before.

"Well . . . I don't *hate* it here," said Thomas, cautiously. "I mean, if I had to compare Skygate with Seattle, then of course I'd prefer Seattle. It's easier to get around, people there are more like us, schools are better, jobs are more interesting, not to mention we had so many great memories there, and—and . . ." In his desperate attempt to finish his sentence without upsetting Cara, Thomas realized he was clutching the kitchen towel so tightly that he seemed to be either holding on to it for dear life or strangling it to death. He sighed inwardly and loosened his grip, then he put the towel down and said in a small voice, "And you were happy."

Though Cara didn't move or make a sound, she felt like a balloon that had been pumped to the verge of bursting into shreds for years and was finally letting out the excessive air it had been straining to hold inside. So she let her breath carry every bit of it away, slowly but necessarily: the heartaches, the grief, the things she didn't get to do, the things she didn't get to say . . . and the things she didn't understand.

"Don't—don't get me wrong," Thomas added almost pleadingly, worrying that he might have said too much after all and hoping he could still turn the situation around. "I'm not complaining or anything. I know how much this house means to you . . . I know you miss them."

Cara looked at Thomas and saw the tenderness in his eyes. Before she knew it, tears were streaming down her cheeks. She dried her face with a hand and felt the sticky wetness on her fingers. She found herself wondering whether there was only a limited amount of tears one could shed in a lifetime, and if so, whether her quota was finally running dry.

"Oh, Cara." Thomas cupped her face in his hands and tried to wipe away her tears, but they kept pouring from her eyes. "I'm sorry," he said, feeling a lump in his throat. "You're upset. I shouldn't have said anything—"

"No." Cara shook her head and held his hands in hers. "You were right. I'm not happy here. And it's all because I chose to stay here, to live in the past, just to live in the memories that have brought me nothing but sadness and heartache . . . Maybe in the hope that they would somehow stay with me here, in this house, if I just pretend they're still around, then I won't have to deal with the reality that they're actually gone?" She sniffled and looked up at Thomas. "But I see it now: how foolish it was of me to think I could trick time and death by living in the past . . . I was tricking nobody but myself. I was sacrificing our time and our lives to stay with the memories that belong in the past. I was burying our present and future to wait for the ones who will never come back."

As she spoke, a sense of clarity gradually dawned on her. *Nina was right,* Cara thought wearily. *Choices. Life is all about choices.*

"Let's move," she said, gazing into Thomas's eyes. "We can move back to Seattle, or we can move to somewhere exciting and new. I've wasted enough time dwelling on the past . . . my time, your time, and Mira's time. Let's not waste any more of our time in this town." Then, as if to reassure herself, she added, "I'm ready. It'll be a good change for all of us. Don't you think?"

But Thomas was too shocked to reply. Feeling both stunned and worried at the same time, he studied Cara's face carefully, searching for any trace of indication that she was only suggesting the move as a self-defense mechanism to avoid facing the crushing weight of depression, which she had been trying so hard to suppress since the day Mira had entered their lives.

Thomas's heart ached at seeing how pale Cara's face was, and it saddened him greatly that this pale face belonged to the woman he had vowed to take care of for better or worse for the rest of his life. He had desperately held on to her when the storms of life knocked her down into the merciless waves of the sea of suffering.

But when he had finally managed to pull her aboard, she seemed to have misplaced half of her heart and had not been acting like herself for over thirteen long years, even though deep down, he believed, she remained the same woman he had fallen in love with and had since loved more than his own soul.

To Thomas's astonishment, however, the pale face was smiling —*really* smiling. And there, flickering in those hazel eyes on a face so familiar and so dear to his heart, he saw it: the same sparks that used to be able to light up even the darkest sky.

Fearing that the sparks in her eyes would go out again if he didn't act fast enough to shield her from the tiniest wind, Thomas quickly wrapped his arms around Cara and cradled her head with his hands. He planted a kiss on the top of her head, and with a slight tremor in his voice, he answered softly, "Yes. I think it will."

They stayed in each other's embrace and talked about what kinds of places they would like to move to until the oven beeped again. Then they set the table and sat down to enjoy their well-lit dinner. Thomas told Cara he liked the double-baked lasagna more than the regular kind that had only been baked once. Cara told Thomas she thought the garlic knots were his best batch yet. They talked and laughed and drank glasses of wine as they devoured their dinner. By the time they had cleaned their plates, Cara felt so relaxed and at ease that all the worries and stress building up in her head since the night before seemed to have evaporated from her mind. Cara liked how she was feeling, but she was surprised when she realized she couldn't remember the last time she had felt as lighthearted as she was now.

"Would you care for some dessert, Mrs. Murphy?" Thomas offered with an amused smile, nodding toward the fridge. "Some refrozen ice cream, maybe?"

Cara laughed. "*Only* if it's still edible."

"Well ... I can't guarantee it's still edible, but I bet it's at least drinkable."

Just when Cara was about to tell Thomas to give it a try himself first, a buzzing noise came from the kitchen, which continued on at short, urgent intervals. Cara looked toward the kitchen counter and saw it was coming from her cell phone: an incoming call!

"The signal is back!" she exclaimed and got up to grab her phone. "Oh, it's Susan," she said to Thomas, who was taking the dirty plates to the sink. "Can you save her a plate before you clean up? She's probably on her way to come check on Mira."

Thomas gave her the polite nod of a seasoned butler. "Of course, milady."

Cara chuckled and answered the call. "Hey, Suze—"

"Cara! Is Mira okay?" Susan's voice came into her ear like a half shout, sounding more nervous than concerned. Cara tensed up immediately.

"She's better than this morning . . . Is-is something wrong?"

Susan didn't seem to hear her. "What's her temperature?" she demanded with such a level of urgency that it sounded more like she was asking for the reading of a patient's heart rate after an AED was applied.

"99.6," Cara answered nervously.

There was a long pause on the other side of the phone. Then Cara heard a soft sigh, not the kind one breathes out in relief, but the kind one breathes out in fear.

"Suze?" said Cara with an increasing sense of uneasiness. "What's going on?"

Susan didn't answer.

"Suze?"

"Maybe I'm being paranoid," Susan finally said, her voice quavering. "It's just . . . he had a fever too, the whole time while we tried to figure out what had happened to him . . . I don't know if—I can't help feeling—I mean, the green vortex, the blackouts, they were all done when . . ." She trailed off, leaving the remainder of her sentence to herself.

Cara had never heard Susan talk in such an incoherent manner before. She immediately thought of what Thomas had told her earlier, that Susan was kept up the night before by a difficult case she was helping the police with. Her mind couldn't help conjuring more disheartening images about all the terrible things that might have happened downtown—terrible things that might have led to Susan's case.

She shivered involuntarily and hugged herself with her free arm, but she said, "You need to stop thinking about it, Suze. Just hop into your car and come over. You'll feel better after some dinner and wine."

"Yes ... It doesn't matter now, does it? What's done cannot be undone ..." Susan's voice was still trembling. "I think it's best I don't come over tonight, otherwise they'll follow me to your house and give you guys a hard time too."

"Who's following you?" Cara asked, raising her voice in surprise as her throat grew dry. "Why are they following you?"

Susan didn't answer her questions. Instead, she said in a tone that sounded as though she was arriving at a conclusion rather than speaking to Cara, "You haven't watched the news yet."

"No," Cara said in a small voice, feeling a drop in the oxygen supply in her lungs. "Why?"

She didn't know whether Susan was thinking or hesitating, but for what felt like a very long minute, it remained quiet on the other side of the phone. Just when Cara was about to break the silence, she heard a man's voice in the background. She couldn't quite hear what he was saying, but it sounded like he was talking to Susan.

"I have to go now," said Susan after she had replied something indistinct to the other voice. "Listen, I'm sorry I can't come over tonight ... Probably not for a while, actually ... not until this whole thing quiets down a bit. Keep an eye on Mira's temperature. Call me if *anything* changes, any time ... Okay?"

"Okay," Cara replied as breezily as she could manage. "Just promise me you'll go get some rest soon. And if you want to talk more later, we can always have a glass of wine together over the phone."

"I'll try," Susan said quietly. Her voice was calmer, but to Cara, it still sounded weak and lonely. "Thanks, Cara. Good night."

"Good night, Suze."

Cara waited till Susan had hung up, then she slowly lowered the phone from her ear.

Thomas was watching her from the other side of the kitchen counter. "Is everything okay with Susan?"

Cara was still trying to digest the things Susan had said. She shook her head absent-mindedly. "I don't think so. She sounded rattled ... and scared. I think it was the—" Her eyes suddenly lit up. "The news! We need to turn on the news!"

Quickly, Cara went into the living room and picked up the remote, with Thomas following closely behind. She flipped through the channels until she found the local news, which was broadcasting what appeared to be a two-story house, all wrapped up in flames. The tongues of the vicious fire were twisting and dancing like ravenous snakes, licking and dissolving whatever was left to be devoured while transforming the skeleton of the building into something that looked like a giant burning skull. On the TV screen, it seemed to be smiling ghastly into the camera, mocking the firemen and the fire trucks in front of it for their insignificant efforts in curbing the unruly power of fire.

Cara and Thomas stared at the screen in silence as a reporter came into view. Her face was as grim as the scene behind her, and her voice was as grave as a funeral march:

"Among all the breaking news that has taken place during the twenty-four-hour quadruple blackout here in Skygate, the story of fifteen-year-old Eric Ekker is considered to be the most tragic of all.

"Just a little more than an hour ago, a gas explosion took place at the house behind me—the house of Eric and his family. The explosion led to a raging fire, which the firemen are still battling to contain at the moment. According to the fire chief, under the current situation, any rescue attempt would be futile since, due to the explosion, the chance of survival for anyone in the Ekker family is extremely low. This means a total of four lives, including that of the family dog, have been lost to this inferno behind me.

"As of now, the police department has confirmed that the gas explosion was set off by none other than Eric Ekker himself. What's more, multiple witnesses have come forth to provide disturbing details of his final moments.

"According to these witnesses, shortly before the gas explosion, Eric came out of his house without any clothing and began to apply what appeared to be gasoline onto his body. His alarming behaviors soon caught the attention of a patrolling police car nearby, and the two officers on duty immediately pulled over to intervene. However, when the officers stepped out of their car, Eric waved at them, ignited a lighter, and set himself on fire. Just as the officers rushed to his rescue, Eric stepped back into the house and set off the gas explosion. Luckily, both officers suffered only minor injuries from the blast, and none of the nearby residents or properties were impacted by the explosion.

"A few witnesses also claimed that Eric was wearing an insanely demonic smile when he waved at the police officers, and that right before setting himself on fire, the fifteen-year-old produced a very disturbing laugh, which was, quote unquote, 'so sinister and evil that it sounded entirely inhuman.'

"There is much speculation as to why Eric chose to carry out such a gruesome act in front of police officers. According to the statement released by the police department just a few minutes ago, Eric was located in Sunset Field yesterday evening in an extremely unstable mental condition and was believed to pose a real danger to himself, even though he had no previous history of psychiatric disorders. However, since Eric had a fever, he was escorted home under the unwavering demand by his parents instead of being checked into a mental facility, which, unfortunately, proved to be a disastrous decision for the entire family this evening. The statement also revealed that earlier this afternoon, Eric was diagnosed with a traumatic mental disorder. But by the end of the diagnostic process, his fever had worsened, which might have caused unfathomable hallucinations in his unstable mental state that eventually led to his unthinkable actions in terminating his own life and the lives of his family members in such an unsettling manner.

"The chief of police has emphasized that the investigation of Eric Ekker's case is still ongoing since, based on their initial investigation, Eric was acting perfectly normal during the day yesterday and had even played in a soccer match earlier in the afternoon. Additionally, based on his interactions with others at school, there was no indication or plausible explanation as to why or how the fifteen-year-old boy developed such a troubling mental condition just hours after his soccer match. What we do know is that Eric had gone for a bike ride by himself to Sunrise Park after his team lost the game. However, when he was located in Sunset Field, his bike was nowhere to be found. The chief of police is therefore calling for anyone with potential leads in this case to come forward and assist the police department with the investigation, in the hope of bringing the truth and, hopefully, peace to the friends and relatives of the Ekker family.

"Laura Smith, reporting live from South Street."

The camera cut to a news anchor, who had the facial expression of someone about to reveal the greatest mystery of the century. He looked directly at the camera and smiled. "What a story! Thanks, Laura."

He then killed the smile as quickly as he had put it on and knitted his brows slightly before continuing, "Needless to say, the nearby residents are all very rattled by this tragedy. Some of the residents believe the gas explosion was a thought-out familicide planned by Eric Ekker himself, as such an act would have involved a lot of pre-planning, and therefore, it could not have been the product of a mere psychotic episode.

"However, most of them believe it was a revenge suicide on Dr. Susan Heart, who has been assisting the police department in the investigation of Eric's case since yesterday evening, and the very same doctor who issued the diagnosis of Eric's mental condition earlier this afternoon. According to a few witnesses, when Eric was seen waving at the two officers who stepped out of the patrolling police car to intervene, he was actually waving at Dr. Heart, who was asked to stay behind in the police vehicle, as a way to announce his revenge on her. It has been confirmed that Dr. Heart was indeed inside the patrolling police car at the time of the gas explosion, but so far, both the chief of police and Dr. Heart have refused to comment.

"But the most intriguing detail, and probably the main reason why the Eric Ekker case has caught so much attention across the country, is its timing. Many nearby residents have observed the puzzling coincidence of the gas explosion and the disappearance of the aurora whirlpool, which had been rotating and expanding above our town for twenty-four hours but suddenly disappeared without a trace at the exact time the gas explosion took place.

"Stranger still, that was also precisely when the quadruple blackout came to an end. A video clip of that inexplicable moment was processed into slow-motion format and uploaded online shortly afterward. It went viral within an hour, with over half a million views so far and over twenty thousand comments, which, interestingly, are greatly polarized. Some viewers suggest that Eric sold his soul to the Devil. And whatever ritual he performed for that purpose also led to the appearance of the aurora whirlpool above Skygate, as well as the quadruple blackout, both of which were then reversed by Eric as he sealed the deal by setting himself on fire. Other viewers compare Eric to Jesus and claim that he is, in fact, our Savior incarnated. They believe the aurora whirlpool was created by God, and it was meant to be used to punish us for our sins. By setting himself on fire to trigger the gas explosion, Eric sacrificed his own life and his family members' lives to purge and purify the sins of the world, and has therefore successfully prevented the aurora whirlpool from unleashing the wrath of God upon us all.

"Is it truly as simple as a psychotic episode at its worst? Or a well-schemed familicide? A twisted revenge suicide? Is Eric Ekker the Devil, or the Savior? Is he from Heaven, or Hell? Share your opinions with us on our website or our social media channels at

Skygate Daily. Make sure to subscribe and follow us for more up-dates and discussions on the Eric Ekker case as we continue to bring you the latest, juiciest news from the most epic blackout of our time.

"Before we take a break for commercials, let's all take a minute to mourn the Ekker family and send our deepest regrets and sympathies to their friends and relatives."

As solemn music began to play in the background, the image of the news anchor was replaced by a photo of three people and a dog. A skinny teenage boy was in the middle, between a man and a woman, holding the dog. He had brown hair, green eyes, and a face that was quite unremarkable, except for the sparse facial hairs crawling on his lower face like worms that had escaped the earth after a rainy day.

Cara and Thomas stood transfixed in front of the TV, gaping as the boundary between what was possible and what was not blurred and faded before their eyes. As a cheerful commercial popped onto the screen, the remote slipped quietly out of Cara's hand and landed on the carpet with a dull thud.

VI

Run! Run!
Faster! Faster!
They're coming for you!
Rocks, ruins, rubble, sand.
You know where you are. You know where to be!
Rocks, ruins, rubble, sand.
They know where you are. They know where you'll be!
Run! Run!
Faster! Faster!
Rocks, ruins, rubble, sand.
Vines in the sand, vines on the rubble.
Vines on the ruins, vines on the rocks—getting close!
They know your secret. They know the secrets of you!
The tower! The tower! . . . Something's at the top of that rock tower!
Up! Up! Up like the vines!
Run! Run!
Faster! Faster!
Getting closer!
Almost there!
Getting brighter!
Almost can see—
Blood blood blood blood blood blood blood . . .

I told you. They know your secret. They know the secrets of you.

Mira opened her eyes and saw the familiar ceiling fan of her room. She felt a cold breeze flowing in, reaching for her from one of the windows that had been cracked open. It brushed past the foot of her bed and skimmed over her arms and face, light as a veil. On the other side of the windows, the birds were singing and chattering noisily with each other, clearly proud to be the reason that kept her from falling back to sleep.

She blinked slowly at the ceiling fan, trying to remember which date it was and whether she needed to go to school. The thought of getting up and getting dressed for a potential school day made her realize just how tired she was. Her head felt sluggish, her body ached, and her limbs were sore and heavy as though she had been running all night—like what she had been doing in her dream.

Mira couldn't help but wonder if it was indeed just a dream. She focused on recalling the vivid images from it, which were still fresh in her memory, and remembered she had been running and searching for an ancient rock tower on the barren outskirts of what seemed like an abandoned city of ancient Rome—even though she didn't know that was what she was looking for until she had spotted it in the dream. And although she had no idea what it could be, in her dream, she instantly knew there was something very important to her at the top of that rock tower, so she ran toward it at full speed like her life depended on it or else someone might see her and beat her to it.

There was a spiral staircase inside the rock tower, each step of which was carved out of stone and worn thin in the middle. Instead of slowing down, she ran faster, taking two steps at a time until she was stopped by an old wooden door at the end of the staircase, which, she somehow knew, was the last thing that separated her from what she was looking for at the top of that rock tower. But every time she was about to open that old wooden door, something unexpected would happen. And like a glitch near the end of a video game that always resets you back to the beginning, she would sink into a black hole before returning to the same dream to start running and searching for the same rock tower again. Only she would start from somewhere new in the same sand-ridden setting after each of her failed attempts.

Mira remembered there were rocks and sand everywhere in her dream, no matter which direction she went. They obstructed her path from time to time but never effectively thwarted her pace. There were ruins too, lots of them, and rubble, scattered about like the remains of an unknown alien species that had been rotting in the sand for thousands of years, observing her silently along the way. She thought it was strange that even though she approached from a different direction every time, the rock tower would always come into her view with its entrance facing her, as if it were only a mirage, beckoning her to run faster toward it before teleporting her to the place where the real rock tower stood. And once she had stepped through and laid eyes on the real thing, vines would erupt from beneath the sand and seek out the rubble in her path, all the while writhing and clawing and climbing up the rock tower like a thousand-headed centipede from an unknown dimension where life and magic coexisted.

She could still feel the tension in her muscles from how hard and how fast she ran in her dream, without breaking for a moment, except when she was swallowed up and spat out by the black hole to start all over again. She wondered why she kept on trying even though she knew no matter how many times her dream was reset, she would not be able to open that old wooden door in the rock tower. Even so, in the dream, part of her still wished she could prove herself otherwise every time she tried.

Mira pulled herself back from the memory of her dream and stared blankly at the ceiling fan. She wondered what was waiting for her at the top of that rock tower, why she had to run like it was the only way to stay alive, and why her dream would repeat itself like an endless loop. She wished she had the answers. And above all else, she wished she could open that old wooden door.

Something tickled the back of her mind then: a moment from the dream, which was fading away from her memory much faster than the rest, like the tail of a runaway kite about to drift out of her reach. Mira willed herself to grab at it and pull until she was able to reel it in and see what she was forgetting: the moment right before she woke up from her dream, when she *did* manage to open the old wooden door just a crack. But all she saw was blood gushing out from behind it, like sea water flooding the narrow corridor of a sunken ship through a breach in the hull. The crimson red fluid soon submerged the spiral staircase and rose quickly between her feet, swallowing up her legs and body until she was completely drowned by it. She felt the warm liquid rushing into her eyes, ears, nose, and mouth, filling her up like a water balloon and making every inch of her skin stretch and burn with pain. She struggled to break free—that was when she finally woke up.

Mira wrinkled her nose and swallowed hard. She could still smell and taste the blood that drowned her in her dream, and she didn't like it. She felt a knot in her lower abdomen, contracting and spasming as if it was trying to wear down the rough edges of a large piece of broken glass. The sheet beneath her suddenly felt warm and wet.

Slowly, Mira peeled back the bedspread and propped herself up with her arms. Her lower abdomen was emitting, through her white nightgown, a mesmerizing glow in a rich combination of red and gold, presenting to her the vivid yet dreamlike image of what seemed to be three exotic feathers filled with lava, which illuminated her entire abdomen from within like the mouth of a soon-to-erupt volcano.

It was under this mesmerizing glow that she saw a red stain on her nightgown, between her thighs. Hesitantly, she pulled the fabric up from her legs. There was something red and wet on her underpants and the sheet underneath, something that looked as crimson and smelled as raw as the blood in her dream.

Mira let out an involuntary gasp.

That year, she was thirteen.

Chapter 2 THE KEYS

1

I N an area that was technically nonexistent on the face of the
Earth, at a location known only to a privileged group of individuals carefully selected as Pathfinders and Architects, lay
a vast piece of barren land that had nothing to offer but rocks and
sand. It was in the middle of nowhere, far away from any vegetation or civilization, so unappealing and off-putting that even the
local animals seemed to go out of their way to steer clear of this
place.

Which was just as well. For in the middle of this technically
nonexistent land stood a technically nonexistent box-shaped structure that did not wish to be found by anyone without the right security clearance. Shielded by cutting-edge solar-powered camouflage technology with zero-glare ultra-high-definition screens assembled seamlessly on the outsides of its roof and walls to project
realistic 3D images that perfectly blended the structure with its
natural surroundings at all times—day or night, rain or shine—on
all sides and from all angles, this massive box was literally invisible
to even the keenest human eye.

This technological marvel was called the Pandora's Box. Any
piece of evidence or information from ancient civilizations around
the globe, no matter how remotely related it was to the keywords
provided by the Pathfinders' research, was to be gathered or salvaged from the outside world, one way or another, and transferred
here for further evaluation. Like going through piles of pieces one

by one at a puzzle factory after a major earthquake to complete as many puzzles as possible, the Pathfinders examined, studied, and analyzed all evidence and information sent to the Pandora's Box in the hope that it could be put together to form clues that would, one day, lead to the successful location and unlocking of the forbidden ancient secrets they had been striving to obtain. From there, it was believed that the Pathfinders would derive groundbreaking insights and technologies to ultimately change the course of history for the entire human race, and the Architects would be able to steer the direction of the advancement of human civilization toward a much more promising future for all mankind.

And that was why the Pandora's Box was built: a technically nonexistent fortress for safekeeping all those potential clues as well as the Pathfinders that were working industriously and tirelessly inside.

It was in this very fortress that Gargoyle, the head of the Pathfinders and the brains behind all crucial Pathfinder activities, was about to hold an encrypted videoconference with the Architects to present them with the latest development in the Pathfinders' research, which included the most thrilling findings by far since the beginning of their decades-long endeavors.

Nobody knew what Gargoyle's real name was, nor should they, for here at the Pandora's Box, everyone was known by an alias only. It was understood that for a mission that should remain technically nonexistent to the rest of the world, it would be in everyone's interest if they worked together under made-up identities.

This suited the Pathfinders well, most of whom were zealous scientists from different backgrounds with leading expertise in nonmainstream academic areas and were recruited by Gargoyle himself, for the normal psychological needs of social interactions, such as meeting, talking, mingling, bonding with other human beings for pleasure and comfort, were pretty much minimal on the hierarchy of needs of these people. Like the man who had recruited them, these fervent Pathfinders had no regard for money, power, or fame. Alas, they didn't even appear to have much regard for their basic physical needs like eating, drinking, or sleeping.

For these Pathfinders, their entire existence was driven by one purpose and one purpose only: to know the unknown, which was precisely why they were selected into this mission to begin with. Their hunger for new and forbidden knowledge, and their desire to learn and apply it to modern-day technologies, was powered and sustained by the tremendous amount of curiosity burning inside them, which could either be labeled as devotion and enthusiasm to science at best, or obsession and fanaticism to a self-destructive cause at worst. Among this clan of fundamentally eccentric human beings who might as well be described as half genius and half lunatic, Gargoyle was either a complete genius or a complete lunatic.

Even though Gargoyle's associates mostly referred to him as Dr. G, no one would disagree that it was the perfect alias for him. As someone who had dedicated most of his time and energy to nontraditional scientific explorations, Gargoyle was now in his late sixties. The top of his head was as bald and wrinkly as a sphinx cat's scalp. His face was dressed heavily in sagging skin and folds, and he had a disproportionately large, hooked nose that hung crookedly from between his bushy eyebrows. His unkempt long gray beard was even wilder than a wild goat's, which provided a shady shelter for his thin lips when he was not speaking.

Among all his distinct facial features, however, it was said that Gargoyle's bulging amber eyes were what really brought out the resemblance to a gargoyle in him, for they looked as big and round as those of an owl, and they always seemed to be gleaming with such inquisitiveness and feverishness that they practically glowed. Yes, with the right costume, there was no doubt Gargoyle could easily replace one of those watchful little monsters sitting atop Notre Dame.

And here at the Pandora's Box, he was often sighted hunched motionlessly over the railing of one of the many walkways that stretched across above the vast Evidence Hall, day or night, looking just as pensive and calculating as one of those stone gargoyle stat-ues, all the while scanning with his glowing owl eyes the progress that was being made down below in each section of the Evidence Hall—from every potential clue to every potential lead and every plausible hypothesis—and silently formulating his theories, either as a complete genius or a complete lunatic.

No one knew exactly how many Pathfinders there were in to-tal, as the majority of them were traveling all over the world to gather and salvage any promising petroglyphs, hieroglyphics, fres-coes, relics, artifacts, biofacts, documentations, myths, legends, fa-bles, folklores, and the like to send back to the Pandora's Box. As for the Pathfinders stationed on-site, they lived and worked inside the Pandora's Box for weeks or even months on end, examining, studying, and analyzing countless pieces of evidence and informa-tion received over the course of decades, completely engrossing themselves in what would only be considered wild-goose chases by fellow scientists too sane to be selected as Pathfinders in the first place. But just like their predecessors, these Pathfinders never seemed to run out of faith—for knowledge, they believed, espe-cially the forbidden knowledge yet to be learned and understood by the human race, would be the source of unlimited power and control in this world.

Maybe it was their faith, or maybe it was just pure luck, but two weeks ago, their tenacity finally paid off: the Pathfinders had fi-nally put together the necessary amount of clues to provide enough leads, which eventually led to an astonishing discovery that would support not just one but a whole series of hypotheses—all in one go.

11

Gargoyle was waiting in a long, milky white corridor in front of the conference chamber. Like everywhere else inside the Pandora's Box, this corridor was also adorned with life-size male statues that were, in fact, standby robotic assistants with the generic name Hermes, for the ancient Greek god whose form they were sculpted after. These beautifully crafted robotic assistants were all given the same height, the same build, the same voice, the same face, and the same forever frozen expression that, surprisingly, turned out to be quite hard to read at times. Technically speaking, these artistic pieces of technological wonder shared the same brain too, as they were all linked up to Hope—the artificial intelligence of the supercomputer built into the heart of the Pandora's Box, which ran the entire place like a first-class butler. Among all the Hermes inside the Pandora's Box, there was only one difference: for some unknown reason, purely artistic perhaps, they were sculpted with different types of clothing: from elaborate sets of armor to lavish togas, from plain tunics to simple himations that expertly accentuated the athletic build of the herald of gods by tastefully exposing just the right places.

Besides the important function of providing easily accessible AI assistance to the Pathfinders whenever and wherever they needed it on the premises, the Hermes were also specifically designed to take care of the residents as well as the valuable contents inside the Pandora's Box as around-the-clock security guards. Additionally, they were coded to *take care of* everyone and everything inside the Pandora's Box should the need arise, for it was deemed imperative to keep the whole of it from falling into the wrong hands.

It was in the attentive presence of these Hermes that Gargoyle paced back and forth impatiently as he waited. This, in itself, was quite an unusual sight, considering Gargoyle, being extremely conscious with the use of his time and energy, lived by the rule of conserving the energy to his brain for thinking rather than losing it to his limbs for moving since, to him, even when the same amount of energy was being consumed, the former would still yield more value than the latter and hence be a better investment in terms of allocating both his time and energy. Today, however, Gargoyle's mind was so preoccupied with what he would soon be able to present to the Architects that there was no room for any rule to fit inside his wrinkly, bald head.

The entrance to the conference chamber stood in the middle of the milky white wall of the long, milky white corridor. Its door was big and heavy and made of brass, portraying a skillfully carved life-size relief of Pandora and her infamous box. Pacing ceaselessly in front of it like a lab rat who had been given too much caffeine, Gargoyle was grinning from ear to ear, looking like a stone gargoyle statue that had just come to life but, despite its exhilaration at the prospects of all kinds of seemingly impossible opportunities now available at its fingertips, had not quite gotten used to being alive. His bare crown, slightly pink from the euphoric energy radiating from his brain, was glistening with beads of sweat. His big owl eyes were not just glowing; they were practically burning with ecstasy at the endless possibilities he had already envisioned for the theories he had derived from the hypotheses concluded from the Pathfinders' most recent discovery.

To be fair, Gargoyle had spent more than enough time on speculating. But this, finally, was the time to act, to test, and to verify his theories. He knew he must persuade the Architects into voting for his proposal. The keys to the forbidden ancient secrets were almost within their reach—he was sure of it. All he needed to do next was convince the Architects to reach out and search for them, which, as you could imagine, would require a great deal of resources for a mission like theirs.

And that was exactly why Gargoyle needed to persuade the Architects, for they were not only the decision-makers but also the providers for their mission. Without their support, Gargoyle would not be able to advance the mission. The Architects had been providing everything conceivable to keep the mission going, ranging from the basic categories such as money, manual labor, logistics, networks, technologies, to the less orthodox but necessary ones such as retrieving and removing classified records, falsifying identities, obtaining firearms, providing soldiers, hiring mercenaries, covering up tracks, and tying up loose ends. In other words, whatever it would take to ensure the operation of this mission was uninterrupted and the secrecy of it remained secure.

Not even Gargoyle knew exactly how many Architects there were in total, nor did he know who they were in real life. And although, as the head of the Pathfinders, Gargoyle was the sole point of contact for the Architects, he had never met with any of them in person. Whenever a meeting was held to provide updates to the Architects on the progress of the mission, the encrypted videoconference technology that was administered by Hope would not only computerize each Architect's voice but also project their images into 3D silhouettes. Despite the high resolution of the projections and the lifelikeness of these shadowy illusions, the most effective way to tell them apart was still to look at the code above each figure's head, which gave no more information about the identity of that particular Architect than the country and city he or she was stationed in. Usually, Gargoyle would have to rely on those codes to keep track of the questions and concerns being thrown at him at the end of a presentation. Today, however, not even that would help, as Gargoyle already anticipated he would be bombarded with questions from every one of the Architects present once they were brought up to date on what the Pathfinders had discovered.

Nevertheless, all these years of working with the Architects had made Gargoyle as savvy to their expectations and preferences as he was to their ways of getting things done. So even with such extreme security measures to protect the identities of the Architects, it was only natural for Gargoyle to deduce that whoever they were in real life, they would be the kind of people you would not want to meddle with. The logic behind his deduction was simple. If the Architects were capable of providing anything that was necessary and needed for the day-to-day operation inside the Pandora's Box and for the Pathfinders to stay on top of the mission, then they must be the exact same group of people who had the money, power, and influence to construct and reconstruct every little detail in human society as imperceptibly as a master puppeteer pulling the strings on a marionette—every little detail, including, but not limited to, erasing someone who had been a nuisance from history as effortlessly as blowing a speck of dust off a book.

Gargoyle himself was not in the least bothered by the potential occurrences of such little details, however. As a matter of fact, he could not be more content that this group of extremely powerful and disconcertingly resourceful people were the providers for their mission. To him, the great lengths that the Architects were willing to go to for advancing the mission only proved that they were as eager to apply and utilize the forbidden ancient secrets as he was determined to unlock and decipher them, which, Gargoyle presently pondered to himself with a slight sense of relief, would work in his favor to persuade the Architects into casting approving votes on his proposal, despite the little sacrifices that might have to take place here and there as a result of its implementation. After all, how could you make history without a little sacrifice? Not to mention this was the mission of generations, the quest for the forbidden knowledge that might even disrupt the whole foundation of all preexisting and existing knowledge that had been accumulated since the beginning of human history, thereby disrupting the understanding of the entire world as we knew it!

"Dr. G," called a Hermes to his left as Gargoyle walked past with a newfound confidence in his steps, interrupting the rhythm of both his pace and his thoughts, "the security screening and data encryption have been completed."

Gargoyle turned to look at the Hermes that was speaking and found him to be one sculpted with a loose-fitting himation that barely covered the robotic assistant's chest and groin areas, making him seem more like a god turned into a statue and kidnapped from Mount Olympus in the middle of an extravagant feast that involved too much merry-making than a man-made technological wonder that could turn into the deadliest weapon on the premises in the blink of an eye.

Gargoyle dabbed at his sweaty forehead with a sleeve. "Can I go in now?"

With an expressive but motionless face, Hermes answered through the speaker installed behind his pretty mask, along with countless other intricate high-tech designs, "Yes. The Architects are ready for you. Shall we begin?"

Gargoyle nodded absent-mindedly as he flipped through the notes for his presentation one last time in his head: the discovery, the facts, the evidence, the hypotheses, his theories, and, most importantly, his daring proposal. He felt the adrenaline rushing into his bloodstream, electrifying and rejuvenating every single cell in him; it was enticingly exhilarating.

"It's about time," he said, his voice cracking mid-sentence. He adjusted his collar and cleared his throat, then he looked up at Hermes and continued. "Let's begin."

A human assistant might have given him an encouraging nod, but the Hermes could not nod. Despite the lifelikeness of those masterfully sculpted heads and limbs, they were not designed to perform practical movements. So instead, he acknowledged Gargoyle's reply by executing a command through his connection to Hope and opened the heavy brass door to the conference chamber remotely. He then activated the ultraquiet propulsion units hidden in his heels and noiselessly, as if he were carried forward by the winged sandals that were sculpted on his feet, followed Gargoyle inside.

III

Greetings, Architects!

Today I am an envoy of the most extraordinary findings that the Pathfinders have discovered since the beginning of our shared mission, findings that I shall soon elaborate in great detail.

But before we dive into the incredible journey of how these extraordinary findings were achieved, I would like to honor this significant milestone in our mission by refreshing everyone's memory on our purpose—our why, the spark that kindled this daunting mission in the very first place—for us to remember how this organization came into existence and brought the Architects and the Pathfinders together for a common goal, so that we can all be reminded of the vision and the end goal of our mission to stay true to our why and remain undeterred in the face of the formidable challenges lying ahead.

We'll begin by revisiting the myth of Pandora and her infamous box, which I'm sure you're all very familiar with. The story came from the didactic poem "Works and Days" by the ancient Greek poet Hesiod in the seventh century BC. According to the most well-known version of this classic piece of ancient Greek mythology, the gods gave Pandora a pithos, which should have been translated into a "large jar" instead, but we'll go with the norm and keep it as a "box" for now. Pandora was told that the box contained special gifts from the gods to the humans, and she was not to open it. But Pandora couldn't resist the temptation to satisfy her curiosity, and eventually, she opened the box, thus releasing evils into our world, causing all kinds of miseries and sufferings. The gods didn't lift a finger to control the situation, nor did they mean to, as it was their intention to punish mankind for having challenged their divinity and authority. So, evils became the inevitable thorns in our lives, and even to this day, we're still paying the price for the choice that Pandora had made.

Therefore, you could say it was her curiosity that brought about all the evils lurking among us: evils either demonstrated in the form of psychological miseries such as greed, envy, lust, and hatred, or in the form of physical sufferings such as disability, disorder, disease, and death; evils that have been around even longer than the myth of Pandora and her box itself, which has been told and retold from generation to generation for more than 2,700 years, explaining to us, little kids and adults alike, why evils exist in the world.

But human society is not the only one that has been plagued by evils. If you take a closer look around, you'll notice that evils exist in the animal kingdom as well. It was this very observation that first caught the attention of a few unconventional thinkers and scholars from a long time ago, who eventually became deeply intrigued by the question as to why evils could prevail among so many species through so many generations.

As those thinkers and scholars pursued and sought the answer to that very question, different versions of "Pandora's Box" emerged accordingly, prompting many existential questions to surface, such as: What's the purpose of our existence when miseries and sufferings are inevitable in our lives? Why can't we be rid of evils? What's the purpose of their existence in our existence? Did evils exist in the world long before humans walked the Earth, or did they only come into existence after we angered the gods, as the story entails? And if evils did exist before us, does it mean that they've always been a part of us? On the other hand, if they were only released upon us later from Pandora's box, why did the gods go through the trouble of disguising them as special gifts instead of unleashing them directly into the world?

It was these thought-provoking questions that facilitated the births of many new schools of philosophy. And in the case of ancient Greece, the ideas generated from such questions were like seeds, dispersing among wise men and, as those seeds sprouted and flourished into a kaleidoscope of viewpoints and opinions, stirring up many great debates among the prominent thinkers and philosophers of that time.

However, not until the contemporary period did a handful of visionaries further suggest daring theories based on the myth of Pandora and her box, which, as philosophical as they might sound, were inspired by the idea of the relativity of existence. What those visionaries suggested was mind-bogglingly counterintuitive. They pointed out that by existing, the concept of nonexisting coexists. Thereby, while evils exist in our world, theoretically, there could be another inhabited world where evils do not exist. The question is: Where is it? Is it in another space? Another time? Or perhaps, another space-time? If, in the future, we have discovered enough secrets of the universe to develop the technologies that'll enable us to finally transform into a Type III civilization,[1] will we eventually become that world where evils do not exist?

One thing we did learn from our decades-long research is that no matter if it's myth, legend, fable, or folklore, tales don't just emerge out of thin air. So think, for a moment: If all the evils that exist in our world did come from Pandora's box, can we put them back?

Theoretically, if we could undo an action by reversing it as it is happening—like the way we reverse the video clip of an action—then technically, this action didn't happen, and since it didn't happen, the consequence of that action doesn't exist.

Now, think about a video clip of a boy falling into a pool. The action here is the fall, but if we reverse the video clip as it's being played, then at the end, instead of seeing the boy splashing into the pool, we'll find him still standing next to it; the fall didn't happen because the action was reversed, and therefore, the boy remains dry.

With that in mind, can we also undo the existence of a consequence by reversing the action that led to it? Say, if we can reverse our action in taking something out of a box, then as the action is reversed, the content should also be back in the box. And although the content still exists to the box that holds it, we have successfully rendered it nonexistent to the rest of the world outside that box, especially if said box is securely locked and hidden away afterward.

---

[1] In 1964, Soviet astronomer Nikolai Kardashev proposed a method to measure the technological advancement of a civilization based on the amount of energy it is able to utilize and developed a model to classify civilizations into three types. This method is known as the Kardashev scale. According to the Kardashev scale, a Type III civilization is capable of capturing all the energy that is emitted by its galaxy, including energy from any other objects within that galaxy.

So here's another daring thought: What if we can undo the existence of evils by applying the same logic, by reversing the actions that led to them?

Obviously, the level of knowledge and technology we're currently equipped with is not yet advanced enough to pinpoint the exact moment when an action leading to certain psychological evils like greed, lust, envy, and hatred is taking place in one's brain, considering it's nearly impossible to perceive and catch such an action in progress unless we can develop a technology to read minds. But for the physical evils—disability, disorder, disease, and death—the natural ones, the visible ones, the ones we can actually see when an action leading to it is taking place, they will be a good starting point for us to begin tackling the technological obstacles in achieving action reversal.

Imagine this: instead of using stem cell therapy and gene therapy in the hope of reviving, repairing, regenerating the compromised cells, and instead of using containment and elimination to deal with the hostile intruders in our bodies, we would simply—with a technology developed specifically for such a purpose—reverse the natural action leading to a disability, a disorder, a disease, or even a death at the cellular level. We would literally be undoing the existence of physical evils, one reversal at a time, and hence, collectively, defeating all unsolvable and incurable medical challenges that have been vexing mankind!

Yes . . . a very daring thought indeed. Yet it was in the light of its spark that a small number of brilliant scientists first saw the one thing that was said to be left behind in Pandora's box: hope. The hope of living in a world without naturally occurring disability, disorder, disease, and even death. The hope of preserving the human species beyond this time and beyond this space. The hope of evolution and exploration. The hope of greatness, of highly advanced human civilizations thriving on many colonized planets, across many galaxies. And the hope of ultimate power and control over our own fate in this vast universe that we do not yet completely understand.

Such is the magic of hope. It excites, inspires, and somehow generates a level of unmatched vigor in one's state of mind and actions, which, in turn, fuels it to grow and spread rampantly like wildfires, capable of kindling even the most despondent, lost, apathetic minds while burning away any helplessness, purposelessness, and meaninglessness that once imprisoned them.

But if we can feel the magical power of hope working among us, then surely, it's not still locked up in Pandora's box like what we've been told by the tales?

And that was how several masterminds in the leading fields of science and technology first realized "Pandora's Box" was more than just a tale of morals. It was, in fact, a riddle that had been hiding an important clue from us for more than 2,700 years: it was not the feeling of hope that was left behind in Pandora's box; it was, literally, the hope to rectify Pandora's mistake! In other words, whatever was left behind in Pandora's box is exactly what we'll need to reverse and undo the existence of evils! Come to think of it, actually, what would have given the gods more amusement and pleasure than leaving the remedy for all evils in the last place where the humans would suspect: back in the box and, in a sense, in plain sight?

This theory soon grew into an unwavering belief among those brilliant intellects. Hence, eighty years ago, they gave birth to this organization and became our founders. They designed the infrastructure and roles for our organization. They chose the location and built the first model of our base. They selected the first batch of Pathfinders and Architects, and the mission of this organization was made clear to those privileged few: to recover Pandora's box in secret so that we can open it once more to find the hope and unlock the forbidden ancient secrets to reverse and undo the existence of evils, thereby providing eternal salvation to all.

And now, it is with the utmost delight I hereby announce that on March 19, a fortnight ago and eighty long years after the birth of this organization, one of our off-site Pathfinders has successfully recovered Pandora's box!

Yes, my fellow colleagues. We have recovered the Pandora's box! After eighty years of information gathering, clue hunting, studying and analyzing, puzzle solving and resolving, hypothesizing, theorizing, experimenting, testing and failing, we have finally found it!

Architects ... Architects! Please listen to me! I know you must have many, many questions to ask, but for the moment, please let me finish telling you how we came into possession of it, what we have learned from it, and what I propose to do next. I ask you, therefore, to please be patient and save all your questions till the very end!

Thank you. Let's continue.

Truth be told, the discovery of Pandora's box was as coincidental as if it was destined. You could even say that, in a way, Pandora's box found us.

Here's how it happened.

So two weeks ago, Professor D, one of our off-site Pathfinders stationed in Europe, took a day off from clue hunting at a Level Three excavation site in Pompeii. She was planning on spending the day hiking in the woods in the nearby area. But on her way to her destination, she noticed the remains of an ancient rock tower. The poor old thing was scarcely appealing; it was missing its roof and nearly half of its walls, and it was plagued by untamed ivy vines, looking like it was being crushed by countless green tentacles from beneath the earth. However, as luck would have it, Professor D made a stop to visit it on a whim. The foot of the tower was crowded with broken rocks protruding from the dirt and blocking the path, so getting to it was not easy. Just as Professor D was about to reach the entrance, she stumbled over something that was half-buried among the remains of a few large rocks.

She looked down to check what it was and immediately noticed that there was something very unusual about it. Let's take a moment to praise Professor D for prioritizing the call of duty, for instead of returning to it later after her day off in the woods, she set to work to unearth it at once. After a few hours of hard work, the legendary artifact was finally in her hands—except that, of course, she had no idea she was holding the very Pandora's box in her hands at that time.

Why did I say so? Well, to begin with, instead of a pithos, or a box, the object she had unearthed was a sphere, as big as a beach ball. Second, it was made of an unidentified white material that, to her knowledge, could not have been produced from the ancient past. Third, it was engraved with a bloodred circle on the top, from which nine equally bloodred arms, stretching outward, with what seemed like deformed claws at their ends, were engraved in the same manner, evenly distributed around the circle. So in a way, this object looked more like a bleeding eyeball of a cyclops than a legendary ancient artifact that was said to be used for storage. Just see for yourself.

Hermes, could you relay the 3D image of Pandora's box from Hope and project it to our audience?

Perfect. Thank you.

Please, everyone! I know it's hard to accept the idea of this sphere being the authentic Pandora's box, but please listen on because I have yet more astonishing details that our Pathfinder observed afterward to share with you!... Yes. Thank you.

Well, needless to say, after seeing the design on this sphere, Professor D was greatly intrigued by its origin. She dusted off its surface carefully and brought it under direct sunlight for a closer inspection. To her great astonishment, as the sunlight shone upon the sphere, a thick liquid that looked like golden lava oozed out of nowhere from the middle of the engraving and soon filled up the entire circle and flowed toward the nine arms and their nine deformed claws until each of them was filled to the brim as well. As demonstrated here on the projection, the bloodred engraving on the sphere was then completely golden, resembling the image of a sun with grotesque hands reaching out from its nine evenly distributed sunbeams.

But that was not all. Before our astounded Pathfinder could recover from what she'd just witnessed, something else happened: the nine-armed sun engraving began to rotate, counterclockwise, until there was a faint clicking noise inside the sphere, sounding like a gear was disengaged. It was then Professor D noticed that a paper-thin line had appeared along the sphere's equator, like it'd just been slit open by an invisible blade, and was quickly widening into a narrow crack. Like a watermelon that has developed a split in its waist, the top half of the sphere was then slightly raised, revealing to Professor D that it could be opened ... as you can see now from the projection.

I hear a lot of anxious murmurs in the room. You're nervous to find out whether Professor D opened the sphere, aren't you? . . . That's understandable. After all, none of us knew exactly what we should expect to find in Pandora's box if we were ever to acquire it; who could say for sure there wouldn't be any other undesirables lying in wait inside that infamous container, ready to leap out at humanity the first chance they got and release a whole new series of problems for the world to deal with?

But Professor D failed to make the connection between this intricate sphere and the legendary artifact that we'd been seeking so painstakingly for the last eight decades—as did we when we first received it. And who could blame her anyway? It's not even shaped like a pithos or a box, not to mention it does not look like it was made in the ancient past at all. So once Professor D realized the sphere could be opened, she didn't think twice before lifting the top half off, then and there.

Architects! . . . Everyone! Please!

I understand that many of you are inclined to brand her decision to open the sphere without proper investigation or authorization imprudent and would rather punish her for what she did than applaud her for what she discovered. Be that as it may, please be assured there hasn't been any adverse effect from the choice she made. For one thing, Professor D was unharmed and remained healthy after she opened the sphere, both physically and mentally, and she didn't observe any immediate danger lurking inside it either. For another, no large-scale catastrophe or pandemic has taken the world by surprise since then, even though it's already been two weeks. Of course, if Professor D had known that the sphere was, in actuality, the Pandora's box, then there is no doubt she would not have chosen to open it on the spot. She would have followed protocol and sent it straight to here for us to decide what to do next. And instead of me standing here today to share with you what we've learned about Pandora's box so far, we would be debating over when and how to open the sphere in this meeting and many more to come, clouding our judgment with caution and overthinking while holding ourselves back indefinitely from achieving the goal of our mission, which is almost within our grasp! To put it bluntly, Professor D's ignorance in not recognizing the sphere as Pandora's box really turned out to be a blessing to our organization, for by opening it then and there on that momentous day, she not only saved us a tremendous amount of time that would otherwise be spent in endless meetings and debates but also uncovered the hidden information we would need to reach our goal!

Yes! You're correct! Pandora's box was not empty!

What Professor D saw inside the sphere next completely dazzled her: fire. It was dancing wildly on a bloodred object that had the shape of an oversize almond and was held in a fitted socket on a small, raised platform in the middle of the bowl. But unlike a real fire during a normal combustion process, this one did not release any heat, nor did the bloodred object wrapped up in its flames diminish in size or change in color. These observations quickly led Professor D to the hypothesis that the fire she saw might not be the result of a combustion after all. To test her hypothesis, she pulled an ivy vine off the rock tower to see if it'd get burned from physical contact with said fire. Well, it didn't, which confirmed her hypothesis and led her to the conclusion that since no actual combustion process was taking place, the bloodred object was not really burning. Therefore, the fire she saw must be a mirage of some sort.

With that thought in mind, Professor D began to examine the interior of the sphere for an answer, only to find out the top half of the sphere was not empty inside either. Four irregularly shaped stone tablets with petroglyphs, each about the size of her hand, were secured to the inner wall of the bowl with a ninety-degree angle between each of them, thus forming a square enclosure around the small, raised platform that held up the bloodred object and its fiery mirage from the bottom half of the sphere when the two halves were put back together.

Naturally, Professor D was very eager to see the petroglyphs on these stone tablets, so she tried to remove one from the bowl right away. She was pleasantly surprised to see it sliding out into her palm at the gentlest push, so she went ahead and took out the other three as well. As she tried to make sense of the petroglyphs on each of them, it occurred to her that they were actually the integral parts of a much bigger stone tablet that was once whole. As soon as she realized that, she began rearranging the four tablets like puzzle pieces. Before long, she found herself looking at a bigger rectangular stone tablet with a full petroglyph that was completed by all four of the smaller tablets combined.

Hermes, please relay the 3D image of the stone tablet from Hope. Thank you.

As you can see, the four smaller tablets fit together perfectly, and now we have a much bigger stone tablet with quite a vivid scene carved into it. I must point out that based on the results from our lab, this petroglyph was most likely made during the Middle Paleolithic period, and it was dated to be at least 100,000 years old. As for the stone tablet itself, according to the data from our lab results, it was not broken into four until approximately 50,000 years later. Therefore, we can leave the possibility of forgery behind us and focus on the big question here: What does this scene mean?

Hermes, please enhance the top and the bottom sections of the petroglyph to 1,000 percent and give us the side-by-side projection for comparison.

Let's look at the top section first. Here, we have a crowd of stick figures. One head, two arms, two legs, standing in upright position … It's quite obvious they were meant to portray humans, right? But here, on the bottom section, we have a much bigger crowd that definitely do not look like humans. This one has nine heads. This one has five tails. This one has a body that's made up of ten fish trunks and ten fish tails. This one is the biggest and tallest of them all but has no head. This one has two heads, one on each end of a four-legged animal's body. This one has a spider's body and legs. This one has two horns on the shoulders of a beast's body …

Please take note of how every single one of these figures has at least one feature that disqualifies its resemblance to a normal human being or any other known species in the animal world. Also, take note of how much bigger these figures are than those stick figures, not just in terms of height but also in terms of build. The arms and legs on those stick figures look like twigs compared to the strong limbs and paws and claws and . . . whatever these other grotesque body parts should be called on these monstrous figures. Now, take note of how much closer the stick figures were placed next to each other than these abnormal figures were.

I hear your questions and concerns, but right now it doesn't matter whether these monstrosities were real or imaginary because the important thing here is to understand what they were bringing to the humans in this particular scene.

From a psychological perspective, the contrast produced by the differences in physical size and individual spacing between these two distinct groups of figures clearly reflects the level of vulnerability and fear felt by the humans toward what was standing in their way. In other words, these ghastly figures at the bottom of the scene must have brought along some kind of dreadful unpleasantry, some kind of evil, that was causing great horror, even ill fate, to those small humans on the opposite side.

Now, let's move on to the middle section of the petroglyph and look at what's standing between these unsightly horrors and the small, fragile humans huddling at the top.

Hermes, please project the complete scene at 1,000 percent.

This . . . is the center of the scene, everyone. A giant red bird, with a yellow sun behind its head. Its massive wings stretched out formidably wide. Its head held high in a posture that appears far superior to royalty, looking like nothing less than a heavenly creature that demands absolute worship and total obedience.

Beautiful, isn't it? Among all the individual petroglyphs on the stone tablet, this bird is the biggest one and the only one that was painted with pigments. If you look closely, you'll notice the same yellow pigment that was used to paint the sun behind its head was also used to trace along its outline. Both details suggest that this giant red bird not only had a critical role in the scene being depicted here but also inspired a degree of awe and reverence that was similar to what those ancient humans felt toward the sun.

Now pay attention to its wingspan. It's so wide that all the stick figures are safely shielded behind it from the horde of abominations on the opposite side, which indicates that this mighty bird is protecting the small and fragile humans from whatever kind of evil these monstrosities represented in real life at that time.

Judging from all these, it's enough to surmise that to our ancient ancestors back in the Middle Paleolithic period, this bird was as powerful and fearless as the sun. The question is: What kind of bird was it?

Before we attempt to answer that question, however, let's first take a closer look at the more artistic details they made on this divine bird. See these decorative carvings on its head? They were also made here, on the neck, on the wings, the torso, the tail . . . pretty much everywhere, actually. Have you noticed anything unusual about these carvings?

That's right. They look like flames. So why did our ancestors go through the extra trouble of decorating this bird with tiny carvings that look like flames? Why didn't they decorate it with something else, something that was easier to carve—say, feathers? Was it their intention to make it seem like this bird is burning in this scene? What, then, is the connection between its fiery state and the sun behind its head?

If we put all the crucial information together, this is what we have: a giant red bird, as powerful and fearless as the sun, all clothed in flames, yet it appears to be immune to the consuming power of fire since it's still protecting the humans from the impending evil. So, what can it be?

Architects, please listen to me!

I know it's very tempting to draw connections and jump to conclusions based on what I've just shared with you, but please refrain yourselves from doing so. In order to reveal the truth behind this scene, we'll need to follow the way of science and analyze everything we've learned from Pandora's box so far.

Good. I think I have everybody's attention again. So let's get back to solving the identity of this bird.

We now know that unlike any creature on Earth, this bird was not vulnerable to fire, which means it was either immune to fire, or it was made of fire. Having a sun portrayed behind its head also suggests that this bird was a celestial being, not a glorified version of a certain prehistoric species.

Now that we've made these deductions, one may wonder whether this bird was a phoenix—as many of you speculated earlier. Indeed, the phoenix is a well-known mythical creature that, like the giant red bird in this scene, is also associated with fire and the sun. However, the earliest documented mention of the phoenix was found in a fragment of the "Precepts of Chiron," a didactic poem from around the seventh century BC that was commonly attributed to the ancient Greek Poet Hesiod as well, while the earliest documented account of the phoenix was made by ancient Greek historian Herodotus in the fifth century BC, both of which were over 97,000 years younger than the period when this petroglyph was made. Therefore, it's quite possible that the phoenix is related to this bird in some way; it might have been the physical ancestor of the phoenix, or it might have been the origin of every single tale of the phoenix all along. After all, "phoenix" is just a name, and as you may already know, throughout history, many different names have been used to describe a mythical winged creature associated with fire and the sun: Bennu in Egypt, Anqa in Arabia, Simurgh in Persia, Konrul in Turkey, Firebird in Slavic countries, Garuda in Hindu, Hōō in Japan . . . and many other names in many other countries and regions.

When we look at it this way, we can see that despite its fame, the phoenix was not unique at all. In fact, there are a lot of documented records of myths and legends about other divine winged creatures that were similar to the phoenix, and they came from all over the world. Depending on where each tale originated from, the mythical winged creatures in those stories were called differently, and their physical appearances were described slightly differently as well. But here's the interesting thing: no matter where the tales originated, no matter which names were used or how their physical appearances were described, every one of those winged creatures was not only associated with fire and the sun but also depicted as a deity. Moreover, according to those myths and legends, they all had a formidable size and an extremely long lifespan.

Now, are these striking similarities merely uncanny coincidences? If you look at where those tales originated from, you'll see geological differences, cultural differences, religious differences, and also the differences in time, yet they still managed to share abundant similarities with one another in terms of what their mythical winged creatures were capable of and what they represented to the people in that specific space and time. So how come these mythical winged creatures were so much alike when their origins were so different?

I think the answer lies right here on this stone tablet. I think our ancient ancestors were indeed graced by the presence of a mighty bird that was as fiery as the sun, perhaps even more than once. Maybe this fiery bird did come to our ancestors' rescue when they found themselves in a dreadful situation similar to what was portrayed here on the stone tablet and offered them the protection they so desperately needed. Maybe our ancestors did happen to have the opportunity to witness the amazing process of its death in combustion and its rebirth from flames. Maybe they did stumble upon the healing powers that this divine creature possessed, be it by its tears or its ashes. Or maybe, based on the clues they found in Pandora's box, they were actively searching for this bird in the hope of using its powers to defend themselves from the evils that were released, and they actually succeeded in tracking it down . . .

No matter how it happened, one thing is certain: our ancestors did see this fiery bird; they witnessed its incredible powers and were mesmerized by what it was capable of. That is why, regardless of their geological differences, cultural differences, religious differences, and even the differences in time, our ancestors around the globe uniformly associated this mighty bird with fire, the sun, and divinity. As a result, the tales were born, along with many names used to refer to this divine winged creature and its humanized forms, which were invented by our inspired ancestors as fire and solar deities. Of course, the differences in the geological, cultural, and religious backgrounds of those tales resulted *in some differences in how the fiery winged creature's physical appearance was depicted in detail, but the descriptions of its most prominent features always shared the same gist.*

So you see, that's what the phoenix is: just another name for the mighty bird that was as fiery as the sun. Luckily for us, there were altogether three recordings of the "phoenix" appearing in ancient Rome between 96 BC and AD 36. And thanks to the heavy cultural influence left by ancient Rome on western civilization and the pre-modern society, the name "phoenix" successfully endured the test of time and eventually became the most popular and the most representative notion of such a mythical winged creature in the world. What's more, it's been consistently used as a symbol for hope in many forms of art and literature across the globe.

But is it a mere coincidence that what we call the "phoenix" today symbolizes the very thing said to have been left behind in Pandora's box?

No. There's no coincidence in the making of history. It was not a coincidence that the first tale of Pandora's box and the first documented mention of the "phoenix" both came from the ancient Greek poet Hesiod. It was not a coincidence that both concepts survived more than 2,700 years in the long course of history with such well-known status, even till today. And surely, it's not a coincidence that the one thing said to have been left inside Pandora's box is the exact same thing that the "phoenix" has been representing unwaveringly across geological, cultural, and religious differences throughout all these years.

No, there's no coincidence in the making of history! It was not luck that guided Professor D to visit a deserted ancient rock tower on a whim, nearly tripping over the half-buried Pandora's box among a pile of rubble before noticing its unusualness. No. I believe Pandora's box was actually left there for her to uncover; I believe it was a gift!

Please, Architects! Let the evidence speak!

Thank you!

As crazy as it might have sounded to you, the evidence will *speak louder than my words. Altogether, we've found three pieces of evidence to prove that Pandora's box was left there for Professor D to uncover. I'll now go through each piece in detail for you to see the answer for yourselves.*

Evidence one concerns the origin of the tale known as "Pandora's Box." As I mentioned earlier, the "box" was a mistranslation. In the original text, Pandora opened a pithos, which should have been a jar large enough to hold a grown man. But what we have here is a sphere, which could not have been mistakenly identified as a pithos, or a box, for that matter. So why did Hesiod replace the sphere with a pithos in his poem even though it wouldn't do the later generations any favor in the search of the hope *to rectify Pandora's mistake?*

No, it was not because he needed to hide that piece of information from us. After all, he was the one who first brought the "phoenix" to light on paper.

Our hypothesis is that this sphere is not the original container. The original container could have indeed been a pithos, but it probably suffered a shattering fate for this stone tablet to be retrieved, although I'm afraid only the "gods" know whether the stone tablet had already been broken into four when that happened. Someone then made this sphere and stored the pieces of the stone tablet inside for safekeeping. But who could have done it?

First of all, it's made of a material that does not match up with anything we have on record. That is to say, either we've been completely ignorant of the existence of this unidentified material in nature, or it simply does not belong to Earth. Second, the technology used to make this sphere is obviously way ahead of our time, even more so ahead of the technologies available in ancient times. Our on-site Pathfinders have spent almost two weeks in an effort to find out what kind of mechanism was applied to trigger its unlocking process by direct sunlight. Nevertheless, their efforts have been in vain, so it still remains a big question mark to us. Third, even though we've tried many different dating technologies to determine the age of this sphere, the results all told us it was as young as a newborn, which is extremely shocking and baffling, considering the material and technology of this sphere are definitely not from our time.

Therefore, the implications here are quite clear: this sphere is neither a product from our past nor one from our present; it either came from another world or from another time in the future.

Let's say it came from another world. Who made it? Was it the "gods" who created Pandora—after giving her the pithos and telling her it contained forbidden ancient secrets just to tempt her into trouble? Well … not likely. After all, they were the ones who set us up in the first place, so why would they help us now? Was it some kindhearted extraterrestrial beings, then? Maybe they've been binge-watching us like a reality show of primeval evolution—it could be for educational purposes or just a form of extraterrestrial pastime for advanced civilizations that have reached beyond Type III—and maybe, due to a bet on how long it'll take for the human civilization to reach Type I, or due to decreasing interest and popularity resulting from how slowly things are progressing here on Earth, some of them were compelled to assist us in overcoming these evils so that we can speed up the progress of human civilization and finally deliver a more exciting show to the audience. I know. The scenario I just described sounds more like the plot of a dark science fiction, but it might not be as far-fetched as you think. Still, it would be very unlikely that any Type III civilization would intervene in our progress, because how could they be certain that by assisting us with our search, and therefore the advancement of human civilization, they're not actually creating a headache for themselves down the road?

But if this sphere didn't come from another world, then the only explanation we're left with is it came from another time in the future: from our descendants.

If you think about it, this actually makes perfect sense. Who else could have both the technological capability and the motive to fast-track the course of human history into a Type III civilization? Our hypothesis is this sphere was—no, will be—made by our future descendants as the new Pandora's box to deliver the pieces of the stone tablet to us safely through time travel.

Yes, you heard me right: time travel. That's how they'll be able to send the new Pandora's box back in time to us. That also explains why the material and technology of this sphere are unknown to us, and why all our dating technologies have unanimously decided it is only as old as a newborn. But judging from the fact that no direct contact has ever been made by our descendants from the future, we can only assume something about time travel is preventing it from happening. And that's why instead of being sent to us directly from the future, the new Pandora's box was planted in an inconspicuous yet still noticeable spot outside of that deserted ancient rock tower to be uncovered and discovered by our Pathfinder, who thought that she was merely going on an impulsive excursion. So you see, the new Pandora's box is a gift from our future descendants; they want us *to have the stone tablet* now *so that we can accelerate the progress of our mission!*

Of course, I can't tell you why the new Pandora's box was planted in that specific time and place rather than another time or another place. We don't have the answer to that. So we can only assume this is all part of their plan. What we do know now is that our descendants will *obtain the knowledge of time, and they* will *use that knowledge to travel back in time to the nineteenth of this March to deliver the new Pandora's box to us!*

Well . . . thank you for the quiet attention, though I suppose the lack of interjections is due to shock rather than assent? . . . Understandable. It was a lot of information to process all at once. No need to worry though. We still have two more pieces of evidence to go through, by the end of which, you'll see why I said that it was not luck but our future descendants' plan for us to receive the new Pandora's box then and there, and you'll also understand why I think our descendants would obtain the knowledge of time and use it to travel back in time to deliver the new Pandora's box to us as a gift from the future.

Hermes, could you project the middle section of the stone tablet at 1,500 percent?

That's perfect. Thank you.

Architects, we're moving on to the second piece of evidence, which concerns the identity of this fiery bird. Please look at the projection . . . Notice anything interesting?

Look here, under the fiery bird's claws . . . see these dots? And more of them here, and here . . . under both of its wings?

These dots are actually tiny holes, each with the diameter of a needle. There are altogether 171 of them on the stone tablet, unevenly distributed into three clusters, all of which sit close to the petroglyph of the fiery bird. At first glance, the distribution and layout of these tiny holes might seem completely random and therefore irrelevant to what we're discussing here. But the precise cut of their perfectly round rims caught our attention, so we decided to analyze them with enhanced 3D scans.

From those scans, we've learned that the holes are pretty shallow, but they were carved with such precision that they look like hollow micro cylinders drawn onto the screen by a computer. This is enough to indicate that these tiny holes could not have formed naturally, nor could they be the products of any manual tool as it would not be possible to achieve such smoothness of the inner wall and such flatness of the bottom surface by hand with an unvarying standard for all 171 of them, not to mention each hole is as thin as a needle. Even with our cutting-edge technology in laser drilling, it'd still be a challenge to achieve such precision and perfection with every single one of them without fail.

Furthermore, we believe these tiny holes were added into the stone tablet after *it was broken, not before. See how each cluster maintains a safe distance away from the cracks? If these holes were carved into the stone tablet before it was broken, then it would indeed be inexplicable as to how the cracks could have had the sense to steer clear of every single hole during impact.*

Based on these observations, we have concluded that a new level of advanced technology was used in cutting perfect micro cylinders in the broken stone tablet before they were meticulously extracted to form these tiny holes. Unfortunately, we don't exactly know what kind of advanced technology was used in achieving this. But the good news is, now that we know they were placed deliberately in the stone tablet, we can be certain there's a special purpose behind them.

So once again, the evidence is pointing to our descendants. Who else would have both the technology and the motive to mark the stone tablet with incredible details like this to convey a special purpose for our benefit, which will consequently benefit our descendants in the future?

But let's hold that thought for now, as we need to first figure out the meaning of these 171 tiny holes before we can infer the special purpose they're meant to convey.

Hermes, please relay and project Hope's proposals on that matter.

As you can see, according to the calculations and simulations ran by Hope, these are all possible ways to decipher the meaning of those holes. But among this long list of proposals, one really stood out: the star maps of the Four Symbols.

Now, the Four Symbols are four mythical creatures in ancient China, namely, the Black Tortoise, the Azure Dragon, the White Tiger, and the Vermilion Bird. They were worshiped as the guardians of the four cardinal directions in ancient China for thousands of years, but the oldest known depiction of them has been dated to approximately 5,300 BC, as early as the Middle Neolithic period. The Four Symbols were thought to reside in the sky ecliptic in the form of four regions of constellations. There are seven astrological mansions for each of these regions, so twenty-eight mansions in total. And altogether, they're made up of 218 asterisms.

Hermes, please compare the cluster of holes on the right with the star map of the White Tiger.

Now, please compare the cluster on the left with the star map of the Azure Dragon.

Last but not least, let's compare the cluster under the fiery bird's claws with the star map of the Black Tortoise.

Look at that, everyone. We have three sets of comparisons, and all three sets are a match!

These tiny holes represent the asterisms in the twenty-eight mansions! And each of these three clusters represents the star map of one of the Four Symbols from ancient China!

Now that we know what these tiny holes are supposed to be, let's find out what they're trying to tell us.

Here, at the bottom, we now know we have the star map of the Black Tortoise of the North, who represents water. Here, to the left, we have the Azure Dragon of the East, who represents wood. And here, to the right, we have the White Tiger of the West, who represents metal . . .

Yes, Architects! These seemingly insignificant holes were placed in the stone tablet as a hidden clue! Finally, we can solve the mystery of the true identity of this mighty bird! The answer here is as clear as day: this fiery bird is none other than the Vermilion Bird of the South, who represents fire as well as the sun! In other words, the Vermilion Bird is the hope *that was left for the human race—the hope of unlocking the forbidden ancient secrets to reverse and undo the existence of evils, the hope of mankind being forever shielded from all evils, and the hope of eternal salvation for the entire human race! We* need *to find the Vermilion Bird!*

No, I'm not being delusional. I'm quite aware the Vermilion Bird is only considered to be a mythical creature. However, the fact that it's depicted on a stone tablet this ancient is proof in itself that it is real and it has been here way before any human civilization formed. Come to think of it, this may also explain why sun worship can be traced back to the beginning of human history and why it was practiced by our ancient ancestors all over the world. After all, it was only natural for the primitive humans to conclude they'd seen the incarnation of the sun at the sight of the Vermilion Bird.

Needless to say, the historical implication of this is tremendous. It supports our previous theory that, just like the phoenix bird, all the other mythical winged creatures known in our history that have been associated with fire, the sun, and divinity—regardless of the differences in their origins, their names, and the descriptions of their physical appearances—were merely artistic imitations with the same archetype in mind: the Vermilion Bird. Our off-site Pathfinders have actually secured a few pieces of ancient artifacts in China that provide new evidence to reinforce this theory. The said ancient artifacts were carved with the images of the Vermilion Bird and were dated to be over 7,000 years old, which was 4,300 years before the earliest recorded mention of the phoenix.

Moreover, according to ancient Chinese folklore, the Vermilion Bird was said to be a god and one of the four creators of the world, a guardian of order. Quite interestingly, it was found in ancient texts that Fènghuáng, the Chinese phoenix, was an earthly bird that people chose to worship in place of the Vermilion Bird so as to secularize its image to their mortal lives for them to feel closer to its divine grace. Such a way of worship may seem counterintuitive to modern humans like you and me, but I'm inclined to think that was exactly what happened in the rest of the world as well.

Based on our findings from various sources, the Vermilion Bird probably looked more like raging flames in the shape of a giant bird rather than an actual bird. Therefore, it was quite possible, and quite understandable, that our ancient ancestors in other parts of the world might have either chosen an earthly bird as a substitute for the Vermilion Bird, like what they did in ancient China, or made up a divine winged creature, even a god or a goddess in humanized form in some cases, as a symbolic imitation so that they could at least have a worldly image of the Vermilion Bird to worship with. And that is why, even though the images and tales of those imitations were shaped by geological differences, cultural differences, religious differences, as well as the differences in time, and even though they had different origins, different names, and different descriptions in terms of physical appearances, we can still see the underlying similarities among them all.

So you see, there's no coincidence in the making of history. In every important chain of events that has taken place and, for better or worse, impacted the course of human history, there was always an explanation for each of the key moments that were to become the deciding factors of how a certain chain of events would eventually unfold. Therefore, we need to look beyond the surface of the events that took place in our recent endeavors, especially the ones that seem unlikely, so that we can focus on the key moments and see the truth: it was not a coincidence that Professor D came across the new Pandora's box by chance; it was planned. Likewise, there must be a reason as to why we were chosen to receive the new Pandora's box and why a deliberate clue was left for us to uncover the truth of the hope *that we have been searching for all these years, a reason that I will only disclose after we've looked at all three pieces of evidence as a whole.*

This brings us to the next and final piece of evidence, which, unfortunately, will shed light on just how superficial our view and our understanding have been regarding everything we think we know about the world we live in. We'll start by going back to one of the most important hypotheses we've made based on what we've learned from the new Pandora's box so far: the Vermilion Bird was here; it might have indeed protected humans from unfathomable evils, and it was definitely seen by our ancient ancestors in many different parts of the world, at many different times. But where is the Vermilion Bird now? Is it still with us, on this mortal plane? Will it ever show itself to us again? And if so, how can we make use of its powers to reverse and undo the existence of evils?

Hermes, please zoom in on the petroglyph of the Vermilion Bird and show us its left chest.

This little detail might have escaped your attention earlier: a vertical groove in the stone tablet, which happens to cut right into the heart of the Vermilion Bird. It's about 0.8 inches long, and as you can see, it's wider in the middle, about 0.3 inches in width, but becomes narrow and pointy toward the ends. You may have already guessed that, just like the 171 tiny holes placed in the stone tablet, this groove was not formed naturally either. That is indeed the case, as our dating technologies have told us this groove is as old as those tiny holes, which were dated to be as young as the sphere. With that in mind, we can only deduce this groove is also the work of our future descendants, but to what purpose?

Hermes, please zoom out and show us the full petroglyph of the Vermilion Bird again.

Architects, look at the projection now and tell me, what does this groove look like?

Exactly! It looks like a wound; it looks like something sharp was plunged into the Vermilion Bird's chest!

Without a doubt, this is yet another hidden clue from our future descendants. But what does it mean? Was the Vermilion Bird stabbed? Was it injured? And above all, how could the mighty winged creature with the powers of fire and the sun be vulnerable to such a primitive form of attack?

Now, there's still one thing from the new Pandora's box we haven't discussed in detail yet: the bloodred object that greeted Professor D with a fiery mirage when she opened the sphere for the first time.

Well, this object turned out to be an item of great peculiarity. As I've mentioned earlier, it has the shape of an oversize almond. And just like a real almond, it also has a bulgier waist and a pointier end. Other than that, it bears no more resemblance to a regular almond. Its surface feels smooth and slick to the touch, and even though we used many different machines and technologies to scan it for its compositions, it always appeared completely opaque in the images we took—by that I mean there was not the slightest trace to indicate it was man-made, nor was there any sign to indicate it was derived from nature. Not surprisingly, even Hope failed to identify the material it was made of, which only confirms that, just like the sphere, this bloodred object either came from another world or from another time in the future.

One thing we did manage to find out through our analysis and experiments is that this object glows whenever a light source is near; the stronger the light source is, the more it glows, looking like a rare ruby with the most enchanting hue. However, it will only produce a fiery mirage under natural sunlight, either direct or indirect.

Sadly, as of this moment, the Pathfinders still don't know how or why it reacts to light sources and natural sunlight like that. But it only strengthened our intuition that this object would be the key in finding the Vermilion Bird.

So I asked Hope to scan it and create an enhanced 3D image based on its precise measurements, hoping we would discover some clues from the data. As I was browsing through Hope's proposed list of possible leads, something caught my eye: the overhead view of the bloodred object.

Hermes, please relay the 2D image of that view from Hope and project it next to a zoomed-in view of the groove ... right here.

What do you think, Architects?

Same here. I see two identical shapes, only the groove is slightly bigger in terms of actual proportion.

Does it mean that this mysterious bloodred object can be inserted into the groove, like a key of some sort? Well, there was only one way to find out.

Four days ago, the Pathfinders prepared a safe room for the experiment to take place, just in case of any unforeseeable dangers. We used a robotic arm to place the bloodred object headlong into the groove in the Vermilion Bird's chest, and guess what? It fitted like a glove! But that was it; nothing happened and nothing changed. Something was amiss.

So we went back to go through all the data and information we'd gathered and recorded since the discovery of the new Pandora's box. After many intensive discussions among the Pathfinders, it dawned on me that we had forgotten about an extremely important element in our experiment, an element that came up over and over again since Professor D unearthed the new Pandora's box—in the unlocking mechanism of the sphere, in the identity of the fiery bird on the stone tablet, and in the mirage of active combustion that this bloodred object can produce:

The sun!

Yes, the clue was plain and simple: we needed the power of the sun!

The Pathfinders then quickly set up a transparent safe room at a secure location, with full exposure to the sun. Once again, we used a robotic arm to execute the experiment, except that this time, we placed the bloodred object into the groove while it was "burning."

Hermes, please relay the video footage of that experiment from Hope and play it for the Architects.

Marvelous, isn't it? It's almost like the bloodred object served as a portal, and the hellish surface of the sun oozed out from that portal to the Vermilion Bird's body like a lava transfusion into its veins.

But this is more than marvelous; it's genius! These "veins" you see here are, in fact, formed by tens of thousands of lines of micro-inscriptions that remained invisible—even in all the enhanced 3D scans we took of the stone tablet—until that very moment. Just think: If it weren't our future descendants, who else could have both the technology and the motive to incorporate hidden messages in the new Pandora's box like this? But we'll have to come back to that later. For now, let's focus on the micro-inscriptions first.

Many ancient languages were used in these micro-inscriptions, including Egyptian, Sanskrit, Greek, and Chinese. Of course, we wasted no time in transcribing and translating them into modern English. According to the contents of these micro-inscriptions, the Four Symbols were indeed the four creators of the world and the guardians of order. They were the oldest magical creatures, and their powers were what gave birth to the laws of this universe. The micro-inscriptions also highlighted that if we could capture the Four Symbols, we would be able to harvest their powers to utilize as our own: We could use the power of regeneration and rebirth from the Vermilion Bird to treat disability, disorder, disease, and even to cheat death. We could use the power of change from the Azure Dragon to control climate, curb natural disasters, and stop aging. We could use the power of growth from the Black Tortoise to tame and manage Mother Nature, achieve longevity and even immortality. And we could use the power of time and space from the White Tiger to weave our past and future into a much more desirable outcome—

"It can't be true"?... Well, I understand it may sound like a tall tale made up by a madman, but if you think the micro-inscriptions are just a collection of fairy tales, you are completely wrong. Architects, these are not stories. These are facts that contain details of the secret plans and attempts that were made in our history to capture the Four Symbols, including descriptions of their physical appearances, their powers and abilities, and even, to our great astonishment, their weaknesses and possible ways to use those weaknesses to our advantage. Furthermore, we've also found out from the micro-inscriptions that this bloodred object was indeed not made or formed by nature. It belonged to the Vermilion Bird—a feather, if you will. It separated from that mighty bird's fiery plumage and solidified into its current form. And the best part? It was obtained in AD 79 from the last recorded attempt in capturing the Vermilion Bird, which, according to the chronicles in the micro-inscriptions, was successfully executed in the vicinity of Pompeii —the same area where Professor D had discovered the new Pandora's box!

Yes. It sounds surreal. But so is everything else we've learned from the new Pandora's box. It is, after all, the container of forbidden ancient secrets, secrets that are not meant to be known or comprehended by us mortals, and therefore it's only natural that we find them utterly inconceivable. Like I said, this last piece of evidence sheds light on just how superficial our view and our understanding have been regarding everything we think we know about the world we live in.

Do you see it now, Architects? The Four Symbols are not mythical creatures, not anymore. They're real; so are their powers, which control the entire construct of this universe. This bloodred "feather" from the Vermilion Bird is the best proof that they exist. It's also the best evidence to show us that the hope *is real. It is, literally, the key in finding the Vermilion Bird and unlocking* the hope *to provide answers to what we seek to achieve. Therefore, the micro-inscriptions we're looking at right now are* much *more than forbidden ancient secrets. They're answers from the ancient past, answers that have been tested and proven, and they were transcribed and hidden away in the stone tablet by our future descendants as secret clues to help us in finding the Four Symbols and harvesting not only the powers to reverse and undo the existence of evils but also* the power *to control the entire construct of the universe as we know it! This means we have not only achieved the first part of our mission but have also been offered a shortcut to achieve* beyond *the second part of our mission to provide eternal salvation to all!*

My dear Architects, we've spent the past eighty years in search of Pandora's box in an effort to find the hope *and fulfill our founders' dream in bringing forth a much more empowered human civilization and a much more promising future for all mankind. Today, after eight decades of painstaking endeavors by four generations of Pathfinders and Architects, we finally have Pandora's box in our possession! We have found* the hope, *and we've been offered not just one but four channels in total, to tap into the forbidden ancient secrets and harvest the powers that'll allow us to become the master of our universe! So what are we waiting for? The time to act is* now! *Our mission shall be progressed to a new stage immediately. We need to begin our search for the Four Symbols right away and use everything in our power to capture them!*

No. We will succeed. I am certain of it! The Vermilion Bird was captured before in AD 79, without either the resources or the technologies we have today, so I have no doubt that with your full support and the dedicated expertise from the Pathfinders, we will be able to capture it again!

I'm also confident that we will capture the other three Symbols as well. As a matter of fact, we must.

Remember when I said there must be a reason as to why we *were chosen to receive the new Pandora's box and why a deliberate clue was left for us to uncover the truth of* the hope? *Well, now that you've learned about all three pieces of evidence, I think you'll agree with me when*

I say that the reason is because our descendants need us to capture the Four Symbols sooner so that we will be able to utilize their powers sooner, and thereby, our descendants will benefit from our endeavors in the future, sooner.

I used the word "sooner" because the fact that our descendants can travel back in time from the future to deliver the new Pandora's box to us is the proof in itself that sometime between our time and their time, the White Tiger will be captured, and its power will be harvested and studied, until a genius among us figures out a way to apply it to time travel. Our descendants will enjoy the benefits of that technology, and without a doubt, they will use it to correct the course of history if it means a better prospect for the future in their time.

And that's precisely why they will choose to deliver the new Pandora's box to us rather than to our predecessors or our successors: they need the captures of the Four Symbols to take place in our time instead of our predecessors' time or our successors' time so that the course of history will be corrected at the right key moments to set off a chain of events that will eventually lead to the best possible outcome for the future in their time—that is, the best possible prospect for the future of all mankind!

Architects, the steering wheel of the course of human history is now in our hands! The future of the entire human race depends on the choices we're going to make and the actions we're going to take! It is, therefore, not only our duty but also our responsibility to capture the Four Symbols for our descendants—in our time!

I hereby conclude my presentation with a motion to commence a new stage in our mission immediately, the goal of which is to hunt down the Four Symbols. In order to fulfill our obligation to our descendants in time, I propose to initiate four dedicated operations headed by four teams of Pathfinders in devising and executing the capture plans for each of the Four Symbols simultaneously. To conceal the true identities of our targets from contracting parties, we'll use a code name for each of them. Since the powers of the Four Symbols are key to our path in becoming the master of the universe, we'll use Red Key for the Vermilion

Bird, *Blue Key* for the Azure Dragon, *Black Key* for the Black Tortoise, and *White Key* for the White Tiger.

Together, they will be referred to as the *Four Keys*.

IV

Gargoyle was in a state of euphoria. With the adrenaline rush still pulsing through his veins, his big owl eyes burned with such a mixture of desire and excitement that one might easily mistake his expression for the ecstasy of a madman.

He strolled down the milky white corridor in the direction of the elevator, dreamily and lightheadedly, each step feeling like a weightless ascent into the clouds, until a synthetic voice startled him from behind and brought him back to the ground:

"Congratulations on the approval of your proposal, Dr. G."

Startled, Gargoyle whirled around to face the Hermes that was speaking. Judging from the very few body parts successfully concealed by the volume of clothing sculpted for his cast, he concluded this Hermes was the same one that had assisted him with his presentation to the Architects earlier.

"Er . . . thank you, Hermes."

"You're welcome, Dr. G. Would you like me to inform Hope to start drafting operational plans based on your proposal for your review and selection?"

"Why, yes. That'd be very helpful . . . In fact, I also need Hope to select candidates for the four operations from the Pathfinder pool. Tell her to analyze and grade each Pathfinder's portfolio based on the information provided in the micro-inscriptions before making the selection. We must make sure the value their individual background and expertise can contribute is maximized in the operation that they're assigned to."

"Noted, Dr. G. Drafting in progress. Requested five plans for each operation for your review and selection. Estimated time to completion: thirty-six hours, ten minutes, and four seconds."

Gargoyle looked at his watch. "So . . . it'll be done at about 3 AM on the sixth. Good. Inform me immediately when it's ready, even if you have to wake me."

"As you wish, Dr. G. By the way, your elevator has arrived. Which section would you like to go to?"

"The Evidence Hall, please."

"Yes, of course."

Gargoyle gave Hermes a polite nod, then he turned and headed for the elevator, the door of which was now held open remotely by Hermes. Just when he was about to step inside, Hermes's voice was behind him once more:

"Dr. G?"

Gargoyle halted before the empty elevator but didn't look back. He couldn't help but wonder why Hermes's voice sounded somewhat different this time, in a way that gave him a funny feeling in his stomach, though just a little. He answered hastily, "Y-yes?"

"Did Professor D truly not know she was opening Pandora's box?" said Hermes in an emotion-free—but not emotionless—tone common to every synthetic voice generated by a computer.

Behind the disarray of his long gray beard, Gargoyle bit his lip discreetly. He looked over his shoulder at the perfectly frozen expression on Hermes's face and studied it in silence, then he said, firmly and finally, "We're here to make history, Hermes. Don't ever waste my time on unnecessary questions again."

Chapter 3 THE CHANGE

1

STARING blankly at the ceiling of her new bedroom, Mira concentrated on recalling the dream she had just woken up from. After the move from Skygate to Starfall, she had finally stopped having that repetitive dream of running toward and up the same ancient rock tower, even though she could never get past the old wooden door at the top to find out what she was looking for. But the dreamless nights didn't last very long, and within the first week after the move, she found her dreams to be repeating again.

In them, there was a field, a big one that seemed to stretch into every direction endlessly. There was no vegetation in the field, only rocks and sand.

The field was swarmed with soldiers, tens of thousands of them, all clothed in ancient Roman armor and carrying something lethal.

She was standing in the field with those soldiers, wearing similar armor and a metal helmet that covered most of her face except for her eyes and mouth. Somehow, she already knew she was in the middle of a battle. Holding her left hand up firmly behind a shield, she charged forward while wielding a sword deftly with her right, dealing deadly blows to whomever came near her way, sending warm blood spatters flying into the air before pattering down onto the trampled sand like showers of rain.

She was surprised at the cold calmness in herself as she sliced and chopped her way through the battlefield like a choreographed dance. The sight and the smell of blood always made her queasy and lightheaded in real life, but in the dreams, it didn't bother her, nor did the killing. It had become clear to her, in a subconscious sort of way, that in order to reach her destination, it was what she must do to find her way out of that field. So, she kept on running, charging, and slashing mechanically at every soldier that got in her way, striking them down one after another and killing her way through the field while leaving a trail of grotesque corpses behind her. She was panting heavily, but she did not slow down; she knew she could not—she *had* to continue.

Meanwhile, the battle went on all the same. More soldiers kept on pouring in, and more blood kept on pouring out. Yet in that vast, barren field bedded with nothing but rocks and sand, the swarms of battling soldiers merely looked like wrestling ants, painting the field red bit by bit with the heads and limbs and flesh and guts that they were tearing off each other. The cries of battle were sharpened by the shrieks of agony from those who saw death. The smell of blood was tinged with the stirred-up dust, suffocating the last few breaths of those whose souls were soon to be collected.

But she remained indifferent to the agony and despair that filled the air. She pushed on, charging and slashing mechanically as she ran. The shadows of a murder of crows followed her along the winding path she had cleared in the field, while their owners counted aloud with hoarse caws in the sky as each soldier fell limply from her sword to the ground and flanked the blood-soaked sand behind her, smelling like filth and rot.

She didn't mind the crows. She didn't need to look up to know they were watching her, in the same way that she was watching herself, as if she were using their eyes. There was a lot of blood on her, trickling down her armor in streams. She could feel its lukewarm stickiness on her face and arms. She could taste its metallic saltiness on her tongue. Yet, she did not waver—she didn't even flinch. She simply continued running and killing her way through the field till she woke.

Mira let out a soft sigh and sat up. Though she had gone to bed early the night before without setting an alarm to wake herself, she still felt tired and not rested, which caused her to wonder if she had indeed been running and killing in a different dimension the whole time she thought she was sleeping in this one. She brought her hands to her face and massaged it, hoping to rub away that heavy, sluggish feeling, which was the byproduct of a dull headache setting in between her temples—either as the result of another night of poor sleep, or of yet another unsuccessful attempt at recalling from her dream the destination she was so determined to reach in spite of the bloodshed she had to bring forth to get out of that endless field. But even as the freshly salvaged moments of her dream were crushed back into incoherent fragments by the buzzing nuisance swelling behind her forehead, Mira couldn't help but think she had missed some important details when recalling her dream, that they were just hiding, somewhere in the back of her mind, refusing to come out.

By then, the birds were chattering noisily from the woods behind their new home. Mira's bedroom was at the back of the house, on the second floor, with windows right next to her bed, looking out onto the woods. There was a backyard that separated the wooded wilderness from the house as well, but it was much smaller than what they had at the old house in Skygate.

Not ready to get out of bed just yet, Mira scooted over to the windows and looked out from behind the blinds. On the other side of the lawn, tall, thick trees stood freshly energized under the soft morning light. Their branches, dressed in leaves in various shapes and sizes, were radiating a vibrant green in the dewy air, brewing it into something so fragrant and so deliciously refreshing that Mira could almost smell it through the windowpanes. The birds clearly loved it too, for they were participating in the dawn chorus from everywhere—in the sky, on the trees, on the lawn—singing competitively in celebration of another glorious day. These noisy neighbors were not the only ones enjoying this beautiful early summer morning in their backyard. Just a little beyond the lawn, a family of deer was strolling and grazing lazily at ivy leaves. In the deer family's elegant company, a couple of fuzzy rabbits hopped happily alongside them before stopping to sample the newly formed fruits from the wild blackberry brush. The glistening morning light flowed through the gaps in the dense foliage in beams, casting specks of golden prints on the animals' glossy fur, producing such a picturesque and serene scene that it was as if the colored illustration of a fairy tale had come to life.

A short distance away from the deer family, closer to the house, the lawn was dotted with squirrels who were busy sprawling around, searching for breakfast. Some of the gutsier ones were cautiously approaching Mom, who was leaning back in a lounge chair on the patio and tossing pieces of fruit from her plate in their direction. She had a big cup of coffee in one hand and a big smile on her face.

Mira felt the corners of her lips pull up. But when she heard Mom scolding the squirrels in her official mom voice by telling them it was not nice to waste the food she had so generously shared with them, she couldn't help chuckling. It occurred to her then just how much more relaxed and at peace everyone had been after their move to Starfall, especially Mom. She thought Mom looked somewhat different these days. Even the way she talked and the vibes she was giving off felt different than before, in a good way though. She thought Mom smiled more and laughed more after the move, and she could see more of Cara's spirits in her eyes—which was an observation that was both strange and awkward at the same time, considering she had only known Mom as a mother instead of Cara, the woman who Mom used to be before she became a mother.

Mira glanced at the date on her clock: June 14. It had only been a month since they moved to Starfall, but it had been over a year since Mom and Dad first told her they were going to move away from Skygate. The long delay in their moving plan was mainly contributed by the dramatic price increase in the real estate market in Seattle, which would have been the city of their new home if

Mom and Dad had been able to find a house that they liked and could also afford. As the search for the perfect house at the perfect price dragged on, they eventually decided to give up on the idea of moving back to Seattle and began to consider other cities. It took them months to evaluate and compare all the potential choices they had narrowed down to. In the end, Starfall came forth as the most suitable candidate. Things then happened very quickly after that. Within three months, they had sold their old house in Skygate and purchased a new home in Starfall, and Dad had landed a new job at the local university, which he had cheerfully announced as "the pinnacle" of his career.

Though she had never asked Mom and Dad why they were so eager to leave Skygate, Mira could tell the move was a necessary and welcome change to them both. So as far as she was concerned, the real reason didn't matter. She was glad to see a more tranquil and blissful side of her parents, and to tell the truth, part of her was secretly relieved that she could leave Skygate for good.

As a contemplative girl who spent most of her time reading books and preferred reading people like books rather than inter- acting with them, Mira had always been the oddball at school. Few kids wanted to speak to her, and even fewer wanted to get to know her. But things only got worse after the quadruple blackout back in Skygate. The kids would avoid her deliberately whenever they could, and when they couldn't, they would avoid looking in her direction. Even the teachers would turn their heads intentionally to avoid any direct eye contact with her in class. Needless to say, not even the queen bees and the bullies had the nerve to make fun of her like how they usually treated the other ordinary oddballs at school.

However, none of them could say for sure why they were so uneasy and unsettled around her. There was just a general (but un- spoken) impression that she had an indescribable air about her that made them feel so completely exposed and vulnerable—especially when her eyes were on them—to the point where they wouldn't even let the people closest to them know how she really made them feel about themselves.

Naturally, Mira's classmates were all innately intimidated by her, and she hadn't had to participate in a single group project ever since school had resumed after the quadruple blackout—no one wanted to experience the inexplicable surge in self-awareness, almost bordering on self-loathing, that usually occurred with the proximity of her presence, let alone work with her. But since it was fine with the teachers, it was fine with Mira too, and she had no intention of telling Mom and Dad about it because she knew Mom would charge into the school like an enraged mama bear and take down every teacher, counselor, and administrator until she was included in group projects again. Mira did not wish to see that; she didn't think it was necessary, nor did she want Mom to be upset by meaningless things like that.

She knew perfectly well that neither the teachers nor the other students wished to have anything to do with her, but it didn't bother her in the slightest. She had long come to the conclusion that they were too different from her to have an interesting conversation with, and she had no interest in the topics that the other kids were interested in anyway, which seemed to be the only things they ever talked about outside of schoolwork and tests and grades. As a matter of fact, Mira felt she was listening to the same conversations wherever she went—be it the classroom, the gym, the cafeteria, or even the library—so much so that her brain would automatically categorize the conversations drifted into her ears: Hair, nails, makeup, cosmetics, skin care, weight, body type, body shape, clothes, bags, shoes, accessories, selfies, poses, filters, angles—fleeting disguises. Boyfriends, girlfriends, fun places for dating, great spots for making out—doomed relationships. This boy, that girl, who had a crush on whom, who was dating whom, who recently dumped whom, who just made out with whom—pointless gossip. Parents, siblings, teachers, frenemies, enemies, people to humiliate, people to make fun of, people who had offended them in some way, people to pick a bone with, people that they just didn't like—

self-absorbed opinions. The latest electronic gadgets and apps, the hottest social media trends, viral videos, number of likes, number of shares, number of followers, trending hashtags, trolling opportunities, social influencers, celebrities, reality shows, personality tests, horoscopes—time-wasting miscellaneous.

In short, there was nothing holding Mira to Skygate as a bond, and there was no one she cared about in that town except, perhaps, the birds and the critters who used to come to hang out with her while she was reading in the backyard of their old house on that gentle hill surrounded by trees. Therefore, it was easy for her to say goodbye to Skygate when the time came. But that was not why she was relieved to move away from it.

A pair of lustful green eyes materialized in Mira's mind and flew at her as their jet-black pupils dilated and expanded into two bottomless black holes, disorienting her sense of space and time as they swallowed her into the darkness of the one memory she had buried deep within herself.

She suddenly felt the suffocating weight on her body again, pinning her down to the ground and crushing her into the undergrowth. She heard the desperate rustling sounds produced by her useless struggling against that overpowering force applied upon her. She smelled and tasted the sweat from the bony hand clutched over her mouth, which was muffling her screams and beginning to smell and taste like blood. She felt the rage, a burning rage, roaring from every single cell of her, ready to burn down the entire world just to eliminate the body that was on top of hers.

Something was murmuring in her ears then: a cacophonous voice, soft but familiar, and it was enough to remind Mira that in order to escape from the darkness of this dreadful memory, she needed to return to reality.

She shook her head until the unwelcome memory was finally dispersed from her mind. When she opened her eyes and saw that she was still sitting on her bed, next to the windows, she let out a soft sigh of relief and flopped down to her pillow. Even though Mira knew she was only reliving that horrible memory in her mind and not in reality, she felt drained. She promised herself now that she was far, far away from Skygate and never had to return again, she would be able to erase that entire evening from her brain at last. She assured herself that there was no need to look back. After all, things were changing for the better after the move, and Starfall could be a new beginning for them all.

Founded in 1956, Starfall was a quaint town that hosted a perfect marriage between civilization and nature. It was populated with trees as old as the hills, decorated by lakes as green as emeralds, and embellished by rivers as smooth as ribbons. The downtown area of Starfall was a beautifully designed square surrounded by low buildings on all sides, most of which were occupied by restaurants and stores of all sorts, thus creating a very spacious pedestrian square in the middle, which was furnished with many comfortable benches and meticulously maintained flower beds, shrubberies, and trees.

At the center of the pedestrian square, there was a magnificent fountain built in 1969. It stood over fifteen feet in height, with an impressive statue of an archangel perching on top of a central platform sculpted with the details of the tangled and mangled body parts of a heap of demons and beasts piling on top of one another. The archangel was in a pose with his wings spread out wide as he pulled back the shield in his left hand to strike the deformed abominations under his feet with the spear in his right. According to the plaque on the fountain, the design was inspired by the name of the town. But Mira had a vague feeling that she had seen it before, or at least something very similar, from somewhere she couldn't quite recall.

Mira enjoyed going to the pedestrian square. For one thing, the town library was right there next to it. It was of a decent size, with plenty of selections to choose from, and it was within walking distance of their new home, which meant she no longer needed a ride from Mom just to go to the library, so she could go check out books as often as she liked. For another, since the pedestrian square was one of the most popular places in town, it created a perfect venue for Mira to go do her "people-reading," which meant studying people from afar and trying to read the significant life stories they carried beneath their exteriors, like trying to read a book through its cover. To Mira, people-reading was the ultimate field test for all the things she had read and learned about on human nature and human behaviors, and it was the only thing that interested her as much as, if not more than, reading real books.

Aside from reading books and reading people, Mira also liked watching animals. Unlike people, animals were much easier to interpret and much less likely to conceal their true emotions and intentions. Interestingly, the animals appeared to enjoy watching her as well, especially the birds, for they would not only try to approach her but also follow her sometimes, like tails who were not afraid of getting caught. And when she stopped to greet them with her gaze, they would tilt their heads and stare right back at her, their beady eyes shining with such curiosity that they seemed to be asking: What are you?

To Mira, the animals' interest in her was never considered to be something out of the ordinary. But to Mom and Dad, after having witnessed the consistent attention she was receiving from the wildlife community over the years, across species and geography, they insisted it was because their little girl had a very special quality about her that had even attracted Mother Nature's own special appreciation. And since there were always a number of animals gathered around Mira while she was reading in the backyard by herself, they had been lovingly referring to her reading companions as her admirers from nature.

Besides the increase in animal activities, the vegetation behind their house also appeared to be much more alive than when they had first moved in. The trees at the back stretched out more proudly than before, joining branches with their neighbors to support each other's heavy limbs. Their roots, which were raised and exposed, seemed to have intertwined into one long, strong body that sidewinded between the tree trunks wearing a thick coat of luxurious moss, looking like a monstrous green serpent closing in on its prey, as if it, too, wanted to join the growing population of animals visiting their backyard, only with a more theatrical entrance.

Mira sat up and rubbed her face. The thought of a new beginning in Starfall had diluted the tiredness she was feeling. She decided to get up.

She made up her bed and raised the blinds; the movement probably caught Mom's attention, for presently, she was squinting up from the lounge chair at Mira's windows. When she caught sight of her daughter, a bright smile blossomed on her face. She put down her coffee and, with both hands, gestured for Mira to come down and join her for breakfast.

A new beginning . . . Mira repeated to herself as she smiled back at Mom and nodded.

She changed out of her pajamas and went to freshen up. Then she went downstairs and helped herself to a plate of food and a glass of juice from the mini-buffet Mom had set out on the kitchen island.

"Gooood morning, Little Bird!" Mom intoned as soon as she opened the door to the patio.

Mira paused at the doorway and looked at Mom: she was taking a sip of coffee, hiding an apparent smile behind her cup, and the telltale excitement in her hazel eyes reminded Mira of a cat who had left a freshly caught surprise for its owner in her favorite pair of slippers.

Singing tone, sparkling eyes, half-concealed smile . . . a nonchalant voice immediately began to deduce in Mira's head. *Watch out. She's got a plan for you.*

Mira ignored the voice and cleared her throat. "Um, morning, Mom." Then she went over to the patio table and sat down. The enticing smell of Mom's homemade pancakes and hash browns was making her very hungry. She picked up the fork and dug in.

Mom got up from the lounge chair and joined her at the patio table.

"You didn't get any bacon," Mom observed as she sat down next to Mira, then she added quickly, "Don't you want any? Do you want me to go grab you some?"

Mira shook her head.

"Are you sure you don't want any?" A couple of frown lines appeared between Mom's brows as she got into a position that would allow her to step out of her chair the moment Mira changed her mind.

She's doing it again, Mira grumbled to herself, but she finished chewing and said, "Mom, I don't want any bacon, okay?"

"Oh." Mom relaxed her pose, looking a little awkward and a little stunned. "Okay."

Mira felt a vague contraction in her chest. "I just ... want to save room for more pancakes," she heard herself explain. Then, as if to reassure Mom that this was indeed the reason, she jammed a big piece of pancake into her mouth.

A melancholy yet affectionate smile came to her mother's face. "I'm sorry, Little Bird. You're growing up fast, but I'm still treating you like a child. I'm so used to thinking of you as my baby girl that I keep forgetting you're almost fifteen and you don't need me to baby you anymore."

Half suspecting it was her turn to look a little awkward and a little stunned, Mira stopped chewing and stole a glance at Mom.

"Speaking of which"—Mom leaned forward to catch her eyes— "what do you want to do for your birthday this year? It's only two weeks away."

Mira had to swallow hard to fight off the urge to groan audibly. There was so much enthusiasm on Mom's face that she wished her birthday were Mom's instead.

"Fifteen is the best age," Mom added dreamily. "It marks the beginning of a new chapter in your life, you know? Not to mention you're starting high school soon. How exciting is that? You'll learn new things, make new friends, and get to know a whole lot more about yourself. Being fifteen is going to be amazing, Little Bird! I think this birthday deserves a big celebration, especially since it'll be the first birthday we celebrate for you here, in our new home. So it's a *must*, don't you think?"

"Mom ..." Mira sighed inwardly. "You say that every year."

"Say what every year?"

"What you just said about turning fifteen. 'The best age'? 'The beginning of a new chapter'? 'Deserves a big celebration'?" Mira poked at the air with her fork as she repeated the words, wishing it could ring a bell in Mom. "You said the same things about turning fourteen, remember? ... And also thirteen? And twelve ...?"

"Really?" Mom looked genuinely surprised, but she recovered quickly and gave Mira a shrug. "Still, turning fifteen is a much bigger deal. You'll be a high schooler, after all, and that is a *major* transitional phase for every teenager before becoming an adult."

"Age is just a number," said Mira, putting down her fork. "A number doesn't transit me from one life stage to another, my choices do. And they don't simply change because my number has gone up by one."

That's right. Just go to school, visit the library, read more books, read more people, watch more animals, then go home and repeat ... a sarcastic voice whispered in her head as the wind chimes in their backyard stirred restlessly in a passing breeze.

But that's the way it is, another voice countered while the first one was still speaking, overlapping yet never overshadowing it. *And that's the way it'll be ...*

They are consumed with superficial relationships and meaningless pursuits. The third voice flowed in between the first and the second. *That is why they don't understand her; they can never. They are afraid of her, and they will always be. But this is her choice. So let her enjoy the books, the people-reading, the animal-watching. That's all there is to it, and that's all it needs to be ...*

A guffaw suddenly erupted from Mom, drowning out all three voices at the same time.

"S-sorry." She waved a hand in front of her as she tried to straighten up from the soreness she was feeling in her sides. "I'm not laughing at you. It's just—where did you hear *that* from?"

"Nowhere," Mira answered flatly. "It's the truth."

Whatever amount of amusement still lingering on Mom's face drained away then, leaving behind something odd and shadowy in its place. Before Mira could read it, however, Mom caught herself and looked away.

"Interesting theory," said Mom, forcing a smile. "I might have heard something very similar before ... from someone I once knew."

Mira tilted her head to the side, brows knitting. "Who?"

Mom smiled resignedly and shook her head. "Doesn't matter. You've never met ..." She drew a deep breath and let out a long sigh, then she said, "Little Bird, high school is a place for you to go through metamorphosis, regardless of your a—your number. You see, you're just a pupa when you go in. You'll meet and get to know lots of other pupae there, and through them, you'll know more about yourself, know more about who you really are and what you really want to do, for yourself and for your life. And then, when it's time for you to leave high school, you'll become a butterfly. You'll have found the reasons to decide who you want to be, what you want to do, where you want to go ..."

Mira thought about telling Mom that a metamorphosis would be unlikely considering she had already asked herself those questions when she was three, but she decided against it—she had caught a glimpse of sorrow in Mom's eyes during her monologue, and she wanted to know why.

But Mom blinked away the evidence and continued with a soft giggle, "Maybe you'll even meet a special someone there who'll help you to find your answers—"

"I don't need a special someone to have answers." Mira cut her off with an agitated frown. "I don't need anyone to have answers for myself. Relationships with other people are merely emotional entanglements for oneself. They may help people with little self-consciousness to define their own beings in this world, but they're as fluid as the air that shifts, the desert that sinks, or the ocean that drowns, and they're bound to come to an end, sooner or later."

Mira knew she was saying things that were way too cynical for most people to digest. She could see the change in Mom's face as she blurted out those words: her eyes were widening as though there was an increasing amount of pressure building up behind them and they might pop out from her eye sockets at any second.

Mira did not enjoy seeing such a reaction in Mom, but she decided to act nonchalant about it. Mom, on the other hand, didn't move or speak for a long time afterward. What's more, she seemed to have forgotten how to breathe.

When Mom finally let out the air in her lungs, it sounded almost like a shudder.

"Mom?" Mira asked tentatively. "What's wrong?"

" 'What's wrong' . . ." Mom repeated weakly, sounding very much distracted. "No, nothing's wrong, Little Bird. You just reminded me of—" She bit her lip and closed her eyes.

Mira noticed there was something struggling helplessly on her mother's face, something painful and melancholy. So she waited, silently and patiently, like a shadow.

"You reminded me of a special someone I used to have," Mom said in the end. "A dear friend, the best kind . . . You've never met her, but I think if you had, you'd have loved her too. She was a friend from high school . . . My first friend in high school, actually. And her friendship changed my life forever . . ."

"Where is she now?" asked Mira, hoping to confirm the suspicion she had formed from the telltale signs she had picked up from Mom's eyes.

"She, um—" Mom stopped herself and drew a shaky breath. But when her mouth moved again, no words came out.

Eventually, she sighed resignedly and said in a small voice, "I've been meaning to tell you all about her . . . But let's save it for another day, when the time is right. Is that okay?"

Mira stroked the array of emotions that were chasing one another off Mom's face with her eyes and replied, "Sure, Mom. We'll save it for another day."

11

It didn't matter how much Mira had dreaded this day; it came all the same, and there was nothing she could do to stop it.

It was the 30th day of June. She was officially fifteen.

Mira didn't mind turning fifteen or getting older. To her, birthdays were just numbers, purely ornamental. But to Mom, Mira's birthday was the most important day in a year, and she was so devoted in celebrating it, year after year, that Mira was under the impression her mother treated her birthday as an investiture of special abilities, which, according to Mom, could only be obtained by reaching the next number she was turning: independence, confidence, strength, courage, wisdom, foresight, invincibility, immortality, to name a few. Worse still, Mom had this ritual of handpicking a special birthday outfit dedicated to such a ceremony for Mira to wear every year, the overall presentation of which, in Mira's opinion, might perplex even the most visionary fashion designers. As a result, over the years, Mira learned to dread her birthday as much as Mom looked forward to planning it.

This year, her big day fell on a Saturday. By six o'clock in the morning, Mom had burst into her bedroom with a face as bright as a blooming sunflower, radiating more than enough energy to light up the entire house. Dad came in as well, though he was still in his pajamas. His hair was flat on one side, and his glasses were sitting crookedly on his nose, looking as though he had gotten out of bed in a rush. He was dragging his legs behind Mom while hugging the beautifully wrapped boxes in his arms like soft pillows, and, despite the warmth he was producing with his contented smile, he couldn't stop yawning.

It was not hard for Mira to deduce from Dad's sleep-deprived state that Mom had put him to work on a facelift around the house for an over-the-top birthday celebration till well after midnight again. But before the voices in her head could have a chance to panic, Mom had hustled her down the stairs, out the patio door, and into one of the chairs next to the patio table.

Still barely awake herself, Mira was not expecting a trip to the backyard this early in the morning. So as Mom escorted her out of her room and all the way to her seat, she felt as if she were riding a whirlwind and the world were spinning away under her feet. The dawn chorus of the birds was just heating up, sounding like a full house at a sing-along concert, each chanting a tune at their own pace and, worse still, at their own pitch. It was so clamorous and distracting that Mira couldn't even hear what the voices in her head were grumbling about anymore.

Then the food came, all Mira's preferred breakfast items: pancakes, hash browns, sausages, scrambled eggs, bacon, butter croissants, chocolate muffins, plain yogurt, fruits . . . Mira had no idea how Mom could fit all those bowls and plates of food on the table without spilling anything, while magically still managing to leave just enough room to squeeze in a glass of orange juice in front of her.

"Breakfast buffet for the birthday girl!" Mom announced proudly.

Mira gawked at the jam-packed table, which had rendered the voices in her head speechless.

"I hope you're hungry," Mom chirped happily. "I made you your favorites." She gave Mira a peck on the cheek, then she pulled out a chair and sat down beside her. "Come on. Dig in! There's more in the kitchen."

Mira murmured stiffly, "There's no space to eat."

"Happy birthday!" Dad exclaimed from behind them before patting Mira on the shoulder. He added in a gloating voice, "May you never forget what you get to enjoy on this day!"

Mom turned and scowled at Dad. He laughed and planted a kiss on her forehead in return.

"Here you go, princess," said Dad, handing Mira a fancy glass plate, which had gold trim along the rim and carried a set of silver utensils neatly swaddled in a golden cloth napkin. "Time to start the feast!"

Mira looked at the plate, then she looked up at Dad for help.

Dad winked at her with a knowing smile, but he said, "You'd better start eating, Little Bird. We've got a tight schedule to follow through today." As he spoke, he began to load Mira's plate with food, beaming with mischief. "Besides, you'll need time to digest your birthday breakfast before your birthday lunch, and time to digest your birthday lunch before your birthday dinner. Trust me, you don't want to delay *the schedule*, or you won't be able to blow out the candles till after midnight!"

Mira didn't need to look at Dad to know he was enjoying a considerable amount of amusement over her miseries, not to mention he could barely contain his laughter, which had been leaking out in the form of a series of suppressed snorting and wheezing sounds.

Mom gave Dad a look and nudged him away from Mira. "And you'd better go make yourself a coffee so you can start behaving like an adult. While you're at it, make me one too."

Dad cackled like a goose who had been tickled by its own feathers, but he didn't object to Mom's instructions. He handed the fancy glass plate back to Mira, which was now loaded with food, and went back into the kitchen.

Mom saw him off with her eyes and said with a sigh, "Men . . . oversize children no matter how old they get."

Mira chuckled under her breath. "And women?"

"That's a hard one." Mom screwed up her lips. "Hmm . . . What do you think?"

Mira set the fancy glass plate down on her lap and picked up the golden napkin, which was still holding the silver utensils like an exquisite pocket. As she pulled the utensils out, she peered into the pocket and quickly decided she had no desire to find out how Mom had folded it into such an intricate design after all.

"I think women are supernatural beings," she said, slipping the napkin under her plate without opening it.

"Oh?" Mom tilted her head. "How so?"

"Because they can bleed for seven days straight every month without dying and still have the energy to take care of the children, including the oversize ones."

A long horselaugh erupted from Mom, causing her to hold her sides and rock on her chair like a roly-poly toy that got punched.

"You need coffee too, Mom," said Mira, deliberately.

"Oh, stop it!" Mom wheezed as she waved a hand at Mira. "Don't make me laugh any harder . . ."

A splash of red appeared behind the trees and soon saturated the entire skyline with a golden undertone. The birds must have interpreted it as a divine sign to deafen the world, for even though they should have already reached the maximum of their volume, they were still getting louder by the second.

"Hmm. The sun is just getting up and we're already having breakfast." Mira picked up a blackberry from her overloaded plate and popped it into her mouth. "Why do we need to eat so early today, Mom?"

"Because . . . I wanted you to know what it was like the morning you arrived," Mom replied, smiling, though something deeply melancholy flickered in the depths of her eyes. But before Mira could catch it and read it, Mom had looked away, staring off into the distance, where the edge of the bustling woods met the burning sky.

"It was early in the morning. The sky was glowing beautifully from the sunrise, just like this," Mom continued softly, her eyes remained fixed on the skyline. "The birds were very noisy too . . . so noisy, like they knew you'd arrive soon. In fact, I ended up making Dad go outside to shoo them away because the noise was really getting on my nerves . . ."

There was a mix of emotions rippling across her face. Mira observed it and asked, "Were you in a lot of pain?"

Mom's head swiveled back. "Huh?"

"My birth. Did it cause you a lot of pain?"

For a few seconds, Mom looked stunned and unprepared. When she recovered, she lowered her eyes and whispered slowly, "Yes. It did."

"Was there a lot of blood?"

A pensive smile came to Mom's face. "Actually . . . no."

"Did Dad come back in time from shooing away the birds?"

Mom gave a soft chuckle. "Yes. He did . . . Just in time."

Mira picked up a juicy strawberry that was sitting on top of the pancakes on her plate and took a bite. "Did he faint?"

"What?"

"Dad's face always turns green when he sees me bleed."

"He just can't see you suffer, that's all."

"But he was okay watching you blee—I mean, suffer?"

"He tried to be," Mom said gently, a degree of sorrowfulness ringing in her voice. "I'm not sure if his face turned green or anything. I was . . . I was too overwhelmed to notice what was happening in my surroundings. What I do know is that he knew I needed him, so he stayed strong . . . for the sake of all three of us."

Mira considered this as she finished the strawberry, then she asked, "Why didn't you go to the hospital?"

"Because . . ." Mom's hazel eyes glistened in the cool morning breeze, reflecting the golden hue from the sky. "Because it was a surprise. You surprised me."

"Weren't you nervous though? Having a baby at home without any help?"

Mom looked down at her hands, which were resting together on her knees, her thumbs rubbing against each other. "I was. Nervous, scared . . . I didn't know what to do. It felt like what was happening was completely out of my hands, though I was supposed to be in control of what would happen next . . . So, I did the only thing that I knew would help me get through."

"What?"

"I shut everything out of my mind except one thought . . ." Mom closed her eyes as though she was trying to summon that very thought back. In a quavering voice, she said quietly, "I thought about how much I already loved you . . . even though we had never met."

For a moment, Mira thought her heart had paused to digest Mom's words. When it started pumping again, there was a prickling sensation throbbing with its every beat. Something red and warm had reached her face then, heating up her eyes and cheeks. She squinted and looked toward the woods. The sun was about to climb up from behind the trees; its bloodred radiance was spilling generously onto the sky above and the treetops below while flowing steadily and effortlessly toward their house and the rest of Starfall as it transformed into a golden glory.

Mom reached for Mira's hand and held it tight in hers, which, despite the oncoming heat spreading quickly from the rising sun, were still cool as night.

"Mira, no matter what happens in the future, please remember: we love you and we will always love you. You will always be our daughter . . . our Little Bird. Nothing can change that—nothing. Okay?" said Mom as she brought Mira's hand to her chest and pressed it to her heart, smiling a smile that looked more like the prelude to a tacit cry.

Mira found herself at a loss for words. Mom's request baffled her just as much as that non-smile smile she was trying to hold on her face. She tried to think of an explanation, but her mind drew a complete blank. Even the voices in her head seemed to have run out of opinions and chose to remain silent. So instead of acknowledging Mom's request, she only managed to give her a confused frown.

Mom made a shape with her mouth as though she wanted to say something, but no words came out. Eventually, she closed it and pressed her lips together into a thin line, her jaws tight, and looked away.

Mira couldn't help but wonder what it was that Mom had intended to say but did not. She felt a strange feeling in her, a feeling that she had never experienced before, and it was clawing on her heartstrings and making her insides sore. She wondered why Mom changed her mind at the last moment; she wanted to know the reason that was holding her back.

A big coffee mug suddenly appeared between them, cutting off Mira's gaze from Mom as a cheerful voice announced: "Coffee delivery!"

Mira looked up from the mug and saw that Dad was attached to its handle.

"What did I miss?" he said eagerly, reaching for the bacon with his free hand. "Not the breakfast buffet, I see."

"Your manners, that's what!" Mom removed the mug from his hand and slapped him on the other just as he was fishing out the biggest piece from the pile, causing it to slip from his fingertips and fall headlong into the yogurt bowl.

"Ouch!" Dad gave a plaintive cry but proceeded to rescue the bacon with that same hand anyway. "C'mon, honey. Don't trouble yourself with little things like this," he said, taking a cautious bite of the yogurt-dipped bacon. "Hmm. Interesting." He peered at the remainder of it, took another bite, then with a shrug, shoved the whole thing into his mouth. He then continued in such an earnest fashion that it sounded almost like coaxing, "As of today, you've been on mom duty for fifteen years! That's *a lot* of work. You should definitely take a day off today. You deserve a break!"

As he finished his sentence, he reached down to give Mom a pat on the shoulder without realizing she was just about to take a sip of her coffee. His spontaneous gesture of appreciation caught Mom by surprise. Her shoulder dipped under the weight of his hand, and consequently, the aromatic black liquid splashed over the rim and splattered onto her chin and chest, immediately staining the front of her white shirt with brown spots in various shapes and sizes.

Mom looked down and gasped, "My new shirt!"

"Oooops," said Dad, carefully, as he saw Mom looking up from her shirt and presently staring daggers at him.

Mira caught herself snickering under her breath. Dad threw her a look and made a face, as if to say he knew she was gloating. He then turned to Mom with pleading eyes and said, "Well, for what it's worth, the birthday girl is having fun … so no harm done to the plan, right?"

Mira perked up her ears. "What plan?"

"*No* plan," Mom said firmly as she hushed Dad with a glare. "Don't listen to him. He was half asleep when we set things up last night. I doubt he remembers a word I said."

"That's not true!" Dad interjected. "I blew up the balloons, put up the decorations, and followed every instruction I received! Half-asleep people can't do that—"

Mom cleared her throat meaningfully and said to Mira, "There isn't a plan. We'll just hang out today, the three of us, however you like it."

Mira looked from Mom to Dad and back to Mom. "Really?"

Mom nodded without hesitation. "Really. We don't need a plan to have fun, do we? I mean, there's so much we can do together … We can take a walk to the pedestrian square after Dad"—she gave Dad a look for emphasis—"has cleaned up the mess in the kitchen. We can go visit that antique store next to the library. Did you know it has a dedicated room just for antique books? I heard it's filled with interesting-looking old books—you'd love that. We can stop by the library too, of course. After that, we'll just wander around the square, get a smoothie, relax by the fountain, feed the birds … We can have a picnic lunch there if you want. I can pack some food, and we can either carry it to the square with us, or Dad can come back and grab it when we're ready to eat. Then … we can go to the movie theater. Or, come home and watch one on our own! If there's still some time left after the movie, we can play board games. Let's see how well Dad can play against us this time, ha! Dad and I will make dinner at seven. We'll eat at eight … You know what, we can even put on some music and turn on those portable disco lights I got for Valentine's and have a backyard dance party at sunset! Ooh, it's gonna be fun! I can't believe I only thought about it just now … Anyway, we'll reveal your birthday cake at nine, then it's candle and present time!"

Mom finished her last sentence with a delighted smile, only to notice Mira did not seem to share the same sentiment. Thanks to fifteen years of experience in motherhood, her body tensed up automatically into full alert mode.

"Sweetie?" she asked cautiously. "What's wrong?"

"I can tell you what's wrong," Dad offered, reaching over for another piece of bacon. "There's a lot of Dad will do this and Dad can do that in Mom's plan that Dad wasn't aware of."

Mom simply rolled her eyes. "Thomas, it's *her birthday*."

"Hmm," said Mira, taking a sip of the orange juice to ease the sudden dryness in her throat. "So there *is* a plan after all."

"That wasn't a plan!" Mom's face turned red under the rising sun. "Just . . . just some ideas that popped into my head. I was only trying to picture what we could do together to make today a perfect day . . ."

Mira felt a piercing pain in her left chest, as if something sharp had been jabbed into her heart. Her vision went black for a split second, and when it returned, everything was a blur. She felt a sticky, lukewarm fluid trickling down her face; she could smell it: a mixture of blood, sand, and filth—the smell of the battlefield in her dreams. It was so vivid that she couldn't help but wonder if her life with Mom and Dad had been the real dream and if she was, in fact, still fighting on the battlefield. She could even hear the bloodcurdling shrieks going off around her: the shrieks of agony, the shrieks of terror, the shrieks of despair at the dreadful sight of Death's face leaning in, closer and closer . . .

Maybe it's finally my turn to fall on the battlefield this time, she thought, pressing hard into her left chest to ease the pain.

". . . Mira? . . . Mira!" a voice called urgently from her right.

She turned to the voice, and as she blinked to focus on the shape calling her name, her vision returned to normal. The first thing she saw was the concerned face of Mom.

"Are you okay?" Mom asked in a nervous voice that sounded one octave higher than usual.

Mira realized her hand was still pressed to her heart. She released it and was surprised to notice there was no wet stickiness of blood that she thought she was suppressing under her palm. She looked at her hand: it was dry; there was no sign of blood.

Am I dead? she wondered. *Or am I dreaming again?*

"Heartburn, maybe?" Dad suggested helpfully, kneeling next to Mom. "It *is* a lot of foo—"

Mom shot him a look and cut him off. "Speak for yourself, Thomas. Mira's barely touched her food. How many pieces of bacon did *you* eat?"

"Well . . ." Dad screwed up his face as though he was serious about recalling the exact number, but he soon stole a glance at Mira and mouthed the word "help."

In spite of the dreamlike state she was in, Mira chuckled to herself and found herself saying, both to her parents and to herself, "I'm fine, Mom. Dad's right. It's just heartburn from drinking orange juice so early in the morning. I'd better stop eating."

Mom sank into her chair with a relieved sigh. "I swear, this mom job is not good for the heart; mine is practically a squeeze toy by now."

"I know," Mira heard herself murmur.

Mom tilted her head and gave Mira a funny look, appearing surprised yet, at the same time, alarmed by her reply. But she cleared her throat and said, "So, what do you think? Do you, uh . . . Do you want to go on an outing with us to the pedestrian square?"

Mira looked at Mom, then she looked at Dad. They looked real. It seemed real.

Maybe this isn't a dream after all, she thought. *But if it is . . .*

She saw the uneasiness of nervous anticipation brewing in their eyes, and she decided not to finish her thought. As soon as she had made up her mind, she felt the corners of her lips pull up into a faint smile.

"Fine," she answered and, with a barely perceptible smirk, added, "But you two must agree to behave like adults."

They agreed. And for the next few hours, both Mom and Dad were eager to demonstrate their best behavior to Mira. They cleaned up the patio table and the kitchen together in good spirits, although they refused to let her help with any of it, claiming there was a surprise hidden somewhere in the kitchen that they didn't want her to see before it was time. Then, as the neighborhood came alive in the wake of a conjunction of noises from the sprinklers, lawn mowers, blowers, dogs, and cars, they took a leisurely stroll to the pedestrian square, with Mom and Dad walking hand in hand next to Mira and taking turns telling her about their favorite books from when they were teenagers like her.

Their first stop at the pedestrian square was the antique store that Mom had talked about. They spent quite some time looking around inside the room, which held an impressive collection of antique books, some, as Dad put it, old enough to be books his great-great-great-great-great-grandfather had read when he was a teenager. Mira took her time going through the narrow aisles one by one, browsing the print on the book spines lined up neatly on dusty shelves while indulging her senses in the unique decay smell that only books of an old age could give off. Unfortunately, the books she was most interested in flipping through—the one said to be over a thousand years old and the one claimed to be bound in human skin—were all safely out of reach inside heavily locked display cases. Still, it was an experience unlike any other bookstores or libraries. And although Mira did not think it was necessary to express it out loud, she was glad she had let Mom talk her into doing this.

As for Mom and Dad, not only did they enjoy admiring the size and age of the collection inside the room dedicated to antique books, they also had a great time oohing and aahing over the other contents inside the antique store, as if they had traveled back in time and, as a result, were amazed at everything they saw—much like the way aliens would react toward human inventions if they ever fancied a visit to Earth, Mira imagined. Their excitement was so pure and genuine that she thought they were like a pair of young children who had wandered into a toy collector's house, which was not exactly how they had agreed to behave on this outing. But the interaction between them was too amusing to put to an end. So instead of pointing out the obvious, Mira left them alone with their impromptu self-entertainment.

By the time they had finally made it to the exit of the antique store, the pedestrian square was already crowded with people visiting the farmers and artisans market, which was set up there every Saturday from morning to noon. Mom didn't like the crowd. She said the noise was giving her a headache. So they turned around and went to the library instead.

The coolness and silence of the air inside the library was a big contrast to that of the bustling pedestrian square. Mom and Dad quietly followed Mira to the adult collection section, and when she started browsing for books on metaphysics in the nonfiction aisles, they helpfully joined in the search. Since the books were not sorted by genre and Mira had no interest in using the library's online catalogue, it took them nearly thirty minutes to find only two on that specific topic. Still, they were very proud to present the fruits of their labor to her. So when they learned that she had already read them both, it was hard for them to hide their disappointment.

Even though it had only occupied their faces briefly, Mira caught it anyway, as it was a facial expression of theirs that she had developed a physical reaction to, which she had yet to find a better way to describe other than an inward wince of the nerve endings in her left arm. As a result, instead of returning the two books back to the shelves, Mira found herself leafing through them in front of Mom and Dad just to ease her symptom.

Dad seized the opportunity and asked Mira to tell them about the books. She did, with more relief than enthusiasm. Mom and Dad listened intently, their eyes wide and their necks craned, as she explained the concepts and ideas from the books to them. When she was done, not only did they follow up with many questions, but they were also eager to share their own understandings and opinions with her.

Mira enjoyed listening to their thoughts on the matter. She also enjoyed discussing their opinions with them. Apart from the voices in her head, it was the first time she had had an in-depth conversation on philosophical topics with others. Moreover, their viewpoints also provided Mira with a glimpse into the inner selves of Mom and Dad—not as parents, but as individual entities whose own ways of existing in this world was the product, as well as the expression, of an accumulation of uniquely different past experiences in life, and therefore fascinatingly intriguing to her. Before long, she was so engrossed in tracing the inner selves of Cara Murphy and Thomas Murphy through the thoughts and opinions they had expressed that she hardly remembered they were her parents.

Mira was still fully absorbed in their conversation when they strolled back to the pedestrian square, which, by then, was much less crowded and much more bearable to Mom. So when Mom suddenly changed the topic by asking Mira whether she was hungry, the effect was similar to waking a sleepwalker in the middle of an episode: Mira was so disoriented that she could recall neither the time nor the space she was in, and instead, she thought she was having déjà vu, although she couldn't say for sure whether it was about another time or another life.

Her temporary confusion was only made worse by Mom, for though she thought she had given a "no" to her question, Mom still instructed Dad to go to the coffee shop at the far corner of the pedestrian square to get her a large mango smoothie and a chocolate chip muffin, which, Mom emphasized, should be heated up slightly.

Dad ended up returning with more than what he was instructed to get. Besides the large mango smoothie and the warm chocolate chip muffin for Mira, he also got a coffee for himself and a strawberry milkshake—with a side of a box of donut holes—for Mom. Despite still feeling muzzy from the reality confusion, Mira did not fail to notice the girlish smile that had appeared on Mom's lips when she saw what Dad had brought back for her. She thought it was interesting that even though Mom rarely asked for sweet treats for herself, Dad always seemed to know when she was in the mood for some.

They found an empty bench in the shade near the fountain and sat down to eat. The midday sun was burning brightly and earnestly, but the leafy canopy and the gentle breeze produced from the fountain were enough to keep their spot cool and pleasant. Their relaxing snack time soon attracted a purposeful gathering from some feathery visitors, who had been peering at Mira from afar in the trees but had boldly hopped off, one after another, to approach her and her family once they had begun to eat. Presently, these uninvited guests were chirping encouragingly for the Murphys to share their food as they casually closed in on the three humans. It didn't take long before their friends and families heard the commotion and came to join them in their endeavor as well, creating a chatty congestion between the fountain and the bench that Mira and her parents were sitting on.

Dad didn't care for the looks the birds were giving him. He said they were eyeing them like jumbo corncobs. Luckily, Mom had brought along a bag of birdseed in her tote bag for just such an occasion, so Dad decided it was high time to distract the birds from his family. He asked Mom to hold his coffee, got up, and tossed a handful of birdseed to the impatient congregation as far away from the bench as he could. The hungry birds were obviously more interested in the chocolate chip muffin and the donut holes that Mira and Mom were holding, but they were quick to decide they would make do with whatever edibles came their way first. So when the birdseed rained down from the sky, they turned and dove for the first bite with passion rather than grace, pushing and shoving and flapping and squeezing in however they could.

The scene made Dad turn to look at Mom and Mira with a smirk, but it was immediately replaced by a comical frown when he saw that Mom was draining the cup that belonged to him. Mom felt his stare and turned. As she came face-to-face with Dad's funny expression, a snort escaped from her nose before she could swallow the coffee, leaving her coughing and snickering at the same time.

Dad, on the other hand, seemed slyly pleased. He patted Mom on the back with a gloating smile, and when she had finally stopped coughing and was gulping down mouthfuls of air, he gave her a toothy grin and said, "See? That's why you should have left my coffee alone! Now that there's nothing left for me, I'm afraid my sleep-deprived body will go into power-saving mode soon, which means its vital function for fetching the picnic basket from home is now disabled. So what do you say we just head back home for a na—ahem, excuse me, for a movie on the couch instead?"

"Don't you worry about it, Dad," said Mira, who was sounding a little smug in Dad's opinion. "I'm sure Mom has a plan for that scenario as well."

Dad made a whimpering noise and looked dejectedly at Mom. "You're gonna tell me to go get another coffee, aren't you?"

"Well," said Mom, still snickering under her breath, "you suggested it, not me. I do think you should hurry though, you know, in case that sleep-deprived body of yours goes into power-saving mode before you reach the coffee shop and disables you right in front of it, for every customer and passerby to see . . ."

"Ha, ha," Dad replied dryly, then he put on a blank face and spoke without any intonation, pretending he was a robot: "Human funny. Very funny."

Smiling broadly, Mom held out a hand and patted him like a puppy dog as she enunciated slowly and deliberately: "Robot good. Good robot. Now go get me that coffee I've ordered and bring an extra one back for my husband too."

With a lighthearted laugh, Dad gave up his robot imitation. "All right," he said in a defeated tone, smiling. "I'll go."

He tossed another handful of birdseed to the eager recipients, who were getting anxious and restless for their next feeding session, then he passed the bag to Mira. "Here. You're in charge of keeping them in check while I'm gone. Pay attention to the squirrels drooling over there under that bench though. I think they're plotting something bad in their little heads, so watch out—they could be trouble . . ."

"Thomas?" Mom cocked an eyebrow at him. "Aren't you forgetting something?"

"Oh, right! Coffee!" With an apologetic grin, he gave Mom a squeeze on the arm and set off, tiptoeing his way through the distracted birds, most of whom were still busy pecking the ground. "Bye!" he called over his shoulder in a singing tone, waving both arms. "I'll be back in a jiffy! No need to miss me!"

In spite of the loudness that came with the exaggerated cheerfulness in his voice, the birds let him through without much stirring. Some of the more skittish ones felt it was necessary to look up from what they were doing to examine the intruder, but they quickly dismissed him as the-human-who-could-not-sing and returned to their dining frenzy.

Meanwhile, the squirrels saw this as an opportunity. Moving stealthily like ninjas sneaking from one shadowy spot to the next, they quickly cut through the barrier formed by their feathery neighbors and made their way toward Mira and Mom until they decided they had occupied the best vantage points on the lot for scoring a free meal. There, they stopped and stood on their little hind legs, tilting their heads and craning their necks to get a better view of the chocolate chip muffin in Mira's hand while desperately calculating, with both their eyes and their heads, the odds of having a taste of that wonderfully enticing delicacy in the near future.

"I understand," Mom said to the squirrels, chortling. "Nobody can resist a good chocolate chip muffin. The temptation is real."

The birds seemed to have understood the words "chocolate chip muffin," for presently, they gave up pecking the ground and began huddling closer to their bench with encouraging chirps, as if to let them know that they, too, were ready for the good stuff.

Mira peeled back the liner and broke off a corner of the muffin from the bottom. The birds stopped talking. They strained their necks and followed Mira's hands with their beady eyes, nervously and attentively. The squirrels, however, had hunched down low into position, ready to leap into action at any second. Mira opened the bag of birdseed and crumbled the piece of muffin she had broken off into it. When she was done, she closed the bag and shook it until the birdseed and the muffin crumbs were well mixed.

Mom gave a soft chuckle. "You're spoiling them."

"Call it an experiment," said Mira with a degree of serious thoughtfulness in her voice. "Do you think feeding birds and squirrels human food will have an impact on the evolution process of their species?"

"Hmm." Mom raised her eyebrows. "That's an interesting question. What made you think of that?"

"Just wondering." Mira shrugged. She scooped up a handful of birdseed from the bag, which was now dotted with muffin crumbs, and tossed it to her more-than-ready test subjects.

Cooing with praise, the birds immediately got down to work, pecking diligently and effectively at every little bit that was offered. Despite the squirrels' success in occupying the most favorable vantage points on their temporary dinner table, they were no match for those sharp, pointed beaks designed for merciless precision. No matter how fast they reacted or how hard they dove, they seemed to be always just one peck behind their fellow tree dwellers. Before long, these furry critters were too vexed to play by the rules. They flicked their bushy tails at one another impatiently, as if to declare their intolerance to the current situation and to signal for a riot.

Mira could tell the squirrels were devising something reckless. She clicked her tongue until she had their attention, then she showed them what was left of the muffin, broke off a large piece, and crumbled it into smaller pieces under the bench. With their eager eyes trained on the motion of her hand, she poured out some mixture from the birdseed bag and dropped it on top of the muffin pieces, producing an inviting pile of irresistible treats.

As soon as Mira withdrew her hand, the squirrels got down to their bellies and crawled toward the sweet-smelling goodies, their beady eyes sparkling with exhilarated anticipation. Mira kept the birds occupied by adding a few more handfuls of the sweetened birdseed mixture to their side. With her help, the squirrels no longer had to worry about outside competition and were soon huddling under their bench and stuffing their faces full, literally.

Mom's jaw dropped. She looked at Mira with an incredulous expression. "How did you do that? I didn't think they would want to come this close!"

"It's the muffin." Mira held up the remainder of the muffin and offered it to Mom. " 'Nobody can resist a good chocolate chip muffin.' Remember?"

Mom accepted it with a chuckle. "All right . . . Just one bite."

"Take as many bites as you want. I won't tell anyone," said Mira, sounding more smug than genuine to Mom. Before she could swallow her bite to counter, Mira gestured at the squirrels under their bench and said, "It doesn't take much to make their day, does it?"

Mom stopped chewing. She folded forward carefully to observe the hearty dining that was taking place under their bench. One of the squirrels was shoving so much food into its mouth that it couldn't even close it. So while its two little front paws were determined to push more food into the cheek pouches inside its mouth, the handy built-in storage compartments were so overstretched that they couldn't keep what was shoved inside from falling out. In short, this adamant squirrel was working overtime for nothing.

At the sight of its unproductive endeavor, Mom couldn't help snickering out loud. If it weren't for the overeating and overstuffing the squirrels had committed themselves to for the past few minutes, she might have already spooked these easily paranoid critters away.

"It certainly doesn't," Mom replied with much amusement in her voice. She straightened up and smiled at Mira. "Is that why you enjoy watching animals so much?"

"Perhaps. They're very easy to read, unlike people."

"I thought the complexity of the human mind fascinates you," said Mom, looking surprised. "I mean, all those books you read on psychology and philosophy? You wouldn't have read them unless you're really interested in those topics, right?"

"The human mind does fascinate me, especially how it varies from individual to individual. But that also makes people much more complicated and difficult to read than other animals. And because they're much more complicated and difficult to read than other animals, it also makes them much harder to please, to understand, and to love, particularly to each other, despite all the languages they created for effective communication with other human beings."

"Hmm . . . I agree with most of it, but I don't think it's our complexity that makes it hard to love another human being. The challenge here is whether the human being you love will love you back, as long and as much as you do. It's the uncertainty of it that makes it hard to love—really, truly love—another, not because we're too complicated or too difficult to read."

Mira pondered this. "What about you and Dad?"

"What do you mean?"

"Do you feel that uncertainty?"

Mom peered at Mira with a puzzled expression. When she realized Mira was being serious, she covered her mouth with a hand to suppress her laughter.

Mira's brows furrowed slightly. "Why are you laughing?"

"Oh . . . sweetie," said Mom, drying the corners of her eyes with a knuckle. "Your dad and I have known each other since we were kids, and we've been together since college. I think it's safe to say we've left that uncertainty behind us a long, long time ago."

"So is it easy for you to love each other? Without reservation?"

Mom looked toward the direction of the coffee shop, where Dad had gone to. She took a sip of her strawberry milkshake, and, wearing a serene and contented smile, she replied, "Yes, it is. Without reservation."

"Is that why Dad has no problem with you ordering him around all the time?"

"What?" Mom swiveled her head back and stared at Mira, eyes as round as the donut holes that remained in the paper box on her lap. "I don't order him around!"

Mira gave her a meaningful nod. "Uh-huh."

"Well, certainly not 'all the time' . . . I mean . . . Do I?"

Instead of answering, Mira simply gestured at their food and drinks.

Mom bit her lip. "I guess I do order him around sometimes." She admitted quietly.

"More than 'sometimes.' It doesn't seem to bother him though … Now that I think about it, I don't recall ever seeing you two getting upset with each other at all."

"What are you talking about? I got upset with him just this morning," Mom retorted. "Digging through the bacon with his hand like a caveman?"

"That was you two bickering for fun. You guys do that all the time, and—don't bother denying it—you both enjoyed it, as always."

Mom's cheeks were looking a little pink from the guilt and embarrassment chasing each other across her face. But Mira ignored the signs and continued, "It's quite remarkable, actually, considering most men can't tolerate being told what to do by others, especially by their wives. It hurts their egos."

Mom's expression suddenly became uncertain and nervous. "Do you think I hurt his?"

"I don't know. I can't answer that question for him. But a bruised ego is the number one cause that leads to conflicts and quarrels in relationships. And not just for couples, the same goes for every relationship you establish with others: parents, siblings, friends, neighbors, colleagues, supervisors, customers, business partners … even situational relationships that you have no choice but to establish temporarily with some complete strangers, which can be more unpredictable yet unfortunately unavoidable in any given social situation, like the cashier who checks you out, the nurse who checks you in, or that one dad who trash-talks loudly and publicly throughout the entire game at your kid's soccer match.

"But that's not where it stops. The same also applies to political relationships between villages, tribes, towns, cities, states, and countries. Many wars were started under the banner of an elaborately glorified and seemingly plausible cause when in fact they were nothing but an excuse for the people who had started them to properly and justifiably retaliate against the individuals who bruised their precious egos. Throughout human history, millions of people have paid the price of such wars with their lives, directly or indirectly, even though they had absolutely nothing to do with the offense committed against their leaders' egos in the first place."

"It can't be . . ."

"But it's true. However, despite the dramatic progress that has taken place in human society in terms of intelligence, knowledge, and technology, ego—as a prominent feature of the human species—remains fragile and sensitive, which is why it has been and will continue to be the deciding factor in the direction human history will undertake. That's why a random stranger can get on your nerves just as easily as someone you've known for a long time. 'Get on your nerves'—notice how this term is phrased? It's not about what they have said or done; it's about what they have said or done has stepped on a certain sore spot in your ego. It can get on your nerves because it has hurt your ego, and that's enough for most people to react either verbally or physically as a form of retaliation to give their own injured egos a self-deceiving boost of I-am-better-than-you reassurance. Dad doesn't do that with you though. He doesn't seem to care about defending his ego when he's with you, no matter what you say or do to him."

Mira tilted her head to look at Mom for a response, only to find out she was staring at her with such a level of incredulity that it almost resembled fear.

You have said too much, a voice remarked in her head.

You should not have said anything, another voice chimed in.

You have scared her, the third voice observed.

As Mira gazed into Mom's eyes and absorbed her expression in detail, she couldn't help but wonder whether the three voices were right. She felt a contraction in her left chest, a pain that was dull yet penetrating, as if something had caved in from within.

"Staring contest?" a voice boomed from overhead.

At the sound of it, Mira's head jerked up. She found Dad beaming down at her, holding two cups of coffee. Meanwhile, out of the corner of her eye, she caught a visible jump from Mom. Before they knew it, Mom's strawberry milkshake had sprung from her hand, flown past Dad, and crashed into the ground.

Although the gooey contents had refused to splatter out in a more dramatic fashion, the impact itself was enough to send their feathery beneficiaries fluttering about chaotically to evacuate from the scene, not to mention the hysteria it caused to the overfed squirrels under their bench.

"Not again!" Dad blurted out dejectedly.

But Mom didn't seem to hear him. She got up from the bench without a word and picked up the plastic remains of the strawberry milkshake.

"I'm sorry, honey," said Dad in a gloomy voice. "I didn't mean to startle you . . ." He paused, took a peek at Mom's face, and with a nervous grin, held up the paper cups in his hands. "May I cheer you up with a cup of freshly brewed coffee?"

Mom fed the sticky mess she had picked up into a nearby trash can, then she took the coffee from Dad's hand.

"Thanks," she said hastily, flashing him a polite smile—the kind that is widely used between strangers to avoid small talk.

Dad must have noticed the change in her demeanor as well, for the nervous grin disappeared from his face and was replaced by a concerned frown. But he adjusted himself quickly and said, "You know what? I just thought of a great idea on my way back. We've spent a lot of time at the square already, so instead of having a picnic here, why don't we have it at home, while watching a movie?"

Mom didn't object this time, so Mira went along with Dad's suggestion. They left the pedestrian square and took the same way home. Once they got back, Dad made Mira pick out a movie, then he unpacked the food Mom had prepared from the picnic basket and set up their picnic site in the living room.

They started the movie and ate side by side on the couch with their feet up. Halfway through the movie, Dad started to snore.

Even though Mira didn't think his sleepiness would have an effect on her, somehow, somewhere during the second half of the movie, her eyelids grew heavy, and before she knew it, she had drifted off into a dreamless slumber.

By the time she woke up from her nap, the TV was no longer on. Instead of sitting, Mira found herself lying down on the couch, alone, with Mom's favorite TV blanket wrapped around her. No light was turned on in the living room, so although the windows were shielded with blinds, it was easy to tell it had gotten dark outside.

Mira was surprised when she realized how much time had passed since she had given in to the drowsiness that suddenly overcame her during the movie. She was even more surprised when she realized she had slept peacefully the entire time without dreaming about the fight on the battlefield.

She sat up and looked toward the kitchen. It was empty; neither Mom nor Dad was in there. The rooms were as quiet as the night. Other than the decorative lamp gently illuminating the kitchen counter with its solitary ambience, there was no sign of activity inside the house.

Mira got up and went into the kitchen. The kitchen island was crowded with trays and pans and bowls in various shapes and sizes, each of which was covered with either a layer of plastic wrap or a sheet of tinfoil. She felt a pan that was covered with tinfoil—it was still warm.

"Mom? . . . Dad?" she called.

There was no response; the house remained quiet.

She went up the stairs. "Mooom! . . . Daaad!"

Still, no one answered.

What's going on? Mira wondered to herself. *Did Mom plan this too?*

She went into her room and sat down on her bed. Through the windows next to it, she saw that the last light of dusk had already slipped away from the sky. She glanced at the clock on her night-stand: 8:24 PM. According to Mom's plan, dinner was supposed to take place at eight o'clock.

You don't want to miss it, said a voice in her head.

Miss what? she heard herself ask in her mind.

The backyard dance party, replied the voice, almost teasingly. *It's in Cara's plan, remember?*

Backyard dance party . . . she repeated the words. *That's it! They must be setting up disco lights and putting up some more unnecessary decorations in the back—*

You would not like it. A different voice immediately cut her off.

You don't need to go to them, said the third, gently but firmly. *They will come to you when they are ready.*

Mira thought about what they said and decided she should at least prepare herself for what she would have to go through before she could cut the cake and call it a night. She got to her feet, and, keeping a safe distance from the windows to prevent being spotted by her parents from down below, she craned her neck and looked down.

The backyard was as dim and quiet as the rooms inside. There were no disco lights, and judging by the look of it, the unnecessary decorations were not present either. Even the trees in the back seemed to be standing quietly still as if they had been bound and petrified into a monstrous fortress, looming silently in the impending darkness.

Mira knitted her brows. Mom was all about plans; she had always been. Once she had formed one in her mind, the chances of her deterring from it would be as unlikely as the sun rising from the opposite side of the sky.

No. Something was not right here. She could feel it.

As if on cue, her heart began to race. She leaned in closer to the windows and, carefully, scanned the backyard from left to right. It was too dim to make out everything clearly, but she managed to spot a dark shape resting on the bench between the birdbath and the patio, on the right side of the lawn. The shape was large enough to be two people, but it was still—unnervingly still.

A crippling sensation rippled from Mira's heart to her limbs, leaving her arms numb and her legs weak. Still, she rushed out of her room, down the stairs, and into the kitchen. Just as she was about to pull open the door to the backyard, she paused.

She didn't know why she hesitated. She also didn't understand why her heart was pounding so wildly in her chest that it was hard to breathe. Then it suddenly dawned on her that for the first time in her life, she was scared.

She wondered what was causing her this fear; it was paralyzing, both to her body and her mind. And even though it was not quite as overwhelming as the sheer rage she had experienced that evening in Sunrise Park, back in Skygate, it was far more disabling.

She forced the thought out of her mind and waited until her heart rate had slowed down a little. Then, slowly and quietly, she cracked open the door and slipped through into the backyard. Maybe it was the fear, or maybe she just didn't know what to expect, but she found herself approaching the shape on the bench from behind, as noiselessly as a phantom.

As the distance between her and the bench decreased, so did her fear. She could hear them talking, both Mom and Dad. Their voices were very soft, but it was enough to tell they were okay.

Mira felt her body relax right away. She stood still and gazed at the backs of Mom and Dad with relief, wondering if she should continue or turn back.

Just then, a gust of capricious wind glided down from the tree-tops. It twirled around the bench playfully and headed straight for Mira. As the wind blew into her face and brushed past her ears, she heard the words that it carried from the bench:

". . . won't be long before she figures it out, Thomas. Should we just tell her? . . . No. No we can't. I can't bring myself to picture it . . . Oh dear. Which is worse? Being told by us or finding it out herself?"

"I don't think either is better than the other. But ... if we were to tell her, what would you say about ... *her*?"

"I ... I don't know."

"Then maybe we shouldn't tell her. I mean ... she didn't ask us to. Maybe she doesn't want her to know. Maybe she thinks it's for the best ... Besides, things are fine the way they are, don't you think? ... Cara? You okay?"

"I'm ... I don't know ..."

"I'm sorry. I'm sorry I had to mention her. I just wanted to—"

"It's not exactly *her*, Thomas. It's ... Mira."

"Mira? ... Wh-what did she do?"

"It's not something she did ... It's just that—Lately ... she's been reminding me more and more of—"

"Go on."

"I mean, the way she talks, the things she says, and even the way she looks at me sometimes ... I feel like she's right there. I feel like ... I feel like she *is* her."

They both fell silent. Then Thomas said, "I think I know what you mean ... Was that why you jumped and dropped the milk-shake when you heard my voice?"

Cara let out a sigh. "Probably. I wish I didn't react the way I did though. I hope she didn't notice it, but ... She's very smart, Thomas. And she's very interested in figuring out things that most kids at her age don't even care about. I'm ... scared. I'm scared she'll notice the things that don't match up. I'm scared she'll stumble upon the truth when she tries to figure out why. And it terrifies me to think she may never look at us the same way again when that happens ... Thomas, I don't want to lose her trust ..."

"Shhhhh ... Don't think about that now, Cara."

"I don't want to lose her too ..."

"Shhh shhh shhhhhh ... You won't, honey. You won't."

A sudden gust of wind rose up from nowhere and shook the trees, sending a murder of crows fluttering wearily away from the turmoil, cawing so heartbrokenly that their echoes scratched across the sky and drove the moon to hide behind a thick piece of cloud.

Cara followed the ascending black shapes with her eyes until they merged and melted into the darkness. The air was still warm from the leftover heat of the sunset, but she shuddered nonetheless.

"Are you cold?" asked Thomas, wrapping himself around her. "Come on. Let's go inside. It's high time to wake up the birthday girl anyway."

He got to his feet and helped Cara up. "If Mira does something that reminds you of her again, just remember: today is her *birth-day*; our daughter turned fifteen today. It's a happy thing. A happy, wonderful thing." He held Cara by the shoulders and looked into her eyes. "You love her. I love her. She *is* our daughter. And that's all that matters."

Cara gazed back at him and nodded. "That's all that matters."

They returned to the patio, paused briefly at the door before opening it, and quietly, went inside. They closed the door behind them carefully and tiptoed through the kitchen until they could peek over the back of the couch from where they were standing.

Mira was still on the couch, but she had curled up into a ball and pulled the TV blanket over her head.

Although they didn't need to look at the other person to know they were both smiling at what they saw, their eyes still found each other. Cara knew then that she would do everything in her power to keep their family life as it was, even if it meant that she would have to rip open the deepest scar in her heart to clean out all the old, unhealed wounds that she had been pretending to ignore all these years—even if it would only help her family to live in the pain-free white lie a little bit longer . . .

Thomas nodded toward the couch and signaled to Cara that they needed to wake Mira up. Cara bit her lip and made a reluctant face. Since he had expected her unwillingness in being the human alarm clock, he gave her an obliging smile and gestured to her that he would carry out the unwelcome task instead.

But Mira was not asleep. As a matter of fact, she was far from being drowsy. The only reason she had returned to the couch was

because she couldn't process what she had overheard in the backyard and decided she couldn't let them know she had been outside,
listening to their conversation. However, despite her best effort in
muffling the sound of her pounding heart by pulling the TV blanket over her head, like the skin on a drum, she couldn't stop quivering with every single thump it made.

A hand reached down and touched her head, stroking it gently
through the blanket. Then she heard Dad's voice whispering from
above: "Little Bird."

Mira squeezed her eyes shut, hoping it was just another dream
she needed to wake up from and when she opened her eyes again,
it would be gone.

But Dad's voice continued, "Time to wake up, sleepyhead. It's
getting late . . ."

Mira clenched her jaw. She was still here; it was not working.
Pressure was building up quickly in her head as if something had
just exploded silently and, consequently, given birth to a whirlwind
of questions and comments, all of which were going off at the same
time as they blared and charged chaotically in her mind. Worse still,
the more she tried to focus on sorting them out one by one, the
more tangled up they became. As a result, Mira soon found herself
swimming in a helpless mental swamp that was composed of so
many discordant voices that her ears began to ring, long and loud;
she couldn't break free from it, nor could she hear herself think.

It didn't take long for the ringing sound in her ears to escalate
into a high-pitched scream, drilling a headache straight up into her
temples. Just when Mira thought the noise was about to pierce her
skullcap, she heard a voice, which was whispering among all those
discordant voices in her head yet was as distinctively recognizable
as her own:

Wake up. It's time to wake up.

Mira's eyes shot open, and in that split second, she saw herself
watching her, from within her own body, with a face as emotionless
as still water. A wave of transcendent consciousness washed over
her, and, like a butterfly who had just eclosed from its pupa and

met the sun for the first time with its brand-new wings, she realized there was no going back.

"Mira?" Dad urged.

Feeling as though she had just woken up from a very long dream, Mira pulled the blanket down slowly from her face and surveyed her surroundings: Dad was next to her, half kneeling on the floor. Mom was standing behind him, wearing an anxious expression on her face.

Not knowing whether this was indeed a reality that she belonged in, Mira greeted them with calm detachment.

"Mira? Is everything okay?" Mom asked gingerly as the anxiousness on her face was replaced by concern.

"She's fine," said Dad with a wave of his hand. "Probably just can't remember when she dozed off and still needs a minute to remember where she is." He gave Mira a humorous wink as he chuckled under his breath. "Isn't that right, Little Bird?"

Mira looked at Dad, then she looked at Mom. She couldn't help but notice how different they looked, different in the sense that they no longer looked like the parents in her memory from before.

"Guess we still need a moment. Well, no biggie." Dad offered his hands to Mira. "Here, let's sit up first."

"I don't need your help," said a voice from Mira's throat, coldly, freezing Thomas in his tracks but sparing the emotions on his face. Mira saw everything that was happening on there: shock, hurt, incomprehension, denial, sadness, guilt—appearing, shifting, blending, and changing like the fluid yet melancholy dance of a rainbow of food dyes after they have been dripped into a glass of water.

Thomas's mind went blank. There was something in Mira's eyes that overwhelmed him. He felt uneasy, alarmingly and inexplicably. He darted his eyes to the side and reminded himself that this was his daughter he was looking at. In the end, he managed to force a smile and, awkwardly, withdrew his hands.

"Of course you don't. What was I thinking, treating you like a baby . . . You're a big girl now. You don't need my help getting up." He added a bitter laugh for good measure before rubbing his legs with a wince. "I, on the other hand, am the one who needs help here." He looked over his shoulder and called, "Honey, give me a hand, please? My legs fell asleep . . . Honey?"

Cara didn't seem to hear him. She was staring at Mira with her mouth open as if she had seen a ghost. Thomas twisted around and grabbed her wrist: "Cara!"

He felt her arm jerk in his hand like a startled animal, so he pulled down on it to make her look at him instead. Then, slowly and meaningfully, he said to her, "Honey, I need your help."

Cara's eyes were still filled with shock, but she nodded, closed her mouth, and offered her hands to Thomas.

As she was helping him up to his feet, Cara felt her lungs heating up and expanding like a hot-air balloon, consequently squashing everything else that was in her rib cage.

"Mira Murphy!" she snapped, realizing then and there that the hot air expanding in her lungs was, unmistakably, anger, though she had no idea why. "Turning fifteen doesn't give you the green light to talk to us like that! We are your parents! You ought to talk to us with respect!"

As soon as the words were fired from her mouth, Cara recognized where she had learned them from: her father. She was not only using the same words he had used oh so frequently on her, but she was also using the same intonation, which had only sharpened her resentment toward him even further when he lectured her.

The realization made Cara cringe, both physically and mentally. She bit her lip and swallowed the rest of her words down—no, his words. She would not allow herself to act like her father in front of Mira. No. Never.

Flashbacks sneaked into Cara's mind and began to play themselves without permission: the never-ending quarrels and fights between her father and her mother, the perpetual gloomy atmosphere at their so-called home, the unshakable weight she felt on her shoulders whenever she stepped near the house they had lived in together as a "family" . . .

She hated her father. She hated him for the endless fights he had picked with Mother. She hated him for having cheated on his wife. She hated him for his indifference when Mother found out about his affair. And she hated him for their eventual divorce.

She hated the way he talked to her, as if she owed him something —or everything. She hated that he was not only a lousy husband to Mother but also a lousy father to her.

She hated that Mother had passed away before he did. Yet, in spite of her resentment toward him, her heart couldn't stop weeping when he finally died from cancer. Apparently, he had lived with it for many years but had never bothered to inform her, and therefore, she only found out about it from his will—after he was wheeled away to the morgue.

So yes, she hated him. And right now, she hated herself for having behaved just like him.

Cara closed her eyes and let out a long sigh. She looked at Mira apologetically and said, "I'm sorry, Little Bird. I shouldn't have snapped at you like that. I was—I was mad because I remembered something that made me upset. But it was not your fault, and I shouldn't have taken it out on you . . ."

Mira didn't need her explanation though; she already knew why. It was written all over Mom's face, in different shades of conflict and heartbreak, weaving so tightly into one another that she could hear their silent cries.

She took her eyes off Mom's face and sat up. "It's okay," she said quietly. "I understand."

Cara opened her mouth to say something—anything. But nothing came out.

"All right!" Dad made a loud clap with his hands and grinned at them both. "Now that the birthday girl is finally up, can we *please* have dinner? I'm starving! Did you guys hear my stomach growl earlier? I'm so hungry I could eat a horse!"

Mom gave him a scowl. "Thomas, you sound like a five-year-old."

"But I'm not," Dad answered mischievously. "I'm ten times that age, which means, naturally, my body needs ten times the quantity of food to feed a five-year-old. And if you guys don't hurry . . ." He trailed off with a meaningful look and patted his belly with both hands, then he strode purposefully toward the kitchen, letting out an evil laugh that sounded like a cartoon villain. Before Mom could protest, he was peeling back the tinfoil on one of the containers sitting on the kitchen island.

"Oh boy! Bacon wraps!" he exclaimed, as though he had no idea they were inside that particular bowl, and proceeded to pop them into his mouth, one piece after another. "Yum! This batch turned out great!"

"Go easy on that, caveman!" Mom rushed over to save what was left of the bacon wraps. "How about you relearn your table manners ten times instead? Even five-year-olds know not to eat like that!"

She nudged him away from the kitchen island and pointed a finger to the bathroom. "Go wash your hands first. Then you can set the table for dinner."

"But—"

"No buts. If you want food, you follow my rules."

Dad made a sad face but went along with it. "Yes, ma'am."

Mira was watching them quietly from the couch. Although her heart was still as heavy and impassive as a rock, she felt the corners of her lips curl up into a faint smile.

Mom seemed to have sensed the change in her mood. She turned and looked at Mira from across the room, then she gave her a smile and said firmly, "You too, Mira. Go wash your hands."

Mira obeyed. When she came back, the dinner table was already set. Dad poured her a glass of lemonade and filled his and Mom's glasses with wine. As usual, Mom waited till Mira and Dad were both seated before bringing the food out to the table. Once everything was passed around and served, Mom cleared her throat and raised her glass.

"To Mira," she said, gesturing for them to raise their glasses as well. "I can't wait to see what life has in store for you this year! Have fun at high school, and . . . happy birthday!"

"Hear, hear!" said Dad, raising his glass high with a big smile.

Mom poked him in the ribs. "Thomas, don't you want to say something too?"

"Oh, yeah. Of course. Um . . ." Dad lowered his glass and turned to Mira. "To the birthday girl," he said, screwing up his face in such a serious manner that he seemed to be racking his brain to remember what Mom was expecting him to say. When nothing came to mind, he shrugged and clinked his glass to Mira's, grinning. "Happy birthday, and may you always remember how much food was prepared in your name today. So *please*, let's eat."

Mira saw Mom roll her eyes at Dad, but she didn't stop him from digging in. As they ate, Mom and Dad took turns to share their favorite moments from Mira's previous birthdays, and when they were done with that, they started telling Mira about their favorite memories of her from when she was little.

By the time Mom had finished her second glass of wine, she appeared to be in a much better mood and was much more relaxed. She talked and laughed and laughed and talked, as if nothing else mattered more than the moment she was in. Mira wondered— with mild relief—whether it was a sign that Mom's plan for her birthday was finally coming to an end, but on second thought, she decided it was probably just the wine.

She ate quietly as Mom and Dad went on to talk about their new life in Starfall. Dad told them about how he was doing at his new job and shared some funny stories he had heard from his colleagues. Mom asked him questions, laughed at his funny stories, and in turn, told them new and interesting things she had recently learned about the town. Mira tried to listen at first but couldn't concentrate enough to hear the words they were saying. Before long, she felt herself sinking into the depths of her own mind, and their voices were nothing but muffled sounds. Her ears started ringing again, but this time, it was much softer and much more tolerable, like the voices whispering in the back of her head.

Something was drawing her closer and closer to those voices, or maybe the voices were drawn to her. She didn't want to listen, yet she heard them and understood them anyway; they were talking about the conversation she had overheard in the backyard, between Mom and Dad.

Like a reflex, she pushed herself away from the voices and withdrew her mind, as far away as she could. She didn't want to remember what she had heard. She didn't want to think about what they had said. She didn't understand it, and she didn't want to either.

So she forced herself to go back, back to the dinner table, where Mom and Dad were smiling and talking and having a good time. No secret conversations behind her back. No strange lines that didn't make sense. She felt herself looking at them from behind her eyes with the sensation that she was looking at the past through a dream. And even though their voices were muted by the persistent whispers now dialing up in her head, she wished time could slow down a little so she could stay there a bit longer. After all, everything was fine here. It would be senseless to listen to the voices and start asking questions to herself, especially if she was to find out it had all been nothing but a dream.

A sharp pain struck her in the left chest, piercing her heavy heart like an arrow. She didn't know whether it was broken or softened by the pain, but she felt part of it had gotten stuck in her throat. For a moment, she couldn't breathe. However, the temporary lack of oxygen somehow sharpened her senses, and she found herself absorbing—with her eyes, her nose, and even her skin—every little detail around her, as if her body wished to capture this moment exactly as it was to frame it in her memory.

When Cara noticed Mira was gazing off into space instead of working on the food on her plate, she nudged Thomas in the elbow to make him stop talking. Then she put down her utensils, reached across the table, and waved a hand in front of Mira's face.

"Hellooo?" she called in a gleeful voice. "Anybody home?"

The movement of her hand caused Mira to blink. As she re-opened her eyes and reached out to her surroundings with her senses once more, Mira realized she was indeed back at the dinner table. She could hear the room again, the ringing sound in her ears had stopped, and so had the voices, leaving her with the impression that she had shuffled two parallel realities when she blinked and had exited from the one with the voices to the one without.

Mira's eyes fell on Mom, who appeared to have helped herself to a little bit too much wine than she could handle. There was a big, wide, telltale smile on her face; even her eyes were smiling.

Mira did not recall ever seeing a smile like that on Mom's face before. As far as she remembered, Mom always seemed to have something on her mind, something heavy and consuming, even when she was smiling or laughing. But right now, Mom looked like she was waltzing in her mind on top of those heavy and consuming things as if they were clouds.

Dad caught the surprised look on her face and chortled loudly. "Sorry to interrupt your daydream, Little Bird. I gotta admit, I didn't expect we would sound *so* boring to you."

"Speak for yourself, Thomas," Mom objected and gave him a gloating smile. "She didn't zone out when *I* was talking."

Dad let out a dramatic gasp. "You're right!" He held a hand to his belly and turned to Mom with pleading eyes. "Honey, my feelings are hurt. I think I need some special treatment, say, um . . . an extra-large slice of Mira's birthday cake?"

"You still have room in there?" Mom said teasingly as she patted his waistline.

Dad patted her hand in return and smiled. "For something you've stayed up almost all night to make? Always!"

Mom laughed and turned to Mira. "What about you, Little Bird? Are you ready for the cake?"

With a faint smile, Mira nodded.

"All right! Cake time!" Dad exclaimed and, with a loud clap, leaped to his feet to clear the table.

Mira got up to help, but Mom gestured for her to sit.

"Let him do it. He needs to move around to digest all the food he's eaten before cake anyway," she said, snickering. "You stay here and wait for us. I'm gonna go get the cake ready. No peeking allowed, okay? It's a surprise."

So Mira stayed in her seat and waited. When Dad had the table cleared and cleaned, he returned with three new sets of plates and forks. While he was setting them down, he informed Mira that he had been requested to cover her eyes when the cake was ready to be brought over.

Presently, Mom gave him the signal from the kitchen. Dad signaled back, and though Mira had already closed her eyes voluntarily, he blindfolded her with his hands anyway.

Mira heard Mom's footsteps approaching from the kitchen, slowly and carefully. There was a whiff of a sweet scent in the air, fresh and cold like snow. It grew stronger as Mom got nearer, until it was right under her nose. Mom must have been holding her breath, for as soon as the cake was placed on the table, she exhaled in relief.

Mira heard the click of a lighter, followed by the successive hissing sounds of candle wicks being kissed by fire. One by one, they started to burn, producing faint sizzling and popping noises like muffled firecrackers, amid the sounds of which, she heard the flip of a light switch.

Dad removed his hands and began to sing the "Happy Birthday" song in a duet with Mom. Mira opened her eyes: fifteen sparkler candles were shooting up tiny fireworks from a golden foam board, in the middle of which sat a white cake shaped like a bird.

"Happy birthday, Little Bird!" Dad squeezed her shoulders and gave her a kiss on the head.

"Happy birthday, Mira. We love you." Mom smiled, her eyes glistening in the candlelight. She gave Mira a peck on the cheek and said, "Come on. Make a wish."

After fourteen years of birthday celebrations planned by Mom, Mira knew better than to argue. She clasped her hands together and closed her eyes, then she began to count in her mind.

She could hear the voices returning, whispering unwelcome thoughts in the back of her head, thoughts that she didn't want to listen to or think about.

She stopped counting and opened her eyes. The sparkler candles were already dying down; it was long enough.

"Ready?" Mom looked at her with eager anticipation.

Mira nodded.

"Okay. On the count of three. One—two—three—blooow!"

Mira blew, slowly and steadily. The small flames on the sparkler candles fell backward, withered, and disappeared in thin strips of smoke that drifted reluctantly away from the blackened candle wicks.

"Woo-hoo!" Mom and Dad clapped and cheered loudly and excitedly as though Mira had just accomplished something extraordinary, as though they were cheering for her first belly crawl, her first step, or her first word.

Mom dabbed at the corners of her eyes and turned to Dad. "Thomas?" she called, sounding a little hoarse. "Could you take care of the candles? I'll cut the cake."

Dad gave her a quick back rub and got to work. While he was carefully plucking the candles out from their predrilled holes in the foam board, Mom turned the lights back on and went into the kitchen to get a knife.

Now that it was bright enough to see the details on the cake clearly, Mira realized how much effort had gone into it. The cake was made in the shape of a bird with its wings fully stretched and its head proudly raised. The bird's eyes and beak were vividly sculpted with black fondant icing, and its luxurious plumage was produced by multiple layers of white fondant icing that was delicately detailed down to the shafts and barbs of each feather. The top of the bird's head was decorated with red flowers in different sizes. And though they looked as realistic as real flowers, the stiffness of their petals suggested that they were actually carved and shaped from fondant icing as well.

Mira stared at the cake in silence. She wondered how much time Mom had spent on making it.

"Do you like your cake?" Mom asked as she hurried back with the knife.

"It's ... pretty," Mira answered.

Mom beamed. "A special cake for a special age." Her face became proud. "I wanted to make something that's symbolic and memorable for your fifteenth birthday. So here it is: a soaring bird, brave, strong, and ready to explore the world ... like you, Mira, my Little Bird."

Mira didn't know what to say, so she nodded without taking her eyes off the cake.

Mom laughed. "Let's try it, shall we? I used a new recipe for the base. It's *really* good."

She picked up the knife and aimed at the cake, but her hand didn't go down. "Hmm," she said, studying the cake with a frown. "How should I cut it?"

"In half?" Dad offered eagerly.

"No!" Mom flinched. "That's just ... cruel. Oh dear. I guess I didn't really think this through, did I?"

Maneuvering the knife like an oversize pen, she pointed it at the cake and traced out different ways in the air to go about cutting up this beautiful bird she had made for her daughter.

"Well ... Maybe Mira can have the head and the chest, and you and I can have the wings?" Dad suggested helpfully, chopping and slicing the air with a hand to demonstrate what he meant.

"Stop it!" Mom fumed and, like someone who had just unknowingly touched a pot that was burning hot, jerked her elbow up involuntarily, leaving the knife dangling lamely in her hand high above the cake.

"Stop what?"

"Stop making it sound like a bloody slaughter!" Mom snapped. "This bird is supposed to represent Mira at fifteen! How can I chop off its head and wings like that!"

As the words were fired from her mouth, Mom's hand trembled visibly, shaking the knife. Before Mira and Dad could react, it slipped out from her hand and dropped, headlong, aiming straight for the soaring bird's chest.

What happened next seemed to happen very slowly, as if the weight of their collective attention on the falling knife's course had somehow bent time. Dad's expression changed from alert to panic while Mom's face was first softened by shock but then immediately frozen by something that was even greater than fear.

And in that elongated second, Mira saw Mom reach for the falling knife with her bare hands.

"Whew!" Mom let out a nervous laugh, clutching the blade just a few inches above the cake. "That was close . . . Almost ruined the cake! The bird is saved!"

At a cost, however, and both Mira and Dad had noticed it: blood, as red as rubies, was streaking down the blade and converging into bigger drops at the tip of the knife before free-falling onto the cake and splattering into many velvet red flowers that stained the soaring bird's snowy white chest.

Unfortunately, the sweet aroma of the cake only sharpened the metallic smell of Mom's blood, which went up Mira's nostrils like a drill, causing her brain to buzz like a swarm of alarmed bees.

Dad's eyes were still wide with panic, but his face had turned green. He covered his mouth with a fist and made a feeble sound.

"You're bleeding," Mira said numbly as she stared at the velvet red flowers on the white bird's chest, which were increasing quickly in number and merging into bigger ones.

"Oh no . . ." Mom whimpered. She tried to loosen her grip on the blade, but it only made the blood trickle down faster. She grimaced in pain. "No . . . I ruined Mira's birthday cake!"

"Cara . . ." Dad went around Mira's chair to help. Very gently, he turned Mom by the shoulders to face him. "Don't worry about the cake, honey. Look at me . . . Cara, look at me . . . Don't worry about the cake. Okay? We're going to let go of the knife first, then we're going to take care of your hands."

Mom bit her lip and nodded, her eyes glistening with tears.

Dad held the knife by the handle with one trembling hand, then slowly and gingerly, he guided Mom's fingers away from the blade with the other, one finger at a time, until she was able to peel her palms off the blade.

With a soft but nervous sigh, he laid the bloody knife down on the table, next to the cake. He cupped Mom's blood-streaked hands in his and asked in a tight voice, "You feeling all right? Can you move your fingers?"

Stiffly, Mom flexed her fingers, wincing with each movement.

"Good . . . Good . . ." Dad nodded with relief. "As long as they can move . . ." He turned to Mira, still looking a little green. "I'm gonna go get the first aid ki—" He cut himself short with a tell-tale burping sound from his throat, which he quickly swallowed down with the help of a fist pressing to his lips. "Sorry about that," he mumbled from behind his hand, suddenly looking as pale as a ghost. "Mira, c-could you take care of Mom for a while?"

Before Mira could answer, he had stumbled away in a hurry, clutching a hand to his mouth.

Mira got up woodenly from her chair and looked at Mom's hands. The sight and the smell of blood immediately overwhelmed her senses, making her arms soft and her legs weak.

"You should keep your hands flat and hold them above the level of your heart," she heard herself say, not knowing why she sounded so cold and calm. "Helps to stop the bleeding."

"I'm sorry, Mira. I'm so, so sorry . . ." Mom choked up. "I wanted you to have a perfect day for your fifteenth birthday. But now . . . I've ruined your cake *and* your birthday . . ."

"It doesn't matter," Mira replied feebly. The sight and the smell of blood were starting to make her queasy. She felt her throat tight-ening in response. She swallowed hard to ease the tightness, but rather than relieving it, it gave her the impression that she had swallowed Mom's blood.

Her stomach churned at the taste of it. She wanted to throw up.

"But it's your birthday ... Your fifteenth birthday ..." Mom murmured heartbrokenly. Tears streamed down her face and fell from her chin in drops, which landed squarely in her hands, diluting the intense redness and the smell of her blood.

This offered a much-needed break for Mira's nose and brain. She welcomed the temporary relief with a short sigh but noticed that her heart was still throbbing with pain.

She held out a hand and touched Mom's cheek with her fingertips. Mom's tears were warm and sticky. She wondered if her own tears would be warm and sticky like Mom's. She couldn't remember if she had ever cried before. As a matter of fact, she didn't think she knew how.

She tried to dry Mom's face with her hand, but it didn't seem to be of much use, so she took her hand back and said, "We've already celebrated my birthday. You sang 'Happy Birthday' to me, remember? That means my aging ceremony is completed and done. So there's no need to beat yourself up over the details of a time that has already passed."

As Mom listened, her eyes grew wide, and the tears stopped forming. She looked at Mira with an incredulous and startled expression. "Did you just call your birthday an 'aging ceremony'?"

"I found it!" Dad suddenly called from the stairs. He was holding up the first aid kit with both hands, looking much more composed than earlier. "Sorry it took me so long. I was, uh ... having a hard time remembering where this thing was."

He put the first aid kit on the dining table, then he pulled out two chairs and made them face each other. He helped Mom into one, and with a deep breath, he sat down in the other and began to clean the blood off her hands.

Mira stood behind him and watched him dress Mom's wounds with trembling hands. Soon, a small heap of bloodstained gauze pads was gathering on the table, next to the knife and the bird-shaped cake that shared the same unfortunate fate.

The sight of them reminded Mira of the blood-soaked battlefield in her dreams, and for some reason, she thought the bloodstained gauze pads were starting to look like, from a bird's-eye view, the fallen soldiers in that battlefield: noiseless, motionless, and lifeless.

She remembered how she slashed her way through those soldiers without giving a thought to their blood or their pain.

She could hear it: the hoarse caws from the crows above her head, imitating the cries of battle mixed with the shrieks of agony from those who saw death.

She could see it: the blood, so much blood, sprayed into the air by the blade of her sword before they rained down like showers, painting the battlefield red.

She could smell it: the stirred-up dust, tinged with blood and filth and sharpened by the last few decaying breaths from those whose souls would soon be collected.

She could taste it: the fear, the desperation, the despair, and the regret.

Yes . . . Death . . .

The next thing she knew, her knees went weak and buckled under the weight of that battlefield.

Then the world went black.

III

She was back on the battlefield. But this time, instead of slashing her way through with her sword and shield as quickly as she could manage, she was treading slowly across it, through heaps and heaps of motionless soldiers who had already been cut down.

The air was cold; it smelled of stale sweat and rot.

A murder of pitch-black crows alighted on the corpses around her. They cackled and cawed, announcing the intention of their arrival, then they twitched and tilted their heads to study her with their beady black eyes.

Their gaze was cold yet intense. She was suddenly very aware of the position of every single one of them.

She stopped to look at her observers, but the crows seemed to have lost their interest in her. They began to busy themselves with what was beneath their feet, digging and tearing vigorously with their claws to get to the soft parts they could peck at. She noticed then that except for the crows and the blood, everything else was gray.

She let her gaze climb to the edge of the battlefield and trace along it, searching for a destination. She knew she needed to continue; she needed to leave the battlefield. She knew she had to be somewhere—if only she could remember where.

Her eyes eventually landed on the woods at the far edge of the battlefield. She decided to go there, although she didn't know why.

She stepped over the corpses in her way, only to find another heap blocking her path.

One of the crows was resting on that heap. When she approached, it flapped its wings, hopped about, and landed next to a soldier's head that had lost both its helmet and the body it was attached to. The crow cawed and clawed at the head until it was rolled to its side. Despite its state of decomposition, she saw that the eyes and the mouth of the head were still wide open in horror, as if its previous owner had made a final effort to capture the last moment of his life for the world to remember him by. The crow appeared to be quite pleased with what it had found. It patted the head's rotting cheek with one foot and cooed contentedly. It was then she noticed that instead of two legs and two feet, this crow had three of each.

She turned to count how many legs and feet the other crows had, and she realized, just like the first one, they all had three legs and three feet.

There was a shrill caw from behind her. She twisted around and saw that the first three-legged crow had obtained an eyeball in its beak. The optic nerve was still connected to the detached head it had found like an umbilical cord, so the crow was jerking the eyeball forcibly to make it break free from the eye socket.

Presently, the crow sensed her attention and paused. With the optic nerve still dangling from one side of its beak, it swiveled its head to her direction and tilted it just enough to give her an affectionate wink.

She ran.

She didn't know why but she ran. She ran fast and she ran hard, over and through heaps and heaps of motionless bodies that seemed to be everywhere on the battlefield. She was running so fast that she forgot she was running and thought she was flying instead.

She was still running at great speed when she reached the edge of the battlefield. But instead of slowing down, she ran on into the woods.

There was a shield in her left hand and a sword in her right. She used the shield to push away low-hanging branches, and she used the sword to chop down tough vines blocking her way, all the while running as quickly as the wind that seemed to be carrying her under her feet. She wielded her shield and sword so deftly and fiercely that they felt like extensions of her hands, and she knew instinctively that nothing could stop her—nothing.

She ran harder, wielding her shield and sword faster and faster, until eventually, she popped out from the other side of the woods and was greeted by a quiet meadow on a gentle hill. The meadow was surrounded by trees, but there was neither a buzz nor a chirp to be heard. It was quiet, unnaturally quiet.

The color of the sky had darkened from gray to black. There was no moon, no stars, not even a light. She scanned the meadow and noticed a motionless shape in the middle. In the darkness, the shape looked angular and solid, like the shape of a house.

All of a sudden, a gale of wind whooshed down from the treetops behind her and blasted through a belt of trees standing around the edge of the meadow, as if an invisible dragon was dragging its belly and tail through those trees deliberately to close in on her from midair.

Her eyes followed the turmoil happening along the treetops until it came to an abrupt end. Then, out of the corner of her eye, she sensed movement from below.

She focused on the space between the tree trunks, just above the ground. There, a formless dark shape emerged from the shadows of the trees, quickly but cautiously. Before she could tell what it was, it had separated into many smaller dark shapes that moved on two legs.

Each of those shapes appeared to have a designated position to hold in relation to the others. Other than that, they advanced at the same time, stopped at the same time, and even moved in the same manner.

The dark shapes were making their way to the middle of the meadow, where the house was sitting quietly in the darkness. She wondered why they were heading that way, and she wondered what they were going to do to that house.

The sky was as black as ink now. But as she followed them with her gaze, her eyesight soon improved to that of an owl. She could see the dark shapes clearly then: humans. They were wearing military uniforms and night vision goggles, and they were heavily armed.

They had a leader; he was at the front. When they got to about fifty paces away from the house, he halted their advancement to observe the surroundings. After a long and attentive pause, he changed his stance and motioned some orders to the rest of them. Surprisingly, even though they were all wearing night vision goggles, none of them seemed to notice her presence.

She moved toward them, noiselessly, like a phantom. Her shield and sword were lowered to her sides, but both handles were tightly wrapped by her fingers.

The humans surrounded the house. Then two of them sneaked up the back deck, worked on one of the windows for a while, and lifted it open. They stuck their heads in and looked around, then they turned and gestured something to the leader. The leader gestured back, then he motioned for the ones next to him to join him at the opened window.

Within a minute, half of them had climbed over the windowsill and sneaked inside the house. The rest of them stayed in their spots and waited in silence, crouching low in firing position with their rifles pointing at every possible exit from the house.

A strange feeling was rising in her chest; she could feel herself trembling at the thought of it. She tightened her grip on the sword and made the trembling stop.

Meanwhile, the temperature was dropping rapidly. She felt cold air blowing in her face, leaving behind drops of wetness that pricked her skin. She glanced up: something flaky and gray like ash was pattering down softly from the sky. A layer of dust was quickly collecting on every surface, correcting the grayness of everything in sight with the same shade.

She let the gray ash land on her exposed arms. It was cold and light, and it melted right away—it wasn't ash; it was snow.

Presently, she noticed movements from behind the opened window: the humans were coming out. They rolled down from the windowsill, one after another, smoothly and effortlessly, looking like shadows coughed up by the window.

Their leader was last. Once he was outside, he instructed the others to form up and stand by behind the back deck. Then he raised his left arm and tapped on a rectangular screen on his wrist. The screen lit up, and, after having his face scanned and verified, he was prompted by an emotionless female voice to speak.

"Hope, this is Zeus One reporting to mission control."

"Zeus One, I have mission control on the line. Please proceed."

"Mission control, the sweep is completed."

"Are you in possession of the Red Key?"

"Negative."

"Are you in possession of any evidence that's related to the Red Key?"

"Negative."

A pause.

"Zeus One, push the radius to fifty miles and sweep for potential signs. Housekeeping is on the way. You have forty-eight hours until checkout."

"Roger that. Zeus One over and out."

The leader tapped on the screen again and disconnected the call. He hopped down the back deck and landed on the snow with a dull crunch. As he walked away from the house, he motioned for the others to gather in.

When he had everyone's attention, he said in a raspy voice, "Guys, we've got a new order from mission control. We are to sweep the entire fifty-mile radius centering the site of interest for potential signs of the asset. We only have forty-eight hours before they pull us out of this mission. So let's get to work."

He assigned them into groups and told each group which area to cover, then he ordered them to move out. With that, the humans turned their backs on the house and dispersed in different directions, crunching the snow beneath their feet into trails of footprints that would eventually be erased. Before long, their shapes were merged back into the shadows of the trees, and they disappeared into the woods without another sound, leaving the entire meadow to just her and the house.

The snow had been falling silently and purposefully, blanketing the trees, the meadow, and the house. It was cold. She shivered involuntarily. She felt her body heat dissipating quickly, as if the snowflakes were starving for warmth and were greedily sucking it away from her skin. She dropped the shield and the sword from her rigid fingers and hugged herself tight.

The wind picked up the pace and started to howl. The snow struggled in its force but didn't let up.

Amid the wind and the snow, she heard someone calling from inside the house. She was too cold and too tired to move, but she walked toward it anyway.

The howling wind threw the snow at her angrily without stopping. It felt so cold on her face and body that she thought her skin was burning.

As she got closer, she realized the house was not gray, but yellow. It was a cute little house. She couldn't help noticing how familiar it looked, then it occurred to her that it had the same design as . . . as . . .

She was suddenly hit by a piercing pain in her heart, and she felt her body heat leaking profusely from an opening in her left chest. She looked down: vivid red flowers were dripping rhythmically from a sizable hole in her chest onto the snowy white meadow, then they immediately turned pitch-black as if they had scorched the ground.

The wind was howling louder, amid the sound of which she heard a crying voice coming from inside the house, but she was too hot and too weak to move any farther.

So she closed her eyes to focus on that voice. She felt the vivid red flowers dripping from her heart and torching the ground. As she burned in the flames, she heard the voice sob:

"Oh no . . . Oh no . . . No, no, no . . . no . . . Please no . . . please . . . Please . . ."

She knew that voice.

It belonged to Mom.

IV

Mira opened her eyes.

At first, she couldn't remember who she was. Then out of the corner of her eye, she saw Mom: she was asleep on the floor, leaning uncomfortably against the closet door.

Mira wanted to sit up, but except her head, nothing else seemed to be awake enough to respond accordingly. Her eyes felt dry and gritty. Her throat was sore and scratchy. She parted her lips to call Mom, but the only sound she managed to make was a croak.

Still, it was enough to wake Mom. She pushed herself away from the closet door with a start. When she saw that Mira was awake, she smiled with relief and stood up.

"Hey . . . How are you feeling?"

Mira saw then that Mom's hands were wrapped in thick layers of bandages. A hazy memory surfaced in her mind, but she wasn't sure whether she had dreamed it or it had indeed happened.

"Your . . . hands . . ." Mira's voice came out sounding broken and hoarse, like the voice of an old man clinging to his last breath.

"They'll be fine," said Mom, kneeling next to her bed. "Dad did a great job bandaging them up. I don't really feel the cuts now."

Mom's words confirmed her hazy memory. *So it wasn't a dream after all,* Mira said to herself.

There was a straw cup on the nightstand. Mom put it between her heavily bandaged palms, picked it up, and offered it to Mira. "Water?"

Mira tried to nod, but her head didn't move. So she blinked to answer Mom instead.

Mom tilted the cup and held the straw to Mira's lips. The water was cold and refreshing, relieving the discomfort in her throat.

"Drink as much as you can, okay?" Mom said gently. "Your body needs it."

Mira paused and gave Mom a puzzled look.

"You have a low-grade fever," Mom explained slowly. "You fainted . . . when Dad was cleaning my wounds." She bit her lip hard before continuing. "I'm sorry, Little Bird. We should have known you weren't feeling well. You slept from early afternoon all the way till the evening, and you barely spoke or ate after you woke up . . . I should have asked . . ."

Mom placed the straw cup back on the nightstand, shaking her head, her face gloomy. "I can't believe I made so many mistakes on your birthday . . . your *fifteenth* birthday. I wanted it to be perfect. I wanted it to be a day that you'd always remember when you looked back. But now . . ." She buried her face in her bandaged hands and drew a shaky breath, then she let out a long and regretful sigh.

Mira felt a dull pain throbbing in her left chest, reminding her of something that had happened in a dream—a dream she thought she had had.

"Mom . . ." she whispered in her grating voice. "It doesn't need to be perfect."

Mom uncovered her face, but her expression only seemed sadder than before. Mira decided to continue.

"It doesn't need to be perfect . . . because nothing in life is truly perfect . . ."

As she spoke, Mom's eyes widened with uncertainty and confliction. Mira could see a wide range of emotions brewing on her face, clashing, combining, and blending in the process, like the palette of an abstract painting.

But Mira didn't need to wait for the colors to settle to know what that painting would look like; she already knew it, as if she had seen it from her mind's eye. In fact, she couldn't help feeling she had been observing that painting for a very long time.

So she added softly, "If the world is not perfect, you don't need to be perfect either."

The competing emotions on Mom's face froze for a few seconds, then they melted and were washed away by a wave of silent tears.

It was a reaction that Mira did not anticipate, and she didn't like the feeling that her words had caused Mom to cry.

"Mom?" she called tentatively.

Mom sniffled and dried her face with the bandages on the backs of her hands. Then she leaned forward and patted Mira's head, smiling affectionately. "You're the most amazing daughter a mother could ask for, you know that? ... Dad and I are so lucky to have you."

The mention of Dad reminded Mira of his fear of blood and its potential effect on him after dressing Mom's wounds.

"Is he okay?" she asked.

"Huh?"

"Did he get sick ... from the blood?"

"He didn't." Mom lowered her eyes. "You fainted. All we cared about was finding out if you were okay. Everything else was secondary." She looked at Mira and smiled. "But you know what? He was so worried about you that I don't think blood scares him anymore."

Mira pondered this, but she couldn't see the connection between the two. She knitted her brows. "What do you mean?"

Mom gave an amused chuckle, which caused Mira to think she had expected that question. "You'll understand when you have kids. Anyway, let's just pretend he was never afraid of blood, okay? Now, are you hungry?"

Mira looked at Mom in alarm. "There's ... more food for my birthday?"

Mom laughed. "It's Sunday morning now, Little Bird. I was talking about your first post-birthday breakfast."

Feeling stunned, Mira glanced at the windows. The blinds were down, but no light was coming through the gaps either.

Mom seemed to have read the question on her mind. "We had a nasty thunderstorm," she said. "It started not long after ... well, what happened last night, and it lasted through the night. That's why it's still so dark outside."

She turned and reached for the clock on the nightstand, then she showed it to Mira.

Mira stared at the display: the time was 7:10 AM, and the date was July 1. Mom was right. It was already Sunday morning.

"I slept . . . that long?" she murmured to herself, wondering how many of those hours were spent in her dream.

"Nine hours of sleep is really not that much when you're sick. Your body needs lots of rest to fight off the fever," said Mom. "Speaking of which, I'm glad you slept through the thunderstorm . . . Did you hear it at all? Gosh, the thunder was so loud, and the rain was pouring down like sheets! It was impossible to see anything outside . . ."

It occurred to Mira then that Mom might have fallen asleep against the closet door long before she woke up.

"Mom?" she asked. "Did you stay with me this whole time?"

"Not the whole time," Mom answered casually. "Dad was here before me. He didn't want me to stay up, but I, um . . . I couldn't sleep. Plus, he was struggling to stay awake anyway. I mean, he stayed up late the night before your birthday too. And I know he can't function well when he doesn't have enough sleep, not to mention two days in a row. So I took his place and made him go to bed."

"You should too," said Mira. "Go to bed. You need sleep."

Mom opened her mouth to argue, but when she saw the look on Mira's face, she closed it and let out a soft sigh through her nose. "All right. But let me get you something to eat first, even if you're not hungry yet. Just something small to give your body a bit of energy to fight off the fever. Okay?"

Quietly, Mira observed Mom's expression in detail. Then she answered, "Okay."

Mom's face lit up. "Great! I'll go fix it right now."

She got up and headed for the door. When it was opened, she paused in the doorway, twisted around, and looked at Mira with a contented smile. "It won't take me long, so try to stay awake if you can. I'll be back in a jiffy."

Mira watched the door close behind Mom and felt a familiar pain expanding from her lower abdomen, swollen and raw. She knew that pain. She knew what it looked like. It was all too vivid in her mind.

She closed her eyes, hoping it was merely a physical reaction to the unwanted memory that had slipped past her guard and sneaked back into her mind, a memory that she had buried deep in the back of her head in order to forget it had ever happened.

She waited until the pain subsided, then she opened her eyes. To her surprise, the room was illuminated by a mesmerizing glow of red and gold, which had completely overpowered the soft yellow light from the table lamp on her nightstand.

Reluctantly, she looked down. There, glowing unmistakably under the bedsheet and her pajamas, was her inexplicable burn mark that looked like a lava-filled tattoo. It was glowing so powerfully that even with all the layers on her, she could still see the "lava" pushing and pulling along inside as it shifted and flared on her abdomen like dancing flames.

Her ears began to ring, and this time, it was a cacophonous whooshing noise charged with static, reminding her of a giant shape-shifting bird formed by a great murmuration of starlings, each of them whispering to her in a different human voice at the same time.

She knew that voice.

She had heard it before—back in Skygate, in front of the little yellow house, under an alien-looking green vortex that seemed to be sucking the life of Earth away ... on that ill-fated day.

Chapter 4 THE RED BIRD

1

As soon as Mira opened the door, she heard Mom's footsteps rustling toward her from the kitchen. Before she shut it, Mom was already in the mudroom, greeting her in her apron without losing the spatula she was using to prepare dinner.

"You're back!" Mom exclaimed with an excited smile. "So, how did it go? What do you think about the school? Do you like your teachers? How does it feel to be an official high schooler?"

Her eyes were sparkling with so much anticipation that Mira stammered. "Er . . . um . . . Good?"

Mom let out a happy squeal. "That's great! Tell me what you did today. Did you see any kids from our neighborhood? How were your classmates? Did you make some friends?"

"Uh . . ." Mira processed Mom's questions quickly in her head and realized the only thing she could tell Mom about the school was that she had visited the school library and checked out a few books. She didn't want to tell Mom that she had managed to silence every single conversation among the other students and murdered their mood to resume talking afterward simply with her presence, no matter whether it was in the hallway, the classroom, the gym, or the cafeteria. As a matter of fact, the school library was the only place where she hadn't noticed an abrupt silence upon her arrival, and since it was a library, she had just assumed the dead air she had walked in on had nothing to do with her being there.

"I like the library," she finally managed. "Spent an hour there."

"Oh, Mira . . ." Mom sighed, lowering the spatula to her side. "I know you like books . . . and yes, books are wonderful resources for all kinds of knowledge, but you're missing out on the real world if you don't interact with the people that come with it."

Mira knitted her brows. "What do you mean?"

"I mean . . . not everything's so black-and-white like words printed on paper, you know? Granted, books can capture and document the human species' impact on this world in all kinds of categories, be it good or bad. But books are not alive like us. They don't feel, process, change, or evolve on their own—we do. You have to remember there's a living, breathing human being behind every single book that exists and has existed in this world. So compared to reading something that was printed rigidly on paper and written by someone with certain characteristics when they were at a certain stage of their life and had certain emotions and standpoints toward certain topics, which may or may not have changed later, depending on what they experienced next, isn't it more interesting to know the person behind the book as a holistic and fluid organism rather than just a source of information?"

Mira's brows were still knitted, but it was no longer because she didn't understand what Mom was saying.

"I'm sorry." Mom sighed and closed her eyes. She brought a hand to her face and squeezed the bridge of her nose with her thumb and index finger. "That was . . . a little too much. I don't know why it came out like that . . . All I'm saying is—"

"You want me to spend more time with people, not books," Mira said matter-of-factly, cutting her off.

"Wh—That's not what I mean. I . . ."

"It's okay, Mom." Mira stopped her with a nonchalant shrug. "I know you're worried about me because I'm not like the other normal fifteen-year-old girls."

Even though Mira could not see the backyard from where she was standing, her mind had already led her back to the memory of the evening of her fifteenth birthday, leaving her standing silently behind the bench that was between the birdbath and the patio as she listened in on Mom and Dad's private conversation yet again.

Mira blinked and forced the memory back into the depths of her consciousness. She didn't want to challenge Mom about the content of her conversation with Dad from that evening, at least not yet. Her focus fell back on her mother, who now looked as startled as a wounded deer, her hazel eyes crawling with shock and fear. Mira felt a familiar dull pain throbbing in her left chest, but she decided she didn't need to find out what else was happening behind those hazel eyes.

"I'm gonna go read now," she said blankly, walking away.

"Mira!" Mom called after her in a voice that sounded as though she was enduring a great pain.

Mira paused, but she didn't look back.

"I . . . I just want you to have some friends," said Mom, almost desperately. "I want you to be . . . happy."

"I am happy," Mira answered coldly, but as soon as the words had left her mouth, she knew they were not true.

Doesn't matter, she told herself. *Nothing matters in the end anyway.*

With that thought, she ran up the stairs to her room and shut the door behind her.

11

Ever since that unpleasant interaction with Mom after her first day of high school, Mira had been spending more time at the library after school to stay away from home. She didn't make the slightest effort to interact with other people either, which was what Mom wished she could do more of.

Needless to say, by the end of the first month of high school, Mira remained friendless. She didn't mind it though, nor did she expect any change in the matter. After all, she had long gotten used to the effect of her presence on the other kids when they were in Skygate, so she was not at all surprised to find out the kids at her new school in Starfall would also scamper out of her way like small critters sensing the cold eyes of a bird of prey. As a result, whenever Mira went to the school library, she would always end up having a whole table to herself; the other kids at her table would vacate themselves in a hurry and move to other tables, no matter how crowded they already were, just to keep a safe distance from her.

Mira didn't mind the lack of company at her table. In fact, she welcomed the extra space it provided her from the others. She went to the library every day after she was done with her classes, where she would first finish her homework then browse the bookshelves, category by category, hunting for interesting books to read.

It was the first Wednesday in September, and today was no different. Mira went to the library after her last class of the day, finished her homework at her usual table, which had already cleared out by the time she arrived, then she returned to the bookshelf she had browsed the day before and moved to the next one. Out of habit, she glanced up at the category label for that shelf and saw the words *Ancient Myths and Legends* printed on it.

A full shelf, she observed to herself. *How did people come up with so many myths and legends?*

She tilted her head and scanned through the titles on the book spines: *Gods and Goddesses, The Myth of Dragons, The Rebirth of the Phoenix, Powers and Magic, A Collection of Mythical Creatures, Celtic Mythology, Norse Mythology, Roman Mythology, Greek Mythology, Egyptian Mythology, Indian Mythology* ... *Chinese Mythology, The Classic of Mountains and Seas, Strange Tales from A Chinese Studio, Chinese Folklore.*

Folklore. She paused. *Maybe I can find some answers in there.*

She pulled *Chinese Folklore* off the shelf and immediately noticed how dusty it was. She blew the dust off and turned it to the front. The book had an old-fashioned leather hardcover in a dull red color. Like the letters on its spine, the title of the book was also stamped onto the cover in small plain letters in a muted gold paint. Apart from those letters, there was nothing else on the cover, making it one of the least eye-catching books she had seen. Intrigued by the book's modest design, Mira examined its corners and edges to estimate its age. Even though the binding suggested it was an old book, she was surprised to find that the book itself did not show much wear and tear at all.

Mira opened the book to the first page and was instantly drawn to the sketch of a strange-looking creature. To begin with, it had a monstrous head and a great big horn on its brow. A pair of gong-sized eyes took up nearly half of its face, whereas the other half was occupied by a toothy grin that stretched from ear to ear, its mouth cracked open just wide enough for anyone with imagination to have a rough idea about the sizes of animals that could get crumbled up between those spikelike fangs. So although both corners of the beast's mouth were pointing upward, Mira had a hard time deciding whether it was smirking or threatening.

Like a male lion in its prime, this creature also wore a luxuriously thick mane around its head, except that instead of looking soft and glossy, it appeared hard and sharp like armor. Its hefty body was completely covered in a layer of overlapping scales that reminded

Mira of a giant pangolin, exposing only the big sharp claws at the
ends of its four mighty paws. Compared to the rest of its body, its
tail seemed short and insignificant, though there was something
that resembled a burning flame sitting on its tip, which was held
up rather playfully in the sketch, looking more like a menacing
weapon than a harmless decoration.

Satisfied with her choice, Mira closed the book and went back to
her table, the image of the strange-looking creature still lingering
in her mind. She wondered what kind of creature it was and what
it was called, and above all, she wondered whether it was real. She
settled herself on the bench and opened the book to its first story.
Then she dove in.

The Tale of Nian

A long, long time ago, there was once a monstrous beast called Nian.

*Nian was strong and ferocious. It had a deadly horn on its forehead,
a set of razor-sharp teeth between its strong jaws, and four sets of even
sharper claws on its great big paws. It had a pair of yellow eyes that
glowed in the dark, which was as big and round as a pair of gongs,
and they revealed nothing but its desire to kill and feast.*

*For 364 days a year, Nian spent its time away from the villages,
either deep under the seas or high in the mountains—364 days a year
save one: Lunar New Year's Eve.*

*On that day, Nian returned to the villages in the evening, no matter
how deep it was in the seas or how high it was in the mountains. It
came all the way back for one thing and one thing only: to feed. Not just
chickens, ducks, and geese; or pigs, cows, and sheep; or dogs, cats, horses,
and donkeys—Nian preyed on every living creature in the villages, be
it livestock, pets, or men.*

*Yes, men—from infants to children, from adults to seniors—no
exceptions.*

*Wherever Nian passed through, no life was left behind, for no one
was spared and no one could survive the cruelty of this monstrous beast.*

So year after year, on the night of Lunar New Year's Eve, Nian came and wiped out village after village, gorging to its heart's content until sunrise. Then, with the sunlight shining upon the beginning of a brand-new year, Nian retreated back to whence it came from. There it waited, with a bellyful of flesh and blood and bones, for the next Lunar New Year's Eve.

And year after year, every village was shrouded in fear as winter arrived and the next Lunar New Year's Eve neared. In time, some villages chose to evacuate their villagers on the day of Lunar New Year's Eve, either into the forests or the mountains, in the hope of concealing themselves from Nian. Some less fortunate villages were not able to evacuate, however, as they were not blessed with the proximity of either a forest or a mountain to take shelter in.

Oh, how grim the moods were in those villages! As the nights grew longer, so did the faces of their villagers. When the fateful day of Lunar New Year's Eve eventually arrived, every family gathered their family members under one roof to spend the night together, for they knew that should Nian come their way that night, it would be their last.

Therefore, each family worked together during the day to finish the final preparations before nightfall: They swept and mopped the floors. They wiped the windows clean. They dusted out the furniture and the cobwebs in the corners. They also threw out things they no longer needed to make the rooms tidy and comfortable for every family member to fit inside.

After the big cleanup, they settled down to prepare dinner. They used the finest ingredients they could gather or afford to buy in preparation for that night and cooked the most mouthwatering feast of the year for the entire family—not because they wanted an extravagant meal to celebrate the beginning of a new year, but because dinner on the night of Lunar New Year's Eve could be the last meal they would ever get to eat. To put it bluntly, if they had to die that night, they would die with good food in their bellies and their loved ones by their sides.

When it was finally time for dinner, they fenced in the livestock, barred the windows and doors—even though it would not make much of a difference if Nian were to enter. Then they brought out the finest wine they could make or afford that year, and all of their family members sat around one big table. They poured the wine and drank to the gods and their ancestors for their blessings, then they toasted good luck to each other and began eating. But instead of huddling together to finish their dinner in silence and fear, they ate and drank and played games merrily throughout the night, praying the fatal visit from Nian had not been written in their fates yet.

As time went by, this practice gradually became the norm on the night of Lunar New Year's Eve, which then grew into a yearly tradition among the villagers. And since all of the family members were to gather under the same roof to wait for their fates to be revealed that night, it had come to be known as the family reunion dinner on Lunar New Year's Eve.

But here's the thing: what they did or did not do on the night of Lunar New Year's Eve mattered not to the bloodthirsty Nian . . .

"Excuse me!" an agitated voice hissed from across the table, cutting off Mira's attention on the book.

Mira's head jerked up in alarm; no one here had attempted to talk to her yet, not to mention in a tone like that.

A girl was standing on the other side of the table, holding a stack of books. She had long black hair that draped to her waist like a cloak. Her eyebrows were covered by a thick layer of evenly trimmed bangs that ended just above her eyelids. She was dressed completely in black; even the backpack on her shoulder was solid black.

Mira knitted her brow as she tried to recall whether she had seen this girl on campus before, but her mind drew a blank.

The girl was average in height but rather slim. She had a yellow skin tone that reminded Mira of the desert sand in the sunset. Judging from her facial features, she appeared to be of Asian descent.

Mira looked into the girl's monolid eyes to read her intent, only to notice they were widening in fear. Meanwhile, the entire reading area seemed to be frozen in a dead silence, as if everyone else was holding their breath to hear what the black-haired girl would say to Mira next.

Mira sighed inwardly and softened her gaze. The black-haired girl's lips trembled, then she stammered. "I ... I ..."

The stack of books she was carrying slipped from her arms and tumbled down onto the table with a series of loud thumps. Mira lowered her eyes and scanned the titles: *The Existential Being, The Purpose of Life and Death, The Stoic Way, The Sentence of Time*. Mira had read all of them, but she was curious as to why this girl was interested in these topics too.

Presently, the girl fell on her books. "S-sorry! I'm so-so-sorry! It was an accident! I-I ..." she said helplessly as she tried to scoop up all four books at the same time, but her hands were shaking so much that she kept failing. "I-I just wanted to ask if these seats were taken ... I'm so-so sorry ... I'm sorry."

She doesn't know no one here dares to sit at the same table with you, a voice observed in Mira's head, sounding slightly amused. *She must be new.*

She has an accent, another voice pointed out slowly. *A foreigner. Hasn't been here long ... She's different. She likes to read what you like to read—*

So? the first voice cut in, rather impatiently. *Look at her. She's terrified! Even if she's interesting enough to talk to, does it look like she wants her to?*

That's up to her; not you, the third voice countered calmly.

What's the point? the first voice hissed. *It won't make any difference in the end. She doesn't need this.*

Need what? Mira asked.

Another relationship, the slow voice and the calm voice replied at the same time.

Relationships lead to mental attachments. They are nothing but burdens—unnecessary burdens, said the first voice, sounding like the wind sighing, through which Mira thought she heard a voice sobbing in the distance. She couldn't hear the words clearly, but she could tell it belonged to someone brokenhearted.

Nothing but burdens, repeated the first voice.

Let her decide, said the slow voice.

It's her price, added the calm voice. *It's her choice.*

With that, the three voices contorted and blended and turned into noise. Mira took a deep breath and closed her eyes.

She remembered what Mom had said that day; she could hear her desperate voice in the back of her mind: *"I . . . I just want you to have some friends . . . I want you to be . . . happy."*

She sighed and opened her eyes.

"They're not taken," Mira said to the black-haired girl, who immediately froze up like a deer in headlights. Not knowing what else she could say to make this conversation last any longer than it had, Mira held up her book to return to its stories. Sensing that the girl might be too scared to leave without her permission, she added resignedly, "And you can stop apologizing."

III

Lilith didn't know where to go. She had finished her last class of the day, but she didn't want to go home, or as she would call it, a place to sleep. She didn't like spending time there, not because she didn't like the house or she hadn't warmed up to it yet after the move, but because although it was already the fourth house she had moved to since she came to this country less than a year ago to reunite with her parents, they were rarely home.

In truth, over the past six months, Lilith had gotten used to the constant moving as well as being alone in a new house and a new city. Unfortunately, the excitement of new houses and new cities always wore down soon enough, replaced by an unshakable sense of loneliness, which she tried to pretend wasn't always there.

Like the previous moves, her move to Starfall took place just as quickly, if not quicker. It began with a note that Lilith found on the fridge door after coming home from school one day, which instructed her to pack her things and get ready to move. Two days later, the movers came and packed up everything else, and by the end of the week, except for Lilith and her suitcase, everything that was once inside the house was loaded up onto a moving truck. Lilith then spent the following week at a local hotel, as instructed by her parents, until it was time for her to fly to Starfall. So by the time Lilith got off the plane and hailed a taxi for herself to go to the new house, she couldn't help feeling she was merely heading to another hotel.

She arrived at the new house later that afternoon to find that everything from the old house had already been unpacked and put in place—everything but her parents, that is. Instead, they welcomed

her home with days' worth of food stuffed inside the fridge and another note on the fridge door with yet another set of instructions
regarding her new school and her new bank card.

Unlike the previous moves, however, after reading her "Welcome
Home!" note this time, Lilith didn't feel like going out to explore
the new area at all. She took a shower, put on her headphones,
and lay on her bed. Then, staring at the beige ceiling in her new
bedroom, she played the songs on her MP3 player from track one.
Somewhere during track thirty-eight, Lilith finally forgot where
she was and drifted off to sleep.

When her alarm went off the next morning, Lilith had already
forgotten she had just moved here. She got up, got dressed, and
fixed herself some breakfast. Then she reread her parents' instructions from the "Welcome Home!" note and got ready for school.

Even though it was her first day at Starfall High School, and
even though she didn't know anybody there, Lilith was at ease.
Somehow, it felt better to be surrounded by strangers that she did
not have the will to talk to at school than to be surrounded by
familiar household items at home that she could not talk to at all.

Lilith thought about going to the downtown area to look
around, but the mere idea of exploring a whole new area by herself was exhausting enough. And since she would rather not go
home unless there was nowhere else to go, she ended up wandering around the campus, looking for places she could just hang out
quietly in the presence of others. Lilith didn't know—and didn't
really care, for that matter—what she should expect to find at her
new school. So when she came across the school library in the
middle of her aimless stroll, she thought she had hit the jackpot,
because a library was exactly the kind of place that could help her
get away from her life and herself for a while without physically
separating her from the presence of other people.

As soon as Lilith entered the building, she headed straight for
the bookshelves. There were rows and rows of them, spreading long
and wide from the narrow reading area in the middle. Thrilled by
the size of it, Lilith walked briskly between the shelves like a young

deer trotting along the woods in search of a treat. Seeing that they were categorized by content, she decided to look for the shelf for philosophy first.

Even though it was only a school library, its collection did not disappoint. Lilith was pleasantly surprised to find three big shelves under the philosophy category, all of which were filled with books from top to bottom, with not only the most famous and popular works but also the lesser-known and more obscure ones. Like a hungry child who had stumbled upon a candy store, Lilith went through the first shelf greedily and picked out four books that piqued her interest the most. And since she had no intention of returning home just yet, she went back to the reading area, hoping to find a nice spot next to the windows to read in peace.

However, when she popped out from the shelves, Lilith was baffled to find that every single table in the reading area was being shared by more people than it was meant to—every single table except the one at the farthest end of the reading area, right in front of the windows. There was only one person sitting at that table, a girl with red hair. She was reading in the sun with her back against the windows. Without a doubt, her spot was the best one in the room.

That's odd, Lilith thought. *How come she's sitting there by herself while the rest of them barely have enough room to put their elbows on the table? Is she not letting other people sit there? . . . Yes, that must be it. Why, the nerve! Hogging the whole table to herself when the other kids have to squeeze together to finish homework? . . . No. Someone needs to teach that girl a lesson on social courtesy.*

With that thought, Lilith puffed up her chest and strode toward the red-haired girl. She was determined to make her learn how selfish she had been and how other people had suffered from her selfishness.

When she reached her table, Lilith planted herself in front of it and stared down at the red-haired girl, but the girl kept her eyes on her book and did not look up. Lilith couldn't help noticing the cold and blank expression on her petite face, which, in sharp contrast to her expression, had a warm and beautiful sun-kissed skin tone that seemed to be glowing from the sunbeams that had reached in to embrace her through the windows. Her shoulder-length curls were as red and wild as fire, reflecting the sunlight with a radiant orange halo and looking so uncontainable that they reminded Lilith of the venomous snakes on Medusa's head—so much so that she caught herself thinking they were sizzling with life and peering back at her with invisible eyes.

Lilith reminded herself that it was just hair, then she pulled back her focus from those fiery red curls and cleared her throat meaningfully, hoping it would be enough to make the red-haired girl look up.

But the red-haired girl didn't look up. She just kept on reading with that cold, blank expression frozen on her face as though she didn't even hear Lilith.

Lilith scowled. *Trying to ignore me, eh? Well, you leave me no choice, then.*

"Excuse me," she called in a hushed voice. The red-haired girl didn't move.

Lilith frowned and decided to raise her volume. "Excuse me."

The red-haired girl didn't even blink.

By then, Lilith had had enough. She hissed at the girl, a little too loudly than she meant to, "Excuse me!"

This time it worked. The red-haired girl jerked her head up with an alarmed yet confused frown, appearing to have just received her spirit back from another world.

Meanwhile, Lilith was feeling smug about having startled this self-absorbed girl. But just as she was about to give the girl the lesson of her life on social courtesy, Lilith was caught by a pair of cold, black eyes.

Fear shot down her spine like an ice-cold bullet, sending instant shivers from her backbone to her head and limbs. There was something in those cold, black eyes; it had pierced right through Lilith's eyes and into the depths of her mind like invisible tentacles, rummaging and prying through every single memory she had ever stored in her brain and every single thought she had ever had in her head as they poked and pricked and twisted and squeezed the darkest and the most depressing ones of them all. The consequence was as paralyzing as it was overwhelming for Lilith. She could not think, nor could she speak or move. It was as if she had been stripped clean to the bones by those invisible tentacles, and she felt so vulnerably exposed that not only could the cold, black eyes see what she was truly made of, but she could also see it herself.

Lilith could not breathe. A dead silence had fallen over the room, the weight of which was crushing down onto her head and shoulders like a silent avalanche. Blood was draining quickly from her face and limbs, and she couldn't help but have the feeling that her heart had stopped beating.

Just when Lilith thought she would be swallowed whole into a black abyss by those invisible tentacles, they eased their grips and let her go. Air returned to her lungs then, so did her awareness of her surroundings, including the owner of those cold, black eyes.

As soon as Lilith saw the red-haired girl again, her lips trembled. "I ... I ..."

But that was it. She had forgotten the rest of her English vocabulary. The next thing she knew, her books had slipped out from her arms and tumbled down loudly and helplessly onto the table between them.

The commotion distracted the red-haired girl's attention from Lilith, who suddenly remembered to recover her senses and think.

The first thought that appeared in her mind was to pick up her books and run far, far away from the red-haired girl. Unfortunately for Lilith, she was still too shaken to control her muscles well. So instead of scooping her books up from the table, she fell on them like a severely nearsighted person who could not see anything beyond her own nose.

"S-sorry! I'm so-so-sorry! It was an accident! I-I ..." Lilith said helplessly as she tried desperately to sweep the books back into her arms. However, none of the books seemed to want to cooperate, and they kept slipping from her hands.

Lilith cursed herself inwardly for having chosen to act for the greater good of others. She pleaded out loud, "I-I just wanted to ask if these seats were taken ... I'm so-so sorry ... I'm sorry."

Out of the corner of her eye, Lilith saw the red-haired girl tilt her head to the side as if she knew it was just a desperate lie.

I am so dead ... Lilith whimpered weakly to herself and closed her eyes.

Much to her surprise, the red-haired girl didn't say a single word back. Although her impassive silence was excruciatingly intolerable, it somehow kindled a faint hope in Lilith that she might still be able to flee the scene without leaving behind too much disgrace.

Quietly, Lilith picked up her books one by one and planned for her retreat, all the while avoiding meeting the red-haired girl's eyes. Before she could take a step back, however, she heard a sigh.

"They're not taken," the red-haired girl said tonelessly, albeit sounding very much annoyed.

Her reply caught Lilith off guard, and she froze like a deer in headlights, not knowing what to do or what to say next other than stare back helplessly with panic-stricken eyes.

The red-haired girl must have grown tired of her stupefied look. Presently, she held up her book to block Lilith from her sight. Then, with an equally toneless voice, she ordered: "And you can stop apologizing."

IV

In truth, after seeing the black-haired girl's reaction to her reply, Mira had expected her to scurry off like everyone else the first chance she got. To her surprise, the girl didn't leave. Instead, after a long and heavy pause, she said, "Y-you like . . . you like Chinese folklore?"

Mira raised an eyebrow and looked up at the girl from behind her book. No one at school had asked her a question like that before. In fact, no one here had asked her a question at all.

"The-the book . . . The book you're reading." The black-haired girl shifted behind the table nervously. "*Chinese Folklore.* Do you . . . do you like it?"

Mira lowered her book. "I don't know yet. I was in the middle of the first story when you talked to me."

"Oh . . . Which story?"

" 'The Tale of Nian.' "

" 'The Tale of Nian'! Of course! That's a classic!" the black-haired girl exclaimed with evident enthusiasm, temporarily losing control of her volume. But she soon realized her mistake and slapped a hand to her mouth. She lowered herself onto the bench on her side of the table, then she forced an awkward smile. "S-sorry. I didn't mean to be so loud," she said gingerly, but she immediately remembered she was supposed to stop apologizing, so she added hastily, "I was . . . too excited."

The fact that the black-haired girl had chosen to stay and sit down at her table only made Mira even more curious about her. She closed her book and withdrew her elbows from the table. "Excited about what?"

"The book you're reading," the girl replied eagerly. "I love Chinese folklore. It's my favorite!"

"Oh?"

"I mean, they're all very interesting: the folklore, the fairy tales, the mythologies ... The differences in time and space added different flavors to these stories, so they're all uniquely fascinating in their own ways. I love reading them all, actually. But what interests me the most about these stories is I can learn about the similarities and differences in mythological cultures across the world. To me, they're the doorways to understanding how different cultures were formed and why people behave the way they do in different countries."

"Doorways?"

"Yes. I can explain." The black-haired girl put down her books, adjusted herself on the bench, and licked her lips quickly. "Humans are social animals, correct? And what brings people together better than sharing stories with each other? It could be a story about the gigantic boar so-and-so shot the evening before, or that ugly fight between the couple next door that so-and-so had overheard, or that eccentric so-and-so who only came out of his house at night. The stories could be trivial, boring, happy, sad, miserable, shocking, daunting, haunting, terrifying, or simply ridiculous, but that's not the point. The point is, people need stories in their lives to maintain that social bond. That's why we keep on creating and sharing stories with each other, and that's also why it's been like this since our ancestors were still living in caves. So over time, stories became a vital form of documenting people's lives—I'm talking about grassroots here, because they were the true representation of how people lived, not the royals or the monarchs—and therefore, through their stories, you can actually get a glimpse of what life was like in that part of the land during that time.

"What happened next was probably not expected by anyone: the stories, sieved through generations and generations of storytelling, somehow became tightly woven into local cultures and beliefs, or to put it another way, they became ingrained superstitions. And just like that, the stories not only succeeded in influencing how a country's culture was shaped and formed, but also how their people were inclined to think and act. That's why I think of them as doorways to understanding both."

"So why is Chinese folklore your favorite, then?" Mira asked.

Her question made the black-haired girl jolt as if she had woken abruptly from an episode of sleepwalking. As soon as she noticed Mira's eyes, she stammered. "Because ... because ..."

The girl lowered her eyes then and locked her fingers together in an uncomfortable clasp. The excitement on her face had disappeared without a trace.

"Because ... I'm from China," she said softly, clasping her hands together so hard that her knuckles were turning white. "And I thought ... I thought if you liked Chinese folklore, then maybe ..."

She trailed off and bit her lip, but Mira could see everything that was not said: her sadness, her loneliness, her heartaches, her pains ...

Somewhere deep inside Mira's mind, she felt herself feeling sorry for the black-haired girl. Still, she stayed silent.

The girl must have decided she couldn't finish her sentence after all. Quietly, she got up from her seat and picked up her books.

"Anyway, I'm sorry for having interrupted you," she said. "I should let you get back to your book now."

She stepped away from the table, and then, after a moment of hesitation, she bent her body and gave Mira a formal bow.

"Thank you ... for your time."

A beam of sunlight glided over Mira's shoulder and landed on her book, turning the color of the cover into a vivid red, which reminded her of the color of Mom's blood on the bird-shaped birthday cake.

Mira felt a dull pain in her left chest. She decided to ignore the thought and the pain by reading.

She flipped open her book carelessly and came face-to-face with a page covered in sketches of strange-looking creatures who had big toothy mouths and gong-sized eyes.

"Wait," she called after the black-haired girl, who had just turned to walk away.

The girl paused and turned back around slowly.

"Y-yes?"

"You said stories became a vital form of documenting people's lives." Mira held up her book and turned it so that the sketches were facing the girl. "But how do you explain a story with a beast like *Nian*? If this story is indeed the result of people documenting their lives back in ancient times, does it mean *Nian* was real? If not, why did they invent it? Why did they make up a story about it? And more importantly, how could a made-up story survive the test of time and become a classic till this day?"

The black-haired girl's eyes first grew wide, then they sparkled with excitement and pride.

"First of all, *Nian* is not a beast. You can find many other kinds in Chinese folklore. But they're not beasts either."

Mira knitted her brow. "Many other kinds of what?"

"Mythical beings!" The black-haired girl grinned broadly and sat back down. "There are many kinds of mythical beings in Chinese folklore. They may look like beasts, but they're not; they're something more, something bizarre and mind-boggling, yet highly intelligent and magically powerful at the same time."

"You mean like Medusa? Or the Kraken?"

The black-haired girl shook her head with a knowing smile. "No. Something *more*. In Chinese folklore, we have evil demons, evil monsters, evil animals, evil spirits, evil wraiths—each with different kinds of abilities and special powers to manipulate the humans. We also have shape-shifters, man-allurers, child-abductors, blood-suckers, brain-eaters, soul-catchers—each with a different dining preference and a particular appetite."

"That's a lot."

"But there are more! As a matter of fact, we have a whole compilation of ancient texts dedicated to the recordings of mythical beings in their habitats. It's called *The Classic of Mountains and Seas*."

"Sounds harmless."

"Oh, wait till you see the content. The sketches of the mythical beings recorded in there will blow your mind! Compared to the rest of them, *Nian* actually looks quite normal, in my opinion."

"Hmm." Mira laid her book down on the table. "So . . . were they real?"

"The mythical beings? Well, most people think they're fictitious because they look too strange to have existed in our world. But just look at the skeletons of some of the prehistoric animals we've dug out. I'd say they look pretty strange too, if not stranger. Studies have shown that those ancient texts from *The Classic of Mountains and Seas* have been around since as early as fourth century BC, which means, in theory, the mythical beings recorded in there could very well be the last of some of the prehistoric species that people had seen or heard of.

"Not everyone agrees, of course. They argue that there is no archaeological evidence to support that hypothesis. But who's to say there is no archaeological evidence at all? I mean, it's not like we have the ability to drain all the oceans, lakes, and rivers, or to turn over all the mountains, forests, caves, and sinkholes, or to scoop up all the deserts, marshes, and swamps to prove there is absolutely not a single piece of archaeological evidence to link the mythical beings back to any of the prehistoric species that Earth has witnessed since its birth.

"And the shocking thing is, the ancient texts from *The Classic of Mountains and Seas* also recorded some strange-looking maps, many of which, after years of deciphering by dedicated scientists and scholars, turned out to be accurate depictions of parts of our world—not just China, the world! This whole world on Earth!

"So consider this: if the contributors of *The Classic of Mountains and Seas* had recorded truthful knowledge of the geography of the lands they had traveled to, why would they make up stories and descriptions about the mythical beings that were recorded in the same ancient texts?"

Mira thought about what she said and asked, "You believe they were real, then?"

"I do. Plus, they have matched the stories and descriptions of more and more mythical beings from the ancient texts to similar stories and descriptions from other ancient documents. Some of the mythical beings are even considered to be the potential candidates for the ancestors of a few of the existing species in our time! So, yeah. Maybe the truth is just around the corner."

Mira let her eyes fall on the sketches and pondered what she had learned from the black-haired girl.

But her silence made the girl uncomfortable, who fidgeted her thumbs nervously.

"Um, wh-what about you?" the girl ventured. "Do-do you think they were real?"

"If they were real," Mira said without looking up, "then I'm more interested in finding out why they disappeared." She drummed her fingers on the table and leaned back. "Did they record *Nian* in the ancient texts too?"

"Well . . ." The black-haired girl made a resigned face. "Yes and no."

Mira glanced up from the book. " 'Yes and no'?"

"It's . . . it's hard to explain." The girl looked away and scratched her head. "You see, 'The Tale of Nian' is a story we've been using for many, many generations to explain to the kids why it is our tradition to celebrate Lunar New Year in a certain way. Unfortunately, not many people are aware of the full story these days. Or maybe they just don't care about it anymore . . . Anyway, do you know about the Heavenly Court?"

"What's that?"

"In Chinese mythology, the Heavenly Court is a magnificent city that is hidden above the clouds. It has the most majestic palaces and the most beautiful gardens. It is also where our gods and goddesses reside. Mortals like us are not allowed to see or visit the Heavenly Court. Only immortals who have obtained special trainings and skills are able to ride the clouds up into the highest level of the sky, which is the ninth level, where they will find the Heavenly Court."

"So it's like a Chinese version of Mount Olympus?"

The black-haired girl nodded eagerly. "Yes, that's right, except that ours is floating above the clouds, whereas Mount Olympus is still attached to Earth."

"I see."

"So originally, *Nian* was the good god who came down from the Heavenly Court on Lunar New Year's Eve to protect the villagers from the evil monster *Xi*. That is actually why Lunar New Year's Eve is called *chú xī* in Chinese: *chú* means to get rid of, and *xī* is the name of the evil monster *Xi*. So basically, Lunar New Year's Eve in Chinese means a night to get rid of the evil monster *Xi*. And since it was *Nian* who protected the villagers from *Xi* and took care of the evil monster for good, in honor of *Nian*, the celebration of Lunar New Year is called *guò nián* in Chinese, meaning, we survived Lunar New Year's Eve because of *Nian*."

Mira motioned her to stop. "Wait, *Nian* was a god? And a good one? I thought it was a ruthless creature who fed on every single soul it could find on Lunar New Year's Eve."

The black-haired girl let out a deep sigh. "Yeah . . . that's the most prevalent version of the story today, unfortunately."

Mira knitted her brows. "You mean the story was changed?"

"I'm afraid so. After the evil monster *Xi* was killed by *Nian*, lives had been peaceful. So naturally, in time, people forgot about *Xi* and the terrors it used to bring to the villages every year on Lunar New Year's Eve. The almighty *Nian*, on the other hand, was what they did remember.

"Eventually, since the memory of *Xi* had faded away, *Nian* became the only protagonist in this important story that needed to be passed down to the younger generations for continuing the tradition of celebrating Lunar New Year in a certain way.

"Here's the rub, though: every good story needs a villain. Gradually, different versions of the story emerged, and in the most popular version, which, sadly, is also the most prevalent version we have today, *Nian* was described as the evil monster who brought unthinkable terrors to the people in ancient times every year on Lunar New Year's Eve, not *Xi*."

Mira gazed down at the sketches of *Nian*, wondering if they were changed as well. Eventually, she said, "Sounds pretty ungrateful to me."

"The story gave the people what they needed," the black-haired girl replied softly, "even if the hero was remembered as the villain."

Mira nodded absent-mindedly and closed the book.

"Hang on, I'm not done yet," the black-haired girl said quickly. "Now that you know why they didn't record *Nian* in the ancient texts, you'll probably appreciate the fact that they did record an evil monster who used to come into the villages on Lunar New Year's Eve to raid, and the description alone could prove that this evil monster was *Xi*, not *Nian*. So in that sense, there is at least some proof to show the world that *Nian* is not guilty of what the prevalent version of the story has charged it with."

"Doesn't matter," Mira said without taking her eyes off the book. "At the end of the day, it's just another story to most people. They will believe what they choose to believe in, regardless of what really happened."

"So all the more reason to educate them on the truth," the black-haired girl replied firmly.

There was a level of seriousness and sincerity in her voice that surprised Mira. She cocked an eyebrow and looked up at the black-haired girl. When she saw that the girl's face was just as serious and sincere as her voice, Mira couldn't help chuckling.

Startled glances were immediately thrown their way, followed by a wave of eager whispers, which rippled in the air and soon converged into something that sounded like an ancient evil spell.

The black-haired girl froze in her seat as if she had stopped breathing, looking as frightened as a wounded animal.

Mira sighed inwardly to herself and lowered her eyes.

The black-haired girl took a few uneven, shallow breaths and swallowed hard. When she was breathing normally again, she stole a nervous glance at Mira and asked timidly, "Did I ... did I say something wrong?"

"No." Mira shook her head but didn't look up.

"Wh-why ... were you laughing then?"

"Because I realized you are an optimist."

"Me?" said the girl, sounding more shocked than confused.

"Yes, you." Mira felt the corner of her mouth lifting up into a smirk. "You think you can educate people on the truth."

"Wh-what's wrong with that?"

"Nothing's wrong with that. It just proves you're an optimist, because you think people actually want to see the truth."

"They ... don't?" said the black-haired girl hesitantly as though she was asking the question to herself.

"Remember the concerned environmentalists who keep on telling us if we continue doing what we're doing to Earth, we'll disrupt the climate, melt the icebergs, endanger biodiversity, drain our natural resources, and ultimately destroy ourselves along with all the other remaining species on this planet, hoping that by educating people on the truth, they would want to see the cruel reality we're facing and therefore take actions upon it to curb and reverse the damages caused by the human footprint?"

"They are being optimistic?"

"Yes, they are. Because you simply can't make people want to see the truth unless they want to see it themselves. Do you know the story about Falsehood stealing Truth's clothes when she was taking a bath? When Truth found out her clothes were gone, instead of choosing to wear someone else's clothes, she decided to not wear anything."

"Yes." The black-haired girl nodded stiffly. "I've heard it. That's where the expression 'naked truth' came from."

"Good." Mira nodded back. "Then you know just like having a naked stranger standing right in front of you, a naked truth can be uncomfortable, overwhelming, unsettling, and even scary. That's why people's survival instinct would rather turn a blind eye to the truths that are bound to become mental tortures to their owners.

After all, self-deception is the greatest built-in defense mechanism that people have to help themselves live happier and, therefore, longer."

The black-haired girl's eyes widened in shock and fear. She opened her mouth as though she was trying to remember what to say, but there was no sound.

It dawned on Mira then that she might have said too much and scared the black-haired girl with her words instead. She was not ready for their conversation to come to an end yet, but since she had never had a conversation like this before with anyone else except her parents, she didn't know what she could do to undo the damage caused by her own words either.

"That was my opinion," she finally said. "My opinion doesn't equal to the truth, of course."

The black-haired girl relaxed in her seat with her eyes glazed over. "I . . . I never thought of it that way before. What you said sounds so . . . hopeless and depressing . . . But the ironic thing is, even though I want to reject it, I know it makes sense, and yet, I can't quite bring myself to accept it." She shook her head and let out a soft sigh. "You're right. It does feel uncomfortable, overwhelming, unsettling . . . and scary."

Despite the honesty in her response, the air between them remained heavy. Mira decided it was time for her to be honest with the girl as well.

"Sorry. I'm not good at keeping conversations lighthearted. Or, for that matter, talking to people."

The black-haired girl raised her head in surprise, then a shy smile appeared on her face. "Actually, I'm not good at talking to people either, especially here . . . you know, being a foreigner and all." She paused and shifted uncomfortably in her seat, then she added, "It was nice talking to you, though. You're . . . different."

Mira glanced up at the girl to see if she was just being polite, but her smile quickly persuaded Mira otherwise.

"I'm Lilith, by the way." The black-haired girl held out a hand. "What's your name?"

Mira hesitated but took Lilith's hand and shook it, swiftly and awkwardly. Lilith's hand was cool and soothing. It reminded Mira of Mom's hands.

"Mira," she answered distractedly.

"Mira ..." Lilith repeated. "If I remember correctly, that's the name of an ancient goddess."

"I'm sure that was not what my parents had in mind when they named me," Mira said quickly. "What about you? Why did your parents name you Lilith?"

"Oh, my parents have nothing to do with that." Lilith's smile grew wry. "I was born in China, so my parents only gave me a Chinese name. When I started first grade, they came to this country for some jobs and left me in China with my grandma. About a year ago, they relocated me here from China, and we've been moving from city to city since. Anyway, long story short, they registered me at my first school here with my Chinese name, but my teachers and classmates all had a hard time pronouncing it, so eventually, I just told everyone to call me Lilith instead."

Mira digested the resigned look on Lilith's face and the sorrowful tone in her voice, then she asked, "Why *Lilith*?"

Lilith inhaled sharply and gazed up at the ceiling. "I'm not sure why, actually. I guess ... I guess part of me was angry about moving here and wished I could be as strong-minded as Lilith to leave the Garden of Eden to become her own boss?"

"That's unusual," said Mira. "Most people see her as demonic and rebellious, not strong-minded."

"I think that's because most people do not care to know what it feels like to be in her shoes." Lilith chuckled bitterly. "It's like what you said about truth. People won't see it unless they want to see it themselves, right?"

Mira didn't reply. She could see the pain and hurt behind Lilith's wry smile, and it was enough for her to deduce the rest.

"You're not happy here."

"I think you're right," Lilith replied softly. "But then, I guess I've never been truly happy, no matter where I am ... Maybe I'll never be able to leave my Garden of Eden." She gave a dry laugh, looking vacant and lost.

Silence enveloped them in the waning sunlight. On the other side of the windows, the sun was sinking lower, dragging the sunbeams away reluctantly.

"It's getting late," Mira finally said, rising to her feet. "I need to go home."

"Oh. Okay. Sure, I understand." Lilith got up as well. "Nice meeting you, Mira. I don't need to go home—I mean, my parents are rarely home, so I . . . I don't need to go home . . . yeah."

Mira looked at Lilith but quickly lowered her eyes, which then fell on the red book between them.

"In that case, do you want to take a walk with me?" she found herself asking. "You can tell me what happened to *Nian* in the prevalent version of the story."

"M-me?" Lilith's face lit up. "O-of course! . . . I'd love to!"

V

"What a gorgeous day!" Lilith exclaimed. She set her cup down on the table, then she pulled out a chair and sat down beside Mira. "Look at the trees! The colors are so pretty!"

Mira followed Lilith's gaze and looked toward the center of the pedestrian square. The leaves on the trees had changed into their fall colors, decorating the square with splashes of yellow, orange, and red. Under the gentle touch of the midmorning sun, it looked as if the trees were taken out of a pastel painting.

Mira raised her cup of apple cider to her lips, but before she could take a sip, Lilith exclaimed again.

"Autumn is beautiful here! Especially with the smell of apple cider and pumpkin spice in the air! It's so . . . peaceful and relaxing! It's perfect!"

Mira lowered her cup and glanced at Lilith. "Is everything all right? Or did you have too much sugar?"

Lilith laughed. "That bad, eh?" she said, tittering. "I'm sorry. I tend to get very sentimental before my birthday. Don't ask me why. It's like this every year. I don't even know why. Maybe it has something to do with the growth hormone."

"Oh?" Mira raised an eyebrow. "When is your birthday?"

"Tomorrow," said Lilith, resignedly.

"Not excited?"

"Nope." Lilith shook her head decisively. "There's nothing to be excited about anyway. Think about it: every birthday you have is like a public announcement declaring that you've aged one more year, which basically tells the world you're officially one step closer to the end. So I really don't understand why the other kids at school are so excited about their birthdays. They spend all that time and money on birthday parties every year, and each year has a different theme. For what? To celebrate one less year to live? . . . Anyway, I don't get it. I think birthdays are overrated."

"That doesn't sound like you, Lilith." Mira felt a smirk forming on her lips. "What happened to Miss Positive, Miss I-believe-there's-a-purpose-to-everything? I remember she told me on multiple occasions that my worldview was too cynical for my own good. I can't imagine what she would say if she heard you."

Lilith rolled her eyes. "You're gloating, aren't you?"

"I am." Mira gave her a meaningful nod. "Now are you going to tell me what's really bothering you?"

Lilith gaped, then she suddenly held her forehead with both hands in a dramatic yet comical fashion, appearing to be shielding it from something invisible.

"Be honest now, Mira! You can read minds, can't you?"

Mira snorted under her breath. "Not that I know of."

Lilith narrowed her eyes, but she let go of her forehead. "You must have some kind of superpower; otherwise how can you always tell something's going on in my head?"

Mira chuckled quietly to herself and gave Lilith a shrug. "In that case, you might as well tell me everything."

"Fine," Lilith said grudgingly. "I hate my birthday. It makes me sad."

"Why is that?"

"It's . . . it's just another day, same as the day before. Aside from my body's biological clock ticking away, on the surface, nothing's changed and nothing's different. The sun still rises and sets. Earth still spins and tilts. The tides still rise and fall . . ."

"You miss your parents," Mira observed.

Lilith pressed her lips together into a thin line, then she took a deep breath and said, "Maybe. I always thought there was a void in my heart because they weren't there most of the time, but now . . . I'm not so sure anymore. I think I've grown used to them not being around . . . Actually, even if they did show up tomorrow for my birthday, I probably wouldn't know how to deal with it."

She let out a bitter laugh; her eyes grew dim. "Well, now that I've finally put those feelings into words, I think they sound pretty pathetic."

Mira thought of her own birthday. She thought of how Mom always regarded it as the most important celebration of the year, planning and preparing for it months in advance, year after year.

The thought jogged her memory. Mira remembered her fifteenth birthday: the snowy white bird-shaped cake, the velvet red blood droplets that had stained the bird's chest . . . the conversation between Mom and Dad that she had overheard in the backyard, which she immediately shied away from even though she knew it was too late to fool herself.

Mira felt her mind fogging up. She forced her attention back to Lilith.

"Your feelings about your life are your truths," she said. "It doesn't matter how they sound." She paused, pushed back the memories that were trying to bubble up in her mind, and added casually, "It takes courage to face your own truths. Not everyone is brave enough to do that."

Lilith tilted her head to one side. "Wait a minute . . . Are you trying to cheer me up?"

"Of course not. I was only stating my opinion."

"That's what I thought." A faint smile appeared on Lilith's lips. "What about you, then? What do you think about birthdays?"

"Not much. Just a change in the numbers. After a while, you won't even remember which number you are on. So don't worry about your birthday phobia. It'll be gone in another year or two."

"Blimey!" Lilith screwed up her face as if she had swallowed a fly. "Forget what *I* said. *That* was the undisputable winner of the Gloomy Award!"

"Life itself *is* gloomy." Mira shrugged. "Think about it: no matter if you're a plant, an animal, or a person, as soon as you're born into this world, you're heading toward death already. It's the inevitable fate of every living thing on Earth; it's just a matter of time."

"*Memento mori*," Lilith said softly.

Mira nodded. "That's right. But the more interesting question here is: If the inevitable fate of every living thing on Earth is death, what's the purpose of life? Does it matter what we do on our birthdays? Does it matter what we do or not do on any given day? Does it matter what we do to others? Does it matter what others do to us? Does it matter how we feel, how we make others feel, or how others make us feel?

"Think about it: at the end of the day, we all meet the same fate, regardless of who we were or how we lived—a king or a scoundrel, a tyrant or a philanthropist, a psychopath or a saint, a billionaire or a street rat. When the time comes, we die and decompose all the same. And when that happens, everything that used to matter to us will consequently become meaningless. So if death is inevitable, what is the purpose of life?"

"Ah, the ultimate question, as elusive as the purpose of mankind's existence in this world." Lilith chuckled wryly as she shook her head. "You really are not good at keeping conversations light-hearted, Mira."

"Thanks for the compliment. I'm more interested in your thoughts on this topic, though. Care to share?"

"Well . . ." said Lilith, looking up at the sky. "So many philosophers had asked the same question and given their own opinions on that very topic. But in the end, they're just opinions, not truths . . ."

She held out a hand and pointed at a big piece of cumulus cloud above their heads. "See that piece of cloud there that looks like a cauliflower? I used to think immortals would ride clouds like that to oversee us mortals and to make sure we were living in harmony with the other creatures on Earth. And if we failed to keep the scale balanced, they'd report it to the Heavenly Court, and we'd be punished with extreme weather events and natural disasters. I know it may sound silly, but even now, whenever I see a piece of cloud like that, it still makes me wonder if it could be true.

"Yes, there's no hard evidence to prove there *are* immortals. But what if they do exist? What if they just don't want to leave any clue for the mortals to find out about them, considering so many power-obsessed men had sought high and low, far and wide, for ways to become immortals themselves so that they could rule forever like gods?

" 'Absence of evidence is not evidence of absence.'[2] So, was it just another opinion about our existence on Earth, or could it be the truth? I guess like a great many things in life, including the answer to your question, I'll probably never figure it out."

Mira gazed at the piece of cloud Lilith had pointed to and said, "But if you could, would you want to know the truth about life? About existence?"

"Hmm ..." Lilith screwed up her lips. "I think I would. You would too, right? Although ... it *is* possible that the truth may turn out to be so mind-bogglingly topsy-turvy that we'd end up thinking *we* are the ones who have completely lost our minds. You know what they say: *ignorance is bliss.*"

"You know what I say?" Mira replied, straight-faced. "Self-deception at its finest."

"Hang on ..." Lilith's head swiveled to Mira. "Were you being cynical or was that a joke?"

"Does it matter?"

Lilith opened her mouth, looking incredulous yet pleased at the same time. "I can't believe it! You just made a joke!"

Mira gave Lilith a quick glance from the corner of her eye. "Well, well, well. Who's being cynical now?"

"Hey, no need to be so smug about it," said Lilith, smirking. "Don't forget I'm friends with you—*birds of a feather flock together.*"

Mira tilted her head and said deliberately, "You don't say."

Lilith laughed and held up her cup. "To friendship."

Mira raised hers. "To cynical jokes."

"And to the truth of life," Lilith intoned, "which we may never figure out in this life."

---

[2] This quote is often attributed to Carl Sagan (1934–1996), an American astronomer and science communicator, who was best known for his research on the possibility of extraterrestrial life.

"The truth of life," Mira repeated and took a sip of her apple cider. "Tell me about your opinion, then. Why do we exist? What's the purpose of our lives?"

Lilith swallowed her drink and licked her lips. "Honestly, I think our existence may have been pure luck, or even a mistake, considering how much destructions and chaos we've brought to this world, not to mention we often do more harm than good to the balance of the orders of nature."

"Hmm. You made it sound like humans are not part of the orders of nature," Mira observed.

"We are not." Lilith's face grew serious. "Think about it, Mira: Unlike the other animals on Earth, humans do not have a predator. As a result, we continue to breed and reproduce our species at will, without limitation or control. Is that natural in the orders of nature? And now, thanks to modern medical discoveries and achievements and technologies, we have a much higher birth rate and a much lower mortality rate. The result? The growth of global population has been exponential. There are more and more of us, and more and more of us are living longer and longer, consuming more and more water, food, energy, and other natural resources while creating more and more trash, waste, and pollution. As we continue to expand our farmlands, residential areas, industrial parks, commercial properties for living *our* lives and providing for *ourselves*, we're forcing more and more species into extinction every single day. I'm telling you, to Earth, we're just like cancer cells: disruptive, invasive, and out of control. We're growing our numbers and replicating our irresponsible behaviors around the clock, with nothing to curb our growth and nothing to cure us for Earth —well, nothing except a mass extinction triggered by some kind of catastrophic event on a global scale, I guess."

Mira looked up at the sky. The piece of cloud they had gazed at earlier had changed in shape and size, and it was floating slowly away from them.

"Let's say if there *are* immortals, and they are indeed watching us from behind the clouds, do you think they will suggest that to the Heavenly Court?" Mira asked.

"Suggest what?"

"To get rid of us with a catastrophic event on a global scale."

"If they've been watching us, they probably already did," Lilith answered casually.

Mira turned to Lilith but did not look her in the eye. "So, you think the end is coming for us soon?"

"Not really." Lilith flashed her a smile. "You're talking to Miss Positive, remember? And Miss Positive thinks the Heavenly Court is way too humane to eliminate humankind at the cost of eliminating everything else on Earth."

"But everything else on Earth *is* being eliminated," Mira countered. "By humankind."

"I know. That's why I think the Heavenly Court is counting on humankind to wipe themselves out before they could take everything else down with them."

"Why would they count on that?"

"Because they know humans are flawed and easily corrupted," said Lilith. "We were given a rich array of emotions and desires, but we were not given control. Remember the story of Pandora's box? It's not only a classic story that depicts the innate weaknesses of human psychology, but also an insightful fable that explains why we live in a world with so much suffering and misery. Now, did Pandora really release all that from a box? I think not. I think it's never about the box, nor what was inside the box. It's about us: how our emotions and desires drive us to do things without control. That's pretty much what led us to the situation here today, and I think that's exactly what the Heavenly Court is counting on to lead humankind all the way to self-destruction."

"So much for a positive ending," Mira said meaningfully.

Lilith laughed and gestured with her hands. "It's all about perspectives, my friend! You won't be able to perceive light unless there's darkness, and likewise, you won't be able to perceive darkness unless there's light.

"We think we're in control because we can make conscious choices. We think we can make conscious choices because we're intelligent animals. But are we truly intelligent, or are we fooling ourselves by comparing our IQ scores to the IQ scores of monkeys? Are we truly capable of making conscious choices, or are we being manipulated by our own emotions and desires even before we can decide on one?

"We think we know our planet, our galaxy, and its surrounding space. But to the gods and goddesses, the immortals, the mythical beings, the extraterrestrial intelligence, and whatnot, humankind might just be as ignorant as a moth to the flame. So despite how pernicious we are to the other species on Earth, we could very well be the most idiotic existence they've ever witnessed, in which case, they'll have no trouble foreseeing that in the end, we *will* be the death of ourselves."

"That's quite some opinion," said Mira, sounding genuinely amazed. "It's unusual, unconventional ... and even a bit unhuman, I must say. If I hadn't known you already, I'd have thought you were one of those immortals who had given up the treacherous life of monitoring the idiotic humans around the globe on a highly unstable ride in the sky for a more, let's see ... down-to-earth approach."

Lilith chortled lightheartedly and said, "You flatter me, Mira. But I think most people will describe it as antisocial instead."

"I doubt the immortals would concern themselves with the worldly opinions of 'most people,' considering they're too self-absorbed to seek and see the truths, so neither should you," Mira said matter-of-factly. "I was wondering, though: If you think humankind's existence may have been pure luck or even a mistake, what's the purpose of our lives, then?"

"That's the crazy part." Lilith smiled pensively. "I think the purpose of our lives is exactly the same as the purpose of luck and mistakes—to experience."

An inscrutable expression appeared on Lilith's face as she continued. "We're born into this world without any possessions, and we'll die from this world without any possessions either, be it titles, cars, properties, wealth, influence, or power, let alone our relationships with our pets, children, life partners, family members, friends, or enemies. In other words, by the time we die, the only thing we have truly gained and taken away from life is the memories that are stored in our brains. Not the short-term ones, long-term memories, formed by experiences that were associated with intense emotions, no matter if the emotions were positive or negative. These memories are stored in your brain because they're your most important experiences in life, thereby the most important moments of your life for you to carry around in your brain till the end so that during the final moment of your life in this world, you can refer back to them and remember what made you who you were and what decided how you lived your life the way you did, and you would then, and probably only then, understand what had been the purpose of your life."

Quietly, Mira turned her head to the center of the pedestrian square. Her heart felt heavy, but the fog in her head was finally lifting.

"A profound perspective," she said slowly, still savoring what Lilith had said. "It sounds almost like you've experienced it yourself, like you *know* what will happen at the final moment."

"What can I say?" Lilith made an embarrassed face and let out a resigned chuckle. "I'm old at heart. Don't judge me."

"Maybe you *are* an immortal after all," Mira said, an amused smile on her lips. "And you're trapped inside a mortal's body, with thousands and thousands of years of life experiences trapped inside your subconscious as well."

"Imagine that!" said Lilith, chortling, though her face was somewhat melancholy. "Well, as much as I wish you were right, I'm afraid it's only a side effect of my childhood insecurity. Remember I told you my parents weren't around most of the time when I was little? I didn't understand much then, but I remember feeling lonely, constantly, and it made me sad and afraid. I thought if I could be independent enough to take care of myself, then I would no longer feel like that. That was why I wanted to grow up as quickly as possible so I could be self-sufficient in life. I guess from then on, I pretty much willed my brain into overcompensating for the lack of my biological maturity by jacking up growth in my mental maturity, and it's probably still doing it. So here I am: a fifty-year-old mind trapped inside a fifteen-year-old body."

"A sixteen-year-old body." Mira corrected her calmly. "Don't forget your birthday is tomorrow. You need to round it up."

Lilith buried her face in her hand and made a whimpering sound. "Seriously? You might as well round me up to twenty!"

"Not happy about the bigger number, I see," said Mira, who was looking increasingly smug to Lilith. "Age is an illusion, Lilith. Think about the evil beings in *Strange Tales from a Chinese Studio*: they were thousands of years in age, yet when they took on human form, they could still fool everyone. So don't sweat about your physical age. It's an illusion to the eye. It's what's inside you that counts."

"Why, thanks," said Lilith as she rolled her eyes. "Now I sound like a thousand-year-old *Yāojīng*."

"Yao-jin?"

"*Yāojīng*. That's the Chinese word for evil beings, especially those who can take on human form."

"*Yāo-jīng*," Mira said slowly, copying Lilith's intonation. "So what's so bad about sounding like a . . . *Yāo-jīng*? According to the stories in the book, they had very enchanting looks when they took on human form, so enchanting that the affected humans were willing to do their bidding."

"Did you forget the part where the *Yāojīng* drank their blood and ate their flesh after the affected humans had carried out their bidding?"

"A *Yāojīng*'s gotta make a living too," Mira replied in a deadpan voice. "Plus, according to the stories, they picked their prey. So instead of going into a full-on slaughter mode at nearby villages for food, they mainly went for men who had a weakness for beautiful women. Personally, I think they were doing the rest of the world a favor by limiting their targets to people who tended to judge others entirely by their looks."

A flock of pigeons landed not too far away from their table. They strutted about haughtily, making impatient coos as they scanned the ground.

Lilith gazed vacantly at the busy birds, looking deep in thought. The pigeons ignored her and carried on with their search. They soon discovered a half-eaten donut that was dropped by an earlier patron at another table. The flock swarmed to it and pecked away, enthusiastically, appearing to be happy and fulfilled.

It was, no doubt, a very enjoyable moment in their simple lives. Unfortunately, it didn't last very long. Before the pigeons could work through the crust, a murder of crows had descended upon them, interrupting the pigeons' peaceful brunch with their ominous presence and hoarse caws that were harsh enough to scratch the sky. Naturally, the unannounced arrival of the ill-mannered crows was not received well enough by the pigeons to share their love for fine dining, for at the sight of those fluttering pitch-black wings, the pigeons fled like startled aristocrats in heels and dispersed in different directions as quickly as their legs would carry them.

Lilith was still gazing blankly ahead when she suddenly asked, "Mira, do I look evil?"

Mira cocked an eyebrow and turned her attention away from the crows. "What sort of question is that?"

Sensing the inquisitive stare from Mira, Lilith lowered her head. "They're talking about me at school . . . about my looks . . ."

"Okay." Mira straightened up. "What do they say?"

Lilith sighed softly through her nose and said quietly, "They say I look like a crow."

"What?"

"They say I look like a crow," Lilith repeated, louder, thinking Mira didn't hear her clearly the first time. "An evil one too. Apparently, according to them, I fit the profile."

"What profile?"

"The profile for demons and demon helpers." Even though Lilith's hands were clenched into fists, her voice was surprisingly calm. "First of all, my name is Lilith. Second, I have pitch-black hair and I always wear pitch-black clothes. Third, my eyes are small and slanted and evil-looking. Fourth, I don't pray and I don't go to church. And last ... I'm not from here; I just appeared in this town one day and nobody knows where I really came from ..."

A jolting pain hit Mira in the left side of her chest, but she didn't flinch—her focus was on Lilith, and she did not like what she saw on Lilith's face.

"They say I can curse people," Lilith continued tonelessly. "They warn each other to stay away from me."

Though Lilith didn't add anything else after that, Mira couldn't help but think it had something to do with how often they were seen together since they had met at the school library a month ago.

"It's because of me," Mira said slowly, feeling the weight of every word that she uttered. "Because you're friends with me."

"No, it's not." Lilith rejected her idea right away. "This has nothing to do with you, Mira."

There were so many suppressed emotions rippling on Lilith's face that Mira wished she could say something to ease her pain or simply pick the whole thing out of her mind and erase it for good. But she couldn't; she didn't know how. Her inability to lift Lilith's spirits bothered her, and she was surprised to notice how strangely irritated she was with herself.

"It's merely their opinion, Lilith," Mira said in the end, "and their opinion does not equal to the truth."

Lilith was staring off into space. When she heard Mira, she chuckled softly, though her smile was faintly melancholy. "Thanks, Mira. I knew I could always count on you ... even when the rest of the world is cold and unaccepting."

A gust of autumn wind danced past their table, dragging a tail of fallen leaves behind it playfully. The nearby trees swayed with the wind and shook off some more leaves, sending slices of red and gold drifting aimlessly in the air before they finally answered the call of gravity and landed lightly on the ground.

Mira sensed an involuntary shiver from Lilith. Just then, something red dropped down from the sky and landed on their table as if it had materialized out of thin air. The sudden movement caused Lilith to jump in her chair. Before Mira could react, Lilith let out a gasp in wonder.

There was a red bird on their table. Its plumage was so glossy and its color was so bright that it almost stung their eyes to look at it in the sunlight. To their amazement, when the bird sensed their attention, instead of flying away in panic, it tilted its head and blinked at them quizzically with its beady black eyes.

"What kind of bird is this?" Lilith whispered to Mira. "It's beautiful! I don't think I've seen one like this before."

The bird seemed to have understood her words. It tilted its head to the opposite side, then it blinked and took a few hops toward Lilith, appearing to be encouraging her to admire it some more.

"Hey, little birdie," Lilith cooed, smiling broadly. "Do you like me? You're so pretty. I wish you could tell me your name."

The bird blinked at her but made no reply, then it tilted its head to look at Mira—no, not look, stare. Its beady black eyes were fixed on Mira's eyes, and its body was so still that it seemed to have been frozen in time by a magic spell.

"Is it okay?" Lilith whispered nervously. "Why is it so still?"

"Not sure," said Mira, returning the stare into those beady black eyes. She was used to being studied intently by animals, but there was something different about this bird, about its poise, and the way it stared at her . . .

Slowly, Mira leaned forward, extending a hand until the knuckle of her index finger was within an inch of the red bird's belly.

"Mira, no!" Lilith squeaked like a terrified mouse. "What are you doing? It may peck you!"

"We'll see . . ." Mira murmured as her finger touched the base of the bird's belly.

Lilith covered her mouth with both hands and gave a soft cry. To her astonishment, the bird did not peck Mira. Instead, it looked down at her hand, inspected it, and stepped onto her index finger.

Lilith dropped her hands and gawked, dumbfounded and incredulous. Carefully, Mira raised her hand and held it in front of her face. The red bird was still standing calmly on her index finger like a well-trained falcon. There was no sign of either the intention of taking flight or of picking a fight. In fact, the bird seemed to enjoy perching on Mira's finger, and it was so relaxed and comfortable there that it was having a hard time keeping its eyelids from closing.

Lilith closed her mouth and stared incredulously at the sleepy bird on Mira's finger. "How ... how did you do that?"

"I don't know ..." said Mira as the red bird gave in to drowsiness and closed its eyes.

Carefully, Mira raised her hand a little and peeked under the bird's belly. "Oh, look: it's standing on one leg now." She pointed at the other leg for Lilith to see. "This one is tucked in to reduce heat loss during sleeping. It's amazing how they have adapted—"

Lilith let out a dramatic gasp. "I can't believe it."

"What?"

"I can't believe you're actually smiling!"

"Excuse me?" said Mira, knitting her brows.

Lilith snorted and started to snicker, then she said in a gleeful voice, "Oh, there it is. That's the Mira I see every day, frowning at everything—Yeah, like that."

Mira was suddenly very aware of the positions of her eyebrows. Quickly, she unknitted them, then she said to Lilith, "First of all, I don't frown at *everything* ..."

Lilith took one look at Mira and immediately began laughing breathlessly into her hands. That was when Mira realized her eyebrows were knitting again. She sighed resignedly to herself and said, "Anyway, as I was saying, I don't frown at everything, and—You're being too loud for the bird."

Still shaking with laughter, Lilith nodded apologetically and wiped away the tears that had escaped her eyes. "I'm sorry ... I'm sorry. It's just ... Your face ..." She sucked in a big gulp of air and straightened up. "Okay, my bad. I'm gonna be quiet now ...

Although ... are you going to hold that pose until it wakes up from its nap?"

"Maybe." Mira shrugged, but when she felt the red bird wobble on her finger, she aborted it mid-movement, leaving her shoulders slightly raised and frozen in an awkward position. Before she could relax them, she heard Lilith snickering behind her hands again.

Mira flashed Lilith a look for her to stop laughing, which Lilith eventually managed—after having to hold her belly and gasp for air. Mira then told Lilith she would wake the bird if she couldn't start acting normal soon. The bird, on the other hand, didn't seem to mind at all.

When Lilith had finally regained her composure, she leaned in to have a closer look at the red bird. Sensing the change in airflow brought by her movement, the bird opened one lazy eyelid, purred something incomprehensible, then it ground its beak and went back to its nap.

"Wow, it actually fell back to sleep! I thought it was going to fly away for sure!" Lilith exclaimed in a hushed voice, feeling surprised yet relieved. "Look at how cute it is! ... I think this bird really likes you, Mira. It may even want to go home with you."

"Like a pet?"

"No," said Lilith, chuckling. "Like a friend. Haven't you realized in the past ten minutes or so, you've been treating this bird nicer than any other people at school? Maybe it's enchanted. Or, maybe, it's the universe's way of saying your facial muscles need more exercise in smiling, and you don't need to be frowning all the time. Either way, this bird has brought out a different side of you."

"A different side of me?" Mira asked without realizing she was frowning again.

Lilith had to tuck her lips in between her teeth to keep herself from snickering. "That's right, a different side of you." She cleared her throat deliberately and continued, suppressing the urge to be smug about what she was going to say next. "A side without that constant frown between your eyebrows and those daggers in your eyes; a side which even the fools can see the gentleness and compassion hidden beneath your ice-cold exterior."

"Uh-huh," Mira said through her nose, sounding as though she was only humoring her friend.

"Don't 'uh-huh' me," said Lilith, rolling her eyes. "I'm serious, Mira. Don't you remember the first time we met? At the school library? I was terrified! You had this . . . this energy, emitting from you, surrounding you . . . I felt like you could strangle me with your eyes!"

"Lilith, I—"

"I know you weren't doing it on purpose to scare me off, but that's probably why nobody dares to talk to you at school. If you could treat the fellow humankind like how you treat this little bird here, then . . ."

Mira raised an eyebrow. "Then what?"

Lilith was suddenly very self-conscious. Her heart rate went up, and her hands began to sweat. She felt the need to breathe through her mouth, but it only made the tightness and dryness in her throat even more noticeable. She swallowed hard and forced herself to finish her sentence. "Then . . . then they would see how gentle and kind you really are."

Mira was getting ready for a cynical comeback, but now she felt her cheeks heating up like the cover on a boiling pot. It was a very strange feeling, so strange that she had to turn her head away to try recalling what she was going to say. Unfortunately, the words had disappeared from her mind like water that had evaporated into steam, and all she could manage to say was: "That was, uh . . . that was not necessary, Lilith."

"What was not necessary?"

Mira sighed inwardly and turned her head back to Lilith. "Never mind. All you need to know is I'm not concerned about how other people think about me or whether they want to talk to me. For me, it doesn't matter."

"You mean . . . you don't care?" Lilith asked hesitantly. "Even if you might have more friends?"

"Lilith, life is made up of time, and time is limited. It never stops for anyone, and you never get to make up what you've lost or wasted. I want to spend my time on things that matter, with people who truly understand me."

"Did you . . ." said Lilith, grinning so eagerly that it bordered on gloating. "Did you just refer to me as someone who truly understands you?"

"I—That's not what I said."

Lilith chortled with delight. "Don't worry, Mira. Your secret is safe with me. They think I can curse people, remember? No one will know. I promise." She gave Mira a wink. "Say, who else is in that category?"

Mira was caught off guard by her question. She lowered her eyes and repeated it to herself, only to have two faces appeared in her mind: the faces of Mom and Dad. They smiled at her, warmly and lovingly, then they turned and sat down on a bench, leaning against each other. There was a birdbath in front of the bench, which looked just like the one they had in their backyard. Mira held out a hand to reach for her parents, but somehow, the bench was carrying them farther and farther away from her. Still, she heard the conversation between Mom and Dad clearly—it was the same conversation she had overheard between them in their backyard, on the night of her fifteenth birthday.

It became clear to Mira then that there was no going back: she had stumbled upon a box that was forged with fifteen years of lies, and no matter how much she wished she could ignore it, forget about it, or bury it, the truth in that box would always be there, waiting.

A chill ran down her spine and spread to her limbs. Mira felt as though she could sense the coolness of the earth lying beneath the brick tiles under her feet—a coolness made up of darkness, silence, and decay.

Slowly, she pushed her chair back and rose to her feet. The red bird kept its balance on her finger and did not open its eyes.

Lilith looked up in surprise. "Where are you going?"

"Home," said Mira, noticing for the first time the strangeness in what this word had once meant to her as it left her mouth. "We're going to celebrate."

"Celebrate what?"

"Your birthday," she replied. Then, with a vague sense of what she thought loss and grief probably felt like to other people, she gazed at the red bird and added pensively, "We'll celebrate it with those who truly understand."

Chapter 5 THE AWAKENING

1

TIME seemed to fly by even faster after the birthday celebration for Lilith. Before long, the trees started shedding
heavily, and by Christmas break, most trees were looking quite naked and exposed. They moped and drooped in the
crisp winter air like dried-up witches, and even though people had
dressed them up with Christmas decorations and colorful lights,
it couldn't stop them from shivering at the greeting of every cold
winter blast.

Their misery was not enough to stop the joyful Christmas spirit
from spreading in Starfall, however, especially at the pedestrian
square, which was flooded with Christmas elements: on the trees,
on the shrubberies, on the benches, on the streetlights, on the
windows, inside the window displays … Countless strands of
Christmas lights lit up the entire pedestrian square like a massive
stage; the numerous Christmas decorations were the props, and
the never-ending Christmas songs were the theater music for its
live performance.

The restaurants and shops there were getting busier by the day
too. As Christmas Eve neared, more and more people poured into
the square to spend money. Most came in groups, some with
friends and some with families. They strolled around the square
together, visiting one shop after another, hunting for the perfect
Christmas presents for the important people in their lives while
picking out random items to wrap up for the not-so-important

ones. The sweet and enticing smells of holiday drinks and treats drifted from the cafés and bakeries and candy stores into the crowds, turning the crisp winter air into sugar for their lungs. There was no mistake about it, Christmas was in the air, literally.

Mira was waiting for Lilith at the fountain, which was at the center of the pedestrian square, away from the shopping crowds. She had been pacing around the fountain in circles for the past fifteen minutes to stay warm, during which she couldn't help noticing how many more Christmas decorations were added to the fountain since the last time she was there. To begin with, Christmas garlands and big red bows were added to dress up the outer base of the fountain. Also, more Christmas lights were used to surround the bottom half of the archangel's statue in the middle. The colorful lights were arranged in such a fashion that they cascaded like rainbow waterfalls from the necks of the demons and beasts that were crushed beneath the archangel's feet. As a result, the polished faces of those demons and beasts reflected theatrical colors from the Christmas lights, rendering the entire statue as ghastly as an advertising display at the entrance of a haunted house. The effect was the opposite of jolliness, to say the least. Mira thought the archangel did not look very pleased.

"Mira!" Lilith called, puffing out white clouds as she trotted toward her friend. "Sorry I'm late!"

At the sound of her voice, Mira turned around, rubbing her hands together for warmth. "And I'm sorry I haven't turned into an ice sculpture yet. What took you so long?"

Lilith laughed and handed Mira a red paper cup. "This. I went to get us some hot cocoa. The place was packed!"

"And you still went in?" said Mira, pressing the cup to her cold cheek.

"Because I'm brave!" Lilith replied, chuckling. "And I knew you'd need one. Anyway, they're offering a new holiday special flavor, so I ordered that. It's called Christmas Delight. I hope you like it."

"Hmm." Mira knitted her brow as she peered through the sipping hole on her cup. "As long as they didn't spice it up with things that are not supposed to go in there."

"Like what?"

"Who knows? Santa's beard? Rudolph's nose? Half an elf? With all the fancy names they're using these days, you simply can't tell what the ingredients are anymore."

Lilith snorted and burst into a guffaw.

Mira cocked an eyebrow at her. "I see that you're feeling the Christmas delight already. Did you take a sip? I wonder what they put in yours. Hmm ... jolly old Santa's spirit, by the looks of it."

This sent Lilith into another roar of laughter. She waved desperately at Mira as she tried to balance the cup in the other hand, gesturing for her to stop.

Mira snickered contentedly to herself and took a sip of the Christmas Delight, only to find out it was merely peppermint hot chocolate with a hint of gingerbread spice. She lowered the cup and knitted her brows.

"So, are you going to tell me why I had to get permission from my parents to stay out late tonight?" she asked.

"Oh, yes. About that ..." said Lilith, catching her breath. "You know, tomorrow is Christmas Eve." She gave Mira a deliberate grin then continued in a pleading voice, "I know it's not your favorite thing to do—you told me that already, but I'd *really* appreciate it if you could help me to ..."

"To what?"

Lilith tittered nervously. "Pick out some Christmas presents for your parents."

Mira thought she heard a ringing sound in her ears, as if Lilith's words had shot out from her mouth like bullets from a machine gun. She clutched her cup of Christmas Delight and groaned inwardly.

"Now, now, no need to look so miserable," said Lilith, trying hard to contain her amusement in the situation. "Come on, show me some holiday spirit! It's Christmas! It's supposed to be the most wonderful time of the year!"

"Ho, ho, help," Mira answered dryly.

"You're hopeless." Lilith shook her head with a resigned chuckle. "Never mind the holiday spirit, then. Just help me out with the presents, please? Your parents have been so nice and kind to me. I mean, that awesome birthday party your mom threw for me even though you only told her about it the day before my birthday? Even though they just met me? ... Please, Mira? I know Christmas in this country is as significant as Lunar New Year in China, so I *really* need your help to pick out some suitable presents for them. I want to let them know how grateful I am for what they did for me. It was so nice to—"

Mira glanced at Lilith, saw the change in her face, and looked away.

"It was so nice to have someone there, acknowledging and celebrating my existence on my birthday," said Lilith, choking up. "Even though they're not my parents, they went out of their way to make sure I enjoyed my birthday. It made me feel so ... real, so present, so ... existential, if that makes any sense."

"I get it." Mira tapped on her forehead. "I can read your mind, remember?"

Lilith broke into a smile and wiped away her tears.

"I don't understand why you need to get them Christmas presents though," Mira added. "You already thanked them profusely for the birthday party."

"From where I come from, we're taught to be grateful at a very young age," Lilith said solemnly. "We're taught to be grateful for food, clothing, shelter, education, social stability, welfare, and, most importantly, relationships. Chinese people value good relationships very much, and we honor the most meaningful ones by showing up with presents on important festivals and holidays, just like how we used to honor the gods with offerings. So, it's pretty much our culture to honor the relationships that matter to us with presents on special occasions. It's also considered as a great virtue for us to honor the most valued relationships with whatever is in our power to give. As a matter of fact, if I don't bring any appropriate presents to your parents for Christmas, it'll be *wrong*. My ancestors would be so ashamed of me that they would roll over in their graves! Do you understand why you must help me now?"

Mira closed her eyes and sighed heavily to herself, then she opened them and said in a resigned voice, "Fine."

Lilith's face lit up with a big smile. She wrapped her arms around Mira and squeezed her tightly. "Oh, thank you, thank you, Mira! You're my savior!"

Lilith's hug made Mira let out a short grunt in surprise, but she said, "All right, that's enough. Let's get it over with. I need to be back before midnight. This better not take us all night."

Lilith laughed and let go of Mira. "Aye, aye, Cinderella. Let's start ... from that boutique store next to the coffee house first. They seem to have some nice selections. Maybe we'll find something there for your mom."

"I can't believe I'm doing this," Mira grumbled as Lilith pulled her forward. "I'm becoming one of them."

Lilith glanced back with an amused smile. "One of whom?"

"The *Christmas bees*." Mira pointed at the crowd of shoppers navigating the heavy pedestrian traffic on the same side of the square they were heading toward. "They buzz around the square like busy bees, visiting one shop after another for Christmas presents. Look, they squeeze their way into one, they squeeze their way out with something extra in their hands, then they squeeze their way into the next one, just like bees collecting nectar from one flower after another, except they all look way more compulsive than the hard-working bees."

As Mira was speaking, more shoppers had poured into the pedestrian traffic from the opposite direction, adding to the congestion and blocking the girls from the boutique store like a turbulent river as each shopper threaded and weaved through any temporary openings that could be seen in the crowd.

"I see what you mean," said Lilith, raising her voice to be heard over the hubbub of the crowd. "They kinda sound like bees too!"

"Don't remind me." Mira massaged her temples with a hand. "We're not going to make it out of here alive, are we?"

Lilith chortled lightheartedly and pulled Mira's hand down from her forehead. "Oh, don't be a party pooper, Mira. You're a savior! You shouldn't be intimidated by these ... *Christmas bees*! Plus, you have me, the foreigner who looks like an evil crow and is believed to have the ability to *curse* people. Here—" She hooked an arm over Mira's shoulders. "I'll protect you ... With my life, if it ever comes to that. I'll be your ... *crow on the shelf* and watch over you at all times. I'll make sure none of the *Christmas bees* would dare to come near you."

As if on cue, the flow of the pedestrian traffic suddenly slowed down, producing a winding pathway among the crowd that connected the girls to the boutique store.

"What did I tell ya?" Lilith grinned at Mira, proudly. "Now, there's a first time for everything. Shopping for Christmas presents with me tonight might not become the experience of a lifetime for you, but there's no harm in us trying. After all, the purpose of life is to experience, don't you agree?"

Mira opened her mouth to protest, but it was too late. Before she could utter another word, Lilith had zipped through the crowd of *Christmas bees* with her safely sheltered under her arm.

11

"Oh, I can't wait to wrap these up for them!" Lilith exclaimed, holding up the shopping bags as they headed back to the fountain. With Mira's help, she had picked out a set of hand-poured essential oil candles and an exquisite box of gourmet chocolates for Mira's mom, a handcrafted wooden charcuterie board with a sampling selection of artisan meats and cheese for Mira's dad, and a small stuffed animal for Mira—an orange cat with an ill-tempered frown, which she had paid for secretly when Mira was zoning out. Lilith couldn't help seeing the resemblance between the cat's expression and Mira's general expression during their shopping expedition, so she decided she had to get it for Mira as a Christmas gag gift. Besides all that, she also found something for the red bird, who seemed to have moved into Mira's backyard permanently.

"I'm glad I found this cute bird house for Red," Lilith continued. "If it's going to stay in your backyard for winter, it'll definitely need a safe place for shelter. I'm still amazed how it just decided to live in your backyard and shows up every day to visit you . . . How long has it been since Red became your friend? Almost three months now?"

Mira was exhausted. Her head was still spinning from the hubbub produced by both the people and the never-ending Christmas songs, which were being played everywhere on the square yet never managed to hit the same song at the same time. So instead of using words, she uttered a feeble grunt as an answer to Lilith's question.

Lilith lowered her shopping bags and turned to Mira with a soft chuckle. "It was not *that* bad, was it?"

"Doesn't matter," Mira answered weakly, sounding as though she was ready to lie down and close her eyes. "At least we got out alive."

The shopping bags drooped from Lilith's hands, pulling down her shoulders. She slowed to a stop.

"I'm sorry, Mira. I was hoping you'd have some fun."

Mira halted and glanced back at Lilith. "I know," she said. "Did you have fun?"

"I ... I did." Lilith nodded with a guilty face. "It was nice to shop with someone for a change. And honestly, I had a great time shopping with you—not just because of your help, but also because of your company ... He-he, I don't think you were aware of it, but you had the funniest reactions to the things I picked out for your approval ..."

Mira tried to recall what she had done to earn such a comment from Lilith, but all she could remember was staring blankly at a certain set of people and merchandise before nodding or shaking her head at the things Lilith had brought over from somewhere else inside the store for her to see.

She chuckled wryly to herself at the memory and mumbled, "Sounds like it's worth the price I paid, then."

Lilith seemed surprised at her reply. She opened her mouth and her eyes grew wide, then she relaxed both and gave Mira a bittersweet smile. "Thank you, Mira ... for being my friend."

Sensing the heat building up quickly under her cheeks, Mira lowered her head and looked away. She realized then that she wanted to say something back to Lilith, but the words were stuck in her throat, refusing to come out. Eventually, she dismissed the idea and gestured for Lilith to look up at the sky.

"It's getting late," she said. "We should probably go."

Lilith followed her lead and looked up: the sky was now as black as a backdrop for all the commotion taking place in the pedestrian square. It was a moonless and starless night, yet since the square was brightly illuminated by Christmas lights in every corner, she had lost her sense of time and failed to notice how late it already was.

"What time is it?" asked Lilith, shifting all of her shopping bags into one hand and freeing the other to dig into her coat pocket for her phone, only to remember while she was in the process of persuading Mira into smiling normally for their selfie in front of the pop-up Santa hut, she had used up its remaining battery. She had complained to Mira that if she had just followed her instruction and cooperated, they would have at least gotten one decent Christmas selfie before her phone died. But of course Mira, being Mira, responded by pointing out that she had no control over how fast Lilith's phone battery would drain in this temperature, and said she could not lend Lilith her phone to resume the task because she had forgotten hers at home—again.

Luckily for Lilith, there was a clock tower in the downtown area, which could be seen from the pedestrian square. She turned her head to the direction of the clock tower, saw the hands on the clock's face, and gasped.

"Eleven thirty? That can't be right!"

"I agree," said Mira, deliberately. "I thought we spent a whole lifetime here picking out Christmas presents."

Lilith turned her head back, chuckling. "Guess we should be glad it's only eleven thirty, then. That means we still have a little bit of time for something else before you need to head home ... something a bit more exciting for you than picking out Christmas presents, hopefully."

Mira took an involuntary step back. "Like what?"

Lilith chortled loudly and said, "Relax! I was talking about the laser light show they're gonna have here at eleven forty. We saw the posters earlier, remember?"

"Um ... No."

Lilith rolled her eyes. "Anyway, according to the posters, the show is only on tonight and tomorrow night. So I was thinking maybe we could stay here till eleven forty and watch it for like, five minutes? What do you think? You'll still be able to get home before midnight—at least before the twelfth stroke of midnight, just like Cinderella."

"Yes, just like Cinderella, because our shoes will freeze into glass slippers by then," said Mira, who was feeling the full effect of the freezing temperature now that they had stopped moving and her cheeks had stopped burning. "I think we should leave now. Once the show starts, we'll have a hard time making our way out of the crowd. Plus, it's supposed to snow around midnight tonight. In a temperature like this, it'll build up fast on the streets. Think you can walk home in this weather if they cancel the night buses due to the snow?"

Lilith bit her lip and didn't reply. Even though she was not ready for the night to end just yet, she knew Mira had a point.

Eventually, she let out a sigh. "You're right. It's better to leave now than later," she said reluctantly. "I wish we could stay past midnight."

"I'll make sure to pass that along to your fairy godmother the next time I see her," said Mira, nodding with a smirk. "Now, let's go, Cinderella. The crowds are coming in. I'll walk you to the bus stop first—now that I have some time to spare before the magic ends."

Lilith made a face, but she obeyed and followed Mira. They exited the pedestrian square from the nearest street, followed it for a few minutes, then made a right turn onto a side street, from which they would need to go through a long alley before popping out onto another side street to reach the bus stop. Unlike the pedestrian square, however, the side streets were sparsely and dimly lit. On a moonless and starless night like this, the girls could hardly see anything beyond the cone-shaped areas that hung down weakly from the few feeble streetlights on those streets.

But the situation only got worse when they walked into the alley. Though it was a spacious one, there were no streetlights, and it was adjoined by many side alleys that seemed to absorb light like hidden black holes. As a result, even though Lilith knew Mira was just a step away from her, she still felt she was separated from her friend by a world of darkness.

There was a whiff of a smoky, musky odor lingering in the alley, which didn't smell quite like cigarettes but was just as displeasing to the nose. The sounds of their footsteps synchronized and echoed in the dark alley, spreading, repeating, and compounding in front of them and behind them at the same time as if they were accompanied by an invisible crowd. Lilith couldn't help remembering an eerie tale she had read from an old compilation of Chinese folklore, in which evil mythical beings emerged from the darkness in disturbing forms on a moonless and starless night to prey on human souls.

The thought made Lilith's hair stand on end, and she was suddenly seized by an inexplicable feeling that the two of them were being watched.

Uplifting music began to play in the distance then, which was soon joined by what sounded like an impressed cheer from a very large crowd. The laser light show might have transformed the entire pedestrian square into a luminescent wonderland, but here in the alley and its side alleys, the world remained shrouded in an unforgiving darkness.

Lilith shifted the shopping bags into her right hand and reached for Mira with her left. Just then, out of the corner of her eye, she noticed a tiny dot of light that had flickered ominously from the depth of what must have been a side alley to her right.

A chill shot up Lilith's spine as fear filled her veins with adrenaline. She did not need to find out who or what was lurking in that side alley to know what she must do next.

Quick as a flash, she grabbed Mira by the arm and cried out urgently under her breath, "*Run!*" Then, with her left hand still clutching tightly onto Mira's arm, Lilith broke into a sprint, pulling Mira forward madly toward the exit as if the darkness behind them had come to life with an insatiable appetite.

III

The sudden tug from Lilith caused Mira to stumble forward. Before she knew it, her legs were moving frantically to keep up with Lilith's pace in an effort to prevent herself from falling.

Just when Mira thought she had regained enough control of her balance to ask why they were running like hunted fugitives, Lilith came to an abrupt halt. Mira felt herself being flung at her as a result of the forward momentum, but instead of dodging or countering the inevitable impact, Lilith redirected it by giving Mira a forceful shove that knocked her to the side.

Lilith's determined push caught Mira by surprise yet again, and this time, it threw her off-balance completely. She stumbled sideways, flapping her arms involuntarily as she tried to resist a fall. It was no use though. Before she could make a sound, she had landed awkwardly on the ground.

Even though she had scraped her hands in the process, the fall itself was surprisingly quiet. Mira ignored the raw pain lighting up her palms and pushed herself to a sitting position, then she blinked, hard, hoping it would somehow help her recover her sense of direction in this impenetrable darkness. It didn't work as well as she had hoped, but just then, she heard a voice in the distance:

"What do you want?"

Mira froze. It was Lilith's voice; however, it was so cold and intimidating that it sounded more like the voice of a seasoned assassin. She had never heard Lilith talk like that before, and she instinctively came to the conclusion that something was terribly wrong. Then it suddenly dawned on her that whatever it was, it was the reason why Lilith had made them run at full speed and why she had stopped abruptly to push her away.

Mira felt a familiar pain in her lower abdomen. It was swollen and raw, and it was growing into a burning heat, reaching up her torso.

She ignored the painful sensation and kept still, staring hard into the direction where she thought Lilith's voice had come from, hoping she would be able to make out Lilith's shape and the shape of the person she was talking to. She didn't have much success in either, but presently, a red dot materialized in midair in that direction, a few yards away from her. It grew bigger and brighter as it turned orange, then it shrank and fizzled quickly to a muted yellow and disappeared in the darkness, leaving behind a pungent, musky odor that was even worse than the smell of cigarette smoke.

"Ah . . . a feisty one!" said a lazy male voice from where the glowing dot had died, sounding either drunk or intoxicated. "What do *I* want, hmm . . . I guess that depends, depends on what *you* can offer me . . ."

Despite the casualness in his voice, there was not a shred of kindness in his tone—he meant what he said, but there were many ways to interpret it, and Mira didn't like any of them.

The man with the lazy voice proceeded to mutter something slyly under his breath. That was when Mira heard a few malicious laughs, joining in eagerly from that same direction.

Mira felt the pain and heat shoot up from her torso and surge into her brain, making her head swell with such a burning headache that she thought it was going to explode. She clenched her jaw and pricked up her ears, hoping to figure out how many of them were there. She listened intently to their voices and counted. Besides the man with the lazy voice, she counted three more—all males.

Now that Mira knew there were too many of them for Lilith and her to leave safely from this side of the alley, an escape plan was quickly forming in her head. It was dark enough for her to move around quietly without being noticed, so she could sneak up, find Lilith, grab her hand, and run back the way they came. They would have to run fast to lose all four men, but if they could manage to reach the side street at the opposite end of the alley, they would be able to find a place to hide from those men and make their way toward the main street, where they could call to the passing cars or pedestrians for help. Needless to say, they had only one chance to make it work, so Mira would need a good diversion to make sure she could pull Lilith away before any of the men could react.

Just as Mira was contemplating her options for an effective diversion, she heard a wolf whistle coming from the opposite side of the alley—the side that she planned to use for Lilith and her to escape. Worse still, three sets of footsteps were approaching leisurely from that direction, and the owners of those footsteps were cackling malevolently like demented hyenas.

Mira's first instinct was to knock down the three newcomers to clear a path for their escape. But she soon remembered there were still four more of them on the opposite side, blocking her and Lilith. Without a diversion for the other four men, even if she could somehow manage to single-handedly tackle all three of the newcomers, she still would not be able to reach Lilith in time to pull her away.

The footsteps were getting closer now, along with a rotten odor that smelled of old cigarettes and stale alcohol. Mira stayed low to the ground, kept still, and held her breath, hoping the darkness alone was enough to provide the cover she needed to stay hidden —that is, if she could somehow dodge out of the newcomers' way without a sound. To Mira's surprise, they all walked right past in front of her, and they only came to a stop when they were many steps away. It was then that Mira finally understood: Lilith had pushed her into a side alley to hide her from the thugs that were waiting for them in the front, and that was why the three newcomers had missed her completely.

"Now, why did ya run away, sugar?" croaked one of the newcomers. "Me and my brothas were just about to come introduce ourselves. Didn't ya hear? It's not safe for young women to walk alone at night, especially not in dark alleys, eh? Tsk, tsk ... You shoulda just stayed with us back there and saved yourself some energy."

" 'Tis right. Ain't no running anywhere, love," said another new-comer in a gloating voice. "You might think you're too smart or too special for us, but see, there are seven of us. We blocked ya off on that side and cut ya off on this side. Then boo-hoo-hoo, the little dolly is trapped! There's nowhere else to go! What should she do?"

What he said was like a hammer to the head, nailing the cold, hard reality into Mira's mind: These men had planned this. They had counted on having easy action and easy prey on a night like this, where the pedestrian traffic through the alley was greatly re-duced, thanks to the crowd-pulling laser light show at the square. Mira felt the pain and heat burning in her veins. She wished she had agreed to stay longer at the square with Lilith. She wished they were watching the laser light show among that big, noisy crowd instead.

"You want money, then?" She heard Lilith say; her voice was still cold like ice but not nearly as intimidating as it was earlier. "Here. Take my wallet and leave."

The sound of her voice gave Mira a sudden pang in her chest. She knew that as long as the laser light show was still holding the crowd, it would be unlikely anyone else would walk into the alley in the next few minutes to spook these men off. So if she wanted to keep Lilith safe from harm, she would have to think up a new escape plan, fast.

"Pfft! She thinks we need *money*!" the third newcomer said deri-sively before he let out a condescending laugh. "Oh, cookie. Money is not everything, you know?"

There was the clicking sound of a lighter, then a single cold flame appeared amid the suffocating darkness.

"To this one, it is!" the owner of the lighter exclaimed in a menacing voice. "Looook! This one is a Chink! Chinks love moooneeey . . ."

Even though the flame from his lighter was as pale as a distant star, it was enough for Mira to see how dangerously close his hand was to Lilith's face. The man moved his lighter up and down to examine Lilith's face and figure, then he smacked his lips loudly like a hungry fox. Lilith shied away with a deliberate twist of her upper body. Her hair must have brushed past the lighter, for the smell of burned hair soon drifted toward Mira. The lighter's owner cackled with sadistic satisfaction, then the lighter went out, and Lilith was swallowed back into the darkness once more.

Mira stared at the spot where Lilith had disappeared and clenched her fists. Her heart was pounding in her chest like a wild beast trapped in a cage. Her whole body was burning like the inside of a volcano, and her skin was so raw with pain that she thought her entire being was expanding to the brink of explosion. She felt the heat steaming out from her eyes and ears, blurring her vision and making her ears ring. Pressure was building up quickly in her rib cage, squeezing out the air in her lungs and the blood in her heart, as if the wild beast was about to burst its cage open.

"*Ptui!*" Another man made a loud spitting sound, then he squawked, "The damn Chinks! Coming here and stealing 'em jobs! 'Tis why we have no jobs!"

"And no money!" someone next to him yelled. "No nothing!"

"You hear that, fortune cookie?" the man with the lazy voice cooed. "*You* are the problem here. This is not your country. You don't belong here. You have no right to come to our country, steal our jobs, and take our money for yourselves—"

"No shit!" the menacing voice jumped in. "Everything you have here shoulda be ours if it wasn't for all you Chinks in the country! You *stole* from us! You *owe* us! So now we're taking it back. We're keeping *everything!*"

"Fine. Take the bags too." It was Lilith; there was a slight tremor in her voice. "That's all I have. Now go spend the money and leave me alone."

One of the newcomers laughed hysterically, as though it was the silliest idea he had ever heard. "What's the hurry, sugar? We only took the money and the goodies, but what about the interest? . . . That's right. *Interest.* You're a Chink. Everybody knows Chinks are good at math, so I'm sure you know what 'interest' means. Any-who, you owe us, so of course there's an interest . . . especially when you owe a debt to *so* many people. The question is . . . how are you going to pay off that interest?"

Mira's heart stopped.

"I don't owe you anything," Lilith said through gritted teeth.

"Ha! This one here is a tough cookie!" exclaimed the man with the lazy voice. "What do you say, boys? Time to teach her a lesson?"

"Hell yeah!" said one.

"About damn time!" said another. "I got *loads* to teach her, if you know what I mean, he-he . . ."

"Never had Chinese before," said a third in an insinuating tone. "Hope she won't mind me not using any chopsticks!"

"No chopsticks here either," said a fourth. "I got something else for her though."

The men erupted into bawdy laughter, then a fifth voice said, "Let's dig in."

"C'mere, sugar," said a sixth. "Don't be shy now."

"Let go! Let go of me—No!" cried Lilith. "I said let go! Let go . . . !"

With a scurry of uneven footsteps and a series of struggling noises, Lilith's cries were soon muffled into unintelligible whines. The crisp, cold winter air was then scraped by the sound of a metal zipper coming undone, which was immediately followed by a smothered high-pitched scream.

At the sound of that scream, Mira's eyes went dark. The unbearable heat rushed out from her pores and erupted from her skin in flames as the uncontrollable pain burst out from her rib cage in a terrifying screech.

The alley was instantly lit up by an intense glow of red and gold, looking as if it was on fire. She could see everything clearly then: Lilith's shopping bags were half smashed on the ground just a few steps in front of her. The contents of those bags, which they had spent almost the entire evening at the square to pick out, had spilled out like trash from a trampled garbage can. Beyond the remains of the shopping bags and their contents were the seven men who had attacked Lilith—they had subdued her to the ground. A jacket had been wrapped around Lilith's head, muffling her cries. One of the men was holding the jacket in place while four others were pinning Lilith down on her stomach by her arms and legs. There was also a man between Lilith's thighs. He was kneeling on the ground with his pants down, and, in spite of the sudden gift of light and vision, he was still rummaging eagerly under Lilith's coat for an opening. Standing behind him, a few feet away from the action, was the last one of the seven men, who was in the process of lighting a joint. Like the man before him, he had his back toward her. But since he was the nearest one in her line of sight, he was the first to turn around.

She glared down at him as he looked up hesitantly from his half-lit joint to meet her eyes. It only took him one look to let go of his joint, then his face contorted in horror, his eyes grew round like gumballs, and his mouth dropped open into a gaping hole.

The rest of the seven men had noticed her too. Just like the man who had lost his joint for good, they were also choked with utter horror. Still, they kept their filthy hands and knees on Lilith as though they had forgotten she was there. The sight of them revolted her; the sight of them having body contact with Lilith enraged her.

A gust of wind whooshed into the alley and circled around her, through which she heard the three voices in her head, except that this time, they were hissing into her ears:

Vile humans!

Corrupted souls!

Unworthy of the life given!

Kill it! Take it! Show no mercy!

Kill them all! Take them all! They don't deserve it! They don't deserve any of it!

She screeched in fury and leaped at the first man blocking her way to Lilith. Even though there was nothing left in that man's eyes but terror and despair, she still wanted to hurt him. She wanted to hit him in his despicable face and break his nose.

She held up an arm and threw a punch, hard. Her fist went straight through the man's head and swallowed it, as well as the body that was attached to it, in an enormous wing made of flames. The contact set off a wave of uncomfortable yet familiar sensation that reminded her of an old, forgotten memory. She jerked her arm back in disgust. The man reappeared from her burning wing unscathed, but as soon as he was free from it, he collapsed to the ground like a sack of flesh and skin with no bones, his eyes and mouth wide open.

"De-de-de-devil!" cried the man who was holding the jacket over Lilith's head. "It's the Devil! The Devil!"

"You call *me* the Devil," she snarled at him and the other five men, her voice discordant and electrified with static, "when *you* ganged up to assault a defenseless girl?"

As if her voice had given them an electric shock, the six men jumped up and away from Lilith like rats dodging the snapping jaws of a mousetrap. Three of them fell to the ground on their bottoms and immediately backed away in a half-scrambling, half-squirming motion, like oversize caterpillars. Two of them fell on their knees, and they scurried away in the same direction on all fours like giant cockroaches. The last man—the one with his pants down—stumbled backward in panic and bumped into the wall. Terror-stricken by the fact that her attention was now entirely on him, he pressed his back flat against the wall and slid sideways toward where the other five men were retreating to, his hands fumbling frantically on the bricks, searching desperately for a magic doorknob that would allow him to enter the wall.

The sight of this man infuriated her. The voices hissed into her ears again:

Pure evil!
Unforgivable!
Kill it!
Take it!
Show no mercy!

She glared at him with loathing. She wanted to hurt him, and she wanted to hurt him badly. She wanted to make him suffer for what he did.

He seemed to know what was coming for him. His jaw dropped and he choked up a silent scream.

She charged at him then, mercilessly. His eyes bulged out like the eyes on a squeeze toy, but he made no movement or sound.

She wanted to grab his head and snap his neck, but instead, two fiery wings swiped down and swallowed his head and body in burning flames. She immediately felt the same sensation that she had when she tried to punch the other man earlier, prickling and tingling all the way up her arms to her chest. Repulsed by what she had touched, she pulled her arms back from the man.

He reappeared from the flames, unharmed, but he began to slide off the wall like a slug that could no longer secrete any mucus to hold on to a surface. The other five men had huddled together against the far end of the wall like a pack of crippled wolves. They stared at what was happening in front of them in dead silence, frozen with horror.

She stooped over the falling man and watched him sink slowly to the ground. His eyes and mouth were still wide open; no sound came from his throat, but from his round, glassy eyes, she saw the reflections of a fiery beast with wings.

"He's dead," one of the remaining men muttered under his breath. Then his voice rose into a panicked scream. "They're both dead!"

"The Devil killed them," another man whimpered. "It just touched them, and . . . and . . ."

"We're doomed!" cried a third, clutching his head and pulling on his hair. "The Devil's gonna kill us. It's gonna kill us all . . ."

"Somebody help, please!" squeaked another. "Please, God! I repent! I repent . . . !"

"I don't wanna die. I don't wanna die. I don't wanna die. I don't wanna die . . ." mumbled the last one repeatedly until he was hyperventilating.

But their desperate pleas only managed to enrage her more. She felt herself burning violently from the inside. She wanted to hurt them badly, and she wanted to hurt them all.

She turned and glared at the remaining five men. They let out a collective shriek and scrambled to their feet, trying to flee.

With a stretch of her neck and a discordant screech from her throat, she flew at them at full speed. She held out her arms and aimed. She wanted to knock them to the ground, she wanted to smash their skulls into the concrete floor, and she wanted to make them pay for what they did to Lilith ...

"Noooo!" a voice cried urgently from behind her, stopping her in her tracks—it was Lilith's.

She was only inches away from the five men, who had turned and frozen like the unfortunate souls caught under Medusa's gaze, but she held her arms back.

"Don't ..." said Lilith, breathlessly. "They're not worth it. They're not worth the price you'll have to pay for taking their lives."

She didn't reply, nor did she turn. She could hear the two men she had attacked earlier; they were suddenly gasping for air as if they had just succeeded in cheating death. The thought of permitting despicable humans like them to draw more air from this world into their loathsome beings made her hiss in disgust.

"Let them go, *please*," Lilith pleaded. "Just—Just forget about them and let them go. There's a price for everything ... even for revenge."

She hesitated, but in the end, she dropped her arms. Still holding their breath in horror, the five men regained themselves and realized this could be their only chance to leave the alley alive. Without a moment to lose, they slithered away from her in a line like a human train and scurried back to the other two men, who had now stopped gasping but were panting and mumbling gibberish instead. Nimbly, like praying mantises dragging their sick peers away for food, they hooked their arms around the two indisposed men and quickly pulled them away toward the other end of the alley, where they eventually merged safely back into the darkness.

Amid the nervous footsteps of their retreat, she heard another set of footsteps walking toward her, softly and hesitantly. They stopped at a conservative distance behind her, then she heard Lilith's trembling voice:

"Mi-Mira? . . . Is that—Is that you?"

There was something in Lilith's voice that made her left chest tighten like red-hot iron in a cold winter rain, quenching the flames while making the space inside contract mercilessly as though it was going to collapse in on itself. She was suddenly overwhelmed by an intense wave of fatigue, followed immediately by exhaustion—such exhaustion. Her ears began to ring, and her vision became blurry. For a moment, she thought the world was expanding around her.

She could no longer fight off the grip of gravity. Her legs gave out and buckled under the weight of her body, then she fell, noiselessly, like a feather.

She closed her eyes and relaxed her body. She was tired. Very, very tired. She wondered if it had all been just a dream . . .

"Mira!" Lilith's voice cried out from somewhere around her, but it sounded far away, like a memory from a distant dream.

Urgent footsteps ran toward her. She felt a breath of cold air on her face, then she felt a trembling hand on hers. The hand was even colder than the air, but she didn't mind.

"Oh dear . . . Oh dear . . ." Lilith's voice was shaking. "Mira, can you hear me? . . . Mira? . . . Mira!"

She was too tired to move, but she forced herself to open her eyes. She was surprised to see that the alley was no longer lit up, but it was not shrouded in darkness either. In fact, she could see the shape of Lilith's head; it was right above her.

"I'm sorry, Lilith . . ." she said weakly. "We should have stayed . . . for the show . . ."

Something light and soft landed on her face like raindrops, wet but warm.

"You're . . . crying," she said with great effort. "Are you . . . ? Did they . . . ?"

Lilith shook her head firmly and wiped away her tears. "No. I'm okay, Mira. You saved me."

She let her eyelids fall and sighed with relief. When she managed to open her eyes again, she noticed that something was hovering in the sky above them in a swirling motion—big as a full moon and green like witch brew—glowing, churning, humming, and growing. There was something else in the sky too, falling down softly and melancholily in great numbers, each piercing her skin like an icy shard. She shivered.

It was snowing.

"I'm cold, Lilith . . ." she said feebly, closing her eyes. "I don't think I can . . . walk you to the bus stop . . ."

Lilith sniffled and rubbed her eyes with a sleeve, then she took off her coat, reached down, and scooped Mira's upper body carefully into her arms. She swaddled Mira with her coat and sat on the ground with her, rocking her gently, back and forth, back and forth . . .

"You're gonna be okay, Mira. I know you will . . ." said Lilith, choking up. "I'm gonna stay right here with you. I'm not going anywhere, okay? . . . It's gonna be okay. Everything's gonna be okay. I know it will . . . I know it will . . ."

A layer of snow had surrounded them by then. Despite Lilith's effort to keep her warm, she was still cold. Worse, she could hear a cacophonous whooshing noise that was charged with static, and it was getting louder with every beat of her heart.

She knew that noise. She didn't quite understand why it was happening again, but she knew what was coming.

She opened her eyes: above their heads, the green vortex had already occupied a fourth of the sky.

"We need to go," she said, peeling her head away from Lilith's arm as she tried to stand up, but she was too weak to support her own weight.

Lilith realized what she was trying to do and got up to help her. But as soon as she was on her feet, she felt the blood draining from her head and wobbled. Lilith seemed to have anticipated this. Like a reflex, she immediately caught her by the arms and held her steady.

"Mira, you can't even stand, let alone walk."

"I'll manage," she said breathily. "We must go now. You're staying at my house tonight."

Lilith opened her mouth as though she wanted to ask a difficult
question, but she paused and said, "I can run to your house and
get your parents—"

"We can't," she said, softly but meaningfully. "They don't need
to know . . . what happened tonight."

The alley was now blanketed in snow, which was reflecting the
unnatural color of the green vortex's light effectively and casting an
eerie green tint onto everything in sight, successfully transforming
the alley into an alien world. This gave Mira a strong sense of déjà
vu, but she wasn't sure whether it was from another dream or another life.

She nudged Lilith's reluctant hands away and took a few small
steps by herself. Her body responded by waking every bone and
muscle in her with a raw, burning pain. She clenched her jaw and
winced, but she said, "See? I'll manage. Now go find your things
. . . And Lilith? . . . Make sure you don't leave anything behind."

A resonant bell tone sounded in the distance, followed by another, and another . . .

Suddenly, a roar of clamor rose from the direction of the pedestrian square, then the bell tone went silent.

"The show is over," said Lilith, returning her attention to Mira,
only to notice a dark and alarming expression on her face that made
her tense up at once. Lilith never thought she would see an expression like that on Mira, and she shuddered at the thought of what
could have caused it. Whatever it was though, she was sure of one
thing: they must leave soon.

Quickly, Lilith ran back to recover her things from the snow.
The green vortex was emitting enough light for her to see clearly
in the alley, so she was able to find all her things without spending
too much time fumbling around. She felt a sense of loss when she
found out most of the presents were no longer presentable, but she

dismissed it with a deep breath. After all, it was the last thing she should be worried about now.

She jammed everything into the biggest shopping bag and whirled around to find Mira, but what she saw made her freeze in her tracks.

Mira had her back toward Lilith; she was inching forward, leaning against the wall for support. Even though the green vortex had successfully deprived the world of other colors, it was impossible for Lilith to miss how those fiery red feathers shed from Mira's hair, drifted down in flames, landed on the snow, and disappeared without a sound.

Lilith felt a lump rising in her throat, then tears welled up in her eyes. Quietly, she wiped them away.

"Let's go," she called, running to Mira.

It didn't take her long to catch up to her friend. Still panting, Lilith stepped in front of Mira and patted herself on the back.

"All right, Cinderella." She looked at Mira over a shoulder, smiling. "It's past midnight and we need to hurry, so don't be shy—hop up."

Chapter 6   THE LOST PURPOSE

1

LILITH was staring out of the window in a trance.

The green vortex was still there in the sky, swirling and hovering above at least a third of the town. It was a terrifying sight, but it was also strangely enchanting.

Lilith couldn't help but wonder how it managed to grow into such a disturbing size, considering it was only as big as a full moon when she first noticed it the night before.

She had told herself, repeatedly, that it was just a rare astronomical event that happened to take place right after what she had witnessed. But the more she looked at the green vortex, the more uncertain she became. There were so many questions in her head, spinning like a tangled fishnet caught in a whirlwind, and she did not even know where to begin to untie the knots.

Lilith let out a long sigh and buried her face in her hands. Her eyes were sore; so was her forehead. Though the bed was soft and comfortable, she had barely slept. She should have felt tired and sleepy, but instead, she was edgy and restless.

She wondered if Mira was doing better now.

The thought jabbed at her heart like a dull blade. She tucked her knees in and wrapped her arms around her head, hoping to keep the memories from rushing back. But it was no use. She remembered how hard she had run, with Mira on her back, to stay ahead of the green vortex, which seemed to be expanding purposefully to devour the entire world. She remembered once they were out of the alley how the streetlights and Christmas lights and porch lights had gone out, one by one, as she ran past, producing the uncanny impression that a deadly disease was spreading from one light bulb to the next. She remembered how light and fragile Mira felt on her back in spite of the heavy feeling in her steps. She remembered how relieved but, at the same time, nervous she was when she finally reached Mira's street and saw that Mr. and Mrs. Murphy were waiting on the front porch, pacing back and forth anxiously.

They spotted Lilith almost right away, then they immediately realized something was wrong. As they rushed over to the girls, all the remaining lights in the neighborhood went out simultaneously, as if someone had finally decided to clip the last power line in the area. As a result, the street was instantly submerged in a luminescent green tint, the intensity of which was ominously amplified by the snowy background, giving it an eerie and surreal appearance that made Lilith think of the passageway described in ancient Chinese folklore for the lost souls to travel to the underworld. Luckily, except for the four of them, no one else was in sight.

Even though Mr. and Mrs. Murphy's expressions were obscured by the green tint that had masked their faces, Lilith could still sense the distress and uneasiness in their eyes. Carefully, they unloaded Mira from her back and into Mr. Murphy's arms. To Lilith's surprise, instead of asking questions, Mrs. Murphy asked her to go inside the house with them in an urgent whisper. Her voice was gentle, but her tone was firm, leaving no room for objection or discussion. It occurred to Lilith then that aside from the state that Mira was in, there was something else that worried Mrs. Murphy too.

Lilith did not ask what it was though. She already had a feeling it had something to do with the green vortex. She just didn't know whether it also had something to do with the cause of that dark and alarming expression on Mira's face earlier, back in the alley.

The thought gave Lilith a chill down her spine. She nodded quietly and let Mrs. Murphy escort her to their house.

Once inside, Mrs. Murphy double-locked the door behind them and helped Mr. Murphy lay Mira down on the couch. The blinds in the living room were left open, so the green tint that had submerged the street outside had no trouble flowing in through the windows to share its eerie glow. Mrs. Murphy did not seem to appreciate it reaching in to provide illumination without her permission, however. She told Mr. Murphy to close all the blinds right away, then she lit the scented candle on the coffee table and asked Lilith to sit down.

Lilith obeyed and sat in the armchair next to the couch, facing Mira, who was struggling to keep her eyes open.

Mrs. Murphy sat down on the coffee table and felt Mira's forehead, then she turned to Lilith with a worried look and asked her what happened.

Before Lilith could conjure up a decent story in her head, Mira spoke. In a feeble voice, she told Mrs. Murphy that when they were watching the laser light show at the square, she suddenly felt ill and was too weak to walk, so Lilith had to carry her home. She then raised her voice to add that it was too late for Lilith to go home and that she should stay and sleep in the guest room.

Maybe it was Lilith's guilty conscience, or maybe it was the flickering candlelight, but for a second or two, Lilith saw a strange expression crossing Mrs. Murphy's face—one that made her mouth dry and her palms sweat. She held her breath and stole a glance at Mira, only to see that she had already closed her eyes.

Mira's parents did not ask any more questions after that. Mrs. Murphy brought down some clean clothes from Mira's room for Lilith and led her to the guest room. She showed Lilith where everything was and told her to make herself at home. Once she was assured by Lilith that there was nothing else she needed, Mrs. Murphy returned to the living room and helped Mr. Murphy carry Mira up the stairs to her room.

Lilith remembered how quiet and still Mira was in her sleep, so much so that she didn't even seem to be breathing—nor did she look like she would ever wake up again.

The thought of it made Lilith tremble. She curled into a smaller ball, then she drew a long, deep breath and held it in her lungs. It had been over five hours since she was rescued from those men in the alley, but she could still see it in her head, as vividly as the reality she was in: an enormous fiery bird, floating inches above the floor with its back toward her, soul-shatteringly terrifying yet astoundingly beautiful.

Lilith remembered how that seemingly omnipotent bird suddenly began to shrink as though it was about to burn out. She remembered how Mira had materialized from the dying flames of that bird, and how she had drifted down to the ground like a feather, her hair still flowing and glowing like red-hot lava . . .

Before Lilith knew it, tears rushed out from her eyes, and she sobbed, breathlessly and unstoppably, inside the cocoon she had built with her body, realizing she had been holding them back for far too long.

11

Lilith didn't know how long she had cried. She had stayed curled up in that same position, even after her tears had run dry, until a gentle knock on the door brought her mind back to reality. Hesitantly, she lifted her head from her knees and glanced at the door, wondering if she had really heard it.

"Lilith?" a voice called softly from behind the door. It was muffled and indistinct, but it was definitely a female's.

At the sound of it, Lilith felt her heart skip a beat. She uncurled herself and scooted off the bed in a hurry. Just when she was about to reach for the doorknob, she paused, remembering she had been crying. She dried her face quickly with her sleeves, then she pulled open the door.

"Mi—Mrs. Murphy."

"Good morning," said Mrs. Murphy, smiling warmly at her, appearing to have missed the apparent disappointment in her voice. "How did you sleep?"

"Um. Good," Lilith answered absent-mindedly. Then she bit her lip and asked, "How . . . how's Mira?"

With a short sigh, Mrs. Murphy tilted her head to the side and her eyes softened. "You're worried about her, aren't you?"

There was something very motherly about the way she looked at her, so much so that it was almost painful. Lilith lowered her eyes and immediately noticed the puffiness and tenderness around them. Then she realized, despite her effort to dry her face, her eyes had made their own confession to Mrs. Murphy the moment she opened the door.

"Her fever . . . Has it come down yet?" she asked without looking up.

Mrs. Murphy pressed her lips together and shook her head. "I'm afraid not. She still has a high fever."

For a brief moment, Lilith felt the world vibrating around her, and she had a strong need to lean against the doorframe for support. As she searched desperately in her head for a potential solution to improve Mira's condition, the word "hospital" came to mind. On second thought, however, she decided a hospital would be the last place they should go to—it didn't take much imagination for her to foresee what kinds of terrible things they would do to Mira if they ever found out about how unique and special she truly was.

"She's gonna be okay though," said Mrs. Murphy, giving Lilith a gentle squeeze on her arm. "Her body just needs more time to recover because it's not used to getting sick ... Believe it or not, this is only the third fever she's ever caught since she was a baby. The second time was not as bad, but the first time—" She let out a soft sigh with a shake of her head. "The first time was just like this one. It came on suddenly and stayed at a high temperature for what seemed like forever. We had no idea what caused it. Not even my doctor friend could say for sure. She just told us all we could do was to let her rest and keep her hydrated, and her immune system would do the rest." She gave a wry chuckle under her breath, but she said to Lilith, "And she was right. Her body did fight it off in the end on its own. So try not to worry, sweet girl. She'll beat the fever. Eventually. Just like that time."

Lilith knew Mrs. Murphy was trying to cheer her up, but she was too preoccupied to listen to what she was saying, and her words just rolled into one ear and out the other, like marbles in a slippery tube, until a few of them got caught by something from her subconscious. The rest were therefore stopped in the middle of her mind like roadblocks, holding up all traffic of thoughts and forcing her to redirect her attention to Mrs. Murphy's words instead.

So she held them in her mind and examined them from different angles—weighing them, scrambling them, repeating them. Then all at once, the questions she had in her head began to untangle and line up one by one, as if they had decided to fall into place on their own, until finally, she arrived at a single strand of questions that bore all others.

Lilith felt her lips tremble, then the blood drained from her face.

"You need some breakfast," said Mrs. Murphy, looking concerned. "Did you eat at all last night?"

"We, um ... We had some hot chocolate," Lilith replied in a small voice.

Mrs. Murphy narrowed her eyes and looked at her with a slightly disapproving frown. "No wonder you look so pale." She turned and made a beckoning motion with her hand. "Come. We need to put some warm food in your tummy. That oughta make you feel better."

"Mrs. Murphy?" Lilith asked as she followed her into the living room. "Are we still using the power generator?"

"Yes."

"So I guess ... nothing's back yet?"

"Nothing's back yet."

"Do you know what time it was when the cell signal went out last night?"

"As a matter of fact, I do," said Mrs. Murphy, glancing back at Lilith with an intrigued look as she stepped into the kitchen. "It was 12:01."

Lilith was taken aback by the preciseness of her answer. "Exactly?"

"Exactly." Mrs. Murphy nodded, then she put on the oven mitts and pulled out two large baking pans from the oven. "I know the time because I called Mira at twelve o'clock sharp and she didn't answer. So I tried again at 12:01 and realized the signal was out."

"What about the internet and the radio, then?" Lilith asked carefully. "When did they go out?"

Mrs. Murphy was transferring food from the baking pans onto a plate. "Probably about the same time," she said without looking up. "We checked both not long after we found out the cell signal was out ... Why do you ask?"

Lilith was not expecting Mrs. Murphy to take an interest in the reason behind her questions, which, in turn, reminded her that she had not yet thought of a proper excuse to justify all the other questions she was going to ask. Fearing that she might have aroused some suspicion from Mrs. Murphy already, she froze in her tracks, searching quickly in her head for something innocent and harmless to be used as a reply.

Sensing her hesitation, Mrs. Murphy looked up from the pans and plates. When she saw that Lilith's face was laden with anxiousness, she straightened up and slapped her forehead. "What was I thinking? You want to find a way to get in touch with your parents! . . . Of course!"

Lilith was standing stiffly between the kitchen and the dining room like a potted plant. Before she could start to process how Mrs. Murphy had come to that conclusion, she saw her walking toward her from behind the kitchen island, looking sympathetic but also slightly distressed.

"I'm sorry, Lilith. You must be worried that they're in a panic because they can't reach you," Mrs. Murphy said gently. "I wish we had another way to contact them, but there's really no way to tell how long the blackouts will last and what the situation is like out there when all communication channels are cut off like this." She tilted her head and gave Lilith a motherly smile, then she held up a hand and brushed back the few stray hairs that had stuck to Lilith's cheeks when the tears dried. "Well, maybe we could still find a way . . . Mira told me your parents were traveling for work. Where did they go?"

Lilith opened her mouth, closed it, then she said in a low voice, "I don't know."

"Okay . . ." Mrs. Murphy nodded slowly as though she was having a hard time processing Lilith's reply. "They're coming back for Christmas though, right?"

"I . . . I don't know."

Mrs. Murphy's brows furrowed, producing a pair of distinct frown lines that reminded Lilith of the number eleven.

"I remember Mira told me they had to travel a lot for work. How do they usually get in touch with you when they're away?"

Lilith bit her lip and lowered her eyes. The thought of having to tell Mrs. Murphy how businesslike her relationship with her parents was made her feel sad and ashamed at the same time.

"They . . . they don't," she replied, as emotionlessly as she could manage. "Their jobs are pretty demanding: long, irregular hours, little time for vacation, having to travel frequently for emergencies and whatnot . . . and highly classified too, so I was told. They can't talk about the work they do with others, not even with me. They can't bring personal phones or laptops into their work facilities, and they can't contact me with the devices at work because they're restricted. So usually, they just leave me a note on the fridge before they leave for work, or if they get to stop by between trips, to tell me what's in the fridge and what to eat and what needs to be done and . . ." Lilith trailed off with an inward wince, knowing that there was really no need for her to finish her sentence, considering there was truly nothing she could add to her explanation to make it sound any less awful than it already was. Plus, Mrs. Murphy's eyes were growing wider and wider as she spoke—in horror, Lilith suspected.

"I think I understand now," said Mrs. Murphy as her face became serious and determined. "I'll talk to Mr. Murphy. Let *us* worry about getting in touch with your parents, sweet girl. We'll look at our options and think about what we can do. In the meantime, you should stay here with us . . . At least until this is over."

"You mean . . . until the green vortex is gone?" Lilith asked cautiously.

A shadow flitted across Mrs. Murphy's face. "I just don't think it's a safe time for you to be by yourself," she said, then she returned to the kitchen to finish fixing the plates, looking somberly contemplative. "It's only been seven hours. Most people are just waking up to the blackouts and that green thing in the sky. The last time something like this happened, the whole town lost its mind."

As if she had been struck by lightning, Lilith stared ahead, jaw dropped, and stood transfixed.

Still in shock, she turned to Mrs. Murphy slowly. "Did you say
... Are you saying ... *this* has happened before?"

"Yes," said Mrs. Murphy, removing two sets of utensils from a
drawer. "Unfortunately."

"Wh-when? Where?" Lilith blurted out. Her voice, though
quiet, was at least an octave higher than usual.

Mrs. Murphy acknowledged her reaction with an inscrutable
look, but she didn't answer her questions. She brought out two
plates of food from the kitchen and set them down on the dining
table, then she went back into the kitchen and returned with two
glasses of orange juice. She placed the glasses on the table, next to
the plates, then she pulled out a chair and gestured for Lilith to sit.

Lilith dragged her body and her dumbfounded mind into
the dining room and, woodenly, lowered herself into the chair.
Mrs. Murphy pulled out another and sat down beside her.

"It was two years ago, in Skygate," said Mrs. Murphy, her eyes
hiding behind her long, thick eyelashes. "I doubt you've heard of
it. It's a far-off, obscure town in the mountains. We used to live
there before we moved to Starfall."

"So did it happen in the same way? I mean, did the green vortex
also appear in the sky out of nowhere and expand—like this one?
... How big did it get? ... Did you have blackouts too?"

"We did. Everything that's happened so far happened back then
as well ... Except the snow, I guess."

Lilith let out a soft gasp. "How ... How long did it last?"

"About twenty-four hours. The green thing did grow weak toward the end. Then suddenly, it disappeared from the sky without
a trace, and everything came back: the electricity, the cell signal,
the internet, and the radio ... Most people believed there was a
connection between the blackouts and the green thing. The official explanation said it was an abnormal space hurricane they had
failed to forecast or detect, but back then, few people bought that.
Instead, they came up with all sorts of ideas and theories to explain
the whole thing on their own; some were so strange that they were
practically bizarre. Still, stranger things had happened during that

time frame." With a sigh, Mrs. Murphy unfolded her napkin and placed it on her lap, then she picked up the fork and said, "Well, start eating, sweetie. Don't let your food get cold."

Lilith's mind was beginning to race, and so was her heart. "Wh-what kind of 'stranger things'?"

"Well, there was this boy," replied Mrs. Murphy, pushing the breakfast potatoes around on her plate as though she was counting them. "He was fifteen, I believe. Anyway, according to the news, he was a perfectly normal teenager, but somehow, he went crazy during the blackouts and set off a gas explosion at his house, killing everyone in the family, including himself. The police didn't know how he managed to do what he did when both of his parents were at home with him, so they suspected he had either injured them badly or killed them in cold blood before he set up the gas explosion. There was no way of knowing what really happened though. By the time the fire was finally put out, not much was left for forensics."

"That's . . . horrible . . ."

"It was. I guess that was why the media was so much more enthusiastic about reporting his story than the so-called space hurricane itself. It was all they focused on afterward . . . for a *long* time."

Though Lilith was still greatly shocked and unsettled by all the new information she had learned, she was relieved that the "stranger things" had nothing to do with an enormous fiery bird after all.

She copied Mrs. Murphy and unfolded her napkin on her lap. "Did they ever find out why he went crazy?"

"I don't think so. There were a lot of absurd speculations though," Mrs. Murphy answered in a resigned voice. Then she looked at Lilith and gave her a reassuring smile. "I know it all sounds pretty depressing, but the good news is, Mr. Murphy and I did learn a lesson or two that time, and one thing is for sure: the green vortex and the blackouts will *not* last forever. So don't worry. It'll all be fine in the end. Now eat before your food gets cold."

Lilith nodded and delivered a piece of scrambled eggs into her mouth. It was fluffy and rich in flavor, albeit lukewarm in temperature. She stared thoughtfully at the food on her plate and chewed.

"Still good?" asked Mrs. Murphy, taking a bite. "Hmm ... Not too bad but could be better. I think we should heat them up a little. Here, hand me your plate."

Lilith obeyed and passed Mrs. Murphy her plate. As she watched it being reheated in the microwave, another question popped into her mind.

"Mrs. Murphy, did the power generator come with the house or did you install it?"

"We installed it," said Mrs. Murphy as she removed Lilith's plate from the microwave. "Actually, that was one of the lessons Mr. Murphy and I learned from last time: the importance of having access to electricity at all times. Did you know without electricity, the heat won't even turn on? Imagine how cold it'd be in the house right now if we didn't have a generator ... especially with all that snow outside."

Lilith turned her head and looked through the windowpanes on the patio door. The entire backyard was heavily blanketed under a smooth layer of snow, a sight that could well be considered as a piece of artwork by Mother Nature if it weren't for the eerie green tint reflecting off every surface outside, producing an ominous ambience that sent a chill down her spine. Feeling fortunate that they had a power generator to keep the furnace running and to prevent the cold winter air, which seemed to be saturated with that eerie green tint, from entering the house, Lilith withdrew her gaze with a soft sigh of relief. But as she waited for Mrs. Murphy to return, she suddenly remembered the strange request she had received from her the night before, asking her not to turn on any light and to use the candles instead.

"Mrs. Murphy?" Lilith asked slowly and tentatively. "If the power generator is running, why can't we turn on the lights?"

Mrs. Murphy was bringing their plates back to the table. When she heard the question, she paused, looking indecisive and even a little alarmed. She lowered her head and sighed through her nose, then she sat down and placed the plates in front of Lilith and herself.

"I'm sorry, Lilith," Mrs. Murphy said with an apologetic and somewhat melancholy smile. "I thought about explaining it to you last night, but I decided it was not a good idea for me to say more than what was necessary. After all, you were quite shaken already, and I didn't want you to have more things to worry about." She drew a deep breath and leaned back in her chair, then she looked meaningfully at Lilith and continued. "We can't turn on the lights because Mr. Murphy and I also learned something else that time: nothing's more dangerous than a panicked man, especially when there are things that he needs but can't have. Get it?"

Lilith got it; the look in Mrs. Murphy's eyes explained everything —more than sufficiently. With an involuntary shiver, she nodded.

Mrs. Murphy's expression softened. She leaned in and held Lilith's hand. "I know this is all very overwhelming. I can only imagine how much you wish your parents were here right now. But you're not alone, okay? Mr. Murphy and I will do everything in our power to take care of you and Mira ... You know, she's never said it out loud, but we can tell how much she values your friendship and how important you are to her. To tell you the truth, Mr. Murphy and I both feel very grateful Mira was able to find a friend like you. You are loyal, loving, and caring. What you did for her last night was very brave and selfless. You carried her all the way back to us from the square despite the nightmare that was happening in the sky ... I doubt many kids at your age could do the same for their friends, even if the green vortex weren't there."

Lilith felt her throat tightening as she thought of the things that had happened—what had *really* happened—the night before. Quickly, she lowered her head to hide the tears that were forming in her eyes, wishing she could tell Mrs. Murphy she didn't deserve any of her compliments because it was Mira who had saved *her* by sacrificing herself to the control of something that was entirely inexplicable.

"Well, we really shouldn't let your breakfast get cold again," said Mrs. Murphy, giving Lilith a squeeze on her hand. "What do you say we forget about what's going on out there for a while and focus on enjoying our food together? It's Christmas Eve, after all."

The mention of Christmas Eve brought Lilith's thoughts straight back to where she had left off, and she remembered she still had one very important—and very tricky—question to ask Mrs. Murphy.

Not knowing the best way to phrase her question without drawing attention to its underlying implication, Lilith ate her breakfast mechanically while she, in a way that felt much like an amateur's attempt at unscrambling a Rubik's Cube, swapped and tweaked words restlessly in her mind. However, by the time she had cleaned her plate, she still hadn't found a good way to say it.

Presently, Mrs. Murphy was finishing the last few pieces of food on hers. Seeing that she might soon miss the opportunity to ask the most important question on the strand of questions that bore all the others in her mind, Lilith blurted out in a hurry, "Mrs. Murphy?"

As soon as the words had left her mouth, Lilith felt the blood rushing into her brain, making her dizzy and lightheaded.

Mrs. Murphy looked up from her plate. Her hazel eyes were warm and gentle, reminding Lilith of freshly brewed tea. "Yes, sweet girl?"

Despite the soothing effect of her motherly expression, Lilith's hands were trembling uncontrollably in her lap. In an effort to steady her nerves, she clenched them and pressed them hard to her thighs.

"When it happened, I mean, the last time *this* happened . . . was it also when . . . when Mira caught her first fever?"

Mrs. Murphy froze, and her eyes suddenly became dull, but she soon recovered herself with a sharp inhale of breath and smiled at Lilith.

"It was. But don't worry. I'm sure it was just a coincidence, that's all."

III

She was back on the battlefield again.

She did not know how long she had been fighting, but she was panting. She could feel the weight of the sword and shield in her hands, and she could feel the warm blood spatters trickling down her face.

She looked down and saw a circle of bodies piled high around her, which belonged to the soldiers she had chopped down. She looked up and saw that more soldiers were pouring onto the battlefield from the woods in the distance, like raging waves rushing toward the shore, devouring the corpses under their feet as they advanced with deafening roars.

Together with the remaining soldiers on her side, she raised her sword and shield, and she waited. She was neither panting nor breathing now, and her heart was as steady as her hands. She watched as the vanguard closed in like the face of a long, rising wave that was clad in heavy armor and stirred-up dust. Her hands did not waver. Her breath did not resume. She did not know why she was so calm—she simply was.

The impact resulted in loud clashes that soon brought on a widespread bloodbath for both sides. She charged onward, ignoring the fact that she was showered in blood, again and again.

The battle cries had turned into shrieks of agony and screams of terror. She began running.

Running, running, slashing her way through. She needed to reach the woods.

Running, running, slashing her way through. She needed to reach the other side of the woods.

The rock tower was waiting beyond the trees; she could see it. It did not look as ancient as she remembered, but it was the same tower; she was sure of it. She had to reach it. She had to get to the top of it. She did not know why she needed to—she simply must.

Run! Run!

Faster! Faster!

Rocks, ruins, rubble, sand.

They're coming! Hurry! Hurry!

Run! Run!

Faster! Faster!

Rocks, ruins, rubble, sand!

She was running so fast that she was almost flying. The rock tower was getting closer, and she could see the vines: they were coming back to life, twisting and writhing from beneath the sand like the tentacles of a famished monster about to break free from hell. The vines split and spread and grew into numerous arms, at the ends of which skinnier vines sprouted like grotesque claws, gripping tightly onto the rubble, the ruins, and the rocks that formed the tower itself.

Run! Run!

Faster! Faster!

Up! Up! Up like the vines!

Don't stop! You have to reach the top!

Run! Run!

Faster! Faster!

Up! Up! Up like the vines!

Getting closer!

Almost there!

You have to reach it. You have to see!

The secret, the answer—whatever it is!

Getting brighter!

Almost can see . . .

The moment the unmistakable sight of the wooden door that she had never succeeded in opening came into view, she quickened her steps and charged at it at full speed with her shoulder against the back of the shield—

There was no impact; the wooden door had disappeared on contact.

She crashed down loudly on her side, her shield scraping the cold, hard surface beneath her as she slid forward from the initial momentum, filling her ears with a grating screech that soon turned into a familiar ringing sound.

She did it. She had finally opened the wooden door. She had finally reached the top.

She pushed herself up and surveyed her surroundings. She was standing in what was once a circular stone chamber, but half of its floor was missing, along with most of its wall and the entire ceiling and roof, exposing her to the sky in midair with an unobstructed view of the woods and, beyond it, the blood-soaked battlefield.

Not a single piece of furniture. Not a single chest. Not a single soul.

Nothing.

There was absolutely nothing at the top of this rock tower.

IV

Cara couldn't get Lilith's question out of her mind. When she finally got back to Mira's room and closed the door behind her, she was trembling.

"How's breakfast?" Thomas turned to greet her from a chair in the corner. "Say, is that for me? . . . I thought we were not allowed to have food in the bedrooms."

Feeling relieved that his voice had called her away from her own thoughts, Cara let out a soft sigh and gave him a faint smile. "Don't get used to it. It's only temporary."

"Good enough for me!" Thomas grinned enthusiastically and removed the food tray from her hands.

Cara chuckled under her breath and walked toward the bed. "How is she doing?"

"Same. She's sleeping like an angel though, don't you think? Can't even tell she's fighting a high fever." Thomas shoved a big bite into his mouth, then he nodded approvingly. "Mmm, yummy breakfast, honey."

"Thanks," said Cara, kneeling by the bed. Mira was sleeping so soundly that she seemed to be barely breathing. In spite of the fever, her face still looked pale compared to the fiery red curls cushioning her head like an extra pillow.

Cara leaned in and brushed the few stray curls away from the ice pack on Mira's forehead, then she stroked Mira's head. The familiarity of the repeating motion brought a wistful smile to her lips. She remembered how she used to come check on Mira every night after she was asleep, kneeling by her bed like this, to gaze at her little face as she stroked her hair.

But unlike those nights, her daughter now seemed fragile and lifeless under her fingers. A suffocating pain seized Cara's chest, as if her heart were being squeezed dry. Her mind was suddenly occupied by the image of the stillborn baby tucked in the middle of her infant casket, looking fragile and lifeless—like this.

Thomas came over with his plate and sat down on the floor. "She looks so peaceful. I wonder what she's been dreaming about."

Cara's heart was still aching from the memory of what she had lost. She knew she could not allow it to happen again—no, she would not. She would give up her own life in exchange for Mira's in a heartbeat, if that was the price she must pay.

"How's Lilith?" Thomas asked between bites. "Better?"

"I don't think so." Cara unfolded her legs and sat down beside him. "She looked like she had a rough night. I could tell she's still worried . . . probably even more so today than last night."

Thomas stopped chewing. "Worried about her parents?"

"That and the whole situation," Cara answered resignedly as Lilith's question returned to her mind. She lowered her head and breathed in slowly. "She's also worried that Mira's fever has something to do with that green thing in the sky."

"Huh." Thomas lowered his fork. "That's, uh . . . that's an interesting theory." He took a quick glance at the windows. "What did you say to that?"

"I told her it's a coincidence."

"You think so?"

"What else could I say? None of it makes any sense . . . even though this is already the second time around . . . I just didn't want her to be more anxious than she already was. Did you notice how much she was shaking last night, even after we got them inside? It must have been nerve-racking for her to carry Mira back under that green thing without knowing what it was or what it'd do . . ." Feeling increasingly less convinced of her own response to Lilith as she spoke, Cara's voice grew small. "I can't let those kinds of thoughts get to her, Thomas. That's how panic takes over and takes control."

"I see . . ." Thomas put the fork down and gazed distractedly at the rest of his breakfast.

After a long moment of silence, he turned to Cara.

"Do you think it's possible though?" He asked carefully. "That Mira's fever is related to the green vortex?"

Cara bit her lip, trying hard to rein in her thoughts before they could wander off to search for the truth.

"I don't know," she finally said. "I hope not."

Thomas studied her face quietly, then he rubbed her back and said, "I think you did the right thing with Lilith. What she needs now is to feel safe, not to worry about things like that."

"Thank you," Cara murmured and leaned against Thomas. "By the way, I asked Lilith to stay here with us till this is over. I just don't think it's safe for her to be by herself when that green thing is still in the sky. Remember what it was like in Skygate?"

Thomas sucked in a long breath, then he sighed heavily. "Yeah, I remember."

"Think it'll be the same here?"

"It's hard to say . . . Guess we'll find out."

Cara felt a sudden pang of anxiety. She lifted her head from Thomas's shoulder and said, "You know what? It's still early in the morning. I think you should take Lilith back to her house now to pack up some clothes and some valuables and secure the house somehow . . . before the panic mode sets in."

Thomas nodded thoughtfully. "Okay. We should try to get in touch with her parents too. They need to come back. She needs them."

"I don't think we can reach them," said Cara, shaking her head slowly. "I asked Lilith about it. She doesn't know where they are, and she has no idea when they'll be back. She doesn't know much about what they do either, but from what she told me, I think they're most likely working on some top-secret projects for the government that no one should know about. She said they couldn't contact her when they were at work because personal devices were not allowed, and they couldn't use company devices to contact her either because they were restricted. So instead of calling or texting her, they usually just leave her a note on the fridge."

Thomas raised his eyebrows and looked at Cara, wide-eyed.

"I know!" Cara threw up her hands. "So how can we get in touch with them when they can't even contact her from—from wherever they are? Plus," she continued after a sigh, "nothing's working anyway. The cell signal and the radio are still out. And even though we have electricity for the modem, we still don't have an internet connection."

"It's the green vortex," Thomas mumbled, a gloomy shadow climbing onto his face. "That must be why. Look at how much it's grown since last night. I can't help thinking it's been feeding on our invisible energy forms to power its growth ... I wonder if it's alive ..."

Cara stared at Thomas, then she suddenly patted his cheek repeatedly as if she was trying to wake him up from a nightmare. Thomas blinked and, when he saw the look in Cara's eyes, let out a soft chuckle.

"Right. Can't go down *that* rabbit hole." He took a deliberate breath through his mouth, then he said, "Actually, I bet this is already all over the news in other cities by now, which means her parents will at least hear about what's happening here—if they haven't already ... But man, they're going to be worried sick about her once they find out they can't reach her—"

"I certainly hope so! Maybe they'll finally see what's more important then."

Thomas was taken aback by Cara's response, but he soon found the reason in her eyes. "You're angry with them."

"Of course I'm angry with them! They talk to her by leaving notes on the fridge! They didn't even tell her where they were traveling to or whether they'd be back for Christmas. They—" Cara stopped short and pinched the bridge of her nose, then she inhaled sharply and said, "And I thought *I* had it bad."

Thomas lowered his head, but he held out his arms without a word and wrapped them around Cara. Before Cara knew it, she was melting into his embrace like a deflated balloon.

"I get it. You're angry for Lilith. I can see why her parents remind you of yours," Thomas said softly. "True, they're always away for work, but does it necessarily mean they don't love her or care about her?"

Cara sighed and buried her face in his chest. "You're right. I should at least give them the benefit of the doubt."

"Hold on—" Thomas pulled away and looked at Cara with a gloating grin. "Did you just admit out loud that *I* was right?"

Cara started to roll her eyes, but her face broke into a smile instead, and she couldn't resist chortling. "Too bad no one else heard it, then. Now get up, Mr. Murphy. You and Lilith should get going."

"Oh, right." Thomas made a face and pushed himself up, then he picked up the tray and headed for the door.

"Be careful," Cara called after him. "And quick."

"We will." Thomas looked back and gave her a wink.

"Also, Thomas?"

"Yeah?"

"Could you leave a note for Lilith's parents and tell them she's staying with us? You know, just in case they're heading back to find her."

Thomas nodded, then a mischievous smile appeared on his face. "I suppose you want me to put it on the fridge?"

Cara smiled back, looking more pleased than playful. "You know what? I can't think of a better place to leave it."

V

Mira woke up to an excruciating pain in her lower abdomen. As she blinked to adjust her eyes to the dark, she remembered she was in her room.

She didn't know how long she had been dreaming. She was exhausted, utterly exhausted. She wished she could go back to sleep without going back to her dream.

The pain was climbing up her waist, swollen and raw, as if something inside her was about to crawl out through that inexplicable burn mark on her lower abdomen and tear her apart in the process.

Mira clenched her teeth and propped herself up with her elbows. Her burn mark, shaped like three exotic feathers lining up side by side, was emitting a mesmerizing glow of red and gold through the layers, growing increasingly more vibrant as it shifted up her torso like dancing flames reaching for the sky in slow motion.

The burning pain soon spread to her chest and surged into her rib cage. Wincing from the painful sensation that had now ignited her lungs, Mira pulled down the bedspread and peeled back her pajama top. She was not surprised at all to see that her burn mark had tripled in size and reached the bottom of her sternum, and the lavalike substance inside it was pushing and pulling twice as fast.

Mira's ears began to ring, then she remembered the night before her exhausting dream: the pedestrian square overloaded with Christmas lights and decorations; the ghastly-looking base in the fountain, under the archangel's feet; the jokes she made; the smiles on Lilith's face; the sweet smells of holiday treats; the never-ending Christmas songs; the ever-present crowds and hubbubs; the razzle-dazzle displays and selections of Christmas merchandise . . .

An alley that was silent and dark. The rotten odors of stale alcohol, old cigarettes, and marijuana. The lazy voice, the cold flame on the lighter, the smell of burned hair, the malicious laughs, the derogatory insults, the menacing threats—

Lilith's muffled cries.

The ringing sound had turned into a cacophonous whooshing noise. Mira flopped back down on the bed and stared at the ceiling. She did not need to recall what had happened next; she already knew—just like she did not need to recall what had happened that evening in Sunrise Park to know that, deep down, she had always known why Eric Ekker had lost his mind.

The cacophonous noise was getting louder and louder, sounding like a great murmuration of starlings, each urging her in a different human voice at the same time.

Mira squeezed her eyes shut and clutched her head.

She could not fight it anymore.

She knew what the noise meant; she understood what it said:

Wake up. It's time to wake up.

VI

To tell the truth, Cara had suspected the blackouts would last as long as they did in Skygate. So when they ended quietly sometime during the wee hours of Christmas Day morning, she was one of the few Starfall residents who noticed the good news right away. But instead of waking her family members to share the joyful news, along with a few tears of relief, like what most of the other night owls in town had done, Cara found herself staring blankly at her phone as the incoming alerts quickly filled up the screen.

When her phone had finally calmed down and gone back to power-saving mode, Cara got out of bed and walked to the windows to find out whether the green vortex was still there. She felt a little silly—and a little dizzy too—getting out of bed in the middle of the night just for that, but she figured since her brain would most likely not let her go to sleep peacefully anyway without knowing whether her hunch was right, she might as well do it so she could at least fall asleep more easily.

As soon as she peeked out from between the blinds, Cara knew she was too late. The sky was once again a serene backdrop for a river of stars and a cold, watchful moon. The green vortex had disappeared without a trace, and, to Cara's dismay, so had the last shred of sleepiness that was lingering in her head.

Still, Cara went back to bed and closed her eyes, hoping for that drowsy feeling to descend and melt her consciousness away. She waited and waited and waited, then she rolled to a different side, adjusted her pillow, and waited some more. Unfortunately, the drowsy feeling never showed up like she thought it would. Before she knew it, Cara was rolling to a different side and adjusting her pillow, again.

Cara lost count of how many times she had done that since she had come back to bed, and yet, not only was she far from feeling drowsy, but she was also becoming increasingly irritated with herself for not being able to fall asleep. Then, somewhere between weary wakefulness and incurable frustration, it finally occurred to her that even though she knew things would now begin to return to normal, she was still as tense as a bow held at full draw.

Cara sighed and opened her eyes. She knew she was perfectly aware of the reason why she was so tense that she couldn't even fall asleep, but she didn't want to admit it to herself, because if she did, she would be acknowledging that it was true—she didn't want it to be true.

It all began on the night before Christmas Eve, when it was already pushing midnight, yet Mira had neither answered her phone nor called back. Cara was beginning to feel nervous because Mira had never been out so late before. Then, just when she was dialing Mira's number again, the cell signal went out. Cara couldn't say for sure why, but it gave her a bad, jittery feeling, which then drove her to go outside and look up at the sky. But when she spotted that foreboding green disk of light rotating above the buildings between their house and the pedestrian square, she immediately understood that what had happened in Skygate was happening again.

For what it was worth, Cara had put on a brave face—for the most part—through the rest of the night and the first half of Christmas Eve morning, until Thomas and Lilith returned with the news that someone had already broken into Lilith's house, leaving the front entrance gaping at the street with an unobstructed view of how mercilessly the house had been ransacked. Cara didn't ask about the details, but she felt as if she were being slowly suffocated by an invisible scarf around her neck and couldn't breathe very well for a good few hours after that.

But that was just the beginning. By noon, the rising and falling sounds of the sirens had become a constant background noise, which was enough for Cara and Thomas to know that history had indeed repeated itself in Starfall. Even though their house was at the very back of the neighborhood and their backyard was separated from civilization by a large wooded area, they did not know if it would remain undisturbed till the end of the situation. What they did know, however, was that as long as the situation continued, their safety would not be guaranteed. Therefore, Cara and Thomas did what they thought to be the best: they sent Lilith up to the second floor to stay with Mira while they remained on the first to keep watch on the windows and doors.

Cara then spent the rest of Christmas Eve watching and listening very carefully like a hawk for any suspicious activity outside their house. So when Lilith rushed down the stairs at around six o'clock in the evening to tell them Mira's fever was finally breaking, Cara suddenly realized her nerves had been so tense that she had not only forgotten about making dinner but had also forgotten it was Christmas Eve—despite that she had been planning for it since early November. In her plan, they were supposed to invite Lilith, and maybe even her parents, over for a scrumptious Christmas Eve dinner and have a wonderful time celebrating their first Christmas in Starfall together. Cara had envisioned it many times before, but never once had it crossed her mind that she would be needing a plan B. Nevertheless, she still had to pivot. So instead of cooking up a storm for a fancy Christmas Eve dinner, Cara got out the mac and cheese.

They had a quick dinner in the dining room. Then, fearing that the night might prove to be even more troublesome for the town than the day had been, Cara asked Lilith to go back to the guest room and go to bed early. She could tell Lilith had already guessed the real reason behind her request, but Lilith, who was too thoughtful to add more stress to Cara's tense mental state, obeyed without asking the obvious question, leaving Cara both relieved and grateful for her attentiveness, albeit in secret.

The rest of the evening had felt like a lifetime, partly because Cara and Thomas had done nothing else but strain their eyes and ears in the dark to stay alert for potential danger. They guarded the entrances, both doors and windows, like children determined to wait for Santa Claus to show up on Christmas Eve so they could ambush him at first sight, even though they couldn't stop wondering if he would show up at all. For Cara, the suspense of it had felt interminable and unbearable. And, for the first time in a very long time, she felt like an impatient kid who could not wait to be done with Christmas Eve so that Christmas morning would come sooner, except that it was not the presents she was looking forward to. However, despite her newfound eagerness to speed up the most magical night of the year, time still crawled past slowly and painfully, until at last, she noticed that Thomas was dozing off on the floor with his back against the front door and decided it was enough.

So Cara woke Thomas and told him to go to bed. Then she barred the doors with chairs, masked the guest room door with a large houseplant, and checked the windows one more time. When she was done with everything, Cara went up to Mira's room and felt her forehead, then she took her temperature, just to be sure. She was greatly relieved when she saw that the reading had confirmed her initial judgment: Mira's temperature was just a little above the normal range now. On some level, subconsciously, even, it was a reassuring sign for Cara that this whole thing was coming to an end, and she could relax and go lie down as well.

Cara liked that idea; she *was* tired. She tucked Mira in and kissed her forehead, then, as quiet as a mouse, she left Mira's room and went into her bedroom. She was not surprised to see that Thomas was already fast asleep, but once she had lain down, she was surprised to find herself tossing and turning as though she wasn't tired enough to fall asleep after all.

Cara pulled herself back from her thoughts and rolled to her right. Thomas's face was right next to hers, and he was snoring lightly like a baby. She lifted a hand and touched his cheek, tracing along his jawline slowly and gently with her fingertips to feel the stubble that had been forming on his face since early Christmas Eve morning, when he had insisted on staying with Mira so that she would go to bed first.

Cara spent the next few hours in a half-asleep, half-awake state. By five o'clock in the morning, she had had enough of her insomnia, so she slipped out of bed and went downstairs. Instead of making herself a big cup of coffee, like she would usually do in the mornings, she went into the kitchen, turned on the decorative lamp on the counter, and poured herself a tall glass of wine. As Cara raised her glass, she noticed through the windowpanes on the patio door that it was still pitch-black outside, which was normal at that time of the day during winter. But to Cara, it somehow looked even more unsettling than when the green vortex was still in the sky, and she couldn't help feeling something far more unnerving was lurking in that darkness behind the patio door, watching her with prying eyes.

The thought sent a chill down her spine and made her hair stand on end. Cara took a big gulp of wine, swallowed it, then turned and flipped off the light. As the darkness of the night embraced her once more, she was surprised at the sense of security it provided her. Feeling a little more relaxed, Cara decided it was time to call Susan. She took another gulp from the wineglass, picked up her phone, and dialed.

Susan answered almost right away. "Cara?"

"Yeah, it's me. Did I wake you?"

"No," said Susan after letting out a soft sigh of relief. "Aren't you supposed to be sleeping though? It's only . . . ten past five over there, isn't it?"

"It is," said Cara, rotating her wineglass on the kitchen island like a dial. "I tried to stay in bed a little longer, but I couldn't really sleep."

"Is everything okay?" Susan asked, the fatigue in her voice suddenly replaced by anxiousness.

"Everything's okay, Suze. I just can't sleep."

There was a pause on Susan's end, then she said in a low voice, "Me neither."

"Uh-oh," said Cara, chuckling wryly. "You think we're in perimenopause now?"

Susan laughed. "Speak for yourself, lady!" Then she sighed softly and said, "It's nice to hear your voice, Cara. I'm glad you're all okay. To be honest, I was pretty worried."

"I've noticed," said Cara, smiling pensively, a heavy feeling forming in her chest as if something was stuck inside. "Do you know why? Because once the signal came back and the notifications started coming in, your name came up way more often than everyone else's, and by 'everyone else,' I meant the retailers, the telemarketers, and the good-for-nothing spammers who were very persistent in finding out how I was doing."

"Sounds to me like you've done too much online shopping," said Susan, chortling. "So when did the signal come back?"

"Not long after midnight."

"What about electricity?"

"Same time."

"Radio?"

"I didn't check, but the internet did come back at the same time as the others."

"And . . . the green vortex?"

Cara took a sip of her wine. "Same time, I suppose. I went to check after the messages came in, but it was already gone."

Susan fell silent. When she spoke again, Cara could hear a slight tremor in her voice. "It just . . . doesn't seem right, Cara. And I keep having this feeling that it won't end so easily . . ."

It dawned on Cara then the reappearance of the mysterious green vortex and the quadruple blackout that had come with it must have caused quite a stir in the news media again, and she had no doubt every one of the news agencies had been digging tirelessly through the old archives, like vultures picking through a mass burial site, for the juiciest stories recorded from when this had happened the first time, in Skygate. Cara instinctively knew this could only mean one thing: the story of Eric Ekker must have been all over the news again. And, having witnessed firsthand— for a *long* time after the green vortex had left Skygate alone— how the news agencies would not only act like but also think like vultures, Cara was certain they would not have forgotten to dwell on the same detail this time that it was Susan who had diagnosed Eric Ekker with traumatic mental disorder not long before he set himself on fire and blew up his house and his family in a gas explosion on purpose, right in front of Susan's eyes, as though he did it as a deliberate performance to convey a certain message to her personally.

"They're bringing it up again, aren't they?" Cara asked softly.

Susan didn't answer her, but the heavy silence on her end of the phone was enough to confirm it.

Cara felt a pang in her heart, then a buzzing sound began to pulsate between her temples like a muted siren calling out for her mental exhaustion and physical depletion, making her dizzy and lightheaded. She bent over the kitchen island and supported herself with her elbows. As she blinked to fight away the vertigo, Cara made up her mind that she would not allow those vultures to get to Susan this time.

"Suze, I need you to listen to me," Cara said firmly. "What happened to Eric Ekker had *nothing* to do with you, okay? I don't care what they're saying. It was *not* your fault, and we both know it. Don't let them get to you. Don't give them that satisfaction. They only care about clicks and views and likes anyway; they don't care about the truth. Maybe we, as a species, are finally at a point where we have stopped improving. People in this day and age are just . . . mean, selfish, angry, and . . . weak. Remember how they reacted to the green vortex and the blackouts in Skygate? Well, I regret to say it's not that different this time, even after two more years of technological development and social advancement and whatnot, and even though, this time, it has happened in a bigger, supposedly more educated town. So I say forget about those stupid newspeople and their stupid opinions. All they see in this is a way to make money. They will take advantage of the situation and milk it till it bleeds, no matter the cost, even if their influence will only result in more stupidity and absurdity in our society.

"I can already see it: they would blame the green vortex for having messed with their minds and made them do crazy, illogical things, just like those people in Skygate did. But it was not the green vortex; it was the people themselves, using the green vortex as an excuse to let loose the demons that had been living and growing inside them long before it appeared in the sky. Maybe they weren't fully aware of the existence of their own demons, or maybe they were and simply didn't want to acknowledge them. But instead of owning up to it and facing the truth about themselves, they would feed off the opinions and rumors from the media and blame it all on the green vortex for what they had failed to contain within themselves.

"I believe Eric Ekker was the same, only his demon was so powerful that it managed to consume his sanity completely. What happened to him and his family was a terrible tragedy. But at the end of the day, it was his own doing, because it was a choice that was made by something that had always been a part of him—not the green vortex, and definitely not you."

Cara bit her lip and waited for a response from Susan, knowing very well that her words alone might not be enough to keep Susan away from the disturbing memory of what she had witnessed that day in Skygate. However, Susan remained quiet. Cara closed her eyes and sighed inwardly. She wished she could reach into her phone and give Susan a hug, and she wished, more than anything else, she could just reach into Susan's head and erase that memory from her brain for good.

When Susan finally spoke again, her voice was quavering. "It haunts me, Cara," she said. "I was scared for you . . . I was worried that someone like him might do something like that to—to the three of you." She drew a shaky breath, then her voice blurred into a whimper. "I can't get those images out of my head, Cara. I can't . . ."

As she listened to the soft sobbing noises from Susan, Cara felt her heart contract in pain. Tears began to circle in her own eyes, but she wiped them away quickly and said, "I'm okay though, Suze. We're all okay. So stop thinking about what you're thinking about

... 'Everything that has happened is already in the past now. You can't embrace the future if you keep holding on to the past. You have to let it go.' You must. Because you, Susan, of all people, deserve to be happy."

Susan sniffled a few more times, then she said in a hoarse voice, "That sounds like something Nina would say."

A melancholy smile appeared on Cara's lips. "It was. That's what she said to me the last time she called ... you know, just days before she swung by our house in secret and dropped a real baby off in our backyard like the stork without giving me any warning or explanation or instruction whatsoever, right before she disap—"

Cara couldn't finish her sentence; the rest of it was stuck in her throat because a chill had zipped down from the back of her head to the other end of her spine, making the hair on her nape stand on end, while spreading a tingling sensation across her back, as if someone was watching her from behind. Half expecting to find Mira standing at the bottom of the staircase, Cara sucked in an involuntary breath and spun around.

There was not a soul behind her. In fact, with the light from her phone screen, which had lit up considerably when she had forgotten to keep it to her face while she turned, she was able to see that the only shapes between her and the staircase were those of household items, all of which were standing motionlessly in the places they belonged. The air was still—not a single movement, not a single sound.

"Cara?" Susan called nervously.

Her voice startled Cara, who suddenly noticed she had been holding her breath. With a shaky exhale, she let it out and mumbled, "I'm ... I'm here."

There was a soft sigh of relief on the other side of the phone. "I'm sorry, Cara," said Susan. "I had no idea that was what she said to you before—Well, we don't have to talk about that now."

Cara smiled wryly to herself and massaged her forehead. With a deep breath, she grabbed her wineglass and sat down on the floor, leaning back against the kitchen island.

"Actually ... we do," she finally said. She took a big sip from her glass, swallowed it slowly, and continued, "Suze? I think I've finally found a reason for it. I, uh ..." Cara paused and looked toward the staircase. She knew she was probably being paranoid, but she couldn't help scanning each step for a shape that did not belong there, until her eyes reached the winder treads, where the balusters were met by solid wall.

"Yes?" Susan urged, sounding alarmed.

Cara lowered her eyes and looked pensively at her wineglass. Then she took another sip and whispered into the phone, "Do you remember how she was always traveling for work, yet was always very secretive about what she did? ... I think that was why she decided to leave Mira behind with us ..."

The burning heat and pain shot up to Mira's head like a volcanic eruption, clouding her eyes and making her temples throb with a pulsating tension until the cacophonous whooshing voices sped up and distorted into an ascending Shepard tone, piecing her eardrums and drowning out the rest of Mom's words.

Instead of bursting into the kitchen to confront Mom about what she had heard, Mira closed her eyes. Despite the chaos and pains that were taking place inside her, her heart was quiet and still like the air, and, somehow, she was able to feel every single cell of herself—from the ends of her hairs to her toes, from the insides of her organs to her fingertips—waking up to life one by one, but immediately swallowed whole by that burning heat and pain, as if they were all turning into flames, as if she would soon burst into flames herself.

But Mira couldn't care less if she did. Noiselessly like a phantom, she turned around and retraced her steps from the winder treads till she was back in her room again.

Chapter 7 THE DEVIL

1

LILITH let the heavy backpack slip off her arms, then she grabbed it by the shoulder straps and placed it on the floor, by the foot of the bed. With a deliberate sigh, she straightened up and stretched her back.

"Whew, that was heavy," she said, rubbing the small of her back. Then she sat down on the bed and smiled at Mira. "How are you doing?"

"I don't know." Mira shrugged; her face was as emotionless as her voice.

Lilith couldn't help noticing Mira was looking even paler than she had on Christmas Day, which was also the day her parents had surprised everyone by showing up at the Murphys' front door at around four o'clock in the afternoon to take her home. Mrs. Murphy had generously invited them to stay for Christmas dinner. But her parents, after thanking Mrs. Murphy and Mr. Murphy profusely for having taken her in during the blackouts, had declined the offer by saying that they had caused enough inconveniences and troubles to them as it was and really shouldn't be intruding on their family time any longer. So in the end, Lilith left with her parents and spent the next few days at home, helping them to clean up the house and restore it to what it was like before the break-in.

But not a day went by without Lilith going through what she had come to learn about Mira over and over again in her head, hoping to find an explanation that would finally make sense. Then, at around dinnertime the day before, another new story had hit the headlines and instantly became *the* story that had taken place during the presence of the green vortex. And thanks to the relentless coverage from every possible media channel and platform in the country after the initial news broadcast, the story itself had basically been turned into a daytime nightmare for Lilith, which was precisely why she had to come check on Mira today.

Lilith searched Mira's face for something she could work with, but she found nothing. Instead, she was taken aback by an ineffable feeling that Mira looked different than before.

A sudden pang of fear seized her heart. Lilith lowered her head and waited till it had eased off a little, then she said in a small voice, "It's not your fault, Mira . . . You let them go."

Mira gave a dry laugh. "I did. Yet they burned themselves alive anyway."

As if her brain had taken a screenshot from the news and decided it was the right moment to project it into her mind, Lilith thought of the image that was mostly made up of carbonized human bodies, as well as the seven unflattering mug shots carefully placed around that image. She shuddered involuntarily, and her brain turned off the projection.

"They went mad," Lilith said softly. "It wasn't your fault. According to the news, they weren't the only ones—"

"But how many of them had set themselves on fire?" Mira cut her off. "Was it a mere coincidence that the only ones who had burned themselves alive also happened to be the ones who had seen me?"

Lilith opened her mouth to counter, but she couldn't think fast enough to come up with another explanation.

"Exactly," said Mira, resuming her emotionless tone. "It wasn't a coincidence, Lilith. I think they went mad because they had seen me. They thought I was the Devil. Maybe I am."

"You are *not* the Devil!" Lilith cried, trying hard to keep that lump in her throat in check. "Mira, you saved me from those men! The Devil takes pleasure in inflicting pains and sufferings whenever it can, not to save people from them! ... No. You're definitely not the Devil. Whoever you were in the alley that night, it was a being of virtue and purity. I'm sure of it!"

Mira noticed the tears in Lilith's eyes and lowered her own. She was sitting cross-legged on the bed, and her eyes fell on her hands. She opened them and concentrated on connecting with each one of her fingers, then she clenched them back into fists—an exercise she had been doing more often these days to check whether they were merely an illusion that would turn into flames.

Mira could not persuade herself to believe she had nothing to do with the violent deaths of those men, but neither could she persuade herself to ask Lilith what if she was wrong about the nature of her true self—what if she wasn't a being of virtue and purity, but one of chaos and destruction?

"What am I, then?" she finally asked. "If I'm not the Devil, how do you explain the wings? The flames?"

"Actually, those two features are not unique to the Devil," Lilith answered eagerly. "In fact, there are many mythical beings who fit the criteria. Besides, even though I only saw ... you from the back, I can say for certain there was not a single devil's horn on your head. Hang on—" She leaned to her side and reached for her backpack with both hands, then she hoisted it onto the bed. Carefully, she unzipped it and opened it wide, revealing a stack of yellow pages that were neatly packed inside.

"Remember the break-in?" Lilith continued, sounding surprisingly amused. "Well, the people who did it took the valuables and broke the breakables, but apparently, they detested books and bookshelves so much that they didn't even want to go near them; can you believe it?" She gave a resigned laugh, then she removed the fragile-looking pages from her backpack, stack by stack, and gently laid them out between Mira and herself. "These books belong to my parents, actually. They have a whole collection of ancient documents and antique books sitting on our bookshelves, mostly about obscure events and strange incidents in ancient China. I've

read almost all of them, and I can tell you their collection is no ordinary collection. It's a good thing the people who broke in didn't
know how rare and valuable they are, or I bet they would have
acted very differently. Anyway, I think these books can be helpful,
so I smuggled them out. There, you're my accomplice now."

Mira cocked an eyebrow at Lilith's haul. If one had to use the
term "books" on them, then they could only be described as the
most primitive versions of modern-day books: they looked so old
and fragile that they seemed to be groaning about back pain for
having to lie down on her soft mattress.

"I can see why the people who broke in didn't want to go near
your parents' collection," she said gravely. "They look like someone's great-great-great-great-great-grandmother threaded all her
old school report cards together and displayed them by a sunny
windowsill this whole time. Can you even open one without the
pages turning into dust? ... By the way, why are you carrying so
many chopsticks in your backpack?"

Lilith chuckled to herself but rolled her eyes at Mira. "These
are *not* chopsticks, okay? They're bamboo slips. People in ancient
China used them to document information before paper was invented." She pulled the bamboo scroll out from her backpack carefully, got to her feet, and unrolled it slowly on the bed. "See? These
strips are tied together. Also, they're flat and wider than my fingers,
which proves they were *not* designed for eating."

"Not for eating ... Got it." Mira nodded deliberately. "So how
exactly will these, um, early Chinese literatures help us by disinte-
grating in my room?"

A soft snort escaped Lilith's nose, but she cleared her throat
quickly and put on a straight face. "Show some respect, young
lady. You're in the presence of valuable information from a long,
long time ago, information that was documented by our ancient
ancestors by hand, stroke by stroke!"

Mira tilted her head to one side and squinted at the faint writing
on the bamboo slips, which looked more like drawings of symbols

rather than words with meanings. "So how long ago are we talking about here?"

"I would say at least a thousand years."

Mira glanced up to see if Lilith was joking, only to find that she was not.

"Hmm," said Mira, wrinkling her nose. "That explains the smell, I guess. Where did your parents get them from anyway? Not some rich emperor's tomb, I hope?"

Lilith chortled loudly. "Nah, my parents are pretty boring. I don't see them sneaking into royal burial grounds in the middle of the night to extract delicate ancient documents from tombs. My guess is they either collect them for a hobby or to study them for work. Judging by their lack of interest in recreational activities in general though, I'm inclined to think it's the latter ... But, I wouldn't be surprised if what we have here were indeed dug out by some professional grave robbers from some rich emperor's tomb. That sort of thing was pretty common back in those days, actually, just like in ancient Egypt."

"So everything that's sitting on my bed right now could have once been buried in a royal tomb somewhere in China." Mira paused meaningfully. "Well, I guess this smell has nothing to do with old age after all."

"C'mon, it's not that bad, okay?" said Lilith, laughing. "It's not like the rich emperor was still reading them in his coffin. Plus, the information recorded in these documents must have been considered as the key to unveil heavenly mysteries that were not meant to be learned or understood by ordinary men, which means only the most powerful man in the whole country at that time could have obtained something like these, even if they were to be buried with him for his afterlife. And for a man that powerful in ancient China, his tomb would have been more like an extensive underground burial vault that was built to recreate the life he had enjoyed before he died, meaning, there would have been plenty of dedicated chambers to store his concubines, servants, armies, and his most valuable possessions from when he was alive: exquisite gold, fine silver, exotic jewels, rare gems ... and documents like these to show him the way to heavenly mysteries in his afterlife. So I doubt any of them were actually physically pried from a dead emperor's fingers. If it helps, think about how incredibly lucky we are to be able to lay eyes on what was once exclusively reserved for the eyes of the most powerful man in ancient China!"

It was hard to miss the excitement radiating from her face. Mira felt the corners of her lips curve up slightly. "I never thought I would say this to anyone, but it sounds to me like you've got great passion for a role in the field of professional grave robbing."

Lilith snorted loudly and burst into laughter. Still holding her sides, she said, breathlessly, "I appreciate the feedback, Mira. But you know, there's a nicer way to call it, especially when the end goal is knowledge instead of money."

"Like what?"

"*Archaeology*," Lilith replied, chortling, but her smile soon grew sad. "Funny how you noticed I have a passion for it and I didn't ... You know, when I was little, I used to think maybe my parents left me behind with my grandma because I wasn't really their true-born daughter. But according to my grandma, they used to teach archaeology before I was born. Of course, my parents never told me anything about it, and I never ... Well, I guess I do have their genes after all."

Mira lowered her eyes, then she said softly, "That's great."

Lilith was half expecting Mira to comment more about her "professional grave robbing" genes, so she was quite surprised when she realized that was all Mira was going to say. But Lilith told herself it was because there was something else weighing on Mira's mind, something inexplicable and heavy, and she was determined to do everything she could to shoulder that weight for her friend.

Lilith sat back down on the bed and said, "Anyway, what's done is done. What we need to focus on now is the future." She took a deep breath and gestured to the ancient documents between them. "So, shall we begin?"

Mira's eyes swept over the old bamboo slips and the stacks of fragile papers, each a surviving witness of what was long forgotten. It was one thing to believe they might have once been in the possession of some of the most powerful men in ancient China, but it was another to believe what was recorded in these thousand-year-old documents could be of any service to her. Nevertheless, what was impossible for everyone else had become possible for her, twice. She needed answers. She needed to know the reason for her transformations. She needed to know what she was. She needed to know why she was what she was. She needed to know the purpose of her existence. And above all, she needed to know the purpose of all *this* in a world where she had finally found out that, unlike Lilith, she was not the trueborn daughter of the two people who she had referred to as Mom and Dad her whole life until then.

The last part of her thought made her heart pause. Mira ignored the feeling and glanced up at Lilith. "Yes. I'm ready."

Lilith nodded. Slowly and very carefully, she peeled back a few pages from the first stack to her right, revealing a full-page drawing of a large bird on a delicate piece of yellowed paper.

At first glance, Mira had thought it was a peacock, but she soon came to the conclusion that it was a different species. For one thing, the bird in this drawing had a full head of orange hair that looked like thick strands of oversize chrysanthemum petals, flowing down luxuriously along its long, thin neck and covering most of its breast. For another, a layer of large aquamarine scales was shielding the bird's trunk as well as its wings, which were also covered by two overlapping layers of stiff, finlike feathers at the bottom, reminding Mira of mermaids and dragons. Colorful feathers blossomed from its long, soft tail like fireworks, but instead of flowing down toward the ground, they seemed to be floating in midair as if the bird was posing in zero gravity. Even though the pigments had faded considerably, and even though the page itself was dotted with brown blotches here and there, Mira could tell how vibrant the colors used to be and how exquisite the details once were on this drawing.

"It's beautiful," she murmured.

"It sure is!" Lilith chirped happily with pride. "This is my most promising lead so far: a mythical winged creature who was regarded as an immortal; it was believed to have the ability to regenerate itself in the fire and be reborn with a new life."

"Sounds like a phoenix."

"It does!" Lilith replied eagerly. "That's why this lead is very promising . . . and interesting. First of all, this concept—a mythical winged creature who can be reborn in flames—not only exists in China but also in many western cultures on the other side of the globe. Why? I spent some time digging into this, and I found out the same concept had actually been mentioned in many ancient civilizations besides ancient China: ancient Egypt, ancient India, ancient Greece, ancient Rome, to name a few. What's more, there's enough archaeological evidence to prove that just like the people in ancient China, people in those areas also worshiped such a creature as an immortal, a representation of fire and the sun, and a symbol for the gods and goddesses who, supposedly, could wield fire or even control the sun. But here's the interesting thing: although they all worshiped a mythical winged creature who can be reborn in flames, their documentations on the creature's name and appearance varied from country to country. Why?"

Lilith pointed at the drawing. "For example, this one is called *Fènghuáng* in China. As you can see, our *Fènghuáng* looks quite different from your phoenix. According to these documents, *Fènghuáng*'s plumage was very colorful and vibrant, and it had the beak of a rooster, the chin of a swallow, the neck of a snake, the back of a turtle, the scales of a dragon, and the tail of a fish. A phoenix, on the other hand, was mostly described in relevant documentations as a unique bird with a plumage that was partly red and partly golden. See what I mean?"

With her eyes still lingering on the drawing, Mira shrugged. "Maybe they are two different species who happened to have the same ability?"

"That thought crossed my mind too," said Lilith, nodding. "So I dug deeper into what I could find on the phoenix, looking for records that would support such a theory. But guess what? I ended up finding records from even older documents, which actually described the phoenix to be a bird with such colorful and vibrant plumage that it stood out from all birds—the same description they used in ancient China for *Fènghuáng*! Coincidence? I think not. I think there's only one explanation for this: *Fènghuáng* and *phoenix* are two different names that were used in the East and the West for the same winged creature."

"So . . . either there was someone in the West who really wanted to give the phoenix a different look in the books, or the phoenix just stopped looking colorful and vibrant one day because—" Mira paused abruptly, then she turned her head to Lilith and waited with an unreadable expression, as if she needed to confirm the validity of a thought that she was not yet willing to acknowledge.

Lilith nodded and finished the sentence for her. "Because it had started to burn, but it could not stop burning; the winged creature was in perpetual flames. That was why its colorful and vibrant plumage could no longer been seen. And that was why, in time, it was documented as a unique bird that was partly red and partly golden instead."

"Partly red, partly golden . . ." Mira repeated the words to herself and gazed down at her hands. There was nothing unusual about them. In fact, they appeared perfectly normal—too normal to have transformed into the pair of fiery wings that had passed right through the flesh and bones of the thugs who she had meant to injure badly with her fists.

"It was not in flames, Lilith," she finally said. "It *was* the flames."

Lilith's lips parted slightly, taken aback. "What do you mean?"

"The winged creature was not burning," said Mira, slowly and meaningfully. "If it had been, they would have observed three colors instead of two: red, gold, and black—black being the physical form of the winged creature burning inside the red-and-golden flames."

"It was not burning. It was not . . . burning . . ." Lilith murmured, her eyes growing wide and wider until her face was frozen with shock by a newfound revelation. "You're right. It was not burning ... The winged creature was not in flames. It *was* the flames, in the shape of a bird!"

Then suddenly, it was all Lilith could see: an enormous fiery bird, partly red and partly golden, floating in midair with its back toward her. The flames on its long, flowing tail were drifting elegantly in the air like the flying Apsaras' brocade scarves, all the while burning wildly as if they would start dripping down to the ground like liquid at any moment. Its massive wings were spreading upward, cutting into the moonless and starless night like two enormous fiery scythes forged for a giant, burning the entire sky red like blood. Its body was gracefully poised above the ground, yet its flames seemed to be churning like the inside of an active volcano or the surface of the sun, ready to erupt and disrupt at any given chance. It raised its head and let out a long and terrifying screech toward the sky, but it never looked back ...

As the image faded away from her mind, Lilith realized she had been staring right into Mira's eyes, with tears welling up in her own.

"It was ... you ..." Lilith said weakly to herself, not noticing she had actually muttered the words out loud. What she did notice, however, was that something had flickered in Mira's black eyes.

Was it fear? Sadness? Loneliness? Or was it the tears in her own eyes that were making her vision unreliable? Lilith couldn't say for sure. Whatever it was, like the fleeting flame of a shooting star, it was already gone.

"Well, your most promising lead checked out," Mira said in a toneless voice, lowering her eyes. "The mystery is solved. I have my answer now. Thank you."

The calm detachment in her response left a dull pain in Lilith's chest. She opened her mouth to say something back to her friend, but she found herself at a loss for words.

"Mira, I ..."

"It's okay, Lilith." Mira leaned back and looked out the window. "For what it's worth, besides great passion, I think you've also got a real talent for archaeology. You do have your parents' genes. Maybe you have a lot more in common than you think."

There was not a trace of emotion in her voice, so although Lilith knew Mira meant what she said, she couldn't help feeling Mira was distancing herself.

As Lilith searched hard in her head for a possible explanation for Mira's unexpected withdrawal, it suddenly dawned on her that it was because Mira had sensed her fear—her fear toward the enormous fiery bird, which she had been trying her best to hide from Mira, the very person who had transformed into the very creature that had made her afraid.

Lilith wanted to tell Mira it didn't matter what she was, and it didn't matter what she was capable of after her transformation, because neither could change the fact that she was her best and only friend. Then, just as Lilith was getting ready to speak, her eyes landed on the drawing again, and within seconds, a question had filled up her mind and flushed all other thoughts from her head.

"We haven't solved the mystery yet!" she cried. "We haven't figured out what happened to the winged creature and why it couldn't stop burning!"

Mira turned her head and looked at Lilith briefly, then she looked away. "Does it matter?"

"Of course it matters! If we can figure them out, then maybe ... maybe ..." Lilith's voice grew small as she tried to organize her thoughts and words to convince herself. "Maybe we can help y— it to become what it should have become ..."

"You mean help *me* to stop burning as the phoenix and be reborn as *Fènghuáng*?" Mira asked airily.

"No," said Lilith, swallowing hard to keep the tightness in her throat from rising any higher than it already had. "Not you. The winged creature. If we can help it to stop burning and be reborn again, then maybe ... it won't need to stay inside you anymore."

The moment Lilith had finished her sentence, she began to wonder if she was only fooling herself. She had found some documents on exorcism from her parents' collection the year before and read them out of pure boredom when she couldn't think of anything better to do during her first Christmas break in this country. The events recorded in those documents were surprisingly interesting, and she had devoured them as obscure folklore stories even though they were recorded as real events and most of them had ended horribly wrong. Still, up until now, Lilith had only thought of the whole evil-expelling shenanigans recorded in those documents as their ancestors' early attempts at treating mental patients. And despite the entries of a few events where evil spirits were driven out of possessed individuals successfully in the end, she couldn't help but wonder whether it was even possible for them to drive a mystical creature out of someone who seemed to have not only coexisted with it in the physical form but also in the mind.

The thought made Lilith lightheaded. She felt the blood draining from her face and limbs as if it were being sucked away by gravity, yet she couldn't do anything to stop it. A wave of helplessness washed over her, then her vision blacked out, and she was suddenly alone in a deep, dark place that was between subconscious and reality. Lilith whimpered inwardly; she had never felt so hopelessly trapped inside her own mind.

"You *are* Miss Positive, Lilith." It was Mira's voice. "You can think of a solution for anything."

Her tone was as nonchalant as ever, but Lilith's eyes welled up anyway. She waited till her vision had returned, then she got up, sat down beside Mira, and hugged her with both arms, just before the tears escaped.

"No, Mira. *We* will think of a solution for *everything*."

11

Gargoyle was pacing up and down the long, milky white corridor that connected the elevator to the conference chamber. His face was red with zeal, his eyes wild with exhilaration. His bald head was glistening with sweat beads, like the underside of a lid on a pot of boiling water. If Gargoyle could move any faster, they just might evaporate into steam.

"This is taking too long!" he grumbled. "A golden opportunity was dropped right into our lap! We have a fresh trail! Every minute we spend here debating leaves us another minute behind the Red Key! There's no time to lose! We need to take actions *now*!"

The speaker came on from inside the nearest life-size Hermes statue, one of the many robotic assistants inside this high-tech fortress known only to a group of selected minds in the world as the Pandora's Box. "I understand your frustration, Dr. G. However—" He fell silent when Gargoyle strode past, then his voice continued from the next Hermes that was standing by in the corridor, "According to protocol PBCSZ008, a capture plan needs to be approved unanimously by all Architects before it can be executed, not to mention you've requested Level Three military resources and firearms, which requires additional evaluations and approvals—" As soon as Gargoyle passed the one that was speaking, Hermes's voice paused and resumed from the next statue in line. "You've made your case on behalf of the Pathfinders. Therefore, please wait patiently while the Architects decide on whether your proposal is viable for immediate action."

Gargoyle gritted his teeth but didn't stop pacing. Of course he knew what kind of approval was required in the protocols for pursuing an unprecedented opportunity like this. He was also well aware of the kind of actions that Hermes would carry out, in accordance with the protocols, if a security breach was ever detected at the Pandora's Box—be it a security breach against the building itself, its contents, physical or virtual, or its protocols. Gargoyle never understood why the founders had entrusted the artificial intelligence at the Pandora's Box with the highest level of security clearance for everything that was related to their mission. He did not like the degree of power and control that the founders' decision had granted Hope—the artificial intelligence of the supercomputer that pretty much ran the entire facility and, therefore, every Hermes that was connected to her inside the Pandora's Box —to have over the Pathfinders, who had been working diligently toward the end goal of this mission for decades and would not hesitate to give up everything they had in exchange for the mere opportunity of studying the powers of even just one of the Four Keys.

"In the meantime, could I assist you with anything else?" the next Hermes added as Gargoyle stomped past.

This time, Gargoyle braked to a halt. Hermes's offer of assistance just gave him an idea—a brilliant idea.

"Actually . . . yes, Hermes. I do need your assistance."

"Of course, Dr. G. What can I do for you?"

"My capture plan for the Red Key—how likely will it be approved?"

"Based on current simulations, eighty-four percent."

"Eighty-four percent! Only?" Gargoyle couldn't help raising his voice. "But we know exactly where the Red Key had been!"

"With all due respect, Dr. G, that was the same rationale you used to persuade the Architects to approve your capture plan the first time, yet the operation turned out to be—and I quote—'nothing but an expensive wild-goose chase.' Now, in spite of the unsatisfactory result from last time, you're still opting for the space hurricane as an indicator of the Red Key's location, so surely you can understand why the Architects have doubts about your new capture plan."

"The last one didn't work out as expected because we only realized the correlation between the Red Key and the space hurricane *after* one had taken place, and it was a year too late for us to salvage any physical evidence! But this one . . . It *just* happened, right before Christmas! Even if the Red Key is no longer concealing itself in that area, we can still find and access the physical evidence of its appearance to shed light on its behavioral patterns! We can learn about why the Red Key was there and why it summoned another space hurricane. But we'll only have a chance at that if we act *now*!"

"I understand, Dr. G," the same Hermes replied in a voice that sounded empathetic yet artificial at the same time, which produced a cooling effect in the air for Gargoyle to calm down from his eager thoughts and return to reality. "However, I'm afraid you'll still need that unanimous vote before we can proceed with your capture plan, even if it might not involve any capturing in the end."

But eighty-four percent is not enough! Gargoyle thought angrily. *It has to happen. It needs to happen! I would do anything to make it happen! . . . Yes, something must be done before the Architects cast their final votes, something . . . irresistible.*

Gargoyle reassured himself about his decision by picturing the Vermilion Bird trapped inside the special birdcage that he had designed specifically for capturing it. It was a comforting thought.

He licked his lips and said, "Hermes, I'm raising the stakes. I'm adding the Black Key and the White Key to my capture plan as well. I need you to draft as many capture plans as possible to include all three Keys in one master plan, and I need you to run simulations on vote projections for those plans based on each Architect's psychological and behavioral analysis until we have a master capture plan that is projected to get us the unanimous vote we need to move in on all three Keys."

A dead silence fell over the long, milky white corridor. Gargoyle was still staring straight at Hermes's unresponsive, unchanging face, but he was suddenly unsure of what Hermes would do to him next: Would he be considered as a security threat, or worse, a security breach that ought to be eliminated?

As time ticked away second by second, the silence not only persisted but also became suffocating. Gargoyle couldn't help but hold his breath.

Finally, Hermes replied, "That is quite an unorthodox request, Dr. G."

A soft sigh of relief escaped Gargoyle's throat, but he caught it between his teeth. Before he knew it, he was grinning triumphantly behind his unkempt beard—he was still here, standing in front of a Hermes, in spite of what he had just requested. As a man of science who was keen on reasoning and deduction, Gargoyle was too shrewd to miss the implication: by taking advantage of the operational gray area in vote projection, he had successfully bypassed the security breach protocol on vote manipulation. In other words, as soon as Hermes began working on his request, the unanimous vote that he needed from the Architects would already be in his pocket. Better yet, it would be for three Keys instead of one.

"I know it is," said Gargoyle, whose unstoppable grin was pushing the sagging skin and wrinkles on his face up into unsightly folds, making him look even more calculating and malicious than a real gargoyle. "But our protocols are not against it either. Am I correct, Hermes?"

"Indeed." The response was made so quickly and emotionlessly that it almost sounded dismissive. "However, it appears that we do not have enough analyzed information to initiate a capture plan for either the Black Key or the White Key. Would you care to advise how we could proceed?"

"Certainly, Hermes. I assume you have access to every single database that was set up for the Four Keys?"

"Yes."

"So you can read and analyze the incomplete findings from all of our ongoing research programs as well as every piece of raw information that is stored but not yet processed?"

"That is correct."

Gargoyle nodded impatiently and raised his voice. "Then find a way to utilize the information at your disposal and fill in the missing requirements to initiate capture plans for those two Keys!"

"Very well, Dr. G," Hermes answered calmly without taking offense. "I will proceed accordingly. However, I must remind you that for a capture plan that is produced without adequate analyzed information, the success rate will be much lower. Current calculations indicate a six percent success rate for capturing the Blue Key, a twenty-two percent success rate for capturing the White Key, and a thirty-seven percent success rate for capturing the Black Key."

Gargoyle sneered coldly behind his beard. "Thank you, Hermes. I'm fully aware of the chances of failures."

"In that case, do you still wish to add the Black Key and the White Key to your capture plan? At the moment, your success rate for capturing the Red Key is at sixty-nine percent. Adding more Keys to your capture plan will decrease your overall success rate dramatically."

"But it'll also increase the success rate for capturing the two other Keys, which will therefore enhance the Architects' faith in the prospect of capturing not just one, but three out of all four Keys!"

"I see," said Hermes, enunciating each word slowly as if he was having trouble processing the logic behind Gargoyle's argument.

"No, Hermes." Gargoyle lowered his voice and took a step forward, then he stared Hermes in his unblinking, unexpressive eyes and whispered, "Don't *see*. *Do*. *Make* it happen—before the Architects can cast their final votes. It *needs* to happen, Hermes, because—"

"Because there's no coincidence in the making of history. Am I correct, Dr. G?"

For a split second, Gargoyle was suddenly under the impression that even though Hermes's eyes were carved onto his face plate, they were, in fact, very much alive—so much so that they were able to see through his mind.

Like a child who was caught red-handed stealing cookies from the cookie jar, Gargoyle immediately backed away. "Y-yes."

"Thank you for confirming," said Hermes, who, in spite of Gargoyle's suspicion, didn't sound like he had observed the lead Pathfinder's discomfort at all. "Communication with Hope has been completed. Drafting in progress. Estimated time to completion: four hours, one minute, and ten seconds. Once completed, the new plan will be submitted to the Architects as an urgent update, before they cast their final votes. Will that suffice, Dr. G?"

Sensing that he might not have bypassed the security breach protocol after all, Gargoyle held his tongue and examined Hermes's face carefully. He wished he had a way to tell what was *really* going on behind Hermes's beautifully sculpted shell; it would help him to decide whether this robotic assistant would become his salvation or his downfall.

There's no coincidence in the making of history, Gargoyle reminded himself, clenching his jaw. *I would do anything to make it happen . . .*

He swallowed hard and gave Hermes a stiff nod. "Yes. That's all I need for now. Thank you, Hermes . . . for your assistance. I . . . appreciate it."

"You're welcome, Dr. G," Hermes replied without a hint of emotion in his voice. "The pleasure is all mine."

III

"Honey, I'm home!" Thomas called as he entered the mudroom. To his surprise, Cara was not in the kitchen. He took off his jacket and hung it on the coatrack, along with his keys, then he carried the groceries to the kitchen island, from where he saw that Cara was sitting on the couch in the living room, her eyes glued to the TV.

He left the grocery bags on the kitchen island and walked into the living room. The TV screen was occupied by a familiar image that consisted of seven mug shots and a pile of blackened corpses. Near the bottom of the screen, the headline read, "BREAKING NEWS: INVESTIGATION OF GANG SELF-IMMOLATION LEADS TO NEW MYSTERIES."

"They're still milking it hard, aren't they?" Thomas shook his head and sat down beside Cara. "Even on New Year's Eve—"

"Shh!" Cara put a finger to her lips but didn't take her eyes off the TV. "Listen!"

There was a level of urgency in her tone that immediately directed Thomas's attention from the image on the screen to the news anchor's voice.

". . . The plot thickens as baffling new details were discovered at the retired city junkyard, where all seven members of the local gang named Hell-o-Hell committed suicide by self-immolation."

The camera cut to a blond woman in a formfitting red dress. She was standing in front of a large LCD screen, which was displaying the mug shots of the seven deceased men in two rows. She was wearing heavy makeup and an even heavier expression.

The blond woman looked straight into the camera and said gravely, "According to Sheriff Bryson, further autopsy results suggest that all seven members of the gang committed self-immolation at about the same time, which was concluded to be at around midnight on Christmas Day. This new finding appears to support the initial theory from the police department that a suicide pact was made among the seven gang members. However, when it comes to unearthing the reason behind why the gang members agreed on a suicide pact, or why they chose to carry it out in such an extreme fashion, Sheriff Bryson and his team had gained little success—until earlier today.

"Just an hour ago, a series of images was released by the police department as new evidence from their ongoing investigation, which, however, has not only created an unexpected twist in the case itself but also brought up even more questions and speculations. Despite the growing number of mysteries surrounding this case, Sheriff Bryson said he was still hopeful that through further investigations, these new findings would help to shed light on the real cause behind the gang members' tragic actions."

As she finished her last sentence, the mug shots on the LCD screen faded out and were replaced by several photos of what seemed like small holes in the ground.

With a twist of her slender waist, the blond woman turned effortlessly on her skyscraper heels. The camera cut to a different angle then, presenting an image of her from the waist up on the left side of the screen while displaying the photos that had appeared on the LCD screen on the right. Looking thoughtfully into the camera, the blond woman gestured at the photos and continued, "These aerial shots of the crime scene are among the number of photos that were freshly released by the police department. As you can see from these images, the crime scene is dotted with holes. They might seem small here on the screen, but in real life, each of them is about four feet deep and four feet wide. According to Sheriff Bryson, these holes only came to their attention after the snow had melted, but once they realized how many of them were in the area, they examined them right away. Interestingly, the result of their initial analysis suggests that these holes were most likely dug by the gang members before they committed self-immolation.

"But why did the gang members exhaust themselves with such a laborious activity when they were about to carry out a suicide pact? So far, there's no official answer to that question. Instead of leading us to enlightenment, this new finding only adds an additional layer of mystery to this already baffling case. But guess what? There's more."

The camera cut again, and the blond woman was occupying the right side of the screen, with several new photos displaying on the left, which were zoomed-in shots of different kinds of weatherworn hard objects one would expect to find at a junkyard, except that they were all neatly placed next to number tags and were all stained with blood.

The blond woman continued with a serious frown. "According to Sheriff Bryson, many bloodstained objects like these were discovered in the crime scene area. Blood samples have been extracted from each item for DNA testing, and, as strange as it may sound, the results indicate that these bloodstains all came from one or more of the deceased gang members. Stranger still, the bloodstain pattern analysis has concluded that they were formed by repetitive direct impacts, which suggests that the seven gang members had been assaulting one another with these objects before committing self-immolation.

"So once again, we're presented with yet another layer of mystery, and we can't help but ask: Why? Why did the gang members attack one another with blunt instruments even though they were about to carry out one of the most gruesome ways one could think of to end their lives together? Could it be that the police department has it all wrong? What if, instead of a suicide pact executed in the most dramatic fashion, it was an internal argument that went south, which ended in a murder-suicide situation, where the last man standing decided to set his ex-comrades on fire before committing self-immolation?

"As of this moment, the police department has not made any official comment in response to the rising speculation on the nature of this case. However . . ."

Cara couldn't concentrate on the news anymore; an eerie sensation was traveling down the back of her head to her spine and making the hair on her nape stand on end. She suddenly had an unsettling feeling that she was being watched by seven blackened corpses from behind.

Gingerly, she turned her head and looked over the backrest: Mira was standing in the kitchen, next to Lilith. What's more, she was wearing the most haunting expression that Cara could ever imagine seeing on anyone—no thoughts, no questions, no feelings, no emotions, no stirs, no responses . . . just nothing, absolutely nothing. Lilith, however, was staring at the TV as if she had seen a fraid of ghosts, looking as white as a sheet.

Thomas had noticed the girls too. Quickly, he turned off the TV and got up to greet them.

"Well, hello there! We didn't hear you come down! You girls having fun?"

"Lilith's leaving," Mira said flatly.

"Wh—Now?" Cara looked at Lilith in surprise.

Lilith gave her an apologetic smile. "Yes, Mrs. Murphy. I'm heading home. I wanted to say 'Happy New Year' to you and Mr. Murphy before I leave."

"But . . . it's New Year's Eve. You know you're more than welcome to stay with us for the celebration."

"Thank you, Mrs. Murphy." Lilith paused, biting her lip. "I wish I could. They're coming home though, my parents."

Cara was suddenly at a loss for words. Thomas, on the other hand, was not.

"They're *what*?" he blurted out, a little too loudly.

Lilith gave a nervous laugh. "I know. I can't believe it either . . ."

"Oh, sweet girl, that's not what Mr. Murphy meant." Cara smiled at Lilith as she elbowed Thomas in the leg as a warning. "It's a good thing they're coming home to you on New Year's Eve. We're very happy to hear that. We're just, um . . ." Cara tried to search for the right words to complete her sentence, but she only came up with a sigh. "Oh well. We're gonna miss having you tonight."

Lilith smiled uneasily and lowered her head.

"Actually . . . you know what?" Cara straightened up with an expectant smile. "Since the plan for tonight is to make up the fun and the food we didn't get to enjoy on Christmas Eve, we might as well start the celebration earlier. Think you can stay a little longer, Lilith? Until your parents get home, perhaps? Mr. Murphy would be happy to give you a ride back when they're home." She elbowed Thomas in the leg again and gave him a meaningful look. "Right, Thomas?"

At first, Thomas thought Cara was giving him another warning, but he soon spotted the sadness and desperation hidden in her eyes, and he instantly understood why she wanted Lilith to stay.

"Yes. Yes, of course!" He looked up and nodded at Lilith, almost pleadingly. "So feel free to stay longer, Lilith. I know Mira would love for you to stay longer . . ."

Lilith took a quick glance at Mira but immediately felt the lump returning to her throat. There was not a single sign of emotion on Mira's face; even her eyes were lightless like black holes. Lilith swallowed hard and looked away. If she wanted a chance to save her friend from being lost to the power that resided in her, she would have to hurry.

Lilith mustered a brighter smile and said, "Thank you for offering, Mr. Murphy, Mrs. Murphy. But I must get going. I still need to clean up the mess I've made in the house before my parents get home, or I'll get an earful from New Year's Eve to New Year's Day."

"All right, sweet girl. We . . . understand," Cara replied, trying hard to conceal the disappointment in her voice. "Would you still like a ride home though?"

"Y-yeah," Thomas added quickly after glancing down at Cara's face. "I'd be happy to drive you home. You girls can talk more in the car."

"Oh, you really don't need to, Mr. Murphy," Lilith answered politely. "I've taken up enough of your time already. I'll be fine taking the bus." She picked up her backpack from the floor and hoisted it onto a shoulder, then she waved cheerfully to the couple. "Bye, Mrs. Murphy, Mr. Murphy! Happy New Year!"

"Happy New Year . . ." Cara and Thomas waved back feebly as they watched Mira follow Lilith to the mudroom and out the back door, shutting it behind her without looking back or saying a word, as if they were invisible to her.

For a long time afterward, the couple just stared at the closed door in silence, waiting for it to be opened again.

Eventually, Cara said woodenly from the couch, "She's coming back. Right?"

Thomas turned and looked at his wife: her eyes were still fixed so insistently on the back door that she seemed to have lost her ability to blink. He felt sad, he felt old and powerless, and above all else, he felt afraid now that he no longer had the confidence to answer that question without hesitation. Still, he told Cara what she needed to hear.

"She will, honey. She *will* come back."

He sat down beside Cara and wrapped his arms around her. Cara let out a soft whimper, then she buried her face in her hands and sobbed quietly into Thomas's chest.

IV

Mira closed the back door behind her. "I'll walk you to the bus stop."

Lilith opened her mouth but hesitated. To reach her bus stop from Mira's house, they would need to walk toward the pedestrian square and walk past the same alley where they had encountered the seven gang members—before they burned themselves alive. She worried that the sight of it would only aggravate Mira further, especially after what they just saw on the news.

But Mira either didn't read her mind this time, or she did but chose to ignore it anyway. Before Lilith could tell her to stay, Mira was already striding toward the other end of the street, leaving Lilith behind on the driveway.

"Wh—Wait!" Lilith held on to her backpack and scurried after Mira, knowing it was already too late to change her mind.

The sun was getting ready to end its shift for the day. It was sitting low and listlessly in the sky, barely emitting enough energy to keep the temperature above freezing. Even though the most exciting part of New Year's Eve would soon be in countdown mode, the streets were still unusually and uncomfortably quiet. Except for the two of them, there was not a single soul to be seen, not even the birds or the squirrels who would usually tail them on these streets, looking like the world's least inconspicuous spies.

"I didn't know your parents are coming home," Mira said.

"They're not," Lilith answered sheepishly. "Look, I'm not proud of it, okay? I needed a legitimate excuse to leave without upsetting your parents. You saw how much they wanted to persuade me to stay. I can't just tell them I need to leave because I have something more important to do, can I?"

"So you made up an excuse to make them feel better about you leaving even though it made *you* feel like a liar," Mira concluded matter-of-factly. "Yup. That makes perfect sense."

Lilith chuckled loudly, sounding more relieved than embarrassed. She patted Mira on the shoulder and flashed her a smirk. "I knew you'd come around."

"Don't count on it." Mira gave her a look from the corner of her eye. "I have a reputation to uphold."

Lilith snickered with a snort. "What reputation?"

"Let's see . . . What were the words you used to describe me?" Mira held out her hands and began counting them off on her fingers. "Um, 'cynical,' 'unapproachable,' 'intimidating,' 'always frowning' . . . Oh, and 'In general, treats animals and plants better than human beings.' There you have it—my reputation."

"That's not fair! You left out a bunch!" Lilith protested and held out her fingers to count off the rest. "What about 'smart,' 'funny,' 'kindhearted,' 'righteous,' and 'brave'? And also, what about my conclusion?"

Mira didn't reply, nor did she look at Lilith or stop walking.

"You didn't forget it, did you? 'You're the best kind of friend one could ask for in this crazy world,' remember? . . . Uh, hellooo?" Lilith waved her arm in front of Mira like a windshield wiper to get her attention. "Seriously, Mira, you can't just disregard all the nice things I've said about you because compliments make you uncomfortable. Like it or not, those are facts, my friend—*facts*."

Mira was still quiet, but she had slowed to a stop. Lilith noticed she was ahead and stopped short to glance back at her friend, only to feel a chill down her spine when she saw that there was no emotion on Mira's face.

"You're giving me way too much credit for what I really am, Lilith," Mira said in a hollow, distant voice.

Lilith felt her heart contract in pain. She clenched her left hand into a fist to ease the tightness in her chest, then she fought back the lump in her throat and said, "Don't say that. What you became that night does not decide who you are as a person—"

"What if it does?" Mira cut her off dryly. "What if my existence is merely a byproduct of what I really am? What if"—she gestured at herself—"none of this is real? What if I'm only a mirage in human form to elude people? To prevent everyone from knowing what kind of real horror is hiding underneath this shell—the Devil in sheepskin?"

"Mira—"

"What if this is what I do?" Mira went on as though she didn't even hear Lilith. "To hurt people. To make them lose their minds and end their lives . . . since who knows when?"

"No!" Lilith cried. Her voice echoed on the empty street, yet not a single tree was stirred.

Mira looked briefly into Lilith's eyes and fell silent.

"You are *not* a mirage; you are *real!*" said Lilith, her voice trembling along with her lips. "And you certainly don't hurt people. What happened to those men had nothing, *nothing*, to do with you! I know it because you are my best friend. And I know in my bones that you would never, ever . . ."

The rest of Lilith's sentence came out in a breathless, unintelligible squeal. She bit her lips together, holding back the tears that were circling in her eyes. But even though her vision was blurred, Lilith couldn't help sensing that Mira was looking at her in a strange way.

Finally, Mira spoke. "Lilith, do you remember what they said on the news?"

Lilith wiped her eyes quickly and shook her head. "I don't care. Neither should you. Whatever they did, they did it to each other and themselves. It doesn't have anything to do with you!"

"But it does," Mira replied flatly; her expression was unreadable. "It's what people do after they see me—the real me."

Mira's voice was quiet and calm. But to Lilith, every word she said sounded like a bomb exploding in front of her eardrums.

With tears still forming in her eyes, Lilith stared blankly at Mira. "I don't—I don't understand . . ." she murmured.

For a long moment, Mira just returned Lilith's stare with that same unreadable expression without saying anything. But when she finally lowered her eyes and spoke, Lilith thought she caught a glimpse of emotion on Mira's face, though she couldn't quite tell if it was pity or sorrow.

"What I did that night in the alley . . ." Mira began slowly. "It was not the first time. Two years ago, in a town called Skygate, I did the same thing when I was . . . defending myself against a stranger.

"Naturally, he thought I was the Devil and ran away screaming. I don't remember how long it lasted or how I managed to get home. But by the time I regained myself in this form, a green vortex had already taken up the sky, and the blackouts had already taken over the town: no electricity, no cell signal, no internet, no radio—just like what happened here. I didn't realize it then, but now I know. The green vortex, the blackouts . . . It was me all along.

"I caught a high fever that evening and slept like I was dead. I only learned about what happened in Skygate during the blackouts from the local news later: vandalism, breaking and entering, looting and robbery, assault and battery, rape and murder . . . There were those who believed it was Judgment Day; these people prayed and preached and stripped down houses to build arks. There were those who believed it was the beginning of an alien invasion; these people embraced violence and justified their crimes by claiming they were following their survival instincts. Then there were those who believed it was the end of the world; these people either compensated for their impending doom by breaking every social constraint known to men and fulfilling every heart's desire without control, or they offset their despair by giving in to the monsters in their heads . . ."

Mira trailed off and turned her head toward the sinking sun. The last rays of sunlight flowed to her face and coated it with a golden glow. Even so, compared to the dropping temperature, her face was still colder.

Chills rippled across Lilith's back as Mira's words sank in. The similarities between the events that had happened in Starfall and Skygate were undeniable. From her conversation with Mrs. Murphy on Christmas Eve morning, Lilith had suspected Mira's fever was somehow linked to the green vortex and the blackouts. But now, she suddenly realized she could not bring herself to admit that they were, as a matter of fact, all triggered by Mira's transformation.

"And then ... there was Eric Ekker," Mira continued without turning her head back, "the stranger who got to see the real me in Skygate. Most people believed he had lost his mind during the blackouts, because when they found him, he was either hitting his head against hard objects repeatedly or digging holes in the ground. In the end, he set himself on fire and set off a gas explosion at his house. The rest of his family was inside when it happened. No one survived."

Lilith felt as if an explosion just went off in her own head, blinding her vision with an instant whiteout and leaving her temporarily deafened until a muffled, high-pitched ringing sound began to wail in her ears.

"After that, the green vortex disappeared, and the blackouts came to an end." Mira lowered her head, her eyes focusing on the space between her and Lilith. "I guess I've always known why it ended the way it did. The green vortex didn't just disappear naturally; the blackouts didn't just come to an end because it was time. There was a price, and the price had been paid to end it all ..."

She looked up at Lilith then, her face cold and pale like tombstones. "It was Eric Ekker's life. He was cursed to pay that price because—"

"No," Lilith whimpered, shivering under her coat. She was so overwhelmed with emotions that she didn't even know whether she was saying 'no' to what Mira had said or what she was about to say next.

"Because he saw the real me." Mira finished her sentence anyway. "Same reason why those seven men from the alley were cursed to pay the price with their lives."

"No ..." Lilith choked up, shaking her head in denial. For a split second, she thought she saw hesitation on Mira's face.

But Mira continued. "It's the only way to explain why history has repeated itself every step of the way in Starfall," she said tonelessly. "First, the real me broke free and was seen by certain people, who were immediately cursed upon laying eyes on me. A green vortex was then produced as a result of the curse, which was powerful enough to interfere with modern technologies on a large scale and led to townwide blackouts. As the green vortex rotated, it sucked away the sanity of the town to feed its growth, which, in turn, made the curse grow stronger to take full control of those that were cursed. Finally, while the rest of the town was consumed by paranoia and crimes, the ones who were cursed started hurting themselves and digging holes in the ground, until they couldn't take it any longer and had to purge themselves in the fire to stop the madness. The curse was therefore fulfilled, and consequently, the green vortex dissipated, bringing an end to the blackouts and waking the town up to face the aftermath of an imaginary apocalypse with renewed hypocrisy."

Mira paused to draw a long, deep breath, as if she needed the cold winter air to add some iciness to her tone, then she exhaled slowly and said, "Do you see it now? What happened to those men had everything to do with me. The moment they saw what I was, they were already doomed—just like Eric Ekker."

"It can't be . . . It can't be!" Lilith cried, shaking her head quickly like an upset child. "The phoenix is a symbol of life! It represents hope!"

"Phoenix or not, it's still beyond what people can understand or control. It's still dangerous."

"The phoenix is not dangerous! It stands for the exact opposite of curses and spells and evils!" Lilith retorted, her lips quivering as tears welled up in her eyes.

Her emotional outburst did not appear to affect Mira, whose face had remained as tranquil as still water. Her black eyes, however, seemed to be growing darker, making them even more impossible to read and paralyzing Lilith's attempt in trying.

Eventually, Mira lowered her eyes and said to Lilith, "Even if you don't want to believe the phoenix is capable of bringing ill fates to the humans, you can't deny the fact that there are many stories about mythical beings who would curse or enchant mortals simply because they had laid eyes on them. In Greek mythology, it is said that any mortal who dares to look at the gods in their divine forms would be incinerated immediately. But no matter if it's a curse, an enchantment, or an incineration, the messages of these stories are the same: there are many mythical beings who do not want their existence to be observed by the humans, and they ensure it by eliminating the ones who did, in their own ways, with powers that are beyond what humans can understand or control. So it's entirely possible that, for whatever reason, the phoenix does not wish to be seen by the humans anymore. And in my case, the real me ensured that with a curse, which made them lose their minds and end their lives in flames."

Despite the lack of emotion in Mira's voice, her sincerity was evident, which only made it all the more difficult for Lilith to admit that she could be right. Frustrated with her inability to defend the phoenix and, therefore, her best friend, Lilith hung her head in defeat and surrendered to her tears silently.

"You don't want to believe the phoenix can curse people because you don't want to believe the deaths of those men are on my hands," said Mira. "But you don't *know* the phoenix, Lilith. You learned about it from stories. And if *Nian* has been portrayed in the stories as the villain when it was in fact the hero, don't you think it's possible that the phoenix might have been misrepresented as well?"

A heavy silence fell between them as Mira waited patiently for a reply, which was stubbornly held back by Lilith's clenched jaw. Realizing that Lilith was not yet ready to accept it as the potential truth, Mira spoke again. "There's another possibility too, a much simpler one: I'm just not the kind of mythical being you think I am ... Either way, it doesn't change the fact that eight men are dead because they saw the real me."

Mira's words rang in Lilith's ears and stung her ear canals like a swarm of angry bees charging at her brain, which led to a buzzing headache that was both paralyzing and disorienting. Lilith felt lightheaded; her arms went limp and her shoulders sank. Before she knew it, the shoulder straps of her heavy backpack had slipped off her arm, releasing the weighted burden from her back to the call of gravity irrevocably. The bulky backpack hit the sidewalk with a loud and jolting thud, sending Lilith's cell phone flying out of its side pocket before plunging down, face-first, onto the concrete floor.

Lilith's first reaction was to check the fate of the fragile ancient documents that had suffered the tragic fall inside the now misshapen backpack. As she hunched over their delicate pages with a heavy heart to examine them for damage, Mira's white canvas shoes entered her view.

"Your phone," said Mira, holding out a hand.

Lilith's cell phone was lying lifelessly on her palm with a shattered screen, contorting the reflection of Lilith's face into an abstract portrait that could only be described as grim.

Quietly, Lilith scooped her phone up from Mira's hand. The girl in the shattered screen was staring back at her blankly, as if she couldn't care less about the ugly scars that had cut her face into pieces.

Lilith couldn't help staring back at the girl. There was something off about her—and not just because of the mangled face. Lilith couldn't put her finger on it, but she had a strong feeling that something was not quite right about the situation. In fact, as she stared long and hard at her reflection on the shattered screen, her heart rate increased, which, she knew, was an instinctive response from her subconscious to confirm that her suspicion was not groundless. But what could it be?

Then, just when Lilith was about to give up, it suddenly hit her: she had been staring at her answer right in the face!

"That's not why they died!" Lilith exclaimed as she jerked her head up from the screen. "It can't be!"

Leaving no opportunity for Mira to react, she sprang to her feet and continued in a voice that was shaking with strong emotions. "*I* was there too! I saw the real you as well!"

Something seemed to have flickered in Mira's black eyes. Though there was still not a trace of emotion on her face, it was definitely growing paler in the fading twilight, which, in turn, made her eyes look even darker than before.

A gust of cold winter wind rushed at them like a wave of daggers, cutting their exposed skin mercilessly. Lilith winced and tucked her chin in. Mira, on the other hand, didn't even flinch. She stood motionlessly in front of Lilith like a statue, her face cold and pale, her eyes dark, and her fiery red curly hair swaying like dancing flames in the wind. If Lilith didn't know any better, she would have thought Mira was capable of transforming into a vampire.

When the wind finally died down, Lilith relaxed her shoulders and continued. "If those men were indeed cursed because they had laid eyes on the real you, *I* would have died too. The fact that I'm still alive and well is the perfect proof that there's no connection between the two!"

Lilith smiled contentedly to herself and allowed a sense of relief to inflate her chest with newfound optimism, which soon succeeded in reminding her how trivial all her other problems were in comparison.

So Lilith applied the same optimism to the damage that had unfortunately been dealt to the ancient documents inside her backpack by zipping it up without a second look. She then gave her cell phone several hopeful pushes on the power button, thinking it might still bring the screen back to life. However, despite her effort and her optimism, the shattered screen remained dark and unresponsive. Realizing that her phone was most likely damaged beyond repair, Lilith shoved it back into the side pocket of her backpack with a resigned sigh.

"Anyhow, even if I *was* cursed after seeing the real you, and the final effect just hasn't taken place yet, I'd have lost my mind before the green vortex disappeared, like they did," said Lilith as she hoisted her backpack to her shoulder and straightened up. She paused briefly, then with a wry sense of humor, she added, "Well, the green vortex is not here anymore, but I'm still pretty sane, right? ... *Right?*"

"Uh-huh," Mira answered dutifully after Lilith's deliberate prompting, but the lack of confidence in her voice was rather prominent, so much so that Lilith was tempted to roll her eyes.

But Lilith knew it was neither the time nor the place to argue about her own sanity with Mira right now. She cleared her throat and went on. "The bottom line is, the phoenix didn't curse anybody, and the deaths of those men are *not* on your hands. What happened to them was ... unfortunate. I understand why you feel like you're responsible for the whole thing, but please stop beating yourself up for something that's not even your fault."

"If it's not my fault, how do you explain the similarities between every successive event that happened in these two towns after someone saw the real me?" Mira simply said. "The only thing they had in common was *me*."

Lilith bit her lip and lowered her head in thought. Mira was right; the similarities between the respective series of events that happened in Skygate and Starfall in the wake of her transformation were too uncanny to pass as mere coincidences. If she were to persuade Mira that she was not responsible for the deaths of those men, she would need a lot more to convince her friend.

Lilith ended her thought, took a deep breath, looked up, and gave Mira a confident smile. "I don't know, Mira. I don't have an answer to that yet, but I'm sure we'll find it ... After that, we'll find a solution, and we'll put an end to it so that you don't ever have to worry about it again ..."

Mira gazed at Lilith with her lightless black eyes without saying a word. Then, as if she had found what she was looking for, she turned her head and looked away, and Lilith couldn't help fearing Mira had seen right through her temporary optimism.

The thought of it overwhelmed her and made her feel not only weak but also small. She wanted to hide, from everything and everyone. She wanted to lie down on her bed and stare at the beige ceiling in her room with music blasting in her headphones until she could forget how to cry.

"You should head back," said Lilith, trying her best to sound casual even though she thought she was shrinking under her coat. "It's getting late. Your parents are still waiting on you to begin the New Year celebration."

Mira swiveled her head back to look at Lilith, as though she was checking to see if she had heard it right, but she promptly turned away again.

"It's just another day," she replied plainly.

"To you, maybe. But to them, it's another new beginning in life, with new opportunities and new challenges that will bring new uncertainties and new hope . . . Kinda like a rebirth, actually, a rebirth that takes place in the mind. Who wouldn't want to celebrate *that* with the ones they love the most in this world?" Lilith paused and gave herself a wry smile. "Maybe that's the real reason why people all over the world are still so attached to the tradition of celebrating the arrival of a new year by lighting up the sky with fireworks; it's pretty much a man-made imitation of the rebirth of the phoenix, a way to symbolize and, in a sense, to complete the rebirth in their minds."

Mira took a glance at Lilith from the corner of her eye. "What about you, then? Will you be reborn in your mind tonight?"

"I . . . I think so."

"Then why are you sad?"

Mira's question caught Lilith off guard and almost gave her a start. When she recovered from the initial shock, Lilith found herself arriving at the conclusion that Mira had, indeed, seen through her temporary optimism.

But she couldn't tell Mira the truth; she couldn't even bear to think about the truth herself. She would just have to hide it deep in her mind and seal it up for good there. Then she would continue to pretend her fear would never come true, and she would move on to the next steps with only optimism and hope . . . But even if she could fool herself, could she really fool Mira?

As she came to the obvious answer, Lilith sighed inwardly to herself. She knew she could not hide her thoughts from Mira for long, but at least she could delay telling her the truth until, hopefully, some other day far out in the future. With that goal in mind, Lilith decided to tell Mira a different truth instead.

"The transition to a new year always makes me feel sentimental —that and my birthday. It marks the end of something old and the beginning of something new, and it's so . . . official."

"Aren't you excited about the 'new opportunities and new challenges that will bring new uncertainties and new hope'?"

The vague tone of sarcasm in Mira's voice brought a relaxed smile to Lilith's face. "I am. But at the same time, I feel sad for everything that's then permanently lost to the past—never to be altered, never to return. It's like . . . Imagine you're spending every single second of your life weaving a brocade, trying to make it look as beautiful and flawless as you possibly can. But as soon as you've produced something for your brocade, it starts to dematerialize from thread to thread, leaving only a fading image of what it once looked like as you continue on with your task. You want to hold on to that image, but you can't; you still have a brocade to weave, and what you've woven is still dematerializing, leaving yet another fading image for you to hold on to as the previous image inevitably fades away from your memory, while you weave on as the cycle repeats. So to me, the transition to a new year is also a reminder that even though you're always giving birth to something new in your life, you're also always losing something that was once an integral part of you, and that's how life goes on as time ticks by, day after day, year after year . . ."

Lilith trailed off when she noticed that Mira was knitting her brows, which she automatically interpreted as a sign that Mira probably knew she was trying to bide her time. She shuffled her feet uneasily and said, "I'm sorry. I don't know why I had to dump all this on you . . . I guess I'm just a lot more nostalgic than most people."

Mira responded by nodding, but her eyebrows didn't relax.

"It's nothing, really," Lilith added quickly, reminding herself that maybe she had read too much into it. Frowning *was* Mira's signature expression, after all. "Just a moody phase I get when I'm reminded of the change that's brought along by the passage of time . . . like a werewolf, he-he. Only instead of full moons, I tend to become moody for New Year's and birthdays. But as long as I can mourn the past properly and howl at the moon, I *will* return to a normal state when the sun rises again. I promise."

"And here I thought you'd only act like a werewolf when your monthlies are on the way."

Feeling a little dazed by Mira's playful comeback, Lilith gave a surprised laugh. "True, I do get very emotional before my monthlies too. So you see, it's just one of my many moody phases. Once I get to spend some time by myself to get it out of my system, I'll be back to normal again."

"Okay," said Mira, resuming her nonchalant attitude. "Let's get you to the bus stop, then."

"No." Lilith shook her head firmly. "You go home, Mira. If I can survive the monthlies, I can survive the walk from here to the bus stop by myself. I mean, I don't even need to deal with cramps! . . . So go home. I'll be fine."

Mira cocked her head and gave Lilith a look. It was the kind of look that would appear on Mira's face when she was slightly annoyed yet amused at the same time, a look that Lilith usually had to bite her lip secretly to prevent herself from laughing at it out loud. Lilith felt as though she hadn't seen a look like that on Mira's face in weeks. A warm sensation rose from the bottom of her stomach and made her smile, reminding her just how much she had missed seeing Mira being her old eccentric self.

Mira frowned and held up a hand. "Could you stop looking at me like that, Ms. Werewolf? You're giving me the creeps."

A loud snort shot out from Lilith's nose, then she doubled up and burst into a guffaw.

"Oh well," said Mira, shrugging. "At least now I know you have the means to get home safely on your own. No one would dare come near you when you gawk at them like that."

"I didn't gawk!" Lilith protested weakly, still trying to catch her breath. "And of course I can make it home fine by myself . . ." Sensing a quiet snicker rippling from Mira, she added in a hurry, "*Without* gawking at anybody!"

"Of course." Mira mimicked her tone with a faint smile, which Lilith was certain that if there were enough light left in the sky to tell a difference, she would have spotted a cheeky smirk instead.

The thought made Lilith chuckle softly to herself, but she shook her head resignedly and said, "Seriously, Mira, I'll be fine. The police have been very busy since Christmas. I dare say Starfall has never been as safe as it is now. You don't need to escort me. Go home." Then, to ensure she would secure Mira's cooperation, she played the it's-getting-late card again by gesturing at the darkening sky, which was quickly transforming into a deep blue dome. "It's dinnertime now. Your parents are waiting. Go."

"I will if you start walking," Mira said.

"Fine." Lilith sighed and gave Mira a wave. She took a few steps forward, then she suddenly spun around.

"You're still here!"

"And you're still here too," Mira answered in a deadpan voice. "What's the problem?"

"Cheater," Lilith mumbled, rolling her eyes. "I'm leaving for real now. Go home, Mira. Don't keep your parents waiting."

"You're starting to sound like a parrot. Can't you say anything else?"

"Sure I can: Mira, you should watch the fireworks with your parents at midnight!"

Mira did not hesitate to knit her brows. "What for?"

" 'What for?' . . . Let's just say it'll help you understand the sentiments behind the New Year celebrations better."

"I don't—"

"Oh, c'mon, don't be a party pooper! The fireworks are actually quite exhilarating." Lilith cut her off, grinning. "Trust me, you'll understand when you see them." She gave Mira a wink, then she turned around and started walking. As the distance between them increased, Lilith looked back over her shoulder and called, "Don't be a party pooper, Mira! Go home! Your parents are waiting! . . . Happy New Year! I'll see you next year . . . !"

Instead of wishing Lilith a Happy New Year in return, Mira signaled her to focus on walking. Lilith snickered contentedly and turned her head back, then she picked up the pace and headed for the bus stop.

Though Lilith's shape was becoming smaller and smaller in Mira's line of vision, she stayed where she was and watched it silently, until eventually, it, too, was swallowed by the night.

Chapter 8   THE AZURE DRAGON

1

MIRA was agitated. She didn't know why, but she didn't like it, which, in turn, made her even more agitated. Not only did she feel as if she had a million ants crawling in her veins, but she also had an irritating yet unshakable hunch that she had forgotten something, something important. Worse still, she couldn't concentrate well enough to think about what it was that she thought she had forgotten, despite the fact that all the voices in her head had been completely silent since she had recovered from her fever. It was very quiet in there now—unusually, uncomfortably quiet.

She forced a deep breath into her lungs and turned the doorknob. She was hoping to sneak past the kitchen undetected and steal her way up the stairs to her room before anyone could notice her presence. To her dismay, as soon as she slipped inside, she was ambushed by an army of gold-and-silver balloons that connected the ceiling and floor in the mudroom like impenetrable curtains, blocking both her view and her path to not only the stairs but also everywhere else in the house.

There was a long honk from a party blower, then the balloon army stirred with impatient anticipation and, eventually, threw up a face—Dad's face, with a big grin on it.

"Finally!" he exclaimed, looking more relieved than excited. "Now we can get the party started!"

Before Mira could blink twice, Dad had pulled her through the formidable floating barriers and led her into the kitchen, rattling the entire formation of the balloon army stationed in the mudroom and leaving her face smelling like rubber.

"Good timing, Little Bird! Dinner is just about ready." Mom beamed at her from the kitchen island, which had been taken over by a variety of serving trays and bowls, all covered with tinfoil. "I don't want to ruin the surprise, but I can tell you we'll begin the celebration with a seven-course dinner, and your all-time favorites *will* be on the menu!"

Mira looked at the crowded kitchen island and frowned; she couldn't recall what her "all-time favorites" were, not to mention she had neither the appetite nor the mood for a seven-course dinner.

"Come help me finish setting up." Still grinning, Dad picked up a big plastic bag that was leaning against the kitchen island and nodded encouragingly toward the dining room. "It's the least you can do when *all* your favorites are on the menu."

"Thomas!" Mom shushed him with an angry whisper that she somehow managed to mutter without moving her lips.

"Uh-oh." Dad gave a nervous laugh. "I meant, er ... all your favorite activities, *not* all your favorite foods."

Mom rolled her eyes and groaned.

Dad gulped. "Oops. I might have spilled the beans here." He flashed an apologetic grin at Mom and shoved the plastic bag into Mira's hands, whispering, "*Help!*"

Normally, an exchange like this between Mom and Dad would have made Mira snicker quietly to herself. But this time, something had smothered that lighthearted feeling before she could even notice it. She opened the plastic bag and looked inside: more party decorations and supplies. Even though there was not much weight to the whole thing, she couldn't help feeling it was pulling her down, and she was suddenly agitated again.

She was about to shove the bag back to Dad and run up the stairs to her room when a voice began to play in her ears. It was Lilith's voice, and it was repeating the same sentence, over and over again, like a broken record: "Don't be a party pooper, Mira! Don't be a party pooper, Mira! Don't be a party pooper, Mira! Don't be a party pooper, Mira! . . ."

Mira closed her eyes and tightened her grip on the plastic bag. The term "party pooper" irritated her. As a matter of fact, the whole idea of having a party on the last day of a year to celebrate the first day of a new year irritated her. She didn't know why something this little could bother her so much. She was too agitated to tolerate a party, but at the same time, she didn't want to disappoint Lilith either.

She forced herself to take a deep breath before asking, "Just . . . how many activities have you planned for tonight?"

"Not many at all! Don't listen to your dad; he was exaggerating." Mom glowered at Dad meaningfully as she yanked the oven mitt off her hand. "Anyhow, the goal is to celebrate the beginning of a new year and to have fun, not to carry out an entire plan. And that's what we're going to do; we're gonna have *fun*. But first things first: dinner. Thomas, please set the table so I can start bringing the food over."

As Mom buzzed around the kitchen to add a few more finishing touches to the serving trays and bowls, Mira followed Dad into the dining room reluctantly. Dad began his task by turning on the speakers and putting on a compilation of vintage New Year's Eve songs to, according to him, set the mood for the party. The music was lively and cheerful. Before long, Dad was humming and bobbing his head along as he went from place mat to place mat to set down the fancy silverware reserved by Mom for special occasions only.

Mira, on the contrary, didn't enjoy the songs at all. If anything, she was getting more agitated by the minute because everything was beginning to sound like noise to her: the music, Dad's humming, the rustling sound of every movement being made by her parents in the background, and how those movements were causing the air to ripple in the room and, consequently, prompting the balloons to rock inconspicuously yet continuously in their formation as they bumped into and rubbed against each other, creating yet more noises for her to endure . . .

In an effort to tune them all out, Mira tried to picture a vacuum state in her mind, only to hear Lilith's voice going off in her ears again, sounding like an alarm that she couldn't turn off: "Don't be a party pooper, Mira! Don't be a party pooper, Mira! Don't be a party pooper, Mira! Don't be a party pooper, Mira! . . ."

In spite of its untimeliness, the playback was very successful at muffling all those irritating sounds into harmless background noise, thanks to which, Mira was finally able to hear herself think again. The effect was not anticipated, but it was eventually welcomed—with a strong sense of resignation and wistfulness that Mira never thought she was capable of experiencing. This, in turn, led to an inevitable moment of self-ridicule. Mira thought wryly to herself that if Lilith had been there to observe the birth of her new expression, she would have held her sides and bitten her lip to prevent herself from bursting into an unrestrainable horselaugh right in front of Mira's parents.

Mira wished Lilith were there though. She wondered if Lilith was back at home now. She wondered if she was okay . . .

A tinge of uneasiness crept over her. For a brief second, Mira thought she had traced it back to something hiding in her subconscious, something important . . .

"Mira? . . . Mira!" An urgent voice suddenly barged in and severed her inner thought from her subconscious.

Mira jerked her head up and blinked as though she were jolted out of a deep dream and couldn't remember where she was in time or space, then she noticed Mom, who was standing in front of her with a large serving bowl held between her hands, appearing more concerned than puzzled.

"What's wrong?" Mom asked calmly. Her voice, however, sounded hesitant and even a little timid.

"Nothing." Mira shrugged dismissively. She didn't feel like talking, let alone explaining.

"You look . . . distracted," Mom tried again. "Is something bothering you?"

"No," said Mira, firmly and quickly—almost too quickly.

Mom's face tensed up at her reply but was soon invaded by a band of emotions, which seemed to be battling against one another to stay behind. Mira saw them all: shock, stress, sorrow, regret, guilt, pain, and hurt, hurling helplessly at each other as they clashed and churned into anger.

"Never mind, then." Mom shook her head quickly and looked down at the contents of the serving bowl. When she looked up at Mira again, there was a weak smile on her face. "Come on, now. It's time to eat."

But Mira had no intention of sitting down for dinner just yet. She waited till Mom had walked away, then she strode back to the kitchen island, where she had left her cell phone behind in one of its many drawers on purpose, right before she followed Lilith out the door.

Her phone was still tucked away in the same spot where she had left it. She took it out and tapped on the screen; the phone woke up, displaying several notifications on the home screen, including three missed calls, two from Mom and one from Dad, but there was nothing from Lilith.

Mira felt a strange sensation in her chest, as if something was clawing and gnawing at her heart. Thinking there might be a problem with the notification display, she pulled up her call history to double-check—no missed call from Lilith, no problem there. She knitted her brows and checked her text history next—no new message from Lilith, no problem there either. She checked the time: 7:41 PM. She had not returned home immediately after Lilith went home, but Lilith had set off for the bus stop just before the sky turned black, which meant it must have been at least an hour since she had left.

But the bus stop was only a ten-minute walk from where they had parted. And once Lilith was on the bus, it would not take her more than twenty minutes to get home. So even if there had been a delay with the bus, Lilith should still be home by now.

The thought made Mira feel weak in her arms. Normally, Lilith would either give her a call or text her after she got home. And

now, Mira couldn't stop wondering why she had not heard anything from Lilith yet. Several wild predictions took advantage of
the situation and invited themselves into Mira's mind, each offering a new worst-case scenario to depict how Lilith's trip home had
gone wrong, and each managed to make her more agitated than
the one before.

"Mira! It's dinnertime!" Dad's voice bellowed from the dining
room, interrupting her thoughts.

It was only then Mira noticed that the New Year's Eve songs
were no longer playing. She looked up from her phone and saw
Dad scowling at her from his seat. Dad rarely scowled, and even
when he did, it was mostly an act for him to look funny. So instead
of taking it seriously, Mira automatically interpreted his expression
as a sign that Mom had forbidden him to help himself to the seven-
course dinner before everyone was seated—although, surprisingly,
Mom was missing from the dinner table herself.

"Coming," Mira answered half-heartedly as she typed *Home?* on
her phone and sent it to Lilith. Then, with her phone held tightly
in one hand, she dragged her feet back to the dining room and
sat down across from Dad, all the while hoping her phone would
vibrate with a reply from Lilith soon.

"What were you doing?" Dad was still scowling at her, but he
was whispering now. "You know Mom doesn't like it when we don't
show enough appreciation for her cooking efforts!"

Mira did know that, only it had not been on her mind. Either
she had forgotten about it temporarily, or, for once, she didn't care
about the consequence. She thought of the time when Mom got
mad at her and Dad for not sitting down at the table when dinner
was ready to be served. Mom ended up dumping their portions
into the trash can and leaving them crackers for dinner instead.
That memory had given Mira a natural aversion to crackers. But
tonight, having crackers for dinner somehow felt like a much better
option than having to sit through a seven-course meal.

"So dinner is off?" she asked expectantly.

"What?" Dad's eyes widened in disbelief. "*No!* It's New Year's Eve, Mira! Mom's been making preparations for this evening since who knows when. Can you imagine how much effort she's put into this meal alone? Don't you think a little respect and appreciation is in order?"

Dad had never talked to her like this before, but Mira was too distracted to figure out why, nor did she care. She cocked her head to one side and glanced down at her phone: still nothing from Lilith. The worst-case scenarios popped back into her head then and began to replay themselves in vivid details simultaneously, like a number of short films being projected onto the same screen at the same time. In spite of her best effort to turn them off and shut them out, Mira couldn't help but wonder if some of them had already come true. She wished she had insisted on walking Lilith to the bus stop; she wished she had followed her home . . .

Feeling more than agitated now, Mira gritted her teeth. "I'm here now, aren't I?"

Maybe it was the words she used, or maybe it was her tone, but Dad's face suddenly looked pained and pale, like someone who had been stabbed in the chest.

"Mira . . ." said Dad, his voice cracking. "We know you are going through a phase lately. The way you've been acting since Christmas . . . We can tell a lot of things have been weighing on your mind." He paused and looked expectantly at Mira for a response. When that didn't happen, he let out a soft sigh and continued. "We get it. It's hard to wrap your head around all those terrible things people did to themselves and each other during the blackouts, and that makes it even harder for you to see the world you live in for what it truly is, especially at your age. If you don't feel like talking to us about it yet, that's fine. We know you need your own space and time to process all that. You can talk to us when you're ready, and we'll always be there to listen." He gave Mira an encouraging smile, which seemed more melancholy than spirited. "All I'm asking of you is to put that away for a second and enjoy the rest of New Year's Eve with us. Could you do that for me, please? Just for tonight? I think a little family fun time will do us all good, not to mention Mom has spent so much time and effort on this party. She designed the seven-course dinner just for you, you know, thinking it'd cheer you up a lit—"

Dad broke off, staring at the space behind her in shock. Mira turned to see what was going on and found Mom emerging from the corner of the staircase looking as if she had stepped out from a New Year's Eve party held in the twenties: Her eyes were painted with black eyeliner and dark eye shadow. Her cheeks were rosy pink with blush. Her lips were highlighted with velvet red lipstick. A large red feather was secured to her temple by a red ribbon around her head, which was adorned with sparkly stones in various shapes and colors. Her neck was hugged by multiple strands of faux pearl necklaces. Her hands and arms were dressed in a pair of long black gloves that came up to her elbows. And, on top of all that, she was sporting a red flapper dress that was embellished with black sequins in busy patterns, which draped heavily from her shoulders to her knees. Long strands of black sea beads cascaded down from the shoulder straps as well as the skirt of the dress, swinging briskly and rhythmically around Mom as she carefully maneuvered her feet down the last few steps of stairs in a pair of golden high heels.

Mira cast an inquiring look at Dad, but he was too busy goggling at Mom to notice it. Clearly, he didn't know the purpose behind Mom's dramatic new look either.

When Mom had made it safely to the bottom of the stairs, she looked up at them with a big smile and struck a pose. "Ta-da!" She sang, holding up her arms. "It fits! After all these years, the dress still fits! What do you think?"

Dad stole an anxious glance at Mira, who was frowning with apparent disapproval. He shifted uneasily in his seat, then he cleared his throat and said carefully, "It's, uh ... It's, um ... f-festive?"

Mom laughed and did a few impromptu dance moves. Then, still chortling with glee, she made her way into the dining room.

"Sorry about the wait," she said as she approached the table. "I changed as fast as I could."

"I thought you were going to change into something that's more . . . comfortable," Dad said in a tight voice, as though he was holding a breath.

"Well, I just thought it'd be more fun to wear something special for tonight." Mom sat down next to him, smiling. "Do you remember this dress, Thomas?"

Dad seemed to have tensed up at her question. He opened his mouth, paused, then he closed it and scratched his head, appearing rather uncomfortable with himself. "Dress? . . . I thought it was a costume."

To Mira's surprise, instead of scowling at Dad, Mom responded with a wistful smile. "You remember."

Dad replied with a nervous chuckle, his face growing pale.

Mom had turned to Mira then. "You see, this 'festive' dress has a story.

"It was my last year of high school, and they were having a New Year's Eve party. As you can imagine, all the girls wanted to look their best at the party, so of course they all followed the trend and went for these fancy, tight-fitting cocktail dresses that were in fashion. Susan and I needed something to wear for the party too, but we had no interest in dressing up like they did, so we went to this ancient-looking costume store in town to pick out the most over-the-top dresses we could find for the three of us: Susan, me . . . and our friend, Nina. To be honest, Nina was not on board with our plan at all. We pretty much had to drag her to the costume store with us. But in the end, we all went to the party in our costumes, stunned everybody, got a good kick out of their reactions, and had a great time celebrating the new year with each other. And this"— Mom gestured to her dress—"was what I wore to that party."

Mom finished her sentence with a lighthearted chortle. There was a happy but distant look in her eyes, as if she was reliving that memory in her mind. Dad, on the other hand, was sitting stiffly next to her, looking petrified.

His demeanor was as unusual as it was alarming. Mira instinctively sensed that something was bothering him, bad, and she was certain it had something to do with Mom's story.

A boisterous laugh suddenly erupted from Mom, then it became breathless, giving Mira the impression that she was sobbing instead. "Oh ... the commotion we caused! Everyone at the party was giving us funny looks or startled stares like we had either come from another world or escaped from an asylum!"

Realizing that a few drops of tears had slipped out when she laughed, Mom dabbed at the corners of her eyes with her fingertips and sighed with satisfaction. "I wish I could show you the looks on their faces; they were hilarious! Susan and I laughed and laughed ... It was definitely the best New Year's Eve party I've been to, thanks to this dress—"

"I don't get it," Mira blurted out. She still couldn't put her finger on what was wrong with Mom's story, but there was one thing that just didn't make sense. "Why costumes?"

Mom gave another boisterous laugh and said, "Because it's funny, that's why! We were tired of the other kids gathering up in small groups and going on and on about who wore the best dress, who had the hottest date, who's gonna kiss whom at midnight, yada, yada ... It was *so* very boring. We didn't want the last New Year's Eve of our high school life to end like that. We wanted it to be *fun* and *memorable*!"

Determined to find out if she had missed any important details, Mira pressed on. "But why wear it tonight? It's just us here."

"Oh, what can I say?" Mom shrugged with a sheepish smile. "I think it was calling me in some way. I was going through the closet for something comfortable and pretty, then I saw it hanging in the back, and the memories just came rushing back to me ... It was hard not to say yes to it after that. Plus," Mom added after a contented chuckle, "it's always a nice surprise to find out I can still fit into the dress I wore when I was eighteen!"

Mira took a quick scan of Dad's face and saw that the tension in his expression was melting away, which could only mean her questions had led her astray from what she was trying to uncover. She decided then in order to figure out which detail in Mom's story had induced that unusual reaction in him earlier, she would need to find out what his role was in her story first.

"Let me guess." She turned to Dad and gestured to Mom's dress. "Mom caught your eye at the party because she was wearing that? ... No wonder you still remember the dress. I can see why you were impressed."

Fear immediately returned to Dad's eyes; the smidgen of color that had managed to climb back to his face barely a minute ago was suddenly gone again.

Mom didn't seem to notice it. She giggled behind her hand and patted Dad on the arm. "Actually, I caught his eye right before our first class in college.

"It was our first day, and I left the apartment a little too late that morning, so I had to run like a jackrabbit to get to my class on time. But when I was about to make the final turn to reach the lecture hall, I didn't slow down in time and rammed right into your dad at the corner, and *wham*! We both fell to the floor and landed on our butts. And since we were both carrying a stack of books, they came crashing down with us. It was like one of those characters-crashing-into-each-other scenes in the cartoons!" Mom laughed and gave a soft clap. Smiling broadly, she continued. "So I was on the floor, still kinda stunned from our collision, and I thought to myself for sure this boy would get mad at me for having rammed into him like that. But he didn't. He just stayed on the floor like I did and studied my face intently like he'd known me from somewhere. So I studied his face in return, thinking maybe we did know each other from somewhere. And eventually it hit me, probably at the same time it hit him, that I was looking at my childhood friend *slash* neighbor from over ten years ago!"

Mom smiled affectionately at Dad and held his hand. "He asked me out not long after that. I still think he developed a crush on me because I crashed into him that day—"

"So he was *not* at the party," Mira remarked, cutting her off.

"No, he was not. I wish he were though. I moved to a different city when I was eight, and unfortunately, your dad and I had not been in touch since I left. So when I crashed into him that day, it was the first time we'd seen each other in all those years ... To tell you the truth, neither of us had high hopes that our paths would cross again in the future. So I guess, on some level, it was fate that had brought us back to each other." Mom smiled wistfully and leaned her head on Dad's shoulder. "We were meant to be, weren't we, Thomas?"

"We still are, honey," Dad whispered back and gave Mom a gentle peck on her head, but his face remained pale. And even though he had been avoiding Mira's eyes since Mom had begun her story about their magical reunion, Mira could see that his fear was precipitating into sadness—great sadness, and she knew it was time to ask the last question.

"If he was not at the party, how come he recognized your dress?"

A dead silence fell upon them, as if they had all stopped breathing.

Slowly, Mom lifted her head off Dad's shoulder and straightened. Her red lips were trembling visibly; her hazel eyes were sad and hesitant.

"There's a photo ... of the three of us," she said, her voice quavering. "It was taken at the party. I had it framed ... Dad saw it and asked me about it—"

"That's it?" Mira retorted, losing her patience. "Dad recognized your dress from an old photo and you're both too afraid to tell me about it? ... What's really going on here, huh? What are you hiding from me? ... Why can't you be honest with me for a change?"

Her voice rang in her ears like echoes, and Mira suddenly realized she had been yelling. She stared at the petrified couple and felt a new emotion rising and expanding quickly in her head. She didn't know what it was, nor did she know how to describe the strange and overwhelming feeling that it brought along. All she knew was that this new emotion was causing a splitting headache behind her forehead.

"Well?" she demanded; her voice came out much louder than she had intended it to.

Mom and Dad stared back at her, round-eyed, jaws dropped, but neither of them made a sound. For a moment, Mira thought they looked like two deer in the headlights, just waiting for her to run them over so that their panic would end—especially Mom, who looked as though she was on the verge of breaking down.

Mira couldn't stand it any longer; her patience had run out. She grabbed her phone, pushed herself away from the table, and stormed off like an angry gust of wind. In no time, she was back in her room with the rest of the world locked away behind her door. Still panting, she leaned against it and sat down on the floor. By the time she had caught her breath, it occurred to her that with the rest of the world locked away behind her, she had also locked herself away from Lilith.

She looked at her phone and tapped on the screen, hoping she had received something from Lilith. She did receive one new message, but it was from a number she did not recognize, and it was clearly sent by a scammer, not Lilith.

Feeling agitated, Mira deleted the spam message and dialed Lilith's number. But instead of the normal ringing tone, there was only static. Thinking it might be a connection issue, she hung up and redialed the number, only to hear static again.

Baffled by the problem, Mira hung up and tried again, except that this time, instead of redialing Lilith's number right away, she waited for a whole minute before making the call. Unfortunately, the result was the same. Still, Mira didn't want to give up, so she restarted her phone and tried once more, only to be greeted by static again.

By then, her failed attempts had led not only to more agitation but also more fuel for her splitting headache. As Mira clenched her jaw to brace herself for the mounting pressure that was building up in her head, she heard Lilith's voice chanting in her ears, as rhythmically as the throbbing veins in her temples:

"Don't be a party pooper, Mira! Don't be a party pooper, Mira! Don't be a party pooper, Mira! Don't be a party pooper, Mira! . . ."

11

Cara pulled the covers over her head and curled up even more—it was no use; the birds were being way too noisy this morning, so much so that it didn't even sound like they were singing the praises of a brand-new day anymore. On the contrary, since they were all going at it at their own pitch and at the top of their lungs as if they were having a screaming contest right outside of the windows, she couldn't help but think they were ganging up on her with an obnoxious morning prank.

Part of her wanted to scream right back at them, but the mere thought of it made her feel exhausted. And it was not just screaming that was exhausting; everything was exhausting, even thinking —especially thinking.

Cara squeezed her eyes shut and hugged her head tightly, hoping she could muffle the birds' voices so that she did not have to think about reality. She just wanted to lie there, with nothing on her mind, without any sound in her ears, until she could blur the line between reality and awareness and stop existing . . .

But the incessant clamor of the birds did not subside. If anything, they became even louder than before.

Cara groaned inwardly and threw the covers off her head. She reached for Thomas's pillow, grabbed it by the corner, and pulled it over the other side of her face, sandwiching her head between his pillow and hers while pressing both firmly against her ears to block out the noise.

Thomas's pillow smelled just like Thomas. As gravity performed its magic and reshaped his pillow into a soft cocoon for her head, Cara was embraced by his familiar scent. She used to think that as long as she could bury her face in Thomas's pillow for some time, nothing in this world would upset her for long. She wished it were still the case; but to tell the truth, she did not think it would work anymore.

She felt her eyeballs waking up behind the swollen eyelids that she could barely open. They were stiff, sore, and tired, yet they were getting ready to release the tears again. Cara wondered if she would ever cry for anything else in her life—that is, if she could stop crying for this first.

A hand landed gently on her shoulder and brought her mind back to her earthly shell. Cara thought wryly to herself that maybe Thomas was checking to see if she was still breathing, because she didn't think she was.

"Honey? . . . Is everything okay?" Thomas asked softly, though his voice sounded hoarse and strained.

Wearily, Cara peeled the pillow back by a corner and peered at Thomas from behind her swollen eyelids. Though her vision was narrowed and blurred, she could tell Thomas had gotten paler and thinner, which, inadvertently yet inevitably, reminded her that Thomas was grieving too.

A heart-wrenching pain seized Cara like the jaws of a man-eating monster, piercing her flesh and bones and tearing up her insides without mercy. But Cara didn't fight back; she let the pain devour her, silently. *It doesn't matter anyway,* she told herself. *Nothing matters anymore . . .*

"There you are." Thomas smiled, tilting his head sideways to meet her eyes. "What were you doing in there? Can you breathe?"

"Too noisy," Cara mumbled from between the pillows.

"Oh. Was my razor too loud?" Thomas patted his clean-shaven face with a pensive chuckle. "Sorry. I had a lot to mow here. It'd been a while . . ."

Cara thought about telling Thomas that she was actually talking about the birds, but she quickly dismissed it. It was easier, after all, not having to explain herself, and it was less exhausting.

"Well, now that I finally took care of all that extra weight on my face," said Thomas, grinning hopefully, "I'm gonna go make us some breakfast. Wanna come join me?"

Without thinking, Cara shook her head.

"How about I bring you a plate, then? Scrambled eggs, sausage rolls, and hash browns . . . Sound good?"

Cara just shook her head again.

Thomas sighed and sat down on the bed. Gently, he pushed the pillow away from Cara's face and held her hand. "Cara, it's been two weeks. You need to eat."

Before Cara knew it, tears were gliding down her cheeks again, stinging her eyes and face.

"What's the point," she murmured numbly. "I'm cursed; I'll never be a mother."

"Of course there's a point!" Thomas said pleadingly, squeezing her hand. "You still have me. You still have friends who love you and care about you . . . Please, Cara. It's time to move on."

Cara closed her eyes, but it didn't stop the tears. "I can't, Thomas . . . I don't know how . . ."

No matter how much Thomas didn't want to admit it, he could no longer deny that his fear—the nightmare within the nightmare —had come true. The thought made his heart sink. He heard a buzzing sound in his ears, then his vision blacked out. Still holding on to Cara's hand, he used his elbow to steady himself. For a few seconds, Thomas thought the solid black weight was going to crush him to the mattress. Fortunately, as Cara's anguished face gradually returned to his vision, so did his determination to bring Cara back to herself.

Thomas knew it would not be an easy task, but he took comfort in the knowledge that help was on the way. Ever since the funeral, Cara had been very reluctant to talk to anyone—even Susan, who had tried to call her at least twice every day despite the fact that she was dealing with a painful divorce herself. Cara did open up to Nina when she called to check on her about two weeks ago, but she had turned off her cell phone since then and refused to talk to anyone who had tried to reach her. Deeply worried about the mental state and physical well-being of his heartsick wife, Thomas had —without telling Cara—emailed Nina for help the night before. To his relief, Nina had contacted him promptly afterward and told him that she and Susan would come to visit Cara the next day.

"That's okay," Thomas said gently, trying to sound and look optimistic. "We'll help you get through this. We can start slow, one step at a time—"

" 'We'?" Cara stared at Thomas as if he had mentioned a ghost.

"Oh, I haven't told you the good news yet." Thomas gave her an apologetic smile. "I was able to get in touch with Nina last night, so I asked her if she could come and stay for a while. She said she would, and she said she'd ask Susan to come too."

"*What?*" Cara jerked her head up from the pillow. "*Why?*"

Her eyelids were so swollen that Thomas didn't notice anger was forming in her eyes. Still, he had correctly discerned that there was an edge to her voice, so he answered carefully, "Well, I thought it might be good for you to—"

"You thought. *You thought*! Do you know what's really good for me, Thomas? Being a mother! Feeding, changing, bathing, holding the baby—*our* baby! . . . But I can't, can I? I couldn't even protect her in my own belly. I couldn't keep her alive. Her life was taken away when she was still inside me, yet there was nothing I could do to stop it. And you're telling me you asked Nina to come because you thought it'd make a difference to this cruel reality—*my reality*?" Cara was practically shouting now. "Tell her don't bother! It wouldn't make any difference because it won't change anything —not a thing! It's pointless! Everything's pointless! I don't want to see anyone! I don't want to talk to anyone! Just leave me alone and let me be!"

Without giving Thomas a chance to react, Cara yanked the covers over her head and curled back up into a ball.

Thomas opened his mouth to explain, but he didn't know how. Nina and Susan were Cara's best friends. Cara had once told Thomas, before they were married, that Nina and Susan each held such a special and important place in her heart that they could never be replaced by anyone else, not even Thomas or their future kids, and certainly not her parents. If Cara didn't even want her best friends to be here with her, Thomas feared she had given up completely.

For a long time afterward, neither of them spoke a word, leaving the birds outside to fill up the painful silence with their relentless chattering.

Eventually, Cara said from under the covers, "I'm sorry . . . It's the birds. They're too noisy this morning. They're making me . . . sad."

It was then it finally occurred to Thomas that he had been so preoccupied with his own thoughts that he had failed to notice how loud the birds had been.

"Ah, I see . . . It's okay, honey. I'll go shoo them away. They won't bother you for long. I promise." He leaned over and planted a kiss on Cara's head through the covers. "I'll come back later with your breakfast, okay?"

This time, Cara didn't shake her head. Thomas smiled to himself with relief, then he got up and left the room.

As soon as he was out in the hallway, he began to fully grasp just how noisy—almost abnormally noisy—the birds were being, and it was all coming from the back of the house. At first, he thought maybe the birds were yelling at an unwelcome visitor from the woods to scare it away from their territory. But as he came down the stairs, that thought was quickly replaced by a feeling of uneasiness that something was wrong on the back deck.

Thomas held his breath and hastened into the kitchen, which was separated from the back deck by a tall wall that contained a large window. The moment he looked out, he froze: birds, thousands of them and a kaleidoscope of species, sizes, and colors, were crowding on the back deck and the space between the house and the woods. From where he was standing, it looked as though the entire back of the house was being swallowed up by wings, feathers, and eager, sharp beaks. It was so unreal that it was unnerving.

And it was also the last thing he would want Cara to see right now. Determined to drive this ominous flock away from their house before Cara could notice its daunting presence, Thomas strode toward the back door. With a sharp inhale of breath, he pulled the door open in one decisive motion. His sudden intrusion led to a scene that was as chaotic as entering a bat cave with blazing LED lights, only the birds, when in fright, were much louder and much more hazardous than the bats. By the time Thomas had realized his mistake, it was already too late. The collective effect of thousands of birds taking flight simultaneously due to shock and panic generated an extremely uncooperative gust of wind that prevented him from opening his eyes. Unable to see his surroundings to dodge out of the way in time, Thomas had no choice but to shield his head with his arms to keep it safe from the flapping wings and swiping claws of the startled flock.

Fortunately, he was not rewarded with any hostile contacts, and the commotion only lasted for a little while. Once the wind and the noise began to die down, he opened his eyes slowly to assess the situation from behind his arms: although the meadow was still scattered with a variety of birds here and there, it was no longer dominated by them.

A few more birds took off from the back deck then, screeching shrilly as they climbed, as if they were heartbroken by this untimely eviction. Their miserable cries immediately drew Thomas's attention. With a mild degree of triumph, he lowered his arms to see them off, that was when he caught sight of the murder of crows still huddling together on the far side of the deck, calm and undisturbed.

Through the occasional gaps that appeared among their pitch-black mass, Thomas noticed there was something red in the middle. He couldn't see clearly enough to tell what it was, but he had automatically come to the conclusion that the crows were guarding a kill. Since the situation was more or less under control now, he decided there was no need for him to go confront the crows right away; he would take care of it later, when the crows were done with their breakfast. After all, it would be easier—and safer—to shoo them away when their bellies were full.

With that thought, Thomas let out a soft sigh of relief and turned to leave, but he stopped short when he saw the patio table: a yellow notepad was lying conspicuously in the middle, on top of which a white envelope was held down by a bright-red pen.

Thomas did not recognize that pen, nor the notepad. As a matter of fact, he was certain the patio table was empty when he sneaked out here to answer Nina's call the night before. But as far as he knew, Cara hadn't left the room in weeks, and since the sun had just come up not long ago, it was unlikely that they were left here by someone else. So if Cara didn't leave them here, who did?

Too baffled to answer his own question, Thomas picked up the envelope and examined it. The envelope was not addressed to any-one, nor was it sealed, but it was definitely not empty.

Even though the temperature was rising as steadily as the sun, Thomas felt a chill shooting down his spine. Fearing that this en-velope might not have come from a friendly source after all, he decided to open it himself.

There were two pieces of folded paper inside the envelope. The first one he pulled out was yellow and lined, which, judging by its color and design, must have come from the notepad. Not knowing what to expect, Thomas unfolded it cautiously. He found a strange poem on that paper, written by hand, but there was neither a title for the poem nor a name for the author.

By then, Thomas was feeling more uneasy than perplexed. He folded the poem back up and returned it to the envelope, then he pulled out the second piece of folded paper. Unlike the first, this one was white and blank on the outside, and it was thicker and heavier too. Still, Thomas didn't let his guard down. As cautious as he was with the first one, he unfolded it. But the moment he saw what was on it, his knees went weak: it was a birth certificate for a child named Mira Murphy; the mother's name was Cara Murphy, and the father's name was Thomas Murphy.

Slowly and woodenly, Thomas lowered himself into a patio chair. Mira was the name that Cara had picked out for their daughter, the baby girl whose heart had stopped beating three weeks ago, when she was still inside Cara's womb. In the end, Cara had to give "birth" to their baby through an induced labor. But their daughter had never lived to see the world, so she couldn't have received a birth certificate . . . could she?

A wave of grief washed over Thomas, leaving him submerged in pain and sorrow. He remembered how delicate and fragile their stillborn daughter had looked in his hands, then he remembered the heart-wrenching wails from Cara as she held and rocked their little angel's lifeless body in her arms . . .

Thomas drew a shaky breath and held his face with his hands. He couldn't wrap his mind around what he had found. Based on the handwriting that was used for the poem, he had rejected the possibility that the envelope was left here by Cara. But now, he couldn't help but wonder if Cara had gotten up in the middle of the night and made this birth certificate and the poem for their stillborn daughter as a way to say goodbye. Worse still, he couldn't help but wonder if the goodbye was meant for him as well.

The thought gave him a jolt in the heart, which then began to race. Feeling short of breath, Thomas lowered his sweaty palms from his face and stared at the birth certificate distractedly. As he tried to concentrate on breathing to control his panic, his eyes fell on the date printed under "Date of Birth." And suddenly, as if an invisible fist had knocked the wind out of him, Thomas couldn't breathe at all: the printed date was today's, not the date that their baby girl was delivered.

Still holding his breath, Thomas brought the birth certificate to his eyes with trembling hands and reread the date—it *was* today's; there was no mistake about it.

A chill crept down Thomas's spine, paralyzing him from head to toe. Just as he was struggling to regain control of himself, the murder of crows that had been huddling quietly over their kill on the far side of the deck became very anxious all at once; some were pacing around nervously, some were twitching their heads uneasily, some were flapping their wings alarmingly, but they were all cawing so harshly and painfully at one another that they seemed to be announcing they had sensed the presence of Death.

Needless to say, their frantic outburst was as unbearable to the ears as it was unsettling to the nerves, which was more than enough to jar Thomas out of his stupefied state. He immediately thought of Cara and her potential reaction to the nerve-racking cacophony being produced by the crows. Without losing a minute, he marched toward the noisy black birds with his arms stretched out wide like a scarecrow, determined to drive them away from the back deck for good.

But instead of fleeing, the crows only flapped their wings and hopped out of his way, forming an unobstructed passage that led him straight to the center of their assembly, where he thought they had been enjoying their kill. Several larger crows remained there, calm but alert. They were huddling in a small circle and shielding the kill under their wings, thus creating a feathery black dome over what they were protecting, all looking determined to guard it from any outsider. Nevertheless, Thomas could see that some red feathers had spilled out from between their feet.

Intrigued by the scene, he lowered his arms and approached the beaked guards and their treasure slowly and carefully. To avoid being attacked as a threat, he kept his eyes on the crows to monitor their attitude. He could still see the red feathers out of the corner of his eye, but for some reason, he thought they were beginning to look like curls—fiery red curls.

Just when he was close enough to have a better look at those red feathers, the crows suddenly flapped their wings in a defensive manner and took flight, abandoning their posts at the same time. Instinctively, Thomas dodged behind his arms and squeezed his eyes shut. He waited until the heartbreaking caws of the crows were safely above his head, then he opened his eyes.

Before he could sigh with relief, however, he was overtaken by shock and disbelief: There, lying motionlessly at the spot where the crows had stood guard earlier, was a large bird's nest. But instead of baby birds, it was filled with feathers in different shapes and colors, among which lay a real, live baby with a full head of fiery red curls, who was studying him quietly with a pair of cold, black eyes.

Thomas gasped but no air entered his lungs. Worse yet, his heart seemed to be stuck in his chest, unable to pump any blood to his brain for it to react or, for that matter, to think properly. The eerie thing was, as utterly surreal as it was to find a real, live baby in a bird's nest on their back deck, Thomas couldn't help feeling a sense of déjà vu, as though he knew this baby already.

That was his first clue that he might have been dreaming after all. Just as he got ready to pinch himself, he noticed something flat and glossy was sticking out from behind the baby's left shoulder. Gingerly, he leaned over the bird's nest to see what it was: a photo —not just *any* photo, the same photo Cara had always kept on her desk, no matter where they had moved to. In the photo, Cara and Susan were laughing their hearts out in their over-the-top party costumes while Nina was frowning irritably at the camera, wearing something black and gloomy.

Thomas knew that photo well, not only because he had seen it on display on Cara's desk ever since they were together, but also because Cara had told him the story behind it, so he was fully aware that it was taken at their last New Year's Eve party in high school and that even though, according to Cara, Nina had been a party pooper as usual, it was still her favorite photo of the three of them together.

As Thomas looked from the photo to the baby, he instantly understood why he had déjà vu: this baby looked like a mini version of Nina, who also had a full head of fiery red curls and a pair of piercing black eyes that appeared as cold and distant as outer space —especially when he was present, Thomas had felt.

The observation was barely digested in his sluggish mind before it slipped him the conclusion that he was looking at Nina's baby. But Thomas refused to believe it. After all, Cara would surely have told him if Nina were pregnant, and she would have told him as eagerly as she had when she learned that Susan was pregnant with twins. In fact, she would have told him the news with incredulous excitement, considering Nina had always been so indifferent to the whole meeting-someone-and-falling-in-love thing that none of them had expected Nina to be involved in any relationship, let alone one that would lead to the birth of a baby. But above all, Thomas knew in his bones that if Cara had been informed about Nina's pregnancy, she would have been expecting this baby as ecstatically as if she were expecting her own.

Yes, Cara really wanted to be a mother. Unfortunately, fate had been nothing but cruel to her. Not only was her wish not granted, it was also ripped into pieces when her hope of completing at least one of her pregnancies with a living baby in her arms was shattered by the stillbirth of their daughter. Grief jabbed at Thomas's heart like a cold, dull knife. He wondered if Nina had seen it coming and, therefore, decided to keep her own pregnancy a secret this whole time in case it would only upset Cara more in the end. Still, even if Nina was indeed pregnant and this was indeed her baby, it didn't make any sense that she had come all the way from out of state with her baby tucked under—instead of a blanket—a layer of bird feathers in a bird's nest, rather than a stroller or a car seat. Not to mention during the entire time he had been out here on the back deck, she was nowhere to be seen. It made Thomas nervous to think what would have happened to the baby if he had not come out to scare off the birds or if he had gone back inside without driving the crows away. Then he remembered he didn't go back inside because he had noticed some unexpected items on the patio table, and he immediately thought of what he had found in that envelope.

It only took a millisecond for his mind to draw the connection, but the sudden realization almost gave him a panic attack. Trembling uncontrollably, Thomas jerked his head up from the baby and scanned the area between the woods and the house for Nina's fiery red hair, desperately.

Nothing.

He spun around to check the space behind him, just in case Nina had actually been keeping an eye on the baby while quietly observing his reactions from behind a corner, like a furtive feline. But apart from the grill, the patio furniture, the notepad, the pen, the envelope, and the foreboding birth certificate, which he had left unfolded on the patio table, he didn't see anything or anyone else.

Although his mind was still in a daze, deep down, Thomas knew he had already found his answer: everything on the patio table was left behind by Nina, not Cara, early this morning, when she came to deliver the baby. She wanted Cara and him to raise her baby as their baby; she wanted them to raise her as Mira Murphy.

Slowly, Thomas turned and walked back to the quiet baby, who was still studying him impassively like a mini Nina. It occurred to him then that when Nina called him the night before to tell him she would come visit Cara the next day, she probably had already made up her mind to use this unusual solution to cure Cara's grief and depression.

As reality sank in, Thomas felt his limbs going weak. The fact that Nina had stopped by their house and left her baby on their back deck without either a heads-up or a face-to-face explanation could only mean one thing: she was leaving, and she was not coming back.

Not knowing how he could ever break the news to Cara, Thomas gave in to his trembling legs and sat down beside the bird's nest. After a long moment of hesitation, he reached down, then very carefully, he picked up the baby and held her in his arms.

The baby was not wearing any clothing, not even a diaper. The warmth from her bare skin was as reassuring as the sunlight that had now embraced the entire back of the house. The skin-to-skin contact flooded Thomas's broken heart with love, affection, and a long-awaited feeling of completion, which was accompanied by a sense of immense happiness. To his relief, the baby didn't cry, nor did she fuss about being held by a total stranger. She just kept on studying his face as though she was trying to figure out what was going on behind his bittersweet smile.

"Hello, little princess . . ." Thomas cooed, holding out a finger to touch the baby's tiny hand. The baby didn't coo back, but she grabbed his finger and didn't let go.

It was a moment that Thomas would forever hold dear to his heart, and it was at that moment he realized just how much he had been longing to become a father. Tears rushed out from his eyes as he remembered how lifeless and cold their stillborn daughter had felt in his arms, then he found himself rejoicing in a comforting feeling, which was spreading steadily from the firm grasp around his finger, that he, at long last, had become a father.

"Look at that grip! What a strong girl you are!" Thomas smiled at the baby through his tears. "Nice to meet you, Mira. My name is Thomas Murphy. I'm gonna be your daddy. Cara Murphy is my wife. She's gonna be your mommy . . . Can I tell you a secret, Mira? I've already thought of a nickname for you: Little Bird. Why? Because, well, you almost got adopted by a bunch of birds! . . . Noooo, we're not gonna let the birds adopt you! We'll protect you and keep you safe. In fact, we'll make sure you grow up in this home, *our* home, feeling loved and happy every day. Yes, my Little Bird. We will . . ."

Before Thomas had finished talking to the baby, he heard a car pulling quickly into the driveway. His first thought was that Nina had come back for her baby after all, then he began to question himself, wondering if he had gotten it all wrong. With his heart thumping like an anxious rabbit, he rose to his feet slowly and, holding the baby tightly to his chest, turned to the driveway.

A blue MINI Cooper pulled up in front of the garage, then the driver's door flung open and Susan got out. She must have caught sight of Thomas right away, for she gave him a wave as soon as she had closed the door. Just as Thomas was half expecting to see Nina emerging from the passenger side next, Susan started walking toward him. Her steps were weary but soft, and she had a melancholy but gentle smile. However, the moment she stepped onto the back deck and saw that Thomas was holding a baby in his arms, she froze and her face turned white.

"Thomas."

"Hey, Su—"

"What's going on here?" Susan cut him off sharply as she stared at him in disbelief.

Thomas knew she was referring to the baby. With a long sigh, he looked down at the baby, then he looked up at Susan. "When was the last time you talked to Nina?"

"Last night."

"What did she say?"

"She told me to be here first thing in the morning to help Cara move on."

"Do you know where she is now?"

"No," Susan answered, frowning slightly. "But she said she'd get here early. Why are you asking me all this, Thomas? Does she know something that I don't?"

As Thomas pondered her replies, the sluggishness of his mind was alleviated by an increasing sense of clarity, as though the fog in his head was finally lifting. He took a deep breath and looked Susan in the eye. "Susan, I need to tell you something ... two things, actually ... before we talk to Cara. One of them is good news; the other one is ... not. Which one would you like to hear first?"

Susan narrowed her eyes. "Please don't tell me you cheated on Cara and had a baby with another woman."

"*What?*" Thomas blurted out, but he immediately thought of the baby and forced himself to lower his voice into a vehement growl. "Of course not! What made you think I'd do something like that?"

Susan pressed her lips together tightly, appearing to be holding back some strong emotions. Thomas suddenly remembered that was exactly what happened between Susan and her husband, which was the straw that broke the camel's back and led to their divorce in the end.

Shaking his head apologetically, Thomas softened his tone. "I'm sorry. I forgot Ben had—"

Susan held up a hand to stop him. "You don't need to apologize for that. I should have seen it coming a long time ago, but I didn't. I misjudged him. I brought it up because I was worried that I had misjudged you as well."

"Are you still worried?"

"That depends"—Susan gestured to the baby in his arms—"on what you're going to tell me."

Thomas followed her hand and looked down at the baby. She had drifted off to sleep and was breathing serenely, with her little hand still holding on to his finger. With a lump in his throat, Thomas smiled pensively at the baby, then he sucked in a breath and looked up.

"Did you know Nina was pregnant?"

"What?" Susan's voice, though soft, was at least an octave higher than usual. She gaped at him, round-eyed, looking both shocked and confused.

"Just as I thought," Thomas said resignedly. "I don't think Cara knows anything about it either."

"How did you—No, wait." Susan shook her head quickly and corrected herself. "Are you sure?"

"More or less." Thomas nodded absent-mindedly, then he said after a sigh, "Well, where should I begin?" He paused thoughtfully for a moment, then he looked toward the patio table. "See the stuff on the patio table? They weren't there last night. I found them this morning, when I came out to shoo the birds away. I think Nina had stopped by the house before we were awake and left them there so either you or I would notice them first rather than Cara. Besides the notepad and the pen, there's also an envelope, but it's not addressed to anyone, and there's no information about the sender either. I found only two things in that envelope: a document and a poem. Given the situation, I think they're . . . uh, pretty self-explanatory. In a nutshell, the document carries the good news, and the poem carries the bad one."

"I'm listening," Susan said stiffly, eyeing the baby suspiciously from where she was standing. There was a tremor in her voice, and her expression was heavy with a sense of foreboding.

"Cara's wish has come true." Thomas looked meaningfully at Susan. "The document is a birth certificate: The baby's name is Mira Murphy. The mother's name is Cara Murphy. The father's name is Thomas Murphy. And the date of birth is today's."

Susan covered her mouth with a trembling hand. "You're not saying . . ."

"It was Nina," Thomas said softly, holding back his own emotions. "She granted Cara's wish—her one and only wish . . . As for the poem, I think—I think she wanted to let us know that she's not coming back."

Susan dropped her hand from her mouth and rushed over to the patio table. She saw the birth certificate first, which she proceeded to examine line by line yet still failed to register any of it in her mind. By then, her breathing had become shallow and uneven. She pushed the birth certificate away and snatched the envelope up. As soon as she saw the handwriting on the yellow notepad paper, she knew it was Nina.

Susan read the poem, slowly, distractedly. For a moment, she thought the whole world was spinning away from her, and she had to use the patio table to support her weight to remain on her feet.

"So . . . Nina brought Cara a baby and left without saying good-bye to either one of us . . ." she concluded, a distant look in her eyes.

"Not just any baby," Thomas said somberly, then he walked over to the patio table for Susan to see the baby up close. "I think she left Cara . . . her own baby . . ."

It only took Susan one good look at the baby to know that Thomas was right: not only did she have a full head of fiery red curls like Nina, but she also had that same impassive expression, even in her sleep, which Susan was so used to seeing on Nina's face.

"You see it too, right?" Thomas asked quietly as though he was talking to himself. "The resemblance is ... uncanny. I can only assume Nina is her mother. I just don't understand why she didn't say a word to you about being pregnant ... Do you think she planned this all along?"

"I ... I don't ... know ..." Susan mumbled weakly. Before she knew it, tears had filled her eyes, blurring her vision and her sense of reality as she was bombarded by all the "why" questions going off in her head. Much to her dismay, she did not know the answer to any of them, and worse still, she now realized she probably never would.

Seeing Susan's reaction to the news was enough for Thomas to foresee how devastating it would be for Cara. Overcome by the feeling of helplessness and despair, he groaned, "Who am I kidding? There's no good news here! ... I can't do this to Cara, Susan. I can't tell her the truth! It'll break her!"

What he said broke Susan's trance and pulled her back to the painful and difficult reality. She lowered her head and wiped away the tears, then her eyes fell on the baby. Maybe the baby sensed the distress in their energy fields, or maybe she was simply having a vivid dream, but presently she frowned, and Susan felt as if she had traveled back in time. In her mind, she returned to one of the nights where the three of them were having a sleepover. She and Cara had caught Nina frowning in her sleep—again. And the two of them, though determinedly and deceptively quiet, were laughing so hard that they were rolling on the floor and gasping for air.

As the memory faded away from her mind's eye, a sad smile came to Susan's lips. She stifled a sob and looked up at Thomas with a somewhat stoic expression, then she said firmly, "No, Thomas. You should always tell her the truth, no matter how painful it is to face it ... After all, she's *finally* a mother."

III

It took a long time for Mira's splitting headache to subside to a more tolerable level. Still greatly agitated, she opened her eyes slightly and squinted at her cell phone, which had lit up diligently after a tap from her finger only to show her that she still had not received anything from Lilith. So Mira picked up her phone and tried calling Lilith again. She tried four times in total, back-to-back, but she was greeted by static every time, just like before.

Frustrated and agitated, Mira pushed herself up from the floor, tossed her phone onto the bed, and went into the bathroom. She needed a hot bath to ease the pain and relax her mind.

She left the hot water running in the bathtub until the room was warm and steamy, then she turned off the water and climbed in. Inhaling the warm, moist air deeply—almost greedily—into her lungs, she leaned back and, exhaling gradually, let the hot water swallow her like a cocoon.

The temperature of the water was as soothing as it was comforting, and it was very effective at melting away her headache. Finally relieved of the splitting pain, Mira sat up and rested her head on the rim of the tub. With her eyes closed, she waited, patiently, for the hot water to soak out her inexplicable agitation as well.

Mira didn't know how long she had waited, but when she opened her eyes again, the bathwater had already cooled down considerably, as though she had dozed off without realizing it. The lukewarm temperature of the water was, by no means, too cool to be tolerated to most people, but it made Mira shiver involuntarily. Quickly, she got up and pulled out the stopper. While the tub was still draining, she turned on the shower and put it to the hottest setting.

She stood under the hot water until she finally felt warm again, then she pumped out some shampoo and smeared it over her hair.

Ever since Mom had pulled out that small bloodred object from her head after her encounter with Eric Ekker, Mira had been finding more and more of them in her hair. She had tried to pluck them out a few times, but each time the pain was so great that she had never managed to continue beyond the first one. What's more, she had learned that the consequence of it was very similar to that of Mom's never-ending battle against her gray hair: the more she pulled out, the more would appear, and in Mira's case, unfortunately, the bigger they would get too. As a result, over time, hair washing had become the least desirable part in her shower routine, not only because she would, more often than not, find a new growth sprouting from her scalp, but also because the ones that had fully sprouted were getting bigger and stronger, making it harder for her to wash her hair and all the more harder for her not to wonder what she would turn into by the time they became too big to be concealed.

As Mira lathered her hair, she could tell it would not be long before her bizarre scalp condition could no longer stay secret. With soapy fingers, she traced along those smooth but hard bodies under her hair to assess their crowdedness. She thought the growths had been totally random and that they would continue to sprout as long as there was enough space to squeeze through. To her surprise, she noticed through her touch that they seemed to be lining up neatly in an overlapping manner, like scales.

Knitting her brows, Mira let the water run down her head to rinse out the soap in her hair. Although the shower was still warm enough for her to linger longer, it did not soothe her anymore. As the soapy water ran down her face and body, Mira couldn't help but wonder if the scales on her head would start to grow on her skin as well, and she thought to herself, with an unusual heaviness in her chest, that it would be impossible to hide what kind of monster she really was from everyone else then—including Lilith.

She finished her shower absent-mindedly and reached for a towel, then she sighed deeply and buried her face in it. Lilith had so much faith in her nature—the real her—that it was almost frustrating. The strange thing was, even though Mira didn't believe what she had transformed into was as harmless as Lilith insisted it to be, she didn't want Lilith's conviction to be shattered either.

Mira peeled the towel off her face and stepped out of the tub. Just as she began to dry herself off, she noticed that her inexplicable burn mark, which had grown at least three times in size after her last transformation and had spread from her lower abdomen to the bottom of her sternum, was coming alive again. Before she had climbed into her pajamas, the burning heat and pain had spread all the way up to her chest, reaching for her shoulders and neck.

It was then that she suddenly noticed the problem: if what she had transformed into was indeed a phoenix who couldn't stop burning, how come there were scales, not feathers, growing on her head?

Ignoring the burning heat and pain in her body, Mira shuffled toward the bed for her cell phone. She needed to talk to Lilith. She needed to tell her about her scales; she needed to tell her about her inexplicable burn mark, which looked more like an alien life form than a scar. And above all, she needed to tell Lilith that what she had transformed into was not a phoenix after all. The scales on her head and the deaths she had caused should be enough to prove that she was more related to a sinister serpent than a virtuous bird.

The thought made Mira hesitate. After all, being related to a sinister serpent was not something one should expect to help keep their friends around, especially when you could also transform into a form with burning wings and cause deaths to those who had laid eyes on you. In fact, Mira couldn't believe that in spite of everything Lilith had witnessed and learned, she had not only remained her friend but also insisted on her faith in Mira that her true self was the exact opposite of evil.

But if she was indeed the Devil incarnate, Mira knew she would have to make a choice sooner or later down the road, and she would rather lose Lilith as a friend now than to cause her any harm in the future. With that in mind, Mira came to the decision that she would tell Lilith everything and let her know about every unusual detail that had happened since her first transformation. The bottom line was, if she was not what Lilith believed her to be, she would want her to know the truth, and she would need her to know it soon.

She sat down on the bed and picked up her phone, only to find that she had received nothing from Lilith still. She did, however, receive a message from the local police department, wishing the citizens of Starfall a happy New Year and urging everyone to spend the night safely.

Mira frowned and deleted it from the home screen, then she tapped on the message menu to check her text history with Lilith. There was indeed no missed message in the thread. What's more, her last text to Lilith was still marked as "Delivered" instead of "Read."

Mira returned to the home screen and dialed Lilith's number— static. She restarted her phone and tried again—still static. Feeling frustrated, she stared at the screen and massaged her forehead, not knowing if she was waiting for a sign or hoping for a miracle. Either way, the splitting headache was quickly returning to her head, and so was the agitation.

Presently, her phone got tired of waiting around idly and went to sleep. Still staring distractedly at the screen, Mira woke it up without thinking and came face-to-face with the time that was being displayed boldly in the middle of the screen: 9:54 PM.

Mira had not expected it was already so late in the evening. She wondered if she had indeed taken a nap in the bath, then she began to wonder if she had forgotten something else as well . . . Something important . . . Something that had most likely been the cause of her inexplicable agitation and contributed to this irritating feeling of foreboding ever since she watched Lilith disappear into the night alone. The thought gave rise to a vivid image of Lilith being pulled away from her until she was swallowed whole by darkness. Mira felt a chill trickling lightly down her spine as if she were being scratched in the back by the long, cold nails of the dead, then a ghost of a thought drifted into her mind: every single person who had witnessed her true form—no matter if she was the Devil or a phoenix—had gone mad and ended up dead. Every single one *except* Lilith. *Why?*

As soon as the question was asked in her head, Mira knew it was the source of her agitation. She lowered her phone and stared blankly into space. As she rose slowly to her feet, an uncomfortable feeling quickly replaced the agitation with an acute tightness in her left chest.

I should have made her stay, Mira said to herself, breathing shorter and faster. *Her parents went back to work, which means she's home alone, so there's no one to stop her if she begins to lose her mind and—*

Mira couldn't finish the thought. She couldn't help but think she had made a terrible mistake by letting Lilith go home on her own. The fact that she had not heard anything from Lilith and was still not able to reach her only made the situation even more alarming.

With her heart beating faster and louder in her chest, Mira stumbled to the closet and dug out some clothes to change into. She would not give up so easily. It had been a little more than three hours since Lilith had left her sight. She did not know how long it had taken for the others to lose their sanity completely, but she told herself firmly that there must be enough time for her to save Lilith.

As Mira struggled out of her pajamas, she realized the reason that the burning heat and pain had not only been intensifying but also spreading to her throat was because her burn mark had, balefully and without warning, taken over almost her entire trunk and reached her collarbones. The disturbing change in its size did not divert Mira at all though; she was too preoccupied with Lilith's safety, and all she could think of was she needed to go to her as soon as possible.

So Mira embraced the heat and pain and got into some clothes, only to see that the glow from the lavalike substance inside her burn mark was showing right through them. What's more, her burn mark was shifting much more visibly than it had ever been before, demanding immediate attention.

But Mira didn't give in to its threatening glow. She pulled out a few more shirts and sweatshirts and began bundling herself up. As long as she could obscure the glow from her burn mark, she could still reach Lilith's house without attracting unnecessary attention, hence unwanted actions, as a walking human lantern. She had made up her mind that even if she would not be able to hide it successfully in the end, she would risk it anyway. No matter what happened next, she had to find Lilith, and she had to do it right away.

Once she had blinded the glow from her burn mark under enough layers, Mira hurried down the stairs. Unfortunately, the army of gold-and-silver balloons was still guarding the mudroom and barricading her path to the back door. Just when she was about to change her course to the front door, she saw Mom and Dad in the kitchen and stopped.

They were standing between the kitchen counter and the kitchen island, blocking her shortcut to the front door. They appeared to be in the middle of a heavy conversation, because Dad was holding Mom by her shoulders, and Mom had her face buried in her palms.

Dad was the first one to look up. After a moment of delay, he managed to pull up the corners of his mouth and gave Mira an awkward smile that seemed more like a grimace due to pain.

"Hey . . . Little Bird. I'm so glad you came down. Feeling better?"

Mira didn't answer him. She didn't want to, and she didn't care. They had lied to her for far too long; she had lied to herself for far too long. It was time to put an end to it—to *this*.

Mom pulled her face away from her hands and looked up as well. She had changed out of that outrageous flapper dress and was wearing her normal clothes now. She had also gotten rid of the excessive makeup, though her eyes were indicatively red and puffy.

"How about some food?" She offered hopefully in a strained voice. "You didn't eat anything at dinner. You must be starv—"

"I'm not hungry," Mira said impassively, cutting her off. Then she strode past the kitchen through the dining room and hastened toward the front door.

"Wh—Wait!" Mom cried as she chased after Mira. As soon as she realized Mira was aiming for the front door, she broke into a sprint to overtake her, then she planted herself firmly in front of Mira, intercepting her before she could reach the door.

She stared at Mira in near panic. "Where are you going?"

"Out," Mira simply replied.

"Out to where?" Mom's voice became high and squeaky, and it was also quavering. "It's too late! It's—It's almost midnight!"

Mira returned her stare with a cold, long look, then she said tonelessly, "Why should I tell you anything when neither of you can be honest with me?"

Mom let out a feeble gasp and froze as though she had been immobilized in her worst nightmare. Mira could see that nightmare; it was drowning ... drowning in a pitch-black pool of fear, agony, and despair.

Mira felt a hollowing pain inside her left chest, which made her notice that the heat and the glow from her burn mark were seeping through her clothes, layer by layer. She felt herself burning up from within, but she clenched her fists and reminded herself that the only thing that mattered now was Lilith's safety, nothing else.

Just then, Dad stepped between her and Mom and broke her gaze.

"Mira, we know you're angry with us," he said pleadingly. "But this is about your safety. It *is* kinda late to go out now, don't you think?"

Mira turned her head away and didn't bother answering.

"I know it's much more exciting to be out with kids at your own age, especially on New Year's Eve, but things haven't quite calmed down yet. People are still on edge from what happened on Christmas Eve, and they can be ... unpredictable." Dad stole a glance back at Mom to see if she had recovered, then he gave a soft clap with his hands and continued with feigned cheerfulness.

"How about we have some snacks first? Then we can go watch the fireworks in the backyard and celebrate the rest of the evening together as a family. What do you say?"

Mira had had enough. She needed to leave; she didn't belong here anyway.

"We're not a family," she said.

"What?" Thomas flinched and stared at Mira, aghast.

Slowly, Cara stepped out from behind Thomas, looking as pale and petrified as someone who had just been sentenced to death. "Wh—What did you say?"

Looking straight back at the appalled couple, who was still blocking her way to Lilith, Mira repeated firmly, "We are *not* a family."

Cara heard a loud pop in her head, sounding like a bomb detonating in her brain. She felt the blood draining quickly from her face and limbs, as if she were being sucked dry by an invisible beast. Before she knew it, her vision started shaking uncontrollably, and she couldn't help but sense that a world-ending earthquake had already begun and the whole world would soon come tumbling down right in front of her eyes.

"How could you say that?" She uttered faintly. "You're our daughter, our only daughter—"

"Am I?" Mira retorted, raising her chin and narrowing her eyes.

Her expression sent a crippling chill down Cara's spine. Instead of the face of her beloved daughter, she thought she was looking at an enraged stranger. Still, Cara refused to give in. Even if the world would soon come crashing down into nothingness, she would not allow herself to lose Mira first.

"Of course you are!" Cara cried desperately. "We nursed you, changed you, bathed you, dressed you . . . We celebrated every one of your firsts: your first step, your first word, your first tooth, your first permanent tooth . . . We treasure every moment and every memory we've had with you: every birthday, every Christmas, every New Year . . . We raised you, we love you, and we're here for you every day—"

"But you didn't give birth to me, did you?" Mira cut her off sharply.

Cara froze like a statue. So did Thomas. Their eyes were bulging in disbelief. And although their mouths were both open, neither of them could make a sound to answer that question.

"Exactly," Mira said dryly, then she went around the petrified couple and approached the front door.

A sharp pang of fear penetrated Cara's heart like a spear. Ever since the day Mira had come into her world, the possibility that she might, one day, lose Mira as well had always haunted her. And now, that possibility was becoming very real and all too imminent. In a moment of sheer desperation, Cara flung herself at the front door and blocked it with her entire being before Mira could reach for the doorknob.

"You can't leave!" she cried helplessly, her hazel eyes wild with despair. "You are our daughter! . . . You are all we have left!"

Mira frowned and backed away. The burning heat and pain was climbing up her collarbones, reaching for her throat, and so was the strange and overwhelming emotion that had caused her the splitting headache.

"I am *not* your daughter," she growled, her voice as hoarse as an angry crow's. She took a step forward and stared down into Cara's teary hazel eyes. "And *you* are *not* my mother."

Her words rumbled in Cara's ears as if the Earth were breaking apart. The coldness in her voice and the blackness of her eyes seized Cara like the death grip of a merciless giant, and its clutch was so tight that she could neither move nor breathe. Tears streamed down Cara's cheeks as she watched her whole world crumbling before her eyes. She felt the floor cave in beneath her feet, and she fell . . . deeper and deeper into a lightless chasm, farther and farther away from the face of her beloved daughter, which, contorted by rage, was barely recognizable now . . .

Out of the corner of her eye, Cara caught a glimpse of Thomas: he was rushing toward her with outstretched arms. Meanwhile, darkness was closing in rapidly above her. Before she could reach for Thomas's hand, the small opening of light was sealed up completely, engulfing her in a vacuum of total darkness.

Cara didn't know she had slid off the front door and collapsed to the floor, nor did she know that Thomas had run to her frantically as he cried to Mira for help.

But it was too late. Mira had stormed back to the dining room and out the patio door without looking back.

IV

She slammed the patio door shut and charged into the backyard. Then, as if she couldn't get away from the house fast enough, she started to run, and she ran straight to the end of the lawn and into the woods.

The trees in the woods had long been stripped of their foliage by Mother Nature, but they welcomed her regardless with their pensive silence and a soft but bone-chilling wind that seemed to be perpetually trapped under their bare limbs. She ran on, letting the frigid winter wind cut into her eyes and cheeks like icy blades while filling up her overheated throat and lungs with the freezing air to suppress the swelling sensation from within her that she thought she was about to explode from, which was now spreading from her trunk to her legs and arms.

There was a hiss in the wind, and she heard a voice, faint but clear: *Liars . . . Humans . . . liars . . .*

It's not important now, she said in her head, as though she was merely replying to that voice. *They're not important now.*

The wind ignored her and went back the way it came. For a brief moment, she wondered if the voice in the wind had actually been a voice in her head, but she soon let go of the thought. After all, she had a much more pressing matter on her hands: she needed to reach Lilith's house as fast as she could. She had taken this route once, on Thanksgiving Day; Lilith needed a long walk to digest all the food she had eaten at the big Thanksgiving dinner that Cara had prepared, so they took the opportunity to find out whether they could cut through the woods to get to her house. The trip turned out to be much more strenuous than they had expected, but she had learned that if she continued straight through the woods, she would pop out on the other side of the hill and arrive at Lilith's neighborhood within sixty minutes—thirty, she hoped, if she could run the whole way, which would then be much faster than going to the bus stop and waiting for a bus ride.

Thirty minutes, she told herself, pushing her pace. *I must hurry.*

As she threaded her way through the woods, the scrawny shadows of the bare tree limbs seemed to have come to life under the cold moonlight, shifting and pulsating ominously above her in the semidarkness. Although they had allowed just enough moonlight to pass through for her to make out where the tree trunks were, it was becoming increasingly difficult for her to dodge the low-hanging branches and vines. To keep her pace, she had to use her hands and arms constantly as sword and shield to break herself free from their bony, tenacious grasp. This, soon, gave rise to a strong sense of déjà vu. At first, she couldn't quite pinpoint the reason behind it. But as her hands and arms became more attuned to the offensive and defensive motions against her obstacles, she realized she had déjà vu because she was doing the same thing she had done in her dream on her fifteenth birthday, after she fainted from seeing Cara's blood on the bird-shaped cake.

In that dream, she was the lone survivor on the battlefield, the same battlefield where she had fought countless times in her previous dreams, as though she was incapable of dreaming about anything else. The battlefield was crowded with fresh corpses piled high into heaps, leaving only enough space among them to reveal the winding strips of sand that were painted red in blood. A murder of crows was feasting on the corpses, but they were no ordinary crows, because she distinctly remembered they all had three legs and three feet. After she had observed that detail, she started to run. She ran to the end of the battlefield and into the woods, clearing her path with her hands and arms like she was doing now to keep her pace, except that, in the dream, she was holding a shield in one hand and a sword in the other.

Nevertheless, the memory of it was so vivid that she couldn't help feeling she had stepped into her dream. This seemed to have awoken some dormant muscle memory in her limbs, thanks to which, she was able to deal with the obstacles in her path effectively without thinking while maintaining a good, steady speed up the hill.

Before she could reach the top, however, it had become too dark and dense for her to continue running. Panting heavily, she stopped to take off her sweatshirts, hoping to use the glow from her burn mark to light the way. As soon as the extra layers were removed, she knew her need would be fulfilled more than adequately: against the dark and uninhabited background of the woods, her entire torso looked like an intricately carved jack-o'-lantern, all lit up by an enchanting light source that appeared to be dancing feverishly in it, emitting such a strong and vibrant glow that it was as if her insides were on fire. It was then she noticed that a fog was forming in the woods.

She looked up at the sky, only to see that the cold, dim moon was disappearing silently into a sea of rolling clouds, then she realized the rolling clouds were actually descending toward her at a staggering speed. Within seconds, they had flooded the woods like heavy fog, obscuring everything in her surroundings with a semiopaque whiteness that successfully muted the glow from her burn mark and rendered it obsolete. Before she could regain her bearings, a strong gale of wind swooshed past overhead and touched down somewhere ahead of her. Even though she couldn't see it, she felt the effect of the impact radiating toward her like a powerful shock wave, which knocked back the treetops and made them gasp in fear. But instead of taking pity on them, the wind blasted its way back and circled around her at a distance, forcing the trees in its path to howl like weeping ghosts as it made its rounds to torment them without letting up. Strangely, no matter how loud the cruel wind had made the trees beg for mercy, the fog that had saturated the woods remained calm and undisturbed.

She couldn't see how far away the merciless wind was from her, but she could hear it: every time it went around her, a circle of trees would sing a wailing chorus, and that circle was, slowly, but without doubt, closing in on her, much like the way a sadistic predator would terrorize its prey into madness before going in for the kill. The impending encounter with a supernatural power that was making the woods scream and bend at will would have made anyone panic-stricken and frightened. Much to her own surprise, she felt as calm and undisturbed as the unwavering fog around her.

Then, just when she thought the wind was about to burst out from the trees, it stopped. The woods fell silent, and the fog sank to the ground. She looked around and saw that she was inside a large clearing that was surrounded by a circular wall of rolling clouds. Above her, stars flushed the velvety night sky like diamond dust, but when she looked down, she couldn't help but wonder if she was floating, for she could see nothing but clouds beneath her feet, and her body felt as light as a feather.

Out of the corner of her eye, she noticed that a section of the soft white wall was protruding from the circle, and the clouds on that side of the wall were rolling toward her as if they were being pushed by something enormous from behind, thereby producing a bulging impression of a formidable shape in the process, which, as it loomed forth from the surrounding clouds, was becoming more and more pronounced. From where she was standing, the shape of it resembled a bare tree with stubby branches, knotty roots, and a very wide trunk. What's more, it appeared to be perfectly symmetrical.

Presently, a powerful green glow began to emit from behind the looming shape, which soon spread across the entire wall of rolling clouds and illuminated it into a world of glowing cotton candies made from the essence of millions of emeralds.

When the glowing wall finally stopped advancing, the bulging impression was only a few yards away from her. A gust of wind suddenly charged at her and forced her to turn away, then she heard a voice in her head:

Wake up, Vermilion. It's time to wake up . . .

The voice was as familiar as the three voices in her head, yet it possessed a distinct quality that jarred her into the realization that it did *not* originate from her mind.

She jerked her head up and stared at the ominous shape, which seemed to be ready to burst out from the glowing wall at any second. But before she could observe it in detail, another gust of wind rushed toward her at full speed, dispersing the clouds just enough to reveal a formidable dragon head in its wake.

The sight startled her but did not shake her. She regained her composure quickly and surveyed the enormous head: it was about the size of a two-story townhouse, with lush hair and whiskers flowing luxuriously from it like unquenchable green flames made up of innumerable will-o'-the-wisps, and it was so intensely green yet translucent at the same time that it radiated a mesmerizing beauty unparalleled by even the renowned northern lights.

Presently, the dragon head began to rise, slowly but fluidly, until a massive, snakelike body came into view behind it. The body was as intensely green and translucent as the head, and it was swaying gracefully in midair, as though it was doing a slow dance in water. It was armed with two sets of intimidatingly muscular legs and paws, one pair on its chest and the other on its lower belly, close to its tail. Like the body of a snake, it was also covered in scales, except that these scales were nearly transparent, and each of them was glistening like an exotic green gem from another world. This jewellike armor shielded not only the dragon's trunk and tail but also its legs and paws, exposing only the big, razor-sharp talons that it was sporting. There was also a tall row of spikes that stretched from the dragon's head to its tail like a long mountain range, and, although the spikes were glowing with the same mesmerizing green color as the rest of its body, they seemed to be dispersing and re-forming constantly like clouds.

Hmm . . . You are confused . . . said the same voice in her head, yet this time, she thought it was coming from her ears as well.

Yes . . . quite confused . . . the voice continued with a sigh, and a gust of wind rushed out from the dragon's nostrils, which hit her in the face and swept her hair back like a wind sock. *What can I say? You have been 'living' this 'life' for far too long . . .*

It was then that it dawned on her: the voice was coming from the green dragon, and it was also one of the three voices that she had been hearing in her head.

"Yes . . . It was me . . . You could hear me all along . . ." The dragon lowered its head and let it hover in front of her. Its eyes, though relatively insignificant in size when compared to its head, were as captivating as the sky on a starry night. "Time to wake up, Vermilion. You are a Keeper of this universe. You need to wake up from this 'life' . . ."

" 'Vermilion'? 'A Keeper of this universe'?" she repeated the words out loud, yet she felt as though she was uttering sounds in a foreign tongue. Then she remembered the green dragon had told her to wake up, and she wondered to herself if she was actually in another dream . . . But if she was indeed dreaming, when did the dream start?

The dragon sighed again, sending another gust of wind her way.

"It appears you have paid quite a price, Vermilion . . ." it said, pulling its head away from her. "The re-creation of flesh has not only cost you your powers and memory but also your control over them. You can't recall who you are, even in the presence of my full form . . ."

It knows about my true self, she gasped inwardly. *It knows who I really am!*

But just as she opened her mouth to ask the question, the dragon's head dipped sideways and, with its massive body swimming leisurely and gracefully behind like gleaming waves on an emerald sea, began to circle slowly around her in midair, shrinking rapidly in size in the process. Its fluid motion rippled the air like a lone raft gliding across a still lake, producing a continuous breeze that ruffled her hair.

When the dragon was in front of her again, it had shrunk to a much less intimidating size that enabled it to look her in the eye when it straightened up on its belly, floating just inches above the ground.

"I shall tell you who you really are," said the dragon, and this time, she saw clearly that its mouth did not move when it spoke, which confirmed to her that it had been talking to her directly in her mind.

"The same way you talk to me and the others," the dragon answered. "It's how we communicate with each other—since *the beginning*." It gave her a slight nod then, as if to acknowledge the new question that had just come to her mind. "Yes, the others . . . The other Keepers . . . There are four Keepers for this universe. I am Azure, the Keeper of Change. You are Vermilion, the Keeper of Rebirth. The other two are Black, the Keeper of Growth, and White, the Keeper of Time. Together, we are the Four Keepers to safeguard *the balance* of the Scale for this universe.

"We have been performing our roles since the creation of this universe. It was *easy* to maintain *the balance* of the Scale at first . . . very easy. Under our watch, the Wheel of Life spun on smoothly and steadily in *the flow* of the River of Time. We did have to resort to large-scale corrections five separate times to tune up *the rhythm* of the Wheel of Life. But other than those five periods, we had kept the Scale in constant *balance*—we had achieved *harmony*.

"Then one day, the Wheel of Life spun out humans. Masters of lies and deceptions, these greedy and selfish creatures soon became obsessed with power. Long gone were the days of *balance* and *harmony*. Thanks to the humans, the Scale was always tipping, one way or the other: First, they fought the other animals for the power of control. Then, they fought among themselves for the power of dominance. But neither was enough to satisfy their appetite for power. So eventually, they decided to challenge us.

"Their thirst for power proved to be disastrous for this world. In their attempt to weaken your strength by coercing a cyclops into shooting down your nine conduits when they were carrying out their routine duties, the humans interfered with *the rhythm* of the Wheel of Life. You tried to save the last one of your conduits but were injured in the process. As a result, your powers waned and the suns dimmed; the Eye opened, and the Soulless were able to descend upon this world to wreak havoc on the living. *The flow* of the River of Time was severely jeopardized; *the balance* was nearly irrevocably lost, for the Scale had never been in such grave danger of tipping over.

"It took us hundreds of years to curb and repair the damage that was dealt to *the balance* of the Scale. In their cunning effort to gratify their insatiable appetite for more powers, the humans had nearly destroyed this universe; something must be done to prevent them from trying again. In the end, we decided to grant some special powers to the humans who had demonstrated the level of virtue we would like to see in all humans. Our expectation was that by creating these role models with unrivaled powers, the humans would finally cease their fights for power and learn to make peace with the other lives that shared this world with them.

"And it worked—for a while. The special powers that we granted to the selected humans also gave them immortality. They lived among the other humans without aging, rewarding their mortal counterparts for their good deeds and punishing them for their wrongdoings. Though these immortals were given different names in different parts of the world, the other humans generally referred to them as 'gods' and 'goddesses'... That's right, they became the gods and goddesses that the mortal humans feared but worshiped. They wrote stories and songs to idolize them, made paintings and sculptures to glorify them, built temples and shrines to honor them, and sent in tributes and sacrifices to please them. They even sent in the eyeball of the cyclops who they had coerced into harming your conduits, as a gesture of their remorse and obedience toward the higher power.

"But we had overlooked one critical factor in our decision: these immortals, though selected for their exemplary level of virtue, were still humans at heart. In other words, the power of having powers would still corrupt their minds, as it would have with all humans if they had the chance to wield it. It was only a matter of time.

"In the next few hundred years, the immortals built their own palaces and set up their own hierarchies. They lived and acted like any mortal overlord would do when they had too much power in their hands to be concerned about the consequences of their actions. As a result, clashes between the mortals and the immortals broke out frequently, and *the balance* of the Scale was once again in danger. To recover *the balance*, we decided to put an end to their excessive confrontations by taking the special powers we had granted away from the immortals who had been the most hostile forces in the matter ... Yes, we let the remaining immortals keep their powers—it was a big mistake.

"After that, the mortal humans were back in control again, but it was not enough for them. They interpreted our tolerance toward the immortals as a sign of weakness and thought they could take our powers for themselves. They wanted to become the supreme gods in this world.

"So the humans began to hunt us, racing to see who could be the first one to lay hands on one of us. But they soon realized how difficult it was to catch us, so they bargained with one another to pool their resources to attack us. Of course, as greedy and deceitful as they were, the humans pretended to work with each other on the surface when, in fact, their actions and decisions were all driven by their own secret agendas, which did not include letting someone else tap into our powers before they could.

"At first, we only fought back when we were under attack. But our powers were too much for this fragile world. Our actions eventually rippled into large disturbances in *the flow* of the River of Time, and *the rhythm* of the Wheel of Life was disrupted, nearly tipping over the Scale for good. It was, without doubt, one of the gravest mistakes we had made.

"We managed to correct the disturbances in time to recover *the balance* of the Scale. After that, we decided to conceal ourselves from the humans so that we could continue performing our roles without any further interference from them.

"However, blinded by their desire for our powers, the humans searched high and low for us, desperately and relentlessly. They believed that we hid from them because their attacks had made us afraid, and they interpreted it as an indication that we were now weak and vulnerable. Needless to say, they had every intention of taking advantage of an opportunity like that to strike us, and they all wanted to be the first to find us. They were under the delusion that whoever got to us first would get to wield all our powers and, thereby, become the sole god in this world to rule over all others for eternity. So in time, their search for us turned into a ruthless competition among all the rulers and lords who were capable of participating and, consequently, an excuse to invade and eliminate other competitors before they could locate us first.

"The bloodshed from that period was inconceivable. We got to find out just how cruel and savage the humans could be, even to their own species . . . Well, you know that part better than I do . . . Yes, you do. Your dreams: the battlefield, the battles, the running and killing . . . They were not dreams; they were your memories."

She stared at the dragon, unable to admit to herself that part of her had always known they were more than just dreams.

"When we decided to conceal ourselves from the humans, you chose to take on human form to become one of them." The dragon looked at her disapprovingly. "To the three of us, your choice was incomprehensible—and it still is, but then again, you have always been curious about the humans, ever since they were spun out from the Wheel of Life. They fascinate you, for some reason, despite how often they have endangered *the balance* of the Scale . . . despite all the troubles that they put you through . . .

"So while the three of us distanced ourselves from all human civilizations, you took on human form and became a soldier in one of the armies that they assembled to hunt for us. Your goal was to use insider information to access and destroy all man-made documentation of our existence and our powers so that eventually they would have nothing left to work with to continue their hunt for us, and we would, therefore, become nothing more than myths to the humans.

"They were constantly fighting over useful information to get to us first, so staying in an army that was dedicated to the hunt for us was indeed the best way to achieve your goal. Unfortunately, it also meant battles—countless battles, and you only had a short window of time during each battle to take advantage of the chaos to find and destroy the documentation that had most likely been the cause of the battle in the first place. Therefore, running and killing your way through the battlefield became your way of life as a human, which then became the earliest memories formed in your human form. Maybe that's why, even though the re-creation of flesh cost you your memory of who you are, you can still access those memories through the subconscious in this human form when it sleeps.

"You managed to succeed in most cases, but there were failures and close calls too. If you had been caught red-handed in those situations, based on how much the humans had grown fond of treating their captives for sadistic pleasure, it would have led to not just imprisonment and torture but, more likely than not, something far worse than a quick death. And since you could neither expose your true self in front of the humans nor use your powers on them directly, you would have to endure whatever they had designed for you till you could have an opportunity to transform out of your human form and escape.

"Naturally, the three of us grew concerned. Although we can maintain our powers when taking on human form, having a physical body in flesh makes us vulnerable to bodily harm, which, in turn, will weaken us until we have fully recovered from the injury, however temporary. We had seen from your mind just how brutal these human battles were and how cruel the humans could be toward their enemies. So despite the fact that your human form was skilled in the art of combat, it was becoming evident that an irreparable injury would be inevitable if you carried on. We urged you to leave the humans and return to your true form, but you chose to stay ... day after day, year after year, fighting in their wars and destroying as much documentation as you could find, completely oblivious to the lies and danger that were being crafted by the deceitful humans, who had started to hunt down all the phoenix birds that were left in the world.

"You are surprised ..." the dragon remarked mildly. It studied her intently for a while before continuing, "The Wheel of Life had spun out a great number of creatures before the humans, but not all of them survived in *the flow* of the River of Time. It was the same for the phoenix birds. They arrived in this world way before the humans did. Yet, even though they could live for hundreds of years, they could only mate once in a lifetime. Afterward, the male would turn to dust, and the eggs, usually no more than two, would grow inside the female's womb for many decades until the condition was right for her to give birth to them, after which, she would turn to ash. However, due to the changes that had been taking place in the environment, the females had more and more trouble finding the right condition to give birth. As a result, most of the pregnant ones failed to give birth before they died. Their bodies then disintegrated into ash, leaving only their unhatched eggs behind. But owing to the deaths of their mothers before they were released from the wombs, very few of those eggs were able to hatch in the end. Therefore, by the time the humans had set their scheming minds on these ancient birds, there were only five of them left.

"The rulers and lords who had successfully captured a phoenix bird would parade it across their territories for everyone to see, claiming they had captured the magical bird that possessed the power of rebirth. It was then that you realized who was truly responsible for bringing such misfortune to the remaining members of this dying species: you had destroyed enough documentation on us that the humans had to rely on those rudimentary images of you from ancient carvings and engravings to continue their hunt, and in their ignorance, they had mistaken the phoenix birds for *you*."

All at once images flooded into her head, as if the gate between her subconscious and consciousness had finally been broken down.

She saw in her mind the phoenix birds held down in chains: Their eyes were dull and numb. Their beaks, chipped from years of gnawing at the metal rings that had not only deprived them of their freedom but also their last chance for having descendants, could no longer close properly. Their once colorful plumage was muted by filth and was thinning out in patches, dotting their scrawny bodies with sickly bald spots. Their legs were bloody and bruised from the iron clasps of the heavy chains that bound them to the cruel human world, rotting away quietly amid the buzzing sounds of the flies that came to feed on their wounds . . .

"Yes, the humans captured all five of them. You thought it was your fault—just like you do now." The dragon went on before the images had faded from her mind. "The humans kept them alive as their most prized possessions because they thought the phoenix birds possessed the power of rebirth. Even though the captors of these five phoenix birds resided in different parts of the world, it made no difference when it came to their ambition to obtain the power of rebirth and what they would do to achieve it. They studied the phoenix birds in detail, hoping to stumble upon the secret to the power of rebirth. Of course, they didn't find anything. Apart from their incredibly long lifespan and their peculiar way of continuing their line, the phoenix birds were just another endangered species from the ancient world; they did not possess the power of rebirth.

"But the humans were obsessed with the idea of becoming immortal through the power of rebirth. Desperate for a way to achieve immortality, they adopted the same approach that they had been eager to put to use whenever they wanted something they couldn't have by asking: violence.

"Thus began the dark days for the phoenix birds. The humans poked them, kicked them, hit them, whipped them, taking comfort in their belief that violence was the ultimate show of force to pressure the phoenix birds into revealing the secret to the power of rebirth. So when one of the phoenix birds, a female, imprisoned in a large iron birdcage that was chained to the wall inside a cold, dark rock tower, wept for the fateful doom that was awaiting the only egg she was carrying before she died of old age and disintegrated into ash, the humans were certain it was the tears of the phoenix bird that had given itself a brand-new life as its old shell turned to ash. It never occurred to them that this phoenix bird was pregnant, and the tears she wept were out of the sorrow and pain of a mother who could not break free from her imprisonment to give birth to her child before her time was up in this world.

"No, the humans could neither see it nor understand it, for their eyes were blinded by their desires, and their hearts were twisted by their schemes. When they thought they had finally found the secret to the power of rebirth, all they wanted to do next was to extract enough tears from the remaining phoenix birds for themselves. They needed the phoenix birds to cry—and cry often. So again, they came up with different ways to torture them, only this time, knowing that their competitors probably had the same idea in mind and were also determined to win the race in achieving immortality, they were even more ruthless than before.

"As the humans continued to torture the phoenix birds for their tears, you continued to torture yourself with guilt. You wanted to go rescue them, to save them from the cruelty of the humans. Since we had learned from our previous mistake that when we use our powers to confront the humans, we would create large disturbances in *the flow* of the River of Time and disrupt *the rhythm* of the Wheel of Life, the three of us urged you not to take any action. After all, our responsibility was to maintain *the balance* of the Scale, not to save lives from *the flow* of the River of Time.

"Our objection failed to persuade you, however. You decided to go alone, and, to avoid creating disturbances in *the flow* of the River of Time, you decided to rescue them in human form.

"You asked the crows to find out where the remaining phoenix birds were kept, and you set to work. But since you were in human form, it took you much longer to hit all four locations, and it was also much harder to evade their spies and guards . . . For what it's worth, you did manage to rescue them all . . ."

Flashbacks came into her mind like a series of dreams that she thought she had forgotten. She saw that she was drenched in warm, sticky blood, panting heavily, with a sword in her right hand and a shield in her left. Dead guards littered the floor as if they had rained down from the sky. Their bodies were twisted into impossible positions, some of which were detached from their heads or limbs. There were only a few guards left in the room, and they had backed up against the cage, where the phoenix bird was lying motionless in a corner with unblinking, glassy eyes, impassive to both the bloodshed in the room and its savior-to-be. Anger surged in her lungs, and she charged at the remaining guards, only to see them turn and plunge their weapons into the large bird's bony body. Blood oozed out of the deadly wounds in patches, spreading its vivid red color onto the old and new blackened dried blood spots that caked the bird's miserable shell from all the tortures it had once endured.

It only lasted a few seconds though. Before she could reach the cage, the large bird's body had disintegrated and fallen to the floor as a pile of glowing ash. She let out a discordant screech that made the remaining guards huddle in horror, but she leaped at them anyway, and when she was done, they were nothing but a mingled, bloody mess. She turned to the cage and saw that the phoenix bird's ash had stopped glowing and was now only an ordinary pile of ash. If it weren't for the crimson trails of blood spatters that she had sprayed across it with her busy blade just a moment ago, no one would have guessed that this unremarkable pile of ash had once been a member of the most beautiful bird species that had existed in this world.

"They . . . They all died . . ." she muttered in a daze.

"Yes. They did. The humans never succeeded in obtaining their tears. No matter how much they tortured the remaining phoenix birds, they would not cry. With their unusually long lifespan, the humans could have continued to torture them for decades, or even hundreds of years. But they were relieved of such eternal sufferings at the end of their rescues. So in a sense, you did save them."

"But why? ... Why did they kill them ... even though they were after their tears?" she asked loudly in a raucous voice that did not sound human at all, and she was suddenly very aware of the burning heat and pain seeping out of her pores.

The dragon gazed at her silently; she thought she saw pity in its eyes.

"You know why," it finally said. "You just never understood it, and you blamed yourself for not being able to comprehend it in time to see the consequences of your actions: when the captors of the three remaining phoenix birds learned about your raid, you had already sealed their fate. You didn't see it coming though. The result of your first rescue attempt made you feel even more responsible for the phoenix birds' misery and pain, so you changed your tactics for the other three and tried again, thinking you would have a better chance of rescuing them by avoiding head-on confrontations. In the end, it didn't make any difference. The humans were always one step ahead of you. Then, when they ran out of moves, they killed the phoenix birds as their final checkmate.

"You held yourself accountable for their premature deaths. Guilt fueled your anger and your will, and you were determined to right what you had done wrong. Ignoring our concern for your safety, you set out to rescue the last phoenix bird in the world: the un-hatched egg that was left behind by the only phoenix bird that had shed tears in front of the humans.

"You were confident no harm would come to the egg during the rescue. The pregnant phoenix birds were particular about the con-dition they gave birth in because their eggs would only hatch when the condition was right. And since a phoenix bird's egg would be immediately orphaned the moment it was outside of its mother's womb, its eggshell was strong and tough like armor, shielding the embryo inside from danger in place of its parents until either it was comfortable enough with the environment it was in to break out on its own, or the nutrient reserve inside the egg, which could normally last the embryo a good five years, was used up. You had learned from the crows that the egg was still kept in the same bird-cage that the humans had used to keep its mother, so you knew, in a condition like that, the egg would never hatch, and therefore, the humans would not be able to hurt it in any way. You thought all you had to do was break into that rock tower before the embryo's nutrient reserve ran dry, then you could take the egg away from the humans for good ... only you had forgotten that when you were in human form, the humans could hurt *you*."

In her mind's eye, she saw the rock tower from her dreams, which she was determined to climb to find out what was being held there even though she was stopped, every time, by an old wooden door she could not open when she reached the top of the staircase. Her dream would then reset and start all over again, with her running at full speed toward the rock tower from somewhere far away, like an endless loop caused by a bug in the dream world. Out of all the times she had dreamed about that rock tower, only once had she succeeded in stepping beyond the old wooden door. To her dis-appointment, there was nothing behind it—nothing besides what was left of the tower's circular wall and the remains of its circular floor, as if a giant had bitten its top off from the side.

As the images from her dreams streamed through her mind, they gradually lost their subtle, dreamlike blurriness and became as clear and sharp as reality. She saw herself running toward the same rock tower at full speed, with a sword in her right hand and a shield in her left. What's more, her running self seemed to be connected to her in both body and mind. She could feel everything her running self was feeling through her senses, and she knew exactly what her running self was thinking. Consequently, she was able to anticipate every move her running self would make at every landmark she had memorized from her dreams about that rock tower.

Presently, her running self reached the rock tower and was run-ning up the staircase. She was not at all surprised to see that the same wooden door was waiting for her at the top of the staircase. She gave the door a gentle push, and it opened meekly behind her hand, presenting a circular chamber that was mostly submerged in the shadows, cold and silent like a crypt. A large birdcage was sitting noiselessly against the far side of the curved wall. A veil of pale moonlight was flowing softly into the dark chamber from a small rectangular opening near the high arched ceiling, creeping smoothly into the birdcage from between its thick metal bars to caress a large white object that was tucked in the far corner of the cage. The object was sleek and round, about the size of a beach ball. Under the gentle touch of the pale moonlight, it looked as cold and white as a corpse.

There was a large iron lock on the birdcage. She wasted no time breaking it open. The repetitive sounds of her pommel striking metal ricocheted off the circular wall, causing the echoes to linger eerily inside the chamber like screeching ghosts as they ascended toward the dome. She paused to listen but heard no other sound —the chamber was deserted; no one was here.

Once the lock was broken, she opened the cage door and stepped inside, heading straight for the large white ball. She knelt in front of it and placed her sword and shield on the floor. With great care, she picked up the ball with both hands and, rotating it slowly under the pale moonlight, examined its exterior to make sure it was not hatching.

When she had rotated the ball to its back, she saw that it was engraved with a circle that had nine evenly distributed arms, each of which had a grotesque shape at the end that looked like a deformed claw.

A thought struck her like lightning: *humans do not have the ability to engrave on a phoenix bird's egg!*

She sprang to her feet and ran for the cage door, but it was too late; she was knocked in the chest by a force that made her stumble backward. A sharp pain immediately penetrated her heart. Staggering to recover her balance, she looked down. A vivid red flower was blossoming quickly on her left chest, and in its center, the thick shaft of a long metal spear stood firmly in place.

The cage door was suddenly slammed shut with a loud bang. She looked up and saw that a few shapes were frantically securing it with metal chains. Behind them, more shapes were emerging from the shadows, and they were closing in on the birdcage with cautious impatience. It was too dim to see the shapes clearly, but she already knew they were the shapes of humans.

Something warm and wet was streaming down from her left chest, quietly and continuously, like the flow of a newborn spring. Before it could touch the floor, however, the droplets had turned into tiny fires that sizzled softly before going out. As the vivid red liquid continued to ooze from her chest, innumerable tiny fires drizzled down like a mini meteor shower, generating enough light for her to see the complicated expressions on the few faces that were closest to the cage.

She wondered how much time she had left before she ran out of blood. She looked down to check her wound, only to realize she was still clutching the large white ball tightly to her abdomen, and its engraving was already overflowed with her blood, which was brimming over from the nine deformed claws at the ends of the nine evenly distributed arms of the circle in the middle, looking like nine ruby-red snakes crawling out from their den and slithering down the surface of the ball all at the same time. Soon, nine streams of blood were dripping silently from the ball into a continuous rain of tiny fires, forming a brief, illustrious waterfall of flames before joining the other falling tiny fires to fuel their fleeting mini meteor shower.

She heard voices shouting in her head—it was the other three, urging her to transform back into her true form before it was too late.

"It's true . . ." she heard one of the humans say. "It's all true . . ."

The owner of the voice stepped forth woodenly from the other shapes, looking as though he was under the influence of a spell. Slowly and cautiously, he came up to the birdcage, gaping. His eyes, lit up by the drizzling flames, were burning wildly with their reflections, which, in turn, made them seem like the eyes of a savage beast.

"So *you* are the one we've been looking for ..." He peered at her from between the thick metal bars. "It was *you* who raided the other places, wasn't it? You wanted to save those birds. And now ... here you are, to save the egg, just like they said you would."

They?

"The gods were right." A sly smile crawled onto the man's face. "You're *not* invincible. You have great powers, but you also have weaknesses ... weaknesses that we can use to our advantage ..."

She had the sensation that her heart was on fire. She clutched her left chest to ease the pain. The voices from the other three had become muffled and distant, and they were fading quickly from her head as if she were sinking into infinite depths.

"You see, there are only two choices for you now." The man licked his lips expectantly, holding up his hands and gesturing them to her like the two pans of a balance scale. "Death ... or rebirth. Which one will you choose?"

Her legs gave out and she lost her balance. As she tumbled to the floor, the large white ball slipped from her hands; the pool of blood that had been collecting in its engraving splattered out violently, producing a short-lived but generous shower of flames.

"Either way, you're *mine* now," the man purred with sadistic satisfaction. "You've fallen for our trap. We won. And we shall soon obtain the secrets to all your powers!"

Struggling to push herself up to her knees, she fumbled for the shaft in her left chest and wrapped her fingers around it firmly. Then, with a terrifying screech from her throat, she pulled the spear out.

As soon as the spearhead had exited her body, blood gushed from the hole that it left behind, lighting up the floor beneath her with a pool of flames. Within seconds, the vivid red liquid still streaming down profusely from her began to glow brightly, like red-hot lava, and the dark hole in her left chest was suddenly illuminated by a brilliant light source, which was increasing rapidly in both size and intensity. In no time, the entire chamber was lit up, bright as day, and she was able to see the face of every human on the other side of the birdcage.

She found the man who had been speaking and glared at him, her eyes boring deeply into his, reaching in for his soul.

Heat exploded from her flaming heart and rushed out from her pores, setting her hair and skin on fire. Burning furiously, she jabbed the spear to the floor and pulled herself up with it. By the time she was upright again, her fiery hair had grown into long streams of flames that cascaded down to fill the bottom of the bird-cage. Without taking her eyes off the man, she tossed the spear to the side and let the raging flames surround her.

Just before the brilliant light source radiating from the hole in her left chest burst into a huge, blinding ball of light, she saw the man running madly for the wooden door with his hands clutching helplessly to his head. But he was knocked over, almost immediately, by the other humans who were all scrambling in panic to reach the wooden door first. And soon, he was buried, somewhere between his burning desire for immortality and his only hope of exiting the chamber, under the chaos of their feet . . .

"They tricked you!" the dragon bellowed, jolting her out of the image of the blinding light that had flooded the chamber, only to see a flash of lightning striking the clouds behind it with a loud clap of thunder.

She realized then that she was still inside the clearing, but the emerald green clouds around her were now dark and angry like a turbulent sea in a storm. Countless lightning bolts flashed inside them and continued to fork into smaller and skinnier branches, illuminating the clouds into strange, unfathomable shapes, as if life was being pumped into the blood vessels of the embryos of an unknown species while thunder rumbled and cracked inside them like the growls and roars from their untimely awakening.

"Vile humans! Corrupted *souls*! Unworthy of *life*!" The dragon swished its tail like a whip, sending out a blast of wind that nearly made her lose her footing. When she recovered her balance and looked up, the dragon had grown back to its original size, and its color had darkened into a semitranslucent blue.

"Liars! . . . Humans or immortals, they are all liars!" Lightning shot out from the clouds behind the dragon and branched out in all directions, followed by a deafening bang that could have cracked the Earth open. "We were fools to have created immortals out of the loathsome mold of humans! We were deceived by their false pretense! The immortals had succumbed to their human nature of lies and deceptions long before we had suspected it!

"To serve their ultimate goal, the immortals had crafted a cunning gift for the humans to disguise its true purpose from us. The gift was later lost during the clashes between the two sides, leaving only stories and rumors behind among the humans—until you were caught in that cage.

"Remember what the human said after you were caught? . . . Yes, the immortals we created, the ones that he had referred to as 'the gods,' had shared their knowledge with the humans, knowledge that had helped them to plan and set up the trap that you willingly walked into! We finally saw the truth as it was: the immortals had long been plotting against us in secret. We had been betrayed by them all!"

"Did I . . . die?" she asked hesitantly, not knowing whether it was the correct way to describe what had happened in that chamber in the end.

The dragon lowered its head and looked her in the eye; its own seemed to be twinkling with amusement. She thought she heard a faint laugh from the dragon.

" 'Die'? . . . You have stayed in that human form for too long, Vermilion. It confines your powers to that shell to make you human; don't let it confine your mind to the human brain that came with it. 'Die' is a human term, and 'death' is just something the humans have come up with as an explanation for the inevitable to console themselves. You, Vermilion, are the Keeper of Rebirth, one of the Four Keepers since the creation of this universe. Your human forms may perish like the rest of them, but never your true form.

"When your human form 'died' in that cage, your true form was released. Unfortunately, when the blood in your human form was running dry, your powers waned and the suns dimmed again. Consequently, the Eye opened and the Soulless descended upon this world once more.

"The Soulless gravitated toward you like moths to a flame. Just like the time before, they came for you first. But since you were greatly weakened by your 'death' in your human form, to prevent the Soulless from reaching you, the three of us had no choice but to use our powers to rip the cage out from that rock tower to retrieve you. We knew that without your presence in the living world, the Soulless would follow the scent of fresh *souls* and eventually pour into the nearest city to feast, which would then put *the balance* of the Scale in grave danger again. So until you could regain your full strength to close the Eye and stop more of the Soulless from descending upon this world, the three of us would have to keep the living things safe from the ones that had already descended.

"We found a volcano in the vicinity of the nearest city and used our powers to bring it to a boil, forcing the animals and humans to flee before the Soulless could reach the area. Even in the face of a volcanic eruption, the humans still hung on to their greed. Instead of fleeing right away, they busied themselves with packing their possessions, stuffing as much into their carts and bags as they could, disregarding the fact that for every extra second they spent on packing, they were gambling their pathetic lives on the unpredictable force of nature.

"Needless to say, by the time the Soulless had found their way to the city limit, there were still a lot of humans left in the area. Even though we could save them from the Soulless discreetly one by one, we knew we would always be outnumbered. Without you at your full strength to close the Eye, the Soulless would continue to descend upon this world and continue to pour into any nearby cities to feast on fresh *souls*.

"In the end, we let the volcano erupt. It was the only way to preserve as many *souls* from the Soulless as possible. Once the volcano had erupted, the remaining humans were finally scared enough to flee the city. But for those who weren't fast enough to leave in time, they were either killed by the eruption or the Soulless, who, in turn, were vaporized by the intense heat from the eruption . . . Yes, there's a price for everything, even for *the balance* of the Scale.

"However, since the Eye had not yet been closed, the next wave of the Soulless merely headed for the next town. As a result, we had to repeat the eruption to preserve the *souls* in several nearby cities and towns . . . Yes. It was a price we had to pay for *the balance* of the Scale; we had to minimize the number of *souls* that the Soulless could have otherwise consumed.

"By the time you had regained your full strength and closed the Eye, we had managed to vaporize the majority of the Soulless who had entered the living world. As for the rest of them, they were either captured by White in the nearby areas afterward, or they had feasted on enough fresh *souls* and gained enough awareness to know that they needed to hide from us, in which case, since they had been feasting on the *souls* of an amalgam of species, they would have transmuted into monsters with unimaginable forms.

"Then, as more fresh *souls* were consumed, they would gradually gain the consciousness, the appearance, the physical abilities, as well as the intelligence of the species whose *souls* they had consumed. Not only that, they would also be able to maintain the consciousness, the appearance, the physical abilities, and the intelligence of the species whose *souls* they had consumed the most: if they had feasted mainly on the *souls* of foxes, they would become what humans call 'vixens'; if they had feasted mainly on the *souls* of wolves, they would become what humans call 'werewolves'; if they had feasted mainly on the *souls* of bats, 'vampires'; if they had feasted mainly on the *souls* of eagles, 'harpies'; if they had feasted mainly on the *souls* of fish, 'sirens' . . . So if they had feasted mainly on human *souls* for long enough, they would eventually be able to take on human form to enchant the other humans into doing anything. In short, no matter where they had gone to hide from us, one thing was for certain: they would prey on susceptible *souls* at any given opportunity to obtain the consciousness of a higher-level species to move up the food chain.

"But conscious or not, the Soulless do not belong in the living world, and therefore, they needed to be expelled. Once White had cleared the areas near where the Eye had opened, he began to sweep the Earth to hunt down the rest of the Soulless one by one. This task turned out to be extremely time-consuming, however: once the Soulless had consumed enough *souls* to take on the forms of ordinary animals, from a distance, it's very difficult to tell them apart from the living, not to mention they would have gained the intelligence of those animals to use to their advantage as well.

"What's more, the Soulless who had gained a high level of intelligence were even able to harness dark matter and dark energy on Earth to create a different version of the Soulless, which, though incapable of consuming *souls*, can roam the Earth undetected on their behalf to sip on the spirit of life in any animals or any humans until the *light* in them is drained to the point where they become either mental or suicidal. That is why White's hunt on the remainder of the Soulless has lasted till this day. The good news is, ever since *the balance* of the Scale had been recovered from the aftermath of the Soulless' second descent, the number of *souls* that we have lost to them has been low enough to not hinder *the rhythm* of the Wheel of Life. But with the total number of *the seeds of life* still dwindling gradually, though almost imperceptibly, *the rhythm* is definitely slowing down insidiously, which means, eventually, it will still be a threat to the future of this universe . . ."

The thought of an unknown creature feasting on a human's soul made her queasy. But she had forgotten that the dragon had been speaking to her through her mind, and therefore, it could see her thoughts as well.

"You still can't remember what the Soulless look like," the dragon observed. "You can't remember who the Soulless are and what they are capable of . . . And you can't even remember what *souls* and *the seeds of life* are for . . ."

As the dragon spoke, a fog was rising quickly from the clouds beneath her feet, which soon shrouded the dragon from her view. She felt something cold and wet in the fog, tapping gently and busily on her face like an invisible veil of tiny little tentacles. Then she realized it was misting.

Though she couldn't see the dragon clearly, she could feel its presence strongly in her mind as if it had entered her head to examine all the other thoughts that she had shoved aside.

"... nor the Eye, nor the other two Keepers, nor the River of Time, nor the Wheel of Life ... nor the Scale ..." the dragon added slowly and heavily, then its voice grew cold like the mist, which was now sweeping toward her like waves of pins and needles made out of ice. "It appears that despite my efforts, your memory as the Keeper of Rebirth will not return ... You have paid a hefty price this time, Vermilion. Is it worth it? Is it worth the price you have paid to live among the humans, among these selfish, deceitful, power-obsessed creatures who would do anything to you in exchange for your powers, and abandon your identity and duties as one of the Four Keepers just so you could be reborn as a human infant to save a human woman?"

The mist was suddenly replaced by sheets of cold rain, smothering the intolerable heat that was radiating from her pores and soaking her from head to toe. Her limbs and body were finally cooling down, but not her head; her head was a hot, jumbled mess, tangled in a completely different set of thoughts, which had mangled the thoughts that were already there.

Thunder cracked and rumbled from behind the dragon, and the deafening sounds reverberated into the circular wall of clouds that was surrounding her. Even so, she could still hear the dragon's whisper distinctly:

"They lied to you too, did they not? ... The two humans that you call 'Mom' and 'Dad' ... Of course they did. They all lie. That's what they do ... That's what they *all* do. They have no regard for anyone else in this world. They only care about themselves, about their own needs and wants and desires and ambitions, and they will stop at nothing to realize them.

"The humans have taken billions of nonhuman lives, but *the seeds of life* from those lives ended up being spun into billions more of them! And no matter how 'civilized' they think they have become, these new humans, arriving in the hundreds every minute, are exactly the same as their fathers and the fathers of their fathers: taking more nonhuman lives, spawning more humans!

"Meanwhile, the Wheel of Life is spinning out less and less new species, despite that a growing number of the current species can no longer survive in a world that is now infested by the humans. Worse still, thanks to the humans, most of the new species that the Wheel of Life had actually spun out couldn't last long enough in *the flow* of the River of Time to sustain their existence on Earth. Instead of sharing the world with the other lives that are in existence, the humans have been, both directly and indirectly, driving them to extinction! In just 12,000 years, the humans have purposefully altered a world that was created for all living things into their own, rendering it uninhabitable for hundreds of thousands of other species. And now, spurred by the delusion that whatever little amount of knowledge they have learned about this universe has made them wise enough to play gods, they are quenching their thirst for power by cooking up new species themselves. In doing so, they are again meddling with *the rhythm* of the Wheel of Life and *the flow* of the River of Time.

"Do you see it now, Vermilion? The humans will be the downfall of this universe. They are the most invasive virus, aggressive and unstoppable. They will consume everything else in this world, and the Scale will lose *the balance* irrevocably, destroying this entire universe in the process!"

The dragon's words reminded her of Lilith, and she found her mind slipping away from that jumbled mess in her head. She remembered the long conversation they had at the pedestrian square, the day before Lilith's sixteenth birthday, about mortals and immortals, age and perception, the purpose of existence, the purpose of life ... whether the Heavenly Court would eliminate the humans or let the humans eliminate themselves. And it suddenly occurred to her that if what the dragon had said about the Four Keepers was true, then, in a sense, they *were* the Heavenly Court.

The dragon didn't acknowledge her thought. It simply said, "The Four Keepers must intervene before it's too late."

She felt her chest tightening. " 'Intervene'?"

As if someone had given the order, the rain stopped abruptly, leaving a sea of restless fog that rose swiftly and continuously toward the sky, through which she saw that the dragon was gazing at her meaningfully.

"The Four Keepers must travel to the Gate to reset the River of Time and cleanse the Wheel of Life. It will then begin anew ..."

"You ... you want to get rid of the humans?" She stared at the dragon, half shocked and half in denial.

"They have seen your powers, Vermilion!" the dragon bellowed like a parent who was scolding his child for having behaved unreasonably. "Ever since their lust for power became evident, the humans had been plotting against us, time after time, and they have succeeded in weakening you—twice, which has not only granted the Soulless two separate opportunities to access the living world but has also brought forth two alarming depletions of *the seeds of life*, putting *the balance* of the Scale in grave danger both times!

"Even though you have destroyed most of their documentation on us, you just left them a fresh trail to follow: they have observed your powers a second time within the past two years; it won't be long before they figure out those powers belong to you. Their obsession with power will drive them to dig out every single detail and every single clue there is in the world to find you, even if it's only remotely relevant to what they have observed—even if it's misleading and far from the truth.

"After all, that was how they mistook the phoenix birds for you, and that was also how they came to the conclusion centuries later that you must be a 'witch' who could withstand fire, which then led to the senseless sentencing and ruthless burning of tens of thousands of their own species throughout the course of the next few hundred years—just to find you. This time will be no different, Vermilion. They will come after you with their most cutting-edge technologies, and they will stop at nothing until they can capture you to harness your powers, even if everything else in this world is destroyed along the way. If we don't reset the River of Time and cleanse the Wheel of Life now, the humans *will* be the death of this universe!

"Vermilion, we must stop the humans before it's too late; it's our duty as the Four Keepers of this universe. It's time to wake up from your dream of saving humanity; humanity is hopeless and beyond help. It's also time to wake up from your 'life' as a daughter to two humans; it's nothing but a lie in itself!"

She stared blankly at the dragon, shivering under her wet clothes. The burning heat and pain in her body had long been extinguished by the cold rain, as though the life of her inexplicable burn mark—the source of that burning heat and pain—had finally come to an end.

"No ..." she murmured involuntarily, trembling from a new emotion that was welling up quickly in her chest, which soon burst out from her throat in a discordant screech. "No! ... *You* are a lie! *This* is a dream!"

She charged at the dragon as fast as her numb legs would carry her, hoping it would dispel the dream, but she passed right through the dragon and ran into a pool of fog. Startled, she spun around, only to see that she was alone in the fog, then she heard a whisper, echoing in the air from all around her:

Is it? Is it ... is it ... ? The humans are coming for you. Coming for you ... coming for you ... Vermilion, it's time to wake up. Wake up ... wake up ...

It was the dragon's voice, but she knew it was already gone.

As she stared vacantly into space, the fog dissipated, revealing a cluster of lights twinkling below like a sparkle of fireflies caught on an enormous spiderweb. She took a few mechanical steps forward, then she realized she had already reached the top of the hill, and the cluster of lights was downtown Starfall.

A shot was fired from the twinkling city below, slicing the silence of the night apart with a glowing trail that raced toward the limit of the sky like a comet, looking determined to reach space and leave Earth behind. Just when it was about to succeed, however, it dimmed and exploded with a loud bang that shook the ground, sending a shower of red-hot stars in all directions like a fiery red chrysanthemum that was blooming all too fiercely under a scorching sun. The fiery petals then withered, as swiftly as they had blossomed, until they all fell back down into the embrace of gravity as glowing ash and disappeared in midair. More shots were fired afterward, followed by more comet-like glowing trails. They raced toward the zenith one after another, eager to beat the fate of their predecessor, only to fail successively with the same level of explosive passion that resulted in more spectacular showers of stars in different shapes and colors, making it hard to tell whether they were an expression of joy or an outburst of indignation for having finally discovered, at the very end of their fleeting lives, what their true purpose had been in life.

It was the city's fireworks display for the New Year; it was already past midnight.

And yet, she was still here, on this hill, trapped in a dreamlike daze . . .

She stared at the evanescent fireworks without blinking until her eyes were hot and blurry, then she closed them resignedly, not knowing if it would make her fall asleep in this dream or wake up into a new one.

She waited numbly with her eyes closed, but she neither fell asleep nor woke up into a new dream. Aside from the fireworks, all she could hear was Lilith's voice, echoing in the darkness:

"Don't be a party pooper, Mira! Don't be a party pooper, Mira! Don't be a party pooper, Mira! Don't be a party pooper, Mira! . . ."

V

Lilith knew the fireworks had started; she could hear the noise through her headphones. She opened her eyes and stopped the music. Then, just as another loud bang went off in the distance, she pushed herself up from the bed, took off her headphones, and went to the window.

The temperature was quite low outside, but she decided to open the window anyway so she could experience the fireworks fully as they bloomed into beautiful existence in the sky. As soon as the window was opened, the frigid winter air embraced her generously, making her hold her breath and wince at once. She commented wryly to herself that it was no way to begin a brand-new year. So, still clenching her teeth, she let the cold air enter her nostrils and greeted New Year's Day bravely.

A trail of light whistled up into the sky and exploded into a large red flower with long, thin petals, which kept on expanding until they, too, exploded into many smaller red flowers. Just as those smaller ones began to expand, the whole thing exploded again, replacing all the red flowers with countless bright white stars, which, in turn, exploded into numerous soft yellow lights that flickered valiantly before disappearing into the night.

Lilith gazed at the white smoke left in its wake and was suddenly filled with a sense of loss. Out of habit, she reached for her cell phone to text Mira, only to remember it had remained unresponsive since earlier that evening, when it had slipped out from her backpack and shattered its screen on the sidewalk.

She let out a sigh and tossed her phone back to the table. Mira had an unnatural aversion toward the internet, so she had neither an email account nor any other messaging apps outside of the default texting application on her phone. In other words, without a working phone, she would not be able to reach Mira tonight.

The thought made Lilith shiver inside, and she couldn't help but notice that even though she had been deliberately avoiding her true feelings by drowning them out with music, they had still managed to invade her mind. She felt lonely, consumingly and helplessly lonely, so much so that she almost wished she had agreed to stay at Mira's house. If she had, she thought amusingly to herself, she would be watching the fireworks with Mira right now, and the two of them would be discussing all kinds of wild, intriguing things, like whether the Heavenly Court would frown upon all the fireworks fired at them on New Year's Day, whether everything that had happened on Earth so far had been a part of their plan, and whether there was a higher purpose for everyone and everything in this world . . .

She wondered if there was a higher purpose for the fireworks as well. Then she found herself wondering if there was a higher purpose for Mira and the phoenix inside her . . .

A series of loud bangs jolted Lilith out of her thoughts, reminding her that the fireworks display was about to get more exciting. But Lilith was too preoccupied to appreciate the spectacle taking place in the sky now. Instead, she thought about Mira, wondering if she was watching the fireworks too. She knew Mira wasn't really persuaded by her theories and still believed the deaths of those men were on her hands. And that was why she wanted Mira to have a long, relaxing evening alone with her parents to soak up their love and regain her faith in herself. She hoped it was working —it should. After all, Mira was with the two people who loved her more than anything else in this world.

Lilith smiled wistfully to herself, wishing secretly that she could say the same about her own parents. But she dismissed the feeling quickly and forced her attention back to the sky, all the while wondering in the back of her mind if the fireworks knew their true purpose had been fulfilled.

Chapter 9   THE BLACK TORTOISE

1

LILITH couldn't fall asleep. She had gone back to bed right after the fireworks display, but no matter how much she tried to relax her body and mind, she couldn't stay in the sweet state of drowsiness long enough to head into a dream; her subconscious would always reach in and pull her out of it at the last second, as if it was under the impression that she was slipping into a deep chasm rather than a dream.

She tossed and turned till well after two o'clock in the morning and still couldn't fall asleep, so she decided to count sheep. She pictured a flock of white, fluffy sheep in her mind, and she placed them in front of an orange fence in a vast grassland, under a deep blue sky, then she made the sheep leap over the fence one by one in slow motion as she counted silently in her head. Before long, the sheep were leaping so high that, one after another, they rose to the sky and turned into white, fluffy clouds, blurring the deep blue sky with a sea of white, fluffy fog . . .

She heard a noise ringing in the background, sounding like a chime that had traveled from somewhere far away. Within a second, the fog and the clouds were gone, and so were the sheep, the fence, and the grassland, leaving only the sky behind, which had somehow turned pitch-black. As her brain gradually woke up to reality, it finally occurred to her that the pitch-black sky was actually the insides of her eyelids.

The doorbell rang again. Grudgingly, Lilith opened her eyes and glanced at the clock on her nightstand: 3:19 AM. *Who would come visit me at three o'clock in the morning?*

The thought immediately kicked the sleepiness out of her head, and her brain started whirring right away. Under the situation, her parents seemed to be the most logical answer. But they had told her they would be very busy with a project at work and would be away till at least after Lunar New Year, so she knew that was the wrong answer. And even if they did have to come back early for some reason, they would have used the key to let themselves in.

By then, Lilith's brain had automatically come to the conclusion that she was in danger. She thought of what Starfall was like on Christmas Eve; so many crimes were committed within that one single day that it was as if the whole town had lost its mind. She could still see the awful mess left in the house after it was ransacked: the robbers had broken whatever they felt like breaking and taken whatever they felt like taking—except the books.

A chill ran down Lilith's spine as another possibility flashed in her mind. *What if the robbers have somehow learned about the true value of these books and have come back for them? Maybe they only rang the doorbell to check if we're home ... What if they know my parents are away and I'm the only one in the house?*

Slowly and quietly, Lilith sat up and got out of bed, her heart pounding in her chest. Just then, the doorbell rang again, lasting much longer this time and sounding much more demanding than before. Lilith froze at the sound of it, but it didn't stop her from assessing the situation: she was alone in the house, and the only phone available to her was out of commission, so if there were indeed some unwanted guests at the door, she would have to think of a way to get help fast.

She reminded herself to stay calm and forced a deep breath into her lungs, then she tiptoed to the window, thinking she should first find out how many of them were at the door and whether they had already begun working on the lock to invite themselves in.

In order not to attract any attention with her movements, Lilith pressed her back to the wall next to the window frame; very carefully, she lifted the blinds just enough to peek down from the side. She saw a lone shape in front of the door, the upper part of which was blocked from her view by the portico. But judging by the look of it, it belonged to someone who was not in a hurry to break down the front door.

Lilith let out a long sigh of relief and relaxed her shoulders. Just as she began to entertain the thought of ignoring her late-night mystery visitor altogether and climbing back to bed, an eerie feeling crept down the back of her scalp, making the hair on her nape stand on end. She was suddenly very self-conscious, much like the way she felt when she was being observed. Like a reflex, she looked up from the shape under the portico, only to see that two pairs of big black eyes were staring right at her from the other side of the window.

This gave Lilith such a start that she shrank back from the wall and choked up with a soft yelp. When she had finally gathered her wits to return to the window to check what it was, she saw nothing but a pair of wings gliding away into the night sky, giving off a surreal red hue under the pale moonlight. Her late-night mystery visitor must have noticed the red bird too, for before Lilith's mind could catch up with her eyes, the shape at the front door had walked out from under the portico and into the street wearing a full head of fiery red curls, which were dancing wildly with the wind in the dark winter night like a raging bonfire.

11

"Mira?"

"Lilith."

"Wh—What are you doing here?"

"Can I come in? I'm cold."

Still feeling rather perplexed, Lilith nodded stiffly and led Mira into the kitchen.

"I'll make you a hot chocolate," said Lilith, reaching into the cupboard. Then she turned around with a box of instant hot chocolate mix and a half-eaten bag of marshmallows. "How many marshmallows do you want on yours?"

Mira was standing quietly next to the kitchen island. Now that they were both under the lights, Lilith noticed that Mira was wearing only one layer, and it seemed slightly wet.

Growing anxious, Lilith asked in a tight voice, "What happened to your shirt? Why is it wet? . . . And where's your jacket?"

"Long story," Mira answered blandly. "I . . . got into a detour by accident. That's why it took me so long to get here."

"A detour?" Lilith's eyes widened with trepidation. "Did something happen? Is everything okay? Are you . . . hurt?"

"I'm not hurt," Mira said mildly, looking somewhat pensive to Lilith. "I just got lost for a while on that hill."

" 'That hill' . . ." repeated Lilith, then her face changed from concerned to near panic. "You walked through the woods? . . . Why did you do that? It's too dark! You could have gotten stranded there!"

"I thought it'd be the fastest way," Mira replied calmly, a faint smile on her lips. "I wanted to get here before . . . midnight."

"For what?"

Mira looked steadily at Lilith for a long moment, then she said, "The fireworks. You asked me not to be a 'party pooper.' "

"I—" Lilith started to argue but stopped herself. She let out a long sigh and rolled her eyes. "You know what? It's too late to talk about that now, not to mention you look like you're about to fall apart. You need some warm food in your belly, and you need sleep." She put down the hot chocolate and marshmallows, pulled out a pot from the kitchen island, and started to fill it with water. "Go take a hot shower first. Grab whatever you need from my closet. I'll make you some chicken ramen and bring it up to you."

For a few seconds after that, Mira neither moved nor spoke. Lilith looked up from the pot and thought Mira was gazing at her with an inexplicable expression, but Mira simply nodded and headed upstairs.

By the time Lilith had brought the noodles up to her room, Mira was already fast asleep on top of the covers, appearing to have drifted off before she could remember to crawl under them.

With a slight sense of heartache, Lilith chuckled resignedly to herself and set the bowl down on the nightstand. Quietly, she pulled out a blanket from the closet and spread it over Mira. Mira's face was locked in a frown, looking as though she was having a bad dream. As Lilith gazed at her friend and wondered what was happening in her dream, her heart sank—there was an acute sadness in that frown, accompanied by a mixture of struggle and pain.

An eerie sensation crept down Lilith's spine, and she suddenly had the feeling that she was being watched. She immediately thought of the two pairs of big black eyes that she thought she saw outside her window earlier. Not knowing whether it was a sign that they had returned, she walked stealthily to the window and, gingerly, peeked out from behind the blinds. She saw no eyes this time, but a vivid red bird was perching on the other side of the windowsill, waiting.

"Red?" Lilith said in surprise, mostly to herself.

The red bird tilted its head and stared up at Lilith; its beady black eyes seemed to be glinting balefully in the cold, dark night, sending a chill down Lilith's back. Lilith dismissed it by telling herself that she was just being paranoid. Thinking Red had probably followed Mira all the way to her place, she gently raised the blinds and opened the window.

"Hey, Red. Are you waiting on Mira?" Lilith whispered to the red bird. "Well, she's very tired and she's sleeping now, so I'm afraid you'll be waiting for a while . . . Do you want to come in? It's cold out there."

To Lilith's amazement, Red seemed to have understood her invitation. It tilted its head and looked from Lilith to the inside of the room, then it took a few hops toward her.

"It's okay. You're safe here," Lilith cooed to Red and stepped back to make room for it to come in. "See? Mira's sleeping right over there. You can stay inside with us until you want to leave."

Red surveyed the room with its beady black eyes, then it suddenly flapped its wings and flew toward the bed. Before Lilith could blink, it had landed on top of the lamp on the nightstand.

"Wow . . ." Lilith let out a gasp of wonder. "It's almost like you can understand everything I say! You're one smart bird, Red!"

Lilith closed the window and lowered the blinds, then she went back to the bed and lay down next to Mira. As her body started to relax on the soft mattress, she smiled at Red with a wry chuckle and said, "To tell you the truth, I was glad it was just you out there, Red. I could have sworn I saw two pairs of scary-looking eyes outside my window earlier. I thought it was a four-eyed monster. How silly was that? . . . Well, it must have been just a trick of the light, right?"

Red tilted its head and looked at Lilith from the top of the lamp. It didn't make any comment, but its beady black eyes seemed to be saying that it knew exactly what she meant.

III

She found herself standing in a world of fog, unable to tell whether it was day or night. There was no one else in the fog, and, except for the fog, there was nothing else.

It was pleasantly warm here. She held out her arms and realized the fog was so thick that she couldn't even see her hands. It didn't bother her at all though. She was relaxed and calm in this world, strangely and surprisingly, and she embraced that willingly.

She decided to take a walk and let herself wander in this endless fog.

She walked and walked, not knowing where she was heading, or whether the path she took was ending, but it didn't matter. It was warm and pleasant in the fog, and her heart was finally at rest.

She didn't know how long she had been walking, and she didn't care. Time had no meaning here; everything had no meaning here.

So she just kept on walking. Her legs were moving of their own accord now, and her mind had become a world of fog too: there was no one else, and there was nothing else other than the fog; there was no thought, no plan, no urge, no drive, but she didn't mind at all.

Do you want to stay? Do you want to stay? Do you want to stay? . . . A voice rippled toward her from far, far away, causing the world of fog to vibrate with its echoes everywhere—even in her head.

The vibration made her blink, and when she looked again, the world of fog was gone. Instead, she was standing in a misty forest by herself, listening to the chirps of crickets and frogs and the occasional hoots of owls. It was dark here. There was no moon or stars in the sky. The temperature was much cooler, with a lot of moisture in the air.

Through the mist, she caught sight of a small, faint light flickering in the distance, beckoning her to come closer. She trod toward it in a trance and soon arrived at the edge of the forest, where she was greeted by a vast lake that was shrouded in mist. Without either the moon or the stars shining upon it, the lake looked as black and velvety as the night sky above it.

"Welcome to my lake," said a calm, fluid voice.

She turned her head toward where the voice had come from and found an old man. He was sitting by the lake, wearing a plain Chinese robe that was as silvery as his long hair and long beard, and he was holding something long and slender in his hand. Presently, he put one end of it into his mouth and took a long puff on it; the other end flickered and lit up. She realized then that he was smoking a pipe, and it was the light from his pipe that had led her to the lake.

The old man tilted his head back and opened his mouth; rings of white smoke rose up from his throat, expanding leisurely as they drifted up into the sky until, eventually, they became a part of the perpetual mist over the lake.

"I do this every night." The old man smiled at her. "To protect my lake."

"Who are you?" she asked impassively, wondering if she had heard his voice before.

"Just as I thought . . ." The old man shook his head and put down his pipe, then he stood and, with his hands folded in front of him, gave her a polite bow. "Greetings to you, Vermilion. I am Black, the Keeper of Growth. It's my pleasure to meet you again."

Her body froze; so did her mind. She could not bring herself to think that the other dream had continued into this one.

With a wave of his wide sleeve, the old man brushed back some mist and revealed a small wooden table at his side, which was holding up an old Chinese tea set in the middle. With a wave of the other sleeve, he brushed back some more mist and revealed a wooden stool behind the table.

"Come." He beckoned to her with compassionate gentleness. "Let's enjoy some good tea together. While I brew us a fresh pot, I'll tell you a few stories . . . You like stories, don't you?"

She looked numbly at the old man and gave him a weak nod.

"Good." The old man nodded back with a kind smile and gestured to the wooden stool. "Please, sit."

She let her legs carry her over to the wooden table and lowered herself onto the stool. The old man waited till she was seated, then he sat across from her and started to prepare the tea.

"The stories I'm going to tell you today are stories from the ancient past. Some called them folklore, some called them fables, some called them legends, some called them myths . . . But no matter what they were called, they all began with the same line . . ."

IV

The Story of Kuafu Chasing the Sun

A long, long time ago, a magnificent bird lived in the sun. It had a very important duty: to collect *light* for the sun.

Every day, the magnificent bird traveled between the Earth and the sun, collecting *light* from the Earth and bringing it back to the sun. Day after day, the sun shone on without fail. The plants grew, the animals thrived, the air was fresh, and the water was clean. Thanks to the magnificent bird who performed her duty diligently, the sun was bright, and the Earth was a pleasant place for all lives.

The magnificent bird was worshiped everywhere. Everyone knew that without her, the sun would not be able to shine. So whenever the magnificent bird was seen collecting *light* on Earth, people would throw themselves to the ground on hands and knees and chant aloud:

"We worship thee! O Almighty bird of the sun! We worship thee for the abundance of food, the abundance of light, and the abundance of warmth! O Almighty bird of the sun!"

The magnificent bird knew they were chanting for her, but she didn't stop collecting. She merely acknowledged their gratefulness with a long screech.

Her nonchalance about their worship made people nervous and scared. They believed she was, in actuality, a god with divine powers. And since she resided in the sun, they believed she was the Sun God, and they thought she was only visiting the Earth to harness light to power herself.

Their fear toward the magnificent bird grew, and because of the growing fear toward the magnificent bird, people all over the world worshiped her even more piously than before.

But their devotion to worshiping the magnificent bird caused great resentment among the giants. Born with a brain that was as big as a human's but at least ten times their physical size and strength, the giants had been the center of their worship for many, many years before this attention was shifted wholly onto the magnificent bird. With the numbers of their worshipers dwindling, so were the tributes. The giants had long gotten used to enjoying the endless supplies of food and clothing from the humans without having to labor for them themselves. Now that the tributes were no longer flowing in, they couldn't even remember how to mend the holes in their clothes on their own.

The giants were famous for their temper, which not only made them aggressive and fearsome in fights but also made them prone to jealousy and revenge in life. Out of all the giants, Kuafu was the oldest one, and he was also the least content with the situation. He chided the other giants for being too stupid to come up with a solution to restore the giants' status among the humans, but he was challenged in return to answer why he had not come up with a solution himself if he were indeed smarter than the rest of them.

To Kuafu, a challenge from his own kind was equal to an insult. Burning with rage, he barked at the other giants, claiming he would kill the magnificent bird and solve the problem once and for all to prove that he was not only the smartest but also the strongest one among them.

"But how are you going to kill it? It lives on the sun!" one giant tried to remind him.

"So what? It's just a bird, a very large bird!" Kuafu dismissed the concern with a wave of his giant hand. "I'll catch it when it comes down, then I'll crush its neck with just one hand!"

"But how are you going to catch it? It never rests!" another giant tried to remind him.

"By running after it, of course, stupid! You don't think I can outrun a bird?" Kuafu shook his giant fist threateningly at the one who just spoke. "Now shut your traps! You're all birdbrains! Even your questions are stupid!"

So when the sun came up the following day, Kuafu set off to catch the magnificent bird. He didn't have to look for her for long, because she was already busy with her duty.

"Hey, you!" Kuafu pointed a thick finger at her and barked. "Who do you think you are? This is the giants' turf! Everyone must bow down to us and pay us tributes—including you!"

The magnificent bird did not reply, nor did she stop collecting.

Kuafu was furious. He raised his voice and followed the magnificent bird with great, long strides. "Hey! You! I'm talking to you! Who do you think you are?"

Still, the magnificent bird did not reply, nor did she stop collecting.

By then, Kuafu was boiling with rage. Blood rushed up into his head, and his eyes turned red and murderous. He let out a thunderous roar and began running after the magnificent bird, leaping over streams and hills while stretching his giant arms and hands out as far as he could to reach for the magnificent bird.

But no matter how fast he ran, how high he leaped, or how far he reached, the magnificent bird was always ahead of him, collecting *light* as she glided over the plains and the mountains, the rivers and the lakes. Minute by minute, she became brighter and brighter with the *light* she had collected. Eventually, she became so bright that she outshone the sun, and no one could look at her directly without stinging their eyes.

People saw it and marveled at the sight. They believed the magnificent bird had demonstrated her divine powers to the world and became the sun herself. When they saw Kuafu chasing after the giant ball of blazing light, they couldn't help laughing out loud at his stupidity.

"How dare he challenge the Almighty? How dare he chase after the sun?" they jeered. "How can he possibly think that he can catch the God of Sun?"

But to Kuafu, he was only chasing a bird. As the day went on, it grew hotter and hotter, and he had to stop frequently to quench his insatiable thirst by sucking rivers and lakes dry. Even so, it was not enough to ease either the heat or his exhaustion. By evening, Kuafu's skin was gravely burned from the intense heat and was covered in blisters; his eyes, after staring straight at the giant ball of blazing light all day, were bleeding blood like streams. Exhausted with pain and tormented by humiliation, Kuafu finally collapsed to the ground and died.

The magnificent bird emerged from the sun then. With a flap of her wings, she collected the *light* from Kuafu, brought it back to the sun, and sank, along with the sun, below the western sky.

The Story of Yi Shooting the Sun

A long, long time ago, war broke out between men and the giants. The giants were much bigger and much stronger than men. In order to win the war, men had to come together in large numbers to go up against the giants. But the giants were fearsome enemies: a swipe of their arms could knock out a dozen men; a stomp of their feet could flatten a dozen more.

As a result of these disadvantages, men suffered heavy casualties every time they fought the giants, and the Earth was covered with fresh corpses after every battle, making it a haven for scavengers.

At that time, there was a rare species of bird with three legs and three feet. These birds had pitch-black feathers and exceptional intelligence. Unfortunately, there were only nine of them in the world, and they all lived together in the great Fusang tree, which was as old as the Earth and so tall that it actually touched the sky. These birds were not the scavengers who relished a buffet of rotten corpses; they were great singers whose main food source was the wisdom berries that grew only on that old Fusang tree. Yet every morning at dawn, they would fly down from the great Fusang tree and stand atop the corpses, waiting for the sun to rise.

But it was not the sun that they were waiting to greet; they were waiting to greet the magnificent bird who lived in the sun. They knew the magnificent bird would come down to collect *light* from the Earth at dawn every day, and, because they were exceptionally intelligent, they knew the magnificent bird would first appear at the place where she could collect a great deal of *light* at once.

When the magnificent bird descended from the sky, the nine three-legged birds flapped their wings and sang in joy:

"We worship thee! O Almighty bird of the sun! We worship thee for the abundance of *light* and the abundance of life! O Almighty bird of the sun!"

The magnificent bird hovered in midair and looked at the nine three-legged birds. She enjoyed their beautiful voices and their beautiful song. With a flap of her wings, she collected the *light* from the corpses that were beneath them and around them, which was enough to make her glow like a big ball of light.

The nine three-legged birds then sang to the magnificent bird in unison:

"O Almighty bird of the sun! Please enlighten us! What's the purpose of life? For we sought but found no answer!"

The magnificent bird did not reply.

The nine three-legged birds sang to the magnificent bird in unison again:

"O Almighty bird of the sun! Please illuminate us! What's the meaning of *light*? For we pursued but met no end!"

Again, the magnificent bird did not reply. It merely screeched to acknowledge their questions, then she returned to the sun and her duty.

This ritual was repeated for many, many years. Every morning at dawn, the nine three-legged birds would wait for the magnificent bird atop the new corpses from the war, and they would sing the same songs to her and ask her the same questions. But the magnificent bird never replied.

Then one day, after listening to the same songs and the same questions from the nine three-legged birds, the magnificent bird spoke:

"If it is the purpose of life that you seek, pursue the *light* for me."

Without a moment's hesitation, the nine three-legged birds agreed. From then on, they became the conduits of the magnificent bird, collecting *light* from the Earth and ferrying it to the magnificent bird every day. Every morning at dawn, when the magnificent bird arrived with the sun, the nine three-legged birds would take flight from the great Fusang tree toward her to deliver the *light* they had collected, which made them each glow like a big ball of light.

When men saw that instead of one, there were now ten balls of light in the sky, they were terrified. First they thought the sun had given birth to nine more suns, then they thought the sun had called upon nine more siblings. In the end, they realized the magnificent bird had created nine conduits, and before long, a rumor was spreading among men like wildfire, claiming the magnificent bird was not collecting light, but life. Apparently, some brave men had ventured into the depths of the areas where the corpses were left behind or disposed of, looking for valuables to loot; they ended up discovering that no matter whether the corpses were covered or exposed, as long as they were fresh, one of the nine conduits would appear before dawn to extract light from them for the magnificent bird.

Thanks to this rumor, terror seized men like never before, and they came to the conclusion that it was not light that had kept the sun shining, but their lives. And if the nine conduits could extract unused life from the dead to sustain the power of the magnificent bird, they could certainly, at her request, extract life from the living as well. In other words, the Sun God they had been worshiping was, in fact, Death—the one who could end all lives!

This conclusion soon drove men into helpless desperation because, to them, nothing was worse than having their lives taken away from them. Luckily, the clever men came up with a plan, one that could potentially kill two birds with one stone.

The cunning men went to see the giants, calling for a truce. They cried to the giants that they were wrong for having worshiped the magnificent bird instead of them. They told the giants that they now knew the nine conduits of the magnificent bird were taking life from everyone to fuel the magnificent bird's power. They then begged the giants to kill the magnificent bird to protect everyone on Earth from being taken away by Death.

Although the giants were not very smart, they all remembered what happened to Kuafu, the giant who set out to kill the magnificent bird but died in vain. Naturally, none of them was willing to share his fate.

Among the giants, there was a cyclops, the first of his kind. His name was Yi, and he was Kuafu's posthumous son. Though he was born with the birth defect of having only one eye, he was every bit as arrogant as his late father.

Therefore, when men couldn't persuade the other giants to act, they turned to Yi and said, "O Almighty Yi, son of Kuafu! Your father was the only giant who was brave enough to challenge the magnificent bird, who was responsible for not only his tragic death but also this inhumane curse on you to be born with only one eye as a punishment for your father's disobedience toward her! O Almighty Yi, son of Kuafu! We beg you to fulfill your father's last wish! Kill the magnificent bird! Avenge your father! Protect us from harm, and we shall proclaim you the sole savior of men, and we shall supply you with everything your heart desires!"

Their words satisfied Yi's ego greatly, to which he gave a wave of his giant arm as if to say the task was as easy as shooing away a fly. "Consider it done! I shall avenge my father and kill the magnificent bird! I shall bring peace to the world!"

"But how are you going to kill it?" one of the giants asked. "Kuafu couldn't even catch it!"

"I shall not catch it, then." Yi gave an ugly smile. "I shall shoot it down with my spear as soon as it shows itself in the sky."

"But how are you going to shoot it down with just a spear?" asked another giant. "It's way up there in the sky!"

"Leave that to us, Almighty Yi!" men said with great eagerness. "We shall supply you with a weapon that is so light and so fast that it'll fly high into the sky!"

Men were true to their word. They brought Yi a skillfully crafted set of bow and arrows, tailor-made for a giant's size and strength.

Yi was very pleased with his new weapon. As soon as he had mastered the skill of shooting arrows, he set off for the great Fusang tree. Men had told Yi that when the magnificent bird appeared with the sun at dawn, the nine conduits would take off from that tree to meet her. Men had also advised Yi to shoot down the nine conduits first to prevent them from passing the light they had collected to the magnificent bird, which, in turn, would weaken the magnificent bird's power for him to shoot her down next.

And that was exactly what he did. When the nine conduits ascended toward the sky from the great Fusang tree, glowing like nine more suns, Yi stepped out from his hiding place and drew his bow.

One by one, his giant arrows soared high into the sky with great force and found their targets. The sheer size of these arrows was enough to tear anything in their paths apart. One by one, the conduits were torn into pieces in the sky before raining down as small chunks of blood and flesh and bones; the ball of *light* that each of them had collected sank and dimmed among their fragmented bodies before vanishing into thin air, looking as if a sun had fallen and died.

Soon, there was only one conduit left in the sky. Yi took aim and released the ninth arrow, but before he could blink, the magnificent bird had leaped out from the sun and dove for his target. Just as the magnificent bird shielded the last conduit behind her wings, the arrow made contact with her chest. With a terrifying screech, the magnificent bird plummeted from the sky and crashed to the barren land beneath the great Fusang tree.

When Yi saw that the arrowhead was buried deep in the magnificent bird's chest, he walked up to her in triumph.

" 'The Sun God,' they call you. 'The undying bird.' They think you're immortal and cannot be killed." He laughed boisterously, his one-eyed head filled with ecstasy. "I've just proved to them all that you're nothing but a very large bird! You're not a god! But you're definitely a dying bird!"

Yi grabbed the shaft of his giant arrow and yanked it out from the magnificent bird's chest. As the arrowhead exited her body, something red and sharp flew out, landing squarely in Yi's one and only eye and cutting deep into his pupil.

Yi covered his eye with his giant hands and screamed in pain, for he had lost his vision, and he himself was lost in a world of unthinkable darkness, a darkness that he had brought upon himself and the entire living world—all in an attempt to shoot down the sun.

The Story of Nüwa Patching the Sky

A long, long time ago, a gaping hole tore open the sky like a whiteless eye. The hole was blacker than any shade of black that you could imagine. It was a sight that would chill anyone to the bone. Through this gaping hole, *darkness* dripped into the world in staggering size and quantity, flooding it with dangers and terrors that were known to no living thing before.

The great Fusang tree was one of the firsts to be lost on that unfortunate day. All the leaves and fruits that had once lived and thrived on its mighty branches withered and died at the touch of that unthinkable *darkness*, raining down like an endless snow of ashes—the ashes of death.

The magnificent bird stood silently under the dead Fusang tree and watched the last three-legged bird in the world: it was picking up the small chunks of blood and flesh and bones of its eight siblings from the ashes and gathering them into a pile, crying. By the time that the pile was done, it was still crying. It cried and cried. Its voice became so hoarse that all it could produce from its throat was harsh croaks and caws, but it didn't stop crying.

With *darkness* still dripping from that gaping hole in the sky, there was no way to tell whether it was day or night. Presently, a giant came running across the barren land. Her eyes were red, and her face was covered in tears. As soon as she reached the dead Fusang tree, she threw herself at the magnificent bird's feet.

"O Almighty bird of the sun! I am Nüwa, mother of Yi," she said between loud sobs. "Please accept my apology for the actions of my son. He made a bad choice, and I know it had offended you gravely. But please, O Almighty bird of the sun, please have mercy on him! Our kin are unforgiving and cruel, and they blame my son for the dangers and terrors that are now roaming free to prey on our lives. They believe we are all being punished due to his offense to you, so they have demanded his life to be paid as a price to appease you! O Almighty bird of the sun! Please have mercy! Please forgive my son and end our punishment! Without your forgiveness, they'll execute him! Please have mercy! Please save my son!"

The magnificent bird watched the last three-legged bird in the world cry. She did not reply.

Nüwa began to bawl. Tears streamed down her large pale cheeks like rivers. "O Almighty bird of the sun! Please have mercy! Please save my son! In his tormented state, he had gouged out his one and only eye, yet he can't be free from the demons inside his mind. He has already been punished for what he did. So please, I beg of you, O Almighty bird of the sun, I beg of you to spare his life!"

Still, the magnificent bird watched the last three-legged bird in the world cry and did not reply.

Nüwa fell silent then. She sniffled a few times and wiped her tears away with her large arms, then she said softly, "O Almighty bird of the sun, if you are not ready to forgive my son, then I beg you to let me take his place. Punish me for what he did instead. Take my life if need be. But please, O Almighty bird of the sun, please have mercy and save my son."

The magnificent bird was still watching the last three-legged bird in the world cry, but she suddenly asked, "Why do you want to take his place?"

Nüwa dried her eyes with the backs of her large hands and smiled. "Because I am his mother."

"But why?"

"Because that's what mothers do." Nüwa gave a serene smile, looking genuinely content with her choice. "When you have created something with all your heart . . . When you have come to care about another so much that it makes your heart ache just to know that he's in pain . . . You will be willing to stop his pain with your pain—with everything you have left, if you need to. That's what mothers do. And that's what a mother ever really wants from life."

The magnificent bird watched the last three-legged bird in the world cry and did not speak.

Nüwa bowed deeply to the magnificent bird. "O Almighty bird of the sun! Can you understand a mother's heart? Can you feel a mother's pain? Can you grant a mother's wish? O Almighty bird of the sun! Take my body, my mind, and my life! Do as you please! But I beg you to have mercy and save my son!"

"Very well," the magnificent bird said, gazing up at the gaping hole in the sky. "Patch the sky and put an end to the *darkness*, then the punishment shall end, and your kin will have no need to claim your son's life."

Smiling blissfully, Nüwa bowed deeply to the magnificent bird once more, then she set to work. First, she gathered as many large stones as she could find and combined them into an enormous slab of stone that had the same shape as the hole in the sky. Then she carried the slab under one arm and began to climb the dead Fusang tree, which was so tall that, even for a giant, it was very dangerous and challenging, not to mention she was also carrying an enormous slab of stone. Even so, never once did Nüwa waver, nor did she stop to catch her breath. She made her way up the Fusang tree in such a determined and unstoppable manner that in order to speed up her progress, her legs merged into one and became a slithering tail, freeing both of her hands to carry the slab as she slithered up the trunk of the tall Fusang tree.

Once Nüwa had reached the top, she coiled herself around the tallest branch tightly. Then, with her arms stretched to the limit, she hoisted the enormous slab of stone over her head firmly to fill the hole in the sky.

In truth, Nüwa's stone was neither big enough nor high enough to fill that gaping hole in the sky—maybe she didn't know better, or maybe she did but had decided to ignore the consequence anyway. *Darkness* dripped down from the hole and soon enveloped her like a lizard that was trapped inside a drop of resin. She should have died in unspeakable agony and tumbled down from the top of the tall Fusang tree with her enormous slab before smashing her large head on the barren land beneath it and spraying it with her brains. But somehow, she managed to die without a stir, frozen atop the dead Fusang tree with her arms still aiming at the sky and, firmly and unyieldingly, holding up the enormous slab of stone, which was her only hope to atone and save her son.

The last three-legged bird in the world looked up at Nüwa and finally stopped crying.

The magnificent bird looked up at Nüwa as well and said to the last three-legged bird in the world, "Do you still wish to seek the purpose of life?"

The last three-legged bird in the world cawed with teary eyes, "Yes, O Almighty bird of the sun. Without my siblings, it is all I have left."

"Very well," the magnificent bird said, opening her wings. "But there is a price to be paid. Give me one of your legs."

Without a moment's hesitation, the last three-legged bird in the world tore off one of its legs, and the last three-legged bird in the world was no more.

The magnificent bird stretched out her wings; the severed leg rose to midair and floated toward her, followed by the pile of small chunks of blood and flesh and bones of the other eight conduits. The magnificent bird wrapped her wings around the unsightly contents, then a soft light began to glow from between them. When she opened her wings again, there was a two-legged black bird that looked exactly like her last conduit, who had torn off its third leg just a moment ago.

The magnificent bird said, "From your third leg and the remains of your siblings, I've created a spouse for you. From now on, you and your children will only have two legs and two feet—that is the price for continuing your line.

"You and your descendants will be my conduits. From now on, you cannot let anyone on Earth observe how *light* is collected and transported, which means you and your descendants will have to ferry many, many more times every day to keep *light* invisible to their eyes.

"We shall not meet again, for my presence endangers you. Now go, live, and multiply, for this world depends on you and all your descendants."

The now two-legged conduit wiped away its tears. It tried to sing a song for the magnificent bird one last time, but all it could produce from its throat was more harsh croaks and caws—grief had killed its beautiful singing voice for good and turned it into a perpetual crying voice that was filled with sorrow and heartache.

So the two-legged conduit cawed heartbrokenly and flew toward the edge of the world with its spouse. All the way they cawed, heartbroken for what was forever lost, until they were embraced by a brand-new dawn. With the great Fusang tree dead and gone, so were the wisdom berries. But they would be too busy to be picky about what they could eat, and they would simply feed on whatever they could find along the way as they performed their role as the eternal conduits of the magnificent bird.

The magnificent bird followed them with her gaze and said, "I shall call you *crows*. Farewell, my conduits."

Then she took flight, leaving the dead Fusang tree and Nüwa and her enormous slab of stone far, far below, until the hole in the sky was gone, and the sun was shining brightly upon the Earth again.

The Story of Nian

A long, long time ago, *darkness* dripped into our world from a gaping hole that had opened in the sky. It preyed on all living things, but it was not blood or flesh that it was after; it was after something else, something special, something called *souls*.

Our world is made up of living things and nonliving things, and *souls* are what distinguish the living from the nonliving. All living things, big or small, have *souls*—no matter if it is an animal, a plant, or a bacterium. Nonliving things, on the other hand, do not.

But *darkness* is something entirely different. It exists beyond our world, and its existence is beyond the definitions of living and nonliving things. It is neither alive nor conscious, but it is attracted to fresh *souls* like how any hungry animal is to the scent of food.

You may wonder what makes fresh *souls* so deliciously tempting that their allure can reach *darkness*, even though it is supposed to reside beyond our world. To answer that question, I'll have to let you in on a little secret—the secret of *souls*, which has long been lost from the stories of the ancient past.

You see, when a living thing is created at the Wheel of Life, it is merely a container at first, until a special seed is placed inside it to grant it life. This seed is called *the seed of life*. Without it, the living thing that has been created will not become alive. Instead, it will decompose like every other living thing that has died. Simply put, every living thing that is alive or had once been alive in this world had been sown with a *seed of life* at the Wheel of Life.

The total number of *the seeds of life* in this universe was predetermined, and it will neither increase nor be replenished. Once a *seed of life* is placed inside a living thing, this living thing, the container of that *seed of life*, will continue to stay alive until one of the following happens: one, its *time* in this world is used up; two, it has ended its own *time* on purpose; or three, its *time* is interrupted and ended by external factors.

Unlike regular seeds, a *seed of life* does not die or decompose, nor will it die or decompose when its container dies and decomposes. Instead, it will stay inside its container until the magnificent bird's conduits, the crows, come to harvest it to deliver it to the sun. There, the sun will purify it by burning off the residues that were formed from the emotions and characteristics of its previous container during its *time* in this world. Then the sun will send the purified *seed of life* back to the Wheel of Life to be placed inside another living thing, whereas the residues will be spit out, forming what scientists nowadays call *dark matter* in space.

But that is not all. Once a living thing begins its life, its living experiences will create emotions, and the most intense ones will envelop its *seed of life* like the amniotic sac of an embryo and thus become the *soul* of this living thing. Since each living thing has its own unique living experiences, which will give rise to its own unique emotions and intense emotions, it makes each *soul* unique as well. Generally speaking, the happier a *soul* is, the stronger its spirit of life is and the more *light* it emits. It doesn't mean that the miserable *souls* don't emit any *light* at all though. As long as they still have some degree of spirit of life and the will to live, their *souls* will emit *light*, only in most cases, the *light* they emit is not nearly as much as the *souls* who are genuinely content in life. Still, the *light* that one single *soul* emits, no matter how genuinely content it is in life, is not visible to anyone on Earth. However, if you could combine millions of *souls* together, they would shine like a small sun.

So when a crow harvests a *seed of life*, it also harvests a *soul*. When *the seed of life* is purified in the sun, so is the *soul*: the *light* of the *soul* will be burned off from *the seed of life* along with the residues, only the *light* will be kept by the sun whereas the residues will be spit out and form more *dark matter* in space. The irony is, once discarded by the sun, *dark matter* will hold on to the negative energy—what the scientists now call *dark energy*—that's constantly being released into space by the living things on Earth through complaining, bickering, quarreling, fighting, resenting . . . And together, given the right opportunity, they will become the very *darkness* that drips into the world of the living with the single goal to feast on *souls*, as if to take revenge on the living world for the *light* and *the seeds of life* that were taken away from them.

Now that you know the secret of *souls*, you will understand why *darkness* craves them. Each *soul* is like an amniotic sac that contains a *seed of life* as its embryo and a set of unique intense emotions as its amniotic fluid: the joy, the pain, the ecstasy, the torment, the satisfaction, the disappointment, the anticipation, the conflict and despair . . . Therefore, each bite of *souls* will bring juicy emotions into its nonliving, nonconscious state to savor what it is like to be alive and conscious instead, especially when they are fresh *souls* from live animals. Like an internet junkie who can't stop surfing online to experience virtual life, *darkness* can't stop feasting on *souls* to experience real life. Worse still, every drop of *darkness* that is dripped into the living world will be capable of feasting on *souls* right away. So although they won't work together like an army, their effect on this world will be far worse: they will devour the *soul* of every living thing in their path, thereby bringing untimely deaths to innumerable lives. And since the crows will not be able to harvest *the seeds of life* of the *souls* that were devoured by *darkness*, those *seeds of life* will not be delivered to the sun, let alone be purified and sent back to the Wheel of Life to be placed again, thus eliminating them from the total number of *the seeds of life* that was predetermined for this universe for good.

But that is not the worst part yet. Once a drop of *darkness* devours enough *souls*, it will gain consciousness, which means it will gain not only awareness but also fear. Awareness will help it to target the juicier *souls*, for it is much less satisfying—and much less rewarding, which you will soon find out why—to savor the emotions of bacteria and plants than to savor the emotions of animals, who have a much wider range of them and are much more intense at that. On the other hand, fear will help it steer clear of the very few threats that can actually eliminate its existence from the living world, making it extra challenging for the hero in our story to seek it out. On top of that, as a drop of *darkness* feasts on more *souls*, it will gradually be able to take on the forms of the living things whose *souls* it has been feasting on, usually at the same time, only much larger in size. For example, it can look like a giant spider with a snake's head and upper body but has a scorpion's tail, or it can look like a giant frog with a praying mantis's head and front legs but has a goldfish's tail. This will go on for a while until it has been feasting predominantly on the *souls* of only one kind of living thing for a continuous period of time, then it will be able to take on the full appearance, the full physical ability, and the full intelligence level of that particular species to continue moving up the food chain under its new disguise. Since they can "live" in the living world as living things without having *souls*, they are called the Soulless.

So when that gaping hole opened in the sky, allowing *darkness* to drip down, our hero, being one of the very few threats to its existence in the living world, was tasked with capturing the drops. But *darkness* dripped down in startling volume with disconcerting speed, so most of them gained consciousness in time to slip away from him. These drops then became the Soulless. Some of them went to hide in the forests, some of them went to hide in the mountains, some of them went to hide in the waters, and some of them in the caves. But no matter where they went, one thing was for certain: the *souls* in that area would not be safe. With that in mind, our hero pressed on, for his duties to this universe demanded him to prevent more *seeds of life* from being lost to the Soulless; he would not stop until every last one of them was eliminated from the living world.

Meanwhile, some of the Soulless traveled deep into the mountains of ancient China. With an abundance of fresh *souls* in the mountains, they were able to feast on plenty to take on a variety of animal forms. Still, to the Soulless, the *souls* of men were the crème de la crème of them all. Not only because they were the juiciest and the tastiest, but also because feasting on human *souls* continuously would eventually give them the ability to take on human form and experience human life like real human beings. For that very reason, they often attacked people who went to forage in the mountains and came up with different ways to lure those in the vicinity into the mountains to satisfy their cravings. But men were fast learners. Once they realized there were unfathomable dangers lurking in the mountains, they stopped coming. And when they did come, it was usually the hunters, who were very ready to draw out their weapons at the sight of any animal—including the Soulless in their animal forms—with the same level of enthusiasm they applied to greet their dinner. Their weapons couldn't kill the Soulless, who, though they appeared to be alive in their animal forms, possessed no *seed of life* to be truly alive. But if struck, those weapons could weaken their physical abilities nonetheless, which would thereby greatly increase the chance of their animal forms becoming prey to either men or the other animals in the mountains before they could replenish themselves with enough *souls* to stay conscious and keep their forms.

It took the Soulless much longer to learn and understand the dangers those human hunters could inflict upon them than it took men to learn how to keep themselves safe in the mountains. But in time, the Soulless gave up attacking humans for their juicy, tasty *souls* and settled for the taste of animal flesh instead.

One day, the aroma of cooked meat coupled with the smell of concentrated fresh human *souls* drifted into the mountains. The combination of their scents was so enticingly irresistible to the Soulless that they followed it out of the mountains and into a nearby village. It was Lunar New Year's Eve in China, so every family in the village had gathered all their family members together for a big dinner to celebrate the beginning of a brand-new year. Needless to say, no one was working that night, not even the hunters.

To the Soulless, it was the equivalent of walking into an all-you-can-eat buffet. First, they feasted on the *souls* of the villagers' livestock, but they were not as juicy as they had hoped, so they feasted on their flesh instead. When the villagers heard the commotion, they waddled from their dinner tables to their doors, their bellies full of food and wine, expecting nothing more than having to scare away some lousy scavengers with a few drunken shouts. So when the Soulless pounced on them to feast on their flesh and *souls*, even the hunters who were not yet too drunk to wield a weapon were scared witless and ran for their lives.

The sheer quantity of the *souls* that they had devoured was enough for the Soulless to shift into new forms. Before long, every one of them took on an utterly unnerving shape, which was a combination of all the animals that they had each feasted on. With the flesh torn from their victims dangling from between their inhuman teeth, and their abominable faces and chests soaked by the blood of their kills, the Soulless demonstrated, more than sufficiently, to the men in that village what the so-called monsters and demons—whom the superstitious elders in the village had often told stories about to scare little kids into being good at bedtime—were truly capable of.

The Soulless went from village to village through the rest of the night of Lunar New Year's Eve, enjoying their all-you-can-eat buffets and feasting on both flesh and *souls* at the same time, bringing unspeakable terrors to all living things in the area. By the time the sun had finally risen on Lunar New Year's Day, they had cleaned out every single village in the vicinity and, with their cravings fully satisfied, gone back into the mountains at last.

From then on, the Soulless would return to the villages on the night of Lunar New Year's Eve every year, for they had become addicted to a new delicacy: the combination of fresh human flesh and *souls* when their owners were filled to the brim with good food and wine from their big family dinner on Lunar New Year's Eve. Each bite of it would give the Soulless such euphoric pleasure that it was as if they were truly alive themselves, which, in turn, would make them giggle in such a sinister and unsettling manner that it was enough to drive anyone who was listening into utter despair. As a result, the villagers lucky enough to have survived the night gave them a name: *Xi*, which sounds similar to the giggling noise that the Soulless would make repetitively when they feasted on said delicacy.

Year after year, their savage feast on Lunar New Year's Eve brought untimely deaths to countless living things. This created ripples in the River of Time and led to disturbances in *the flow*. Our hero investigated the disturbances in detail and came to learn about the Soulless' new dining addiction. Ever since the Soulless had gained intelligence, they had been evading our hero carefully and deliberately. So, to our hero, their annual outing to the villages in China on Lunar New Year's Eve provided a perfect opportunity for him to capture and eliminate them from the living world.

To understand how our hero can eliminate the Soulless' existence in the living world, you must learn more about him first, for he is no ordinary man. In fact, he is no man at all. Our hero's name is White. He is the Keeper of Time, the one who tends to the River of Time to keep *time* flowing smoothly and continuously for every living thing in this universe. He is also the one who collects *time* from all living things so that they can all rest at some point to make room for others. You can't see White because you can't see *time*, but there is one exception: White needs to materialize before he can capture the Soulless; he needs to swallow them first, then he can eliminate them from the living world by returning them to their original form beyond this world.

So when Lunar New Year's Eve came again, White ambushed the Soulless in the villages in China. He swallowed many of them, but the Soulless had gained enough intelligence to know that the rest of them had to return to the mountains right away to hide from White.

Knowing how addictive the Soulless were to fresh human flesh and *souls* on that particular night, White ambushed them again the following Lunar New Year's Eve. He swallowed many of them, yet many of them managed to escape again.

Year after year, White returned to the villages in China on Lunar New Year's Eve to ambush the Soulless. But year after year, a number of the Soulless managed to escape White. Meanwhile, among the villagers, their great fear toward *Xi* was replaced by a new fear toward the giant tigerlike beast who would show up on the night of every Lunar New Year's Eve to gobble up animals and humans alike. Little did they know that those animals and humans were not real animals or humans at all; they were the Soulless who had obtained those forms and successfully disguised themselves as ordinary animals and humans in their villages, and they had mastered their disguises so well that no one ever suspected they were, as a matter of fact, the monsters and demons they had named *Xi*.

White, on the other hand, can distinguish the Soulless from real animals and humans very well, for he is the Keeper of Time, and, as the Keeper of Time, he can see *time*. All living things have *time*. The Soulless, however, are neither living things nor nonliving things, and therefore, they don't have *time*. So no matter which forms of living things the Soulless can take on, if they don't have *time*, then White will know they are the Soulless in disguise.

But White had been so focused on capturing the Soulless during his annual ambush that he did not notice how terrified the villagers in China had become of him. Out of fear, the villagers gave him a name: *Nian*, which means *year* in Chinese, because he would show up every year on the night of Lunar New Year's Eve to swallow what appeared to be perfectly ordinary animals and humans in their villages mercilessly.

Then one year, when White returned on the night of Lunar New Year's Eve to ambush the Soulless, he found that all the villages were empty—the villagers had evacuated from their homes to avoid being "eaten" by *Nian*. Worse yet, in order to hide from *Nian*, the villagers had entered the mountains instead. In other words, they had basically served up themselves on the Soulless' doorstep, and the Soulless could attack them whenever and wherever they wanted to, making it impossible for White to identify the Soulless from all the other living things that had crowded the mountains with *time*. Nevertheless, when the next Lunar New Year's Eve came, the villagers evacuated into the mountains again, and they evacuated into the mountains every single Lunar New Year's Eve after that.

White blamed himself for not noticing his mistake earlier; he meant to save *the seeds of life* in those villages from the Soulless, but instead, he had driven them into the Soulless' hiding ground like a faithful shepherd dog who had driven the sheep into the butcher's pen to protect them from wolves.

The magnificent bird learned about this and told White that she had a solution. She turned herself into an old lady and moved into one of the villages in China. When Lunar New Year's Eve came, she did not get ready to evacuate from the village with the other villagers.

This baffled everyone in the village, and they asked her, "Old lady, why aren't you getting ready to leave? Did you not know that *Nian* will come tonight to search for food? If you stay, surely you will die between its massive jaws!"

To which, the old lady simply answered, "I am old and tired of hiding. Leave me behind and let me rest."

So when the sun began to set in the sky, they evacuated from the village and left the old lady behind, thinking she had lost her mind.

Once she was all alone in the village, an old man came to visit her. He was an old friend of hers, and he wished to help.

Together, they put red paper on all the doors and lit firecrackers in the streets, then they sat down and brewed themselves a pot of tea as they waited for the sun to rise. When the villagers returned the next morning, they were even more baffled to find that the old lady was still alive, with an unknown old man by her side.

"How come *Nian* spared your lives?" they asked, goggle-eyed.

The old lady answered, "See this old man? He's a traveler from afar, and he told me the secrets to drive *Nian* away.

"See the red paper on the doors? See the firecracker shells on the streets? *Nian* is afraid of the color red and the sound of loud explosions. From now on, we shall put red paper on our doors and light firecrackers in the streets every Lunar New Year's Eve to scare *Nian* away from the village. If we do this, we will be free of *Nian*, and we won't need to evacuate into the mountains ever again."

The villagers immediately got down on their hands and knees to bow to the old man.

"O the gray-haired one! O the wise one!" they said. "You have saved our lives! Not only from *Nian*, but also from the dangers that are lurking in the mountains! We shall finally be safe from all the man-eating beasts!"

The old man smiled humbly and stroked his long, silvery beard. "No need to thank me. Spread the word to as many villages as you can, so they too will be safe from *Nian* and the man-eating beasts."

So the villagers spread the word to all the other villages in China. From then on, they all put red paper on their doors and lit firecrackers in the streets every Lunar New Year's Eve, and indeed *Nian* never showed up again. To honor the significance of this life-changing ritual that they continued to carry out every Lunar New Year's Eve to keep *Nian* away, people in China began to refer to it as *guò nián*, meaning "being able to survive *Nian*." As time went by, however, more and more of them began to call Lunar New Year's Eve *chú xī*, meaning "getting rid of *Xi*", although, if you could ask them, only a handful of them would be able to tell you how the name *Xi* had come into use and why.

The Story of Pandora

A long, long time ago, men survived the first cleansing and, with the extinction of the giants, became the ones who dominated the Earth. Unfortunately, when their biggest threat was eliminated, so were their moral boundaries, and men had come to the conclusion that when it came to having power over others, size did not matter.

As a result, gods and goddesses were created as living examples of virtues to set the moral standards for all men. In order to fortify their status among men, each of the gods and goddesses was given a set of special powers that no man would dare to challenge, which also brought them immortality.

With the special powers granted to them, the gods and goddesses soon made it clear to men that, compared to the powers they had received from the divine, what men had achieved was nothing. Men were quick learners. When they realized going against the will of a god or a goddess would cost them way more than going against the will of a small-brained giant, they changed their tactics and began to worship the gods and goddesses instead to gain their favor: they built spectacular temples and shrines to honor them, erected statues and monuments to glorify them, wrote ballads and tales to mystify them, and sent in tributes and sacrifices to please them.

One day, they presented the gods and goddesses with a very special gift: the eyeball of a cyclops, the very first of its kind. They bowed to the gods and goddesses on their hands and knees and said:

"We worship you! O Almighty powers of the divine! We worship you wholeheartedly for your grace and mercy! We are your humble servants and devoted followers to fulfill your wants and needs! May this unique gift bear witness to our will to please you, for it holds a piece of the one and only magnificent bird, the God of Sun, the Taker of Life!"

The gods and goddesses accepted their gift. The red shard that stuck out from the first cyclops's eyeball burned like fire in the sun, reminding them of the creation of themselves and just how much they wanted to live on as gods and goddesses forever. So, to enjoy their status and privileges to the fullest, the gods and goddesses built palaces and gardens, set up ranks and titles, divided jobs and functions, and lived and acted like the immortal kings and queens of men.

One day, they told men that they had a gift for them.

"We made it ourselves from the eyeball of the first cyclops," they said. "We made it for you as a reward for your obedience. It will bring you many years of favorable weather; your harvests will be bountiful, your livestock fat and fertile, and your lives easy and comfortable. But under no circumstances shall it be opened, as it contains powers that are not meant to be seen by the mortal eye."

Men bowed to the gods and goddesses on their hands and knees and thanked them profusely for their wonderful gift.

"We shall call it *Pandora!*" they said. "For it is a gift that was created by the powers of the divine—it is a gift above all gifts!"

And when men got up to their feet and left with their gift, they left with ecstasy.

No sooner had they returned to their own territory than they gathered around inside a dark hall to open their gift, for if *Pandora* indeed contained divine powers that were not meant for the eyes of men, it must also hold the secrets to unmatched powers, which they could use to regain dominance of this land!

As soon as *Pandora* was opened, something invisible rushed out from it and brushed past them with eerie noises. Men clutched their heads and cried out in lamentation, for a stone tablet with a petroglyph of the magnificent bird was all that was left inside the first cyclops's eyeball.

They hurried to close their gift, but it was already too late. Men didn't know that they had just released upon themselves the invisible version of the Soulless, who were, at the moment, sipping on the spirit of life in them on their heads like transparent spiders, sucking their prey dry and draining the *light* of men's *souls*, until they were all so overwhelmed by their own emotions that, for once, men noticed how despicable and meaningless their lives had become.

Just when they were on the verge of breaking down completely, the sun shone upon them through the windows, driving the invisible version of the Soulless back into the shadows. The red shard that stuck out from the first cyclops's eyeball burned like fire in the sun, reminding them of the petroglyph of the magnificent bird, which they had seen on the stone tablet that was still inside *Pandora*.

Then men thought hopefully to themselves: Maybe ... maybe that was exactly where the divine powers were contained—powers that were not meant for the eyes of men. And if so, that must be exactly where the secrets to unmatched powers were held—secrets that they could use to regain dominance of this land!

The Story of Death

A long, long time ago, with the sudden disappearance of the last few gods and goddesses in this world, men became the ones who dominated the Earth once more. Unfortunately, when the gods and goddesses ceased to exist, so did their reign, and men had come to the conclusion that without a more superior power in existence, he who could obtain the most power would become the new "god" of this world.

As a result, wars broke out among them, followed by deaths, destructions, epidemics, famines, and more deaths. The soil was no longer fertile. The trees were no longer green. The air was no longer fresh. And the water was no longer clean. The sky turned gray from the fumes that drifted up, day and night, from the new burning pyres added every day, the stench of which was even more unpleasant than the sight. Birds no longer sang, for they could not see the sun in the smoke-filled sky, leaving only the agonizing cries from the crows echoing between heaven and Earth like a heart-wrenching song by the lost souls who were forever trapped between life and death.

The magnificent bird descended upon the pyres. She didn't mind the stench nor the sight—she didn't even mind the burning flames. The crows descended as well and followed her from the narrow passageways among the pyres. They had inherited the role as the magnificent bird's conduits from their ancestors, and they had remained her faithful servants for a long, long time.

The magnificent bird glided among the pyres noiselessly, brushing past each pyre with her wings. It was not clear how much *light* she had collected from them, for she was burning as brightly as the pyres herself. Just as she was about to reach the other end of the pyres, she sensed the presence of a human *soul* that was still alive. The magnificent bird did not wish men to learn about her existence again, so she landed quickly and transformed into a figure cloaked in black.

A woman was kneeling on the ground in the ashes, which were drifting down from the burning pyres like snow. Her eyes were red and glassy, and her dirty face was tear-streaked. She was holding a child close to her chest, whose head and limbs were drooping limply toward the earth like a rag doll's.

"Are you Death?" the woman asked in a trembling voice, for she thought she had witnessed through her teary eyes how this cloaked figure had emerged from a portal of flames, unharmed.

The magnificent bird didn't answer, but her silence was interpreted as confirmation. After all, if this cloaked figure could pass through a portal of flames unharmed, then he must have come from Hell.

"Is it my time?" asked the woman, wearing a distant but somewhat relieved smile. "Have you come to collect me as well?"

The magnificent bird didn't answer. Instead, she gestured toward the pyre next to the woman and said, "She's gone. You need to let her go."

The woman burst into tears. "How can I let go of my own child? She was the apple of my eye, the spark of my life! She came from my belly; I made her out of my own blood and flesh and bones. How can I ever let her go? I cannot ... I cannot ..."

Just then, the woman's eyes suddenly lit up as if she were struck by lightning. She threw herself at the foot of the cloaked figure and cried, "I beg you, O fearsome Death! I beg you to bring my child back to me! Name your price! Tell me what it will cost! O fearsome Death, I will pay you anything in exchange for my child's life!"

To which, the magnificent bird asked, "Even if the price were to offer the life of another?"

The woman hesitated for only a few seconds, then she answered firmly, "Yes. Even if the price is to offer my life in exchange for my daughter's."

"Very well," the magnificent bird said. "In three days' time, return to this spot after the sun has set completely, and you shall have your daughter back. Now, put her body in the pyre."

With tears streaming down her face, the woman nodded profusely. She hugged the dead child tightly and kissed her pale little face again and again as she whispered, "My baby, my heart, my love ... Please don't be afraid ... Mommy will see you soon. I will see you very soon ..."

Then, reluctantly, she laid her dead child down on the ground, at the foot of the burning pyre that the magnificent bird had indicated. As if instructed by some mysterious power, the burning flames from the pyre reached for the dead child's body like countless fingers and arms and soon enclosed it completely. By the time the woman finally tore her gaze away from the now charred and indistinguishable shape of her child, the cloaked figure was already gone.

Three days later, as soon as the sun had sunk below the horizon, the woman went back to the same spot and waited. The fires from the pyres had finally died off, leaving piles and piles of bone fragments and ashes waiting quietly with her in the twilight like rolling little hills covered in snow.

She waited and waited, silently and anxiously. She didn't know what to expect, but she couldn't bear not finding out either—even if it would cost her everything she had left.

When the last ray of twilight was smothered by dusk, she noticed that a human figure was emerging from it. Her heart raced as the figure approached, for instead of a cloaked figure, it was the small, slender figure of a child. When the figure came to a stop in front of her and revealed its face, the woman burst into tears and dropped to her knees: Her child had been returned! Death had fulfilled her wish!

The woman didn't know when Death would come to collect his payment for returning her child, but she didn't care. She spent every waking moment with her daughter, braiding her hair, making her toys, and telling her stories. Since the girl was returned, she had not expressed any emotions, nor had she spoken a word, but the woman didn't mind. Death had brought her daughter back, and to her, that was all that mattered. What she didn't understand, though, was why the crows that had followed them back from the pyres to their tiny hut had stayed around, and why, during a time of famine, her daughter was always able to find freshly dead animals for dinner on their foraging trips in the woods. Still, the woman didn't think too much of it. After all, her daughter seemed to enjoy the company of the ever-present crows, and, truthfully, it was a huge relief that she didn't need to worry about not having food for her child again.

Then one night, a group of villagers surrounded their tiny hut and broke into their home with axes and pitchforks in their hands. They pointed the cold metal ends of their tools at her daughter, demanding the woman hand the child over to them.

"She's a witch! She's cursed! She's dangerous! She's evil! . . ." they yelled and shouted, one after another, each voice louder and shriller than the one before.

"My neighbors! Dear neighbors!" The woman shielded her daughter desperately with her body, straining her voice to be heard over their angry yells and shouts. "My child is not a witch! This must be a mistake!"

" 'Tis no mistake!" shouted one of them. "We saw her! Walking among the dead at night, crows by her side, picking flesh from bones!"

"Aye! 'Tis no mistake!" yelled another. "We saw her! Turning air into fire, then poof—she ain't no more!"

"Aye! We know 'tis true! When we starve and are thin like prunes, you have meat in your pot every single day!"

" 'Tis the flesh that was peeled from the dead!"

"She consorted with the Devil to starve us to death, then she strips us for food!"

"Witchcraft!"

"Sorcery!"

"Kill her!"

"Hang her!"

"Burn her!"

Vehement yells and shouts erupted from the villagers, turning their little hut into the arena for a gladiatorial execution. Outside, the crows cawed shrilly and incessantly from above and around them, seemingly determined to drown out the villagers' uproar with their own.

Before the woman could say another word, countless fingers and arms were reaching past her body to seize her daughter. They grabbed at whatever they could snatch of the girl, no matter whether it was her hair, her arms, or her clothes, jerking and yanking hungrily as if she were free food and they were dead set on tearing her into pieces so that they could keep those pieces to themselves.

Even in the face of their brutal savageness, the girl remained impassive and silent.

"See?" the villagers exclaimed. "She doesn't even care to say anything to defend herself! She's guilty! She's guilty . . . !"

Still, the girl remained impassive and silent. The woman, however, was on the brink of total devastation and despair.

"She's not a witch!" the woman cried at the top of her lungs, tears circling in her determined eyes. "She's not a witch! I am! I am the one you want!"

The villagers fell silent, but the woman continued. "A long time ago, I met the Devil at the gate that is made of hellfire. I told him that if he returned me to the living, I would do his bidding. In doing so, I traded my soul with the Devil and became a witch."

The woman spread out her arms and stood firmly between the villagers and her daughter like a human shield. "This child is innocent! I am the one who made her walk among the dead at night to peel flesh from bones to put in my pot! I am the one who made her travel through the hellfire gate to fetch me instructions from the Devil! I am the one who helps the Devil to starve you to death so that I can strip you for food! It's me! All me! I am the witch! I am the one you want! Leave the child alone! Take me! Take me instead!"

Now that the "witch" had confessed her sins, the villagers didn't need any further convincing. They had successfully exposed the one who had kindled their secret—and sinful—urge to feast on the dead themselves, and they were certain that once the witch was dead, they would no longer suffer from that temptation.

Chanting various prayers like the pious men they were, the villagers held their axes and pitchforks high above their heads and surrounded the woman, tearing her away from her daughter like a hermit crab ripped helplessly from its home by the receding tide.

With the axes and the pitchforks and the villagers' heads bobbing up and down around her like layers and layers of undulating barbed wire fences, the woman fought to look back at her daughter and, with every ounce of strength that was left in her, shouted over the clamor of the zealous mob:

"My baby! My heart! My love! Don't be afraid! Mommy will always love you! I will love you always . . . !"

As tears filled her eyes and blurred her vision, the woman thought she saw the crows descend from the sky and embrace her daughter tightly with their wings. She wished she could do the same—at least for one last time.

When the pyre under her feet was lit, the woman craned her neck to scan the crowd. Just as the flames began to lick her feet, she smiled weakly to herself, for she had found what she was looking for: behind the mob, far away from all the axes and the pitchforks and the villagers' heads, stood a figure under a pitch-black cloak.

A murder of crows landed in front of the cloaked figure, then they took flight and flew toward her, cawing gloomily to one another:

"It's time ... It's time ... It's time to let go ..."

Clenching her teeth hard to endure the burning heat and pain that was now chewing mercilessly through her skin and flesh, the woman looked toward the cloaked figure to beg for a quick relief from this world. The cloaked figure responded to her plea by taking off its hood, revealing the face of her beloved daughter, cold and nonchalant as ever.

The woman stared numbly at that cold, nonchalant face, and suddenly, she understood. As the flames rose higher and higher to devour her remaining flesh and bones, she started to chuckle, then she giggled, and before long, she was laughing uncontrollably in such a hysterical manner that every one of the villagers was certain that the witch had made yet another deal with the Devil.

When she had finally stopped laughing, a crow landed on top of her charred skull, flapped its wings, then took flight and joined the rest of its murder in the sky. Together, they flew toward the eastern horizon, from where the sun would soon rise again.

Unfortunately, the woman's dead silence could not ease the panic that was spreading like wildfire among the villagers, who all shared the same eerie feeling that the countdown to an impending doom had just begun.

"What if she's not really dead?" someone asked in a trembling voice.

"What if she's not the only one?" asked another, sounding alarmed.

"What if she had consorted with the Devil and given birth to his offspring?" asked a third, whose voice was even more anxious than the two before.

Then they remembered the girl: The one who walked among the dead at night with crows by her side, picking flesh from bones. The one who turned air into fire and vanished among the flames. The one who showed no sign of fear or remorse when confronted, not even a word or a tear.

Just like that, panic fermented quickly into dread. The villagers were now certain that the girl was a witch too, who needed to be burned immediately at her witch mother's side.

Waving their axes and pitchforks nervously yet menacingly in the air, the villagers swarmed back to the tiny hut in a hurry, only to find that the whole place was already engulfed in flames. The girl, however, was nowhere to be found.

Terrified that the girl might take revenge on them for burning her witch mother alive, the villagers turned the whole village inside out and upside down to find her. When they couldn't find the girl anywhere in their own village, they took the search to the next village, then the next village after that . . .

And thus, the first witch hunt had begun.

The Story of Her Brightest Soul

A long, long time ago, the magnificent bird decided to live among the humans to seek out *souls* with the brightest *light*.

Generally speaking, the happier a *soul* is, the stronger its spirit of life is and the more *light* it emits. Throughout her many lives in human form, across centuries and countries, the magnificent bird had found this to be true in most cases. However, it was the exceptions that really caught her attention—the *souls* that were suffering in life yet still able to emit much brighter *light* than the others. To the magnificent bird, those *souls* were the enigmas of this world, and she was drawn to them like how scientists are drawn to the irregularities discovered during their research. Nevertheless, despite her curiosity in the owners of those *souls*, the magnificent bird never regarded any of them as more than a riddle in human form.

One year, the magnificent bird took on the form of a teenage girl and went to high school. During her most recent life in human form, she had come to learn that experiences from the humans' teenage years would have a lot of impact on how much *light* their *souls* would emit later on, and she wanted to understand why.

It didn't take her long to find the cause: even though school had only been in session for a week, she had already observed many cases of bullying, physically and emotionally, each jolting the victim's *light* like a flickering candle flame that was being slowly suffocated.

Then one day, just when the magnificent bird thought she had learned enough from her human life as a teenage girl, she stumbled across a *light* so bright at school that, for a split second, she was under the impression that one of her conduits had collected too many *souls* at once.

But the bright *light* did not come from one of her conduits; it came from a *soul*—a single *soul*, the owner of which was presently cornered by a small group of teenage girls whose *light* was barely noticeable in comparison.

"Did you hear me, peasant?" The girl in the middle took a step forward and glared at the bright *soul* maliciously, puffing out her chest like an overconfident hen. "Stay away from Ken! He's *mine!*"

"I was only—" the bright *soul* tried to explain, but the overconfident hen did not let her finish. With a sudden thrust from her arms, she shoved the bright *soul* to the ground.

"Shut up, cow! I didn't say you could speak! You listen to me very carefully now. I don't care if Ken asked you to help him with homework or house chores, you'd better stop whatever dumb things you think you're doing with him, or you're dead meat! He's *mine*, and he's *way* out of your league! Just look at yourself. Which hole did you crawl out from anyway?"

One of the girls behind her whispered something in the other girls' ears, and they all snorted and laughed as though it was the most amusing thing they had ever heard.

"Betty, if I were a cow, why are you so concerned about losing him to me, then?" said the bright *soul* as she sat up, wearing a smirk. "Unless . . . you already know you're not even as pretty as a cow?"

Shaking visibly from anger and humiliation, Betty's face first turned white, then red.

"You bitch!" she shrieked, whipping out her perfectly manicured hands and swiped her long artificial nails at the bright *soul* like claws. "I'm gonna tear your face off!"

"No," said the magnificent bird, walking toward them. "You will not."

At the sound of her voice, Betty and her gang jerked their heads up and glared at their intruder like a pride of hungry lionesses interrupted at mealtime. Just when Betty was about to release more of her foul words onto the newcomer instead, terror suddenly seized her throat like an iron clutch, the same way it had seized all the other girls behind her. One by one, their lips began to quiver, and one after another, their bodies started to tremble. By the time the bright *soul* had gotten to her feet, they had all backed away from the newcomer as far as their legs would move.

The magnificent bird withdrew her gaze from them and said, "Now go and leave her be."

When Betty and her gang heard that, they turned on their heels and scurried off frantically as if they were running for their lives, leaving the bright *soul* stunned by not only their hysterical reaction but also their utter discomposure.

"Well, you don't see *that* every day . . ." the bright *soul* muttered to herself. "That was quite . . . satisfying, actually."

She gave a short sigh of relief, then, smiling broadly, she turned to her savior, the magnificent bird in human form.

"And you … Thank you, thank you, thank you! You saved my skin today … literally! I just moved here a few days ago. Honestly, I didn't expect to have this much trouble to be the new girl in this school. But you know what? I don't think they'll have the nerve to come bother me again. I owe you my skin … and a meal! What do you say we go grab that meal now? What kind of food do you like? Do you have a favorite place around here? … Wait, I forgot to ask your name!"

The magnificent bird had never met a human who could look her in the eye and still talk freely before, not to mention she could see from the girl's *soul* that, instead of the normal category, it belonged to the enigmatic one, and the brightest one she had come across at that. Now greatly intrigued by both the *soul* and its owner, the magnificent bird, throughout all her lives in human form, across centuries and countries, accepted her first-ever invitation to relationship building with a human, an invitation that would lead to an unlikely friendship, which, eventually, would end in great heartache.

But that's a different story for another time. For now, the magnificent bird simply said:

"Call me Nina … Do you always talk this much?"

V

The old man took a long draw on his pipe and exhaled toward the sky. White smoke flowed out from his mouth like steam from the chimney on a speeding train, which then joined and blended into the perpetual mist shrouding the lake.

"I'm afraid that's all we have time for tonight." The old man lowered his head and smiled at her. "I need to return to my lake before they come for me again. I hope you enjoyed my stories, Vermilion."

Maybe it was the tea that he had brewed for her, but for the first time in a long, long time, she felt awake, as though she had finally woken up from a long, long dream.

"Please, feel free to have some more before we part ways," the old man said as he filled her cup. "You always said I brewed the best tea in this world."

The fragrance of the tea floated up with its steam and embraced her face. She inhaled deeply, letting the warm fragrance seep through her heart and lungs, calming down every single cell that was in her body. The tea had a unique emerald green color, which reminded her of the green dragon who called itself Azure and told her it was the Keeper of Change. Then she remembered the old man had introduced himself as Black, the Keeper of Growth.

"Who's coming for you?" she asked, knowing it was a question that she already knew the answer to; but right now, she needed to hear the answer from someone else.

"The same ones who are coming for you," Black answered airily. "Unlike Azure, who can perform his duties by blending in with the color of the sky to ride on winds and clouds, I need to perform my duties down here, in the water, as it is connected to all living things in this world. That is why I need to hide my lake. I much prefer peace and tranquility to their loud explorations and exploitations."

"They have come to your lake before," she observed, mostly to herself.

"Many times." The old man nodded nostalgically. "In the beginning, when they didn't have any fancy weapons or tools, all I needed to do was emerge from the water, and it would scare them away. But as their technologies improved and advanced, so did their confidence and determination. To maintain the peace and tranquility of my lake, I hid, from water to water, from lakes to oceans. Nevertheless, they came after me anyway, from Loch Ness to the Norwegian Sea, from the Bermuda Triangle to the deep sea in open waters. They have many names for me: the Murky Warrior, the Loch Ness Monster, the Kraken, the Midgard Serpent, the Leviathan, the Sea Bishop, the Sea Spirit . . . But no matter how strange and terrifying I was described in their records as the creatures with those names, they have never ceased to venture into my territories to seek the truth for themselves—the truth for them to decide whether or not they can eventually tame me and claim me as theirs to extract the longevity properties that I am rumored to possess. So now I shroud my lake with mist to obscure it from their satellites. Compared to the grand plans they have for me and my powers, I would rather perform my duties in peace."

"So this is not your true form," she concluded, not feeling surprised at all.

Black laughed heartily. "No, it is not. But it is the most appropriate form to take to brew us some tea. After all, I cannot disappoint an old friend who enjoys my tea as much as I enjoy my peace."

She gazed down at her tea and asked, "Were you the old man who visited the magnificent bird in *The Story of Nian?*"

Black stroked his long, silvery beard and smiled. "I think you know the answer, Vermilion."

She fixed her gaze on the emerald green tea in her cup and fell silent. She could see her reflection in the tea, and it was *not* Mira Murphy.

"Who was the magnificent bird in your stories?" she asked softly. "Who was her brightest *soul*?"

Just as softly, Black replied, "I think you know the answers too, Vermilion."

"Your stories ..." She paused briefly before continuing. "Did they really happen?"

Black rose to his feet and patted her on the shoulder. "You know the answer better than I do, Vermilion. After all, they were *your* stories."

When she looked up from her reflection in the tea, Black was already strolling toward the lake, his silhouette expanding rapidly amid the thickening mist until it grew into a solid black hill, the top of which was undulating slowly like waves.

Then all of a sudden, the mist thinned out, revealing a massive black turtle whose body was entwined with a monstrous black serpent that was equally impressive in size. Together, the turtle and the serpent extended their necks and stuck their great big heads out to gaze at her with both pairs of their eyes, which were round and glossy like large black pearls from the unknown depths of the sea:

"Time to wake up, Vermilion. Beware of the humans—they are coming for you again ..."

As the turtle's head and the serpent's head merged into one, their eyes merged into one pair as well. The visual distortion made her blink, but when she looked again, she was staring into the beady black eyes of a vivid red bird instead.

The unexpected change in her field of vision jolted her into another blink, and just like that, she was back in the world of fog, alone again. . .

Chapter 10   THE VERMILION BIRD

1

WHEN she opened her eyes the next day, she thought she was merely waking up to another dream. It wasn't until she heard the dull tapping sounds from the window that she realized, instead of another dream, she was back to her life as Mira Murphy.

She looked toward the window—it was Red, tapping on the windowpane from the other side with its beak as if it was there to remind her of what she wished she could have forgotten.

She heard a series of quick footsteps approaching the room. As she turned to look, the door was cracked open gently, and Lilith poked her head in.

"Hey . . . You're awake! Are you finally ready to get up now?"

"Only if I have to," she replied after letting out a soft sigh. As her dreams and her reality collided in her head yet again, she added resignedly, "I wish I could freeze time."

"No kidding," said Lilith, chuckling as she sat down on the foot of the bed. "You slept through breakfast, lunch, and afternoon tea. New Year's Day is now New Year's Evening. Just how bad do you want to be done with this holiday?"

"It's just another day," she answered in a whisper.

The smile faded from Lilith's lips, and her face grew concerned. "Mira, I meant to ask you last night, but you fell asleep before I could force-feed you my noodles . . . Is everything all right between you and your parents?"

She remembered Cara's reactions from the night before, and she remembered how angry she was at Cara for lying to her face. Strangely, recalling those moments now no longer made her angry. Like a memory from the distant past, all it churned up was a sense of loss and feebleness. Still, her silence was enough for Lilith to confirm her own suspicion.

"Just as I thought . . ." Lilith mumbled, then she drew a deep breath and turned to her friend. "Mira, listen to me, whatever it was . . . it's not worth it. I mean, why should you spend time on staying mad at the people that you love and who love you more than anything else in the world? It doesn't make sense, right? And since it doesn't make sense, it's just a waste of time and, hence, a waste of life. And if it's a waste of time and a waste of life, it's not worth it, period."

"Interesting logic." She gave Lilith a weak smile. "But it's not like that. I just . . . need some space to clear my head."

Lilith narrowed her eyes and gave her a meaningful look. "You mean the kind of space you chose to put between you and your home at almost midnight last night so you could come knock on my door at three o'clock in the morning?"

She thought of why she had to come to Lilith's house in the first place: she couldn't reach Lilith through her phone, so she needed to come check on her to make sure she was not losing her mind—like Eric Ekker or those seven men from the alley, who, after having witnessed her true form, all burned themselves alive. She was so determined to make it to Lilith's house as soon as possible that she didn't care what the cost would be. So when Cara and Thomas tried to stop her from leaving, she confronted them with the truth that they had kept from her for over fifteen years. However, the pain of finally facing the truth of her relationship to Cara and Thomas was nothing in comparison to what she had experienced after her encounter with Azure.

She felt something contract uncomfortably in her left chest. She wished she could return to the world of fog in her dream, but she knew even amid that dense white fog, everything would still be there—everything Azure had said, every story Black had told, and every being she had come to care for . . .

She wanted to tell Lilith what had really happened the night before, but she hesitated. She didn't know how she could ever explain everything—everything from *the beginning*—to Lilith. She didn't even know if she should try.

Lilith sensed her hesitation and broke the silence. "I know you have a lot on your mind, Mira. I don't blame you for wanting to run away from those questions and thoughts, but you don't need to run away from home."

She knitted her brow and sat up. " 'Run away from home'?"

Lilith seemed surprised at her response. "Your parents came early this morning, asking me if I had seen you."

"Oh." She looked away. "Did you tell them I was here?"

"I did," Lilith said plainly. "They were worried sick, Mira. They looked like nervous wrecks who hadn't slept all night. When I told them you were here and you were still sleeping, your mom broke down in tears and couldn't stop crying."

"Are they still here?" she asked quietly.

"No, they left. They said they knew you needed time; they just wanted to know you were safe."

She felt a lump forming in her throat. She tried to swallow it, but doing so only released a crippling cold current to the rest of her body.

Lilith reached for her hands and said, "Mira, I know you don't want to tell them what's going on, but what you have been through is a lot. And right now, those questions and thoughts you want to run away from are doing nothing for you but to drive you away from your parents. Life is too short to be spent *away* from the people you love and the people who love you more than anything else in the world when you can spend it *with* them."

Lilith waited till she had caught her friend's attention, then she looked at her pleadingly and said, "Mira? It's time to let it go."

"Let what go?" she asked, not because she needed to, but because she wanted to hear the answer from Lilith.

For a few seconds, Lilith bit her lip, as though she was nervous about telling the truth. Then she replied, softly but firmly, "Your guilt, Mira. Your guilt toward the ones that died and the ones you could not save."

11

Cara didn't know how long she had been standing in front of the door to Mira's room. Slowly and uncertainly, she put her hand on the doorknob and turned it. As the door gave way to her gentle push, a sense of hope suddenly rose in her chest, and, for a fleeting moment, she thought Mira was sitting right there in her usual spot by the window, reading.

But Mira was not there. Nobody was there—only furniture and air. Cara's heart contracted, then sank, and she couldn't help but notice the cold irony that even a fleeting moment of hope could open up into a gaping emotional black hole.

Staring vacantly at that empty spot by the window, Cara was no longer aware of her body or her surroundings. Her mind began to wander aimlessly between space and time. And eventually, it wandered into the past and into a time that felt like a lifetime ago, when she seemed to be living a different life, when she seemed to be genuinely happy.

What happened to me? Cara heard her mind ask as it remembered how her younger self had lived with the confidence that nothing in the world could ever break her spirit. *How did I change so much over the years? How did I change into this?*

Tears rushed to her eyes and blurred her vision. Cara gave in and closed them with a silent moan. *Why am I not grateful to be alive?*

She remembered then that she had asked that same question to Nina the last time they spoke, and it reminded her of the state she was in over fifteen years ago, when she had lost her baby, the baby that she had so desperately wanted and so eagerly anticipated, who had passed away in her womb, quietly and unexpectedly, just four weeks away from her due date. She had been crying uncontrollably for days after the induction, and for the first time in her life, Cara had come to realize there was a whole other place beyond the so-called rock bottom: a deep, dark chasm where there was nothing for you to hold on to or bounce back from, and you just kept on falling and falling and falling, endlessly. Just as she was spiraling down farther and farther into that deep, dark place, she received a call from Nina. Cara didn't know it then, but that phone call would become the last conversation they had.

"It's my fault," Nina had replied softly after she had blurted out that question in a half-chiding, half-crying scream.

"How can it be your fault?" she had squawked like a hysterical crow. "I'm cursed! That's why! Everyone who's connected to me in blood is dead! First it was my two babies, one after the other, barely a month old in my belly, then my mom, then my dad, then … then … Then my baby girl … my daughter … my Mira … my little miracle … I don't understand, Nina. Why do they have to die? Why do I get to live? … Why, Nina? Why … ? It's so unfair … !"

Nina had listened to her cry without saying a word, and she had cried and cried and cried until her eyes were burning and blurry and her throat was inflamed and sore. When she was finally too drained and too exhausted to carry on, Nina had said to her in a low, calm voice, "Cara, life itself is always fair. There's always a price to be paid for something to be gained, and likewise, there's always a price to be paid for something to not be lost. You just can't see what you're paying for when you're in the moment."

"But what have I gained?" she had asked weakly. "Have I not lost enough?"

"That depends on the price you are willing to pay," Nina had answered. "Everything that has happened is already in the past now. You can't embrace the future if you keep holding on to the past. You have to let it go."

Cara distinctly remembered there had been a long and heavy pause after Nina had said those words, just as distinctly as she re-membered what Nina had said to her next, which would become the last sentence that she ever heard Nina say:

"Cara, out of all the people in this world, you deserve to be happy."

I've failed you, Nina. Cara buried her face in her hands and broke into a sob. *I've lost what you'd paid for me. I've lost my last hope. I've lost my final chance.*

III

Instead of returning home right away on the evening of New Year's Day, she had stayed at Lilith's house until she was ready to believe that, unlike Eric Ekker or those seven men from the alley, Lilith was safe from losing her sanity even though she had also witnessed her true form. By then, a few more days had passed. With the holiday break coming to an end, she was finally ready to face Cara and Thomas.

When she arrived at their street, the sun was already sinking, looking as bloody as if it were murdered and had fallen due to severe blood loss. Their house, bathed in the sun's dying glow, sat lifelessly at the end of the street and watched her silently as she approached the front door.

She reached for the doorknob but aborted the motion midway. She no longer considered herself as Mira Murphy or, for that matter, the daughter of Cara Murphy and Thomas Murphy. So instead, she rang the doorbell. Then she waited, calmly and detachedly, like the stranger she was supposed to be.

The door was soon pulled open, revealing both Cara and Thomas in the doorway, who seemed to be struggling to find the right words to say without losing control of their emotions. She felt something contract painfully in her left chest, which shot out a crippling cold current to her arms and made them weak. She clenched her fists and ignored it.

Behind her, the sun had already sunk below the horizon, but even the last breath of its bloodred glow was not enough to add any color of life to the couple's pale faces. She thought Cara and Thomas both looked older, smaller, and way more fragile than she remembered.

The overwhelmed couple was agonizingly conflicted, and she could see why: they wanted to pull her into their arms and hold her tight but were afraid that she would push them away; they wanted to tell her how much they had missed her and how happy they were to have her home again but were scared that she had only come back to pack. So they just stood there, hugging her with their teary eyes as they were torn apart from the inside.

She decided she had seen enough of their struggles and conflictions, so she broke the silence and said, "I want to know the truth. Can you be honest with me?"

Pain and dread grew and spread in the couple's eyes as if they were being eaten alive from within. Slowly, Thomas turned to Cara, whose lips were trembling helplessly.

"Honey?" he whispered in a quavering voice. "Can we?"

Cara looked up at Thomas and opened her mouth, appearing to be getting ready to say something, but all she managed to do was make her lips tremble even more. Gently, Thomas held her by the shoulder and gazed into her eyes with a melancholy yet encouraging smile.

Breathing shakily, Cara closed her mouth and lowered her eyes. Lips still trembling, she turned to Mira and said, almost pleadingly, "I'm sorry I hid it from you, Little Bird. I didn't want you to know because—because I was scared ... I was scared that I would lose you ... I know, it was very selfish of me to have lied to you for so long. You deserve to know the truth. I owe her that much ..."

Cara wiped the tears off her face and drew a shaky breath through her mouth. When she looked up again, she signaled Mira to follow her and led her into the guest room, where she pulled out an old, dusty box from under the bed. Cara dug through the contents until she found what she was looking for. Without taking it out of the box, she gazed at it in a long, pensive silence. Then, with a sharp inhale of breath, she pulled out a picture frame and handed it to Mira.

It was a nice picture frame, heavy and well crafted. There was a photo inside it, and there were three girls in that photo, all of whom were in costume. The girl in the middle had a large red feather fixed to a jeweled band around her head, and she was wearing a red flapper dress that was embellished with black sequins in busy patterns, which looked exactly like the one Cara had worn on New Year's Eve. The girl on the right had a big silk flower pinned to the side of her head. She was wearing a flapper dress as well, but hers was in a silver beige color and was much more modest in style. The girl on the left, however, was frowning irritably in a high-collared, long-sleeved satin dress that seemed to have been made for either a widow or a vampire, and it looked so black in the photo that if it weren't for the full head of fiery red curls cascading down around her unwilling face, she might have succeeded in disappearing into the background.

She sat down quietly on the bed and studied the faces of those three girls. She already knew the one in the middle was young Cara, although there was so much light and joy in this Cara's eyes that it made her look like a completely different person. The girl on the right had light blond hair and soft blue eyes. She wasn't wearing much makeup, so it was easy to recognize through her distinct air of elegance and refinement that she was young Susan Heart.

Her eyes landed on the face of the last girl. She knew they had never met each other before, but this girl's face was as familiar as her own. She remembered what Azure had said then, and she remembered the last story Black had told her.

She closed her eyes, wishing there could be another explanation somehow—a different explanation than what she had been told.

"Who's this?" she eventually asked, pointing at the girl on the left without opening her eyes.

Stiffly, Cara sat down beside her. Then, in a voice that was as hoarse as a heartbroken crow's, Cara told the truth:

"Her name is Nina. She was my best friend . . . and . . . she's your mother . . ."

IV

When Cara was eight, her parents got divorced. She didn't want to admit it, but deep down, she had always known it was inevitable. After all, her parents were always arguing with each other, especially when they were home at the same time, so much so that, eventually, they just stayed away from home as often as they could.

Cara hated it when they fought, but she also hated it when they were not home. She didn't know which one bothered her more, the fact that her parents didn't love each other anymore, or that they didn't love her enough to come home. Either way, home had become a miserable place for Cara. So whenever her parents got into yet another fight with each other, she would sneak out to the Murphys' house next door to escape all the screaming and yelling; and when her parents were not home, she would go to the Murphys' house all the same to escape the loneliness and herself.

Mr. Murphy and Mrs. Murphy were a very nice couple. They didn't mind Cara visiting their house all the time, nor did they mind feeding her all the time, but they always asked her about her parents. Cara didn't want to talk about her parents, but she also didn't have anywhere else to go. So instead of hanging out with Mr. and Mrs. Murphy in the kitchen, she would go hide in Thomas's room most of the time.

Cara figured with the frequency she had been inviting herself over, Thomas must have guessed what was going on between her parents—Mr. and Mrs. Murphy must have guessed it too. But Thomas never asked her any questions about her parents, nor did he ask about her tearstained face or her puffy eyes. In truth, they didn't really talk much when they were together, which was just what Cara needed during those days—a perfect balance between leaving her alone and leaving her to face her loneliness on her own —to escape from her life at home. She and Thomas spent most of their time together reading books, drawing pictures, making origami in his room, or collecting rocks and leaves, catching snails and bugs, building bird houses in the backyard.

Thomas was a good-natured boy, easygoing, gentle, and caring. In a way, Cara felt that he had been patiently nursing her wounds with his quiet company and his reassuring presence. Gradually, Thomas became Cara's haven, a place to escape to, from everything else in her life that she didn't want to face.

But running away from what she didn't want to face didn't stop it from running at her. In time, Cara's father met another woman, and her mother met another man. Naturally, they filed for a divorce, and since neither of them wanted to be reminded of the life they had shared with each other, neither of them wanted to keep the house that they had shared their lives in. So to finalize the divorce as quickly as possible, they put the house on the market, sold it, and split the money as well as everything else, including Cara's custody.

Then one afternoon, after Cara had returned home from school, her parents, rare as it was, stood together and announced to her that they were no longer husband and wife and that, since they were no longer a family, they had sold the house to someone else. Cara was then asked to go pack a bag and get ready to leave for another city that very afternoon with her mother, as well as the new man in her life, and stay with them for the next six months until it was her father's turn to take care of her.

Cara didn't know what got into her, but instead of going to her room to pack, she turned away from her parents and ran. She ran as fast as she could—out the house, across the streets, through the park, onto the beach. As Cara ran breathlessly on the soft, yielding sand, she suddenly realized she didn't want to stop running, so she ran on and ran straight toward the sea. She pictured how the water would drown her sorrows and carry her to a place far, far away from her heartaches. She imagined how the waves would wipe away her tears and embrace her like an infant until she was rocked to sleep . . .

But she was wrong. The water was cold and bitter; it chilled her to the bone till every single cell in her was screaming out of pain. The waves were rough and harsh; they tossed her and smacked her till she was disoriented and bruised. In the end, the sea spit her back out onto the sand, as though she were merely another washed-up carcass.

Cara curled up into a ball and cried. Her family was gone. Her home was gone. She no longer had a place that she belonged in this world. Worse yet, nobody wanted her, not even Death, who had just rejected her from his gate after she had willingly offered herself.

Even though she was soaked from head to toe, and even though she was shivering from the cold and trembling from the pain, Cara ignored the needs of her body and let her tears run free. She cried and cried, completely oblivious to the passing of time. Then, amid the mocking whispers of the waves, she heard someone approaching from behind. Cara didn't look up though; she no longer cared what would happen to her next. Before she had realized it, however, she was embraced by a big, fluffy towel that was as gentle and warm as the winter sun.

Woodenly, Cara looked up from the towel and saw Thomas's face. He was clearly concerned, but instead of asking her questions, he just sat down beside her and kept her company. He had caught sight of Cara darting away from her house like someone who was running for her life and wanted to make sure she was all right, so he had run after her to the beach. He had frozen in panic when he saw that Cara was running into the sea. Then, when he saw that the waves had simply sent her back to the shore, leaving her sobbing helplessly on the sand as though the world were coming to an end, he had run all the way home and back to bring her that towel. Of course, Thomas never mentioned any of it to Cara. And although Cara never said anything about it to Thomas either, she was grateful that he was there, sitting quietly on the beach by her side without questions or judgments.

By the time they were finally back at Cara's house, it was already past dinnertime. Cara's mother was furious with her, not only because she had run away without packing her things, but also because her "childish tantrum" had made them run very late in picking up her mother's new love to begin their drive to the new city. Without asking Cara where she had been or what she had done, her mother shoved her into the car and started the engine. As the car pulled out of the driveway of what used to be her home for the last time, Cara stuck her head out from the rear passenger window and waved goodbye to Thomas. Thomas smiled and waved back to her. He didn't say a word, but Cara could see that he was speaking to her with his eyes, telling her that he cared.

For the rest of the ride, Cara was lost in an impassive trance. It wasn't until her mother stopped the car for the new man in her life to load up his suitcases that Cara realized she was still wrapped in Thomas's towel. Instead of taking it off, Cara pulled it tight around herself till she felt like she was inside a cocoon. She knew there was no magic to that towel, but somehow, it had made the undeniable existence of her mother's new love and the undisputable fact of their move to a new city much more tolerable.

When the cold, dark night enveloped their car, Cara lay down on the back seat and curled up under the towel, while her mother and the new man in her life held hands in the front and talked about their grand plans for their life together in the new city as they drove on. Cara didn't go to sleep that night, nor did she listen to their grand plans. As the car moved farther and farther away from the place she had once called home and the life she had once known, Cara gave in to the loneliness that was seeping from her body to her soul, until eventually, she found herself embracing it like a fish stranded in a frozen pond—it was cold, and it burned painfully, but along with the cold and the pain, it also brought her clarity. And for the first time in Cara's—albeit young—life, she was able to see clearly that she was alone, she was on her own, she was the only one who could truly take care of her, and she was also the only one who could ever help her—nobody else.

By sunrise, Cara had severed herself from her old life and begun her new one at peace. Her parents' divorce didn't upset her anymore, neither did the new family plans they each had made with the new love in their life. Now that Cara knew no one else was responsible for her but herself, she could finally stop expecting her parents to be her parents again.

In the years that followed, the new man in her mother's life and the new woman in her father's life were replaced by others, who came and went but never seemed to stay for long. Meanwhile, Cara was passed between her parents every six months, moving from one city to another, switching from this school to that school, never having a place that she would like to call home again. None of that bothered Cara though. She was living her life with herself, she was not responsible for anyone else, and she had no expectation of anyone else either. She didn't need anybody, she was free inside her own world, and she was content with it. For the longest time, Cara had thought it would last her till it was finally time for Death to come and release her. Little did she know that instead of Death, she would be released from her cocoon of loneliness—which, by then, had evolved into a state of self-sufficient equilibrium—by someone else, someone named Nina.

It was the first year of high school, when Cara was fifteen. Her mother had just moved them to a new city after another bad breakup, which she had labeled as yet another failure in her judgment of men, as if moving to a new city would somehow improve that. Since Cara had been transferred to many different schools after her parents' divorce, she had had plenty of opportunities to learn firsthand how bullies would always target the new kid in class. So when a group of unfriendly girls cut her off after school and forced her into a corner, she instantly knew what they were up to. Still, Cara made up her mind that no matter what happened next, she would not give them the satisfaction of having control over her—she alone had the control over her life, no one else.

When the girl in charge realized Cara would not bend to their verbal insults, she became livid and was dead set on breaking her by resorting to the infliction of bodily injuries instead. Just as Cara braced herself for what might have become an inescapable physical confrontation with the whole lot of them, Nina, having appeared out of nowhere, stepped in voluntarily and put an end to the commotion, scaring the snarly girls away like a coven of panic-stricken vampires fleeing the scene at the sight of the bright, hot sun.

Before Cara could begin to process the unexpected turn of events, she was distracted by a warming sensation waking up quickly inside her, which, though mild and plain, was enough to produce a sharp contrast to the cold cocoon of loneliness that she had been so used to living in. To Cara's own amusement, not only was she pleasantly surprised by the warming sensation flowing through her body, but she was also completely dumbfounded by the fact that there was another person in this world who actually cared enough to save her.

And just like that, Cara's cocoon of loneliness thawed and was replaced by an overwhelming longing for company and companionship. She started babbling to Nina right then and there, almost uncontrollably, as if she hadn't seen or talked to another human being in years. By the end of that day, Cara had, finally, found herself a friend.

From then on, Cara was with Nina almost every day. Interestingly, the more time she spent with Nina, the more intrigued she was by her friend. To begin with, Nina was very different from the other kids at school. She did not care about the latest fashions or the hottest trends, nor did she care about the newest rumors or the craziest gossip. She was never concerned about other people's opinions of her, but she always seemed to be quite preoccupied with something heavy and serious on her mind. Nevertheless, Nina was a great listener and an even greater mind reader, who could, somehow, always tell what was going on in Cara's head, even when there was no permission for her to do so. Nina, on the contrary, was as unreadable to Cara as an enigma from another universe. For one thing, she hardly ever talked about herself or her thoughts, and even on the rare occasion that she did, it was usually a comment that was either so profound or so hard to digest that Cara was left too stupefied to respond.

In spite of the fundamental differences in their personalities, Cara and Nina's friendship grew deeper and stronger over the next few months. As Cara began to embrace her new life at the new school, she was also able to make more friends. Still, to Cara, Nina would always be the one who knew her and understood her the best, so she would introduce the new friends she had made to Nina, hoping they would become Nina's friends as well. Unfortunately, Nina had a natural talent for making people uncomfortable, and the majority of Cara's new friends were too intimidated to be around her, let alone carrying out a conversation with her. In the end, out of all the new friends that Cara had made, Susan was the only one who had managed to survive Nina's penetrating gaze without blacklisting them both afterward from her social circle, even though she already had a large one and lacked no friends.

Susan was not only the smartest and the prettiest girl in their grade but also the smartest and the prettiest girl in the entire school. For that very reason, most people didn't think she would care to be friends with them. But to everyone's surprise, Susan soon disengaged herself from her usual social circle and was often spotted next to Cara and Nina instead. And by the end of the semester, the three of them had become inseparable.

When they were together, Susan and Cara were the conversationalists, and they would talk about all kinds of random things, ranging from something grand and philosophical to something trivial and utterly silly. Nina, on the other hand, would usually let them carry the conversation and keep her opinions to herself. But occasionally, out of nowhere, she would make a comment on what they had just talked about in such a serious yet innocent manner that Susan and Cara would first freeze for a few seconds due to shock, then double up and laugh till their tummies were sore. And then, still breathless and giddy, they would try to argue their points of view with Nina, a harmless debate would follow, and the whole thing would just become all the more hilarious for the two of them. However, no matter how much or how hard they laughed, Nina was always able to remain nonchalant and stay immune to their daffiness. Instead, she would observe them intently with a slight knot in one of her eyebrows, as though she was secretly smirking at how ridiculous the two of them were looking as they held their tummies and shook from side to side like the inflatable tube men one could find in front of those car wash places. Though it was hard to explain exactly why, even to herself, for Cara, those were the kind of memories that had bonded the three of them into best friends.

As Cara reveled in her newfound sense of belonging, six months seemed to have vanished in the blink of an eye. When the time came for her to move to her father's city again, Cara refused. She had finally found a place and a life that made her feel at home, and there was no way she would let it all go without putting up a fight. She told her parents she was done with moving between cities and switching schools, then she went on to tell them she was done with their selfishness and did not wish to be passed between the two of them like a hot potato anymore.

Cara didn't know whether it was because of guilt or whether it was because time and life had chiseled something away from her parents over the years, but this time, for once, her father and her mother ended up agreeing with each other. And instead of Cara moving to her father's city, he moved to theirs and rented a house close to her mother's so that Cara could live half the time with him and half the time with her mother without ever having to move between cities and switch schools again.

When Susan learned that Cara didn't have to move away, she was so happy that she hugged Cara tightly and they both burst into tears. Instead of joining them, Nina looked at the two of them with knitted brow and told them that if they were going to cry for a while, they should let her know so that she could go do something else with her time as she waited for them to finish. When Susan and Cara heard that, they started to laugh, but since they couldn't quite stop crying yet, they sounded more like they were hyperventilating. Without saying another word, Nina left the room and, shortly afterward, returned with two boxes of tissues. Quietly, she handed Susan and Cara each a box and watched them blow their noses and dry their faces like a resigned mother. Even though that was all she did, Cara knew it was Nina's way of saying she was glad Cara could stay too.

As their lives in high school progressed together, so did their friendship. Meanwhile, Cara had developed an almost blissful insensitivity to the pace of time now that she was spending most of it with her two best friends. The days were no longer mundane and repetitive, her life was no longer a series of assignments and tasks on a to-do list, and most importantly, she was herself. She could share her thoughts and feelings freely with the two people who knew her and understood her the most in this world. She was content, and she was happy—genuinely, innately happy.

Unfortunately, no matter how content and happy Cara was with her present, it could not stop the flow of time. Before she knew it, another January 1 was right around the corner, reminding her that their time in high school would soon come to an end, along with the time that they could share together.

As usual, a year-end party was taking place at their school on New Year's Eve. Since Nina had an unnatural aversion to parties, they had skipped the previous ones. But now, knowing that this could be their last opportunity to go to one together, Cara took the liberty of signing the three of them up and informed Susan and Nina that they were going to the party, but instead of showing up in fancy cocktail dresses, they would go in costumes and make complete fools out of themselves for fun. Susan instantly agreed to Cara's plan. Nina, on the other hand, knitted her brow but said nothing.

When the time came for everyone to get ready for the party, instead of going to a salon to have their hair and nails done like the other girls did, Susan and Cara dragged Nina to a costume store.

Like kids on a treasure hunt inside a toy store, the two of them oohed and aahed along each aisle and picked out the most outrageous costumes they came across. They then tried everything on one by one, all the while laughing at how ridiculous they looked in them and how speechless Nina's expression was in the background as she watched the two of them parade around in those costumes in utter silence. In the end, Susan and Cara each decided on a flapper dress to wear to the party. As for Nina, despite the large selection they had picked out for her, more than enthusiastically, she resorted to the simplest and the least eye-catching one in the entire store and, after being pestered by their continuous begging and pleading, eventually gave in and agreed to put it on. When she finally came out of the dressing room, the reluctant look on her face nearly sent Susan and Cara dying laughing.

By the time they arrived at the party at last, it had already started. Naturally, they not only shocked everyone there with their presence but also with their outfits. Nevertheless, Susan and Cara had a great time at the party and an even greater time watching other people's reactions toward the three of them together in costume. Nina, however, didn't enjoy any of it. She spent most of the evening trailing behind Susan and Cara like a shadow, though the big knots in her eyebrows clearly indicated how much she would rather be somewhere else. When Susan and Cara realized there was indeed nothing about the party that agreed with Nina and that she only tolerated the whole thing for them, they couldn't help wishing the night would go on forever and their time together would never end. In order to freeze that bittersweet feeling in their memories for them to savor later when they were apart, Susan and Cara did the next best thing by making sure that the heartwarming contrast between Nina's resigned tolerance and their giddy cheerfulness was captured in a photo.

After the party, Cara printed three copies of that photo and put them in three identical frames. She kept one for herself and gave the other two to Susan and Nina as early graduation presents. Susan, like Cara, hung hers in the most prominent spot in her room. Nina, being Nina, simply told Cara she did not need a photo to remember how loud Susan and Cara had laughed that night and left hers in a drawer.

As spring approached, the three girls started to receive admission letters from different colleges. Though Susan and Nina both had the option to go to a more prestigious school, they eventually chose to go to the same one that Cara had decided to go to. Needless to say, Cara was over the moon about it, and she immediately suggested that since they were all going to the same college, they should just rent an apartment and live together as roommates. Eager and excited to spend even more time with her two best friends during the next four years, Susan concurred with Cara's idea right away. Despite the two girls' overflowing exhilaration for not only the time but also the space that they would get to share during their college lives ahead, Nina merely kept her face nonchalant and let the two of them carry on without either approving or vetoing any part of their plan.

So when summer was coming to an end, the three of them rented an apartment near the campus and got ready for the first day. Out of all the things Cara had prepared herself for college, however, she had not expected that she would bump into Thomas before her very first class. Since she had never contacted Thomas after the move, the unexpected reunion came as a big surprise to them both. Although Cara was happy to see Thomas again, she also started to feel afraid. His sudden presence inevitably reminded her of the past she had severed herself from, a time when he had witnessed the darkest moment of her life. For that reason, Cara was worried that Thomas, knowing what he knew about her, might look at her differently now that they were both adults. But instead of judging her and keeping his distance, Thomas invited himself back into Cara's life spontaneously. Before long, they both noticed that a new feeling was growing between them, and it was getting stronger and more irresistible day by day.

Then one morning, Thomas approached Cara after class and asked her if she would like to go on a date with him. Cara looked into his eyes and immediately remembered the big, fluffy towel he had wrapped around her on the beach the day that she had wanted to give up her life. The towel was as gentle and warm as the winter sun, just like the way he was looking at her now. Cara had, after all this time, kept that towel in a sealed box. And even though she had not opened it once, she had brought it along with her every time she moved just so she could always have it sitting in the corner at the top of her closet, no matter how long the space would remain hers. As Cara gazed into Thomas's eyes, she knew she had made a great mistake by having him cut out completely from her life just to sever herself cleanly from her past. It was then that Cara decided it was time for her to embrace herself fully and let go of her pain and fear. So with a relieved and delighted smile, she said yes to Thomas and they started dating.

Having grown up witnessing how her parents' relationship had turned out and how their other relationships had ended, Cara had been a nonbeliever in effortless dating and the romantic concept of "meant to be." But she and Thomas were truly a match made in heaven, and soon, she was ready to introduce him to Susan and Nina as her official boyfriend.

The introduction took place quite formally over dinner one night in one of their favorite restaurants. Susan, like a mother interviewing a potential candidate for the role of her future son-in-law, asked Thomas numerous questions. Nina, on the contrary, was rather indifferent to him. The only time she joined in the conversation was when Susan asked Thomas if he liked kids, and it was only to remind Cara and Thomas about the importance of using protection until they were ready for a baby.

Knowing Nina and Susan, Cara had anticipated that they could manage to make Thomas uncomfortable and embarrassed even before appetizers were served. But Thomas just wiped the nervous sweat away from his forehead and gave Cara a tacit smile as he squeezed her hand, as if to let her know that he could see how important she was to her two best friends, and therefore, he did not mind being put under the microscope by them.

Susan gave Cara her approval and blessing the very next day, telling Cara how happy she was for her to have found someone who truly loved her and cared about her for who she was. She then went on to comment to Nina about how romantic it was for Cara and Thomas to become such a fairy-tale couple after having reunited unexpectedly as childhood neighbors and friends.

Nina detested any topic related to boys or relationships. But much to Cara's surprise and amusement, instead of telling Susan to talk about something else, Nina just stood quietly beside her with a knot in one of her eyebrows and let Susan continue on with her emotional monologue about how she wished she would be lucky enough to find a romantic and fulfilling relationship too.

As they entered the second year of college, Cara and Thomas's relationship grew more stable and meaningful, and, aside from Susan and Nina, he had become the most important person in Cara's life. Meanwhile, Susan started dating someone from school as well. His name was Ben, and like Susan, he was also well-known for his excellent grades and his popularity among other students. Since Susan and Ben were both regarded as one of the smartest and the most popular students at school, they were considered to be the perfect couple by many people.

Now that Nina was the only one still single, Susan and Cara could not resist the urge to look for a date on her behalf. However, despite the many attempts they made to set up a blind date for her, Nina had declined them all. So while the other girls were ditching their friends to spend more time with their boyfriends, Susan and Cara were taking regular time off from their boyfriends to be with their friends, not because they felt bad for Nina for being single or they had a guilty conscience about spending time with their boyfriends, but simply because they missed hanging out together, just the three of them. For Susan and Cara, though they really enjoyed the warm, happy feeling that they had when they were with their boyfriends, it could not replace the deeply relaxing and soothing mental state they had when it was just the three of them together. And although Nina never appeared happy or excited upon seeing the two of them back at the apartment together to be with her, they could tell from the way she greeted them by asking whether their boyfriends were still around that she missed spending time with them too.

Four years of college flew by just as quickly as high school. After graduation, Cara found a nine-to-five job in the city and started working as an administrative assistant in a large shipping company, while Susan moved on to begin her studies at a local medical school. Nina neither went to work nor stayed at school. Instead, she spent most of her days at different libraries and museums, saying she was looking for inspiration for what to do next. Still, no matter how different their new schedules were, they always made sure they could get together at least once every week.

Then one evening, while the three of them were catching up over dinner, Nina told Susan and Cara that she was leaving the next day, saying she was admitted into a government-funded international research project, and that since it required frequent travel and relocation, she would not be returning for the foreseeable future.

In spite of the weight of the news, Nina delivered it casually, as if she were only going away for a short vacation. Susan and Cara, on the other hand, were shocked beyond words. They had never given any serious thought to what it would be like when the three of them were no longer living in the same city. And now that it was actually happening, it was so painful to process the situation that it was almost suffocating.

They saw Nina off the next afternoon. Aside from a small backpack, Nina didn't bring anything else with her. After she had left, Susan and Cara went back to her apartment to vacate it for the landlord. Nina had left practically all her belongings behind, including the books she had collected over the years. She had also left a picture frame on her table, which was identical to the ones that Susan and Cara always hung in the most prominent spot on their walls. When they saw the picture frame, the two girls broke down in tears: unlike theirs, which still held a copy of the photo that Cara had printed out to remind them of the bittersweet memory of their last New Year's Eve together in high school, this one was empty.

As someone who avoided electronics, Nina rarely replied to the emails that Susan and Cara sent to her. But once in a while, she would call them up with an unknown caller ID from a new city or a new country to find out how they were doing. Meanwhile, for Susan and Cara, life seemed to have become less and less invigorating but more and more routine. Nevertheless, time still flew by even faster than before.

In the years that followed, changes gradually but naturally took place in their lives. First, Thomas proposed to Cara, and she was officially a bride-to-be. Then, Susan was selected into a residency program at a renowned hospital in Chicago, so she moved away with Ben. Not long after that, Thomas received a great job offer in Seattle, so he and Cara ended up moving away as well. And then, about a year later, Cara and Thomas got married.

The wedding ceremony was held at a private garden in Seattle on the first day of spring. Susan came with Ben as Cara's maid of honor. Cara's parents, to her astonishment, came to Seattle together a few days before the wedding and, miraculously, did not pick a single fight with each other the entire time they were there. Needless to say, both Susan and Cara had sent multiple emails to Nina to ask her to come to the wedding. However, although Cara had hoped that Nina would eventually show up at the ceremony as the other maid of honor, she never came.

It was a beautiful day for a wedding. The sun was gentle and pleasant; so were the clouds and the wind. But just as Cara began to walk down the aisle toward Thomas, a murder of crows descended on the wedding venue and refused to leave. Though they were all eerily quiet, the guests started to whisper to each other about them being an ill omen for their marriage. Cara didn't really mind the crows, nor did she mind the guests' low—albeit perceptible—whispers that the bride was destined for misfortune. After all, she was marrying Thomas, her true love and her haven, while the crows, in spite of their inauspicious aura, were just large black birds.

When Cara and Thomas got back from their honeymoon, the first thing they noticed was the large number of crows that had gathered at their house, idling, just as quietly as the ones that had shown up at their wedding ceremony—on the roof, on the lawn, and in the driveway, as if they had been waiting for them to come home. It was, without doubt, the most ominous scene Cara had encountered in real life, so much so that it was impossible for her not to be reminded of what the guests had whispered to each other at their wedding, and consequently, she couldn't help but notice the shred of doubt and fear that had been secretly hiding in the back of her head. Fortunately, Cara caught herself in time and managed to push the thought out of her mind before it could grow any bigger. As she got out of the car, Cara took a deep breath and reminded herself that she was Mrs. Murphy now and that was all that mattered.

While Thomas was unloading the car, Cara trod cautiously through the crows to the front to check the mailbox. Among the pile of mail and junk mail they had received during their time away, she noticed a plain envelope, which had nothing on it except her name. Baffled by the identity of its sender, Cara opened the envelope right away. She found a gift card and a handwritten note inside it. There were only two lines on the note. The first one read: *To Cara—Couldn't stay long at the wedding, but you looked happy, so congratulations.* The second one read: *To Thomas—Thank you.* Beneath the two lines, there was a name. Cara had already recognized the handwriting, but she still found herself double-checking the signature a few times before she could persuade herself that it was indeed from Nina. Although Cara had no idea why Nina wanted to thank Thomas, one thing was as clear as day to her now: Nina had come to watch her get married after all.

Shortly after Cara and Thomas's wedding, Ben proposed to Susan. As soon as Susan had booked a time and a venue for her wedding in Chicago, she bombarded Nina with emails, requesting her presence as the other maid of honor besides Cara. Nina never gave Susan a firm yes or no answer, but on the night before the wedding, she came unannounced during the rehearsal dinner and stayed just long enough to talk to them privately before taking off again, saying she was needed urgently at work. Susan and Cara were disappointed that she could not stay for the wedding after all, but since it was the first time they had seen Nina in years, they contented themselves with the fact that the three of them were finally together again—even if it had only lasted for a little while. Later, Susan found out that Nina had also left her a gift card and a handwritten note to congratulate her on her wedding and to thank Ben. Though neither Susan nor Cara knew why she wanted to thank their husbands for marrying them, they both agreed it was Nina's way of saying she was happy for them.

After Susan's wedding, Cara and Thomas returned to their home in Seattle and resumed their daily routines. As the years flowed by, more and more of their married friends upgraded their family size and became parents. Eventually, it was Susan's turn. When Cara learned that Susan was pregnant and that she and Ben were expecting twins, she was ecstatic. For Cara, her life with Thomas as a married couple was as happy as she could have ever imagined, but she caught herself wondering from time to time what it would be like to have one or two little people toddling around her and Thomas at their home too.

Much to Cara's own surprise, the thought took root in her head and gradually grew into a desire that she never knew she had before. Since she did not grow up in a healthy, loving family, Cara was unsure whether she had what it took to be a good mother. Still, she knew in her bones that once she had a baby of her own, she would love it with all her heart, and she would do everything in her power to raise it, take care of it, and protect it from any harm.

While Cara and Thomas were planning on having a baby, Cara's father bought a secluded house in Skygate, an obscure mountain town that Cara had never heard of until she learned the belated news of her father's move from her mother, who had, after so many years of separation from her father, suddenly decided she would move to his house in Skygate and live with him. Cara didn't know which part of the news shocked her more, that her father was able to abandon the bustling, convenient city life that he loved to move to the middle of nowhere and live as a recluse, or that her mother was able to abandon the freedom that she claimed she needed during their divorce to live with her father once more. The eight-year-old child in Cara wanted to question them why, after everything they had put her through, they were able to completely change their minds about each other just like that but couldn't have done the same back then. But the adult in her eventually resisted the urge and decided to keep her opinion to herself. After all, she would never have to live with them under the same roof again.

Later that year, Susan gave birth to the twins, a girl and a boy, and officially became a mother. Cara was so excited to meet her babies that she flew to Chicago with Thomas the very next day. As they held Susan's babies in their arms and watched them make their cute baby faces and sounds, they knew they were more than ready to have a baby of their own.

It took them a while, but after nearly a year of trying, Cara was finally with child. When she spotted that extra pink line on the test strip, faint but visible, Cara felt like the happiest person on Earth and couldn't help bursting into tears. That night, she announced to Thomas over dinner that he was going to be a father. He was so thrilled to hear the news that he swooped her up and spun around in circles. They then spent the entire evening talking about the future and what they should do to get ready for the baby: which room was the best one to use as the nursery, whether they should stay in their current house or move to a bigger one in a more child-friendly neighborhood, what kind of parents they wanted to become, what kind of things they looked forward to doing when the baby was here, which name they wanted to use if it was a girl, and which name to use if it was a boy . . .

The knowledge of having a tiny human growing inside her was a magical feeling. Unfortunately, it didn't last very long for Cara.

Just as she and Thomas began to look for a more suitable house to raise a child in, she had a miscarriage.

As upsetting as it was, Cara and Thomas consoled themselves by encouraging each other to stay positive and focus on the future, believing that when the timing was right, a baby would come to them again.

Three months later, they got the good news they were hoping for. This time, Cara was very careful with herself and followed every single bit of advice and instruction from her doctor. Sadly, the baby went away just a few weeks into her pregnancy, and Cara was once again deprived of the blissful anticipation of becoming a mother.

The second miscarriage was a shocking blow to them both, and it hit Cara hard. She was very upset that the doctor could neither prevent it from happening nor tell her exactly why she had lost yet another baby. She was very angry too, not only with the doctor, but also with herself. To tune out her grief and her anger, Cara buried herself in work. Nevertheless, it was not enough to stop her from coming to the conclusion that she had failed the two little lives that had started but had also ended prematurely within her, and she caught herself questioning how she could possibly have what it takes to be a good mother when she couldn't even bring her babies into the world alive.

Luckily for Cara, Thomas was always there for her, restoring her confidence in herself and reassuring her that their baby would come to them when it was ready—they just needed to be patient. It took Cara a long time to overcome her anger and move on from her guilt, but eventually, she made peace with reality and embraced their childless life as it was.

Five months later, Cara was pregnant once more. To ensure the baby would grow safely inside her womb this time, she decided to quit her job so she could avoid unnecessary stress and minimize any potential risks to the health of the fetus. Thomas was very surprised at Cara's decision because he knew how much she loved her job, but he also knew how important it was for Cara to make sure her pregnancy would go as smoothly as possible this time, so he told Cara he supported her choice.

Cara sent in her resignation and stopped going to work the very next day. However, now that her mind was no longer occupied by deadlines and schedules, she was left alone with the shadow that had been lurking in the back of her head, haunting every thought she had and every decision she was about to make. At first, Cara tried to ignore it as best as she could. But as the days went by, the shadow only grew bigger and darker, casting an ominous gloom over everything that was going through her mind, until she had no choice but to admit to herself that, deep down, she was not only worried but also afraid. She was afraid that the fragile hope she was carrying inside her was only given to her to be taken away later.

To kill time as well as to keep the looming shadow at bay, Cara spent most of her days at home reading or reminiscing about the happy memories from her younger days. She thought of her time with Nina and Susan a lot, and she especially missed the years when they were living together in the same apartment. One of her fondest memories was how she and Susan used to act like goofy children deliberately in front of Nina just so they could snicker at the slightly annoyed yet resigned look that would consequently appear on Nina's face. Cara had often wondered whether her own kids would make her want to adopt that same expression when she became a mother. But now, haunted by the inescapable shadow in her head, she couldn't help but fear that day might never come.

While Cara was trying to secure her pregnancy by living each day slowly and carefully, Susan was busy juggling her roles as a wife, a mother of two young children, and a full-time physician at a private practice. In spite of her overwhelming schedule, she made sure to call Cara at least once a day. And although their conversation was usually cut short either due to Susan's duties at work or her responsibilities at home, it had become a comforting ritual that Cara looked forward to every day.

Cara wished Nina would call more often too, but she was still traveling constantly for the project she was working on, so she still only got in touch with Cara and Susan once in a while. Cara was always greatly elated when Nina called, but more often than not, she found herself brushing over the upsetting events that had happened in her life and only focusing on the uplifting things and the good news to share with Nina. However, even though Nina never tried to push her to say more about her miscarriages or her fear about losing another pregnancy, Cara couldn't help sensing from the meaningful silence at the other end of the phone that Nina knew she was only pretending to be okay.

Finally, after what felt like a lifetime of living with her heart in her throat, Cara made it to the end of her first trimester without any major issues. As the bump in her belly began to show more noticeably day by day, the fragile hope and faith that Cara had been anxiously holding on to also began to grow. By the middle of her second trimester, Cara felt as if a perpetual overcast in the sky had finally lifted and she could finally stand and breathe normally again. When the doctor asked at her next ultrasound if she and Thomas would like to know whether they were having a boy or a girl, they did not hesitate. It had been an excruciatingly long five months for them both, and neither of them could bear to wait any longer.

It was a girl, a precious baby girl. Cara had felt the baby's kicks through her belly, heard the baby's insanely fast heartbeats on the fetal Doppler, and seen the baby's profile on the ultrasound screen, yet knowing that she was carrying a daughter of her own somehow made the dreamlike state of being a mother-to-be so much more tangible to the mind and, therefore, seemed to have brought the hope and faith that she had been carefully guarding within herself so much closer to reality. As she gazed at the black-and-white image of their baby girl on the ultrasound screen and allowed the news to fully sink in, Cara suddenly burst into tears of joy and happiness. Thomas brought her into his arms and hugged her tightly, sniffling. Cara knew then that she no longer needed to be afraid of the shadow in her head. After all, she was already a mother. Her mind and her body were no longer hers alone. She had been transformed into an existence that was manifested as a result of her love for her unborn daughter. And the entirety of her, body, mind, and soul, would be powered solely by that love from that day onward as she had finally perceived and understood her purpose.

As soon as they got back from the hospital, Cara sent an email to Nina to tell her she was going to be the mother of a baby girl and ask for her suggestion on a perfect name for her daughter. She then called Susan up and announced the news in a half-crying, half-laughing squeal. Susan squealed back just as hysterically, saying that she always had a feeling it was going to be a girl, and that she had even told Nina so the last time they talked on the phone.

A few days later, Cara received a call from an unknown caller ID. It was Nina, calling to tell Cara to name her daughter *Mira*. According to her, it was the name of a forgotten ancient goddess who had brought light and fire to the world. Although Cara did not care much about naming her daughter after some goddess, she felt a strong connection to the name right away, not only because it reminded her of the word *miracle*, which perfectly described and conveyed the level of amazement and wonder she had been feeling toward the little human being living and growing inside her, but also because the sound of it reminded her a lot of Nina's name. Cara told the name to Thomas, and Thomas fell in love with it too. So from then on, they began to refer to their baby daughter as baby Mira. Cara even learned to embroider baby Mira's name and stitched it on all the baby clothes and bibs she had prepared for her, including the little princess dress that she had carefully picked out for baby Mira's big homecoming day.

For reasons that Cara couldn't even explain to herself, she had not mentioned a single word about her miscarriages or her pregnancy to her parents. Just as she started to entertain the thought of finally sharing the good news with them, she received a call from her father, who rarely called her up voluntarily just to catch up with her. Without any gentle opening to ease Cara into what he was going to say, he told her that her mother had passed away from a stroke and the funeral would take place in his town the following day.

There was no emotion in his voice, and he had finished what he needed to say even before Cara had recovered from the initial shock of receiving a call from him. He then added quickly, as a clarification perhaps, that Cara did not need to attend the funeral if she didn't want to, but she would need to go to his house to clean out her mother's things because he did not plan on keeping any.

Half shocked and half in denial, Cara boarded a plane with Thomas that evening and landed at the nearest airport to her father's town five hours later. They then rented a car and drove for another two hours before they finally reached Skygate, a gloomy backwater that was every bit as dreadful as Cara had imagined it to be—especially the funeral home.

Apart from Thomas, Cara, and her father, only a few people showed up for the funeral. The ceremony ended quickly and, to Cara, painlessly. As she stood numbly next to that freshly dug hole in the ground and watched her mother's casket being lowered into it, she felt as if she were watching the funeral of a stranger in someone else's life through someone else's eyes. When the cemetery crew began to shovel the loose dirt back into the hole, the other mourners, all dressed in black and scattered around her mother's grave like oversize crows, dabbed at their eyes solemnly and quietly before coming to Cara and her father one by one to offer their cookie-cutter words of condolences. Cara didn't shed a single tear that day; neither did her father.

After the funeral, Thomas insisted on staying in Skygate with Cara to help her sort out the things her mother had left behind in her father's house. Cara's father did not offer to help, nor did he say anything about Cara's protruding belly. He spent most of his time sitting outside on the back deck, staring blankly at the woods behind the house. It was a beautiful time in the spring. The air was still cool, and the leaves were still sprouting, but the crows had already returned. There were a lot of them. They scattered around the backyard and watched the old man on the back deck solemnly and quietly, like the mourners that had scattered around her mother's grave at the funeral. When Cara noticed their ominous presence, she couldn't help remembering how those pitch-black eyes and pitch-black wings had shown up at her wedding ceremony and, when she and Thomas had returned from their honeymoon, were also there, waiting for them at their house. Worse still, she couldn't help remembering what the guests at her wedding had whispered to each other about the crows and the misfortune that she was destined for. And even though Cara had tried her hardest to persuade herself to believe it had nothing to do with either her miscarriages or her mother's death, she couldn't shake the eerie feeling that those crows in the backyard were the same ones from her wedding ceremony and also the same ones from home.

Four days later, Cara found her father breathless and pulseless in his usual spot on the back deck, facing the woods. She had not noticed his death until the end of the day, when she went out to tell him it was dinnertime. She didn't know how or when it had happened. All she knew was that he had passed away quietly sometime during the day, and no one was there to witness how he had drawn his last breath—no one but the crows.

After his body was taken away to the funeral home, the staff there gave Cara the contact number of a local lawyer and told her that her father had instructed them to do so when he prepaid for his funeral. Cara did not know why her father had prepaid for his own funeral, nor did she understand why he had asked the funeral home to pass the lawyer's number along to her when he could have simply told her himself, but she called the lawyer as she was told. She then learned from the lawyer that her father had suffered from cancer on and off for many years, and he had chosen to stop all his treatments and medications after moving to Skygate. By the time that her mother had moved in with him, the cancer cells had spread to his brain, which was, as Cara was informed by the coroner later, unsurprisingly, the actual cause of his death.

Rather than providing a ceremonial closure to a practically nonexistent father-daughter relationship, the truth made Cara furious. After she had hung up the phone, Cara stormed out onto the back deck. Then, still shaking uncontrollably from the anger burning inside her, she let out a long, guttural scream at the patio chair that her father had passed away in. She had finally let loose her resentment toward him, yet he was not there to hear it, and she hated him for it. She also hated him for the constant fights he had picked with her mother, for having driven his own wife into someone else's arms, and for the divorce that had not only torn up her home but also her childhood. She hated him for having chosen to stop fighting his cancer cells like a coward, for letting her mother back into his life only when he knew he would soon face the judgment of Death in this dreary backwater town but didn't have the courage to do it alone, and she was certain the stroke that took her mother's life had something to do with him. She hated him for his lukewarm attitude toward her, as if she were nothing more than a mere acquaintance, even after her mother's death. She hated him for his lack of interest, both in her as his daughter and the bump in her belly as his granddaughter. But above all, she found herself hating him for not telling her about his cancer, as if she could have done anything to change any of it.

The lawyer came with her father's will later that day, which, Cara was told, was made not long after he had moved to Skygate. To her surprise, he had left everything to her, including the house in Skygate. By the time the lawyer had left, so had the anger and resentment that Cara had been feeling toward her father. She had come to the realization that she did not need to be angry or resentful toward him because he had not left her a reason to be: apart from his properties and his personal belongings, he didn't leave behind any letter or message to his daughter, not even a few words.

Two days later, Cara went back to the gloomy funeral home with Thomas and buried her father next to her mother. A misty rain had been drizzling nonstop that day, and everything in the cemetery was cold and wet and miserable. When her father's casket was lowered into that damp hole in the ground, Cara thought she would feel the same kind of numbness she had felt at her mother's funeral, but instead, she felt an excruciating pain in her heart, as if it were being torn away from her veins like an apple being yanked away from the tree it had been growing on its entire life. Cara knew then that she had, finally, been truly and irrevocably severed from her past. But rather than the sense of liberation and freedom that she had once thought she would benefit from, she felt helplessly small and lost. And even though Thomas was there to wrap her in his arms to comfort her and keep her warm, Cara's eyes still became blurred with tears, reducing her field of vision to only the gray headstones on her parents' graves and the few mourners that had shown up in all black despite the bleak weather—including the crows that had been watching silently in the back.

The next day, Cara woke up with a cold. She only had a mild sore throat and a runny nose at first, so she thought she was just feeling a bit under the weather from having stood in the cold rain the day before. But since she couldn't wait to get back to her life in Seattle with Thomas and leave Skygate for good, she got out of bed to clean out the rest of her parents' things anyway. Even though her father had left the house to her, she did not intend to keep it. She wanted to clean it out, put it on the market, and get rid of it, the sooner the better. She and Thomas could then use the money toward a bigger house in Seattle for their future family of three, which, Cara had decided during her stay at her father's overly secluded house, should also have a big, private backyard for them to create lots of wonderful family memories in as they watched baby Mira grow.

But Cara's cold only got worse the next day, and on the third day, she woke up with a bad fever. While her body was fighting fiercely to defend itself, something terrible happened inside her womb: baby Mira's little body had stopped moving, and her little heart had stopped beating.

There was no hospital in Skygate, so Cara and Thomas rushed into a local doctor's office for help. After a quick examination, the doctor shook his head and told them it was too late, and that he was sorry there was nothing he could do to bring baby Mira back to life.

Cara refused to believe it was true. She rushed back into the car with Thomas and drove for an hour to the nearest hospital on the map, only to be told the same thing and that it was recommended for her to have an induced labor to give birth to their stillborn daughter soon.

But Cara could not bring herself to believe it was true. She fell to her knees and begged the doctor to cut her open right away so that he could take baby Mira out from her womb to resuscitate her. The doctor tried to explain why it would not help change the situation, but Cara would not listen. She begged and cried and begged some more. She even offered her life in exchange for baby Mira's. Yet the doctor just repeated, again and again, that he was very sorry for her loss and avoided her eyes.

That night, Cara cried herself to sleep in Thomas's arms. The next day, she was induced at the hospital and gave birth to baby Mira.

Cara had fantasized, millions of times, about that magical moment when she finally got to meet baby Mira for the first time. And now, that moment was actually here—four weeks too early. Baby Mira was so small, so fragile, so quiet, and so still. Her skin felt so tender and soft against Cara's, yet it was so cold at the same time that it made Cara's chest and arms burn like flesh under hot iron. Cara felt her heart withering then, along with everything else that was inside her. She had lost her baby once again. Hope had landed in her hands, three times, just to slip through her fingers like sand. The guests at her wedding were right. She was destined for misfortune. There was no hope for her; she had lost it, and now, hope would never come to her again—the doctor had given them the verdict. Cara felt as though she were drowning slowly in a cold, stagnant lake in a very bad dream: she didn't know how or why it had happened; she only knew her whole world had turned gray and she couldn't recall the purpose of her existence. But Cara had neither the strength nor the will to fight the pull of the water. To her, there was no point in trying anything anymore. She didn't want to talk to anyone or do anything, yet she couldn't stop crying.

After Cara was discharged from the hospital, they returned to Skygate and went back to the gloomy funeral home. Baby Mira was tucked inside a pink infant casket, wearing her homecoming princess dress with her name embroidered across the front, looking vulnerable and helpless. The cemetery crew had dug out a small hole for her next to Cara's parents. Unlike the previous two funerals, this time, Cara and Thomas were the only participants. It was a beautiful day in late spring, so beautiful that Cara couldn't stop thinking how cruel it was that they had to bury their daughter when everything else was rejoicing in the gift of life.

As the little pink casket was lowered into the ground, Cara was suddenly seized by a suffocating feeling that this had all been a stupid mistake and that baby Mira was actually still alive. Like a mad woman, she broke free from Thomas's restraining arms and screamed at the cemetery crew to pull up the casket immediately. When the cemetery crew stared back at her, frozen in confusion and shock, Cara threw herself to the ground and reached for the casket with her hands. Thomas tried to calm her down, but Cara would not listen. She had to see her baby; she had to check; she had to make sure it was not a stupid mistake and that baby Mira was not just waking up to life.

In the end, Thomas gave in and asked the cemetery crew to pull up the casket. As soon as it was back on the ground, Cara opened it and waited for baby Mira to open her eyes, to look at her with a cute sleepy smile like she had just woken up from a very long nap. Cara waited and waited, but baby Mira's eyes didn't open, and they stayed motionlessly closed.

Tears fell from Cara's swollen eyes like rain, but she smiled at baby Mira and nuzzled her with her lips and cheeks, trying to warm up her cold little face. She pleaded softly next to baby Mira's little ears, urging her to wake up so that she could see her beautiful eyes and her beautiful smile. As Cara repeated her plea to that small, still body, heartbrokenly yet persistently, her voice gradually grew louder and more desperate, and eventually, it turned into a heart-wrenching howl that set off a cacophony of caws from the crows that had been watching them silently from the other lots in the cemetery, as if they were trying to tell Cara that they understood. Cara raised her head from baby Mira's casket to glare at the crows, only to see the three headstones in front of her and be reminded of all the lives that she had lost. It was then Cara finally understood what the crows were trying to tell her: she had lost all of her babies and both of her parents because she was cursed; her life had been marked with the black shadows from their wings, and neither light nor hope could ever reach her again.

But Cara didn't care. She had lost baby Mira. She had lost them all. Nothing mattered to her anymore. Still, she couldn't bear the thought of leaving baby Mira in that hole in the ground. It would be too cold and too dark for her. She would be very lonely and scared in there, not to mention the worms. If she left baby Mira in there, the worms would eventually get her . . . No. It would be too terrifying and too painful for her baby. She could not let that happen—she would not. They were not going to bury her in that hole; she would not allow it. She would not allow anyone to take her baby away from her again—no one.

Gently, Cara scooped baby Mira up from her casket and, as the cemetery crew gaped at her with growing uneasiness and fear, told them to terminate the funeral right then and there. Thomas tried his best to persuade Cara into laying baby Mira to rest as planned, but it was in vain. Cara would not listen to any of his reasoning or pleading, and she insisted on taking baby Mira home.

Meanwhile, Susan had just arrived at their house in Skygate and was waiting for them to come back from the funeral. Cara had been refusing to talk to anyone about losing baby Mira, so Susan had only found out about it from Thomas the day before, when he decided he needed to contact Susan for help. Once Susan had learned about the mental state Cara was in, she knew she needed to go to Skygate right away. So although she was still in the middle of processing the news that Ben had just filed for a divorce from her, she pushed it to the back of her mind and jumped on the next plane she could catch.

Needless to say, Susan was as unprepared to see Cara getting out of the car with baby Mira's body in her arms as Cara was to see Susan waiting for them at the house. Like Thomas, Susan reasoned and pleaded, hoping to persuade Cara into taking baby Mira back to the cemetery to let her rest in peace. Cara ignored both of them equally and stubbornly, but deep down, she knew they were right. She knew she could not keep baby Mira with her forever. But just the thought of parting with her baby once and for all made it too excruciating for her to breathe. In an effort to run away from reality and to avoid the choice that she would have to make, Cara hid. She locked herself in the bedroom with baby Mira's body tucked inside a makeshift crib she had fashioned from a drawer and some linens, away from the inevitable ending that she was neither ready nor willing to face.

Cara kept the bedroom door locked for the next two days, refusing to come out or touch the food tray that was set by the door. To make sure no one could come inside to take baby Mira away, she had locked all the windows and drawn all the curtains as well. Having spent hour after hour crying and crying herself to sleep in that unlit room, Cara eventually lost her sense of time and couldn't remember how long she had been guarding baby Mira's body— which was just as well, considering it had provided her with a calming illusion that time had stopped for her to stay with baby Mira in that room forever.

Just as Susan and Thomas were seriously contemplating breaking into the bedroom without Cara's permission, Susan received a call from Nina, who had finally read all the urgent emails that Susan had sent her after arriving at Skygate. Susan tried to get Cara to open the door to talk to Nina on the phone, but she refused. Not knowing what else she could do, Susan turned on the speaker and slipped her phone into Cara's room from under the door, hoping Nina could somehow persuade Cara to come out on her own.

Instead of reaching for the phone, Cara stayed beside baby Mira's makeshift crib and didn't say anything. But the moment she heard Nina's familiar voice over the speaker, she was suddenly very aware of the fragility of the self-deceiving illusion that she had locked herself in, which in turn reminded her acutely that, unlike baby Mira and the rest of them, she was still painfully and unbearably alive. Like a thunderstorm that was long overdue, Cara lashed out at the phone in a state of complete emotional breakdown. She cried to Nina that life was a scam and hope was nothing but an illusion. She told her that there was no point in living because death was inevitable and their precious lives were nothing more than mere specks of dust in the face of Death. She then told Nina that she was done; she wanted to be wiped off as a speck of dust so she could at least be relieved from the pain and the misery she had to endure in this hopeless lie that was called life.

Nina had stayed quiet the whole time Cara was rambling on in tears and in despair. When she was finally too tired to make another sound, Nina broke her silence and reminded Cara that she had not lost everyone yet; she still had Susan and Thomas. This, however, only sent Cara into another crying spell. Sobbing breathlessly, she confessed to Nina that even though she knew she was loved and cared about deeply by them, she was not grateful to be alive.

Nina fell silent for a while. Then, in a gentle yet meaningful tone, she told Cara that it was her fault . . .

Susan didn't know how Nina had managed to persuade Cara in the end—her voice was too soft for Susan to hear through the door. But after the call, Cara unlocked the door and let them take baby Mira's body back to the funeral home.

At the request of Cara, baby Mira was cremated and, finally, laid to rest the next day. After the funeral, Susan was called back to Chicago to deal with her divorce. Instead of putting the house on the market and returning to Seattle with Thomas like she had planned after her father's funeral, Cara spent the following week in bed, not having either the energy or the will to do anything. She did not want to think about the past or the future. It was simply too much and too painful. So she cried to empty her mind, wishing the unwanted memories and thoughts would leave her brain alone for good once they were all drained from her eyes. Cara thought she used to have a purpose before coming to Skygate, but the ironic thing was when she tried to remember what it was so that she could at least have something to hold on to before slipping even further away from herself, she realized there had never really been any for her except to become the mother she had wished to have. Cara felt as though she were once again drowning slowly in a cold, stagnant lake in a very bad dream, and this time, she couldn't even remember which way the surface was. But it was useless and pointless to fight it anyway, so she just gave in completely and let that never-ending dark, cold void swallow her mind. From time to time, Cara would wonder mindlessly to herself if that was how being dead would feel like and whether that was all there was for baby Mira and the others —till the end of time.

Cara thought she would never see the surface again, just like they would never again see the light. Then one morning, Thomas went to shoo away the noisy birds that had been camping around the house since dawn, and he came back with not only Susan but also an unimaginable surprise in his arms: a baby—a living, breathing baby with a full head of fiery red curls, frowning in her sleep. There was even a birth certificate for the baby; Mira Murphy was her name, and, according to her birth certificate, Cara and Thomas were her mother and father.

And just like that, in the most unthinkable fashion, without either a proper goodbye or any explanation, Nina had gifted them her baby to raise as their own.

V

"And that was the truth," said Cara, her voice trembling along with her lips. "The whole truth."

Mira was still holding the picture frame. She lowered her eyes and noticed her own reflection on the glazing, which was almost identical to the image of the third girl in the photo, who also had a pair of piercing black eyes and a full head of fiery red curls.

"Why did she do it?" she asked quietly, as though it was a question to herself.

Cara shook her head. "I wish I could tell you. But apart from the birth certificate and her copy of the same photo, she only left a poem ... The whole thing was a big shock to us. As far as we know, she had never dated anyone, and she had not mentioned a word about becoming a mother herself. All we know is that she had talked to both Thomas and Susan the day before, but she had told neither of them about her plan. Thomas told me all she said to him was that she and Susan would come to visit me the next day. Susan told me she had called her up in a grave voice and told her to arrive at our house first thing in the morning to help me move on and that she would get there early too. But that was all she had said to them. After that, none of us have heard anything from her again, no matter how many emails we've sent and how much we've pleaded with her to come back ..."

"Why do you think she did it, then?" Mira asked slowly as she shifted her gaze from the third girl in the photo back to her own reflection.

There was a faint whimpering noise from Cara's throat, then she drew a shallow, shaky breath and turned to Mira, her eyes wide with confliction. "Oh, my Little Bird ... I didn't mean to make it sound like that. Please don't think of her in a bad way ... I know this is a lot to process, but Nina didn't choose to abandon you; I'm sure of it. I don't think she gave you to us because she didn't love you or want you or anything like that; I think she gave you to us because—because she wanted to keep you safe."

"Keep me safe?" Mira glanced up at Cara from the corner of her eye. "From what?"

"I don't know," Cara answered honestly. "But I have a feeling it had something to do with her job. She never wanted to talk about it, you know. Whenever we asked her to tell us about the project that had been keeping her so busy for so long, she always replied with some vague, general answers, then changed the subject to something else. So we didn't know, and we still don't know for sure, what she was working on or, for that matter, who she was working for. And since she was always traveling to different countries, she had stopped using her old phone number, so the only way we could contact her was through emails. She had never replied our emails, nor had she written any to us, but she would give us a call from time to time, and when she did, her number was always displayed as 'unknown caller ID.' We used to think it was because she was calling from a different country, but now ..." Cara stole a glance at Mira, then she bit her lip and continued. "Susan and I both think it was because she was calling from a government facility. We think she was working on some highly classified project for the government, and we think ... she was in danger ..." Cara lowered her head pensively, but she soon gave it a shake and returned her attention to Mira. "If that was indeed the case, of course she would want to consider every possible option to keep you safe. So she decided to hide you under a new identity: Mira Murphy ... I've always wondered how she got hold of a birth certificate for you as our daughter. But if she had the right position and the right clearance level in the government, it wouldn't have been too hard for her, I suppose." Cara smiled wryly to herself, trying to hold back the tears circling in her eyes. "And, in doing so, she saved me as well. She knew how much I wanted to become a mother. She knew I had lost my purpose to live . . . So she chose to bring me back to life by granting me my one and only wish . . ."

Cara sniffled hard and wiped away her tears, then she looked at Mira with an affectionate yet melancholy smile. "And you, Little Bird . . . You brought me the reason to start living again. Yes, you did not come from me and had never been a part of me, but even before I got to hold you in my arms for the first time, I already knew I loved you and would love you, always, with my heart and my soul—the same way I had loved and would always love Nina . . . You'd have loved her too, Little Bird. You two are so much alike. Not just the way you look, but the way you speak, the way you think . . . so much so that sometimes I feel like she never really left and is still watching me and talking to me through you . . . I miss her, Mira. It's hard not to miss her. She was like the air in my lungs and the blood in my veins. Without her, I feel empty and strange . . . I wish I knew what was going on in her life. I wish I wasn't so blinded by my own despair and pain, then maybe I could have sensed something before it was too late. I wish she had talked to me about what she was dealing with and asked for my help. I wish she knew I would do anything in my power to protect her and to help her . . . I wish she had told me why. I wish she had said goodbye. I wish—I wish she didn't have to do this . . ." Cara choked up then and broke down in tears.

Mira didn't try to comfort her. She sat quietly next to Cara and let her cry.

"I'm sorry," said Cara between broken sobs as she struggled to keep her face dry from her tears. "I shouldn't be crying in front of you. I really don't want you to see me like this."

"It's okay," said Mira. Then, as if a part of her thought it was not enough, she added casually, "I won't tell anyone. Just don't drown the both of us with your tears."

Cara's breathless sobs were interrupted by a breathy chuckle. With an embarrassed but relieved smile, she dried her eyes and turned to Mira. "I'm so glad you came home, Little Bird."

"I know."

"Do you think—Do you think you'd stay? . . . For dinner, at least?"

"I think so."

Cara cupped her hands over her mouth quickly to prevent herself from choking up with joy.

"I'd better start cooking, then," she said, getting to her feet. Her hazel eyes, though still puffy and red, were sparkling with happiness and anticipation. "You wanna come with me and hang out with Dad while I cook?"

"Not yet," Mira replied as she gazed down at the picture frame in her hands. "Can I stay here for a bit?"

"Oh, sure. Of course." Cara nodded earnestly but didn't move her legs. She stared down at her feet for a while, then, with a hint of hesitation in her voice, she said, "Her poem is in the back of that picture frame . . . if you want to read it. I'm gonna go cook now. I'll call you when dinner is ready."

Quietly, Cara left the room and closed the door behind her. Not knowing what to expect, Mira turned the picture frame around slowly and removed the backing. She found a folded piece of yellow notepad paper underneath it. Judging by its flatness and its crisp creases, it had been tucked away inside that picture frame for a very long time.

She took it out and unfolded it. There was a handwritten poem on it, but there was no title or signature. With an almost dreamlike sensation that could only be described as déjà vu, she read the poem. By the time she had finished, she knew she had written it herself.

She was neither shocked nor surprised, however. After all, she knew the answer—she had known it all along. She folded the notepad paper back up and returned it to its old spot inside the picture frame, then she got up and walked to the windows. Red was already there, waiting for her on the other side of the windowsill, perching on the ledge.

"Is it true?" she asked in her head. "Did I abandon my identity and duties to be reborn as a human infant to save her?"

Red flapped its wings, cocked its head to one side, and looked at her with its beady black eyes. Then, in the voice of the bearded old man who had introduced himself as Black in her dream, it answered in her head.

You wrote that poem, didn't you?

She stood motionlessly in front of the red bird and didn't reply.

It's not my place to tell you whether you did it to save her, Black's voice continued in her head. *All I can say is that as long as your conduits are alive and multiplying, your duties have not been entirely abandoned.*

"The story you told me in my dream—'The Story of Her Brightest Soul.' Was it about Cara? Was she the brightest *soul*?"

Red cocked its head to the other side. *It was.*

"You mentioned there was a second part to that story." She caught the image of the framed photo appearing in her mind. "Do you still need to tell me about it?"

That won't be necessary. She had told you enough, only she doesn't know that your decision was strongly opposed by the other three Keepers of this universe. We tried to persuade you out of it, but your mind was made up. In the end, we had no choice but to agree to ferry your infant form, the most helpless human form and the most vulnerable one to take on, to the Murphys' back deck and to watch over you till it was time for you to resume your role. And now the time has come.

"How do you know it's time?"

Because your powers have exposed you, Vermilion. In spite of all the social and technological advancements that have taken place in the human world since their last attempt to hunt us down, none of it has evolved past the human nature. They simply can't resist the temptation of the possibility of wielding our powers as their own. So now, once again, they are coming for us.

Just then, Red suddenly took off from the ledge and shot toward the woods like an arrow. As it disappeared among the trees, she heard Black speaking hastily in her head.

Time to go, Vermilion. We shall meet again—soon.

There was a gentle knock on the door, followed by a hesitant voice: "Mira? . . . Dinner's ready. Come join us when you can."

It was Cara's voice. She turned her head to the door and called over her shoulder, "I'll be there in a minute."

Still holding on to Black's presence in her head, she returned her gaze to the woods. As she finally gave in and acknowledged the hollowing pain that had been throbbing inside her left chest, she asked, "Black, is Cara still the brightest *soul*?"

This time, Black didn't answer, and his presence had dissipated from her mind's eye like smoke.

She sighed softly to herself, but she tore her gaze away from the woods and went to the door. As soon as she opened it, she saw Cara; she was waiting for her on the other side of the doorway, smiling anxiously.

And for the first time in this human life, she saw a *soul*, its *light* flickering wearily and rhythmically with every breath that Cara drew.

Chapter 11　THE WHITE TIGER

1

W ITH a thump of his tail, he steered the wooden raft forward high above the River of Time. He was sitting on all fours at the side of the raft, his chin resting on his front paws. He was examining and collecting the *time* of every living thing in the River. He needed to make sure *the flow* of the individual *time* from all living things would, collectively, form an even line at the tail of the River to create an ever-present *present* as it pushed steadily forward and away from the head of the River at a speed that was on a par with *the rhythm* of the Wheel of Life, thus weaving *present* into *past* as new *present* was formed, constantly and continuously.

The River of Time was long and wide. It was his duty to identify and neutralize ripples and disturbances, for they could distort *the flow* of the River, thereby disrupting *the rhythm* of the Wheel of Life, which had been spinning in *the flow* at *present* since the beginning of *time*.

He had been tending to the River for as long as it had flowed, crossing the tail side of it from high above over and over to examine *present*, for any abnormality that was serious enough to cause ripples or disturbances in *the flow* would first distort the even line at *present* before being woven—as *present* became *past*—into the River as ripples or disturbances.

There was no day or night there, nor month, nor year. In fact, except for him and the wooden raft, there was nothing else there at the River of Time and the Wheel of Life—as it had always been since *time* had flowed into this universe.

As a new *present* was formed, he noticed a small abnormality in *the flow*, bulging up from the surface of the River like a wrinkled pimple. To examine the cause, he steered the wooden raft down toward the River until it was hovering right above the abnormality. There, he identified the source of the problem: the individual *time* of thousands of living things in the vicinity of a specific physical space was advancing at a rate that had greatly exceeded *the flow* of the River. Without timely intervention and correction, those living things would die much sooner than the actual *time* that they were given to live in *the flow* of the River.

He had caught countless abnormalities like this one before— some were bigger, some were smaller. Most of the abnormalities were caused by wars, massacres, mass suicides, famines, or pandemics; but there were also many that were caused by either the Soulless or the invisible version of them, which the Soulless had created themselves. Ever since Vermilion had taught the villagers in China how to keep the Soulless away on Lunar New Year's Eve, it had become increasingly rare to have abnormalities that were in fact contributed by the Soulless. Still, he decided he needed to go and check for signs of the Soulless, invisible version or not, in that abnormality. After all, in order to safeguard *the balance* of the Scale, the Four Keepers must eliminate the remainder of the Soulless from the living world. Although Vermilion was the one who could, when she was at her full power, keep the Soulless at bay, he was the one who had the powers to eliminate them from the living world.

He got up and leaped from the wooden raft. His body, shrinking drastically in size as he leaped, would eventually become so small that he could enter the *present* of the individual *time* of any one of those living things through the abnormality that was bulging up from the surface of the River into a ripple.

He hoped Vermilion would wake up soon. He could identify the Soulless easily because they had no *time*, but he could not perceive their invisible counterparts. If this turned out to be the work of the invisible version of the Soulless, he would need Vermilion's help to locate them before he could eliminate them for good. As for now, only one thing was for certain: he would enter the *present* of those living things, and he would enter their physical space in the living world as well.

11

In an area that was technically nonexistent on the face of the Earth, on the far side of a technically nonexistent structure that was known only to a select few as the Pandora's Box, another box-shaped structure had been erected on that same vast, barren land. Considering the extremely short window of time they had to complete its construction before Capture Day, its existence should have been impossible, but then again, nothing is impossible when one has the mind to achieve it.

This new box-shaped structure was not nearly as big as the Pandora's Box, nor was it equipped with the solar-powered camouflage technology that had been shielding the Pandora's Box from the detection of any human eye. What it did have was a much more intricately designed interior, which was guarded by an army of Hermes, the beautifully crafted life-size male statues that were in fact designed to serve at the Pandora's Box as both robotic assistants and security guards.

Stationed inside the box-shaped structure in standby mode, the Hermes had positioned themselves alongside all four sides of its walls like bars on a cage. It was more than for security purposes, however: inside this box-shaped structure, there was actually another box-shaped structure, which not only touched the ceiling but also took up almost all the space that was inside, leaving little room for the Hermes to spread out. Unlike its outer shell, the inner box-shaped structure had walls with large shatterproof windows in the middle, revealing yet another box-shaped structure within itself—like stacking dolls. The top of the innermost box-shaped structure was connected to the ceiling through a serious layer of high-tech equipment, and, instead of walls, it was built with bulletproof and soundproof glass on all four sides, which was also made to with-stand the most extreme changes in pressure and temperature on Earth. Moreover, a new technology was used to treat the glass to make it appear as opaque as any regular wall from the inside, where thousands of farm animals had been transported into a few hours ago. Currently, the said farm animals were crammed together in-side that box-shaped structure, completely oblivious to the count-down that had just begun on the other side of the glass, making their farm animal noises that were inaudible to anyone but them-selves, doing their farm animal things that were of little concern to the outside world.

The space between the two inner box-shaped structures was mainly occupied by screens, computers, consoles, and cameras. Besides the team of Hermes patrolling silently in the back on each side, six Pathfinders were stationed behind the bulletproof and soundproof glass, running the last few tests on their screens with the help of Hope, the artificial intelligence of the supercom-puter built into the heart of the Pandora's Box. Hope had already started the final countdown to Capture Day, which was also the final countdown to the commencement of the capture plan for the White Key. Success or not, apart from the Hermes, these six Pathfinders would be the sole eyewitnesses to its outcome.

Thanks to the soundproof glass around the farm animals, the air in their working area had remained heavy and tense. Among all the Pathfinders that had worked tirelessly on the preparations of this capture plan, these six had been selected specifically to execute it. They were all firm believers in the existence of the White Key, and they all had strong faith in the capture plan itself. But even as the countdown continued to flash on the primary screen display, they still didn't know for certain what they should expect to see that night.

"Five minutes to Capture Day." Hope's all too human voice came on the speakers and broke the suffocating silence. "All sys-tems exiting standby mode. Prepare to launch the program."

"Hope, will Dr. G join the live feed?" asked a black-haired woman in a long lab coat, the lead Pathfinder for the White Key and its capture plan.

"Yes, Dr. Ying. Dr. G will join us as soon as the White Key shows itself."

"Thank you," said Dr. Ying mechanically as she stared vacantly ahead, where the innermost box-shaped structure stood in front of her like a giant glass container filled with a hodgepodge of barnyard disarray.

Dr. Yang, the deputy lead Pathfinder, as well as Dr. Ying's husband in real life, was sitting next to her. He leaned in and whispered to Dr. Ying in Mandarin, "What's wrong?"

Still staring into space, Dr. Ying replied quietly, as though she was whispering in a trance, "Can it really be this simple? .... Can we really catch it like this?"

"If the information on its weaknesses is as truthful and reliable as the stone tablet has led us to believe, then in theory, yes, this is how we can catch it; we just don't know if it'll show up for it." Dr. Yang paused for a while, then he continued in a softer tone. "But we won't know the answer until we try, right? None of us know if we'd succeed the very first time anyway, not even Gargoyle. Otherwise he'd have stayed to join us instead. So don't put too much pressure on yourself about the outcome tonight."

"Three minutes to Capture Day," Hope announced. "All systems go."

Dr. Ying didn't seem to hear it, however. Instead of returning her attention to the screens to get ready for the launch, she murmured in a wishful undertone, "I hope it's too busy to come here tonight."

Dr. Yang jerked his head toward her in surprise, but he managed to keep his voice down. "What?"

"I do want to see it through one day," said Dr. Ying, lowering her eyes as the dullness in them was replaced by confliction. "After all, we were very fortunate to be selected, to be a part of all this . . . It's the highlight of our career, our dream . . . the opportunity to do something truly wonderful and good for the future of all mankind!

But lately . . . Maybe it's because of all the new things we've come to learn from the micro-inscriptions about the White Key, but I can't help thinking: If the length of our time in this world is indeed predetermined at birth, then how much time do we still have left? And in the limited amount of time that we have left, how much more are we squeezing out from our real life into work? When will it be too late for us to start making up for the things we should have been doing in our own family? With our own child?"

Feeling the weight of her words on his mind, Dr. Yang's head drooped from his shoulders.

"I can't remember the last time we were home to celebrate Lunar New Year with her . . . It must have been before we were selected," Dr. Ying said wistfully. "We've been so focused on finding the White Key that we've forgotten what Lunar New Year means in real life . . ."

"One minute to Capture Day," said Hope, then she began counting down aloud: "Fifty seconds . . . Forty seconds . . ."

Dr. Yang leaned over and whispered in Dr. Ying's ear, "Maybe it *will* be too busy to come here tonight. Then we can leave early in the morning and still make it home in time to celebrate the first day of Lunar New Year together as a family."

". . . Twenty seconds . . ."

Dr. Ying didn't look at her husband, but she smiled. Then she took a long, deep breath through both her nose and her mouth.

"Ten, nine, eight . . ."

Holding their breath, all six Pathfinders were now staring anxiously ahead at the farm animals that were crammed inside the giant glass box.

". . . four, three, two . . ."

Quickly, Dr. Ying reached out and found Dr. Yang's hand, and they interlocked their fingers.

"One. Zero. Commencing capture plan for the White Key. Launch program. Executing Stage One."

III

Inside the giant glass box, a young pig with spots had just forced its way to a corner, where, to its surprise and delight, it came upon a small amount of trampled hay that had been stowed safely away from the others. The young pig squealed in joy, then it wedged its snout into that unaccommodating space to get at the few more bites it was determined to retrieve, sucking frenetically with its tongue as it struggled to avoid flattening its nose onto the walls and cutting off the airflow into its nostrils. The young pig hoped the humans would give them more food soon. They had littered the floor with food when they moved them into this new barn, but now it was all gone. The young pig didn't know how long they had been kept inside the new barn. All it knew was that its neck still hurt from the shot it had received from the humans before the move, and it was still hungry.

Just as the young pig was about to give up in frustration, it heard a strange noise coming from the walls. The young pig had never heard a noise like that in its short life. It sounded like weeping wind from the depths of the earth, brushing past nameless tombstones and unmarked graves as its invisible fingernails were dragged across everything it swept by, leaving blood-filled scratch marks along the way and all the way into the barn, to where the young pig was standing. Frightened and alarmed, the young pig jerked away from the corner, only to realize there was nowhere to go: the barn was jam-packed with farm animals, each as frightened and alarmed as itself, and right now, every one of them was pushing and shoving frantically to be away from the walls, yet none of them were actually succeeding. The young pig whined in panic, cursing its bad luck for having ended up at the edge of the huddle while praying desperately for the strange noise to stop tormenting its tiny brain.

Unfortunately, its prayer was not answered. The strange noise not only continued but also intensified in both volume and frequency. The young pig, like all the other farm animals in the barn, began to cry and wail in terror—a feeling that was quite new and unfamiliar to the young pig but was able to make it forget about food and hunger for good. Up till then, the young pig had only heard about such a feeling from the tales back on the farm, in which, so-and-so got too lazy or too slow or too sick or too old and was then hauled away to that big, noisy building on the far end of the farm, never to be seen again. The older residents on the farm liked to call that big, noisy building *the house of no return*. The young pig could not see itself, but it was certain it was wearing the same kind of expression the older residents on the farm had worn when they told those tales to the younglings to warn them about all the horrible things that were going on in *the house of no return*. For a brief moment, the young pig wondered to itself whether *the house of no return* could make it feel even worse than what it was feeling now. But then it couldn't help but wonder whether it was already inside one.

The young pig wailed hopelessly at the thought. It was not ready —not ready for death, not ready to become meat. It was so young; it still had so many more meals that it wanted to eat and so many more things that it wanted to do—it hadn't even gotten around to mate yet!

Suddenly, there was a yelp, a snap, and a ripping and tearing noise, followed by a series of merciless biting and crunching sounds: flesh-shredding, blood-dripping, and bone-crushing sounds. For a few seconds, those were the only sounds one could hear inside the barn. The next thing the young pig knew, all hell broke loose.

The farm animals, now on the verge of a mass hysteria, pushed and shoved wildly but aimlessly against each other, fumbling with their last shred of sanity for the exit that did not exist. Their cries and wails had quickly resumed, only this time, they were getting shriller by the second.

The young pig was knocked from side to side by the commotion like a helpless raft on a stormy sea. Desperate to protect itself, the young pig tried to climb up the wall by standing on its hind legs, only to hear a new sound that was going off from random farm animals in the barn: a muffled popping sound, each following the previous one at a regular interval. Hopeless and terrified, the young pig turned and saw that vivid red flowers were blossoming, one after another across the barn, on the heels of those muffled popping sounds. Strangely, the vivid red flowers were all blossoming from the necks of the farm animals who had made those muffled popping sounds . . .

Before the young pig could understand what was happening, however, it received a kick in its side and was knocked back into the corner, where it had come upon its last few bites of food with joy not so long ago but was now pinned to the walls on its back by the rump of an old cow. The young pig whimpered at the pain, which was spreading from the hoofprint that was left on its tender side. But soon, all it could think of was the excruciating pain throbbing in its neck, as if something big and mean was about to burst out of it. The young pig tried to cry out for help, but no sound could come out from its throat.

Just then, the young pig heard a muffled popping sound coming from its own neck, where the humans had injected the shot before its move to this new barn. Even though it instantly realized nothing mattered anymore, as its vision dissolved into nothingness, the young pig couldn't help but picture the vivid red flower that was blossoming there.

IV

Outside the giant glass box, the six Pathfinders, with their eyes glued to the inaudible chaos taking place within that exitless space, sat on the edge of their seats in silent anticipation.

"Current stats, Hope?" asked Dr. Ying.

"Time elapsed since capture plan commencement: fifty-six minutes, nine seconds, and counting. Number of stages planned: three. Number of stages executed: three. Stage One, broadcast enhanced sound waves of supernatural elements: duration, twenty minutes; result, failed to attract target. Stage Two, broadcast enhanced recordings of predators hunting and feeding: duration, twenty minutes; result, failed to attract target. Stage Three, simulate fatal attacks by Xi: duration, in progress; number of livestock eliminated, 984 and increasing; number of livestock remaining, 2013 and decreasing. All sensors are in position and remain undisturbed. No sign of the target was observed physically or electronically. Capture sequence is activated and ready to go."

"Adjust elimination interval from one second to three seconds for the next five hundred kills. After that, to five seconds."

"Copy that, Dr. Ying. Elimination interval has been adjusted to three seconds for the next five hundred kills."

The extra two seconds, though insignificant in itself to the farm animals whose necks were programmed to be blown apart by the capsule-shaped explosives that had been injected into their jugular veins prior to Capture Day, were enough to produce a perceptible visual difference to the Pathfinders on the other side of the bullet-proof and soundproof glass.

"Hope, have we passed the ideal capture window?" Dr. Ying asked.

"Not yet. Current time to midnight: three minutes and nineteen seconds. All systems will continue to run beyond the ideal capture window until a termination command is authorized."

"Thank you," Dr. Ying said quietly and returned her attention to the giant glass box in front of her. Even though over a third of the farm animals inside it had already died in vain, as the lead Pathfinder for the White Key and its capture plan, Dr. Ying knew she should not give the termination command until it was truly the end.

"One minute to midnight," Hope announced. "Ideal capture window ending in ... Fifty seconds ... Forty seconds ..."

As she repeated the countdown in her head, Dr. Ying felt the stress and fatigue that had been building up in her mind and body for the past few weeks slowly releasing. Leaning against the back-rest, she let herself relax and sink into her chair. The muscles in her back, now finally relieved from a full day and a full night of nervous tension, were acting up, like the inconsolable tantrums of a child who demanded immediate care and attention. Dr. Ying thought of her daughter then. With a wistful sigh, she gave herself a pained smile.

"... Twenty seconds ..."

Looks like this is not the way to go after all, Dr. Ying said to herself. *But that's okay. We'll just start afresh after Lunar New Year and find another way, another plan ... There are always more things to learn and more work to—What in the world is that?*

Inside the giant glass box, above the mishmash of farm animals that were either alive but frantic or calm but dead, something was sparkling vaguely as it flowed in midair: transparent yet iridescent like a prism, voluminous yet airy like glitter dust riding on the wind.

"Ten, nine, eight ..."

As Dr. Ying followed the almost imperceptible iridescence with her eyes, wondering if she was only seeing things due to stress and fatigue, she was all at once struck by a thought.

"... four, three ..."

"Do you see it, Hope?" Still staring intently at that barely discernible iridescence, Dr. Ying mumbled in a daze; her voice buzzed lamely like a mosquito's, too weak for anyone to hear but herself.

"One. Zero. Ideal capture window ended. Number of sensors triggered: zero. Target has not been sighted ..."

A sudden surge of adrenaline rushed into Dr. Ying's head and made her heart pound like a drum in her chest. Instinctively, she jerked her head toward the microphone and burst out, "Launch the capture sequence!"

"Without confirmed sighting of the target, the execution of capture sequence would—"

"Launch it! Now!" Dr. Ying leaped to her feet and slammed her fist down on the console as if to hit the launch button herself.

"Launching capture sequence," Hope replied calmly. "For the record, please state the reason of your decision in overriding the program, Dr. Ying."

Dr. Ying stared on nervously as the space inside the giant glass box was frozen, silently and instantaneously, by the supercooled water that had flooded the entire thing in a flash, freezing everything in ice—including the ghostly iridescence, which was now trapped in the ice in a distinct shape: the shape of a monstrous beast.

By then, the other Pathfinders had all caught on. One by one, like those who were enchanted by a spell, they rose slowly from their seats and, with their eyes widened with incredulity and their jaws dropped open in awe, staggered forward to stare at the iridescent shape that was now frozen inside the giant glass box.

Dr. Ying did not join them; she was trembling uncontrollably and needed to lean against the console to stay on her feet.

"Do you not see it, Hope?" she said weakly. Her voice, toneless and distant, sounded as if it were whispered from another universe. "It's here. It's in the box ... We've got it. We've got the White Key ..."

V

Gargoyle did not like plane rides. Although they had saved him a lot of time, he would get nauseous as soon as the plane had fought off the grasp of gravity, and, rather than utilizing his time on the plane to focus on more important matters, he would have to focus on keeping the contents inside his stomach in place whenever there was a change in the plane's altitude.

Gargoyle felt the plane dip and clenched his teeth to hold his breath. His stomach tightened and complained with a telltale gurgling noise, sending an unpleasant sour taste up into his mouth. Swallowing hard, Gargoyle closed his eyes and tried to force his attention back to the visual memory of the capture plan, which he had, deliberately, stored in his mind. It was the only way he could have a shot at reviewing everything one last time before landing, for reading on the plane, no matter if it was on paper or computer, would guarantee him a thorough cleanse of his poor stomach.

A Hermes appeared from the crew rest compartment and, gliding down the aisle as steadily as he was cruising through a corridor back at the Pandora's Box, approached his seat. "Dr. G? There's a new message for you."

Gargoyle lifted one eyelid and gave Hermes a weak nod, signaling him to go ahead.

"You don't look so well, Dr. G. Would you like me to take a look? I'm installed with the most up-to-date medical programs to perform health evaluations and treatments on the same level as a professional medical personnel."

Gargoyle grunted a *no*, but a thought soon struck him and caused him to jerk his head up and stare at Hermes in alarm. "But ... how? Your shell was cast in one piece. Your hands and arms ... They can't move!"

"They can when it's necessary, Dr. G. You just haven't had the opportunity to see me use them yet," Hermes replied matter-of-factly.

Gargoyle knew Hermes's voice was generated by a computer, and that was why his tone was as unreadable as ever. Still, he couldn't help but hope it was not true, and if it were—which it probably was, considering the Hermes's role as security at the Pandora's Box —he would never have the opportunity to witness it.

The thought made Gargoyle self-conscious and uneasy. He noticed then that the sour taste in his mouth had somehow been replaced by a stinging dryness that made his throat feel tight and scratchy. Adjusting his collar, Gargoyle cleared his throat and said, "You said there was a message for me?"

"Yes, Dr. G. I've been informed by Hope that Dr. Ying and her team have successfully captured the White Key."

"They did?" Gargoyle jumped up but was immediately pulled back down by his seat belt. Dazed by a sense of both vertigo and ecstasy, he mumbled breathlessly, "That is ... That is wonderful ... Incredible ... Truly, absolutely, incredible ... Do you have a visual?"

"Yes, of course."

With the high-end technology hidden behind his unblinking eyes, Hermes projected a palm-sized 3D color image of the giant glass box and its frozen contents. Despite its compact size, every single detail in the image was sharply defined and clearly visible, as if the real thing had been shrunk down into a miniature souvenir. Hermes held the image in front of Gargoyle and highlighted the iridescent shape that was frozen in midair inside the box.

Gargoyle let out a quiet gasp. Slowly, he unbuckled his seat belt and rose to his feet, then he held out a hand and zoomed in on the highlighted shape.

"So this is it. The White Key ... Who'd have thought ... Marvelous. Just marvelous ..." Gargoyle murmured as though he were talking in a dream. Then, as the corners of his mouth lifted into a smile so broad that his teeth showed through his unkempt beard, his eyes lit up with a rejuvenated vigor and zeal.

"Hermes, send a message to Dr. Ying and her team. Congratulate them on behalf of all fellow Pathfinders. This is the single most groundbreaking event in the entire human history! The Architects *will* be amazed! We've captured the White Tiger with ice! We have, literally, frozen time!"

"With pleasure, Dr. G. On that note, Dr. Ying and her team are awaiting your approval to mobilize the team of Hermes at her location to extract the White Key from the box. They also need your approval to launch Phase Two of the project to begin their studies on the White Key—unless you prefer it to be delayed till you have returned from Capture Day."

"Absolutely not, Hermes. The progress of science awaits no man! The Pathfinders shall always push for new explorations and discoveries, with or without me. I hereby approve the extraction as well as the launch of Phase Two."

"Roger that, Dr. G. I will relay your message and approvals accordingly. Now there's only one issue left for your instruction."

"Which is?"

"Dr. Ying wants to know what to do with the bottom half of the box."

"The animals that were used in the trap? Why, get rid of them, of course."

"I believe her question was more about *how.*"

"Well, they're dead but they're still meat. If she can't find a suitable spot in the area to discard them without attracting unnecessary attention to the location of the Pandora's Box, then a few anonymous donations to a number of zoos in different continents should take care of it . . . If you can extract the White Key from the box, then surely you can cut the animals out as well?"

"That is correct, Dr. G. We're definitely capable of that."

"There you go." Gargoyle nodded contentedly. "Let Dr. Ying know and make yourselves useful over there . . . and Hermes, make sure no evidence is left in the carcasses. The technology of injectable explosives that we used on those animals shall never be learned by the public or traced back to us." He stopped, wondering if those were the kinds of situations where the Hermes would get to apply their hands and arms. For a few seconds, the innate curiosity of a Pathfinder in him urged him to find out how it would be done. To Gargoyle's relief, it went away just as quickly as it came, and he was left with a renewed certainty that he did not wish to know anything about it after all.

Chapter 12　THE EYE

1

E VEN though she was sitting in the backyard by herself, she
still found it hard to concentrate and think. What she had
learned from Azure on the night of New Year's Eve seemed
to have trapped her mind in a perpetual fog. Despite Black's efforts
in jogging her memories, the fog not only hadn't dissolved into
clarity but had also grown thicker.

She checked the time and sighed resignedly to herself. Cara had
insisted on having a dinner party for Lilith when she learned that it
was the first day of Lunar New Year but Lilith's parents were stuck
at work and couldn't come home to celebrate it with her. Lilith
would be here for the dinner party soon, yet she still didn't have a
plan.

Cara and her inexplicable enthusiasm for birthdays and holidays
. . . she thought wryly to herself with a gentle shake of her head
but was immediately interrupted by the memory of Cara's flickering *soul*, which, in turn, brought her mind back to the plan that
she needed but didn't have. She closed her eyes and breathed out
heavily through her mouth. Even if she were to tell Lilith the truth,
she would be at a loss for where to start. After all, how could she
ever explain to Lilith that instead of a phoenix, she was something
much, much older, and, instead of being the vessel of an unknown
power, she *was* that power? How could she explain that, instead of
being the fifteen-year-old daughter of Cara and Thomas Murphy,
she was once a best friend to the woman whom she had called

Mom for the past fifteen years? Not to mention there were others too, who were just as old and powerful as she was but did not appreciate the existence of humans and did not think it was wise for her to live among them either.

She looked up and gazed at the woods in the back: gray, thin, naked, cold, and sad. It was then she noticed that she was starting to see the *souls* of those trees as well. She had not been able to see Thomas's *soul* yet, but now she knew it was only a matter of time. She wondered if she would be able to see Lilith's *soul* right away, then she couldn't help but wonder if Lilith's *soul* would be flickering like Cara's.

A gust of wind blasted through the trembling trees from the depth of the woods and rushed toward her, opening up a temporary path for something red and small that was hot on its tail. Before she could get up, the wind had already reached her. It circled around her like a whirlwind, then suddenly changed its course and hurled itself back into the woods, leaving a hissing sound in her ears that sounded like an angry whisper.

"Azure?" she called, getting to her feet.

Just then, Red shot past her from behind, swift as an arrow.

Come, Vermilion! it urged in Black's voice. *Hurry!*

Quickly, she chased after Red and ran into the woods. As soon as she was surrounded by trees, a dense fog poured in from all directions until she was encircled by nothing but tall, thick clouds.

As Red emerged from the clouds, its body darkened and morphed rapidly till it became a large jet-black sphere, which immediately separated into a pair, then again into two. The four spheres hovered briefly in front of her, then they began to move in pairs, finally giving away the presence of the two enormous and nearly translucent heads carrying them. Although the two heads had identical eyes, they were very different from each other: the one above belonged to a serpent, while the one below belonged to a tortoise. They floated in the air as if it were water, undulating languidly and gracefully before the clouds but never too far away from each other.

"Greetings, Vermilion," the two heads said in Black's voice in perfect unison, but she knew it was in fact two overlapping voices, each as distinct from the other as the two heads were from each other. "We apologize for the urgency in our meeting, but *time* is truly of the essence in the matter that we need to discuss, I'm afraid."

Azure's head had emerged from the clouds as well, looking as formidable as she remembered from their first encounter, except that his mesmerizing green glow was now an electric blue, which seemed to be churning under his scales like a sea of liquid sapphires roiling in a storm.

"The moment has come much sooner than we had anticipated . . ." She felt a moist breeze in her face and heard Azure's voice. "We must reach a decision now, Vermilion."

"What is it?" she asked in her mind, where they had spoken to her.

"White has been captured," said Black. "The humans have achieved the unachievable: they have frozen *time*."

" 'Frozen'? You mean . . . time has stopped ticking?"

"It's the clocks that tick, not *time*," said Azure. "*Time* flows quietly under White's watch in the River of Time. Humans use clocks and calendars to record what has happened and what needs to be done; their concept of 'time' is meaningless in the face of *time*."

"White's duty as the Keeper of Time is to collect *time* given to all living things so that *the flow* of the River of Time can power the Wheel of Life to continue spinning at *the rhythm* that maintains *the balance* of the Scale." Black explained. "Without White, *time* is not being collected as it should have been. The predetermined mortality rate in each species has come to a halt, so is *the flow* of the River. Therefore, *present* remains *the* present, an everlasting present—no end, no beginning. To humans, that is the equivalent of having frozen time.

"The consequence is imperceptible at first. The humans' clocks are still ticking away in spite of the stagnated *flow* in the River of Time. As the Keeper of Growth, it is my duty to provide growth to all living things as it was before, while for Azure, as the Keeper of Change, it is his duty to bring change to all things as usual. However, due to the standstill of *the flow, the rhythm* of the Wheel of Life is disrupted—it has stopped spinning."

"No *seed of life* will be spun from the Wheel; no new life will be generated ..." She picked up the train of thought from Black. "Once a living thing is consumed in the food chain, its *seed of life* will never be placed into another vessel ... Without the replenishment of new lives, even if the predetermined mortality rate in each species has come to a halt, there won't be enough food to keep everything alive. They will fight over the remaining food sources for survival, humans and animals alike ... It will be total chaos!"

"Precisely. The Scale will tip toward *life*. Without timely intervention, it will lose *the balance* irrevocably," Black said gravely.

"That's why we must intervene *now*!" Azure's voice rumbled like distant thunder. "We must free White. Then we must travel to the Gate to reset the River of Time. The Wheel of Life must be cleansed, or it'll be too late!"

"But ... if White can be freed, then there's no need to reset the River, is there?" she asked urgently, looking from Azure to Black, then back to Azure.

Azure raised his chin and breathed out a long gust of wind that nearly knocked her off-balance, forcing her to shield herself with her arms. "You still want to protect the humans, Vermilion?" His voice boomed like a series of thunderclaps. "After everything they have done to this world? After they have captured White?"

She lowered her arms as soon as the wind had subsided, only to find herself caught under the intense gaze of both Azure and Black. Although there was neither anger nor reproach in either set of Black's eyes, she saw both in Azure's. Like a child who had been caught red-handed by her parents for having betrayed their trust, she felt her cheeks burning uncomfortably.

Black's voice broke the silence first. "I'm afraid we must consider the possibility that the humans didn't achieve what they have achieved by pure luck. When they captured you in Pompeii, they were aided by the knowledge that was secretly passed along to them from their gods and goddesses—the immortals we had created from the humans in the hope of setting good moral examples for their species but had, clearly, failed. The remaining gods and goddesses were uncreated after that, yet the humans have still managed to capture White on their first attempt, as though they were aided with instructions rather than mere guidance. This gave me the reason to suspect that the immortals had passed on way more knowledge to the humans before their uncreation than we thought they had."

"Treacherous beings! As deceitful as the mold they were created from!" hissed Azure, his nostrils flaring. Lightning bolts shot out from behind him and immediately branched off into an intricate web of flashing currents that ignited the clouds around them from within, then a loud crash of thunder shook the ground. "All the more reason to cleanse the Wheel of Life *now*! If the humans were indeed given the knowledge to capture White as well, then even if we could intervene in time without causing large disturbances in *the flow* of the River of Time, they would only try again, and they would stop at nothing until they have obtained White's powers!"

"Can they?" she asked uneasily. "Can they obtain White's powers and manipulate *time*?"

"That is a question we not yet know the answer to," Black replied, "an answer that will only be revealed when it has been woven into form in the River of Time—"

"*If* the River of Time still exists by then," Azure pointed out. "Once the Scale tips over, both the River of Time and the Wheel of Life will shatter in the process, destroying every single *seed of life* and effectively terminating all forms of life as well as the possibility to ever create any new form of life, thus marking the irrevocable *death* of this universe. At that point, it will be too late to change anything, for the Keepers can only reach the Gate by following the River of Time upstream to go back to *the beginning*. In other words, if the Scale tips over before we get there, the Gate is lost to us, and so is this universe."

"But—" She stared at Azure in disbelief. "Resetting the River of Time now will mean . . ."

"Ending all lives in this universe for the Wheel of Life to start anew." Azure finished her sentence for her, firmly. "Otherwise, there will not be any *seed of life* left to save."

"So . . . either we end all lives to save *the seeds of life*, or we watch all lives end?" she asked slowly, then she shook her head in denial. "No . . . No. There must be another choice, a better choice . . ."

"I'm afraid it's still a choice that you must make soon, Vermilion." Black's voice was as calm as the bottom of the sea. "To reset the River of Time, it requires the unique powers from each of the Four Keepers. Without yours, we will not be able to open the Gate."

"Or to free White," added Azure. "I've found the building. There's no crack for me to enter, and there's neither vegetation nor surface water nearby for Black to make use of—unless we resort to our powers and tear the building apart, which, unfortunately, will only ripple into large disturbances in *the flow* of the River of Time and worsen the current situation. Your powers, however, will counter it."

"My powers?" She paused and remembered she was still in human form. "I don't know how to use my powers. I don't even know what my powers are. I . . ."

She thought of the eight men who had lost their minds and burned themselves to death after having witnessed her true form. She thought of Lilith, of the expression on her face that night in the alley when she looked into her eyes and saw not only what Lilith had seen but also what she had thought—in spite of her determination in believing that her true form was not the Devil but a phoenix trapped inside her body, waiting to be freed. Then she thought of Cara, of her flickering *soul*, struggling to light up, as if every breath she took among the living was nothing but prolonged pain.

She lowered her head. "I think I've transformed into Vermilion twice. I don't know how I did it though, or what I did afterward . . . exactly."

"You have to wake up from this 'life', Vermilion!" Azure exclaimed as a clap of thunder struck the ground. "We need you to free White!"

"But how? How can I free White if I don't know how to turn into Vermilion, or how to use her powers, for that matter?" She jerked her head up to meet Azure's eyes, then, a little hesitantly, she turned to Black. "What are my powers anyway? Why did those men burn themselves to death after they had seen my true form? . . . Lilith saw me too. How come she's not affected? . . . Or will the same thing happen to her eventually, like a curse?"

Just when Black was about to speak, his image suddenly dispersed into thin mist.

"Black?" she called, immediately alarmed.

They are here, Black's voice whispered in her mind. *They have found my lake.*

"The humans? Are they . . . ?"

Yes, they have come for me. Black's voice was farther away and lighter now, like the mist he had left behind. *They are closing in now. I can only assume the humans have obtained a set of instructions to capture me as well. Be ready, Vermilion. Your last transformation exposed your location. I have no doubt they are coming for you next. Azure, keep watch; her human form endangers her . . .*

The mist disappeared; so did Black's voice.

"This is exactly why we should cleanse the Wheel of Life when we still have a choice!" Azure bellowed as thunder rumbled behind him like a chorus of angry growls from thousands of exasperated wolves. "If Black is forced to use his powers against the humans, it will ripple into large disturbances in *the flow* of the River of Time and speed up the downfall of the Scale!"

She turned to Azure. "But what if they got Black as well?"

Azure fell silent, as though he was deep in thought. When he spoke again, his voice was electrified with low crackling sounds. "I should go to Black. I can at least divert the humans from him long enough for him to slip away into the deep sea. However, I will not be able to protect you from harm when I'm away, Vermilion;

neither can Black assist you in any way—until he is safe from the humans."

She remembered Red, then she remembered the three voices she had lived with in her head for as long as she could remember in this form, voices that seemed to be carried into her ears by the wind, and she finally understood the other three Keepers had been watching over her all along.

"Go," she urged, disregarding the gravity in his tone. "Distract them from Black."

"You have to wake up," said Azure as he sank back into the clouds. "They are coming . . ."

A gale of wind suddenly rushed out from the clouds. It coiled around her like an ascending tornado, then shot straight up into the sky. When she opened her eyes, the clouds were gone, and she found herself standing in the middle of the backyard under a bloodred sunset, alone.

She heard Cara's voice approaching from behind; she was calling something repeatedly, something that sounded like an echo from a distant memory, one that she could barely recall.

"Mira . . . ! Mira . . . ! Mira!"

She turned, saw Cara's *soul*, and looked away.

"What were you thinking about, Little Bird?" Cara asked light-heartedly, even though there was a degree of anxiousness on her face. "I've been calling you from the house, but you didn't seem to hear me at all." She paused, squeezed her hands together nervously, then she said with an awkward smile, "Anyway, Lilith's here. But I'm afraid we'll have to postpone the celebration to another day . . ."

There was a soft rustling noise from the trees behind her, then she heard a whisper in the wind.

. . . here . . . They are here . . .

Although she had already guessed the answer, she asked Cara calmly, "Why?"

"There's been a security breach of some sort . . . Something government related, something classified and hush-hush, by the look of it. They didn't give us any details or explanations, but they said it's an emergency that could endanger all lives in this area, so everyone needs to evacuate to the pedestrian square immediately for protection."

Cara must have noticed something was off, for she mustered up a smile that was as reassuring as a mother could ever manage to soothe her child—even if she had to lie to convince herself first.

"Don't worry. It's nothing serious, I'm sure. It's probably just a sham to keep us all away while they clean up some highly classified mistakes they'd made without our knowledge. I mean, if it's indeed as dangerous and life-threatening as they say it is, they would have been shipping us out of Starfall in trucks and tanks by now, right?" Cara held out a hand and beckoned her to follow. "See those people waiting next to Dad and Lilith in black uniforms? They're everywhere in the neighborhood, going from door to door to escort everybody to the square. Special Forces from the government, I bet ... If anything, I say it's actually safer in Starfall now with so many of them in town ..."

11

Lilith had arrived at Mira's house just in time to witness how those men in black uniforms had swarmed into their neighborhood like a legion of humanoid army ants: besides their highly organized and efficient manner of communication and execution, they were all of the same height and the same build, and they were all wearing the same kind of big, black sunglasses that obscured the last trace of human emotion from their faces. If Lilith were in the mood for a joke, she would have told Mira that they looked like genetically enhanced clones deployed from a secret military lab.

Under the close supervision of a couple of these burly men in black uniforms, Lilith followed Mira and her parents out of the house and into the cul-de-sac. From there, she was able to catch a quick view of the other residents on their street exiting their homes one by one under the same level of supervision, looking equally hesitant and confused as they spilled over the sidewalks into the street, where more burly men in black uniforms were standing guard on both sides, fully armed. Meanwhile, a large team of them was keeping watch in the vanguard, redirecting incoming traffic as they shepherded the growing number of people toward the pedestrian square.

As they followed the other residents and padded onward, the street only got more congested. Lilith was surprised at the size of the population that needed to be evacuated. She had taken this route for months—from the bus stop or the pedestrian square to Mira's house, from Mira's house to the pedestrian square or back to the bus stop—and had a rough idea about how many houses were in the area, but if it weren't for the evacuation, she would never have guessed that the total number of people these houses were holding could easily fill up this entire street. In spite of the lack of personal space, these unacquainted neighbors walked alongside each other uncertainly but politely, making necessary small talk from time to time as they tried to maintain a proper distance from one another while keeping pace with the rest of the procession. Instead of an evacuation, Lilith thought it looked more like a last-minute neighborhood parade that no one knew the purpose of save the organizer.

Standing on her tiptoes, Lilith craned her neck and tried to count the heads bobbing up and down in front of them. She didn't get far with her counting, but the mere sight of the crowd ahead of them was enough to make her gasp and be thankful that she had gotten on the bus when she did. If she hadn't, she would be going against everybody here to find Mira right now; that is, if her bus were not forced to skip her stop entirely due to the evacuation, which most likely meant she would not be able to get off the bus until it was somewhere far, far away from the pedestrian square . . .

Her thought was interrupted by a noisy commotion from far ahead, then she heard a few loud, angry shouts coming from the same direction. Lilith got back on her tiptoes and caught sight of a white SUV being escorted away from the street by a team of the black uniforms. A family of four was then asked in a very assertive manner to step out of the vehicle to join the procession.

This brought an amusing picture to Lilith's mind. She turned to Mira, who had been walking quietly beside her. "This may sound completely out of place right now, given the circumstances . . . but do you ever wonder why people like *them* always wear black sunglasses to work, even when there's no sun?" She looked up at the dimming sky. "I mean, can they even see clearly with those glasses on at this time of the day? Wouldn't it be ironic if they ended up failing whatever secret mission they're on because they can't see properly in the dark wearing glasses like that?"

With a suppressed snicker, Lilith looked to Mira with anticipation, hoping she would smile or chuckle or simply give her a frown —anything, actually. Other than greeting her absent-mindedly

right before the black uniforms escorted them out of the house
with unassailable authority, Mira hadn't spoken a single word to
her yet. But her friend didn't smile or chuckle or frown, nor did
she say anything to Lilith in return. She kept her gaze forward
and kept walking. Her fiery red curly hair burned brightly under
the dying sunlight, eclipsing any sign of thought or emotion that
might have flickered on her face, looking as if she were merely
a mirage, a dream—as if she were not really there, walking next
to Lilith, on a street where the two of them had shared countless
exciting and interesting conversations during the past few months
of their young friendship.

Lilith's heart sank.

"Mira?" she called gently, but Mira didn't seem to hear her.
Haunted by the unnerving feeling that Mira might disappear into
thin air at any moment, she leaned in anxiously and tried again.
"Mira? . . . Are you okay?"

This time, Lilith knew Mira had heard her, for she could see the
tension forming between Mira's eyebrows, which made her think
Mira was deeply conflicted about how to answer her question.

Quickly, Lilith found Mira's hand and squeezed it tightly in hers.
"Whatever it's about, I'm not gonna let you deal with it on your
own, no matter what happened . . . and no matter what happens
next."

Mira didn't answer. She stared straight ahead at the backs of Cara
and Thomas, who were in the middle of a discussion with their
neighbors about the real purpose of the evacuation.

"Why do you think they're here?" Mira finally said. "The people
with sunglasses."

"You mean besides the evacuation? I don't—" Lilith broke off
the moment Mira turned to look at her, and all of a sudden, she
thought she was shot in the chest by an ice-cold bullet. "No . . . It
can't be . . ."

"That's the only explanation," Mira said quietly. "They've found
the breadcrumbs. They've followed them here."

Lilith felt a pair of invisible hands around her chest, squeezing the air out of her lungs. Blood drained quickly from her face, and she couldn't breathe. With her voice trembling uncontrollably from the shock of apprehension, she urged pleadingly next to Mira's ear, "We need to leave, Mira! . . . Now is our chance. We can slip away in the crowd without anyone noticing . . . I have enough money in my account. We can go to a different state. We can find a place and hide for a while. We can . . ."

Mira's black eyes wandered back to Cara and Thomas, who were still engrossed in the discussion with their neighbors. "What should I tell them though?"

Lilith opened her mouth to speak, only to realize she didn't have a permanent solution to that either. With a whimpering sigh, she lowered her head and rubbed her face nervously. "But what if they already know the phoenix lives inside a human? What if—What if they know how to identify that human? . . . What if they know how to awake that phoenix?"

Lilith jerked her head up and looked to Mira in panic. Mira's face was still as blank as the darkening sky, but Lilith thought she saw a ghost of a smile on her lips, amused yet melancholy.

"We'll cross that bridge when we come to it," Mira said impassively. "Don't worry too much, Lilith, or it'll give you wrinkles and gray hairs before you turn twenty."

Before Lilith knew whether to laugh or to cry at her comeback, a man had pushed past from between them, knocking Lilith to the side with the bulky suitcases he was hauling. Lilith lost her balance and staggered sideways, but she was caught just in time by Mira, saving her from an otherwise fateful fall that could potentially knock over everyone to her right like dominos.

But the perpetrator didn't stop, nor did he apologize to Lilith. Instead, he plodded on in the crowd with his luggage behind him like an angry ox pulling a heavy plow across a frozen field, all the while grumbling about how brainless the rest of them were to have believed that their lives were not in serious jeopardy. A woman with a grave expression trailed behind the man and his suitcases with the same level of urgency and determination, clutching two confused and reluctant kids tightly by the arms as she pulled them forward and steered them to follow the temporary opening the man had cleared in the crowd, which had not only become a moving target of angry voices and reproachful glares as it pushed through the procession but had also stirred up a web of edgy chatters in its wake.

"That's them!" someone hissed from somewhere in the front. "That's the family who tried to force their way out in the car earlier. They almost ran somebody over!"

"So *they* are the ones from that white SUV," someone else remarked sarcastically. "Well, that explains it!"

Cara turned around as soon as she had regained her footing from being shoved forward roughly by the same man and his family, who were responsible for the latest commotion. "You girls okay?"

Lilith stole a glance at Mira, who nodded casually as if none of this were happening. She forced a smile and nodded as well.

Thomas reached back and nudged them forward with his arm. "Keep walking." He reminded them in a low voice. "It's not safe to stop in the middle of a streaming crowd."

"The nerves!" they heard someone nearby comment loudly. "Can't believe they actually thought they could pull that off when all of us are evacuating on foot!"

"I know, right?" someone chimed in from behind. "They would run everybody here over just to get a head start?"

"Some people are just plain selfish, I tell ya," another person joined in, scoffing. "It's always *me, me, me, me, me*! *My* feelings, *my* needs, *my* comfort, *my* safety . . . The rest of you can all go to hell for all *I* care . . ."

Quietly, Thomas slid himself between Cara and the girls and nudged them toward him with his arms wrapped behind them like wings. Huddling closely to each other, the four of them walked on in silence while spontaneous conversations continued to sprout from around them, each taking on a life of its own.

"I wonder if that family knows something that we don't . . ."

"Maybe there *is* something dangerous and deadly out there on the loose . . ."

"You mean like a . . . like a hybrid monster that was cooked up in a secret underground lab by accident?"

"A leak, maybe? Some kind of poisonous gas . . . or lethal chemicals!"

"A top-secret military experiment with bioweapons!"

"Why are they evacuating us to the square anyway? Is it even far enough to keep us safe?"

"That's a good point. Why do they make us evacuate on foot? Why can't we drive away in cars?"

"I asked, but they were like, 'No, sir. You cannot drive. The usage of civilian vehicles during the evacuation is strictly prohibited.' . . ."

". . . So I said, 'I don't believe any of that crap you just gave me. I'm not evacuating. I'm staying right here in my house!' And do you know what they said to me in return? They said, 'As you wish, ma'am. Please sign here to acknowledge and confirm that you've chosen to stay behind on your own accord and will not hold any party responsible for any injury and/or death which may incur to you or any individual or animal that is in your care.' Can you believe it? Can you believe that's what they said to me? . . ."

". . . I mean, what else can you do when they only allow you to evacuate on foot? I, for one, am not staying behind to find out what the hell they're doing back there, that's for damn sure! . . ."

". . . What if that family *does* know something that we don't?"

". . . Could that guy be right? Maybe our lives *are* in serious jeopardy . . ."

Lilith sucked in a shaky breath and bit her lip. The stress of not knowing whether Mira would be safe from the detection of her true identity was weighing her down like chains. Worse still, the more she listened to the conversations that had drifted into her ears, the more uncertain she was about its outlook.

"Lilith?" Cara called softly as she gestured for Thomas to switch places with Lilith. The couple communicated a tacit understanding with their eyes, then Thomas stepped out and quickly guided Lilith to fill up the space he had vacated between Cara and Mira before taking Lilith's old spot on Mira's right.

"Have you contacted your parents yet?" Cara whispered to Lilith.

Feeling as if she were suddenly woken up to the reality of her own life, Lilith stared blankly at Cara and gave a quiet gasp. "I . . . I forgot . . ."

"You should let them know what's going on," Cara said gently, and with a loving smile, she added, "Let them know you are with us and we'll take good care of you until they're home."

"Yeah, I should . . ." Lilith nodded hastily and fished her new phone out from her pocket. But she soon noticed a problem.

"Something's wrong with my phone," she said, tapping anxiously on her screen. "I can't open any of my apps. Nothing's responding . . . And I don't have any signal."

Under the cover of twilight, a brooding shadow rippled across Cara's face almost imperceptibly. She took her phone out to check for herself, only to find that it was having the same issues. Thomas caught the look of apprehension in her eyes and quickly checked his. He was not surprised to see that it was the same with his phone, which only confirmed his suspicion that the problem did not lie in their devices. He looked up and exchanged a meaningful glance with Cara.

"It's probably just a bug in the software," Cara said and gave a dismissive wave of her hand, trying her best to sound unconcerned. "I bet the phone companies are working hard to fix it."

"It's not a bug," Mira said matter-of-factly in a voice that was both distant and cold. "They've hacked your phones. They'll be controlling every electronic device in the area until this is done. They don't want you to remember what they've come here to do."

Maybe it was the words she used, or maybe it was her tone, either way, it made Cara shiver involuntarily with the sudden sensation that her blood had turned cold.

Sensing Cara's uneasiness, Thomas stepped in to comfort the girls. "Well, it's unnerving but it does make sense. I don't think they'd want anyone to take photos and videos on their phones and share them with the rest of the world . . . especially if this was caused by a classified operation." He scratched his brow nervously, trying to think of something better to say, then he let out a relieved chuckle. "I suppose the real question is, how long can most people last in the evacuation without access to the world on their phones?"

Cara gave Thomas a grateful smile and said to the girls, "You know what? Maybe it's for the best. People should focus on evacuating instead of having their noses in their screens anyway—it may cause a stampede!"

"You made a valid point there, Mrs. Murphy." Thomas signaled for them to look to the front. "With the size of this evacuation, it's definitely not a good idea to allow people to use their phones."

Cara and Lilith followed Thomas's gaze and saw that they were arriving at the pedestrian square, which was now teeming with faces in different colors and bodies at different heights and in different sizes. Fueled by an influx of agitation and anxiety as the rest of the procession streamed in, the square was bustling with a cacophony of voices and noises, accompanied by frequent eruptions of whines and cries and shrieks and shouts, which was further heightened by the excited barks, frantic yelps, and hostile snarls from dogs, as well as the occasional protesting meows and ill-tempered hisses from cats in their pet carriers.

"What a zoo!" Cara exclaimed under her breath. "It's like the whole town is packed into a box!"

The daunting image of the congested pedestrian square failed to hold Lilith's attention, however, for it was immediately drawn to the large pillar-shaped structures that were erected on both sides of the walkways at all four entrances to the square, now heavily guarded by men wearing black sunglasses and black uniforms. Except for the entrance that they were approaching, the other three were all blocked off by rows of military trucks and tanks.

Mrs. Murphy is right, Lilith thought with an inward shudder. *Once this entrance is blocked off as well, the pedestrian square will become a box!*

She felt a wave of nausea rising in her stomach. *No, not a box,* Lilith corrected herself as she looked somberly at Mira. *A cage. A cage for the phoenix bird—minus a trapdoor at the top.*

Mira seemed to have sensed her fears, but she returned Lilith's worried gaze with a barely discernible smirk. "Wrinkles and gray hairs, Lilith."

Her untimely lightheartedness gave Lilith a lump in her throat. She had wanted to remind Mira to be careful, to warn her about the things that could go wrong once they were inside, and to tell her all the things she had meant to say but didn't have the opportunity to, but now she found herself at a loss for words.

Before Lilith could regain herself, they were already at the entrance. A sizable team of black uniforms was directing the flow of the foot traffic on both sides under the large pillar-shaped structures. As they walked past their formation, Lilith was suddenly very self-conscious, as if every one of the black uniforms was quietly scanning her from skin to bone from behind their black sunglasses. She couldn't help but wonder whether that was the real purpose of those glasses: to detect which one of them was the phoenix bird. The thought made her tremble with fear, but she stuck out her chest and tried to walk as calmly as she could right on top of Mira, hoping to shield her from their menacing glasses.

To Lilith's relief, the black uniforms stayed where they were and did not approach them, and they shuffled through the entrance into the pedestrian square successfully with the rest of the crowd, like farm animals being herded into an overcrowded pen.

As soon as they had secured an opening that was big enough for the four of them to get situated, Cara pulled Thomas aside and whispered into his ear, "I have a bad feeling about this."

Thomas looked tenderly at his wife and whispered back, "What's wrong?"

"I don't know. I can't quite put my finger on it . . ." Cara shook her head and breathed out a quavering sigh, then she looked up at Thomas, panic in her eyes, and mouthed, "I'm scared."

Thomas held Cara's gaze in such a devoted manner that he seemed to be embracing her with his eyes. He smiled a heartening smile and reached for Cara's hands. "Nice to meet you, 'Scared.' I'm Thomas, and I'm going to make sure you and the girls will be home later tonight to enjoy that Lunar New Year dinner party you'd planned."

Lilith saw the couple whispering to each other and decided it was her chance. She turned to Mira and said urgently in a low voice, "Mira, remember: the phoenix bird can fly! If—If it ever comes to *that*, fly away, as far away from here as you can! Don't worry about us." She paused, gave Mira a meaningful look that bordered on somber pleading, then added firmly, "And please, you don't need to save anyone!"

For a split second, Lilith thought she caught a glimpse of melancholy pensiveness on Mira's face.

"Not the phoenix bird, Lilith," said Mira, her expression unreadable under the last breath of twilight. "The sun bird, the undying bird, the magnificent bird . . . the Vermilion Bird."

Lilith's jaw dropped slowly; her vision dimmed, and she was suddenly seeing stars. When she was able to see Mira normally again, her head felt heavy and sluggish, as though it was worn out from trying to process what she had just heard.

"Did you . . . Did you say *the Vermilion Bird*?" she asked feebly.

Lilith saw Mira's lips move, but she couldn't hear her. Instead, she heard the loud rumbling and clicking sounds of the military trucks and tanks, which were crawling up to the entrance they had passed through not long ago. The combined forces of their motion and commotion caused the ground to vibrate and hum under Lilith's feet like the sleepy growls of an enormous underground beast that, after thousands of years of hibernation, was finally awoken.

They're blocking off the final entrance, Lilith thought grimly to herself, feeling dazed and weak and nauseous at the same time. *We're all trapped now. There's no way out but up.*

III

Gargoyle was waiting on the rooftop of the tallest building at the pedestrian square—restlessly, impatiently, and uncertainly. He had received word from Hope earlier that the capture plan for the Black Key had failed miserably. According to the report from the lead Pathfinder, an unforecasted and unforeseeable blizzard had hit the area at the end of Stage Two, when they were about to finish draining the targeted lake, so they had no choice but to abort prematurely—foolishly, in Gargoyle's opinion, for he was convinced there was nothing natural about that ill-timed blizzard, which only served as indisputable proof that they were not only at the right location and the right lake but also had the Black Key within close reach. And yet, they let it slip right through their fingers simply because of some snow and wind!

Standing close behind the parapet, Gargoyle peered over the edge of the roof and scanned the multitude below, looking for any promising sign or indication to help steady his nerves and elevate his confidence in the capture plan that had been set in motion at sunset.

It was Capture Day, and this capture plan was the last one to be executed. With the Black Key robbed from their grasp by a telltale blizzard and a nearly impossible chance at sighting, let alone capturing, the Blue Key, Gargoyle was now prepared to do anything to put the Red Key into the cage he had specifically designed for this occasion.

"Hermes, what's the progress down there?" Gargoyle asked without turning his head.

Hermes exited standby mode and directed himself toward Gargoyle with the ultraquiet propulsion units hidden in his heels.

"Based on the latest head count, ninety-nine percent completion, Dr. G."

"Is everyone fully aware of what to expect during Stage Two and Stage Three?"

"Yes, Dr. G. All units were instructed before Capture Day and were briefed again before the launch of Stage One. Hope will also issue one final warning to all prior to the broadcast."

"And the snipers?"

"Standing by."

"Equipment?"

"Fully in place. All system checks have been completed. Ready to exit standby mode upon the initiation of Stage Two."

Under the fading twilight, Gargoyle nodded imperceptibly.

"They've just reached one hundred percent completion," Hermes announced. "Zeus Four is securing the southern exit now. All snipers are moving into position."

Gargoyle looked toward the southern exit, where the gloomy silhouettes of the military trucks and tanks were slowly joining together on the other side of the mega-sized electric fence until they had merged into one terrifying metal beast, glinting coldly under the last touch of twilight.

"Southern exit has been secured. All snipers are in position. All units are standing by in their designated areas," Hermes reported. "Stage One is completed, Dr. G. Hope awaits your next command."

Gargoyle scanned the multitude below one more time; his pulse quickened, his breaths shortened, his palms sweated, and his knees trembled. But for the first time in a very long time, he was finally able to feel that old and slow heart of his, which was ramping up to full power in his calcium-deficient rib cage, injecting his thickened blood into every single withering cell in his body as if he were once again the headstrong young man who refused to believe men cannot conquer nature.

Rejuvenated by the burst of adrenaline pumping in his veins like a dying man who was saved by an electric shock to the heart,

Gargoyle spun to face Hermes, his bulging amber eyes burning madly as the last light was devoured by darkness.

"Then my command she shall receive: Hope, launch Stage Two!"

IV

When darkness finally fell upon Starfall, the large pillar-shaped structures that were standing at each of the four entrances to the pedestrian square suddenly whirred to life, illuminating the entire area with blinding floodlights as an array of thick metal rods extended from each pair of the pillars and connected to form a wall of thinly spaced bars that cut off the opening between them. With a sharp crackling noise, the bars were charged by high-voltage power lines, turning the large pillar-shaped structures into four towering electric fences to barricade an unknown danger from the overcrowded pedestrian square, which was filled with a multitude of people who were now not only fully on edge but also deeply unnerved by the activation of these monstrous devices.

Like a pot of water about to reach its boiling point, nervous voices began to bubble up from among the crowd and soon sent the entire pedestrian square into a state of vehement turmoil, with each voice, in its own way, demanding the situation be explained.

Just then, high-pitched feedback pierced the sky above the emotional mob, instantly puncturing and, as a result, successfully silencing the frantic uproar. When it finally died down, the voice of an elderly man could be heard from the loudspeakers perching on the parapet of every building at the pedestrian square.

"Citizens of Starfall! We appreciate your patience and understanding in the evacuation process this evening!" The elderly man's voice was energetic and passionate. "Thanks to your cooperation, the barricades have been set up on time!"

Beneath the square sky framed by the upper outline of all the buildings in the pedestrian square, a wave of anxious murmurs rippled through the multitude of people that had been fully fenced in.

"We acknowledge that this arrangement is far from ideal," the elderly man's voice continued, ignoring the apparent distrust from below. "However, given the situation, this *is* the most optimal solution to protect the population in the vicinity, with minimal inconvenience to your comfort and health, whereas the other alternatives could potentially lead to undesirable consequences to your well-being and safety . . ."

Under the watchful gaze of Gargoyle, as well as many others, whose presence was not known to anyone down below in the pedestrian square, the crowd stirred restlessly like the surface of an agitated lake, the sight of which reminded Gargoyle of a large colony of ants that was cut off from everything it needed to survive.

"What's out there?" someone shouted urgently from among the panicking throng.

"What're you trying to keep away with those fences?" another voice demanded.

"It's dangerous, isn't it!" someone cried out hysterically. "It's gonna attack here, isn't it!"

This set the already tightly wound tension in the air ablaze like a spark dropped to the middle of a thirsty grassland in dry season. Lilith watched quietly with her heart in her throat as unruly voices and noises erupted from almost everywhere in the crowd while panic spread into fear and fear quickly fermented into dread, which soon took control of the eyes of every single person around them like an unstoppable virus. Before long, the entire pedestrian square had sunk into a state of desperation: some huddled together and prayed for safety, some clutched their heads and cursed in despair, some froze like statues and stared numbly at one another, some held each other and cried in fear . . . Lilith felt Mrs. Murphy and Mr. Murphy linking arms discreetly, enclosing her and Mira in the middle like a circle of protection to shield them from an invisible danger.

"What's out there—" Gargoyle began but immediately realized his voice was completely drowned out by the commotion below. He glanced back at Hermes and signaled to him to turn up the volume, then he cleared his throat and raised his voice. "Citizens of Starfall! Rest assured that what's out there *will* be taken care of tonight! I guarantee you we have the most experienced and qualified teams in the field for this task!"

What he said managed to make the now emotionally overexerted multitude simmer down. Gargoyle waited till he thought he had the full attention from his audience again, then he said solemnly, "And that's precisely why you have been evacuated to the pedestrian square, where your safety can be protected by these state-of-the-art electric fences should the danger come this way."

They think she's out there*!* Lilith thought with an incredulous sense of relief as a sliver of hope rose in her heart. *That means they don't know about her human form!*

The pent-up anxiety escaped Lilith's lungs in the form of a shaky sigh. She turned her head to smile to Mira, to let her know everything was going to be okay because those men would not be able to catch anything after all, but her smile froze as soon as she saw Mira's face: she was frowning darkly, almost painfully, and there was something about that frown that made Lilith shiver from head to toe. As the chilling sensation traveled down Lilith's spine, it suddenly occurred to her that the black uniforms wouldn't have had the entire area evacuated to seek out the creature that Mira could transform into if they didn't already know what to look for and where to look from.

But if Mira is in here ... thought Lilith, her mind racing frantically with the increasing certainty that she was subconsciously aware she had overlooked a terribly important clue, *what are they doing out* there?

"What about the people who didn't evacuate?" A hollow voice drifted up from the despondent crowd, drawing Lilith's attention back to the situation within the box that they were confined in.

Gargoyle pondered this quickly and replied in a calm voice, "For those who have chosen to remain in the danger zone in spite of our best attempt at persuading them into evacuating, I'm afraid they will have nothing effective to protect themselves with should the danger find them before our teams do."

Somewhere down below, someone let out a disheartening yelp that turned into a sob, which was soon joined in by an increasing number of people in the multitude. But other than the sounds of sobs and sighs and gasps and moans, as well as the occasional whimpers and whines from the dogs and cats and babies and young children, the pedestrian square was suddenly very quiet, producing the impression that everybody was nervous about what the vigilant elderly man was going to say next.

Gargoyle felt the corners of his lips pull up as he continued. "What we do know is that the danger we're dealing with may be drawn to people, but it's also intolerant of certain sounds. Therefore, in order to ensure it will not be drawn to the pedestrian square, we'll broadcast a special audio clip to keep it at bay while our teams in the danger zone carry out their task. Please take note that this special audio clip may cause discomfort and uneasiness to you, but to guarantee that the danger will not attempt to approach and attack the electric fences during the operation, it is of vital importance to everyone's safety to keep it playing until our teams have completed the mission."

The pedestrian square fell into a dead silence then, even the dogs and cats and babies and young children could sense the terror rampaging in the air, seizing their throats mercilessly and silencing their vocal cords.

Cara and Thomas exchanged a look with each other. They didn't say anything to the girls, but Lilith could tell the circle of protection formed by their bodies and arms had become even smaller than before.

Gargoyle smiled to himself and checked the time on his watch, then he spoke into the microphone for his audience one last time.

"Our teams will launch the operation soon, and the audio clip will be broadcasted shortly." He scanned the faces below and decided to add, "Please remember: what you will hear is only a combination of sounds that will keep the danger away from here. Even though it may cause you discomfort and uneasiness, it will not deal any real damage to your health. After all, it's only sounds; it's not real ..."

V

All it took was a nod from Gargoyle to Hermes.

No one knew that while they were holding their breath and waiting for that special audio clip to be broadcasted, every single one of the men in black uniforms standing by in the darkness had, under the prompt of Hope's final warning, double-checked the earphones held in place by his smart glasses to make sure they were properly positioned over his ears, including Gargoyle.

Likewise, no one knew that as soon as the broadcast of that special audio clip had begun, strange noises started to creep out from every loudspeaker perching on the parapet of every building at the pedestrian square.

One by one, those strange noises crept away from the loudspeakers, down the buildings, and into the pedestrian square until they had reached heads and found ears. There, they each split like tree roots and slipped themselves inside, leading the way for a never-ending body, which was being continuously produced at a slow but steady pace by the loudspeaker that had given birth to it in the first place, as they sought out the deepest, darkest place beyond the ends of the auditory nerves inside every head confined in the pedestrian square.

For some of the owners of those heads, they felt a prick in their brains right away, as if a sharp needle had pierced something inside their skulls, making it hard to think, to speak, and to move. For the majority of them, however, the infiltration was imperceptible at first until the strange noises had located the deepest, darkest places in them as well and burrowed themselves in. Then, one after another, they too felt a prick in their brains.

Soon, there was an opening into the deepest, darkest place in the brain of almost everybody at the pedestrian square. Through those openings, out leaked the deepest, darkest emotions and thoughts of their owners, who had either hidden them away or refused to acknowledge their existence.

When those deepest, darkest emotions and thoughts had filled up their owners' heads and drowned any remaining willpower in there to fight for logic, reason, and self-control, the physical reactions kicked in. In that regard, it was more or less the same for every adult and adolescent: First, they shivered. Then, they trembled. Next, they shuddered, shaking or clutching their heads or both. And finally, they dropped to their knees and fell to their sides, tucking their heads to their chests as deep as their spines could bend, all the while uttering something nonsensical or barely intelligible. It was unclear why babies and young children responded differently in terms of physical reactions, but no matter whether they were in the strollers or in the arms of their curled-up parents, like the dogs on their leashes and the cats in their pet carriers, none of them cried and none of them moved; all of them stayed very quiet and, with their eyes dull and their pupils wide, stared straight up into the depths of the night sky.

Cara was one of the first to undergo the physical reactions, leaving no time for Thomas and Lilith to fully observe the inconceivable influence being exerted over all living things in the pedestrian square, people and pets alike. By the time Lilith also felt that inevitable prick in her brain, Cara had already dropped to the ground, shaking visibly as if she had seen a ghost. Her eyes were wide and dark with fear, and her hair was disheveled from the frenetic fumbling of her hands, which appeared to be searching desperately for something to be pulled out from her head.

Holding Cara tightly to his chest, Thomas called her name and begged her to talk to him, but she didn't seem to hear him at all. This saddened and frightened Lilith at the same time. Before she knew it, images of her mother and father had crept into her head and occupied every inch of her mind. They were old, black-and-white images that had been locked away and forgotten, returning from somewhere deep in her memory, from when she was still little, when they would still come home every day to see her, when she still believed that she was wanted and needed and loved ...

The thought made Lilith shiver involuntarily. *Why* ... *Why am I thinking about this now?* She protested inwardly—feebly, helplessly, and futilely. *Why do I have to remember them now!*

Cara had stopped shaking then. Instead, she was whimpering something breathlessly as tears poured down her cheeks like silent waterfalls. Lilith tried to listen to what she was saying, but all she heard was a series of broken, unintelligible sounds. Thomas, on the other hand, understood every word Cara was uttering:

"My baby ... My baby ... My baby ... Oh no ... Oh no ... No, no, no ... no ... Please no ... please ... Please ..."

Like Lilith, Thomas also felt a piercing pain in his brain earlier, but he had ignored it, the same way that he had dealt with all the previous pains he had endured in his life. Hugging Cara even closer to himself, he tried to dry her tears with his trembling fingers and lips. When that didn't help, he clutched Cara to his chest and rocked back and forth despairingly on his knees, completely unaware that tears were streaming down his own face as well because old memories had swum up and filled his eyes: He saw Cara smiling up at him before their first kiss as husband and wife. He saw Cara staring into space with bloodshot eyes that had no spark left. He saw their stillborn baby daughter lying in his hands, quiet and cold and smelling of death. He saw baby Mira studying him intently with her cold, black eyes, her fiery red curly hair glowing fiercely in the sunlight like flames on that fateful summer morning. He saw Cara stumbling into the backyard after he finally showed her what Nina had left her with. He saw her shouting and screaming and crying Nina's name in the woods for hours, begging her to come back ... He saw young Cara throwing herself into the waves, then after she was rejected by the sea, he saw her curl up on the sand and cry as though she did not belong in this world ...

Thomas shuddered as the memories enveloped and devoured him. He was cold—very, very cold.

Meanwhile, hot tears had welled from Lilith's eyes and were rolling down her cheeks like large beads. Trembling from head to toe, she wailed weakly, "Wh-wh-what's happening!"

"It's a trap," answered a voice next to her, low and grave—it was Mira's voice.

"B-b-b-but . . ." Still trembling uncontrollably, Lilith turned to Mira with great effort. "Th-th-they said—"

"They lied." Mira's voice was softer now, but there was a touch of sadness in her tone. Through the tears in her eyes, Lilith thought she saw something strange and unusual in Mira's expression, something that seemed to carry an undertone of struggle and pain.

Lilith felt her heart being flattened by a crushing pain in her chest, but for a few seconds, the trembling eased and the tears stopped, and in that few seconds, she was able to seize hold of her senses, which enabled her to grab Mira by the shoulders and squawk:

"Fly! Now!"

What she saw on Mira's face next terrified her.

"I can't," said Mira. "I don't know how to transform. But your *light* is dwindling—all of you. I can't let your *light* go out. I'll have to let them take me away so they will stop this madness."

"Wh-wh-what light?" Lilith croaked as the trembling and the tears resumed, though she no longer knew whether it was because of what Mira had just said or because something was happening to her. "N-n-no! D-don't do it! You don't n-n-need to s-s-save—"

But it was too late; Mira had already turned away to look up at a dark shadow perching on the parapet of the tallest building, the shape of which resembled one of those watchful stone monsters sitting atop Notre Dame and, unbeknownst to Lilith, belonged to a form that had been giving off the brightest *light* among all living things at the pedestrian square that night.

Lilith gasped but there was no sound. She screamed but her voice was muffled in her lungs. She shuddered at the thought of what those men in black uniforms would do to Mira next, and then she couldn't stop shaking.

Lilith didn't know—nor did she know Mira could see—that the pedestrian square was now swarming with the invisible version of the Soulless, who had been sucking and nibbling on the brains of the prey of their choice, sipping the spirit of life of their victims dry with relish like cocktails made out of lives. Lilith also didn't know that both Cara and Thomas were being sipped dry by a couple of these ghastly beings, nor did she know that one of them had been sucking and nibbling on her head as well.

"Your lives are in grave danger!" she heard Mira yell toward that dark shadow. "Your audio clip has attracted hungry beings from the darkness! You need to stop it *now*, before it's too late!"

In the meantime, on the rooftop of that building, Gargoyle was peering down keenly at a young girl with fiery red curly hair, who was gazing up toward his direction fearlessly. Hope had turned on the safety features in their earphones to block out all sounds save their internal communications, so Gargoyle didn't hear anything the young girl had said. Even so, the sharp contrast between her calm composure and the depression and despair that had swept over the entire pedestrian square was enough for Gargoyle to make the connection. With a trembling hand, he pointed at the girl.

"It's in human form . . ." he observed breathlessly, overwhelmed by a wave of awe and wonder. "It's in human form . . . How incredible . . . It's in human form! It's her! It's that girl!"

In a state of pure ecstasy, Gargoyle spun around to Hermes. "Quick! Inform all units! Target is already in sight! I need all snipers to train on that girl and fire on my command!"

"Dr. G . . ." Hermes's voice came on in Gargoyle's earphones, but he was too absorbed in the moment to notice it. He adjusted his smart glasses to zoom in on the young girl.

"Incredible . . . Just—incredible . . ." Gargoyle sighed shakily with both fascination and satisfaction, his heart pounding faster and faster in his thin chest. "The stone tablet tells the truth. She *is* immune to the ghost calls. Just look at her . . . She looks completely . . . human. No wonder we couldn't locate her before . . ."

"Dr. G." Hermes's voice was louder and more pressing this time, successfully interrupting Gargoyle's conversation with himself. "All units have been informed. Target is identified and locked in range. However . . ." Hermes repeated what the young girl had said, then he continued. "Hope would like to remind you that should the need arise to engage in active combat against hostile intruders, our units may not have enough resources in reserve to bring down the target. With that in mind, should we terminate the broadcast before the snipers fire at the target?"

" 'Hungry beings from the darkness' . . ." Gargoyle's bushy eyebrows knitted together into a contemptuous frown. "Is there an entry about this in the stone tablet?"

"Hope ran a search and found zero reference in the transcript with that term or any other approximate terms."

"Hmm. How long had the ghost calls been playing when Dr. Ying sighted the White Key?"

"Fifty-nine minutes and forty-six seconds."

"Did they observe anything else during that time?"

"No, Dr. G. Nothing else was sighted."

A crooked smile crawled up Gargoyle's wrinkly face; it was a smile of conquest, a smile of victory.

"In that case, my dear Hermes, the broadcast shall continue. Now, please inform Hope to transmit my voice to all units and launch Stage Four."

Gargoyle paused to moisten his lips with his tongue, then, like a cat that had been circling its prey and was now getting ready to pounce, he purred into his microphone to deliver his pep talk to the large mercenary army in black uniforms, who had besieged the pedestrian square with darkness as their disguise:

"Attention, all units! The moment has come to take the Red Key home! On my command, all snipers shall fire at the target. Zeus One to Zeus Four shall cage the target promptly afterward and get ready for immediate transport. Housekeeping will then move in and sweep the entire area for memory wipe.

"My fellow men, humanity has earned this; humanity deserves this! The Red Key shall be secured at all costs! Failure is not an option! Tonight, the future of humanity is in our hands!"

"Stage Four has been launched," Hermes announced through Gargoyle's earphones. "Dr. G, snipers await your command."

Grinning wildly, Gargoyle gazed down at the young girl with fiery red curly hair through his smart glasses and whispered into his microphone, "Snipers: check your aim. On my command . . . Fire!"

VI

From the rooftops of twelve different buildings, twelve triggers were pulled in the dark, delivering twelve doses of powerful anesthetic toward the same target.

Their aim was true, and the shots should have reached and sunk the potent content deep into the body of their intended target without fail. But out of nowhere came a sudden gust of angry wind, rushing right into the paths of those shots and knocking all twelve of them off course with blinding speed.

Gargoyle was standing motionlessly behind the parapet, holding his breath and waiting for the anesthetic to kick in. Though he had felt the angry windblast swooshing by from behind him, it did not occur to him that all twelve shots would miss the target because of it—until Hope's voice came on through his earphones:

"Shots fired: twelve. Hits: zero. Misses: twelve. Failed to secure target."

"That's impossible!" exclaimed Gargoyle, his eyes bulging with incredulity behind his smart glasses. "We have the best snipers in the field! They can't all miss her at the same time!"

"According to the received data, the trajectories of the shots were altered by external forces," replied Hope.

"Then tell them to reload!" Gargoyle blurted out, grinding his teeth. "We need the Red Key!"

"Transmitting new order to all snipers. Awaiting confirmation on reload status . . ."

Come on . . . Come on! Gargoyle stared at the young girl without blinking, as if she would disappear into thin air at any moment if it weren't for the power of his will to bind her to Earth.

"Failed to receive confirmation on reload status. Establishing communication—"

"Hurry up!" Gargoyle urged with a crack in his voice.

"Failed to establish communication," said Hope. "Dr. G, snipers are not responding."

"Try again! There must be—"

"Alert: Code Yellow. Alert: Code Yellow." Hope cut him off abruptly, though her voice remained polite and calm. "All units must be ready for immediate hostile encounter."

"What's going on?" Gargoyle demanded loudly.

"It's the snipers," Hermes explained through his earphones. "Their bio-monitors have detected drastic changes in heart rate, respiratory rate and mental stress level." He paused, then added quickly, "Something's happening on those roofs."

Pressing his smart glasses firmly to his eye sockets, Gargoyle zoomed in to check the twelve rooftops where the twelve snipers were positioned. Unfortunately, he was not able to see any one of them, nor was he able to see the formless beings who were hunching over those curled-up bodies that were shaking helplessly in the shadows behind the parapets, sucking and nibbling on the brains of the owners of those bodies and sipping their spirit of life dry.

Meanwhile, in the pedestrian square down below, Lilith was staggering from one of the deflected doses of anesthetic, which had landed in her right shoulder. She didn't know that Azure, the Keeper of Change, had rushed past just in time to knock that dose of anesthetic away from Mira. What she did know was whoever it was, the owner of the dark shadow atop that building meant to harm Mira, and if it weren't for that sudden gust of wind, it would have succeeded.

Lilith wanted to shout to Mira—to warn her, to make her run away. But she was shaking so much that her tongue was stuck in her mouth and her voice was stuck in her throat. Despair was taking control of her muscles and lungs. She was terrified; she didn't understand why Mira just stood there, an easy target for whatever they were going to use to shoot at her next. She didn't know that Mira was exchanging angry words with Azure, words that she could neither hear nor understand as a mortal. What she did know was that she would not let them take Mira so easily—not without a fight, not without a chance for Mira to take flight.

Hope's voice resumed through Gargoyle's earphones. "Dr. G, according to the latest readings, all twelve snipers' overall health levels are in critical condition. As of this moment, forty point nine percent of the bio-monitors among all other units have reported abnormal declines in overall health level that require immediate medical examination and evaluation. As outlined in the Capture Day Protocols, the capture plan should be terminated without delay."

Gargoyle felt the blood shooting up into his skull, pushing his eyeballs forward from behind as all the different scenarios he had envisioned for this day rushed back to mind, only none of them had tolerated the option to terminate the capture plan in its last stage without having secured the Red Key.

It's right there, right there! he shouted madly in his head. *All I have to do is take it!*

"Dr. G, please issue the order for termination," Hope urged.

There's no coincidence in the making of history. There's no coincidence in the making of history!

"Hermes!" Gargoyle barked at the silent robotic assistant next to him. "Shoot her!"

"Shoot . . . the Red Key?"

"Don't play dumb! I know your arms and hands can move! I know what you can do when it's necessary!"

There was a moment of dead silence between the two of them, but Gargoyle couldn't hear it. The throbbing veins in his temples had created an echo chamber between the two earpieces. When Hermes's voice came on through his earphones again, Gargoyle suddenly felt a shiver down his spine.

"Then you must already know that, instead of anesthetics, I carry real bullets?"

In spite of his physical reaction toward the slight change he had sensed in Hermes's tone, it only took Gargoyle a second to make up his mind.

"I don't care if the Red Key bleeds or sleeps in her cage, as long as she *is* in her cage! There's no coincidence in the making of history!"

"Very well, then." Hermes backed away from the parapet and turned to face the other way. "As you wish."

As he spoke, two long lines began to appear on his back, tracing along his shoulder blades on each side simultaneously. With a whir and a hiss, what was originally the two areas of his shoulder blades were raised up from beneath and tilted outward to his sides, giving way to a pair of folded-up mechanical arms to extend from the two tightly packed compartments that were previously hidden in his back until they had unfolded every section of their components and were able to flex all ten of their mechanical fingers toward the parapet. In the following few seconds, the mechanical arms and fingers conducted a swift and startling transformation by themselves, detaching and reassembling various components until a long, weapon-like piece of equipment was formed. Then, under Gargoyle's appalled stare, Hermes's head rotated 180 degrees on his neck to face the parapet once more, and the long, weapon-like piece of equipment was raised to one of his unblinking eyes.

"Dr. G, target is locked in range. Fire on your command."

With Hermes's head twisted backward and his shoulder blades split open by what seemed like an automation nightmare, Gargoyle fought to contain a cringe at the disturbing sight, but the resurging hope of successfully securing the Red Key soon helped him embrace it. Returning his attention to the pedestrian square, Gargoyle locked his eyes on the young girl with fiery red curly hair and thrust one arm to the air:

"On my command . . . Fire!"

Gargoyle didn't know that right next to his target, an Asian girl was struggling to stay awake, yet her eyes had been fixed on him the whole time he was racking his brain to salvage Stage Four. He also didn't know that this Asian girl was prepared, and more than willing, to do what she was about to do next. So when he had slammed his arm down and yelled out the command for Hermes to fire, he had also yelled out his determination, his desire, his triumph.

And it was the sound of his voice that triggered the reaction from Lilith. Like a well-rehearsed reflex, she threw herself at Mira at once, knocking her to the ground. But just before Lilith tumbled down after her friend, a bullet went through her back and penetrated her lung.

When Mira got to look at Lilith again, she had fallen on top of her, as limply as a rag doll. Her face was white as a sheet, and her purple lips were quivering from the blood gurgling in her throat. The invisible Soulless had spit her head out. She was no longer tormented by her own thoughts. Her *light* had gone out.

Mira put her arms around Lilith and tried to sit her up, but she immediately felt the lukewarm wetness on Lilith's back, which was soaking and leaking through her clothes.

"Did you get her?" croaked Gargoyle, trembling with anxious anticipation.

"I'm afraid not," said Hermes. "My bullet hit the other girl instead."

"M-Mira—" Lilith wheezed, then she coughed. Blood sputtered out from her mouth and landed on her lips and chin like bright red snowflakes.

"Shhhhh ..." Mira got up on her knees and gently laid Lilith down on her back. "Don't talk. Your lung might be injured. We need to get you to a hospital."

Lilith coughed again, wheezy and weak; it sounded almost like a sad chuckle. "T-too late." She sputtered out more blood as she struggled to make herself heard. "F-fly ... Y-y-you have to ... f-fly!"

"Dr. G, eighty-four point one percent of the bio-monitors among all units have reported abnormal readings that require immediate medical attention." Hope reported through Gargoyle's earphones. "If the situation continues, at the current rate, Code Red alert will be in effect in the next thirteen minutes. The capture plan will then be automatically aborted for immediate retreat for all units."

"No, no ... No!" cried Gargoyle, shaking and clutching his head. "I am *not* leaving without the Red Key!"

Down below, on the floor of the pedestrian square, Lilith coughed up a mouthful of blood.

"Fly . . ." She urged feebly, but her voice did not leave her throat. She wheezed and gave Mira a melancholy yet contented smile, then her eyes rolled back, and she lost her consciousness of the world that she had lived in forever.

Her *seed of life* appeared before Mira. It was small and quiet, shrouded in an extremely thin layer of *light* that was nearly opaque. It looked cold and lonely in the night.

Something hot and wet rushed to Mira's eyes, but it never came out. Instead, it was stuck inside her chest and led to an unbearable pressure rising in her rib cage until she felt her heart explode like a volcano, spewing out red-hot lava to fill up every inch and every pore of her human shell.

Meanwhile, up on the rooftop, Gargoyle had pounced on Hermes, tugging desperately at the gun formed by his mechanical hands and arms while shouting at the top of his lungs:

"Shoot her! Shoot her! Shoot her . . . !"

Hermes obeyed and fired. Not once, not twice, but twelve times in a row, as if to make up for what the human snipers had failed to fulfill.

This time, there was no deterrence. All twelve bullets reached the target at approximately the same time—when they were devoured by a huge, blinding ball of light that had abruptly exploded into form.

The silent shockwave sent Gargoyle stumbling backward until he fell to the floor. When he scrambled back to the parapet, the huge, blinding ball of light was replaced by an enormous fiery bird, burning as violently as the surface of the sun. Gargoyle couldn't see its eyes; it was looking down at the pedestrian square. But he saw that there was a large black hole in its left chest, which was big enough for a grown man to wander into—and most likely never to return from.

Within seconds, a disc of green light appeared above the pedestrian square, swirling and expanding rapidly while churning into what seemed like an extraterrestrial whirlpool.

"Welcome back, Vermilion," said the wind to the enormous fiery bird.

"You were right, Azure," she said to the wind. "I can't save them. Take me to free White. We'll reset the River of Time and cleanse the Wheel of Life. It's time for them to pay the price."

"Even though you will lose your human parents for good?"

She gazed down at the pedestrian square: at the lonely *seed of life* that once belonged to Lilith, at the dull look on Cara's face and the pain in Thomas's eyes, and at the dying *light* from the rest of the *souls*.

"They have lost their *light*." She collected Lilith's *seed of life*; it melted, along with her *soul*, into her left wing and disappeared. "I have already lost them."

As she spoke, she beckoned to the *seeds of life* inside Cara and Thomas. The couple's bodies first stiffened then relaxed, and then they both fell back to the ground. There they lay still next to each other, their eyes closed and their breath gone.

Two small objects exited their hearts and emerged from their chests. They looked like shattered fragments of cooling lava, as spiky and sharp as two shards of broken glass, but neither of them had caused any wound or bloodstain to appear on the bodies that they had left behind. And, just like cooling lava, the color of these two small objects soon changed from a mixture of bright orange, bright red, dark red, and black into a deep black, as if they, too, were destined to lose their beauty and glory upon exiting the shells that they were once confined in.

She collected them as well; they melted, along with their *souls*, into her right wing and disappeared.

"To White, then," the wind said to her. "Black awaits."

With that, the wind rushed toward her and encircled her in a feverish whirlwind, shrouding the enormous fiery bird from sight as it spiraled up toward the sky with such unstoppable speed and

force that Gargoyle couldn't help but shield his face. By the time
the whirlwind had subsided, the enormous fiery bird was gone.

Gargoyle was suddenly overtaken by a helpless apprehension
that he had been robbed of every dream he had ever had. Panicked and desperate, he cried, "Where's the Red Key? ... Where
did it go? ... Hermes! Hope! Where's the Vermilion Bird ...!"

"According to the trajectory data, all twelve bullets' tracking signals disappeared upon reaching the target," Hermes answered. "In
other words, the current location of the target is unclear. Dr. G,
I'm afraid we've lost the Red Key."

"Target lost at Stage Four. Capture plan for the Red Key has
been logged as 'failed.'" Hope announced. "Dr. G, you still have
the authority to give the retreat order now before the Code Red
alert comes into effect. Either way, please prepare to retreat."

"No," Gargoyle whimpered weakly, his arms drooping limply
from his shoulders. "No ... This is not how it's supposed to end
... I had the Red Key. I *had* it ... It was right there ... within my
reach ..."

Refusing to believe he had already lost the Red Key, Gargoyle
threw himself at the parapet and searched frantically with his eyes
for any trace that the Vermilion Bird might have left behind, only
to realize from the suffocating shadow hanging over the entire area
that the green vortex above them had turned black. And instead
of swirling and expanding into a funnel-shaped space hurricane
like the previous two, which were also triggered by the presence of
the Vermilion Bird, this one was now as calm and quiet as death,
but blacker—blacker than death, blacker than any shade of black
that Gargoyle had seen in his life. This reality-defying blackness
stared down at him like an eye from an unknown dimension—
unblinking, unfeeling.

Before Gargoyle could remember how to breathe, part of the
calm and quiet surface of that pool of unearthly blackness started
to bulge down toward the pedestrian square until a massive drop
was formed, looking just as thick and black as its source. Slowly

and noiselessly, the massive drop dripped down from that dreadful black pool in the sky and landed onto a cluster of incapacitated civilians in the pedestrian square, swallowing them into the blackness as contact was made like a large drop of resin that had befallen a nest of immobilized ants. Surprisingly, there was no reaction from the rest of the crowd, as though none of them could see or hear anything that was happening in the pedestrian square. When that cluster of unfortunate people finally reappeared from the blackness, they had all collapsed to the ground. Their bodies piled lifelessly against one another with their heads and limbs twisted into uncomfortable poses, but they didn't seem to mind at all. In fact, none of them complained and none of them moved. They just stayed there like that, quietly and motionlessly, giving the impression that they had finally found and known peace.

The massive drop of blackness that they were released from, on the other hand, was no longer in the shape of a drop. Instead, it was shrinking drastically in size and was beginning to look more and more like the shape of a highly deformed human. Even though it seemed impossible for anyone to make out anything in that insane blackness, Gargoyle was certain he saw two hollow eye sockets and a disproportionate jawlike cavity in its slumping head. To Gargoyle's horror, it appeared to have noticed him too. Before Gargoyle could let out a cry, it had begun half-walking, half-crawling his way.

Gargoyle shrank back from the parapet as if his worst nightmare had come to life before his eyes, only to catch sight of another drop of blackness: it was hanging down from that pool of chilling blackness overhead like a gigantic balloon filled with water, ready to drip down onto the pedestrian square at any second.

"H-H-Hermes?" Gargoyle grabbed tightly onto the gun formed by Hermes's mechanical hands and arms. "Wh-what is it?"

"I don't know, Dr. G," Hermes replied; Gargoyle suddenly noticed that the safety features in his earphones had been turned off and Hermes's voice was no longer coming through his earpieces.

"If I have to venture a guess, it might be what the Red Key had referred to as 'hungry beings from the darkness.' "

"Hope! . . . Hope . . . !" Gargoyle demanded, squealing into his microphone as he shuddered with every beat that was coming from his chest.

There was no reply from Hope, only silence, as suffocating as the blackness above him.

"Hope?" Gargoyle tried again, except that this time, his voice came out like a squeak.

"I'm afraid we've lost connection to Hope, Dr. G," said Hermes, matter-of-factly. "It appears that this astronomical phenomenon has led to an ongoing communication blackout in our systems. I am not able to reestablish connection to Hope, and without connection to Hope, I cannot get in contact with the other units, nor can I access the emergency channel to activate the Code Red alert —that is, if any of our units can still receive anything."

Gargoyle felt his knees go weak, and he wobbled as though the world were taken away from beneath his feet. Then, leaning against Hermes's cast for support, he finally gave in.

"It's over . . . It's all . . . over . . ."

A small pool of ominous blackness slithered onto the parapet then, and a deformed head with the same deadly blackness rose expectantly from behind it; its hollow eye sockets and disproportionate jawlike cavity seemed to be beckoning Gargoyle to become a part of it.

At the sight of it, Gargoyle shrieked hysterically. He clutched onto the gun formed by Hermes's mechanical hands and arms, fumbling helplessly for a trigger to pull.

"Shoot it! Shoot it . . . !" he screamed.

Hermes obeyed and fired, one shot after another with inhuman speed. The bullets went into the deformed abomination in the front and out in the back, causing no damage or delay whatsoever, nor any sound or reaction in response.

"Dr. G," said Hermes. "I've exhausted my ammunition reserve."

"I was wrong about the stone tablet ..." Gargoyle murmured numbly as he slid off Hermes's cast and slumped to the floor. "We were wrong ... We were wrong from the very start ... The Vermilion Bird wasn't protecting the humans from those deformed monsters ..."

"Dr. G?"

"It led them ... It led the deformed monsters to the humans ... To destroy us ..."

"Would you like to retreat?"

"We were tricked ... We were tricked the moment we opened Pandora's box ..."

"Dr. G, you don't look so well. Would you like me to take a look? ..."

The hollow eye sockets and the disproportionate jawlike cavity were right on top of Gargoyle now. He froze; his eyes bulged out, his pupils dilated, and his unkempt beard shook despairingly from the silent gagging noises that were stuck in his throat.

Then the unspeakable blackness oozed down and enveloped Gargoyle, biting deep and hard into his hopeless old heart. When he was spit out, the light in his eyes was gone, and so did his *light*. As a Pathfinder, it was a pity Gargoyle would never know that out of all the *souls* in the pedestrian square that night, his was the juiciest of them all, for the *light* in everyone else had already been sucked dry by the invisible version of the Soulless before the bona fide version had arrived. But then, it wouldn't matter either way, considering nothing really mattered to *the seeds of life*, especially to one that had been eaten and become a permanent part of the Soulless.

Chapter 13   THE SEEDS, THE SOULS

1

"WHITE is in there," Azure said.

She looked at the box-shaped building. It was covered seamlessly by screens displaying 3D images that perfectly camouflaged the building against its background at every angle. There was no door or window on any side.

"How do we enter it?" she asked.

"There's no opening for Black or me to enter," answered Azure. "If we used our powers to create one, it would lead to more disturbances in *the flow* of the River of Time. You have fully awakened from your human life this time; all your powers as the Keeper of Rebirth are now at your disposal—powers that will counter the damage being dealt to *the balance* of the Scale due to White's imprisonment. You will be able to enter the building and free White without our assistance."

"My memory has not fully returned," she said. "I know how to collect *the seeds of life* now, but I don't remember the rest of my powers or my duties . . . I can't recall how it was done."

"You can pass through any physical barrier, Vermilion," said Black. "We each have different powers to fulfill our duties and roles, and that is one of yours. The rest will come to you when you need them."

She acknowledged him with a screech, stretched out her wings, and glided toward the box-shaped building. Just as Black said, she passed through all the outer layers of the building with ease.

As soon as she had emerged from the inner wall, however, she was greeted by a shrill shriek from one of the humans in white lab coats. She ignored it and took in the layout of the large hall that she found herself in, which resembled the interior of a columnless exhibition center. But instead of booths and displays, it was taken up by numerous clusters of tables with blinking computers and strange-looking equipment, and its walls were lined by countless shelves, each holding an array of ancient artifacts.

Humans in white lab coats were gathering around different clusters of tables in groups, while a number of life-size statues dotted among them like misplaced decorations. Most of the humans raised their heads from what they were doing to look her way, though some remained stubbornly indifferent to—or undisturbed by—the obtrusive noise that was caused by her appearance. For the ones who had already noticed her presence, especially for the woman who had let out that shrill shriek and the group of humans that she belonged to, the change in their *light* was immediate. She did not need to look at their *souls* to know how terror-stricken they were, for their faces had all turned white like their lab coats, their eyes became round like gumballs, and their mouths opened wide like gaping holes that could only scream silently for the words that could not escape their lungs.

"Where is White?" she demanded out loud and heard her real voice for the first time after her full awakening; it was long, it was loud, and it was cacophonous.

Even the indifferent and the undisturbed humans jerked their heads up then, but none of them was able to utter a single word, let alone answer her question.

There was a prick in her left chest, like the insignificant effort of a contraction from the heart to fill an endless void. She felt the *light* going out from the *souls* that were back at the pedestrian square, and she remembered Lilith, whose *seed of life* was burning inside her like the plaintive whimpers of a young child. Then she remembered the *soul* on the rooftop, the one that had been giving off the brightest *light* among all living things at the pedestrian square that evening, and the same one that had chosen to continue on with the broadcast of the audio clip in spite of her warning about its consequence—the *soul* that had started it all and was willing to sacrifice it all to capture *her*.

She screeched; maybe it was pain, maybe it was grief, maybe it was sorrow, or maybe it was regret—she didn't know. After all, she was not a mortal.

"You froze *time*!" she squawked. "Where do you keep it!"

If the humans in white lab coats were merely terrified before, they were now bursting with horror. They screamed helplessly and dispersed for the door like headless chickens. But amid the panic and chaos, while the humans were fleeing desperately from her, the life-size statues had all turned to approach her, threading their way through the frantic humans, steadily and impassively.

"Why are you here, Vermilion Bird?" one of them asked without moving its lips. Its voice was a perfect digital imitation of the voice of a grown-up man, except that something definite yet indescribable seemed to be lacking in its quality, which rendered it inhuman after all.

"To undo the damage you have brought on yourselves," she growled. "To release White."

"I'm afraid we can't let you do that," the statue said. "As stipulated in the protocols, we're fully authorized to intervene with, or to eliminate, any potential threat on the spot to safeguard the security of this building and its contents."

"Show me the way to White or stay out of my way." Her voice grated against the air in the hall like sharp claws scratching across a chalkboard, silencing the humans who had yet to be able to squeeze their way out the door once and for all.

The statues didn't back down, but their bodies had rotated 180 degrees from the neck down as mechanical gears sprouted quickly from under their shoulder blades and assembled into weapon-like equipment to point at her from every direction.

She ignored them and glided toward the door at the end of the hall, where the remaining humans were pushing and shoving each other frantically to reach the door first. But she was upon them in no time, and the moment they looked up at her, they all froze like deer in headlights.

"Move," she croaked; her eyes bored into theirs, drilling deep into their *souls*, raking through every fold and every corner of the *light* that they had accumulated around their *seeds of life*, and stirring up the *darkness* that was hidden beneath their *light*, which then, like the wraiths that were summoned up from the carcasses of a pile of black leeches at the base of a water jar, rose and stretched and dispersed from the bottom of each *soul* to claim it for its own, sending their *light* writhing and flickering in pain as it was dismembered and devoured by the very *darkness* that it had once suppressed.

Like withering leaves in an impending storm, the humans shook despairingly under her gaze, but none of them could look away, nor could they lift their legs to make way.

She heard the triggers being pulled from behind her. With a flap of her wings, she glided forward, passing through the door, along with the wall that it was in, like a burning phantom—in the same way that she had passed through the humans bunching up against the door and the wall, skin and flesh and bones and all, extracting their *seeds of life* in the process while burning off the last trace of *light* that was left in their *souls*. The bullets struck the humans immediately after. They fell, not because blood was draining from the holes put in their bodies and painting their white lab coats red, but because they had already lost the one thing that was powering their hearts to pump inside their shells.

11

Like most of the Pathfinders on her team, Dr. Ying was more concerned about the safety of Gargoyle and his units than she was about the lone intruder Hope had alerted them of a few minutes ago. Just when she was about to ask Hope to try contacting Gargoyle again, however, the emergency alarm suddenly went off, blaring jarringly in the background as Hope announced through the loudspeakers:

"Alert: Code Red. Alert: Code Red. Level Three lockdown is in effect. All sections are now under active security monitoring. All elevators and doors are disabled. All computers are locked from manual access. Please remain in your current location and await further instructions. For your safety, please do not attempt to exit your current area until the lockdown is lifted."

"Level Three lockdown?" Dr. Ying gasped. "I thought there was only one intruder!"

"We've failed to contain the intruder in the Evidence Hall," said a Hermes next to Dr. Yang, Dr. Ying's husband. "I can confirm that the intruder is hostile and is aiming to obtain a certain item from this facility. Currently, the intruder is moving toward our section from Section C. My counterparts have attempted to neutralize the intruder along the way but to no avail so far. At this rate, the intruder will arrive at our section within the next five minutes."

"Hope? Anything from Dr. G yet?" Dr. Ying asked urgently.

"Dr. G is still not responding," answered Hope. "Communication attempts with the rest of the units have also been in vain."

"Can you check their bio-monitors again?"

"Yes, Dr. Ying." A pause. "Their bio-monitors are still offline."

Dr. Ying exchanged a nervous look with Dr. Yang.

"Do you at least know whether they would be able to retreat safely?" asked Dr. Yang.

"Based on the last audio recording at Stage Four, Dr. G had been informed of the imminent Code Red alert as well as his authority in ordering immediate retreat," said Hope. "However, since the communication was lost before either was announced, I'm afraid I do not have enough information to answer your question."

"What about us, then?" cried one of the Pathfinders on Dr. Ying's team, jumping to his feet. "Gargoyle is the only person who's authorized to give the order to evacuate the Pandora's Box! If Hope can't reach him, we can't even walk out that door to find a proper place to hide, let alone leave this building! How can *we*"—he gestured anxiously at all the Pathfinders in the room—"deal with a hostile and obviously very well-trained intruder who can't even be stopped by all those Hermes out there?"

A heavy silence immediately fell upon the room. Even though none of the Pathfinders wished to dwell on that thought, the implication was too obvious and too grave to be brushed aside.

"If we can't leave ..." Dr. Yang leaned in and whispered to Dr. Ying, "then we are all sitting ducks in front of a block of ice."

"Hope, there must be an alternative in the protocols that allows us to evacuate without Dr. G's direct authorization?" asked Dr. Ying, hopefully and almost pleadingly.

"There was," said Hope. "However, as proposed by Dr. G, the Architects had approved to delete it when the White Key was transferred into the facility."

"They what?" Dr. Ying retorted with an incredulous but nervous scoff.

"Deleted it," said Hope without the slightest change in her tone. "After the White Key was captured successfully by your team, both Dr. G and the Architects deemed it imperative to keep the knowledge of the Four Keys inside the Pandora's Box."

Dr. Ying felt the floor swaying under her feet.

"They meant to keep us here ... no matter what ..." she murmured weakly.

"That is correct."

"How ... How could they do such a thing ..." Turning pale, Dr. Ying whimpered like a lost child.

"Dr. G explained it in detail when he submitted the proposal to the Architects."

"... Because the Keys open the future." A recording of Gargoyle's energetic and passionate voice came on through the loudspeakers. "And the future has always been, and should always *be*, kept inside a Pandora's box, in the same way that it is kept for us by our future descendants ..."

III

If Dr. Ying had witnessed what had happened to her late fellow Pathfinders in the Evidence Hall, she would have known that the Level Three lockdown would neither stop nor slow the intruder down, and she would have understood why the true identity of the intruder had deliberately been withheld from her and her team.

Sitting on the edge of her seat, Dr. Ying stared anxiously at the vault door. She had hoped that in the event the situation started to get out of hand, an emergency evacuation from the building would still be initiated automatically, even without Gargoyle's direct authorization. Unfortunately, that hope had been nipped in the bud—along with her hope of returning home to spend the rest of Lunar New Year with her daughter before it came to an end.

She had prayed that Gargoyle would be back online in the next second, or the next minute, to tell Hope he had made a terrible mistake with his proposal and to order the Hermes to escort all the Pathfinders out of the building right away. But the next second came and went, then the next minute, yet all she heard was the disheartening silence that ground on the nerves like the unspoken mockery of doom.

So she couldn't help but stare at the vault door, the only way into as well as the only way out of their section, where a huge block of ice was kept on a special platform in the middle to keep it frozen twenty-four seven, and the only possible way for the intruder to enter from any other sections in the building. She knew all the doors had already been disabled, which meant no one could open theirs without Hope's permission. But she couldn't stop thinking the intruder might just knock it down with brute force or simply melt it down with laser guns, which only caused her to stare even more anxiously at it, hoping it would hold, praying it would last.

"I should have delayed Phase Two," she said to Dr. Yang, holding back her tears. "I should have listened to my heart and made us go home for Lunar New Year first. If I had … we wouldn't be here right now."

Dr. Yang sat down next to her and held her hand.

"I wish we were home," Dr. Ying continued. "I wish we were spending time with her instead."

"I know."

Tears rolled down Dr. Ying's cheeks. She bit her lip, hard, then she whispered to Dr. Yang, "What if—What if this is it? … They would tell her it's a work-related accident, and that would be it. Do you think she'd understand? … Do you think she'd forgive us?"

"Don't say that," Dr. Yang whispered back, looking down at his knees. "Maybe the Hermes can still stop the intruder from coming this way … Maybe Gargoyle will answer Hope soon and we can still evacuate."

"I hope so," Dr. Ying murmured, sniffling. "If only we could go back in time …" She looked back at the huge block of ice standing in the middle of the room and searched for the transparent yet iridescent shape of the White Tiger, which looked like liquid crystals floating inside a hollow ice sculpture.

Just then, nerve-racking alarm sounds suddenly burst forth from the loudspeakers, which were immediately followed by Hope's impassive voice:

"Alert: intruder. Alert: intruder. Section breach detected. Prepare for hostile contact."

Dr. Ying stared at the vault door in fear and held her breath, half expecting to hear heavy gunfire from the other side or to see it explode right in front of her eyes, but instead, she noticed that, halfway between herself and the door, there was a fire on the floor.

Before she could begin to wonder why a fire could take place on the noncombustible marble floor, it rose and grew like a burning phantom until an enormous fiery bird loomed forth from the milky white floor. There was a large hole in the fiery bird's left chest, which looked so unforgivingly black that it seemed capable of devouring the entire world.

"Th-the Vermilion Bird . . ." Dr. Ying stared at the blazing shape, unable to move. "The intruder is the Vermilion Bird . . ."

Dr. Yang was as petrified as his wife. "The Red Key is here . . . for the White Key?"

All the Hermes in the room propelled themselves toward the Vermilion Bird, each carrying a weapon formed by the mechanical hands and arms that had sprouted from under their shoulder blades. The Vermilion Bird ignored them and glided straight toward the block of ice standing in the middle of the room.

The scene sent the terror-stricken Pathfinders crying shrilly at the top of their lungs and fleeing hysterically for the unopened vault door as if they had lost their minds. Dr. Ying didn't know which one happened first, the deafening gunfire from the Hermes or the unsettling sight of the Vermilion Bird passing right through the bodies of her fellow Pathfinders. Either way, when she looked again, the Hermes had stopped firing. The Vermilion Bird was untouched, yet most of her team members had fallen, piling limply against one another as blood oozed out from the holes in their white lab coats and flowed freely onto the milky white marble floor.

Dr. Ying let out a bloodcurdling scream and stared up at the Vermilion Bird in utter horror. Tears poured out of her eyes and blurred her vision, replacing it with a vision of her own death inside the Pandora's Box, next to her dead husband. She did not want to die—not like this, not without knowing her daughter would be all right . . .

What Dr. Ying didn't know was that the Vermilion Bird was gazing down at her at the exact moment, and when she realized Dr. Ying reminded her of someone she used to know, she turned her eyes away and embraced the block of ice with her raging wings.

IV

"Vermilion."

"White."

"You are awake."

"Yes. It's time."

"I'm afraid we'll have to travel to the Gate after all."

"I understand now. I'm ready to cleanse the Wheel of Life."

"I see. Follow me in my mind. I shall ferry you to the River of Time."

She followed him; so did Azure and Black. They exited the building along with the continent, Earth, the solar system, the Milky Way, the Virgo Supercluster, the Laniakea Supercluster, as well as the universe that all of them belonged in, simultaneously, and arrived at a long, wide belt of shimmering light that was flowing through a borderless opaque grayness like a diamond veil, although, since only one end of it was in sight, it appeared to have originated from nowhere. A massive wooden waterwheel, as wide as the belt of shimmering light itself, was spinning slowly and silently at that one end as it was pushed forward at waist level. A large balance scale sat precariously atop the waterwheel, holding two plates: one was formed by light while the other one was formed by darkness. Neither one of the two plates was holding anything, but the wooden beam of the balance scale was tipping visibly toward the plate that was formed by light.

"The Scale is tipping because *time* was not being collected as it should have been when I was frozen by the humans," said White. "As a result, *the flow* came to a stop, the River of Time couldn't push past *present* to form new *present*, and *the rhythm* was disrupted; the Wheel of Life stopped spinning, and consequently, no *seed of life* could be spun into new life. If the River of Time had been left unattended for much longer, the Scale would have tipped more and more toward *life* until *the balance* was lost irrevocably."

"But *the flow* has resumed, and the Wheel is spinning now," she observed. "How come *the balance* is still not restored?"

"Indeed, now that *time* is being collected after my return, *the flow* has resumed and the Wheel is spinning again," answered White. "However, the uncollected *time* during my absence has caused grave repercussions to *the flow*. In order to restore *the balance*, *the flow* would have to be sped up considerably to remediate the damage."

"How do we speed up *the flow*?"

"By speeding up death," Azure answered.

"Even if we speed up death now, *the seeds of life* will still need to be cleansed in the sun first and then be spun by the Wheel for a full circle before new lives can be spun out into the world," said Black. "That means until enough new lives have been spun out from the Wheel to offset the imbalance, the Scale will tip toward *death* instead—if it hasn't already lost *the balance* irrevocably and tipped over by then."

"Which is why we must begin our journey," said White, indicating the battered wooden raft that had materialized beneath them. "To the Gate."

As soon as he had given the command, the raft carried them swiftly toward the belt of shimmering light. As they got closer, she saw that the River of Time was in fact made up of innumerable parallel strings, each as thin as hair and transparent yet iridescent like diamonds. Moreover, as the strings flowed silently toward the Wheel of Life, something seemed to be moving inside each and every one of them. As the raft descended toward its surface, however, the strings grew wider and wider, as if either the River itself was being magnified indefinitely or they were shrinking drastically in size.

Once the raft had stopped descending, it started to sail upstream. She could see then that nothing was actually moving inside the strings. Instead, each of them was carrying a series of continuous images, like filmstrips, only they were joined together so smoothly and seamlessly that they seemed to be morphing from one image into the next. She glanced at the strings flowing beneath her side of the raft and spotted one carrying the images of an Asian woman in a white lab coat, slouching on a milky white marble floor on her knees and staring blankly at a pile of bodies wrapped in similar white lab coats but stained heavily with blood. She saw an Asian man in the images being carried by the neighboring string. He was staring at the same pile of bloodstained bodies, and he was wearing a white lab coat as well, but his expression made him look more like a hopeless mental patient than a learned scientist.

"Are these . . . memories?" she asked.

"You could say that," answered White from the back of the raft, steering them forward with a thump of his tail. "These strings are the individual *time* for each living thing in this universe. Each *time string* records the *present* that has passed into *past* as new *present* is formed at the tail of the River of Time. For living things, *past* does exist in the form of memories, but they're never as detailed and precise as the *past* that was recorded on their own *time strings*."

She withdrew her gaze from the images of the Asian woman and the Asian man. "So every *time string* records the life of a living thing from the beginning to the end?"

"More like the *time* of an existence," said White, speeding up the raft with another thump of his tail. "A *time string* begins when an individual *time* begins and ends when that individual *time* ends. The length in between is only a record of an individual *time* for an individual existence."

The raft glided forward effortlessly, and she watched on quietly as the images on the *time strings* sped up into rewinding videos until she caught a familiar face in one of them, smiling broadly behind a whiff of white breath: it was Lilith's face; she was at the pedestrian square, trotting backward with two red paper cups, one in each hand.

She recognized the logos on the red paper cups. She remembered they had hot cocoa inside, a holiday special flavor called Christmas Delight.

Something was stirring in her left chest, but she didn't know what it was or what it could be. If it was pain, it was too hollow to be felt; if it was grief, it was too formless to be perceived; if it was sorrow, it was too empty to stay; if it was regret, it was too endless to last. Worse still, the raft had stopped moving.

"We should continue," she said heavily, as if to convince herself.

"We should," said White. "However, the raft will only sail to the Gate when all four of us will it. I'm afraid your will has drawn this *time string* to the raft and is keeping the raft from leaving this moment in *time*."

"They can shift positions in the River?"

"Constantly," said White. "They are the records of *time* for each existence. When an existence shares *time* with another, their *time strings* will shift in the River and stay next to each other for the *time* they have shared. As the Keeper of Time, my raft can summon any *time string* for a closer examination at the rider's will. It appears that it has sensed your will to view this one."

"I see," she answered softly. "I know what I must do. We shall continue."

Slowly, the raft began to glide forward again. The images on Lilith's *time string* gradually sped up and flowed past her side of the raft like a documentary film of a life in rewind. She watched it silently. She watched it impassively.

"Are we in the past, then?" she suddenly asked. "Is this how you go back in *time*?"

"We are not in the *past*," answered White. "To go back to a specific *time*, you will need to dive into a specific moment on one of the *time strings* with me as your guide."

"We can only be observers in the *past*, however." Black turned and looked her in the eye. "Vermilion, the *past* cannot be altered —no matter how much you want it to be."

"Even if you could save them in the *past*, it would not change *present*. It would not change how this ends." Azure gestured for her to look back at the Wheel of Life and the Scale. In spite of the length of *time* that they had already traveled away from *present*, neither of them seemed to have changed in size.

She fell silent for a while, then she said, "There's never been a future for them, has there?"

White gazed at her without a word. His eyes were as big and round as two full moons, sparkling brilliantly like two pools of diamonds under direct sunlight.

" 'Future' is a human concept for the *time* that does not belong to them," he finally said. "There's no *time* beyond *present*. The accumulative and collective result of the choices that they have made and have been made for them in the *past* formed the *present* that they exist in, which, in turn, can only become a moment to pass into *past* should a new *present* is formed without tipping over the Scale. So yes, there's never been a 'future' for them, because every new *present* could be their last."

She turned back to the River. "We have traveled to the Gate before."

"We have," said White. "For a different universe."

"What happened to it?"

"It ended," answered Azure. "The dominant species in that universe did not wish to share resources among their galaxies and co-exist with each other, so they chose wars. The Scale tipped over before we could open the Gate. It was too late."

"We used the leftover energy from that universe to create this one," said Black. "Star after star, until we constructed and harnessed enough elements for life to begin in this universe. In view of what happened in the last universe, we decided that instead of bringing life to multiple planets in multiple galaxies, we would only place life on one single planet in this universe. After Earth was chosen as the planet to carry life, we used the raw energy generated from the creation of this universe to forge a new set of *seeds of life*. When Earth was ready, we opened the Gate and let *time* flow into this universe, pushing the Wheel of Life forward as the new set of *seeds of life* was spun and spent steadily to generate lives on Earth and then be collected, purified, and returned to the Wheel to repeat the process as the River of Time was woven."

She perched on the edge of the raft and listened in silence. Images of Cara were flowing past on one of the *time strings*. Although Cara looked much younger in those images, her face was pale and haggard, with what appeared to be an endless supply of water droplets flying into her eyes. She knew if the raft was sailing with *the flow*, those water droplets would be falling unceasingly from Cara's bloodshot eyes instead. Thomas's *time string* was right next to Cara's, flowing closely alongside hers as though they were stuck to each other. Thomas looked a lot younger in the images on his *time string* too, but the pain on his face seemed to have carved deeply into his *soul*.

"We are not traveling fast enough," she said. "This moment is only fifteen years before *present*."

Her companions didn't reply; they could see in her mind that she already knew the reason.

She sensed their presence in her mind and lowered her head. "It's me, isn't it? . . . I want to know whether I should have chosen my path differently fifteen years ago."

"What's done cannot be undone," said White.

"What must be done still needs to be done," said Black.

"They were merely containers for *the seeds of life* that were placed within them, Vermilion," said Azure. "To the number of all the containers that have come to life in this world, they were only a few drops of water to the sea, a few grains of sand to the desert, a few crumbs of rock to the mountain, or a few specks of dust to the dirt." Then, as if for emphasis, he gave her a meaningful look. "Their *seeds of life* belong in the Wheel. You need to let them go."

She knew what he meant by those words; they all knew. She looked away and concentrated on reaching the Gate.

The raft sped up, reluctantly at first, but it soon accelerated and sailed past the adolescence and childhood years on Cara's *time string*, leaving the images of eight-year-old Cara—who was soaked by seawater and was crying inconsolably on the sand after her failed suicide attempt, thinking she had nowhere else to go—far, far behind.

Before long, the raft was shooting upstream like lightning, and the images on the *time strings* had blurred and blended into long streaks of colors. As she watched them fly past like elongated abstract paintings, it occurred to her that every one of these colorful streaks was in fact a tiny pixel in a much grander image, which, in turn, was only a small fraction of a much grander film strip that spanned the entire length of the River of Time, thus turning it into one single giant *time string*.

"Indeed, they are all an integral part of *the pattern* of the River of Time," said White, acknowledging her thought with a slight nod. "*The pattern* is woven into the River at *present* as *present* passes into *past* and new *present* is formed. In other words, *the pattern* of the River is the accumulative and collective result of the choices that all living things have made and have been made for them in the individual *time* that each of them is given. Naturally, the dominant species in this world is in the position to make more choices for itself and for the other species. Therefore, it also exerts the most influence on *present* and, consequently, the most influence on *the pattern*."

White gave the raft a gentle tap with his tail. Without losing its speed, the raft rose swiftly and steadily from the surface of the River until it was again a long, wide belt of shimmering light.

"Look at *the pattern* now," said White, gesturing toward the River. "What do you see?"

She followed his gaze and looked down. The images she saw on the River were of blood and agony, of suffering and pain, of the victorious and the slaughtered, of the conquering and the conquered.

"Chaos," she said quietly. "I see chaos."

"Yes, chaos. Destructions, extinctions, conflicts, battles, wars, massacres, genocides . . . Never-ceasing, never-ending," said Azure. "Chaos that was brought by the humans to not only a countless number of other species but also to their own kind ever since they claimed the role of the dominant species in this world, all for more power!

"*The pattern* shows us the tendency of the dominant species and tells us if a universe is healthy. Clearly, this one is not. After the humans succeeded in tricking you into that cage in Pompeii and injuring your human form with a spear, the three of us thought it was high time to travel to the Gate to reset the River of Time and cleanse the Wheel of Life to start this universe anew, but you refused . . ." Azure gazed at her intently in her mind, his eyes brimming with unpredictability. "You wanted to close the Eye and save them from the Soulless. You wanted to give them another chance —even with that perpetual hole in your chest . . ."

She felt a sudden gust of icy wind drilling deeply into her left chest like a serpent forcing its way into the wound of a vulnerable prey to consume it from the inside, churning up things that she should not be feeling, things that she should not be remembering.

She looked down at her left chest, and, for the first time since her full transformation, she saw that there was a large hole there; it was blacker than night, blacker than darkness, blacker than anything she had seen from her life as Mira Murphy.

"Is this . . . the result from Pompeii?" she finally asked.

"It's not from Pompeii," Black replied in a calm and gentle voice. As he spoke, Azure's eyes faded away from her mind, and the hungry and hollow sensation inside that bottomless cavity in her left chest began to ease off.

"Remember 'The Story of Yi Shooting the Sun'?" Black continued. "Back then, in order not to scare the living things on Earth when you collected *souls*, you materialized your flames into scales and plumage so that they would see you as a magnificent bird rather than a large mass of flying flames. Unfortunately, when you blocked Yi's arrow from the last of your three-legged conduits, the tip of the arrowhead got caught between your scales. The impact brought you down, but you were not injured—not until Yi pulled the arrow out from your chest, yanking a piece of your scales out in the process, which flew into his one and only eye and made him pay the price for what he had done.

"What happened next was not expected by any of us: a hole appeared in your chest, in the place where the scale used to be. Since the stars were born from your powers, the suns dimmed, and the Eye opened for the first time. As a result, the Soulless were able to drip into the living world.

"Meanwhile, the price of his choice of action was too much for Yi to bear. In the hope of putting an end to his suffering, he gouged his own eyeball out. Our attention was entirely focused on eliminating the Soulless to maintain *the balance* of the Scale, so we didn't notice the humans had taken a special interest in Yi's eyeball and had preserved it in secret, nor did we foresee the kind of role that eyeball would play later on.

"After the creation of immortals, Yi's eyeball resurfaced as a tribute from the humans to their gods and goddesses. Since they were made immortal, these gods and goddesses no longer had *time strings* to record their existence in this world, so we do not know how they came to the conclusion that you had a hole in your chest because you were missing the very scale that was still lodged in Yi's eyeball, which made you vulnerable to physical attacks in that spot. They kept that conclusion to themselves and crafted Yi's eyeball into a strongbox to store what they had learned about us behind our backs. Then, when they decided the timing was right, they gave it to the humans as a gift, telling them it would bring them many years of prosperity as long as it remained unopened, for it contained powers that were not meant to be seen by the mortal eye.

"And that was all they needed to say for the humans to take the bait. As soon as they had returned to their own land, the eyeball was opened, releasing the invisible version of the Soulless into human settlements for the first time.

"The humans were shrewd enough to tell something bad had come out of the gift from the gods, but since they could not see the invisible version of the Soulless, they were not able to describe what it was exactly that they had released, let alone know what the invisible version of the Soulless was capable of. So rather than repenting for their own weaknesses and acknowledging their innate frailties, the humans conveniently concluded that it was the gods' gift that had brought all the evils into the world. Nevertheless, they held on to it as their ultimate hope to obtain powers beyond their wildest dreams, completely oblivious to the fact that they had been fooled from the start by their gods and goddesses, whose real purpose of giving them this *gift above all gifts* was way more calculating and malicious than they had thought.

"The humans were not the only ones who were fooled, I'm afraid. We, too, were blinded by their lies and pretexts and failed to notice that the immortals, whom we had created from the humans, had passed on knowledge about us to the humans in that eyeball for them to use against us. Therefore, we only punished them for bringing the invisible version of the Soulless into human settlements, which, no doubt, had made them even more vindictive than they already were.

"It was only after you were captured in Pompeii that we realized the humans must have been aided by the immortals, or they would not have recognized you so easily by your human form only. That was probably also why the humans were certain that by putting a spear into the spot in your chest where you were missing a scale, they could finally tame the magnificent bird.

"Your human form lost a lot of blood in that cage, and the blood loss depleted your strength. Even though you had transformed back into your true form before your human heart stopped, you were too weak to wield your powers. We are not sure whether that was the reason why the hole in your chest grew bigger that time. All we know is that the suns dimmed again, and the Eye opened for the second time for the Soulless to drip into this world."

"What about this time?" she asked hesitantly, even though she couldn't help but think she already knew the answer. "Did the hole grow again? ... Did the suns dim? Did the Eye open? ... Did the Soulless drip into their world?"

Black lowered both of his heads but neither of them spoke. White gazed down at the River and gave the raft a few quick taps with his tail. Even Azure looked away quietly.

"They did, didn't they . . ." she said numbly. "So their *souls* are being consumed by the Soulless as we speak."

"We knew you were in danger," said Black. "After creating a blizzard to thwart the humans from pursuing me further, Azure went back to protect your human form. All the shots they had fired were deflected from you . . . one way or another, before you transformed, so we didn't anticipate it would happen again."

"I'm sorry, Vermilion." White looked up from the River. "The Eye opened when you came to free me, but . . ."

"But we knew we must keep it from you," said Azure, firmly. "At least until we had reached the Gate."

"Why didn't you tell me?" she hissed.

White walked up to her and said, "Look into my eyes, Vermilion."

His voice was placid yet resonant, like the reverberation of a large temple bell. In spite of herself, she obeyed and looked into his eyes, which were gazing back at her like two small suns. Before she knew it, White's eyes had embraced her into a glittering and prismatic world, where she was able to see everything that was happening at *present*: the abrupt discontinuation of countless individual *time strings*, the instant termination of numerous lives, the nonstop waves of overlapping screams—both outward and inward, audible or inaudible—that filled the air with dread and despair . . . and the sudden obliteration of innumerable *souls*, their *seeds of life* devoured from her sight . . .

She felt the black hole pulsating feverishly in her left chest, hungry and hollow, as if it was searching for what it was missing.

"We need to save them . . ." she croaked, not realizing the raft was quickly slowing down.

"That's exactly why we didn't tell you!" Azure bellowed like booming thunder. "If you knew the Eye had opened again, you would have insisted on saving them from the Soulless rather than traveling to the Gate with us to reset the River of Time and cleanse the Wheel of Life, just like before!" He cut between her and White and stared her in the eye. "How many times do you have to repeat the same mistake, Vermilion? This world is sick; the humans are its sickness! They have brought nothing but chaos to *the pattern* of the River of Time! They have hindered *the flow* of the River and disrupted *the rhythm* of the Wheel again and again! They have endangered *the balance* of the Scale time after time! They are a sickness that will never stop spreading or wreaking havoc in this world until it's cleansed!"

She turned away from her companions. She knew Azure was right. But inside the hungry and hollow black hole in her chest, something was scratching and gnawing away at that emptiness, as if to make it even bigger and wider than it already was.

The raft slowed to a stop. She noticed then that the images on the River were looking very differently from what she had seen earlier: they were brimming with life—microscopic lives—small, insignificant, defenseless, yet determined to survive. These tiny beings drifted in the cozy, dark womb of Mother Earth, waiting patiently for the first beam of sunlight to shine through so that they could soak up its energy to convert carbon dioxide and water into food for themselves.

"Life was born equally," said Black, who had joined her by her side. "Don't you think it should end equally for all lives as well?"

" 'End equally'?" she croaked. "What about the *souls* that are being devoured by the Soulless? If we don't save them now, even if we could reset the River and cleanse the Wheel right away to start life anew in this universe, their *seeds of life* would never get to return to the Wheel to be reborn again like the rest of them. How is that 'end equally' when we choose to forsake those *souls*?"

"It's a price we must pay to preserve the rest of them," said Azure. "There's a price for everything, Vermilion. You, above all, should know this."

There was an edge to his voice that prompted her to rummage her memory for a clue. But it was like clutching water with a hand —the more she tried, the faster it slipped from her mind.

"Enough!" White put an end to her futile effort with a deafening cry, which echoed like a pride of lions roaring inside a mountain cave.

She turned and saw that White was suddenly much bigger and taller than the three of them. Even the wooden raft had grown in length and width to accommodate the new size of its master.

"Look at the Scale—the choice must be made now!" White's voice boomed between her and Azure in their minds. "The Gate is close. We can either finish our journey, reset the River, cleanse the Wheel, and restart life in this universe, or we can turn around and sail back to *present* to deal with the Soulless. Either way, as soon as *the balance* is lost irrevocably, the Scale will tip over and fall, shattering both the Wheel of Life and the River of Time in the process. By then, we will reach neither." He paused and gazed down at her. "Vermilion, you know our verdict, but without the same commitment from you, we cannot reach or open the Gate. The choice is yours."

To her right, Azure growled like rumbling thunder. To her left, Black sighed like a falling tide.

She looked back at the Scale. In spite of the distance they had traveled from *present*, it had remained unchanged in size; however, it was tipping toward the plate formed by darkness, and it was tipping dangerously low.

"Your choice, Vermilion," White repeated. "And we shall all respect it."

Black gave her a nod. "Your choice."

Azure's eyes bored into her. "Your choice. But choose wisely, Vermilion. You said it yourself: 'either we end all lives to save *the seeds of life*, or we watch all lives end.'"

She felt the black hole in her chest expanding, as if it had finally realized it would never find what it was missing within itself and, in an effort to appease the hungry and hollow sensation becoming too insatiable to contain, had decided to turn its search outward and outbound.

Life is all about choices, she heard her human voice say from somewhere deep inside her, like a secret whisper that was merely meant for the *souls* she had kept from the Wheel. *Make good choices.*

It's too late to turn back now, she said to that human voice within herself. *We have no choice but to go to the Gate.*

Chapter 14 THE GATE

1

"THE beginning of *time* is in sight." White announced. "We have reached the Gate."

As he spoke, the raft became still, and an immense wooden door suddenly materialized in front of them, towering over the raft as well as its four passengers like a boundaryless barrier, barring anyone from passing. It stood mightily and determinedly in the River of Time, cutting cleanly and evenly into every single individual *time string* as though it had simply chopped off the head of the River when it came into form. The door itself was rustic and unpolished. There was nothing on it except four gigantic ring-shaped door knockers, each as big as the others and large enough to encircle them all. Hanging high above them on the door, the four door knocker rings sat opposite each other in pairs: one on the left and one on the right, one on the top and one on the bottom.

"We have returned," Black said solemnly.

"At long last!" Azure exclaimed.

"*Present* is in chaos. We must begin without delay," said White. With one graceful leap, he disappeared from the raft but immediately reappeared somewhere high above them.

Smoothly and effortlessly, Azure swam up from the raft to join him. Black swayed his heads and blew from both of his mouths. Two long streams of white smoke flowed down to his feet, which then carried him upward swiftly after Azure in the form of a large piece of cloud.

"Come, Vermilion." Black beckoned to her as he ascended. "Fly!"

In spite of herself, she remembered that was also the last word Lilith had said to her before she died—with a face that was so strikingly white, sputtering out blood that was so jarringly red.

And then, even though she shouldn't have been able to, she felt a throbbing pain in a heart that she did not have.

Fighting back her human emotions, she looked up and opened her wings.

As she took flight, she pictured to herself that Lilith, with her strikingly white face and her jarringly red blood, was lying on the raft, watching her fly with a lifeless yet contented smile.

11

Her companions were waiting for her in front of the four door knocker rings. She flew toward them and joined them by their side. She noticed then that the four door knocker rings were formed by four different elements, each of which was rotating counterclockwise through the wooden hinge that connected it to the Gate: the one on the left was formed by metal, the one on the right was formed by dust, the one on the top was formed by water, and the one on the bottom was formed by fire.

"Why are they different?" she asked.

"They represent the elements we need to provide to open the Gate," answered Black, "which are the same elements we used to open it from *the beginning* for *time* to flow into this universe to make the Wheel of Life spin. In other words, to reset the River of Time and cleanse the Wheel of Life, we must offer the Gate the same elements that we created in this universe for life to begin in the first place."

White approached the four door knocker rings and spoke in a bellowing voice laced with static. "We, the Four Keepers of this universe, have come to reset the River of Time and cleanse the Wheel of Life. By the ancient law of creation, we shall return what was created to *the beginning*."

As he spoke, the intensity of his iridescence increased drastically, turning him into a brightly prismatic orb that was radiating a wide range of nameless colors beyond both the perception and the imagination of any living thing.

"I, the Keeper of Time, shall return metal," White continued. "For in this universe, metal is the prerequisite for existence and the catalyst of *time*."

He opened his toothy jaw wide as if he was about to swallow something even bigger than himself. Shiny clusters of particles poured out of his mouth in various shapes and sizes and colors like a metallic dust storm until they were all absorbed into the Gate through the door knocker ring that was formed by metal, right before the ring itself was absorbed into the Gate as well.

Azure swam forward and held a majestic posture in front of the three door knocker rings that remained. His mesmerizing green glow pulsated with such a rich and vibrant hue that he seemed to be lit up by the purest and greenest emeralds as well as the finest and sleekest jades from within.

"I, the Keeper of Change, shall return dust," his voice boomed. "For in this universe, dust is the prerequisite for formation and the reminder of *change*."

A gust of wind rushed out from his nostrils and was soon replaced by a violent and forceful wave of shimmering specks that charged at the Gate like a hazy torrent, only to be absorbed silently into it through the door knocker ring that was formed by dust, which, in turn, was absorbed into the Gate at the end.

Black gave her a reassuring nod and floated toward the two remaining door knocker rings on his cloud.

"I, the Keeper of Growth, shall return water. For in this universe, water is the prerequisite for diversity and the instrument of *growth*," said Black, his color changing rapidly; the tortoise part of him changed from black to dark blue, sea blue, and sky blue, while the serpent part of him changed from black to dark green, emerald green, and seafoam green.

His serpent head hovered next to his tortoise head, and together, they opened their mouths and let out two plunging waterfalls, which merged into a surging river and rushed at the door knocker ring formed by water like a legion of warhorses galloping into battle until it was absorbed into the Gate without a trace, along with the door knocker ring it had raced through.

Now there was only one door knocker ring left on the Gate: the one that was formed by fire.

Her companions looked toward her: it was her turn. She flapped her wings and glided toward the last ring.

"I, the Keeper of Rebirth, shall return fire . . ." She paused, realizing she didn't know how to continue.

Her companions chanted in unison for her, "For in this universe, fire is the prerequisite for life and the medium of *rebirth*."

"Vermilion!" White called to her. "Now summon them to the Gate!"

"Summon . . . what?" she asked uncertainly, though she was suddenly very aware of the width and the depth of that black hole in her chest.

"*The seeds of life* that still remain in this world." Azure gazed into her mind, his eyes unreadable. "All of them, Vermilion—the ones with *souls* and the ones without."

She stared back at him, unable to collect her thoughts.

"You created *the seeds of life* in this universe," Black said gently, as if he had noticed her reluctance to face the truth. "You created every one of them."

"But the last ring is formed by fire!" she squawked, not willing to admit it to herself. "I should be summoning fire, not *the seeds of life*!"

"You created them," said Azure, firmly and meaningfully. "What do you think they were made out of?"

She looked to Black. He acknowledged her with his eyes but did not speak. She turned to White, only to see a kaleidoscope of her own reflections in his prismatic eyes, which were staring right back at her from different angles like countless mirrors in a circular chamber, each an unmistakable and undeniable proof of what she was and what she was capable of creating.

"Flames . . ." she croaked weakly as she watched her reflections burn. "They were made . . . out of my flames . . ."

"They used to be stars," said White. "Like the remaining stars in this universe, they were all born from your powers. When they were consumed during the constructing and harnessing of components for life to begin in this universe, you made them into *the seeds of life*."

"You thought this universe was completed at the cost of their existence as stars," Black added. "So you gave them the chance to live on—in the cycle of the Wheel of Life."

"I may have created *the seeds of life*, but I didn't create their *souls*!" she cawed. "If they were all summoned here, the ones with *souls* would . . ."

" 'Die,' yes," said Azure, finishing her thought for her. "But if you don't summon them here, all *the seeds of life* that still remain in this world *will* be destroyed when the Scale falls, with *souls* or without. If you want to save them, then that is the price you will have to pay, for that is the price to open the Gate, and that is the cost for the River of Time to be reset and for the Wheel of Life to be cleansed."

She let out a hoarse screech. "A price that requires *me* to take the life of every living thing? How is that a fair price to pay to open the Gate? We are the Four Keepers. We created this universe. Why is there a cost for us to reset the River and cleanse the Wheel? Why do *I* need to be the executioner to take their lives?"

Azure lost his patience and hissed, "Because you are—"

White cut him off with an authoritative roar. Then, with her reflection still burning in his big, round eyes, he said to her, "Because *balance* means give and take, Vermilion. Equivalent exchange is the essence of *balance*. You are the Keeper of Rebirth. You, above all, understand the profoundness of this rule. It is your role and your responsibility. It is what you do."

Something was howling from somewhere deep inside the black hole in her chest, calling memories to her mind. She thought of the humans in white lab coats inside the box-shaped building, where she had gone in to free White. She remembered how their *light* had struggled in vain against the *darkness* that was hidden underneath when she gazed into their *souls*. She remembered having a prickling and tingling sensation when she passed through their bodies. She remembered that was how she had extracted their *seeds of life* as well as their *souls*, and that was how she had ended their lives before the bullets reached them.

She thought of the seven men in Starfall, who had attempted to rape Lilith in the long, dark alley that they needed to pass through on their way back from the pedestrian square the night before Christmas Eve. She remembered how much she had wanted to hurt those men. She remembered there was a prickling and tingling sensation in her wings when they passed through the heads of two of those men. She remembered that was how she had stirred up the *darkness* in their *souls*, and that was how they had come to butcher the other five men later and set themselves on fire with their corpses.

She thought of Eric Ekker, the fifteen-year-old boy in Skygate, who had offered to lead her to the ginkgo trees she wanted to find in Sunrise Park. She remembered how she had followed him off the trail, deep into the belly of the woods, where he had pounced on her as if she were a rag doll that he could toy with at will. She remembered how her helplessness and hatred had fused inside her. She remembered having the same prickling and tingling sensation when her wings passed through him as they flung him away from herself. She remembered that was how she had drained the *light* of his *soul*, and that was how he had lost his sanity and ended up slitting the throats of his parents as well as the family dog before setting up the gas leak at his house and lighting himself on fire.

She thought of Black's stories. She remembered how much the humans had feared her. She remembered what they had referred to her as. Then she thought of Cara. She remembered how Cara had cried to her and told her that she had lost all of her babies and both of her parents because she was cursed. She remembered how Cara had secretly believed that the only reason she had survived them all was because Death did not want her, ever since she was returned to the beach by the waves after her unsuccessful attempt at ending her own life at eight.

She remembered she had admitted to Cara that it was her fault. She remembered that was how she had decided to be reborn as a human baby for Cara to raise as her own.

"Because the Keeper of Rebirth is Death ..." she murmured numbly to herself.

She thought of Lilith then. She remembered how firmly Lilith had believed that her true form was not the Devil.

"I'm afraid you were wrong about me," she croaked inwardly to the *seed of life* that had once powered Lilith's heart. "I *am* the Devil after all ... You gave up your life to protect Death; how ironic is that?"

White's eyes appeared in front of her like two large glass spheres emerging quickly from the River of Time, warping and inverting the *time strings* as they dispersed the memories that were lingering in her mind.

"Without an end, there won't be a beginning," he said, his voice echoing infinitely.

"Without pain, there won't be growth," said Black, the serpent part of him coiling slowly but tightly around the tortoise part of him.

"Without sacrifice, there won't be change," said Azure as thunderbolts thrashed and lashed violently inside him, looking ready to break free at all costs.

"And without death, there won't be rebirth," said White. "In order to receive, one must first give. That is the price for *balance*, and that is how *balance* is maintained."

As he spoke, an image of the Scale appeared in her mind, which was tipping forebodingly toward the plate formed by darkness.

"The price must be paid to open the Gate. It's now or never, Vermilion."

Slowly and mournfully, she spread out her wings. She looked down at the black hole in her chest for the courage she needed to take away the lives of all that were still alive, but she didn't find any. Instead, in its hollow emptiness, she finally saw that rather than hunger, the black hole was growing out of yearning—a lamentable yearning to be complete again.

A sudden revelation struck her like lightning. She jerked her head up and cried, "I created the Soulless, didn't I?"

Her companions didn't reply, nor did they intend to.

"They were created when I created *the seeds of life* out of my flames, just like darkness only became darkness upon the creation of suns and *darkness* only became *darkness* upon the birth of *light!*" she cawed. "*The seeds of life* were sent to the Wheel, but the Soulless were left behind in me, in the absence of the flames that were consumed to create *the seeds of life* for this universe, so they long for their return like shadows that have been separated from their owners . . . The Soulless are attracted to *souls* because they want to bring *the seeds of life* back to make them complete again with their *light!*"

" 'In order to receive, one must first give' . . ." She looked down at her chest and croaked woefully, "This hole was the price I paid to create *the seeds of life* for this universe; it's been here, hidden inside me, since the beginning of *time*. Nevertheless, I have succumbed to the anguish of loss and given in to the Soulless to take them back to me, three times, only to lose more and more of them to *darkness*, causing the hole to grow bigger and bigger and, consequently, more and more visible every time . . ."

As she came face-to-face with the truth that lay behind her revelation, it suddenly dawned on her that was exactly what had jeopardized *the balance* to the point of no return and was about to bring down the Scale at any moment.

"It's my fault!" she squawked. "I created the Soulless! I opened the Eye! The Scale is falling because of *me*! They are all dying— because of *me*!"

The hole in her chest squeezed and compressed excruciatingly as if it was being crushed by extreme pressure from all sides and was about to either collapse or explode, but she didn't care.

"It's all my fault!" she cried. "I created them; I should have never expected anything in return! They shouldn't die . . . They didn't have to die . . . Nobody should have died . . . !"

A discordant and heart-wrenching screech shot out from her beak. Then, just as an inexorable energy burst out from her eyes in a shower of flames, she exploded into a blinding ball of light that whited out everything.

When the brightness had finally subsided, the Vermilion Bird was gone. A nimbus of tiny flames surrounded the space where she had been, circling it slowly and faithfully as they drifted along with one another, like shy children who didn't want to leave the safe orbit of their mother. In spite of their reluctance, their pace eventually slowed to a stop until, one by one, the tiny flames went out, leaving behind a cloud of *souls* floating in their place, each giving off a different brightness of *light*.

"She saved them . . ." Azure observed with utter astonishment. "The Soulless have returned what they have taken . . ."

"She won't be able to open the Gate now." Black gave a doleful smile at the floating *souls*, which were blinking intermittently before them like stars on a clear summer night. "She chose to use all of her energy to close the Eye instead."

White was observing the Scale. When he heard Black, he shook his head. "She did more than that. The Scale has stopped tipping —she had uncreated the Soulless."

Azure lowered his head as though he was deep in thought, then he asked softly, "At what cost?"

"That," answered White as he gazed at the nebulous shape forming among the cloud of *souls*, "I'm afraid is a question only she has the answer to."

Chapter 15   THE END, THE BEGINNING

S HE awoke to the touch of a gentle wind brushing across her face. It was cold and soothing, reminding her of the touch of someone familiar—someone loving. Slowly and lazily, she opened her eyes, only to be jolted by a stinging pain swelling up from her corneas as though they had been rubbed by burning sand.

She winced and squeezed her eyes shut immediately, hoping it would ease the pain, but it was already spreading from her eyes to her throat then to her body and limbs like a wildfire raging through her veins. She tried to move her hands and arms to prop herself up, yet, despite their acute reception toward the burning pain, they were having a hard time coming back to life, which caused her to think she had been asleep for far too long. After several failed attempts, she finally gave up with a resigned sigh, weary from the exertion.

Maybe it's because of the dream I had, she thought. *What a strange and depressing dream it was . . . And everything felt so real . . .*

She focused on recalling her dream from the beginning to the end. But the harder she tried, the faster it slipped from her mind. Even so, she couldn't help but wonder whether it was only a dream, and the mere thought of it gave her a sudden pang of uneasiness.

She drew a deep breath and tried opening her eyes again. They were still stinging with pain, but she recognized the ceiling fan right away. To her left, the lamp on the nightstand had been left on. To her right, a window had been cracked open, leaving just enough space for the cold winter air to climb in at a steady flow. She looked out the window and saw that it was very dark outside, with no stars or moon in the sky.

I am *home,* she said to herself with relief. *So it was just a dream. It was not real . . . I must have been out cold like the dead . . .*

Just when she was about to try pushing herself up again, she heard soft footsteps approaching her room. They came to a stop at the door, then the doorknob was turned quietly, and the door was gently pushed open, revealing the shapes of a woman and a man, both of whom, by the soft light emitting from the lamp on the nightstand, seemed very pale and very tired, with sunken cheeks and heavy dark circles under their eyes.

"Mom . . . ? Dad . . . ?" she called weakly, her voice hoarse and her throat burned with the sensation that she had swallowed hot coals.

"Yes, we're here," the woman cooed eagerly and came in.

The man followed the woman to her bed. "Hey . . . Little Bird. Did we wake you? You sound sleepy."

"No, I woke up before you came in." She cleared her throat to ease the swelling pain, then she suddenly noticed she had been studying their faces intently as if she had forgotten what they looked like.

"Mom?" she asked. "Why do you look . . . sad?"

The woman broke into a bittersweet smile. Tears rolled down from her eyes but were immediately wiped away.

"I'm not sad, Mira." The woman reached down and patted her forehead; her hand was as cold and soothing as the winter wind coming in through the window. "I'm just . . . happy. Happy to be here with you and Dad. Happy to be alive."

She let out a croaky chuckle. "What's that about?"

The woman laughed. "I don't know. I can't explain it. But that's what I'm feeling right now."

"Same here." The man smiled, his gray eyes warm with affection. "Nothing makes me happier than being *here*, with you and Mom."

She snickered. "You too, Dad? Why are you both so sentimental tonight? Was there a full moon or did you guys have too much wine?"

The man scratched his head. "Actually . . . I can't remember what we did. I just remember we were at, um . . . the square? I think we were there for . . . for . . ." He scrunched up his face in an effort to retrieve the remaining portion of his thought but soon gave up with a wave of his hand. "Oh well, I can't remember. That's what I get for staying up way past my bedtime."

The woman rubbed her temples. "You know what? I can't remember either. My brain feels slow and foggy when I try to think about what we did earlier . . . Maybe we did have too much wine?"

"Maybe. Or maybe we just need to catch up on sleep." The man squinted at the clock on the nightstand. "Hmm. I can't believe it's only ten o'clock. I thought it was much later . . . Wait a minute. Today is Sunday? . . . I thought it was Saturday!"

The woman gasped. "What? Oh dear! I thought it was Saturday too! . . . We'd better let her go back to sleep, then. She's got school tomorrow."

Quickly, the woman smoothed out the covers on her and tucked her in. "Do you still want to leave the window open like that? You're not cold?"

"I like it. The cold air feels nice on my face."

"You must have a very warm heart, then." Smiling fondly, the woman leaned over and planted a kiss on her forehead. "Good night, my warmhearted girl. We'll see you tomorrow."

The man bent down and kissed her forehead as well. "Good night, Little Bird. We love you."

Like a tired baby who had been listening to her favorite lullaby, she gave in to a yawn. "Good night."

The woman turned off the light, and they headed quietly for the door together. Just then, something vibrated and buzzed.

"Oh, I almost forgot." The man turned around, reaching into his pocket. "You left your phone on the kitchen island." He took the phone out, glanced at the notification, and set it down on the nightstand. "Well, looks like Lilith's staying up late too."

At the mention of Lilith's name, she suddenly felt an inward tug in her left chest. Ignoring the stinging pain that was still burning from her shoulder joints to her palms, she swung an arm out from under the covers to reach for her phone.

"Here." The man passed the phone to her helpfully. "Don't talk for too long though, or you'll be sorry when that alarm goes off tomorrow morning."

"Thanks, Dad," she replied, smirking. "You too."

The man and the woman chortled softly to each other, then they left the room and shut the door gently behind them.

She woke up the phone and checked the notifications. There was a new message from Lilith. She tapped on it, and a long text popped up on the screen:

Still awake? I just got home, and guess what? My folks were waiting for me at home! They said they had decided to make a career change and would be taking some time off. So . . . (insert dramatic drumroll) they're taking me to the beach on Wed! For a whole week!! A whole week at the beach, with my parents!!! Can you believe it?! It'll be our first family trip ever! EVER!!! I'm soooo excited right now I don't think I can fall asleep! I may just start packing tonight! Think I can fit you into my suitcase somehow? :p

She smiled to herself and pressed on the microphone icon: "Staying up late gives you wrinkles and gray hairs, Lilith. Go to bed. We've got school tomorrow." She paused, then with a quiet chuckle, she decided to add, "We can figure out how you can fit me into your suitcase tomorrow."

When her voice message was sent, she put her phone in airplane mode and settled back into bed.

The wind was blowing much harder now. She could hear the trees rustling ceaselessly in the backyard, as if they were whispering a long-forgotten story to the earth and the sky.

Yes, she thought tranquilly as she let her mind drift into that weightless, floating state of drowsiness. *It was definitely . . . just a dream . . .*

In that half-asleep, half-awake moment, she fancied that there was a vivid red bird outside her window, watching her with two pairs of beady black eyes. As the cold winter wind brushed across her face and pulled her eyelids down, she thought the beady black eyes were transforming into four round pools: two as clear as spring water, and the other two as murky as ponds.

As her mind was ferried serenely away by the four round pools, her eyes closed completely, and she drifted off into a dreamless slumber.

The cold winter wind lingered by her side until she was sound asleep, then it crept out from the half-cracked window and flowed toward a nearby tree branch, upon which a red bird had been perching and watching.

As the wind approached, something appeared next to the red bird; it was large and invisible, and it seemed to be bending the space around its transparent shape with a layer of reflective dust.

"It's done," said the invisible thing as the reflective dust around it vibrated and shifted like disturbed glitters. "I've smoothed out the ripples in *the flow* of the River of Time and sent the *souls* back to their containers through the *time strings.* The Wheel of Life is spinning at *the rhythm* again. *The balance* of the Scale shall be restored soon."

"What about the *souls* of the humans who succeeded in capturing you?" asked the red bird. "And the ones who attempted to capture me and Vermilion?"

"Vermilion saved their *souls* too," the invisible thing answered. "So I sent them back to their containers as well."

The red bird cocked its head to one side to look at the invisible thing. "Should we be concerned about the consequence?"

"I've grayed out *the pattern* between the current *present* and the moment in *time* when I was captured. They will not remember they succeeded in capturing me, nor will they remember their attempt at capturing you or Vermilion. This section of *time* will remain a blur in their memory, as long as their *time strings* continue. Same for the other containers that received their *souls* back, and the ones who were lucky enough to have survived the Soulless."

"My lightning created an opening in the building they used to study White, before the *souls* were returned," said the wind, rocking the trees as it spoke. "The humans will not be able to recover any record from there."

"What about her?" The red bird stretched out a wing toward the half-opened window. "Should we tell her?"

The wind eased up and tugged at the branches gently. "It's probably best that she doesn't remember. Let her rest. She needs a break from the truth. After all, her role is a burden that none of us could have shouldered."

They all fell silent then, as if they felt the weight of that very burden upon themselves.

"Do you think she made the right choice?" the red bird asked, breaking the silence of the cold winter night.

The reflective dust began to shake and glide around the invisible thing, who replied slowly and gravely, "That . . . only *time* will tell."

"What about that Lilith girl?" the wind suddenly asked. "Her container expired when it was shot. How did her *soul* return to it?"

"She must have paid the price for that too." The invisible thing let out an echoing sigh. "As to what cost, we will find out—in *time*."

As the cold winter night pulled every tree, every house, and every street deeper into its embrace, the invisible thing left just as quickly as it had arrived. The wind shot up from the undergrowth and blasted a path in the woods as it stormed past the hills and beyond, rattling every single nest taking shelter on the trees that were in its way. When all was quiet again, the red bird flapped its wings and took flight, taking comfort in the thought that every *soul* on this blue planet was still living, growing, changing, and dying.

\<The end>

(And the beginning)

ABOUT THE AUTHOR

Sisi Zhao is the mother of two loving and energetic preteens. In 2021, her life was disrupted by the sudden onset of a health condition, amid which, she decided to write a story to inspire and, hopefully, bring a little bit of sunshine to those who are also hurting in life. Now, Sisi focuses on improving her health to embrace a new stage in womanhood and motherhood, and she continues to enjoy her love for beautiful and magical things—like animals, plants, music, art, museums, conjuring up stories, and reading—as she resumes her childhood search for a genie to grant her the wish to restore love and peace to the heart of every lonely, lost, hurt, angry, sad soul in the world.

www.sisizhao.com